Anne Goring was born in Manchester and lived there until she married. She travelled with her husband to Singapore where they lived for six years before returning to the UK to live in South Devon. She has previously had published a number of articles, short stories and four romantic novels.

A Turning Shadow

Anne Goring

KNIGHT

First published in 1993
by HEADLINE BOOK PUBLISHING

First published in paperback in 1994
by HEADLINE BOOK PUBLISHING

This edition published 2001 by
Knight an imprint of Caxton Publishing Group

10 9 8 7 6 5 4 3 2 1

ISBN 1 84067 375 3

Printed and bound in Great Britain by
The Guernsey Press Co. Ltd, Guernsey, C.I.

Caxton Publishing Group
20 Bloomsbury Street
London
WC1B 3JH

But that the Sun still in our half Spheare sweates;
  Hee flies in winter, but he now stands still,
Yet shadowes turne; Noone point he hath attain'd
  His steeds will bee restrain'd
    But gallop lively downe the Westerne hill;

John Donne

Chapter One

It was a winter's afternoon when I first met Nicholas Fox. Only, of course, I did not then know his name nor that the meeting in so bleak and wild a place and in such dreadful circumstances was to be the first and that the pattern of our lives would be so fatefully interwoven.

My only concern was the cold and misery of our situation. I was fearful of what lay ahead, distressed beyond reasoning by the events of recent weeks and desperate to keep a cheerful face for Ben's sake.

'How far is it now, Jo?' he asked every few moments and I tried not to be sharp with him. I hated to see the look of crumpled distress that came to his face when anyone spoke angrily. Even if the anger were not directed at him, the sound of raised voices set him trembling.

I stopped for a moment to catch my breath. The sunken lane was little more than a rut burrowing between great hedge banks and now rising in its rambling way up yet another slope. Bare rock thrust up through earth that fell away to pits full of ice. I dreaded to think what it would have been like had the weather been milder and the lane awash with clinging red mud. As it was, we made a sorry spectacle, unwashed and travel-stained as we were, faces pinched from exhaustion and the constant battle with the wind that now,

1

ominously, carried a few swirling snowflakes. The sky held that purplish-yellow gloom that betokened worse to come. And it would be dark within the hour.

The bags we carried contained everything we possessed in the world. Little enough, but with every step seeming weightier to tired, aching muscles. A short cut, the farmer had said. Perhaps Devonshire miles were extra long, like Irish miles. We had been trudging for what seemed an age. But the farmer had been kindly and that had been a gift in itself, for to be penniless and homeless I had quickly learned was to earn nothing but suspicion and frowning looks. The rare helping hand was as precious as a nugget of gold in a sack of coal.

''Tis a rough sort of path,' he'd said, 'but 'tes shortest.' His weatherworn features had crinkled in concern. 'You hurry now, maid, and you'll be to Falconwood afore dark. I must be off home or I'd take 'ee round t'other road. But I daresn't linger. There's dirty weather coming.'

I wished I had a shilling to give him, but I could only smile and thank him for his kindness. The ride on his cart, along with a crate of hens and a couple of pigs, had been as good as in a fine carriage to anyone as long on the road as we had been. When he waved his whip and disappeared round a bend in the road that seemed scarcely wider or less pitted than the one we now trudged so wearily, I felt an overwhelming sense of isolation.

No creatures stirred in the deep hedge banks which rose steeply above us, closing us in. There was no friendly smell of wood smoke that might have betokened a cottage nearby, only the salty tang of the sea on the harsh wind that rattled the leafless branches above our heads.

I shuddered. As much at our situation as at the bite

2

of the wind. I had talked myself into believing that we would be made welcome. Grandfather, when he saw for the first time his two remaining grandchildren, would be moved to forgive and forget. That thought had sustained me over the last weeks, but certainty was sliding and slithering away as we stumbled along the lane, leaving only a hollow, nervous apprehension.

'Is it far now, Jo?' Ben asked. 'Will we be having supper soon?'

'Soon, Ben,' I said, hoping it was true.

We puffed wearily up the slope. I tried not to notice that my cloak was already speckled with snowflakes. Pray God we reached some habitation before a blizzard started in earnest. Pray God, too, that it was Falconwood, for even Grandfather could not turn us away in such weather.

Increasingly in evidence, I noticed, was a smell. No, not a smell, a stink. It came thickly on the gusts of wind. The stench of rot and corruption. Ben tried to muffle his face in his upturned collar.

'I trust that is not the aroma of Falconwood's midden,' I said to make him smile, 'for I fear we shall be sorely tried by it.'

But it was not a midden smell. It was the stink of decaying flesh. A sheep, perhaps, fallen into a ditch and decomposing there.

We came to the top of the hill and suddenly we had a view.

The hedgerow on our right turned away to enclose a field. The lane branched here, one arm meandering off towards a copse, the other skirting a stretch of open land studded with furze bushes. This heathland sloped towards cliffs. Beyond was the sea. Grey and sullen and wind-lashed.

But we did not look at the view. Ben stepped close to me and I laid a soothing hand on his arm, though

3

I was feeling far from calm myself. For above us, placed at the junction of the two paths so that no passer-by could miss it, stood a gibbet and the source of the stench. Chains creaked in the wind, tattered remnants of clothing, and worse, fluttered like grim flags under the darkening sky.

I turned my head, sickened. I had never in my life seen a public hanging. Papa had been sternly against such spectacles, though many people found them a source of great entertainment. The barbarous practice of exhibiting the hanged corpse of a criminal as a warning to others, he had said, and I fervently now agreed, was gruesome in the extreme. To come across such a sight in such a place seemed a peculiarly potent omen.

I almost jumped from my skin as something moved at the foot of the gibbet. In the fading light, I had thought a heap of rags lay in the grass. Now I saw the shape of a man spread face downwards, bare hands clawing into the turf, shoulders heaving.

The wind, having no barrier, was strident here. He had not heard our approach, abandoned as he was in an ecstasy of weeping. The thing in chains, swinging slowly to and fro, had one mourner at least.

Then I saw, lashed to the gibbet post, a rough sign.

ISAAC FOX, AN INNOCENT MAN.
FRANCIS KERSWELL DID THIS.

Underneath was a crude wreath fashioned of holly and fir branches. The red berries glistened like drops of blood against the shining green leaves and I stared at them before my eyes again sought the rough sign.

Francis Kerswell. My grandfather's name. Isaac Fox? Something stirred in my memory. Something Mama had told me. But it fled, shocked, as with one swift movement the man on the grass leapt up to face us with all the menace of an aroused and dangerous animal.

A young man of perhaps five and twenty, a mere handful of years older than Ben, but so very different. His features were distorted and blotched with grief, but the grey eyes under the thatch of wild black hair glinted with fierce intelligence. He was tall. I had to look up at him, for once made to feel of an average, womanly height. That alone was enough to press home our vulnerability, but there was as well such an air of barely controlled violence in his look, in his lean and muscular frame, that I became rooted with shock and fright.

Somehow, though my knees trembled, I found words. Silly, inconsequential words.

'Such dreadful weather! We have been travelling for so long and we are still not within sight of our destination. Tell me, pray, in which direction is the village of Starcombe?'

He took a step nearer, fists clenched. I tried not to flinch, fixing a polite smile on my frozen lips.

'I keep telling myself it will be in sight round the next bend, but here we are close to the sea and not a rooftop in sight.' I heard my voice, over-high, strained. I paused and swallowed. His head was thrust forward, his eyes glaring into mine, yet I had the odd feeling that he looked through me, saw something other than an ill-dressed, grubby girl. 'Well, sir,' I rattled on in the same desperate tone, 'if you cannot help us then we must chance this path across the common there and trust it leads us right.' Cautiously I took a sideways step. 'Good day to you, sir.'

His hand lashed out, whip-like in its speed. Fastened itself on my wrist above my worn glove so hard that I almost dropped my carpetbag and could not prevent myself squeaking in fright.

My cry seemed to bring him abruptly to his senses. He blinked, shook his head, almost as though trying to clear himself of a nightmare. Abruptly he let go my wrist.

'Forgive me,' he said. 'I was not . . . that is, I was distraught.' All that wild energy was visibly draining from him, taking the blood from his face. 'Your path lies through the trees. The village is down the combe beyond the wood.'

His voice was a surprise. Deep and without the broad dialect that had made the farmer's speech almost incomprehensible. Though there was a softness there, a not unpleasing cadence to his speech that contrasted strangely with the flat northern tones I was accustomed to. I realised that he was no ragamuffin either. His coat and breeches were plain and sturdy.

'I must have frightened you,' he said in a low voice. He gazed incuriously at Ben, shrinking behind me, then gestured at the gibbet. 'And this is a foul thing for strangers to come across.'

'But worse for those who knew the poor soul,' I said quietly.

'He was . . . my father.' The words came slow. Dragged out of pain and despair . . .

Snowflakes whirled between us. The wind caught my cloak and flapped it wildly.

'I have been away in America.' The words ground out of him as though he could not hold them back. 'I return to this. To my father convicted and hanged for a crime he did not commit. To our house occupied by a new blacksmith. He has left nothing, that bastard, Kerswell. And all because of old grudges that have festered in his black soul.'

He was not speaking to me but to himself. If we had

6

not been there I believe he would have cried it to the air.

'Frank Kerswell shall pay for this. I shall be back and take my vengeance.'

Again I saw the violence, the menace, in his eyes, but I realised that it was not directed at my brother and me, two feeble, defenceless travellers, though his words again stirred apprehension in my heart. What manner of man was my grandfather to rouse such hatred? This man upon whose charity I was about to cast myself?

I said, shakily, 'Sir, I know nothing of you or your circumstances, but I, too, have known the loss of my parents recently. I comprehend and respect your grief.'

'Thank you,' he said, then added bitterly, 'I trust your people died in their beds and not at the end of a hangman's rope.'

'My mother of the smallpox, sir, along with my two sisters. My father of a broken heart. And if you think that makes it easier to bear than your own loss, then allow me to disabuse you.'

He looked at me properly then. Really looked. What he saw brought the first hint of softness to that bleak face. In a way that was worse than his rage, for I knew Ben and I were a sorry-looking pair. He so shambling and dull-eyed. And myself, well, I wished, not for the first time, that I was pretty and dainty like Mama and my sisters and not a gawky, plain beanpole dressed unbecomingly in garments that bore all the bedraggled evidence of our long journey. I wished, too, that I was older than my seventeen years, to command authority and respect instead of pity.

He said, softly, 'I have given offence. I beg your pardon.'

I bowed my head stiffly in acknowledgement.

He looked around, as though aware for the first time

7

of the snow-laden wind. 'The snow is settling fast. You had best be on your way. Do you seek friends in Starcombe? Relatives?'

Even now, I do not know why I spoke so openly. I knew nothing of this stranger except that he hated my grandfather. And, human nature being what it is, that hatred might so easily have channelled itself upon us. But, strangely, my fear had evaporated. Perhaps it was that in some way our mutual grief overcame the dark and unnatural manner of our meeting. More likely it was mere physical exhaustion that dulled my senses and caused me to speak without a thought to the consequences.

'We are headed for a house called Falconwood. The person we seek is Francis Kerswell, the man of whom you just spoke.'

I heard the quick intake of his breath, saw the black brows lift in shock and the shoulders under the broad-cloth tense.

'He is a . . . a relative of my mother, sir,' I said, recovering my wits in time to prevent myself speaking of a closer kinship. 'We have no other family in the world. We are come to seek his charity.'

'Then I pity you.' His mouth twisted bitterly, then his narrow, unreadable glance went from Ben to me and he said in a gruff voice, 'But surely not even he could be so iron-hearted as to turn two such waifs, his own kin, from the door in weather like this.' He seemed to struggle with himself for a moment, then with an exasperated sigh, he whipped the bags from my numb, cramped fingers. 'I know the shortest route. It will save you a steep descent into the village and a worse climb out of it. Make haste now and follow me.'

He shook off my feeble protests as a dog shakes raindrops from its pelt. 'By the look of you both, you'd be like to end up dead in a snowdrift as at your destination. I'll not have that on my conscience.'

He walked fast, Ben and I stumbling after him. The light was going, all landmarks obscured by whirling snow, yet he strode out strongly as though finding his way by instinct.

We zigzagged through a tangle of furze bushes. My boots slithered on the white speckled grass. I fought for balance, choking on a giggle that was almost a sob. He glanced round sharply, and, almost immediately, set down the bags.

I feared I had offended him and he was now about to leave us stranded, but he merely pointed ahead and I saw that we were on a path still visible under its coating of snow.

'I must leave you here.' Again that bitter twist of the lips that marked his smile. 'I fear my face would not be welcome at Falconwood. It is scarce half a mile now.'

'Thank you,' I said. 'You have been more than kind. Especially when your . . .' I broke off. I could not mention that dreadful gibbet. 'When it is such fearsome weather,' I amended weakly.

He seemed to understand and he smiled again. This time the smile touched his eyes and white, slightly crooked teeth showed between his lips, giving his bony face an unexpected charm. He held out his hand.

'I do not even know your name, but I am Nicholas Fox.'

'Joanna Howarth,' I said, putting my hand in his as formally as if we were being introduced in some cosy drawing room instead of being buffeted by a steely wind with snowflakes tangling in our clothes. 'And this is my brother, Ben.'

He nodded gently to Ben who looked at him with fearful eyes and said, 'Jo, is it far now? Are we nearly home?'

'Nearly, Ben,' I said.

9

'I hope that is the truth of it,' Nicholas Fox said half to himself. Then he bowed over my hand and released it. 'Perhaps one day we may meet in more pleasant circumstances. Perhaps not. But I wish you well, Miss Howarth.'

'And I you, Mr Fox,' I said.

We parted then but I looked back as I walked, watching his tall figure become hazy and insubstantial through the veils of falling snow. I knew in my heart he was returning to the place where we had met. The echoes of his grief, his aloneness, seemed to spiral back at me on the wind and I held them to me in silent recognition.

Then I silently wished him Godspeed and trudged on to Falconwood.

Two stone gateposts loomed up out of the dusk. They flanked ornate iron gates and I hoped desperately that they were unlocked for the walls looked impossibly high to climb. They creaked open at a touch and we hastened up the curving drive. Ben still crying, 'Is it far, Jo? Is it far?'

'Here we are, Ben,' I said, cheerfully, with an inward sinking. 'Journey's end at last.'

There was not a welcoming light to be seen in the black bulk of the house. No friendly candlelit windows, no sound of voices. It took all my courage to lift the brass knocker on the heavy oak door. I knocked. And again, louder. Then a third time, a regular hammering that sounded as panicky as the thudding of my heart. After an agonisingly long interval there came the sound of bolts being drawn and the door opened a crack to reveal a candle held high by some person who hid all but one eye and a straggle of unnaturally orange hair behind the door.

'Well?' the woman demanded. 'What is it?'

I said, 'I wish to speak to Mr Francis Kerswell.'

'Then you have made a wasted journey. He is away and not like to be back tonight in this weather.'

'It is a private matter,' I cried, seeing the door begin to close. 'A family matter.'

'Come back another time.'

In desperation I thrust against the closing door. There was surprisingly little resistance. The door swung inwards as the person inside staggered backwards. When I went to help her to her feet I saw why. She was a mere sparrow of a woman, with black eyes that snapped furiously at me. She was arrayed in a motley and garish assortment of old-fashioned garments composed of satin and taffeta and hung about with shawls and gauzy scarves. On her head was the highest and most elaborate cap I had ever clapped eyes on. I righted the candle and handed it to her.

'I apologise—'

'Apologise!' she screeched. 'Be off with you this instant.'

'I cannot and will not,' I said, with a calmness I was far from feeling. 'If you will allow me to explain—'

'Explain? What is it that is so urgent? Got into trouble and come to Mr Kerswell's door in hopes of a purse of shillings? You'll get nothing here, I tell you.'

As she was talking I had pulled Ben inside and closed the door. With my back to it I said, 'I am Mr Kerswell's granddaughter. This is his grandson. We are penniless. If when our grandfather returns he wishes us to go, then we will do so. Until that time, I ask that we are given food and beds for we cannot go a step further.' As I spoke I knew it was true. The days of travel, the lack of food, the cold now combined to send alarming waves of weakness through my limbs. 'Pray show us to the parlour, if you please.'

In any other circumstances I would have laughed at

11

the expression on her face. Her mouth hung open. Her eyebrows, plucked and painted in a high arch, rose in a nest of wrinkles almost to meet the lowest frill of her cap. The patches of rouge on her cheeks stood out like fire beacons.

'Grandchildren? But that cannot be!'

'Our mother was Ellen Kerswell who married Arnold Howarth.'

'*Ellen*. But . . .' She broke off and mumbled the name over to herself, then gave a great cackling shriek of laughter. 'Well, 'tis the best laugh I've had in an age.' She thrust the candle at my face. 'Aye, I can see it. You've a look of him. The nose, for sure. And not to your advantage. Nor the size of you.' The candle swept towards Ben, who shrank back. 'And this one. Has he no voice for such a grown fellow? What's amiss with him, eh? Eh?'

I said, coldly, 'My brother is tired, as I am. When we are refreshed I will answer any questions you may put to me.'

'Oh, hoity-toity, aren't we, miss, for someone claiming to be destitute.' She cackled again. 'I shall like to see his face when he sets eyes on you. Indeed I shall! Oh, 'tis a fine joke and he telling everyone his only daughter dead almost on her marriage bed all those years ago.' Abruptly she turned away, calling, 'Make haste then, don't stand as though you were stuffed,' and set off at a fast pace on totteringly high-heeled slippers.

We passed no lighted rooms but a fire glowed dully in the kitchen where she led us.

She dug at the embers with a poker and set a pan of milk to warm while I wearily removed my cloak and bonnet and helped Ben out of his damp overcoat. A loaf of bread, a crock of butter and a half cheese were thumped down on the table and I sank to a chair,

12

scarcely having the energy to saw slices from the loaf as she commanded. The coarse bread and cheese tasted like a banquet. I choked over the milk, which she had laced with brandy from a flask that she carefully extracted from a deep fold in her peculiar garments, but felt the glow of it kindle in my veins. In a little while, the feeling returned painfully to my toes and fingers and the trembling in my knees subsided.

Then, having built up the fire, this little scarecrow of a woman drew up a chair and peered closely into my face, her button-black eyes full of malicious glee.

'Now, tell me how you came here. Speak up! Speak up!'

I said, carefully polite, 'May I know who you are, ma'am?'

She smiled slyly. 'My name is Amelia Alice Lightbody. Is that enough for you? Is it?' She did not wait for an answer. 'But perhaps it is *what* I am you would like to ask, but you have been raised too civil to put it straightly. Well, it may be in me to tell you and there again it may not.'

Was she some mad old relative, kept out of kindness? A servant grown eccentric with age?

I said, 'Ma'am, Miss Lightbody, these are family matters. I should not like to speak out of turn.'

'Ah, but is that not the most amusing way to go about things? To speak out of turn? It has landed me in a mort of trouble in my time, but what fun. What fun!' She sighed, all the wrinkles in her face running together. Without animation, her face was mournful as a monkey's. 'No fun nowadays. 'Tis a county of bumpkins. When I think of the theatres and the masques and the intrigues ... But that was London.'

Brightening again, she cried, 'You come from London perhaps, or near?'

'From the north,' I said. 'We lived in Sheffield last. Before that, Leeds and Manchester.'

She dismissed such obscure places with a wave of her clawed hand and said, in her erratic way, holding up her chin in a grotesque parody of some society beauty, 'Do you think me pretty?'

It was impossible to answer, as she knew very well. She chuckled. 'I know, I know. I am fit only to be a gargoyle on a church wall. But once, ah, once, I was very different. I was dainty and pert as you please with yellow curls and a wit as sharp as a pin. I cared not a fig for anyone's opinion. That was how I was when your grandfather saw me and oh, we had such good times together. It was he persuaded me to come here, all those years ago. More than twenty.' She hoisted a yellow striped shawl round her skinny shoulders. Bits of fraying silk wafted to the flagged floor and stirred there in the draughts. She leered, showing small discoloured teeth. 'Damme, we scandalised the lot of 'em. All the bumpkins. But now 'tis like a dream. I am his *housekeeper*, Miss Hoity-toity, his *housekeeper*. I warm his bed no more, for what lusty man could draw heat from this bag of bones.' She pointed her finger and tittered. 'Lor', 'tis an age since I saw a girl blush! Do I embarrass you?' Then with a sharp change of tone, 'Come now, speak up. I am in charge of this establishment in its master's absence. And, besides, I am all the family that he has acquired in the years since your mama left in a hurry. Does that not give me the right to know? Eh? Eh?'

I meant to give her the merest outline of our circumstances. But somehow with the brandy lulling my senses, the food comforting my stomach and the now roaring fire sending a cosy glow into the kitchen, I found my tongue loosened.

As perhaps she had planned. For she was no fool, this eccentric old woman with the peculiar clothes, and I was but a green girl.

My papa was on a walking tour of Devon when he came across my mama. She was Ellen Kerswell, then a headstrong miss of twenty. She literally fell at his feet when her horse was startled by Papa's sudden appearance over a churchyard wall. He had been making notes of interesting memorials and, characteristically, had not noticed the approach of horse and rider before he vaulted the wall to continue his walk. Mama, furious, had berated him soundly but Papa had seemed more concerned with his scattered notes than with the plight of a young woman who was obviously unharmed.

It was a new experience for Ellen Kerswell to be ignored. It was a new experience for Papa to meet such an outspoken young woman. Once he had gathered his papers and she stopped cursing him, they took stock of each other. Within minutes they were sitting on a tombstone sharing Papa's luncheon pasty and exchanging life histories.

Papa's walking tour came to a premature end in that churchyard. He found lodgings in a nearby hamlet and instead of garnering colourful anecdotes for a slim volume to be entitled *Some Curiosities, Ancient and Modern, relating to the County of Devonshire*, he spent his days courting Ellen Kerswell. For a courtship it rapidly became. It was the attraction of opposites. An attraction that was to last through many trials until their death.

The only stumbling block to the smooth progress of the courtship was Grandfather. Having been alerted by a cottager who wished to put himself in his master's good books, Grandfather stalked the unsuspecting pair to their favourite grassy nook. His rage was a sight to

15

behold when he came across his only daughter clasped to the bosom of a stranger.

Mama had related the story to us many times, laughing as she did so, still wearing the look of that beautiful, reckless girl who had captured Papa's heart.

'Go on, Mama,' we would urge. 'Tell how Grandfather locked you in the house and sent men to drive Papa away and he hid in an oak tree like King Charles.'

So she would tell with great dramatic effect how she had suffered imprisonment in her bedroom because she was already betrothed to Jonathon Lapthorne who had money and property conveniently adjacent to the Bascombe acres.

'It was an arrangement our fathers had agreed upon when we were children,' Mama said airily. 'But when I met my dear Arnold, he made all the horse-smelling young men of my acquaintance seem boorish in the extreme. Why, they had not a thought in their heads beyond setting their hounds on foxes or blowing some innocent bird from the sky with their guns. Merely to talk to your papa was to discover a world I knew nothing of.'

A rose-glow world of ideas and idealism, of debate and discussion, of books and poetry. But when Mama knotted her bedsheets and escaped under cover of darkness to Papa's embrace, she could not foresee that her Arnold was a man doomed to champion unpopular and unprofitable causes. And that the very unworldliness that had drawn her to him would make for an uncomfortable and lifelong acquaintance with penury. But as the lovers fled north they were confident that love would smooth their way and soon bring a recalcitrant parent to heel. A severe case of over-optimism on both counts.

Once they were ensconced in lodgings at Bristol, Mama wrote to inform Grandfather that she was mar-

16

ried to a perfect gentleman whom he would welcome as his son-in-law once he knew of his sublime and tender nature. Papa enclosed a note swearing to cherish his bride whose beauty and intelligence had quite overwhelmed him. Both bride and groom begged for understanding and forgiveness.

Grandfather's answer was brief and addressed solely to Papa: 'Sir, your letter is incomprehensible. I have no daughter. Any chit claiming a relationship to me is an imposter.'

There were further letters from the young couple. To no avail. Grandfather did not answer them.

'But though we regretted his decision to ignore us,' Mama declared, tossing her black curls, 'what really mattered was our happiness, our future.'

It was at this point that an errant pang of sympathy for my unknown grandfather crept into my thoughts.

'Do not trouble yourself over him,' Mama said, when I admitted my feelings. 'He was ever a proud and arrogant man. He would never heed my wishes. He deserved to be left alone.'

'But did you not have many pretty dresses, and your very own horse to go riding as you wished and a puppy?'

Mama's eyes flashed dangerously. 'And you think these things important?'

'I think,' I said, unwisely, 'that I should very much like to own a puppy, but I did not mean that precisely, Mama.'

'Then what *precisely* did you mean, Miss Impertinence?'

Too late I saw that, once again, I had managed to annoy her. 'It is just that Grandfather seems to have lost all his family,' I stammered. 'Grandmama who died young ... My uncle, your brother, who was drowned, then you, Mama. For he must have loved you to give you the things that he did.'

Phoebe cried, 'Oh, stop interrupting, Jo. You are spoiling the story.'

'Joanna will have her say. However hurtful and unfair her words.' The scorn in Mama's voice shrivelled me.

'But I did not—'

'Be quiet,' Phoebe hissed, pinching me.

I winced and fell miserably silent. However I tried, I always seemed to draw Mama's displeasure.

Ben, ever my champion, said cheerfully, 'Ah, but admit it, Mama, Jo has a point. Grandfather was generous with you.'

Mama's glance softened as she regarded him. She took his teasing lightly. For her, then, he could do no wrong. It was only later that she could not bear to look at him for the anguish it gave her to remember him as he was.

'It would appear so, to an outsider,' she agreed. 'That was precisely the effect he desired.' She clasped her hands together in a dramatic gesture. 'In private he was a ruthless man, determined to have his own way in everything.'

Ben caught my eye and winked. I knew he was thinking, as I did, that perhaps Mama had inherited more of Grandfather's nature than she realised.

'Tell us about when Papa had his pocket picked,' little Rose piped up.

So Mama related once more all the adventures they had encountered. She was a born storyteller. She made all the right pauses so that we held our breath in anticipation of some disaster to come. She made us shout with laughter and choke back tears. Their marriage had held plenty of both.

The loving couple had delayed in Bristol only to await the summons to Devon for a poignant reconciliation. When this was not forthcoming, there was nothing to be gained by remaining. They made first for Shrewsbury where Papa's parents lived, their welcome making up for Grandfather Kerswell's recalcitrance.

I have a vague memory of Grandpa and Grandmama Howarth. A recollection of soft voices and warm arms, though by the time I was seven they had both died. Grandpa was a country doctor, so devoted to his duties that he could never turn away poor folk from his door and was half the time impoverished himself. Papa was very like him in manner and looks. Both had the same dreamy blue eyes set upon distant horizons, the same kind smiles and gentle attention when they listened so that you imagined what you were telling was more important than anything else in the world.

Papa and Mama could not impose upon these good people for long, so it was off to Stafford where Papa had the temporary post of tutor to an earl's son. Our progress through the country, on the tail of Papa's various modes of employment, was marked by the birth of children. Phoebe was born in Stafford, Ben in Lichfield where Papa had a brief and disastrous dabble in a printing business. I was born in Liverpool (an investment in shipping was to bring us certain riches) and Rose in Chester (a splendid idea for a novel which gave us children an idyllic summer running wild along the banks of the Dee). Mama miscarried twice in Derby (during the setting up, establishment and demise of a school wherein the fees of rich pupils would cover the education of deserving poor children, save that the poor came in quantity and the rich not at all) and again in Manchester (a weekly newspaper for the benefit and improvement of the labouring classes).

It was a gypsyish life that we took quite for granted, the pattern always the same: Papa's enthusiasm for the new enterprise, the upheaval of house-moving – all too often a moonlight flitting – the exuberance of the first weeks or months, the gradual disillusion, Mama's sharpness as money became in short supply, the quiet, urgent whisperings behind closed doors as creditors grew pressing... then the whole cycle beginning again.

In my eyes Papa could do no wrong. I loved Mama but my feeling for her was always coloured by knowledge of my inadequacy. I was not pretty with curling dark hair like Rose or graceful and accomplished like Phoebe. I was far too tall and thin with ugly frizzy hair the colour of rusty iron. I had some small talent at painting and sketching, but if I attempted to sing in company, diffidence reduced my voice to a squeak. Though I liked music, my fingers were incapable of mastering any instrument. The knowledge of my unnatural height and excessive plainness made me too shy and gauche to be an easy dancing partner. I had all Papa's enthusiasm for books but Mama was not pleased that I too often chose to evade the household duties by escaping to some quiet place and losing myself in whatever story was currently capturing my imagination. Her disappointment in me whom she loved least of her children made it easier to understand why she blamed me for what happened to Ben. But it made it no easier to bear the burden of guilt her rage and sorrow laid on my young shoulders.

Papa loved me unstintingly and I adored him. From the time I could walk I was his shadow. I was early acquainted with the coffee houses where he met his acquaintances and where I was regarded with tolerant amusement. Wherever we were, Papa seemed to draw to himself the same kind of friends. Sincere men, earnest in their desire to improve the lot of mankind – animal kind on occasion. They spoke movingly and fluently against the slave trade, capital punishment for minor offences, the employment of young children, bull and bear baiting – a hundred and one burning subjects that touched their conscience. They were men who took the time and money that might have been better spent on their wives and children and squandered both on dreams. They had neither the influence nor the strength of purpose of true reformers. Men of words rather than action, and even those words, when printed into pamphlets, found few admiring purchasers. And while they debated so fluently, black men still knew the hell of the middle passage, animals were torn to death on street corners for men's amusement and hungry people died for stealing a loaf of bread.

But this I see only with hindsight. Then, I thought Papa and his friends most noble gentlemen, our frequent moves when Papa's private philanthropy became too much for his means more exciting than inconvenient. He could do no wrong in my eyes. Nor in Mama's.

We left Manchester and crossed the Pennines into Yorkshire, new territory, because none of us could bear the place after what happened to Ben.

It began, so innocently, with one of Ben's escapades. He was a cheerful boy, bright and eager to please, but with a streak of devilment that would have its way. Phoebe always considered herself too grown up to indulge in apple scrumping or sneaking illicit rides on the back of heavy wagons. Rose was too young to be included, so being closest to Ben in age, I was the one who was his sometimes giggling, sometimes terrified, usually eager co-conspirator. But that day, that awful day, when Ben urged me to go with him to Knott Mill Fair, I was reluctant. It could have been premonition but I think it was more due to the sore throat and aching head that betokened an imminent head cold.

Mama had taken Rose and Phoebe to the

dressmaker. Ben was recovering from the cold I was now suffering from and was bored. I had been left to hemming sheets turned side to middle and we were alone in the house, save for our one maid whom we had heard sneaking up the attic stairs and whose snores now reverberated through the thin walls.

'Joan will tell Mama,' I said uneasily.

'How will she know? We shall be there and back before she wakes.'

'But my head aches and Mama made you promise that you would keep clear of the fair.'

'Oh, stuff! We shall only look. Just the veriest peep.' He tossed a penny in the air. 'Come on, Jo. I'm sick of being cooped up.'

Against my better judgment I went. He made a great game of it, as always. We had to run through the house pretending we were evading Boney's soldiers, then leap to our imaginary mounts and gallop through the streets to the fair. We could hear the noise of it from the house and, as we drew close, the cries and shouts and screeching music were too tempting for a lively boy who had been confined to the house for several days.

Eyes sparkling, he snatched my hand and plunged into the crowd. There was plenty of free entertainment to be had. We wandered from booth to booth, laughing at the antics of the showmen as they tried to entice people inside, sniffing the heady pungent aroma of hot pies, Bury puddings, toffee apples, trodden earth, strong ale and sweating bodies.

Only when a nearby clock boomed the hour did we realise that the afternoon had fled.

'Mama will be home,' I cried, tugging at Ben's coat. 'Hurry, Ben. Hurry.'

Oh, God, that we had sauntered. But we did not. We went in a tumbling rush, panting and laughing, taking no heed of the man who stood at the fringe of the fair, in hope of catching passers-by along

Deansgate. He had a flaming torch in one hand which he swept about his person, apparently to extol the properties of some elixir that would miraculously prevent burns.

At the moment we reached the road a wretched old horse pulling a laden two-wheeled cart found energy enough to shy and rear as the bright flame startled it, before collapsing dead between the shafts. The cart and its load overturned.

One wheel spun crazily away from the chaos. A crate of screeching fowl missed me by inches. The torch carrier was felled by a basket of cabbages and rose strewn with green leaves to exchange curses with the driver.

I was fascinated by the exchange and turned, giggling, to speak to Ben.

The laugh choked in my throat.

The cartwheel had spun past me and smashed against a wall. On its way it had caught Ben and thrown him to the ground. He lay very still as though sprawled in sleep.

I could not believe that he was badly hurt. I shook his shoulder, turned his head. Then I saw the crushed bone, the sodden hair and the blood that ran in bright streaks to a growing puddle.

I cannot remember the details of the time after that. I know that the torch bearer proved to be a kind man who organised a litter of some sort to carry Ben home. I remember Papa's white face as he pressed coins into his hand. And Mama's screams.

The rest has blurred. I have an impression of a darkened house and unnatural silence and a voice sobbing on and on. Mine? Mama's? Phoebe's? Perhaps all three. It could have been weeks or months before Mama faced me, her eyes blind with tears, her voice curiously detached and cold.

'The doctor says it is unlikely that Ben will recover.

He will remain as he is for the rest of his life. Do you know what that means, Joanna? He will have to be cared for as if he were a baby. He may never walk or talk or recognise us again.'

I could not speak. I stared at her in sick fascination.

'My son is as good as dead to me. My dear and only son.' Her voice broke. I made to go to her, but she drew back and her eyes were cruel. 'You see what you've done, Joanna? You were expressly forbidden to go near the fair and you disobeyed me. Well, perhaps this will curb your headstrong ways, for your punishment will be to look at your poor helpless brother and realise the grief you have brought to this house.'

'But I—'

'Excuses, Joanna? Come, let me hear them. You failed to hear my instructions? You were kidnapped by a masked intruder who carried you bodily to the fairground? You fell asleep and, while unconscious, walked there all unaware?'

The acid of her sarcasm could not wound more than my own passionate regret for what had happened. And later, when Papa who judged more fairly tried to console me, I could hear the words but not take in their meaning. He told me I should not blame myself, but who else was there to blame? Not Ben. Not now.

I was scarcely thirteen years old, but all childhood fled on that fateful day of the fair. I grieved desperately for Ben and flung myself into caring for him, sitting by his bed for hour after hour, talking, reading to him, willing him to look at me with recognition in his eyes. I helped Mama to move him and feed him and bathe him. She was stonily silent during these interludes, doing what she had to with chilly efficiency.

She had always hated sickness, but to employ a permanent nurse would have been more than Papa's unstable finances could stand. I knew, too, from the way she averted her eyes, that to be constantly reminded of what Ben had become was deeply distressing to her. So more and more I took Ben's care upon myself.

'You do too much, child,' Papa chided gently.

'Ben needs me. I must do it.'

'But Ben does not . . .' he waved a vague hand, 'that is, he cannot know who is about him. Phoebe should do more.'

'Phoebe does not care as I do. I shall get Ben better.'

'Oh, my dear, how can that be? The doctor said—'

'He will get better,' I said, fiercely. 'Already he can move his arms and legs and almost raise himself unaided. Soon he will be able to feed himself and walk again.'

I had to make myself believe it, yet progress was so painfully slow that even I, striving to make every small advance a victory, came perilously close in the early months to despair. But the victories came. The day he sat up unaided, the first time he struggled to feed himself, his attempts to walk and, gloriously, when he turned his head as I read to him and smiled and said, 'Jo. Kind Jo.'

I was elated then and I swallowed the tears in my throat and hugged him, some of the melancholy that had haunted me since the day of the fair lightened. Ben really would get better now!

But that sort of advance was rare and I learned to live with disappointment. I learned to live, too, with Mama's indifference. How could this dull-eyed, shambling youth bear any resemblance to her darling, lively son. She withdrew from him – and me – more and more, concentrating her energies on Phoebe and Rose. Life went on, leaving us in a kind of backwater. Ben and I, circling round and round like dead leaves in an eddy, while the main current rushed busily past us.

We had several moves in those last years in the north. Phoebe's constant complaint was that as soon as she had made friends she must bid them farewell. All the same, she enjoyed the challenge of new faces – especially those of the young men who were drawn to her dark, glowing beauty like candle-witched moths. Our chronic shortage of funds never deterred Mama from making a show. Occasionally Papa was moved to mild protest but with an airy wave of her hand she would insist Phoebe must have a new bonnet, and breadths of muslin for new dresses were a necessity. She had a way with tradespeople that had them falling over their feet to serve her. What they felt when their accounts remained unsettled troubled me greatly. I could never pass the establishments Mama frequented without averting my eyes lest some irate butcher or haberdasher accost me and demand settlement.

But Papa, dear, unworldly Papa, ended it all. Mama's bold extravagance, Phoebe's bright beauty, Rose's quicksilver charm.

He was collecting material for a new book, which excited him greatly. 'It will be a major work,' he explained. 'A complete list and description of all the occupations in the town. Think of the benefit to future historians, for I shall fully relate all the particular detail in the lives of humbler folk. I am sure I shall be able to interest a reputable publisher in the work.'

I feared that like most of Papa's literary ventures he would end up paying to have it printed privately and the copies would remain gathering dust on the book-sellers' shelves. But I had not the heart to dash the light of enthusiasm from his spirit.

How I wished that I had. If I – someone – had dissuaded him, he might not have visited the home of a shoemaker and spent several days in his workshop, observing and questioning. The man's wife was a har-assed woman, caring for two sick children in an upstairs room. Only when it was discovered that they suffered from the smallpox did Papa hasten away.

Too late. The infection was already upon him. He took it mildly, recovering quickly. Then Phoebe sickened, and Rose. Mama and I fought a long, grim battle doing our best with blisters and emetics and cooling compresses to counter the raging of the fever, the ugly progress of disfiguring postules. By the time Phoebe, unrecognisable, crop-haired, had lapsed to a last coma, Mama was down with the first rigors.

Within a week they were all three dead.

A month later Papa followed them. Though the doctor said it was a lung fever that had taken hold while he was in a weakened state, I knew that he had merely let go of his slack hold on life. From the moment he had heard Mama's last faltering breaths, he had been a husk, a shell of a man. Without Mama his life was purposeless.

It was ironic that Ben and I should have survived. Two lame ducks. Ben was able to look after himself, to do errands if everything was explained to him carefully. In his own way he was happy. I had my wits, thank God, but little else to commend me. Mama's acquaintances failed to call again after bestowing their deep sympathy upon us. One or two of Papa's friends made encouraging noises. A position as governess might be found, they thought, or maybe a companion to some elderly person. For me. For Ben there could be nothing so comfortable. Someone spoke of an asylum and was grievously offended when I rounded on him.

'Never! I will not let him go somewhere to be kept prisoner and made an object of ridicule.'

'What else is there?' the gentleman enquired, huffily. 'The lad has no intelligence. You must earn your living. Ergo, the prudent course—'

'I shall find a way. You may take yourself off if that

is all the sense you are prepared to speak.'

He was shocked by my anger. I, who had always been so quiet and retiring, was equally amazed. But if I did not champion Ben, who would? I could not bear to think of us being parted. All we had left in the world was each other.

Later, when I was alone, I wept as I went about the sorry task of clearing Papa's study, all defiance gone in a wash of despair. My tears dripped onto bundles of useless yellowing manuscript that must be burnt and on the covers of books that must be sold. We were deeply in debt. Furniture, carpets, Papa's library, Mama's jewellery, all must go to settle the bills. There was nothing left for Ben and me. My mind was too numb with sorrow to contemplate any sort of future except that we must stay together.

It was when I turned over Mama's few trinkets that the idea came to me of finding Grandfather. Among the ear-bobs and buckles was a delicate necklace. Tiny pairs of scalloped leaves linked by a fine gold chain. Mama had worn it often and it had survived the more penurious times when other more showy items had to be sold. Her father, she said, had given it to her on her sixteenth birthday and perhaps, despite her scorn of him, some sentiment did still linger, for she had kept it when other things – her sable tippet, her enamelled patch box, her silver scissors – had gone.

I looked at its supple length glinting in the lamplight, then closed my fingers over it. Its true owner, my mother, was dead. Phoebe, the eldest daughter, would have inherited it. But Phoebe was gone, too.

I, like the necklace, survived. And perhaps the hand of providence was in that for, had Phoebe been the one to live, she would have had no compunction in shutting Ben away in an asylum. He had become an embarrassment to her, to be shooed away out of sight of her friends.

I unfastened the clasp of the necklace and, slowly and carefully, put it about my neck.

I looked at myself in the speckled mirror above the mantel. Thin face, tight pale mouth, frizz of rusty hair. But I did not see my features, only the thread of fine gold lying on the cheap black of my mourning dress, remembering how it had lain round Mama's white throat, remembering who had given it to her. Grandfather Kerswell, far away in Devonshire.

I resolved two things at that moment. Not to sell the necklace and to seek out my grandfather. Surely if he still lived he would not cast his daughter's orphaned children from his door. He was our only hope.

The fire had fallen to red ash and I was aware of having said far too much. A drowning tiredness weighted my limbs and I struggled to keep my eyes open.

'How long have you been travelling?' Miss Lightbody asked, then answered her own question, 'A good long while, from the looks of you.'

I shook my head. I could scarce recollect how many days. I knew that few of the nights had passed in the poor lodgings that were all that we could afford; for the rest, it had been barns and stables and once under a hedge.

'We are very tired,' I said wearily. 'Perhaps you would be good enough to show us where we may sleep . . .'

'Oh, so you think I shall allow you to stay, do you, having warmed my ears with such a sorrowful tale of misfortune?' Miss Lightbody thrust her wizened face close up to mine. 'I'm no soft touch, you know, Miss Beanpole.'

An odour of old woman and lavender water and

brandy gusted over me. I wanted nothing more than to spread my arms on the kitchen table, cushion my head on them and sleep, sleep . . . but I held her glance as well as I could.

'And what would my grandfather say,' I said, 'if he found that you had cast his grandchildren out into the snow? Listen to that wind. Even a dog would not be banished out of doors on such a night. My grandfather—'

'Your grandfather,' she answered, tartly, 'would not even have let you into the house, my fine lady. Had he been here, he would have set his men to drive you off his land.'

Disbelief must have shown on my face.

'You think I spin a tale to frighten you? Well, you shall see. You shall see. Yes, indeed, you may stay. But pray do not think me touched with pity for your predicament. I have learned through my long life to have pity for no one except myself. No, it is for my own amusement. It's been many a day since such a diversion has come my way. A fine entertainment is in store.' She rose in a flurry of drooping silks and trembling fringes and reached for a candle. 'Follow me, the pair of you. You shall enjoy the best the house has to offer. The rooms have not been used in many a long year, but a little damp won't come amiss, eh? Eh?'

She scuttled out on her tottering heels, Ben and I trailing in her wake. Up a narrow staircase, along a panelled passage. She paused at a cupboard where shelves of linen stood in order.

'Get what you will,' she ordered impatiently. 'You must make your own beds. I gave the sluts the half-day, idle wenches, mother and daughter, and insolent to boot.'

Muttering under her breath she tottered to the end of the corridor, made a great clanking with a bunch of keys and flung open a door.

I saw, in the flickering light, heavy furniture, faded blue hangings looped round the bed and the window where dark flakes slid down glass that was already opaque with frost patterns.

'Her room,' Miss Lightbody said. 'Ellen Kerswell's bedchamber. Locked up and never used since she left. 'Tis fitting that her daughter should sleep here.' Her button-black eyes glinted with malice and mischief. 'As for you, boy,' she said to Ben who stood gazing blankly around, 'you shall have the room that belonged to your Uncle Philip, Ellen's brother that drowned. Come! Come!'

She urged Ben into the adjoining chamber, sending light flaring into dark corners as she lit more candles.

'What do you think of it, boy? Eh? Speak up? Is it not grand?'

Ben looked helplessly at me. 'Jo? Do we sleep here this night, Jo?'

'Yes, Ben,' I said. 'We are at journey's end. We shall be comfortable here.'

'I should not count on it,' the old woman hissed.

'Thank you for your assistance, Miss Lightbody,' I said as politely as I was able. 'We shall manage now.'

'Indeed you will, miss!' she answered sharply. 'I'll not be running at your beck and call.' Then she made an elaborate, quivering curtsy, smirking up at Ben and fluttering her seamed eyelids in a grotesque parody of flirtation. 'But this lad now. Well, I'd have seen the time when I should have willingly run at his bidding. Such a fine set-up young man, for sure. Had I been forty years the younger, even twenty, I should have made it my business to teach you a few wicked tricks, as I did your grandfather. Aye, and he was only one of many who sought my favours. I had my pick and I always chose the handsome ones, no matter that they had not a sensible thought in their head. A lack of wits never displeased me. Physical beauty was ever more important. So transient it is. So soon the smooth skin sags and bones grow stiff.' The candle fluttered as she sighed gustily. 'And then we are trapped within our bodies. Forced to watch it decay, while inside the youthful spirit bursts to get out and when it cannot, becomes despairing . . .'

Her voice fell to a lament. I did not know which oppressed me more, Miss Lightbody salacious or Miss Lightbody maudlin. What I was sure of was bone-deep weariness and the icy dampness of these upper rooms. I interrupted the flow of now almost tearful utterances with a brisk, 'Do not let me keep you, Miss Lightbody. The air is very chill here.'

She snapped her jaw shut, glaring at me malevolently.

'Tchah! Such manners. When I was a girl I should have been whipped for interrupting my elders and betters.' She held the candle high to light my face and with another swift change of mood let out a cackle of laughter. 'Well, one must make allowances. For to be sure, there'll be no string of admirers falling at your feet. I have it in my heart to feel for one so plain.' But there was no warmth in her voice, only the lacing of malice that characterised all the old creature's utterances. 'Very well, then. I shall leave you. I bid you good night. You will need your rest if you are to face Frank Kerswell on the morrow.'

With that final sally she tottered off. As the last papery rustle of her ancient skirts and the uneven click of her heels died away, it seemed that the passage was whispery still with fading echoes.

I suppressed my shivers with action. I saw Ben settled and returned to the chamber that had been my mother's. The wind howled at the casements and icy draughts sent the candle flame bending and twisting like a tormented creature. I undressed with numbed fingers and crept into my nightgown. The bed welcomed me with soft musty arms. My thoughts whirled mindlessly. Papa, my sisters on their deathbeds, the trials of the journey, Amelia Alice Lightbody. Faces loomed and faded then blackened to the dark release of sleep.

My last conscious memory was of that foul object hanging in chains on the cliff top and of Nicholas Fox crying, 'Frank Kerswell shall pay for this. I will take my vengeance . . .'

Chapter Two

I stared, bewildered, at the sagging tester above my head, inhaling unfamiliar odours of dust and cold and mildew before the webs of sleep cleared and recollection rushed back. I turned my head to the window, the source of the dazzling light that stung my eyes. The reflected brilliance of sun on snow lit the dingy ceiling and flooded the neglected room with a transient illusion of brightness.

When the sun went in, it would not be such a cheerful place. The looped hangings round the bed were threadbare, the silk cushions on the chairs split, the long mirror on the damp-stained wall tarnished and blurred with dust. Cobwebs stirred softly in every corner and soot was heaped in the rusty grate. Neglect indeed. Years of it.

I got out of bed, the biting air bringing goose bumps to my bed-warmed flesh. I pulled the coverlet from the bed – raising a veritable fog of dust as I did so – and swathed it round my shoulders for warmth while I made a circuit of the bedchamber. Closer inspection revealed signs of hasty abandonment. Slippers kicked aside on the hearth, drawers half open spilling out their contents. I touched yellow lace and frail silk. A large press was crammed with gowns that spoke of the fashions of my mother's girlhood. A carved box on the dresser stood open and empty. Had this held her

35

jewellery? I touched the necklace at my throat. Easy to carry when she made her flight, when all the clothes she had owned would have been an encumbrance. She had taken but one small valise, she had told us, throwing it down to the shrubbery below before she made her escape.

I went to the window and struggled with the rusty catch. After a moment or two the window jerked open, sending a cascade of snow from the window ledge.

The angled roofs of outbuildings jutted out not two feet below the window. An easy descent for a nimble girl. Beyond was a yard, or a garden – impossible to tell when everything was blanketed with snow – surrounded by a low wall.

Icicles hung from the eaves, stiff and unmelting though the sun was already above the cliffs and the sky as blue as a dunnock's egg. The air was bitter. The wind had eased but the sea still roared beyond the ragged cliff edge, its sparkling surface fretted with foam.

I wondered if the snow would keep Grandfather from home today. Perhaps, I thought hopefully, we should have a day or two to recover from the journey before we confronted him. With the sun so brilliant and a good night's sleep behind me, I found it easy to be optimistic about the outcome, despite the warnings we had had about Grandfather's cold and vengeful character. He would be shocked, of course, to find us here, he might even be enraged, but surely he could not do other than welcome his orphaned grandchildren. I dismissed the shadows cast by that dreadful gibbet. Isaac Fox had probably been a scoundrel who had deserved his fate. His son, naturally bitter and distressed, had needed to find a scapegoat for his father's death.

I closed the window. I wanted to be out in the icy

air, walking, exploring, testing my new surroundings against the stories Mama had told us. The orchard where the pigs ate the windfalls, the cove where she and her brother, my Uncle Philip, had learned to swim, the kitchen gardens where they had stolen the early raspberries, the walled herb garden that my grandmother had planted and which, after her death, Philip and Ellen made their special hiding place, playing among the overgrown clumps of rosemary and sage and fennel and the fast-rooting weeds . . .

I had a sudden sense of closeness to my mother.

It was a strange sensation, something I had rarely experienced when she was alive. I had so desperately wanted her to love me as wholeheartedly as she did my brother and sisters, but she had only ever shown me, at best, a somewhat impatient affection. Yet here, standing in her room, in the house she had grown up in, I felt a deep awareness of her presence, as though I might turn and catch her regarding me with one of her rare conciliatory, affectionate looks. Hear her clear, light voice saying, 'Bravo, Joanna. You have done well to get this far. I had not thought you capable but you have spirit. Perhaps there is something of me in you after all. I wish you well, my dear.'

Idle fancies. Yet I was heartened as I wrapped myself in my still-damp cloak and went in search of water to wash away the grime of the journey.

Ben lay as one felled when I peeped in at him on my way to the kitchen. This room, that had been my Uncle Philip's, bore no signs of neglect. The bed hangings were crisp and clean, the furniture polished, the silver inkstand and the silver-backed brushes on the tallboy winked in the sharp light. Ben had slept in more savoury surroundings than I.

I closed the door softly and went downstairs to the kitchen.

37

At my appearance a puddingy, straggle-haired girl stirring porridge over the fire dropped her ladle and set off screeching. Another woman, older, greyer, but with the same pudding-like features, burst in from the scullery wielding a broom handle like a sword.

It was evident that Miss Lightbody had not bothered to acquaint the servants of our presence.

I embarked upon an explanation, raising my voice against a tide of incomprehensible Devonshire dialect. I finished by requesting that hot water be taken to my room. The pair looked at each other, then at me. The older woman said, 'But 'tedden natural. 'Er's bin dead over twenty year. On 'er marriage bed, master said . . .'

I assured her that my mother had been alive until a short time ago but as they continued to gawp and mutter, keeping well back from me as though from a dangerous wild animal, I went to the hob and seized the kettle.

'Find me a jug, if you would be so kind,' I said. 'I shall take the water myself.'

'Master's to Kingsbridge,' the woman said. 'What'll he say when he comes home? 'Tes fair mazed I am.' But she un-mazed herself enough to reach a white pitcher from a cupboard. I poured the hot water into it and escaped, hearing the rising pitch of exclamation and excitement as I went. I heard, too, at the end of the passage, a faint scutter and glanced round in time to see a wisp of skirt disappearing round the corner. Miss Lightbody, I thought wryly, had started her day with a little eavesdropping. The little scene had probably been entirely to her satisfaction.

I washed piecemeal in the rapidly cooling water which I poured into the dusty flowered china basin on the washstand. It was a luxurious feeling to be clean all over. I dried myself on my petticoat and threw it with the rest of my grubby undergarments into a heap in the middle of the carpet to be dealt with later.

I brought out clean clothes from my bag and put on a grey wool dress which was the warmest garment I had. Wrapped once more in my cloak I slipped downstairs and drew the bolts and turned the ancient key in the lock of the massive front door.

The snow was deeper than I thought, but I picked my way round the outside of the house which, by daylight, proved to be built of a warm greyish-pink stone bearing a tracery of leafless creeper. It was a low, rambling house which looked as though it had grown over the centuries from the slope of tree-crowned land on which it stood. A solid house, enduring and sturdy, yet not repressively so. The gabled windows, the clusters of tall chimneys, the unexpected corners and angles of its walls gave it an almost rakish attraction.

It was an attraction that struck me forcibly and quite suddenly, so that I caught my breath. And some deeper, instinctual emotion stirred within me as I stood by the garden wall, heedless of the snow beginning to seep through my worn boots. Recognition. As though the house and I were, on some hidden level, already bound together. That it had been waiting for this moment to welcome me.

I shook myself and laughed. Foolish fancy, borne of all the many stories Mama had told of her childhood at Falconwood. Of course I felt that I knew it. Yet as I slithered on my exploration of the stables and outbuildings, I could not rid myself of the feeling that the house was a warm, physical presence watching over me with benevolence.

Nothing stirred in the stable yard save a flock of small fluffed up birds, made brave by hunger so that as I walked among them they merely hopped or ran a safe distance and began foraging again. Ben would be pleased to see them. He had spent many hours at our last house feeding sparrows and starlings and pigeons that came to our window. But here there were blackbirds and throstles and a fat robin, even a flock of colourful goldfinches. The stables were empty. Two startled cats leaped from a manger and fled for safety into the rafters. They were all that moved.

At the end of the stable yard a gate gave onto an orchard, the old trees crooked under the burden of snow. Beyond would be the track that led to the cove, but my feet now were painfully cold. I would not explore further today. There would be time enough.

I hugged my cloak about me. I leaned on the gate, looking between the trees to the snowy waste that was the headland and the glittering sea beyond.

Then, slowly, I turned as if compelled to look again in wonder and respect at the house. We were home, Ben and I. Home at last. And to such a place. My joy and relief knew no bounds.

It was four days before my grandfather returned.

I spent the time as usefully as I could. I tackled my bedroom with broom and duster, learned the geography of the house, took Ben for brisk walks outdoors and tried, with notable lack of success, to strike up some kind of communication with Mrs Beer and her daughter Bessy. They continued to regard me with suspicious sullenness. My requests for cleaning materials were met with flat refusal.

''Tedden allowed,' Mrs Beer muttered. 'Master'll not let'n touch that place.'

'Miss Lightbody has given me the use of the bedroom, though it is scarcely fit for habitation . . .'

''Er 'adden the right. Doors been locked these twenty years,' Mrs Beer said flatly. ''Tedden for me to go against master's orders.'

'I shall take full responsibility,' I said, striving for

patience. 'I merely wish to set the room into some kind of order.'

But she stubbornly refused to give me any assistance. I had to invade the scullery and find what I wanted for myself. She followed me round, muttering all the time of the retribution that would be heaped upon us all when my grandfather returned.

I strove not to take such gloomy prognostications to heart.

Had I been older and wiser, I might have listened more carefully and been better prepared for what was to come.

The inside of the house was as solid and as fetchingly rambling as the outside. The furniture was mostly old and heavy and dark, the furnishings shabby. It was obvious that Mrs Beer and her daughter took good enough care of it, but there was still a lack of small personal touches – a vase of flowers, a pretty ornament pleasingly displayed, a carelessly abandoned embroidery frame or sketchbook – that betokened a chilling lifelessness, the lack of a warm and caring hand. Miss Lightbody dwelt, I learned, in a room on the upper floor and whatever her mysterious occupations, she kept them well hidden. The chairs in the larger parlour sat squarely about the empty fireplace as though no one ever pulled them close to a cheerful blaze. In the adjoining room the long dining table loomed, darkly polished, stark in an uninviting cavern of faded red velvet and antique oak.

The pleasantest room was a small parlour at the back of the house. It looked out onto what, in summer, might be a formal garden backed by a tall stand of trees, the view framed in threadbare rose silk curtains. There were two or three comfortable chairs, a pretty marquetry table, a walnut writing desk and, on one wall, a faded silk hanging showing scenes of oriental characters amid flowers and bright coloured birds.

Although the air was as damply chill as the rest of the house, the aspect of this room was decidedly more feminine. This was the place, I felt, that had belonged to the women of the house. Here was where my grandmother, my great-grandmother, had written their letters, seen to their household accounts, read to their children, gossiped with their friends. I could see myself taking possession. Sitting by the open window in the summer, smelling the scent of roses wafting from the garden. Or toasting muffins over glowing coals on storm-laden winter days. So rosily did I contemplate my future. So mistakenly.

I resolved that when Grandfather returned I should request that the chimney be swept and a fire lit. Had I not already had a disastrous and sooty experience with the fire in my bedroom, I might have ordered the fire to be lit there and then, but some of Falconwood's unused chimneys must not have been swept for years.

The only other of these rooms to be heated by a fire, apart from the kitchen and, presumably, Miss Lightbody's lofty abode, was Grandfather's study. But it spoke so strongly of his presence that I felt I could not presume to warm myself there. There were racks of guns, a large desk scattered with papers, a high-backed leather armchair, a number of glass-fronted cupboards cluttered with all manner of jumbled objects, discarded boots by the fender, jars of tobacco, a crumpled brocade smoking jacket . . . I only once peered round the door and hastily retreated, the smell of stale pipe smoke and Macassar oil seeming to create an alien and forbidding atmosphere.

During these two days I saw little of Miss Lightbody. Having admitted us to the house and prised out our story, she now appeared to have abandoned us. But I was often conscious of being watched. I would turn quickly to see a door closing, a skirt whisking away round a corner or catch the patter of footsteps running ahead of me beyond the angle of the staircase. For one so decrepit she was surprisingly nimble.

With Mrs Beer for ever hovering at my elbow in an aura of disapproval and Miss Lightbody's somewhat unnerving, not-quite appearances, I could not feel at ease in the house. It was also exceedingly cold. Despite the layers of garments that we wore, Ben and I still shivered in the fireless rooms. So we stayed outdoors as much as possible, tramping and slithering through the crisp blown snow, returning with glowing cheeks and enormous appetites which were well satisfied by Mrs Beer's truculently produced dishes of bread, potatoes and cold bacon. To anyone with more dainty tastes such fare might have seemed dull and coarse, but it was a long time since Ben and I had fed so sturdily. And it was no penance to eat in the warm kitchen, even if we must shift ourselves from the range of Mrs Beer's mutterings and grim looks as soon as we had finished.

On the third afternoon the thaw set in. The wind veered south and brought a soft mizzling rain. I awoke the next morning to the sound of gurgling and dripping and the rush and thud of the last snow sliding from the roof.

By noon the snow was shrinking to dirty grey clumps under hedges and walls. Under the lowering sky even the view from the small parlour was dismal. An expanse of tussocky grass and blackened vegetation. If the smooth lawns of my imagination had ever existed, they were long gone wild and neglected.

But at least Mrs Beer did not dog my footsteps today. There was an air of bustle, and a smell of baking and roasting that betokened the return of the master of the house now that the weather had eased.

43

I settled Ben in his room copying the alphabet onto a slate. A new step forward this. I had hoped that in the coming months we might advance to words and sentences. And, oh, if Ben could be re-taught to read and write I should truly begin to believe I had won the battle that had been so long and slow. I could not sit with him today. I was unbearably restless. I was anxious and excited and apprehensive in equal measure. And, above all, I wanted to face Grandfather before Mrs Beer or the elusive Miss Lightbody met him with exaggerations and complaints.

I dressed myself neatly for the coming interview in the thin mourning gown which, alas, was my newest garment as well as the most appropriate, and scraped back my hair as best I could into a tidy knot. I feared I had grown another unbecoming inch or two in recent months. The sleeves of the dress now ended above my wrists and though I was mostly as skinny as Mrs Beer's broomhandle, the bodice had become somewhat constricting. I thought, with the ghost of a smile, that Phoebe would have had no grounds now to declare that I should always have to pad my bust.

I wandered restlessly about the downstairs rooms, my ears pricked for the first sounds of Grandfather's arrival. Now that our meeting was so close I seemed to hear nothing in my head but the unkind words spoken of him. By Mama, by Nicholas Fox. The chill of the rooms seemed to sink into my flesh, my bones.

I was suddenly afraid.

In the event I did not see my grandfather return.

Ben had grown tired of the tasks I had set him, so I needs must sit with him in his room and keep him amused, telling him over and over that it was far too wet to walk out of doors to feed the birds and the stable cats.

Then, all at once, I heard the booming of a man's voice, the banging of doors.

I leaped to my feet so suddenly that Ben jumped and cried, 'What is it, Jo?'

I said soothingly, 'I must leave you for a few moments. Stay here and look through your book until I call you.'

I smoothed my hair and pulled down my cuffs with fingers that trembled as I went softly downstairs. There was no mistaking where Grandfather was. With a sinking heart I heard his booming tones, along with a high thin voice acting as a counterpoint. Miss Lightbody had got to him first and was in his study no doubt regaling him with the tasty scandal of our arrival. Even my knock on the door did not interrupt the excited flow of conversation. The door was ajar. Taking a deep uneven breath, I pushed it open and stepped over the threshold.

The voices cut off as though sliced with a knife.

They stood before a fire that snapped and blazed and drew wisps of steam from the coats of the two great muddy dogs that lay panting across the hearth. Miss Lightbody had dressed grandly for the occasion in a towering wig that threatened to topple, with its many varied ornaments, to the shoulders of a monstrously flounced taffeta gown. But I registered only the briefest impression. My eyes were for the man whose height and authority dominated the room.

A mane of white hair that might have once been the same rusty colour as my own; a curving beak of a nose above a mouth set in a grim, tight line; a pair of pale eyes that raked me over with chilling displeasure.

My grandfather.

The dogs heaved themselves up and came towards me. I put out my hand to the inquisitive damp noses, but Grandfather growled, 'Jupiter! Rex! Back, damn

45

you!' The dogs slunk away and sprawled once more on the hearthrug.

Miss Lightbody tittered. 'I told you, Frank. I told you she has the Kerswell look.'

'Hold your tongue, you lying chit!'

'But look at the height of her. And that nose! 'Tis the clearest likeness I ever did see.'

'Hush your noise, woman!'

'Your daughter was reckoned a beauty,' said Miss Lightbody, quite impervious to his commands, 'but this one is not made in her mould, I'll be bound. Poor wench, to be so saddled with her grandfather's looks as to be poor stakes on the marriage market.'

'What's that to me, you fool? I have no daughter or granddaughter. This . . . this conniving madam thinks to get money from me by fraudulent means. But I'll have none of her.'

I tried not to flinch under that quelling stare. My voice shook, sounding girlish and thin, as I said, 'Sir, you do me great wrong. My mother was Ellen Kerswell, your daughter, who eloped with Arnold Howarth and married him. I am Joanna Howarth.'

'My daughter is long dead.'

'If you wish for proof, see, I have the necklace you gave to her on her sixteenth birthday.' His eyes followed my hand as I touched the gold chain at my neck. Emboldened by his silence I rushed on, 'We . . . my brother and I . . . have been left orphaned. My father, my mother, my sisters – all gone. I had no one to turn to, no money, and I could not put Ben away so I thought of you and we have travelled from Yorkshire, a long and arduous journey, sir. I thought you might be glad to see us, having been so long estranged from your daughter. I thought you might shelter us—'

'You thought many things, seemingly.' His voice was as stony and biting as the east wind that had raged over the countryside these last days. 'All of them wrong. I repeat, my daughter is dead. She was dead to me the moment she defied me and left this house to make her own path. I wish no truck with you, your brother or your simpering tales of poverty.' He thrust his head forward like an eagle that has its talons in a rabbit and now would tear it to shreds of flesh. 'Do you hear me? There is no shelter, no charity for you under my roof. I have had enough deceit about me to last me a lifetime.' His voice sank to a harsh whisper. 'I will not let another generation of ingratitude and treachery into my house to torment my old age.'

I was aware of Miss Lightbody's bright, black gaze, the glee on her monkeyish face. I wished I could share her pleasure in the drama, instead of feeling a sick sense of defeat and hopelessness.

'But could you not employ us?' I said desperately. 'I would do anything... labour in your house... or perhaps you have friends who could help us...'

He had half turned away. Now he swung back, coat-tails flying. 'Are you deaf, girl? Did you not hear me?'

'I heard you, sir, but—'

'Allow me to spell it out for you in clearer terms. I will not tolerate you in my house or on my property. I wish you to leave. So take your bags and your brother and remove yourself.'

'But where...?'

'That is not my concern. You may cast yourselves off the cliffs, for all I care. Do you understand? Do you?'

For a moment I closed my eyes. And it seemed that in those seconds all the terror, the guilt, the misery of the last years and months consumed my spirit. This final rejection was more than I could bear. I was sick of struggling, weary of the burdens I had carried for so long, tired of the unhappiness that had taken my childhood. Everything welled up in an emotion both unexpected and unfamiliar. It was rage. Hot, tearing rage.

Rage against the death of my family, against Ben's accident, against my mother who had not loved me enough, against my own inadequacy in the face of the poverty that had driven us here, to this final rejection at the hands of a wicked old man with a heart of flint.

It burst out of me. I stood there and blazed at him, no longer caring what he must think of me. I held nothing back. I told him that he was a vengeful tyrant, a monster! I also believe, I am ashamed to admit, that I cursed him heartily in words that a well-brought-up young lady should not have known. And when I had done I was as breathless as though I had been running and so drained that my knees trembled.

'Bravo!' cried Miss Lightbody, clapping her mittened hands. 'Such temper. Lah, Frank, you must see now that she follows you even in this particular. A veritable chip off the old block, eh? Admit it, man. Admit it!'

Grandfather's response was to raise his hand, his eyes alight with temper. He would have knocked me to the floor, I am sure, had not the door creaked open behind me. Instead, his hand stayed raised, fixed, as though it belonged to a statue, as he stared beyond me, all the angry colour draining from his face.

I felt a timid touch on my arm and there was Ben.

'Do not look so troubled, Ben, dear,' I said shakily. 'There is nothing to fear.'

'This is your grandson, Frank,' Miss Lightbody cried. 'There now, is he not a well-set-up young man? A little lacking in the top storey but 'tis no disadvantage as any clever woman will tell you.'

Grandfather did not seem to hear her. He seemed transfixed, his face almost as white as his hair, all the deep-etched lines and wrinkles standing clear about his eyes and mouth. In a matter of seconds he seemed to have aged twenty years.

Even Miss Lightbody, prattling on, eventually took note of his silence and said, 'What ails you, Frank? Do you suffer an attack of the bilious cramp? I'll wager you caroused last night with the Pascoes and ate too much rich food. You know how it upsets you, so you have but yourself to blame. Come, seat yourself, and I'll fetch you some peppermint water.'

But he shook off her hand and turned away. He went to the hearth and leaned against the high carved mantel. Staring down into the flames, still with his back to us, he said in a low voice, 'Leave me, please.'

Miss Lightbody was puzzled. She looked from me to Grandfather and back again.

'I wish to be alone,' he said, muffled, tired. Then, like a weary old man, he glanced up at me and said, 'You – and your brother – may stay until I decide what is to be done.'

He was still contemplating the blazing logs as we slipped from the room.

Within the hour Mrs Beer trudged upstairs with the message that we were to eat our meals from now on in the dining room instead of the kitchen and master had ordered that if there was anything we wanted we were to say so.

I was bewildered, for I was certain that after my stormy outburst I had quite lost any chance of gaining his interest or affection.

'Why, 'tis the boy, of course!' said Miss Lightbody, as we seated ourselves for dinner that afternoon. 'I might have known it. Harry Beer, ignorant as he is about anything but horseflesh, saw it as soon as he clapped eyes on him. Frank keeps the portrait by him, but I've seen it a time or two and, damme, he's right, the likeness is there. And all the time I thought the sight of you might soften him, you running true to the Kerswell looks.'

I looked at her blankly.

'The boy. Your brother,' she said with impatience. 'He is the image of his uncle that drowned.'

'My Uncle Philip?'

'Of course, Philip, you addle pate. Have I not just said so?'

'And this . . . this has been enough to soften Grand-father's heart?'

'By all accounts, Frank doted on him. The son and heir.'

I thought of my mother's tales of her childhood. She, too, had adored her brother and we had laughed many times at their escapades together.

I said, softly, 'How sad that he drowned so young.'

'They say Frank was never the same man afterwards.'

'With his death and Mama running away I suppose it is understandable that Grandfather turned bitter. And there was then no woman to share his grief, my grandmama having died.'

'Ah, yes, the lovely Harriet,' she said slyly. 'Another source of trouble.'

'Trouble?'

But Mrs Beer and Bessy entered at that moment and placed several dishes before us. No bacon and potatoes now, but roast fowl, boiled parsnips, buttered greens and a golden-brown pie that emitted a herb-scented muttony steam.

'Will Grandfather not be joining us?' I enquired, indicating the place presumably set for him at the head of the table.

'I doubt it,' Miss Lightbody said. 'He mostly eats solitary. This table is only set for company once in an age.' She looked about her in satisfaction, giving a great cackle that caused Mrs Beer's expression to darken. 'And even if 'tis a damp and chilly chamber, why, it will find that idle daughter of yours something to do, to set a fire in the hearth. What say you, alewife? Eh? Eh?'

Mrs Beer merely turned her back and went from the room, muttering inaudibly. When she returned later with Bessy to clear the empty dishes and replace them with a fat currant dumpling, an apple pastry and a brown dish filled with thick crusted yellow cream, she announced loudly to no one in particular that she and Bessy was skivvying for no upstart female who was no better than she should be and if fires was to be laid then it was only on master's ordering of it. Having delivered this speech she marched out again.

Miss Lightbody cast a derogatory 'Alewife' at Mrs Beer's departing back. Then, seeing my expression, cried, 'These peasants have no notion of polite manners. They must be treated as the donkeys they are. I have always done so or my life would not be in the slightest tolerable.'

From which I gathered that these contentious exchanges were an everyday matter and not to be taken with any seriousness.

We made enormous inroads into the pudding, crowning it with generous dollops of the rich yellow confection that Miss Lightbody explained was clotted cream made commonly in the county by scalding rich milk in shallow pans over a slow flame.

Ben beamed at us as he laid down his spoon. 'I liked it all, Jo,' he said.

I laughed. 'So did I. We have landed lucky after all, though I did not think so earlier.'

'Ah, luck,' Miss Lightbody said. 'An unreliable element, I have always thought. Never to be depended upon.' She leaned towards me confidentially. 'Perhaps your grandpa thinks to fatten you up for slaughter, like the cattle he keeps in his fields.' She gave my arm a sharp pinch. 'And you need some fattening, mark my

51

words. Should you like that, eh? Eh? To be made into a plump pie with a nice tender crust?'

She rolled her bright black eyes towards Ben and I said, hurriedly, lest he be taken in by her nonsense, 'You are outrageous, Miss Lightbody. Such a thing to say.'

'Of course I am outrageous. It is a more interesting thing than to be dull and commonplace. Besides, if I had not decided to be outrageous, I should long have wilted away in poverty.' Then, abruptly, 'And I suppose you would wish to know the scandal about your late grandmother?'

'I am not sure that it is proper—'

'Fiddlesticks! You want to know about your family and I am the one to tell you, for Frank is close as an oyster. And if you wish to know how I learned it, it is because I have made it my business to find out.'

I strongly suspected that listening at keyholes might be among Miss Lightbody's methods, but curiosity overcame my scruples.

'It goes back to Frank's boyhood,' she said, 'and his friendship with a lad that became rivalry. Bitter rivalry. You see, they had both fell in love with the same girl, Harriet Tucker, but Frank was the son of Falconwood and his friend was merely the son of the village blacksmith. Harriet was a prosperous farmer's only child and Frank's father saw the future acquisition of lands adjoining his as a valuable asset. The marriage was arranged when they were scarce out of the schoolroom, but not to Harriet's entire satisfaction for she had a fondness for the blacksmith's lad. However, she was an obedient girl, and sensible. Life in a humble cot, however romantic, bore no comparison to life as wife of the future squire. She went into marriage with her eyes upon Falconwood, her body promised to Frank, but her heart set upon another. Even as she made her vows, she was doubtless scheming how to contrive assignations with her would-be lover, even though he frustrated her by removing himself into the next county for several years.'

'But how can you say this?' I burst out laughing. It was so scurrilous as to be comic. 'You could not know how or what she felt.'

'I know because I am a woman and have seen the ways of the world,' Miss Lightbody snapped. 'It is the curse of Eve that we are at the mercy of those who would use us to their own advantage, but a woman of sensibility and intelligence may usefully contrive to make the best of any situation in which she is placed. Now, hold your tongue, chit. You know nothing about Harriet Kerswell and I have come to understand her well. She determined to have Matthew Fox—'

'Fox, did you say?' I could not help the interruption.

'You have heard the name? 'Tis a family whose fate is much intertwined with the Kerswells'. Even into the next generation. Your mother's brother lost his life through the intervention of one Isaac Fox.'

It was a gibbet in the swirling snow I was thinking of, but I nodded, remembering now my mother's stories. 'Mama did not speak of it much, for it grieved her, but I recollect that she told us—'

'Yes, yes,' Miss Lightbody said impatiently, 'but that is to run ahead of my tale. I don't care to be interrupted.'

So I sat meekly while she related with relish, and a great deal of highly coloured detail, the happenings of half a century ago. Of my grandmother who had loved one man and married another. Of Matthew Fox who married a village girl scarcely a week later, some said out of despair, and took himself off to seek his fortune with the herring fleets in Cornwall, returning to the smithy only when his father became too frail to continue his work. Within weeks of his return, Miss Lightbody insisted, he and my grandmother were lovers. 'She had done her duty by Frank, producing two healthy babies. Matthew's wife had died giving birth to their son, so a fine-looking woman whom he had lusted after through his youth was temptation enough. The time was ripe. They met on the cliffs and in the woods.' She cackled. 'Collecting botanical specimens, they called it, both having a love of nature.'

'Perhaps it was the truth.'

'Then you're greener and younger than I thought,' she cried. 'What red-blooded man would take a married woman alone into woodland glades other than for dalliance? Child, you have much to learn. And 'tis certain your grandfather did not believe such weak excuses. He came across them when they thought him safe in Exeter on business. He fell on Matthew Fox and such a fight they had, it is still spoke of with awe, having been witnessed by two villagers keeping themselves hidden because they were about the business of poaching Frank's rabbits.' She sighed hugely. 'But I should like to have seen it all myself. I once was took to see the great Mendoza and such a spectacle it was I have never forgot it. The crowds cheering and cursing, two valiant men pounding each other till blood ran free and bones were broke and both staggering from exhaustion. Such bravery. It made the heart swell and the senses tingle.'

'But what happened between Matthew Fox and Grandfather?' I prompted.

'They were too close matched to make either one the victor. It was Harriet throwing herself between them that ended it. She came back here with your grandfather, swearing her innocence still, and Matthew went back to the forge. Frank and Matthew never spoke to each other again. Some years later a tinker's horse brought in for shoeing bolted and trampled him.

Some said that Frank had bought the horse, knowing its evil temper, and bribed the tinker to take it to the forge. But the tinker disappeared and Frank denied all knowledge of him or the horse.'

'And Grandmother?'

''Tis said she was never the same after the fight and Matthew's untimely death. From all accounts, she had been a cheerful girl, if fond of her own way, but the spirit went out of her. She became dreary as a frost-blighted summer flower and brought a decline upon herself. Silly wench.' Miss Lightbody eyed me slyly. 'I should wager you are not made in her mould. You would have more spirit than to die because you were blighted in love, what say you?'

'I have never been in love,' I said, 'so I am not in any position to judge.'

'Oh, hoity-toity. Then tell me what you think of my tale, eh? Do you not think it romantical in the extreme?'

'I think it very sad,' I said. 'I am sorry for Grand-mama if she was not married to the man she loved. And I am sorry for Grandfather for it is clear he was deeply hurt and embittered by the experience.'

'Embittered!' she cackled. 'You would not have said so had you known him at the time I first met him. A roistering rake-hell who set the streets of London alight in the weeks he was there and many a society miss agog to be the second Mrs Kerswell. But I reckon he thought nothing to milk-and-water misses. He was a man who needed standing up to. Which was why I took his fancy and he mine.'

'But he did not marry even you, did he, Miss Lightbody?'

For a moment her face looked crushed, like a wrinkled old walnut, and something other than malice flashed briefly in her eyes.

'No, he did not,' she said with a touch of wistfulness.

'And I do confess I should have wished it.'

'I – I am sorry,' I said. 'I spoke too hastily.'

She waved her hand, taffeta flounces all a-tremble. 'Do not blush, girl. By Satan's fire, you spoke the truth.' She looked mournfully into distances I could not see. 'We were young when we met, in our prime. I think till his wife's treachery he had been faithful enough. Content with the managing of his estates for the benefit of future generations of Kerswells. Many's the lecture I had on his ancestry. He was ever high-nosed because Kerswells had been here long before Norman William.' She tittered. 'I confess to being secretly much impressed. After all, what was I but a bastard out of the Westminster stews? Making my fortune in the way I knew best, by virtue of my beauty and wits—' She broke off, grinning archly. 'Ah, but 'tis he of whom we speak. My own fortunes are not of interest to Kerswell whelps. Where was I? Ah, yes, Frank cuckolded, then bereaved of his faithless wife, so he ups and makes merry elsewhere whenever he pleased.'

'And met you?'

'Indeed so. When he was at home he remained the dutiful country squire, devoted to his children and to the making of money on his estates. Elsewhere, his true nature was let rein. And a hot-headed, lusty rascal he was. Yet there was caution in his soul. His wife's treachery had cut him deeper than he realised. With his son's death, his heir, his daughter's elopement, caution became twisted into something very different. Like separate elements being brought together and tempered to hard, cutting, killing steel. Aye, I saw the difference when he sent for me. And I came posthaste, unthinking, glad only that now we would be together. Perhaps, in my foolishness, I thought we might even marry, and I respectable, respected at last . . .' Her voice died. In a shuddering movement she drew her shawl about her in a flurry of moulting fringes. 'He was past caring what people thought. He set me up in this house, his fine doxy, his pretty trollop, to scandalise his neighbours. He would not marry again, he said, nor breed children, for there was no thanks in any of it; only sorrow and ingratitude. He cared only that he should please himself.'

'And . . . and Isaac Fox, Matthew's son?' The clank of chains in the bitter wind, the tainted air, a grieving figure in the swirling snow, *Isaac Fox, an innocent man. Francis Kerswell did this.* 'How did . . . that is, what was his involvement in my Uncle Philip's death?'

'Tchah! What proof had Frank? True, the boat that foundered was young Isaac's and a mere cockleshell that should not have been out on such wild seas. But it is the way of youth to seek excitement and challenge. It was Isaac being saved while Philip was took onto the rocks and dashed to death that festered in Frank's soul. That and the fact that by his own neglect his son had bred a friendship with the Fox whelp. A bad conscience breeds twisted thoughts, betimes.'

'But I thought Grandfather doted on Philip.'

'He did, but he was away much and the tutors that came and went could not oversee a high-spirited lad for every minute of the day. He and Isaac Fox were of an age and for ever up to mischief. Had Frank been here . . . well, the tale might not have had a tragic end. But there 'tis.'

'And Grandfather was revenged on him in the end,' I said, without thinking. 'And so cruelly.'

Her eyes sharpened. 'What do you know of that, eh?'

'The . . . the gibbet. We passed it. Someone had put a notice there, telling who it was and that Grandfather was responsible.'

'Had they indeed? Well, Isaac Fox had friends . . .

and a son, though I had not heard he was returned from his travels.' She was suddenly bored, pushing aside her empty plate, gathering her skirts.

'But why was he hanged?' I said quickly, for it seemed important that I should know.

She shrugged. 'An exciseman was battered to death and Isaac caught close by with blood on him. Hanged for murder, he was, though he swore he'd only stopped to try to aid the man.' She forestalled my next question with an impatient look as she rose from her seat. 'There are many about here who make a comfortable living from the business of fetching French brandy and tobacco across the Channel.'

'A smuggler!'

'There'd be few houses that don't benefit along this coast, if 'tis only a cask to keep their mouths shut. The good villagers of Starcombe are no exception.'

'But why should Grandfather be implicated in his death?'

'Mercy me, why should I know or care?' She began to totter from the room, her heels clicking unsteadily on the boards. 'Perhaps he planted the evidence or told the militia where to look . . . Then there is James Pascoe, Frank's friend, who is the magistrate who sent the villain to the assizes. Perhaps there was some friendly collusion. Whatever the means of it, Isaac Fox is getting his just deserts in heaven or hell. And if Frank it was who was the means of despatching him there, the book is closed. 'Tis all at an end and the final debt paid. The Foxes will trouble the Kerswells no more, and vicee versee. And a pox on all scheming men, I say.'

The clicking of her heels died away, but I sat staring down at my plate. Within the faded flower-patterned rim I seemed to see the dark, grieving face of Nicholas Fox.

58

'Frank Kerswell shall pay for this. I shall be back and take my vengeance.'

If Miss Lightbody supposed it was all at an end, I did not. I felt in my heart that my grandfather had still to reckon with Isaac Fox's son.

I saw Grandfather once in the following days. I was summoned to his study where he questioned me closely about the circumstances of Ben's accident and his progress since. The interview was conducted coldly and at the finish Ben must be fetched to be scrutinised closely before we were dismissed.

Beyond that, we were left to our own devices as if he were not in the house. No more messages came via Mrs Beer and when we met Miss Lightbody at mealtimes, all she could tell us was that Grandfather was up to something.

'Oh, come,' I said, ever hopeful, 'it is surely that he is unaccustomed to having us here. When he settles to the notion he will be sociable with us, I am sure.'

'I should not bank on it,' she said darkly. 'There's been too much tooing and froing. Harry Beer sent off with messages hither and yon. And Frank himself disappearing for hours on end. Aye, he's planning something, I'd wager on it.'

Her look made me uneasy, but I tried to believe that whatever it was would be for our benefit. Our fortunes were improved for the better already. If he needed time to adjust to the idea of grandchildren, that was understandable. Meanwhile we would accept the shelter we had found at Falconwood with gratitude and relief. In due time Grandfather would reconcile himself to our presence.

The days slipped by. When it was fine we went for rambles along the cliffs, sometimes accompanied by one or other of the dogs who seemed to have taken to

Ben, bounding to greet him, feathery tails swishing. Ben was delighted. He saved titbits for them and spent hours grooming them with an old brush while they rewarded him with blissful looks and great wet licks. The two horses, now that they were back in the stable, must also be visited daily and petted and the stable cats coaxed twining and yowling from their secret corners. Mrs Beer's husband, Harry, who seemed to act as groom, handyman and valet to Grandfather and had returned with him from Kingsbridge, regarded us dourly from whatever task he was about. He was, though, more communicative than his wife. It was from him I discovered the names of the headlands we could glimpse on our walks. The bold ridged dragon's back of Start Point to the east, Prawle Point and Bolt Head to the west, and that the pair of grey hawks that we glimpsed swooping and gliding at the cliff's edge above the cove were peregrine falcons. The falcons of Falconwood. I looked out for them with particular pleasure after that, in the romantic belief that perhaps the ancestors of these same birds had once spurred some distant forebear of mine to name his house for them.

It was from Harry Beer, too, that I learned that Grandfather owned all the land and the farms hereabouts and had an interest in shipping, in partnership with a Mr Aggett of Kingsbridge. On the rare occasions when he had to visit Kingsbridge on necessary business with his lawyer or Mr Aggett, he would dine, before returning home, with an old friend, Mr James Pascoe, who lived on the outskirts of the little market town.

'But master, 'ee don't like stayin' away from 'ome, no more do I,' Harry said tetchily. 'An' now, miss, I must get on – and young master, go careful round Sultan there. 'Ee's not to be trusted.'

But Sultan was docile as a lamb with Ben; it was only if I ventured to stroke the velvety nose that his eye rolled menacingly.

It was strange, this instinct that Ben had developed for animals. Before his accident he had merely had a boy's admiration in a showy horse to be seen on the streets or a passing desire to own a dog. Now he displayed a fearless trust that dogs, cats and horses alike seemed to sense and return. They were gentle and affectionate with him as though they recognised and understood that here was someone who had no conception of malice or cruelty.

Once we went down to the village, past the tiny church on the hilltop, where the bones of the Kerswells lay in neglected tombs in the overgrown churchyard, to the huddle of cottages clinging to the fringes of the sea at the foot of the deep grassy cleft that was Starcombe. The few people that were about answered courteously enough when I smiled and bade them good morning, but I felt how they watched and whispered as we went on. A few young children followed us to the stone quay but they were too shy to speak. The fishermen mending their nets, who had been laughing and chaffing, fell silent at our approach. I felt that the villagers knew all about us and what they knew was not to our advantage. I was glad when we retraced our steps up the steep hillside.

I was content to let time drift. As the days passed I began to feel lighthearted, almost a child again. Once, in an excess of high spirits, I flung wide my arms and danced on the high and lonely hilltop, much to Ben's astonishment. Then he laughed and joined in clumsily. We pirouetted and bowed and made up steps with only the wheeling gulls to watch. We danced to the rush of the wind and the pounding of the sea and no orchestra ever provided sweeter music.

After we collapsed, exhausted, on a boulder that thrust from the rabbit-cropped turf, I cried, 'We shall be so happy here, Ben. How could we be otherwise in this beautiful place? Grandfather will grow to love us and you will become quite well again!'

'I like it here, Jo,' Ben said happily. 'I like Jupiter and Rex and Sultan – and shall we give the cats names, too?'

'Of course we shall,' I said.

We walked back to Falconwood in solemn discussion as to the merits of Mouser or Tiger, Tabby or Punch, names I privately thought none of the vagrants in the stable yard would ever acknowledge. But I was delighted that Ben was able to take such interest. I had not seen him so animated since the runaway cartwheel had ended his youth and mine.

It was a symbol, I felt, of the direction our life would take here, and who could blame me for feeling so? We had been prisoners of an unhappy fate for too long. I needed hope now and the prospect of release from the guilt that had been my constant companion.

So when I saw the stranger riding towards the house, I had no foreboding. Merely a curiosity as to Grandfather's visitor. We arrived in the stable yard as he was dismounting. He glanced at us and put a question to Harry Beer, who mumbled something before leading the horse away. The man removed his high hat and bowed.

I smiled and Ben stopped, nervous as always in the presence of strangers.

The man – he was, I guessed, something over thirty and dressed in neat but shabby black – bid us a pleasant 'Good afternoon' and regarded Ben with some interest. 'So this is Benjamin.' When I nodded, surprised, he went on, 'Mr Kerswell's description was most accurate. A fine-looking young fellow. I am Clive Chadwick, d'you see.'

'I am sorry, but—'

'The tutor Mr Kerswell has engaged for his grandson.'

'Tutor?' I was taken aback.

'Do you look after the lad? A governess, perhaps? A nurse? Mr Kerswell did not mention any such person, but naturally in the unfortunate circumstances there must be someone of that sort . . .'

'I am Mr Kerswell's granddaughter,' I said. 'Ben is my brother.'

Astonishment warred with embarrassment on his undistinguished features. 'I pray your forgiveness. I have spoken out of turn. Mr Kerswell did not mention—'

'Do not distress yourself, Mr Chadwick,' I said. 'It was a natural enough mistake. I must look sorely muddied and windswept after our walk.'

The flush on his cheeks deepened as he took in with a quick sweeping glance, hurriedly removed to some safe spot above my head, my cracked boots, darned gloves and antiquated bonnet. But he swept off his hat once more and said, gallantly, 'Indeed the wind is blustery today, Miss Kerswell.'

'Howarth,' I corrected gently. 'My name is Joanna Howarth. We are the surviving children of Mr Kerswell's daughter.'

Confusion again overtook him. 'I was sure Mr Kerswell . . . that is, I think the name he mentioned . . . dear, dear, such a dreadful mistake.'

'Let us begin again, Mr Chadwick.' I held out my hand. 'How do you do. I am most interested to learn that my grandfather has engaged a tutor for my brother.'

He took my hand gratefully. 'I am delighted to make your acquaintance, Miss Howarth.'

As we walked to the house he informed me that this was merely a preliminary visit and he was expecting to take up his appointment the following week. 'I am indeed pleased to see how solid and gracious the house is and how agreeably situated,' he said. 'Where I have been these last two years – at Sir Henry Mallingham's – the hall is set in a hollow that gathers a great deal of mist and damp. And though the parkland is very fine, I have a taste for wider, more natural scenery. I feel I shall be most at home here. Most at home.'

'I trust so,' I said politely. 'Was your previous engagement with young children?'

'Quite young. I have become known, you see, for my work with, er, more difficult pupils. I expect that is how I came to Mr Kerswell's notice.'

'By difficult do you mean backward?' I asked, frankly.

He glanced at me and then at Ben ambling at my side.

'Sir Henry's Oliver was not exactly backward,' he said carefully. 'But then he was not the brightest of boys. Still, I brought him on favourably. He is able to go away to school now and if he applies himself he will not disgrace himself. Not at all.'

'As you see, my brother is no longer a child. He is almost nineteen. But before his accident he was bright and intelligent. I should like to think that someday he will be as he was.'

'Of course you do,' he said. 'Though I could not make promises upon that point, you may trust me, Miss Howarth, to do my very best to encourage every aspect of his higher nature. I find the prospect a challenge. I do indeed.'

'He has a gentle disposition,' I said. 'He will never respond to a heavy hand.'

'My touch will be of the lightest. I have never believed that even the cleverest intellect could prosper to its fullest under a harsh regime.' His smile was warm. 'Those of lesser brilliance must be allowed to proceed at a rate which suits them best and with constant stimulation of their often wayward attention. This is not a mere theory, let me assure you. I have put it to the test and proved its worth.'

I felt reassured. The idea of some strict authoritarian figure bearing down on Ben was repellent. But a person such as Mr Chadwick professed to be – and his kind and courteous manner confirmed his words – might be just the one to restore Ben fully. He had knowledge and experience whereas my own efforts, though well meant and loving, were necessarily amateurish. If I had brought Ben so far, what might not Mr Chadwick achieve?

I was elated as I showed Mr Chadwick into the house. Grandfather had been making plans as Miss Lightbody suspected, but they were purely to our advantage. I was touched by the evidence that behind Grandfather's stern and remote manner he did care for us after all.

Mr Chadwick's visit lasted over two hours. For most of that time he was closeted with Grandfather in his study, but before he left Mrs Beer, surly as ever, brought him to where Ben and I sat in the small parlour. I had discovered that the afternoon sun made the room pleasant, even though Mrs Beer was still refusing to speak to Grandfather about having the chimney swept and a fire laid.

I was patching a shirt of Ben's. Ben was looking at a book of fables which he much loved. He was chuckling over the pictures of the animals but when Mr Chadwick came in, he put the book down and moved to sit by my side on the sofa.

Mr Chadwick ignored Ben, picked up the book and seated himself.

'Why, how splendid,' he said. 'I do so like these little tales. The hare and the tortoise is very droll.' And in his light, pleasant voice he began to read. Ben kept his eyes down at first but after a while, as Mr Chadwick read the familiar story, he smiled and looked up.

When he finished, I said, 'Do please read my favourite, Mr Chadwick. The fox and the grapes.'

Mr Chadwick turned the pages. 'I do not seem able to find it,' he began, 'perhaps you could . . .'

'I will show you,' Ben said, rising eagerly. He took the book, found the page, pointed out the woodcut that headed the tale, then quite unselfconsciously drew a chair next to Mr Chadwick and prepared to listen.

It was admirably done. My estimation of Mr Chadwick rose as, the acquaintance established, he carefully drew Ben out, teased him a little, made a small joke so that he laughed.

I watched them together as I sewed. I had not seen Ben so easy with anyone for a long time, though it was true that most people either ignored him completely or frightened him with loud hearty voices. But Mr Chadwick hit exactly the right note.

Presently he said, 'Well, Ben, I must leave you now but I should very much like to return and bring you some more books to look at. Should you like that?'

'Will there be pictures of dogs and horses?'

'Most certainly. And I have some puzzles and games that you may find pleasing.'

'Then I shall like that very well,' Ben said.

Mr Chadwick rose. 'Will you shake my hand, Ben?'

After a moment's frowning thought, Ben slowly took the proffered hand, then shook it heartily and beamed. It was almost as though some far off memory of such an action had been triggered. So much, I thought, blinking against the sudden sting of grateful tears, was locked in his mind waiting for the right word, the right time to be released. And Mr Chadwick might well be the one to do it.

'Until Monday, then, Miss Howarth,' he said.

'I look forward to it,' I said warmly.

'And I, Miss Howarth,' he said. 'We shall do very well, I think. Very well indeed.'

The room next to Ben's was prepared for Mr Chadwick. The old schoolroom at the back of the house was also set upon by Bessy and scoured vigorously. I noted that in all this time no one had set foot inside my room, though Ben's was attended to daily. When I asked Mrs Beer about it she pursed her lips and said, 'When master says so, it'll be done. But master 'ee 'adden said nothin'.'

'Have you asked him?'

''Tedden my place. 'Tes never been opened, that chamber, till 'ee come.'

'But Miss Lightbody said—'

'That's as mebbe. 'Tedden right is all I knows.'

And nothing more could I get from her. Not that I worried unduly. I quite enjoyed putting the room in order. It was sadly in need of a thorough spring-clean and new hangings at the window and the bed, but I took pleasure in sorting out my mother's clothes and trinkets and bringing a gloss to the furniture. I took the rugs into the garden and beat them soundly, creating a choking fog in the process, and brought primroses and violets in from sheltered places under the hedges to set in bowls on the windowledge. I had never known spring flowers so early but the soft damp air must be particularly favourable here. Indeed, there was already a feeling of spring, though it was only early February. In the north we should have still been locked in winter. Here buds fattened, birds squabbled over territory, magpies gathered twigs to add to last year's great untidy nest in a thicket beyond the stables.

I would have thanked Grandfather for engaging Mr Chadwick had the opportunity arose, but he still avoided us, spending long hours locked in his study or riding out on Sultan. On the occasions when we did meet, he barely acknowledged me, his curt greetings were for Ben alone. I might not have existed. I did not know whether to be vexed or amused. Time, I thought, would bring us closer and I should do all in my power to please him when he unbent enough for me to discover his likes and dislikes.

Mr Chadwick arrived. He did not seem to have many belongings beyond boxes of books, but he brought something far more valuable. A lively mind and pleasant wit. Mealtimes became cheerful occasions. Having been reliant upon Miss Lightbody's scurrilous and meandering tales as a form of entertainment, it was gratifying to be able to take part in discussion on all manner of interesting subjects. He reminded me in some ways of Papa. Yet he was less dreamy, less studious, more interested in putting his theories on education to the test rather than writing learned tomes on the subject. I looked forward to the long quiet evenings which were now enlightened by Mr Chadwick's presence, though Miss Lightbody scowled and sulked. 'Such dull talk. Who cares to hear of dry-as-dust books and the goings-on in Parliament?' I think she was put out because she was not the centre of attention, though she did her best to make herself so. She appeared at each meal in a different garb, each more weird and ornate than the last. Her face bore a layer of thick white powder. She was patched and rouged and incredibly grotesque.

Mr Chadwick treated her with grave courtesy and not by the flicker of an eyelid did he display astonishment. I think he saw her as an elderly wayward child who might be won over with patience and kindness. From the gleam in Miss Lightbody's eye I did not envisage such an easy victory. I suspected that, as with the feud with Mrs Beer, Miss Lightbody would get much sly enjoyment from pitting her wits against Mr Chadwick.

The third morning after Mr Chadwick's arrival began like any other of the new routine. Ben and Mr Chadwick were closeted in the schoolroom, Miss Lightbody in her mysterious chamber on the upper floor. The house was very quiet. I had been picking over my mother's wardrobe wondering if I might adapt some of the gowns to my own use, when Bessy and Mrs Beer appeared together at the door.

'Master wants you,' Mrs Beer announced. 'In his study.' There was something about her voice that made me look at her sharply. Was it suppressed excitement? Triumph? No way of knowing, for her face was as puddingy as ever.

'I shall be down in a few moments,' I said.

'You'm to go now. This minute. Partic'lar, he was.'

Behind her, Bessy fidgeted and blinked at me through her straggly locks of hair. She held her hand over her mouth as though she did not want me to see that she smiled, though I could tell that she did.

'Something of urgency, then?' I said. I did not know why I delayed. Why with slow, casual movements I returned the dresses to the press. But some inner sense suddenly made me alert.

''Tedden anything I knows of.'

'Very well.' I waited for her to go, but she stood there, her arms folded over her bosom. 'Thank you, Mrs Beer,' I said stiffly.

I went to the door. She stepped back to let me pass and then quickly moved into the room as I left it, Bessy scuttering after her.

'So you are to clean my room?' I said, pleased.

'Just you leave it to us, Miss Howarth.' There was still something I did not understand in her tone. Was

69

it the slight, mocking emphasis on my name? I had a foolish urge to pull her away from the room and order her to the kitchen, but it was not my place to do so and Grandfather was waiting.

I hurried off, pausing at the head of the stairs to look back. Bessy, watching me go from round the doorpost, suddenly jerked as though her mother had pulled her away.

The dogs rose to greet me as I tapped at the door and went into the study. For once Grandfather did not call them off. He was sitting in his big leather armchair by the fire. Without speaking he pointed to the chair that faced him across the hearth. I sat down.

I tried not to fidget as I prepared in my head the little speech of thanks I would make for his kindness in giving us shelter and engaging a tutor for Ben. I thought I might mention the matter of chimney sweeping and fires in the cold rooms and if it was permissible to make use of Mama's old clothes. I should also wish to ask if there were any way I could be useful to him. I had been accustomed to help Mama about the house and kitchen and I would willingly turn such skills as I had to ease the burden on Mrs Beer.

Grandfather fixed me with his flinty stare. Then, with slow, deliberate movements, drew a watch from his waistcoat pocket.

'The time is five and twenty minutes before ten o'clock,' he said. 'When the hands reach the hour you will leave this house.' With the same slow care he placed the watch on the table at his side. 'You will be taken to a place where you may pick up the Exeter coach. In Exeter you will go to the address written on this note.' He indicated a long paper which lay folded and sealed beside the watch. 'It is the home of two ladies who are in need of a young companion. I have accepted this position on your behalf. You will take up your duties there today and fulfil them to the best of your ability.'

The conciliatory words I had meant to speak died stillborn.

'You will,' he continued, 'be obedient, willing and docile at all times. If you are not and if your behaviour proves untrustworthy or headstrong in any way I shall be straightway informed. You will then forfeit the right to see your brother until such time as your conduct improves.' He paused, head lowered, cold unblinking eyes never leaving my face. 'If, by your demeanour and general worthiness, I consider it suitable, I shall allow your brother, accompanied by his tutor, to visit you at a time convenient to myself and the Misses Polsham into whose charitable care you are now to be placed. I shall only permit these visits if my grandson, Benjamin, is not distressed or set back by any hysterical or injudicious action on your part.'

Again that weighty silence fell. I was too stunned to break it as my shocked mind strove to understand.

'I have decided that Benjamin's place will, from now on, be here with me at Falconwood.'

I found voice enough to whisper, 'And mine?'

He gave a short, dry laugh. 'Think yourself lucky that I have let you stay so long.'

'But . . . but you cannot be so cruel!'

'Did you not bring the boy here in order to place him under my guardianship?'

'But to part us . . . Ben needs me!'

'Does he? You have money, then, to pay for the doctors to be consulted, his schooling?'

'Money does not buy love and devotion,' I cried.

'You forced your way into my house.' His voice was harsh. 'You begged for my charity. Well, now you have it. Your brother will have the best that money can buy.

71

You are of an age to earn your keep, so I have made arrangements accordingly.'

More than ever he reminded me of a great bird of prey, wings darkening the body of its victim. There was no pity in his face, no feeling, only the implacable weight of his will.

'The women of this family have proved a treacherous breed. I have no reason to expect from you anything but deceit and mischief-making. I want no more of it here at Falconwood to curse my old age or poison Benjamin's young mind.'

'So I am to be punished for what has happened in the past?'

He tapped his watch with a horny fingernail. 'Time runs on. Mrs Beer will have packed for you by now. I wish you to remove yourself quietly from this house.'

I was doubly shocked as I grasped his meaning. 'I . . . I am not even to say goodbye to Ben?'

'For his sake I have let you stay until he was settled. For his sake the break will be clean and quick.' A thin smile touched his mouth. 'Mr Chadwick will soon replace you in his affections, my dear. In no time at all he will be cut free from the abominable influences of his past.'

I had an odd feeling, then, as though his words, the tone of the interview, were prompting me towards a course of action he had envisaged from the beginning.

There was a leaden weight in my breast that I must ignore. I must think, think. There was danger here. It was almost as if something in the very air cried out a warning. The fancy came, fleeting, tenuous, that the shades of the women my grandfather spoke so harshly of – my grandmother Harriet, my mother – stood at my back willing me to take care.

I searched his face, seeking some clue. The smile that twisted his mouth was born of contempt and a deep, fixed bitterness. No tears of mine would ever touch him, nor my anger.

I saw it. Sharp and clear. The thought leaped into my mind forcing a calm path in the welter of my emotions. That was what he wanted. Tears, rage, hysterics. Anything that would give him an excuse to part me for ever from Ben.

Grandfather hated me. He hated me because I was a woman, because I was my mother's daughter. Ben he would cherish because he was reminded of the beloved son he had lost prematurely. I had no part whatsoever in his schemes. I was a nuisance he must dispose of as cheaply as possible and if I made a fuss he would turn me off without a qualm and never let me see Ben again.

It would please him indeed if I danced to his tune, if I made it easy for him to dispose of my 'abominable influence'. But what must I do?

Fight. But how? What weapons had I? My mind ticked over clear and sharp. He had imposed conditions upon me. I must accept them. Penniless as I was, I had no other choice. But as to the future, who knew what that offered? I had to hold to the hope, with dignity and composure, that someday I should be reunited with Ben.

Quelling the turbulence of my spirits, I said, meekly, 'Very well. I shall do as you have arranged. I shall go to Exeter.'

I watched him closely as I spoke. The glint of surprise in his eyes made me thankful that I had heeded the warning of my instincts – or that of the shades that slipped away now, beyond my consciousness, their work done. I had taken the right course. But I would not go without showing some spark of courage.

'I have two small requests to make of you, sir.'

'I scarcely think you are in a position to make

requests. Obedience is all that is needed.'

'They are simple, sir. Easily granted.'

'Well?'

'I should like to be kept informed of Ben's progress. If Mr Chadwick could write—'

'Out of the question. I will not be paying him to write reports,' he growled. 'Nor are you to pester him with letters. Do you hear?'

He meant to turn the knife indeed. I did not shift my gaze from his nor betray by the flicker of an eyelid how keenly the blade bit.

'And the second request?'

'That I may make my farewells to Ben in person.'

'I have said—'

'You have said that the females of this house are schooled in deceit, but *I* do not wish to slip away in an underhand and deceitful manner as though I had something to hide, which I have not. But perhaps you, sir,' I said deliberately, 'are ashamed by your *arrangements* so as to want me to sneak off without witnesses.'

Anger flared scarlet in his cheeks. My nails felt as though they might draw blood from my palms, but I pressed on.

'I am not given to hysterics. More than anything I love Ben and wish only for his happiness. I should not like to leave him grieving, as I assure you will happen if I just disappeared as though the east wind had carried me off. Remember, sir, you scarcely know your grandson. Credit me at least with that knowledge.' My voice teetered on the edge of distress. I paused, then went on, barely above a whisper, 'I shall make our parting as painless as possible and leave him in good spirits.'

I was willing his permission. How could I go without saying goodbye to Ben? Despair took the last shreds of pride.

'Please, Grandfather,' I begged, 'allow me this one small concession. I give you my word that I shall not upset Ben in any way.'

For a moment I thought all was lost. Then, impatiently, he clenched his fist and thumped the table.

'Five minutes only,' he barked. 'Not one moment longer. And if there is the merest hint of upset I shall personally remove you.'

I flew from the room before he could change his mind. It was a small victory against the greater loss. I kept it close for courage as I raced up the stairs to the schoolroom.

Ben, I think, barely understood. He took my reassurances in bewilderment, looking from me to Mr Chadwick as I told him that from now on his tutor would be his friend and guide in my place. I said that I must go away for a little while – a lie, but how could I say other? – and that he should visit me soon.

Mr Chadwick, who had been told of my departure but an hour since, shook my hand and said in a troubled voice, 'I did not think Mr Kerswell meant – that is, I am sorry, Miss Howarth, that you are to leave, but you may rely on me. I shall care for your brother as if he were my own.'

'I know you will, Mr Chadwick,' I said, my throat tight with tears. I could not help but say that Grandfather had forbidden him to write to me but if there was any chance, any chance at all, I should so much like to hear how Ben progressed.

'But of course,' he whispered back, patting my hand.

'I do not wish you to find yourself in any trouble with my grandfather . . .'

'Trust me to be discreet. My mother lives in Exeter. We may manage some communication through her.'

'I cannot thank you enough.'

The expression in his kind brown eyes almost overturned my shaky composure. My face felt as if it had been starched with the effort of maintaining control.

'I shall endeavour to keep your memory fresh in your brother's mind,' he said earnestly. 'You will not be forgotten, even if communication is difficult.'

Time was running out.

I gave Ben, my dear brother, a swift hug, kissed his cheek and fled.

Mrs Beer and Bessy, looking well pleased, stood outside the closed door of my bedroom, my bags at their feet. With a smirk, Mrs Beer turned the key in the lock.

''Tes to be shut up again,' she said. 'Master's orders.'

So my mother's room, briefly brought to life, was now closed away again, left once more to the spiders and the dust. All traces of my short occupancy would soon be gone.

Bessy handed me my cloak and bonnet. My hands shook as I put them on. I picked up the bags and walked to the top of the stairs. I heard a cackle of laughter as I descended. Miss Lightbody, shrouded in cascading plumes and ragged lace, leaned over the banisters. 'I told you so, you foolish child. I told you he was plotting and you would not heed.'

I could not answer. I shook my head in despair.

'No matter,' she cried. 'No matter. 'Tis not for you, this place. You'd not be happy here. Frank would not allow it. Better off with the old maids in town. Better by far, you see.'

She meant to offer comfort perhaps, but I was beyond comforting.

I was well away from the house, jogging along on the back of the spare horse, Harry Beer ahead on Sultan, when I allowed myself to think of all that I had now lost. Mama, Papa, my sisters and now my gentle brother.

We came to the place where the gibbet swung its noisome, foul cage in the sea wind and I remembered the young man abandoning himself to grief in the snow. Now the bare turf bore no crude evergreen wreath. Nobody mourned for Isaac Fox today.

Nobody mourned for me, either, and I felt as dead and abandoned as the fleshless bones that rattled against the metal chains that bound them.

I breathed a silent prayer as we passed, then fixed my glance on Harry Beer's uncaring back.

Of the jolting miles to the turnpike I remember nothing. My eyes were blinded by the soft, cold rain that mingled with the tears that would no longer be denied.

Chapter Three

All I clearly remember of those first weeks at Torre Crescent was the cold; of being chilled to the marrow of my bones. Though there was physical misery enough in that stern house and chilblains blossomed in itchy, painful welts on my fingers and toes, this was more an inner chill, a deadly exhaustion of the spirit that seemed to isolate me from my surroundings. I listened, I moved, I spoke, I ate, but it was as though I functioned with the stiff, unthinking acceptance of a clockwork creature and the real person, the warm, human, living spirit was locked in ice and unable to break free.

I could not even feel despair. Or perhaps it was that I did not dare to for fear that I might break entirely under its weight. I had nothing left to me. I had lost everybody I loved and the grief was beyond enduring. So I locked it away, along with my tears, in my ice-bound heart and turned a dull obedient face to the world.

The Misses Fanny and Olga Polsham, daughters of the late Mr Nathaniel Polsham, Elder of the chapel of the Strict Followers of the Gospel of God, a minor and now defunct religious sect, had been born and lived out their genteel lives at 6 Torre Crescent, a severe red-brick iron-railed house constantly invaded by the clangour of bells within and without. The cathedral tower could be glimpsed over the nearby

79

rooftops, the small pink-stoned chapel of St Perran crowded the end of the close, and there were other churches round about, each marking the passing hours with close or distant boomings from ancient spires and towers; summoning the faithful to worship with joyous paeons, tolling sonorously for the dead, accompanying solemn processions to the assize courts or announcing cheerfully the arrival of some visiting dignitary. The demanding tongue of Miss Polsham's handbell was a continuous, intrusive counterpoint.

The sisters were above sixty, the elder Miss Polsham being an invalid with an obscure complaint which revealed itself in vague and profuse symptoms – aches, weakness, megrims, palpitations – and to which Miss Olga referred reverently as 'My Sister's Trouble'. Yet Miss Polsham, the invalid, was as pink and pigeon-plump as her sister was thin and grey and faded, though that was perhaps hardly surprising for Miss Polsham ate better than anyone in the house. It was she for whom the sugared almonds which she claimed aided her jaded appetite were fetched by Miss Olga each week. It was she who must have the best of any dish served up by the old crone who ruled the kitchen. The breast of chicken, the fruit jellies, the egg custards. Miss Olga and I must survive on a far more frugal regime.

Neither lady seemed to notice that the food we ate was generally boiled, baked or stewed to ruin by the cook, Mrs Caunter, an ancient grey-whiskered woman, a survivor from the late Mr Polsham's time, who lived in a dark room off the basement kitchen and terrorised the one maid with fearful bellowings that could be heard in the parlour. Neither Miss Polsham nor Miss Olga ever professed to notice anything on these occasions and continued whatever they were doing – crocheting, napping, reading aloud – to a background accompaniment of roarings from Mrs Caunter and snivellings from the maid. Perhaps they had become so used to it over the years that, like the sound of the church bells, they did not hear it any more.

At any other time I would have found it distressing in the extreme, especially on the day I came across the maid on the stairs as I was on my way to Miss Polsham's room to fetch her a different shawl. (It was never the right one – this one too warm, that one too heavy, the other too thin; some days she changed her mind with such frequency that I near wore a path with my feet in the stair carpet.) There had been a more than usual prolonged bout of basement bellowing and the maid, a fair-haired wisp of a girl, was weeping noisily into the linen cupboard on the landing as she returned freshly ironed sheets to the shelves.

"'T'weren't my fault that I dropped the dish, miss,' she sobbed. 'She never said 'twere that hot I'd burn my fingers when she passed it to me.' She held up her hand so I could see the pink, blistered skin. 'Did it a-purpose, miss, 'er did. 'Er's always up to they sly tricks, then puttin' the blame on me. 'Taters and gravy all over the floor and me to clean it up – and 'aving to pay for the broken chiney. 'Tes wicked and cruel an' I shan't stand it much longer. Mark me, miss, I'm for off when I can get another place.' She mopped her tears on her apron and added darkly, 'I was warned 'afore I came about this house. Can't get a maid to stay long, nohow. Allus choppin' and changin'. Allus will be as long as that old besom lives.' Then, perhaps aware she'd said too much, she eyed me worriedly. 'You won't say nothing, miss, will 'ee? 'Bout what I just sez. Not to the ladies. Else they'll be putting me off without a character.'

Had I been my normal thinking self, I should have been indignant on the girl's behalf and stirred myself to try and help, to intercede with the dreadful old cook, or at least bring the girl's plight to the notice of my employers. But it was a measure of my new state of mind, the dull, emotionless pit into which I was sunk, that I did not care. I merely assured her of my silence and proceeded upstairs, my conscience undented, my heart unmoved.

I performed all my duties in the same careful, lifeless way. I rose, shivering, at six. The only fires permitted in the house were in the kitchen, the parlour – but only half an hour before Miss Polsham came downstairs – and Miss Polsham's bedroom. I washed in cold water because Miss Olga considered that young persons benefited from its bracing qualities, and in the early weeks in the dark, for my candle must last the fortnight. By six-thirty I must present myself in the fireless dining parlour along with the maid and Mrs Caunter. Here Miss Olga took morning prayers standing at the lectern that had been her father's and looking very much like the small painting of him, thin-lipped and austere, that hung above the mantel. Miss Olga read a passage from the Bible or a portion of one of her late papa's sermons from one of the bound volumes that stood in rows behind glass doors, the only books resident in the house beside the Bible. Prayers were long, Miss Olga being much given to extemporaneous harangues with her Maker over any general and particular wickedness that might have caught her attention.

Mrs Caunter interspersed these offerings with loud, wheezy 'Amens'. I kept silent, head bowed, as Miss Olga's voice droned on, my thoughts only on the agony of not being able to scratch my chilblains in Miss Olga's presence and with the hope that my empty stomach would not grumble too loudly. I had already suffered the embarrassment of being prayed over for allowing the disgrace of both these unseemly actions to mar this reverent time.

Released from prayer, Mrs Caunter and the maid went back to their basement and presently Miss Olga and I, seated silently at the table, waited for breakfast to be served, after which my daily duties began – attending to the physical wellbeing of the invalid and helping Miss Olga in any household tasks she considered unsuitable for the maid or too onerous for herself.

'A heavy breakfast, indeed any sort of over-rich meal,' Miss Olga had informed me on my first day, 'is a burden to the digestion and causes an unfortunate sluggishness in the intellect. My dear late papa upheld the principle of a light, plain diet as being highly beneficial to the whole system. I have proof of this in my own unfailing good health and alertness of mind. You will feel the benefit yourself, Joanna, in good time.' She eyed me up and down, her lips a tight line. 'I expect you have been grossly overindulged in the past or you should not have grown to such an ungainly height. Still, a low, sensible diet may yet prevent any further growth.'

Breakfast was scarcely worth the fervent grace Miss Olga read over it. Nor any other meal. I sometimes feared that the food I ate was barely enough to keep me alive, let alone growing. Not that I cared. Perhaps I should fade away altogether, I thought dramatically, and die and be glad of it.

Breakfast consisted of a bowl of thin milkless porridge and a dish of weak tea, the leaves sometimes of the third or fourth brewing. Dinner was taken at twelve – vegetables boiled pale and watery, a small portion of gristly stew, or a wing of a fowl that had probably expired of old age, or a minute fillet of fish followed by a sliver of cheese and a biscuit. At supper a glass of buttermilk accompanied the slice of bread and hog's pudding, with the added indulgence of a careful paring from the apple pie that would reappear for at least three more evenings, or a meagre dish of tapioca pudding.

I was permanently hungry and perpetually tired. From the time I arranged Miss Polsham's breakfast tray – a coddled egg, hot toast, butter and strawberry jam, a pot of coffee kept hot over a spirit stove – to the time I helped her to bed, I was scarcely allowed to sit down except to read to her or to engage in some urgent household mending.

The sameness of the days added to my sense of living in a cloudy limbo world. Whatever the short-comings and eccentricities of my upbringing, there had always been excitements pressing upon us, new vistas unfolding. Papa's precarious financial ventures might bring sorrow as much as joy, but there was ever an air of optimism and cheer about him so that we gladly followed where he led. Mama's brisk, sharp spirit kept us all attentive and eager for what the future might hold. There might be arguments, escapades, even dreadful disasters such as Ben had suffered, but each brought its own particular challenge, a sense of purpose.

Now there was nothing. The ladies lived quiet, reg-ular, dull lives and I with them. I did not go out of doors but I did not regard the house as the prison it was. The ice had such a hold on me that I was not even mildly curious as to what lay over the doorstep. Miss Olga, now that there was someone at hand to relieve her of the burden of her invalid sister, would depart on little errands – sewing silks to be matched at the haberdashers in the High Street, bargains to be sought in the market – or remove herself into the garden where she seemed to spend many hours potter-ing with a trowel and trug basket. I endured within and did not even notice that frosty winter had been replaced by a mild, blustery spring.

Miss Polsham did not care for visitors, they brought on her palpitations. Indeed, there was little sign that the sisters had any friends and no relatives were ever mentioned, save for Mr James Pascoe of Kingsbridge, a distant cousin, and his children, an unmarried daughter, Susannah, and a married son, Blandford. So the only visitor was the doctor who called regularly upon the invalid, Miss Polsham. Once the necessary interview had taken place, he was given a careful measure from a bottle of Madeira that Miss Olga kept under lock and key in the parlour sideboard and a slice of the rich fruit cake saved especially for the occasion.

It was Dr Barlow, a bluff, middle-aged man with kindly brown eyes behind small thick eyeglasses, who set in motion the events that were to crack the ice that bound me.

It was late April and the parlour blinds were drawn against the rays of sun that had begun to creep across the rooftops each morning and threaten the carpets with the dire possibility of fading. The doctor sat by the empty hearth in the carved chair tacitly dedicated to the male sex, it having been the chair in which the late Elder Nathaniel had sat to compose his sermons. I do not think that the doctor appreciated the honour, for he was careless with cake crumbs, which had to be meticulously brushed from the upholstery after he left, and was for ever shifting his weight as though in discomfort or picking at the carved armrest with an impatient fingernail so that the wood must later be inspected for scratches.

Miss Polsham, as usual, lay on the day bed swathed in rugs and speaking in the palest of voices only when directly addressed. She wore an expression of patient suffering, an expression particularly in evidence during the doctor's visits and likely to be replaced by one of frowning sharpness when he had gone. Miss Olga and

I perched on small hard chairs ready to wait on the doctor should he be persuaded to eat another slice of cake or drink a further glass of wine.

The atmosphere was heavy with the mixture of unease and deference that the doctor's visits seemed to inspire in the Misses Polsham, as though this booming male presence brought intimidating echoes of a different world into the quiet house.

'Will you not join me, ladies?' Dr Barlow had enquired, as he usually did, when refreshments were pressed upon him.

'Indeed no, doctor,' Miss Olga had replied. 'My sister had her eggnog only moments before you arrived and I do not care for refreshment so close to the dinner hour.'

Her normal answer, usually accepted without question, but today when the doctor was seated, glass in hand, he regarded me over his eyeglasses and said, 'And you, Miss Howarth, will you not indulge?'

'Oh, I think not,' Miss Olga put in with a nervous laugh. 'It would quite spoil her appetite.'

'Really? Is your appetite then so poor, Miss Howarth?' he asked.

'Oh, no . . . that is . . .' I hesitated, aware of a stiffening in Miss Olga's back. 'I do not think I should . . . so late in the morning.'

'Nonsense!' Dr Barlow said gruffly. 'You need flesh on your bones, child. Here, allow me.' He sprang to his feet, cut a generous wedge from the rich cake, placed it on his own plate and pressed it into my hand. 'Eat up, now!' he ordered, jovially. 'Every crumb.'

He did not sit down but stood over me, sipping his wine, unheeding of Miss Olga's gasp of astonishment and the way Miss Polsham's eyebrows rose in surprise.

As my teeth sank into the first delicious mouthful, I almost closed my eyes, wanting to savour the taste, but

I ate as neatly and quickly as I could, not easy in the circumstances with all eyes upon me, and smiled my thanks as the doctor reached forward to take my empty plate.

He beamed at Miss Olga, though there was an edge to his voice as he said, 'It is a pity that Miss Howarth has quite lost the roses in her cheeks since she came to the city. I think perhaps she is too much indoors and I would suggest that a brisk walk in the fresh air at least once a day is indicated.' He hovered over the sisters, paternal, encouraging, dominating. 'And you must take no nonsense, dear ladies, about lack of appetite. Young girls get silly fads and fancies. What Miss Howarth needs is good wholesome food. Let her eat as much bread and butter as she can, and plenty of eggs and fresh creamy milk and butcher's meat will soon have her looking bonny again.' In a coaxing tone, but inviting no disagreement, he went on, 'We would not want to see the child decline into a consumption, would we now? We who are older and wiser must take matters into our own hands for her own good.' He bowed to each lady in turn. 'I will bid you good day, Miss Polsham, Miss Olga. I hope to see you both in favourable health next time I call and I trust Miss Howarth will by then have begun to regain the bloom of youth.'

When I saw him to the door, he murmured with a wry smile, 'The good Elder Nathaniel has much to answer for regarding his esteemed diet, so often urged upon me by Miss Olga. She herself seems to come to no harm through it and Miss Polsham has cleverly managed to avoid submitting to it, but for a young person – most unsuitable.' His eyes were shrewd and kindly. 'The ladies, I believe, are not deliberately heartless. It is merely that they reflect their own upbringing which was strict. Indeed, one might say harsh. I believe that their stepmother, who might have provided a gentler feminine influence to bear on their father, was herself greatly lacking in maternal affection and it is my experience that children raised so hardily often reflect a certain severity of character in adult life. So we must be tolerant and make allowances, yes indeed.' He nodded briskly. 'I have done my best for you, my dear, but you must play your part too. I have some inkling of your history and understand that there has been much suffering in your recent past. If I had an elixir to remove the grief, I would give it to you, but alas there is no such thing and I can only recommend that you look to the future and do not let yourself sink too low in spirits.'

He slammed his old-fashioned bicorn hat on his balding head and marched down the steps, turning as he gained the gate to wag his finger at me and say loudly, 'Fresh air and exercise, remember! That is an order! Good day, Miss Howarth.'

For the rest of the morning Miss Olga was purse-lipped and indignant but at dinner there was a glass of milk, a small crock of butter and half a dry-looking loaf by my plate.

'If you feel the necessity, Joanna,' Miss Olga said, tartly, 'you may help yourself, but do not come crying to me if you suffer from indigestion later. Dr Barlow means well, I daresay, but his ideas are not always of the soundest.' She attacked her piece of bony salted cod as though she wished it were Dr Barlow himself she speared with her fork. 'Why, I clearly remember the summer he insisted that he lend us a bathchair and his man to push it, so that my sister might take the air. It was a disaster! She was shook to bits by the cobbles before she reached the end of the crescent and she was so overcome by the heat and the smell of drains in High Street that she near fainted and had to be brought straight back home. She was in a fever for a week and suffered abominably from pain in her back for months afterwards.' Miss Olga nibbled the impaled flake of fish triumphantly. 'Even Dr Barlow had to admit his little experiment was a failure.'

'He seemed very insistent that I go out,' I said, 'but if you think otherwise . . .' I did not really care either way.

'No, you must do as he says,' she said, quickly and uneasily. 'He can be quite forceful when crossed. Indeed, if it was not that *my* dear papa always thought highly of *his* father, old Dr Barlow, who inherited a modest fortune and was always generous with donations to the chapel, then I would dismiss him and have another physician attend us.' She sighed. 'But there again, that would be upsetting to my sister who cannot stand change of any sort.'

She wore her air of a woman much put upon for the rest of the day, especially when in the late afternoon she ordered me to put on my cloak and told me where to find the shoemaker.

'If you are to have outdoor exercise, I will not have you wandering purposeless about the town. There is a pair of boots I have left for repair. Inspect them carefully for any fault before you accept them and make haste back for I have a mind to have the parlour curtains down and replaced with the summer ones and the girl will need help.'

So ungraciously despatched, I left the house and took my first uncertain steps towards the recovery of my health and determination.

Within a week I was well acquainted with the area round about Torre Crescent, the cathedral and the High Street. Miss Olga despatched me on errands once, sometimes twice a day, rain or shine, and with each journey I began to feel less apprehensive, more daring about taking a different way home.

Exeter, like Chester where I had once lived, still had much of its ancient Roman wall standing. It drew a firm red line around the hill on which the city stood, though houses and streets had long since burst out from these confines to spill untidily onto the nearby slopes. I would dawdle my way home through the warren of medieval streets that surrounded the carved and pious splendour of the great, pale cathedral and once or twice followed fashionable sightseers into the soaring magnificence of the nave. My parents had been casual in the matter of churchgoing for us children, Papa, indeed, being inclined to question the need for what he termed 'superstitious practices', yet I found myself unexpectedly awed as my glance was drawn upwards from the carved columns marching down the nave to the flowing tracery of the fan vaulting in the dimness of the roof. It was more than mere appreciation of the workmanship of those ancient masons, but as though centuries of worship had soaked into the stone and now gave off an invisible, yet palpable, sense of reverence.

All over the city there was a great richness of medieval and Tudor houses, some fallen on hard times and being replaced with fine modern terraces and crescents, others now swarming slums where I had been warned not to set foot. The River Exe curled round the southern walls, and beyond were the rolling Devonshire hills, lushly green.

Despite myself, I began to note the interesting features of the buildings I passed.

Papa had once written a series of articles for his paper on the ancient architecture of the town of Manchester. I had wandered with him round narrow alleys of the old Shambles, the Roman remains at Castlefield, and half-timbered inns and, infected as always by the

90

enthusiasm of his interest, had picked up a little knowledge. Now I found myself more than once thinking, 'What a splendid piece of Tudor carving, I must tell Papa . . .' then bringing myself up short and swiftly fixing my thoughts on something else. I would not, *must* not, think of the past. There was pain there, suffering. Better that I stay unthinking, uncaring, locked in ice.

Then from one moment to the next all that was changed.

One morning I cut through the alley curving along the wall of St Perran's, and a woman stepped from behind a buttress, blocking my path.

I realised I had seen her before, loitering in the crescent. A woman in respectable black with a deep-brimmed bonnet shadowing her face.

For a moment I was alarmed, then laughed at myself for she was half my height and elderly and I had nothing to offer any thief or beggar, as she could see for herself.

'Miss Howarth?'

I was taken aback. 'How do you know my name?'

'From my son, Mr Clive Chadwick, who is tutor to your brother.' She smiled. 'Oh, but I am so relieved to meet you at last. I knew where you lived and I had your description – and my son described you most clearly – but though I have watched often, I did not see you until this week.'

'Mr Chadwick,' I breathed faintly. The name sounded strange, foreign, on my lips.

'I have letters from him,' she said, dipping into her reticule, 'which he asked me to keep until I should meet you.'

I stared dumbly at the package she put in my hand. There seemed to be a tight band round my chest preventing me from breathing.

'Miss Howarth? Are you well? You have gone quite white.' Mrs Chadwick's anxious face peered up into mine. 'Oh dear, perhaps I should not have startled you by appearing so suddenly.'

'I . . . I think,' I said carefully, 'that I must sit down for a moment.'

For all she was so spare, Mrs Chadwick had a strong arm. She wrapped it about my waist and urged me into the church, which was empty and cool and filled with the smell of dust and dead flowers.

I sat in a pew near the door until the dizziness passed, Mrs Chadwick chafing my wrist. Eventually I was recovered enough to assure her that the fault was not hers.

'I have tried not to think . . . about . . . about Ben. Now, it all comes back . . . and I do not know if I can bear it.'

'My dear, my dear, I understand,' was all she said and we sat quietly for a while, her hand clasped tightly about mine, while I felt the warmth of her calm presence steady me.

Presently I managed a wan smile. 'I have not yet thanked you. You have gone to great trouble to bring me these letters.'

She brushed away my thanks. 'I am pleased to have the opportunity to help. I think it unfeeling of your grandfather to cut you off so completely from your brother.' She hesitated. 'Are you comfortable in your situation? Are your employers kind? My son is most anxious to know how you fare and I shall be writing my weekly letter to him tonight.'

'I . . . I am settled,' I said, shortly, unable to say more for to speak of the bleakness of my existence might again undermine my composure. She squeezed my hand and gave me an understanding glance. 'Oh, but if you write to Mr Chadwick,' I said quickly, 'will you please thank him for the care he gives to Ben . . .'

'But you must thank him yourself!' Mrs Chadwick exclaimed. Again she delved into her reticule and withdrew a scrap of paper. 'My address. It is not far from Sidwell Street. I shall be glad to enclose any letter of yours with mine.'

I stayed only a little while after she left, then I followed her, too bemused even to open the letters, into the sunshine.

I did not have a chance to open the package until late that night.

When Miss Olga had locked and bolted the front door and I had seen Miss Polsham settled in her first-floor bedroom, I was allowed to climb the uncarpeted flight of stairs to the half-landing above and my own cramped quarters.

For once its limitations did not weigh on me. The meagre view of roofs and chimneypots from the one tiny window, the narrow bed with its thin blankets and faded coverlet pressed against one wall, the rickety washstand and tallboy against the other, with scarcely space between to house the moulting rag rug that was the only ornament the room possessed. I was concerned only to retrieve the package from its hiding place under the mattress.

I lit the candle with trembling fingers and carefully unfolded the letters. The first was dated three weeks after I had left and was the shortest.

Falconwood, March 1822

Dear Miss Howarth,

I have taken my mother into my confidence and she being a person of the greatest sensibility and discretion will do her utmost to ensure that my letters reach you privately and I trust that this communication will go some way to relieving your mind, which must be greatly troubled, as to the wellbeing of your brother.

I intend to employ the utmost frankness in my correspondence as I am sure you would expect nothing else, so I must therefore say that the first days were not easy, your brother being in much distress and constantly asking for you. Indeed, at one stage, I feared his pining might reach injurious proportions. However, I am greatly relieved to be able to tell you that Ben is now very much his old self, his appetite and cheerful spirits restored and that eccentric person Miss Lightbody has proved an unexpectedly valuable ally, setting herself to amuse and divert your brother – and diverting herself into the bargain, I fancy, for I think she has been lonely in this house for a long while and is growing to appreciate a change of company . . .

The tears so long confined began to drip onto the paper. The ice barrier at last was melting as the vivid, searing pictures I had long striven to subdue sprang into my head.

I saw Ben's puzzled misery and felt it the twin of my own. I saw my grandfather's hawkish, cruel expression and felt the bite of anger and a dark, curdling bitterness. And above all I felt the raw ache of loss so strong that I flung myself onto the bed and muffled my face into the pillow lest the sound of uncontrollable sobbing disturb the untroubled sleep of my employers.

When the storm of weeping was over, I mopped my eyes and read the other two letters which spoke hopefully of doctors visited, of medications and treatments to be tried, of cheerful incidents in Ben's day. Then I blew out the candle which I had allowed to burn extravagantly low and, clutching the letters to my heart, stood by the window.

A sickle moon hung in the sky above the chimney-pots. Almost unconsciously, as I had so often done in childhood with a giggling Phoebe and Rose, I curtsied three times to the new moon and wished. Long ago it had been for foolish things, some toy, an outing, a picture book. Now my wish was for strength. Strength to go on. Strength to bear whatever the future might hold so that Ben and I would someday be permanently united.

And I made a vow.

The ice had not quite melted. A sliver of it remained, cold and steely in the deepest recesses of my mind. Perhaps it would never go. Perhaps I did not wish it to, because it would keep my vision clear, reminding me of this moment, when I knew that I had lost Ben because of my own frailty, because I was poor and powerless and therefore vulnerable to the wiles of men like my grandfather.

So I made my vow silently.

From this moment on I would use my wits to improve my situation. I would fight with all the courage I had to better myself and to provide myself – and those I loved – with protection against the cruel manipulations of others.

And however remote or foolish that possibility might seem, I was filled with the conviction that I could make it happen.

My eyes felt heavy and puffy as I went downstairs the next morning but my steps were surprisingly light, even though I had received something of a shock as I tumbled blearily out of bed.

I usually gave the small spotted mirror above the washstand the briefest of glances to ensure that I was tidy before I left my room. This morning I was about to remove my nightgown when I glimpsed this barely recognisable figure in the glass and froze in astonishment.

I had never been plump, but now I saw why Dr Barlow had been concerned about my health. I was desperately thin. My wrists, my collarbones jutted bonily from the confines of my cotton nightgown. There were bluish hollows beneath my cheeks and at my temples. My eyes, normally a colour between grey and green, looked huge and dark in their bony sockets and the scattering of freckles across the bridge of my nose seemed to emphasise the pallor of the stretched, almost translucent, skin beneath. Even my hair seemed to have lost its normal frizzy ebullience and lay in lank waves around my shoulders.

I was considerably shaken. My spirits might be restored by the making of new resolutions, however laughable or unattainable they might seem by daylight, but my physical recovery would not be so swift. And I realised that it was entirely due to Dr Barlow's perceptiveness that I had been drawn back in the nick of time from a final descent into a dark and sickly pit of self-pity and despair. For if he had not ordered it, I should not have gone out of doors, encountered Mrs Chadwick and received the news of Ben that burst the barrier of ice that imprisoned me. I should still be lost, perhaps for ever, in that unfeeling, limbo world, trapped within this gaunt, haunted creature who stared back from the mirror.

I breathed a silent prayer of thanks to Dr Barlow as I dressed. Life *was* worth living, painful as it might be to face up to all that I had suffered. I was young, blood coursed strongly in my veins, I had a purpose. I was alive! And I rejoiced.

For the first time since I had come to this house my

shoulders were not bowed wearily as I listened to Miss Olga droning through the ritual of morning prayers. Instead I stared around, my newly awakened senses keen and alert.

I smelt the familiar closed smell of the dining parlour. Beeswax, dried lavender and the faint underlying tang of camphor that hung about the whole house against Miss Olga's deadly enemy the moth. I heard the wheezy rattle of Mrs Caunter's bronchitic lungs and the rustle of the maid's cheap lilac print skirts as she shifted her feet in boredom. And I looked at Miss Olga afresh, watching her colourless lips move in prayer, seeing the lines of discontent etched deep into her parchment yellow cheeks, the thin grey hair drawn tight under the plain cap, her slight frame encased in a snuff-coloured morning gown, faded under the armpits and darned at the hem.

Yesterday, I had thought her hard and forbidding and authoritative. I had submitted myself to her as I submitted myself to the situation my grandfather had forced upon me, with dull resignation. I had never been truly aware of her as a person. This morning, with my newly clear vision, I saw her not as a flat, stiff image, like her father's portrait, but as a rounded three-dimensional figure. There she stood, a plain, shabby woman, with a past that had perhaps been harsh and unloved, a present that consisted of pandering to her sister's whims and maintaining the dreary round of a limited existence and a future that held nothing but the slow encroachment of old age.

What else could I do but feel sorry for her? And because I did, I felt my fear of her slide away.

Indeed, as she reverently closed the Bible and preceded me into the dining parlour across the stretch of red and blue Turkey carpet I said, impulsively, as I might have spoken once within my own family, 'Such a lovely morning, Miss Olga. I shall be glad to take my walk today. Perhaps you would care to join me, for you were saying yesterday that Miss Polsham needed new nightgowns and I could help you choose the stuff and carry it home for you.'

Her head jerked round. The fire irons might have leaped from the hearth and addressed her, so alarmed and astonished was her look.

I, too, felt a ripple of nervous apprehension. I was no longer the girl I had been yesterday. That docile, obedient, near-silent person had gone. My own true personality had resurfaced. Miss Olga might disapprove of such a puzzling and disturbing metamorphosis, yet I could not turn back the clock, nor could I go on pretending to be what I was not.

I thought about it as Miss Olga said grace and as I shook out the starched napkin, I said, frankly, 'Miss Olga, I owe you an apology.'

Her look of alarm deepened. 'Apology? Why? What have you done, girl? Is something broken? If it is, you shall pay.'

'No, no! It is just that these last weeks I have been so lost in my own misery that I fear I have not been at all myself. It was the enforced separation from my brother, coming so soon after the loss of my parents and sisters that drove me into such a dreadful state of gloom.' Despite my efforts to maintain a cheerful tone, I could not help adding, bitterly, 'I thought my grandfather would be willing to forget past grievances when I begged his charity on behalf of my brother and myself, but he is a hard man. His attitude has added greatly to my grief.' I looked Miss Olga straight in the eye. 'But I realise now that it is both unhealthy and unfair on those around me to dwell on what cannot be undone. I shall try to be more cheerful and amenable from now on, for I am sure that my sorry face and gloomy disposition must have been something of a trial for you and Miss Polsham.'

Miss Olga was clearly taken aback. I thought, with a flicker of amusement, that she had probably not even noticed or cared about me or how I went about my duties as long as I did as I was told.

'Well, Joanna,' she said, uneasily, choosing her words with care, 'I . . . I shall try to overlook any, er, deficiencies that may have occurred since you came and trust that your future conduct may be . . . improved.'

The maid hurried in with the bowls of porridge and placed them before us. The small interruption gave Miss Olga time to gather her wits and her safe, comfortable opinions and quote me at length about the duties of young persons to their elders.

'You must understand, Joanna,' she said as I poured the jug of thin cream, which now appeared by my plate each morning, over my porridge, 'that your poor brother is of an age when it is no longer fit that he should be ruled by womenfolk. My cousin Mr James Pascoe, your grandfather's friend who kindly arranged that you should come here, explained the situation most clearly and we of the gentler sex should always be prepared to defer to the wisdom of those meant by nature to have authority over us.'

'Even if we feel that to be wrong?'

Her smile was condescending. 'Feminine inexperience and youth are no match for the intelligence and scope of the masculine mind which by its very nature is able to embrace the wider issues.' I felt it might have been the late Elder Nathaniel quoting from Miss Olga's lips. 'Humility, obedience and meekness are virtues that men honour most in a woman.'

I stifled a sigh. I felt that none of those so-called virtues applied to me.

'Some women never learn this lesson, even within the tender confines of matrimony,' Miss Olga went on. 'I remember my dear papa had great trouble with another of the elders of the church whose wife had become corrupted from the reading of unsuitable books.' She lowered her voice. 'By one Mary Woolcraft, I believe.'

'Could it perhaps be Mary Wollstencraft?' I queried, remembering all too well the lively family discussions that had taken place when Papa had once read aloud to us the *Vindication of the Rights of Women*, in order, he said, that we girls should learn of the harder part that women had to bear in society, and the contempt in which most men viewed any hint of equality in the female sex.

'Possibly, possibly,' said Miss Olga. 'What I am certain of is that dear Papa swore that should ever my sister or I be found in possession of so much as a paragraph of that lady's writings, he would personally lock us out of the house.'

The last spoonful of porridge almost stuck in my throat.

'And the elder's wife?' I asked quietly.

'As Papa pointed out, she received her just deserts. She left her husband, taking her infant children with her, because she said he had married her merely to get possession of her fortune and he had treated her unkindly.' Miss Olga's nostrils flared. 'A terrible scandal! Though of course her husband followed her and literally snatched her children out of her arms when she was about to make her escape on the Falmouth packet. A fearful wailing and weeping she made, and the children likewise, they not knowing any better, but he had a stout man with him and they carried the children off and left her to suffer whatever deserved retribution should fall upon her.'

100

'And what did?' I asked, my fingers clenched stiffly about the spoon.

'The last I heard she was a mad old creature to be seen often at the gate where she had used to live, begging passers-by to tell her where her children were taken. Though they were long grown and gone and her husband moved to Berkshire.'

'How dreadful,' I whispered. 'The poor woman.'

Miss Olga frowned. 'I was young when the event occurred and, like you, expressed some sympathy towards the woman and the innocent children, but Papa took the trouble to explain to me that the marriage bond is sacred and vows of love and obedience made in the sight of the Lord cannot be put lightly aside out of convenience. It is so easy, you see, Joanna, to get into the way of assessing a situation wrongly when one is young. It is always best to listen to the judgment of those older and wiser than oneself.'

I looked at Miss Olga's self-satisfied expression, unable to speak for sudden anger and knowing that any comment I made to the contrary would not move her. It was clear she had not even one pitying thought for that poor, lost, heartbroken woman.

I cut a slice of bread from the heel of the loaf and buttered it fiercely, wondering how I could go on living under the same roof as such an unfeeling woman, let alone be a dutiful companion. But my anger slowly faded as I thought of what Miss Olga's life had been, cooped up in this house. Had she ever had the chance to form an opinion of her own? I could not believe that she had ever been granted that particular indulgence. She had been taught to repeat, parrot fashion, the prejudices of her elders so that she had come to believe them as sincerely as if she had dreamed them up herself.

In a way, that was almost as sad as the tale I had

just heard. The chance to air her views seemed to have put Miss Olga in an expansive mood. She now considered my earlier, impulsive request.

'I do not care for my sister to be left for too long . . . but as you say, the morning is fine . . . I shall try to arrange to be free by half past ten when you may make yourself useful by accompanying me to Tucker's.'

'Of course, Miss Olga,' I murmured, half regretting making the suggestion.

'I have always found them reliable and not too fanciful as regards prices. If there is anything you wish to purchase today,' she added graciously, 'I shall be pleased to give you my advice and make sure that you make a suitable choice.'

'That is most kind of you,' I said cheerfully, 'but I cannot make any purchases because I do not have any money. I spent what little I had on our journey to Devon and of course my salary is not due until the end of the month.'

Miss Olga looked quite disappointed. I realised that few people must ever ask her advice upon anything and she had relished the prospect.

A solution immediately presented itself and was out before I stopped to think that she might take offence.

'I do have need of new strings for my summer bonnet as the old ones are nearly frayed through. If you could see your way to advancing me a small amount on my salary, then I would be most happy to take your advice on their purchase.'

I held my breath as her frown deepened, wondering if I had gone too far. But after a moment she said, dourly, 'I would not wish to encourage you to live beyond your means, but in the circumstances . . . I could possibly see my way to advancing you, say, five shillings against your first quarter's wages. Now shall we compose ourselves to prayer and ask a blessing on the meal we have eaten?'

Five shillings was scarcely a fortune, but it seemed so to me as Miss Olga counted out the money into my palm. My first earnings. I felt a thrill of excitement that did not leave me through the long session in Mr Tucker's dark tunnel of a shop as bolt after bolt of cotton and fine lawn was unrolled and rejected until Miss Olga found the exact quality at the right price. And I had never known the choice of new bonnet strings to be so thoroughly testing a matter. The shabby cream straw seemed scarcely worth the fuss, though eventually we – or rather Miss Olga – settled for a length of narrow brown velvet ribbon which being the last of the roll might be bought at a discount.

'And enough there to make a trimming, too,' she said triumphantly as we emerged into the breezy sunshine.

I smiled with genuine amusement; she was so pleased with herself that her long, sallow features bore the look of a cat glutted on cream.

'I should never have managed so well on my own,' I said, with truth.

'Of course not,' she said, sounding satisfied. Then, with a return to her usual tartness, 'Come now, we must make haste back or you will be tempted to spend unnecessarily now that you have money to burn. Foolish habits are all too easily acquired by idle young girls.'

I wondered, idly, as we walked briskly back to Torre Crescent, if Miss Olga had ever had the urge to acquire any foolish habits. Or indeed if she had ever been young. It was hard to imagine either possibility.

That night I took two shillings and placed them in an old leather pouch in which my father had once kept his pipe tobacco. There were dark brown shreds still clinging to the inside and the sharp, familiar smell of it almost undid me, so clearly did it bring back an image of Papa bent over his desk, his pipe clenched between his teeth, the scratchy sound of his pen speeding across the paper.

I gritted my teeth. 'This is just the beginning,' I said aloud. 'Two shillings only, but soon it will be more. Much more.' I fastened the pouch. I had brought it with me out of sentiment, but now it was a talisman in my hands. It seemed to represent Papa's loving, gentle spirit just as Mama's necklace, which I always wore under my dress, reminded me of her proud, impatient temperament.

I hid the pouch along with Mr Chadwick's letters under the paper lining at the bottom of a drawer in the tallboy, hoping that Mama and Papa watched over me from whatever heaven they occupied and approved my high-flown plans.

Perhaps they did. A week later, I met the girl who was to become my first true friend in Exeter and I could not help but fancy that some benevolent fate had arranged for our paths to cross.

Chapter Four

... and I conclude by once again thanking you
for your kindness to my dear brother and remain
hopeful that it may not be too long before I have
further news of him.

I added my respects and my signature and folded
the paper into a small square that might unobtrusively
be included with Mrs Chadwick's own letter.

Early morning light made a pearly lustre of the sky
above the rooftops. I had struggled to raise the sash
window – whether I should ever be able to close it was
another matter, the frame was so stiff and swollen with
damp – but I had lain all night with the touch of the
cool, night air on my face and now the morning breeze
streamed in, tumultuous with birdsong. The rustle of
the breeze, the joyous sounds of the blackbird making
his territorial claim from the damson tree, sparrows
twittering in the eaves, gave me a sense of being part
of the wider, freer world outside this house of elderly
women.

For several days I had been rising early, enjoying
this hour when I might have the leisure to read one of
the few favourite books I had brought with me or
mend stockings or merely indulge in daydreams.

This morning, the letter to Mr Chadwick completed
and the means of getting it to Mrs Chadwick a problem

for later, my drifting thoughts turned to the women who had previously occupied this narrow little cell. I wondered if any of my predecessors had heard the spring birdsong with lifted spirits. Had they forced open the window to sniff at the breeze rolling down from the green hills? Or had they resolutely kept the window shut against all temptation to look beyond the narrowness of an existence they must endure without complaint?

There had been several ladies who, in the ten years since Mr Nathaniel Polsham had passed away, had occupied the position of companion to the Misses Polsham. None seemed to have stayed for any length of time or left any impression of their character in the house.

I could not help thinking of my mother's room at Falconwood, how the very air breathed of her presence, how her vivid character sprang from the fripperies and ornaments cluttering the shelves, the once-pretty bed hangings, the curtains. Even if the room had been polished and bare and tidy, it would still have cried out that it was *hers*.

I myself might move out of this anonymous little cell today and though I had been here for three months, no one would ever be the wiser. Oh, my books were ranged on the top of the tallboy, my hairbrush and comb on the washstand, my clothes neatly ranged in the drawers, but the room remained itself. Anonymous, dingy, uncared for except by the briefest of attentions by the maidservant.

I uncurled myself quickly from the bed and tucked the letter to Mr Chadwick carefully within the glove I should wear today. Then I surveyed my room with a calculating eye, slowly pacing it from door to window and back again, noting its narrowness, its height, its every fault and reckoning how the fault could be rectified or disguised. And once more at the door I leaned my back to it, smiling at the sudden thought that this was exactly what Mama had used to do when she walked into any house that would be ours, however temporarily. Exhaustion from the move and the journey would seem to slip from her. She would raise her head eagerly and gaze round at a dingy hallway, a dark parlour, a dismal bedroom and immediately endow it with possibilities.

'Why, Arnold, this room has the most splendid proportions,' she would cry. 'I do believe it will catch the morning sun, so our blue curtains would look most splendidly cool – with only a little alteration, I am sure. And the chiffonier there with the blue Spode vases at either end – oh, and that gloomy corner is just the place for the japanned screen. Rose's sampler that she embroidered so beautifully will hang just *there*. And perhaps we could re-cover the wing chair – a satiny stripe perhaps. How splendid it would look by the fireplace. Do you not see it, girls? We shall be perfectly comfortable here.'

We saw. We agreed wholeheartedly. For we knew that Mama had an instinct for these things and even if Papa were to lead us into a barn with an earth floor, Mama would have it decked out and draped fit to receive the most genteel visitors in a trice.

'Nowhere is so bad that it cannot be improved! Think of that, girls, when you have establishments of your own. A most unpromising room can be transformed by rearrangement of furniture, by harmonising the colour of drapes and hangings and upholstery or the clever hanging of pictures.'

My room was scarcely the establishment my mother had envisaged but my residency here might be a long one. It would make my life more pleasant if I had a comfortable and cosy place of my own to retire to.

Nowhere is so bad that it cannot be improved.

The room was made to look narrower because of the positioning of the furniture. If the bed were put across the end wall under the window it would alter the perspective, give an illusion of breadth. Then the tallboy and the washstand could be arranged closer to the door.

I longed for the japanned screen! Mama had always valued it as being a most useful item for disguising an ugly corner or dividing a uselessly large area into comfortably private and manageable sections. It would have been a great asset in here, but of course it had gone to the saleroom, along with the boxes of curtains and swags of material, old shawls and counterpanes that had always travelled with us about the country, ready to be pulled out, cut down, patched up or dyed and hung afresh at windows, over beds or thrown with apparent carelessness – and with clever effect – over a sofa to hide a threadbare spot or across a scuffed table on which might stand an elegantly arranged vase of leaves and garden flowers to make even the most critical caller's eye brighten with admiration.

I had nothing with which to begin my campaign of alteration. And the room cried out for colour and warmth. The bedcover might once have been blue but years of laundering had turned it ashy grey. The rag rug was composed of black serge scraps, the hessian backing showing in the worn patches. There was a cheap cream blind at the window when clearly a hanging of some bright material would be most beneficial – maybe a heavy drape that would keep out the draught in winter but the pole long enough so that the curtain could be pulled back to allow the summer breezes to blow in . . . perhaps a sunny yellow, and a coverlet for the bed to match . . .

Castles in the air. I chuckled at my grandiose ideas when I had scarcely a penny to my name. But in time . . . And surely there was nothing to stop me moving the furniture?

I could have begun enthusiastically wrenching it about there and then, but I had already heard the maid moving on the creaky attic floor above. It was time I washed and dressed, and in any case I had better be cautious and ask Miss Olga's permission. Perhaps there was some unwritten rule about the deployment of furniture that I might unwittingly transgress.

But I should find the means to brighten my room, I promised myself. To make it mine, as my mother's Falconwood room was hers, as any house she had lived in had borne the aura of her strong personality.

However cheaply it had to be done, I should leave my mark upon this room and, who knows, maybe even on the house itself.

But not today. Miss Olga was clearly in no mood to be tackled on any matter, let alone the frippery one of furniture. She had suffered all night with the tooth-ache, her cheek was swollen and her temper consequently very short. I could do nothing to ease her suffering or otherwise please her. Not to be outdone, Miss Polsham declared that she felt she was sickening for a summer cold and would stay in bed. It being the maid's half day I was the whole afternoon running up and down stairs from Miss Polsham's room to the parlour where Miss Olga sat wreathed in the scent of oil of cloves with a hot bran pack to her cheek. Then down to the basement, time and again, to beard the cantankerous Mrs Caunter in her den in order to secure a supply of hot drinks and nourishing titbits for the elder sister and soothing possets for the younger.

Worse was to come. The maid returned early from her half day and announced, defiantly, that she was to leave at the end of the week.

"'Tis Harry Drew, see, he and me bin walking out a

109

fair while and now he'm got word his uncle died and left him a cottage and a pig an' money besides so 'e's setting up on his own – as carpenter, if you please, Miss Olga, at which he'm very skilled. And there's nothin' to stop us being wed which we'll be d'reckly.' She stopped to draw breath and rushed on, as though she had rehearsed it thoroughly beforehand. 'And my Harry says 'tes no matter about a character, miss, if 'tes puttin' you out so long as you pays up what you owes me, for I shall have no need for to go out workin' no more, 'im bein' comfortable and me 'avin enough to do lookin' after 'im from now on . . .'

Miss Olga's nostrils flared angrily. She caught out of the welter of words the ones most guaranteed to set her already inflamed nerves on edge. 'You have the face to stand there and demand wages, girl, when you are prepared to leave without any thought to the distress and inconvenience you are causing to your employers?'

'I'm owed this week's wages, miss, an' if I work to the week's end, 'twill be four and ninepence by my reckoning.'

'And nothing by mine!' Miss Olga snapped. 'For you shall pack your bags and leave this very hour. You are dismissed for . . . for ingratitude and insolence!'

'But I never—'

'Not another word!' Miss Olga looked so fierce, the girl stepped back uncertainly, her lip beginning to quiver.

'You'm . . . you'm a heartless old baggage!' she cried. 'An' . . . an' I'll be glad to go away from all the old miseries in this 'ouse.' She threw her apron over her face and ran sobbing from the room.

Miss Olga clutched her cheek and closed her eyes. 'To think that I have harboured such impertinence under my roof,' she quavered. 'It makes me feel quite distressed, and I am already in such pain.'

I looked at her coldly. I clenched my teeth against the words that wanted to spill out. That poor girl's life had been made a misery by the harassment of the dreadful Mrs Caunter. She had worked long hours for a pittance and had never been seen by the Misses Polsham as anything other than a lowly creature whose feelings need never be considered.

I said, quietly, 'Miss Olga, I believe the girl has worked hard and faithfully until today and deserves more than to be dismissed so summarily. I know your toothache is painful and it is understandable that today you should be particularly upset that she is to leave, but in all fairness, could you not see your way to letting her have something of what she is owed? She is to be married, after all, such a joyous occasion . . .'

Miss Olga's eyes snapped open. 'You get above yourself, Joanna,' she said. 'I do not need your recommendation. The girl has condemned herself out of her own mouth. She has been encouraging a follower against my specific ruling to the contrary.'

'But in her free time—'

'The decision is mine and mine alone. I will brook no interference on your part.' She pursed her lips and added, 'Pray remember that if your conduct is anything other than willing and obedient I shall be obliged to inform your grandfather. You will then lose the chance to see your brother. Now take yourself upstairs and make sure that the impertinent chit does not pack anything that is not hers in her baggage before you see her off the premises.'

I had thought myself beginning to grow a shell against hurt, my new spirit of endeavour armouring me cheerfully as I went forward to a bright, if hazy, prospect of betterment. My will alone, I felt, was enough to make a happier future possible. I had almost convinced myself that Miss Olga might grow, if not to like me, at least to appreciate my efforts to please her, but now I felt my resolve shudder as the realisation that I was still vulnerable came sharply home to me.

I could not pretend. The Misses Polsham and my grandfather had me exactly where they wanted me. I had no defence against the threat of permanent banishment from Ben.

It was a thought that turned my hopes to ashes, my anger to bitterness as I followed the maid up the stairs, pausing only to enter my room and snatch a few coppers from my precious hoard.

I pressed them into the maid's hands. The maid! I still thought of her with the detachment with which I had viewed her when I was imprisoned in ice. She had a name. She was a person.

'Emily, it is all I can give you, but it will buy a ribbon or a posy for your wedding day. I wish you well.'

'Oh, miss.' She held the coppers in her palm, then said fiercely, through her tears, 'You should get away. You'm too nice. They stingy old bitches'll wear you down in no time at all.'

'Not me,' I said. 'Not me, Emily.'

But watching her leave the house, her few possessions tied in an ungainly bundle, I could not but envy her.

Miss Polsham remained bedfast for the next few days. Though she was given to a continuous moaning about her aching head and congested lungs, her round cheeks remained defiantly rosy, her skin cool and the bouts of coughing which greeted my every appearance sounded decidedly false. Not that I had time to dwell on what I was beginning to regard impatiently as her play-acting. I was far too busy. Miss Olga was genuinely in agony with the toothache and refused to call in Dr Barlow in case he decided to draw the tooth.

Having an all too clear memory of a childhood encounter with a tooth-puller – a most painful and bloody experience – I could sympathise. Whether from inheritance – Mama's teeth had been white and firm – or the regular cleansing of my mouth with toothpowder when it could be afforded, soot and salt in leaner times, I had not been troubled since and I thanked heaven for it as I reheated bran packs and tried, in vain, to take her mind off the pain.

I brought up the matter of engaging a new maid but she waved me aside. 'I cannot put my mind to it now. In a day or two, when I am recovered. We can manage until then.'

Indeed we could, for I was ordered to undertake most of the maid's duties. In addition to my normal tasks I hauled hot water and coals upstairs, brought the slops down and emptied them into the privy at the end of the garden, scoured chamber pots, polished furniture, strewed the carpets with tea leaves and brushed them up along with the dust, kept the brass fender and fire irons polished and would have rubbed up the front door knocker except that Miss Olga thought it would not do for me to be seen by the neighbours to be skivvying out of doors.

And to cap it all there was Mrs Caunter to be faced each time I entered the gloomy kitchen.

'There's all they pans to be scrubbed, don't 'ee forget,' she would snarl, jerking her whiskery chin towards the scullery. Or vegetables to be scraped. Or water to be fetched from the pump. 'Miss Olga, she do say you'm got to give I a hand. I shall tell 'er if you don't.'

'Yes, *yes*,' I would cry, hastily preparing trays for the invalids or making camomile tea to Miss Olga's exacting standards or whisking past with the slop pail. 'I shall be back shortly. Just give me time . . .'

There was never enough time. It sped past in a blur of exhaustion. My letter to Mr Chadwick remained in my glove. There was no time for pleasant walks. I really did now feel myself to be a prisoner for I realised how much I had come to depend upon and enjoy my strolls in the town.

Then one morning Miss Olga took prayers, which had become somewhat curtailed, at her usual lengthy pace, adding fervent thanks for the relief of suffering. The swelling on her face had gone down considerably, she even managed a tight smile as she informed me that she was considerably recovered. 'Though when you have cleared the breakfast dishes, Joanna, you may run to the druggist for a further supply of oil of cloves in case the pain returns. And there are one or two other errands you may do, for I shall not venture outside while the wind still holds a chill.'

The air felt like cool fingers against my cheeks as I walked thankfully away from Torre Crescent. Sunlight spilled across cobbled gutters and flagged pavements, limned overhanging eaves and rosy pink stone. I did not hurry, even though Miss Olga had warned me not to dawdle. I strolled past the cathedral, delighting in the antics of the pigeons strutting and preening on the grass of the cathedral yard and, above the tower, the gulls wheeling in from the river, a dazzling white against the blue of the sky. Never had freedom felt so sweet.

I threaded my way through a narrow alley, pausing with pleasure when I reached High Street to view the bustle of the market. It was the last Friday in the month when the largest and finest of the markets clogged not only High Street but most of Fore Street sloping down to the bridge over the river. Stalls were ranged two deep in front of the shops, many of which

114

had sensibly barricaded the lower part of their windows against accidental breakage. Panniered horses, men pushing handcarts, pony traps and carriages made slow progress in the narrow thoroughfare left to them. The sound of hooves and wheels and boots on cobbles made a continuous background clatter to the cries of impatient chairmen demanding passage, stallholders calling their wares, the jeers of urchins tormenting a drunkard penned for an hour's punishment in the Guildhall stocks and the distant bellow of the crier describing a stolen pocket watch. There was a ripe smell of cheese from a nearby stall, a tang of crushed straw and sweating horse, a waft of lavender water from a group of fashionably clad ladies swaying past, a less agreeable waft from a heap of horse droppings.

I sniffed it all in happily and plotted my route through the crush.

'Go round carefully and find the best prices before you purchase,' Miss Olga had instructed me. 'No more than two and threepence for the brace of fowls, mind, and if butter is above tenpence, buy only a pound.' She had shaken her head, tut-tutting as she doled the money into my palm. 'Fourpence ha'penny for salt is a disgrace, but you must go to Cross's and watch that his assistant gives you fair measure.'

That would take no time at all, then I could go in search of Mrs Chadwick's house and deliver my letter.

I made to step out but a tug at my skirts jerked me to a halt. I turned sharply to see a filthy scarecrow at my heels. I pulled my skirts out of the clawing hand, and instinctively guarded my basket, as Mama had always cautioned us to do after having her purse snatched once by an apparently crippled beggar woman who had instantly dropped her crutch and disappeared at great speed. Even so, I was inclined always to feel pity rather than fear for most of the beggars pleading for coins on street corners. Dull-eyed women with scabby infants at their breast, aged cripples, stick-limbed children and men, the flotsam of the war with the French, forced into destitution and beggary. I had seen many of them on the journey south – the lamed, the blinded, the horribly maimed. Heroes once, when Boney and his French hordes threatened the British populace, conveniently forgotten in the seven years since the war had ended.

But this was no old soldier or sailor, merely a young girl, barefoot, ragged and persistent, dogging my heels as I began to walk away and pleading not for money but for work.

It was not so much the request, but the sound of her voice that made me turn and regard her sharply.

'Miss, please, miss, I'll do anythin'. I'll work 'ard, I promise. I'm mebbe small, like, but I'm strong an' 'onest.'

'Where are you from?' I asked.

She had brightened seeing my interest, her eyes shining with hope through the grime of her face. Now her lids came down, but not before I had seen the flash of fear.

'From . . . from Bristol town, miss,' she said dully.

'And before that?'

'Nowhere afore that,' she said, too quickly. 'Allus lived there till me mam died. I bin travellin' since, lookin' for work. If you know of anybody wantin' to tek on a fine, strong, willin' orphan lass then I'd be in your debt, miss.' She chanced a glance up at me and, apparently encouraged by my expression, added, 'I'm fifteen, I reckon, an' I learn quick.'

I said nothing for a moment. I couldn't. It was her accent that touched me with unexpected nostalgia. So homely and familiar and alien here where people spoke with the rounded, sometimes incomprehensible,

Devonshire burr. It pointed the girl to be a liar, of course – she was no more from Bristol that I was a Dutchman – but I wanted, suddenly, to know why. Her accent was from the north. South Lancashire, I guessed. But there was something – some intelligence – in those bright, pleading eyes that reached out hungrily for understanding and struck an answering chord in my heart.

'What work have you done before?'

Again her glance slid away. She said, vaguely, 'Lotsa things, miss. Field work and such . . . but I'll learn anything right quick.'

'And your name?'

'Lily, miss,'

'Do you have a character?'

Her face went blank. 'Character, miss?'

'From your previous employers. To say that you are what you say you are. A good, honest worker.'

The fear flooded back into her eyes. For a moment I thought she was going to run. Her scarecrow limbs tensed, her face crumpled with such sick distress that I instinctively cried, 'No! Don't go! I will try to help you.' I caught her wrist, my mind racing. 'I think I may be able to find you work. Come with me.'

She tried to pull free of my grasp, wary, I could see, at this sudden benevolence.

'Where to, miss?'

'You must trust me,' I said urgently. 'If you are sincere in wanting work then I may be able to find you a place. But hurry.'

'I dunno . . .'

'I have no time to waste.' I released her hand. 'If you want to follow me, you may. Otherwise, you must take your chance elsewhere.'

I knew nothing of her beyond that she was a liar, and a poor one, yet somehow I felt her need as I had once known my own when Ben and I were on the road and every kind word was a rare and blessed event.

She blinked at me like a wary, desperate kitten that wants to cuddle into the proffered hand yet fears the sudden, vengeful blow. But, out of desperation perhaps, when I began to walk away she followed me.

I found Mrs Chadwick's house in a plain terrace of respectable houses. Thankfully, she was at home.

'I have brought a letter for Mr Chadwick,' I said, out of breath from my haste when she opened the door, 'but I have a favour to ask, and it is most impertinent when you have gone out of your way already to help me, but if I might have a moment of your time . . .'

She regarded me with a calm, welcoming smile, that reminded me a great deal of her son.

'Come inside and tell me all about it,' she said.

So I dragged a bewildered Lily inside, and told Mrs Chadwick of my plan.

I was very late back at Torre Crescent. The rush of confidence I felt when I saw Lily, scrubbed until her skin glowed pink, evaporated as Miss Polsham viewed the pair of us.

I could not have believed such a transformation could have been affected in the short time I was absent making my purchases. I had merely asked that Lily be allowed to make herself clean and tidy, but she had been stripped and washed from head to toe, her hair had been cut short ('There was nothing else for it,' Mrs Chadwick had whispered regretfully. 'It was knotted with filth and crawling with lice. I should see, dear, that she uses a toothcomb regularly from now on . . .') and new, if well-worn, clothes had been found for her. A bodice one of Mrs Chadwick's apprentices had grown out of, a patched skirt, hastily stitched to fit, an apron and cap and even a pair of cracked ancient boots discovered and fitted with new laces. 'You have worked wonders, Mrs Chadwick,' I had cried in astonishment, and her three young apprentices giggled, having been called in to help in the transformation.

I had not known that Mrs Chadwick was a dressmaker. And a successful one, to judge by the busy state of her front parlour which was her workroom – trestle tables bearing a rainbow of materials, half cut out dresses, paper patterns piled in heaps, cottons and needles and scissors in wooden trays, coloured engravings of ladies posed in the latest fashions pinned to the walls.

'I have interrupted your work. I am so sorry. I did not realise.'

Mrs Chadwick waved aside my thanks and my apologies. 'It has been quite a diversion,' she said gaily. 'Has it not, girls?' Another chorus of affirmative giggles. 'The poor child looks the part at least. I just hope that the Misses Polsham will find her suitable.'

But Miss Olga was too busy berating me for my lack of consideration in staying out so long to give Lily more than a cursory glance. And when she did eventually pause to scrutinise her, it was with so contemptuous a look that my heart sank.

Lily was clearly scared, but she had the presence of mind to bob a respectful curtsy and launch into the story I had drilled into her as we raced home.

'Please, miss, I'm an orphan returned to my birthplace in order to obtain parish relief, but I'd sooner work and earn a livin' wi' God-fearin' folks. An' I'll work hard and long, miss, and do everything to please.'

'An orphan, you say? Do you have no relatives at all?'

'Don't remember me dad, miss. Me and me mam was on us own livin' in a little place near here, Exeter – till she died, that is, miss – 'cos I remembered how we used to pick stones in the fields and frighten crows

119

from the corn . . .' This I had not heard. I had a feeling that it was the truth she spoke, out of nervousness, but she stopped this rush of information, suddenly wary, and bobbed another curtsy. 'So when I couldn't get work up north, in Bristol, that is, miss, I thought meself to come back 'ere and look for a place.'

Miss Olga was only half listening. I could almost see her mind ticking over. An orphan, young and untrained. A good saving on wages, no home to run to with tittle-tattle, no importunate followers. But without a character . . .

'And you say, Joanna, that you got into conversation with the girl in the market?'

'She appeared honest, Miss Polsham, and eager for work . . .'

'And you are, of course, experienced in the interviewing and hiring of servants,' she said with heavy sarcasm. 'So that you instantly perceived these qualities and decided to bring her to my attention.'

'In order that you might be saved the cost and bother of advertising,' I said brightly.

'How very thoughtful,' she said. 'In that case, I shall make you entirely responsible for her behaviour. You,' she said, turning back to Lily, 'will be given two weeks' trial. If I find you suitable, your wages, in view of your age and inexperience, will be five pounds a year and your keep. You will have one half day off a month when it is convenient. Miss Joanna will show you your duties.' Then, to me, 'Should breakages occur or other discrepancies come to light during this trial period, you will forfeit any costs from your own salary. You will also incur my very grave displeasure. Is that understood, Joanna?'

I swallowed and nodded. I knew exactly what she meant. She held the threat over my head like the sword of Damocles. If the scrawny orphan I had impulsively decided to befriend proved to be dishonest or clumsy or impertinent, I should pay for it. Not only with money. She would have the greatest delight in informing my grandfather.

Miss Olga had everything to gain and I everything to lose. The thought raised her spirits greatly. She was almost amenable for the rest of the day.

'Now,' I said grimly, 'the truth, if you please, Lily.'

The household was in bed and I sat with Lily in her attic room. This was merely a space separated from a lumber room under the eaves by rough boards, the stacked furniture and dusty trunks clearly visible between the gaps in the planking. I sat on the one chair, Lily on the pallet bed. The only other furniture was a deal cupboard on which stood a ewer and basin. There was no blind at the slit of a window, no rug on the floor.

It was bare and uncomfortable and Lily was in heaven.

'Eh, it's grand, isn't it, miss?' Lily sighed, ignoring my demand. 'A proper bed all to meself. I'm clean all over – and such lovely new clothes.'

'Lily! You heard what Miss Olga said. I am to be responsible for you. You owe me the truth. Now, where do you come from. Manchester? Or somewhere close to it?'

I held the candle closer to her face. In the flickering light her eyes were those of a startled rabbit caught in the beam of a hunter's lantern.

''Ow did you know that, miss?'

'Because I have lived there and you have the dialect in your voice.' I placed the candle on the uneven floorboards between us so that the light played less starkly upon her, then said gently, 'Whatever the tale you have to tell, and however bad it is, I swear it will

121

not go further than these four walls.'

So the story came out and a sad and sickening one it was.

Her name was Lily Walker and she held a memory close to her heart of a childhood in the countryside near Exeter.

'There was a pond wi' ducks an' geese. An' fields all round. Me dad was a sailor drowned at sea but we was happy till Mam was took of a fever and I was put in the poorhouse. Then a gentleman come and took us children off, some no more than five years old. To a better life, he said, to learn a trade an' mek plenty o' money. We was proper excited . . .'

Lily was nine years old then. She went on a long journey through the mists and rain of autumn, packed with other children in an open wagon. The 'gentleman' had been scouring the southern parishes for apprentices to be taken into the cotton mills. The lucky ones went to places where the owner took some interest in the children's welfare.

Lily was not lucky.

For six years she starved on a diet of onion gruel and oatcake, dragged from her few hours' sleep by blows and kept awake at the machines by sadistic beatings. Some of her fellow slaves faded and died. One girl lost her reason from being hit on the head too often, another flung herself into the black pit where the mill wheel churned after the owner's wife had whipped her for giggling in her presence.

'You sorta got used to it, miss. I cried a lot at first, an' then I stopped 'cos it was no good. So I started to think me dad wasn't really drowned and one day he'd come and fetch me away an' we'd go and live in a nice 'ouse and nobody'd ever box me ears or shout at me again. I was always hopin' like. Of a Sunday mornin' when we was marched to church, I'd look out for a stranger 'anging about. A sea-going man wi' a tarred pigtail, who'd look at me and know I was his daughter. But there wasn't never nobody. Only country folk, who looked down their noses at us. It were a nice place, though, where t'mill was. In a valley wi' a river running through. We saw children paddlin' in the river sometimes in t'summer. We was never let, though. There were never no time for skylarkin'. An' we was allus dog tired any road up.'

Hope finally ran out when she saw her best friend caught by her long hair in the winding gear and smashed, screaming, to a bloody pulp. She faced the fact squarely that there was no one who would come to her rescue. There was only one way of escape.

After her shift the next night, Lily straggled behind the others and hid herself behind a stack of bales in the mill yard until the watchman moved from the gate to relieve his bladder behind a bush. Then she flew, silent as a grey wraith, under the arch in the high stone walls and out onto the moors.

Somehow she survived, though there was already snow ledged among the tussocky grass, twice narrowly missing search parties, for an apprentice was a valuable commodity and must be found and severely punished lest others take it into their head to run off. She drank from streams and raided farms and outhouses for food, growing canny and bold. Once she stole a skirt and pinafore spread out to dry on a garden hedge.

'Proper respectable I looked after that. For a bit, any road, till I'd wore 'em day and night for a month or two.'

They were the vermin-ridden rags Mrs Chadwick had stripped off her.

Lily made her way steadily south, picking out of her memory the names of the places where the wagon had rested overnight on its journey to the mill. Finding a day's work here and there – on a farm, at an inn – telling the tale of how she was an orphan going to find relatives in Exeter, fearful of staying too long anywhere in case it was suspected she was a runaway apprentice.

'I'd 'a' killed meself any road rather'n go back to t'mill,' she said in such a matter-of-fact voice that I felt chilled at the certainty that she would have done so. 'An' I was beginnin' to get desperate that I'd never find work and someone would suspect sommat. Now I find meself here, in this grand house . . .'

Her voice trailed off. She gazed round in wonder at the bleak garret, the soft light thrown by the candle catching the roughly cut edges of her brown hair in a blurry, golden nimbus. Then she faced me and said in that same flat voice, 'So there you 'ave it, miss. I don't doubt you'd get a fine reward if you turned me in. I'm a runaway and a thief. I've stole food an' I've stole clothes. An' I've lied.' She held up her scarred, rough hands with their broken nails. 'But it's not me true nature. These is honest hands as didn't want to steal nothin', 'cept I had no choice. An' I lied because I was right frightened. But you give me a chance, miss, an' I'll work until I drops. I'll not let you down.'

There was a moment's silence, then, impulsively I reached out and held her hands tightly in my own.

After that we sat there for a long time, sometimes talking, sometimes lost in companionable thought, as the candle guttered extravagantly to its end.

There were two long weeks to get through and I died a thousand deaths on Lily's behalf. Though she was eager and sharp, she knew nothing of household duties or nice manners. Her world had been the noisy, stinking hellhole of the mill where orders, oaths and blows followed in quick succession. In the overcrowded apprentice house where the children slept three to a bed in dormitories with barred windows, the slatternly woman who prepared their food and occasionally shifted the dirt from one corner to another had scarcely been an example of domestic efficiency. Lily had to learn everything from scratch, with either Miss Olga standing over her, chivvying and scolding, or Mrs Caunter's malevolent eye watching for the smallest mistake.

I did my best to school Lily in her duties and to distract Miss Olga when I saw that Lily was clattering the best china as though it were the tin bowl and mug she had been used to, or about to bounce up the stairs two at a time, or when I heard the sound of cheerful whistling as she scrubbed the front step.

'But why mustn't I whistle, Miss Jo?' she asked, bewildered.

'It is not *done*,' I hissed. 'Whistling is for rough street boys.'

'Well, rough is what I am,' she grinned, 'even if I'm not a lad. Should you like to hear me whistle proper? I could allus make meself heard better'n mill hooter—'

'No, *no*. Lily, you must be quiet and decorous or Miss Olga will put you off.'

'What's dec'rus, miss?'

'Well, obedient, proper, decent, especially in view of the neighbours.'

'But I does everythin' I'm told. An' you're keepin' me decent, Miss Jo, findin' clothes an' that. I can't see as that stops me from showin' that I'm right pleased to be livin' here.'

I sighed. 'Could you not perhaps hum quietly to yourself, instead of whistling?'

'I'll try,' she said. 'But sometimes it just bursts out o' me, the 'appiness . . .'

That was the touching, shaming thing. That Lily's life had been so unpleasant before that servitude in

Torre Crescent was a positive delight. She was even undaunted by Mrs Caunter.

'Bless you, miss, if you'd 'ad ole Bradshaw as your overseer for six year, you'd've learned the ways of folks wi' mischief on their mind. He was up to all sorts. He'd cause trouble then blame it on some lad 'e'd got it in for. I seen many a one forced to work wi' an iron weight tied to his ankles 'cos Bradshaw 'ad a down on 'im. An' he were fond of lifting the big girls' skirts wi' 'is cane to look at their legs then 'ee'd complain as they were lewd and wanted punishing. He'd tek a strap to 'em – and to t'lads as gawked and laughed same as 'e did.'

'Did you not complain?' I exclaimed, shocked.

'Who'd've listened to us? Any road, I learned not to catch his eye when he were in that mood.' Her grin was wide as though these grim memories were nothing. 'So I'm too fly where yon slow owd cook's concerned. Like yesterday. I saw her 'ide a broken old plate among t'dishes I was about to wash in t'scullery. An' she stood at me back, ready to pounce when I come to it. So I just says as I can smell burnin' and a cinder must've jumped out o' t'fire an' she scuttles off to see to it. Then I hides the plate in me drawers and chucks it down the bog-hole when I goes to piss. She couldn't say nowt about me breakin' a plate then wi'out givin' herself away, could she? An' if she accuses me of stealin' it, where's the evidence?'

'Not bog-hole, Lily,' I quavered, faintly. ' "Necessary" or "privy" if you must mention it. And please, *please* never speak of . . . of relieving yourself or of . . . well, undergarmets, in the hearing of our employers.'

My imagination rioted. I thought of the expression on Miss Olga's face if Lily ever used such earthy terms to her in so blithe and unembarrassed a way. As for

Miss Polsham, such phrases falling upon her ears would cause her sensitive nerves to jangle fit to rival the cathedral bells.

I could not help it. I could not remember when I had last given in to laughter, but now I was helpless with it.

Lily Walker's presence in the house was proving a tonic in more ways than one. I just prayed that she would not do or say anything too outrageous, so giving Miss Olga cause to turn her out.

But Miss Olga was no fool. What Lily lacked in manners and experience she made up for tenfold in willingness and a seemingly inexhaustible appetite for hard work. She scurried round the house like a miniature whirlwind, a smile always ready to break out, her cries of 'What next, miss?' echoing after her. And to see her absorbed in her polishing, elbows going like pistons, was a sight to see. Never had the brasses gleamed so brilliantly, the window glass sparkled so finely or such a deep, mellow glow been raised on the furniture. If she was still gauche in the matter of waiting on table, or a touch too familiar when showing in Dr Barlow by telling him he looked hot and mithered as she took his hat, then that was something time would rectify.

And if her fate did hang in the balance, then Dr Barlow tipped it in her favour.

'Well done, Miss Olga,' he said heartily, interrupting her as she related rather sourly my part in bringing Lily to Torre Crescent. 'It takes a generous nature to take in an orphan off the street, but then when have the daughters of Mr Nathaniel Polsham ever been behind in charity?' Pleased colour tinged Miss Olga's parchment cheeks and the doctor turned his head as though to contemplate the wine in his glass. I was the only one who could see his eyelid drop in a distinct wink. 'You will soon have her trained to your exacting standards, for there's intelligence there if I'm any judge. And I must congratulate you on the improvement in Miss Joanna here. Your kindly attentions to her are already paying dividends. Why, she is a different girl already! There is colour in her cheeks and a lively look to her that speaks of good nourishment. And those troublesome chilblains quite gone, which is a sign that the whole constitution is less languid. Keep up the good work, dear lady! I shall look to see continuing improvement when next I call . . .'

So Lily's fate was sealed. Miss Olga, preening with undeserved compliments, had found a true treasure. And I a friend.

On the first day of June, Miss Olga doled out my first quarter's salary, less the five shillings she had previously advanced. I placed three sovereigns into my father's tobacco pouch and hoped, by careful expenditure, to make the remaining fifteen shillings last until September.

But there was the matter of keeping myself respectably clothed. Lily had come to Torre Crescent with nothing but what she stood up in – and that due to Mrs Chadwick's generosity. Miss Olga had supplied her with the minimum of two cheap print dresses, caps and aprons, but that was all Lily could expect. I passed on what stockings and undergarments I could, cut down and darned and patched though they were. Now it seemed that my precious hoard must be raided to keep us both decent.

I reviewed my sparse wardrobe with something approaching despair. The weather had turned warm and I sweltered still in wool and flannel. I had hopelessly outgrown the three summer dresses which had originally belonged to Phoebe. Last year, with false hems and the letting out of seams and darts, they had served well enough but now they were so tight I could not fasten one button and so short as to be indecent. I gave every spare moment to the unpicking and reworking of the sound material and I discovered a stall on the market where secondhand clothes were sold. There I searched for bargains, quickly putting aside my initial reluctance to delve among the sometimes grubby goods. I do not know whether Mama would have been horrified or amused to see her daughter haggling with the stallholder over a voluminous striped gingham skirt or an old-fashioned hooped net gown, considerably torn in places but with a silk underskirt that had possibilities for reworking. Certainly the Misses Polsham would have been shocked. But I took good care to be discreet and felt that as Miss Olga never thought to enquire about Lily's circumstances or mine, I did not owe her an explanation.

Mrs Chadwick understood. More than once when I called, there was a small bundle of leftover material for me.

'Some scraps, my dear. You may work them into patchwork, perhaps. Oh, and here are some bobbins with a little thread still left upon them that I have no more use for.'

They were more than scraps. A collar and cuffs might be made from one piece, a chemise lengthened with another. I was grateful that I was in possession of at least one or two respectable gowns when at last the news came that I had been so long awaiting.

The letter had been at Mrs Chadwick's for more than week before I had chance to collect it.

The weather had been hot and the fruit in the garden had ripened.

'We shall pick gooseberries today, Joanna,' Miss Olga said, 'then you may assist Mrs Caunter in the

129

preparation and making of the jam. Then it will be the turn of the redcurrants . . .'

Despite my wearing the old cotton sunbonnet kept on a hook by the scullery door for just this purpose, the sun turned my nose pink and brought up a rash of freckles on my face and arms as I picked the fruit. But I enjoyed being in the garden as much as I loathed being in the sweatily hot kitchen. Miss Olga, too, was at her most content out here. The garden, I realised, was her especial pride and it was as groomed and colourful as any small plot could be. Apart from the fruit bushes and the apple and damson trees, the space within the high protective walls was given over to flowers. She fussed over the roses and geraniums, stocks and verbena, lavishing upon them far more care and attention than ever she seemed prepared to give to any person, even her own sister. I smiled to watch her shabby figure, shrouded in an old wrapper, trowelling and clipping and watering in dedicated silence. I could almost imagine she communed silently with the plants, perhaps even poured upon them whatever love still stirred in her gaunt, grey soul.

The making of the gooseberry jam and redcurrant jelly was a particular penance. Mrs Caunter, exceedingly cantankerous, set me to stirring the vast jam pan over the fire. My face was soon as scarlet as the blaze and runnels of sweat soaked my bodice.

'That 'en't set yet,' she'd bawl as I tried to be helpful by testing the jam. 'You'm no idea! Needs another five minutes. Now git from under my feet and see as that young imp o' mischief 'as scalded they jars proper . . .'

Then the last jar, thankfully, was sealed with egg white and tissue, capped with oiled paper and laid upon the pantry shelves. I straightened my aching back and returned to the parlour. I should have liked nothing more than to sit quietly for an hour with a book or some sewing. But Miss Polsham wished me to go to the druggist for cooling powders.

'It is the heat, I am overcome with it,' she said tetchily. 'And the smell of the jam has pervaded the house, so that I feel most sickly . . . No! Do not draw the blind, the sun will be right in my eyes.'

'But if I opened the window a little—'

'I cannot bear a draught, as well you know,' she moaned. 'Now pour me a glass of barley water and I think I may force myself to eat a slice of bread and butter, cut very thin with a scraping of the new jam. I have scarce had a morsel to eat today I have felt so enervated and I may say my condition has not been helped by your conduct these last few days, Joanna.'

'My conduct, Miss Polsham?' I queried, puzzled, pouring barley water from the jug to the glass at the table by her side. Though it was within easy reach of her plump hand, she had been too weak – or too idle – to help herself.

'I have been most abominably neglected – no, do not protest. I have scarce had half the attention given to me for which you are paid most handsomely.'

'But the jam. Miss Olga said—'

'Of course, the fruit has to be preserved. But not at the expense of my health. You should have been constantly alert for my bell, instead of which every time I rang it seemed that Lily was the only one within earshot. And a bouncing, clumping creature she is to be sure, and impertinent, too, for she always insisted that you were too busy to attend upon me and being too ill to argue I had to put up with her ministrations . . .'

The complaining voice droned on. I was deeply grateful to Lily for shielding me for a little while from its constant nerve-grating whine. I would thank her later. We would laugh over it. But now I was tired and hot and sticky and had to fight an impulse to pick up

131

the jug of barley water and pour it over that nodding, lace-capped, selfish head.

One day, I thought fiercely, it will all be different. One day I shall be free and independent.

One day.

Sometimes that day seemed so far away as to be unattainable.

Despite my weariness I almost ran to the druggist so that I might snatch a few moments to call at Mrs Chadwick's. I opened the letter she had for me and scanned it quickly as I walked back to the High Street. Then stopped, clutching the paper to my breast, the complexion of the long wearisome day suddenly changed.

Ben and Mr Chadwick were coming to Exeter! I was to see my dear brother at last!

I wanted to dance and shout right there on the street. I felt a great foolish beam spread across my face. I scarcely felt the cobbles under my shabby shoes I was so elated as I dodged round the knot of men gathered jovially at the door of the Swan Tavern.

A face swam out at me. A face known from the dark edge of dreams I sometimes had. Dreams of fear, of distress, of falling snow and bitter wind. Dreams from which I woke crying out and full of fear.

I stopped short. Recognition was instant.

Nicholas Fox.

And a very different Nicholas Fox to the distraught young man whose brooding image still haunted some inner corner of my mind.

The despair and distress of that winter's afternoon might never have been. He looked, today, the very picture of a man who had not a care in the world. As I watched, he threw back his head in laughter, showing the strong brown line of his throat above a carelessly knotted cravat. One hand tapped lightly in emphasis on the shoulder of a plump, dandified man in a canary yellow coat as he continued speaking. Doubtless some ribald tale if the sly grins of idlers hovering within earshot were anything to go by. At his other side was a villainous-looking man, built like a house end, broken-nosed and with a gap in his grin where a tooth was lost.

The tale ended. A roar of laughter broke out.

And Nicholas Fox turned his head and saw me.

For a moment his glance held mine, sharpened. His dark eyebrows lifted in surprise and, distinctly, I saw the flash of recognition in his eyes and the way he caught his breath as though he was about to speak.

I smiled at him, foolish with excitement because of my secret news and pleased, perhaps, to see that he, too, had made his recovery from the desperate grief I had understood and shared for a brief time on that bitter winter's afternoon. I wanted for a few heady seconds to run to him, to tell him all that had happened and that I knew, now, why he had cautioned me about my ruthless grandfather. I wanted to know how he had fared these last months and what his plans were and if he was still intent on revenge. I might even have taken a step towards him . . .

The dandified man at his side spoke, went unheard and turned impatiently to see what held his companion's attention.

It was like a door slamming in my face.

Nicholas Fox's glance was suddenly altered. It swept over me, past me. Cold, indifferent. He had seen me, recognised me, cut me dead.

Slowly and deliberately he turned away, sweeping a careless brown hand across the dandy's shoulders, so that he, too, turned his back again, merely bestowing on me a passing incurious glance.

They walked into the tavern and I gathered my wits and pressed on homewards, all the joy the letter had brought oddly muted. Which was quite ridiculous. Why should it matter that someone met so briefly and at such a dreadful time should now choose not to acknowledge me? Perhaps it was that I had unexpectedly jolted his memory of a day that he preferred to forget. Perhaps he now wished to put all that talk of revenge behind him and my sudden appearance had embarrassed him.

Or perhaps he had discovered that I was closer in kinship to Francis Kerswell than I had chosen to reveal on that wild afternoon.

Hatred of the Kerswells was bred in his bones. His grandfather, his father had suffered at Frank Kerswell's hands.

I was tainted with that same ancestry. I was the granddaughter of this man he had every cause in the world to hate. Therefore I was to be despised and ignored.

It was a thought that took some of the brilliance from the clear and sparkling summer afternoon.

Chapter Five

'We are to have visitors,' Miss Olga announced after prayers a week later. 'My cousins the Pascoes are to call this afternoon.' Her tone was martyred. She had intoned a long, gloomy passage from the Book of Job, as though to set the tone of the day: '. . . man dieth and wasteth away . . . and thou destroyest the hopes of man . . . his flesh shall have pain and his soul within him shall mourn.' The phrases rolled with gloomy relish off her tongue. Then she dismissed Lily and Mrs Caunter, closed the Bible and turned away, flinging at me, grudgingly, as an afterthought, 'And your brother and grandfather will be in the company, Joanna.'

An air of unease had hung over the house for several days, ever since a note had been delivered by a liveried servant. Lily told me he was Mr James Pascoe's footman. 'Right cheeky article,' she declared. 'Looked down 'is nose proper snotty when 'e handed me the letter, then tried to pinch me arse the minute me back was turned.' She giggled. 'So I stepped on 'is foot real hard. Bent the buckle on 'is fancy shoe. He didn't 'alf cuss. Mebbe it'll learn 'im to keep 'is 'ands to 'isself in future.'

Miss Olga did not condescend to inform me what was in the note, but both she and Miss Polsham grew increasingly tetchy. Had I not been forewarned by Mr Chadwick I would have been bewildered by my

135

inability to please them in any particular. But guessing that it had something to do with Ben's visit and that perhaps some arrangements had been made for me to have some meetings with him, I tried to be patient.

And now I was to have my reward.

'We shall need extra chairs down from the attic,' Miss Olga announced. 'Really, it is most inconvenient, so much company at once. Of course, dear Cousin James always calls when he is staying in Exeter to see if there are any repairs or such to the house that we may be in need of. And dear Blandford and Susannah and Blandford's wife Jane – if she is in good health – usually call separately to pay their respects. But to come all together! And with your brother and his tutor and your grandfather! That is six, and if Jane accompanies them, seven! And gentlemen will want more substantial fare than bread and butter with their tea. The last time Blandford was here it was winter and he would insist on toasted crumpets which we had to send out for, at great inconvenience and expense . . . Oh, and they know my sister is not to be over-excited or she will become feverish.'

'Could not Mrs Caunter prepare sandwiches?' I suggested brightly. 'And there is time, surely, for her to make a few pastries. The new jam would make excellent tartlets and there is still half a fruit cake left which could be cut up small and nicely arranged—'

'As you are so full of useful ideas,' she snapped, 'you may speak to Mrs Caunter yourself and offer her your assistance. Now please ring for Lily and accompany me to the attic.'

I dutifully followed Miss Olga upstairs, wishing too late that I had not spoken so hastily. Confrontation with Mrs Caunter was never a pleasant prospect. It was something, I had grown to realise, that Miss Olga herself particularly avoided.

The attic was dark and silent and shrouded under dustsheets.

'Why, there are some pretty things here,' I exclaimed, peering under a dustsheet and forgetting the prospect of battling with Mrs Caunter in my surprise at finding an oval mirror in a gilt frame that was most delicately carved with a design of twining leaves and smiling cherubs and several framed oils of half-naked nymphs sunning themselves in a forest glade. Even through the dust the colours shone clear and cool and delicate.

'French and most unsuitably crude and frivolous for the house of respectable people,' Miss Olga said, 'as my stepmother pointed out when she had them removed up here. My mother brought them with her as part of her dowry. My maternal grandfather was a Guernsey man who owned a fleet of merchant ships and collected a great deal of what Papa considered to be tasteless curios from foreign places. Now, where were those chairs put?'

'These them, Miss?' Lily queried, peering round a pile of boxes. 'Sorta bandy gold legs they got and right mucky—'

'That will do, Lily,' Miss Olga snapped. 'Hold your tongue and help Miss Joanna move the boxes.'

There were six chairs, which looked to be of the same style and period as the mirror. By the time we had them out, our hands and the sacking pinafores we had prudently pinned over our gowns were grimy and Miss Olga even more out of temper.

'The silk covering on the seats has quite rotted through on two of the chairs. The rest will have to do, though they will look sadly out of place among the better pieces downstairs.' She sent a frowning look round the attic. 'Heaven knows what moths and other harmful creatures may be breeding to spread into the rest of the house. Your first duty when you return from jaunting with your brother, Joanna, will be to supervise Lily in the turning out and thorough cleansing and ordering of this attic.'

'Then I am to be allowed to go out with him?' I said eagerly.

Miss Olga compressed her lips. 'It is most inconvenient, but your grandfather has requested it, and naturally my sister and I feel obliged to give our consent.'

'I am most grateful, Miss Olga,' I said meekly, hardly able to control my delight. I felt pleased, too, at the prospect of turning out the attic. If she thought it was a punishment, she was wrong. I rather liked the thought of discovering what treasures lay hidden and forgotten up here. 'Oh, and if I may mention it,' I said as she stood at the foot of the stairs while Lily and I struggled down one at a time with the chairs, 'should you have any objection if I rearranged the furniture in my room to make it more convenient?'

Lily chose that moment to stumble on the stairs, distracting Miss Olga into a flurry of recriminations.

I added, quickly, seizing the opportunity, 'Perhaps there may be items in the attic – valueless items, of course – that with your permission I might also borrow.'

I was not sure that she properly heard my last request, but I was not fool enough to repeat it.

She waved away my query with an impatient, 'Do what you like, girl. Just do not bother me when I have more important things on my mind. Lily! Watch that you do not knock the banisters!'

It was all I needed.

Despite all that there was to do, the hours passed with agonising slowness. My emotions swung back and forth like the pendulum of a clock from the heights of joyous anticipation to the depths of doubt. I so longed to see Ben, yet we had been separated for so long that I feared he might now regard me as a stranger. Mr Chadwick was his closest companion, Grandfather was the benefactor who showered him with everything he could wish for – which mostly seemed to be an ever-growing menagerie of animals. What had I to offer him now, except my love? That might now to him seem a poor and unwanted thing.

Mrs Caunter blew to a rage that set every grey whisker on her chin trembling when I carefully put to her my suggestions for refreshment. She wheezed her refusal in no uncertain terms.

'Make pastry? At this hour? 'Tes ridic'lous. Bread 'n' butter's allus been good enough for company afore.'

'But it is a large party, with several gentlemen, Mrs Caunter, surely—'

'Don't you give me no argument, miss!'

'But I would help, Mrs Caunter. Miss Olga especially asked me to give you every assistance.'

'Hah!' Mrs Caunter folded her arms across her stained pinafore. 'You want fancy articles, you best get on and make 'em. I 'en't got the time wi' dinner on the go.' She turned her back on me and went to stir the pot of greasy mutton stew over the fire.

I took her at her word, which brought down another cascade of fury on my head.

'What you doin' in my pantry? And who tol' ee to go peeking in the dresser and movin' my things?'

'Mrs Caunter!' I snapped back. 'If I am to make pastry I have to find where you keep butter and flour and the rolling pin, and I must have some room on the kitchen table.'

Lily chose that moment to come bouncing in from the garden with pails of water from the pump.

''Ere, Miss Jo, I knows where everythin' is.'

Mrs Caunter aimed a cuff at her head. 'You meddle yourself wi' your own business. There's a stack o' pans to be scrubbed in the scullery an' if they're not done in five minutes I'll take the broom handle to ee.'

Lily winked cheekily and dodged away, reappearing with everything I needed.

'You young toad,' Mrs Caunter screeched. 'What did I tell ee?' Her face was purple, the veins on her forehead standing out like wriggling worms. Then suddenly her hands flew to her chest and she staggered back to fall into the upright chair by the range, her mouth opening and shutting like a stranded fish.

Lily and I both ran to her.

'A glass of water, Lily. Quickly!'

I chafed Mrs Caunter's hands. She tried to push me away but there was no strength in her arms.

'What is it, Mrs Caunter? Are you in pain?'

'It'll go,' she gasped. 'Allus does . . .' The colour had drained from her face, leaving it ashy grey.

Lily brought the glass and presently Mrs Caunter was able to take a sip.

'You have had this pain before, then,' I said, gently. 'Should you not speak to Miss Olga about it?'

'No!' Her colour and her ill temper were returning. 'Naught to do wi' anyone else. 'Tes just the heat an' bein' tormented by girt fools!'

'But you looked so ill, Mrs Caunter. Surely it would do no harm for Dr Barlow to take a look at you.'

'Don't ee go spoutin' none upstairs, d'ye hear?' Her whiskers quivered alarmingly and, fearful of her taking another swooning fit, I agreed to say nothing.

But some of the fire had gone out of her. She moved cautiously round the kitchen after that, as though frightened that the mysterious pain would strike again, and apart from grumbling continuously under her breath she made no more protests at my presence in the kitchen.

'I seen her like this afore,' Lily confided. 'Went all white and near dropped a pan on 'er foot.'

'If she is ill, she must be persuaded to see the doctor.'

'Not 'er,' Lily said. 'Stands to reason. She's scared the old biddies upstairs'll turn 'er out if she can't do 'er work, and where else would she go? She's got no family, no friends. She bin 'ere that long that the only way she'll leave and me get a bit o' peace is if they carries 'er out feet first.' She grinned. 'Don't look so worried, Miss Jo. She's a cantankerous ol' bat, but I'll watch out for her and do me best to 'elp her where I can.'

In the end all was prepared in good time. The tartlets were overbaked because I was not used to the range, but at least the pastry did not defy the teeth as Mrs Caunter's did. They looked well enough when set out on a tray with the sliced fruit cake. There were sandwiches of both cucumber and plain bread and butter and of a quantity to satisfy the gentlemen. Lily was primed in her duties. The chairs in the parlour – the gilt chairs looking frivolous among the dark, solid shapes of oak and mahogany – were arranged to Miss Olga's satisfaction. Miss Polsham lay amid cushions and shawls on her day bed practising an air of invalid languor. Miss Olga and I sat nervously at the embroidery she insisted was the only activity permissible with company due.

The sound of the front door knocker made us start and it took all my strength of will to remain in my seat until Lily opened the parlour door to admit the guests.

The room was suddenly, overpoweringly, full of strange faces, loud voices. As I curtsied and smiled, acknowledging the introductions, I barely saw these strangers. My eyes were only for Ben, shyly clinging to Mr Chadwick's side, as once he had clung to mine.

For a moment, pain stabbed, fierce and sharp, then I forgot it as Mr Chadwick gently urged Ben forward.

'See who is here, Ben. Did I not promise you that you would see your sister today?'

I saw him through a blur of tears. Saw his frown, the slow moment of incomprehension – then the lighting of his face as his innocent, childlike, beautiful smile broke out.

'Jo? It is Jo!'

'Oh, Ben, my dear . . .'

It was as much as I was allowed to say. No polite formalities for my brother. He crushed me in a great bear hug and I, regardless of the others, flung my arms round his neck and held him close.

'Ben! Come now! Sit here by me.' Grandfather's harsh voice split the silence that had momentarily descended on the company.

Ben reluctantly released me and as I fought to control the happy tears I saw to my embarrassment that our reunion had drawn every eye. Curiosity, amusement, sympathy, condemnation, even a flicker of distaste – I saw how each person reacted before glances fell away and conversation resumed.

Mr James Pascoe seated himself at my side. He was a short, round gentleman, looking fit to burst out of his straining coat.

'And how does Exeter suit you, Miss Howarth?' he asked after we had exchanged polite pleasantries.

'It is a fine city,' I said, absently, as I watched Ben staring round in some puzzlement as though wondering why he was made to sit here with all these bewildering people. I silently blessed Mr Chadwick who had stationed himself behind Ben's chair and put a reassuring hand on his shoulder from time to time.

'Hah! Then I would be obliged if you would pass your opinion to my daughter,' Mr Pascoe said. 'For ever since she spent a time in London, she has found Devonshire considerably dull. Do you not tell me so every day, Susannah?'

'Of course, Papa.' Susannah Pascoe laughed prettily. 'But perhaps Miss Howarth has visited London and knows for herself. You have had the benefit of living in a great many places about the country, I understand.'

'Mostly in the north,' I said. 'I have never visited London.'

Mr Blandford Pascoe leaned forward. 'I have not been to the north but I fancy your face is familiar. We have met somewhere, perhaps? A ball? A soirée?'

'Perhaps it is the family likeness,' his wife, Jane, put in softly. 'I can very much see the resemblance to Mr Kerswell.'

Blandford Pascoe bared small discoloured teeth in a smile. 'Ah, Jane, you have an opinion, do you? Speak up, my dear, so that we may all share it.'

Jane Pascoe coloured and lowered her lashes. 'It . . . it was just that I saw it . . . right away . . .'

'How very observant of you, but in this case, as so often, I fear you are quite wrong in your assumption.'

'Do not tease poor Jane,' Susannah cried, 'for Miss Howarth does truly have the look of the Kerswells, and it is hardly likely that you have met before, for Miss Howarth has surely not mixed in society.' A small pause, in which those sparkling eyes seemed to assess and dismiss my striped gingham gown as if she knew it was cut from a voluminous skirt bought secondhand and a person wearing such a thing could never be expected to move in circles where she and her brother might be encountered. 'No, Blandford, you have probably confused Miss Howarth with some other.'

She herself sat poised on the gilt chair like a pretty

143

butterfly at rest. Her golden hair hung in bunched ringlets about the smooth oval of her face. Her beribboned bonnet was in the latest mode. Her flower-embroidered lemon gown was made of the finest silk. She was, I guessed, eighteen or so, her brother a few years older. He was handsome enough though the pallor of his complexion and the petulant twist to his full red lips gave him a dissipated air. He was as showily groomed and dressed as his sister. His thin brown hair was arranged in careful tendrils, his high linen stock was elaborately tied, his pale green coat fashionably tight and cut to reveal the revers of a pink silk waistcoat. I did not take to either of them and I felt sorry for Blandford's wife, Jane, who sat between them in her silvery grey gown like a frail mouse poised nervously between two elegant predatory animals.

Thankfully, attention then switched from me. Miss Olga asked Jane Pascoe how her little daughter fared. Her husband brushed the question aside before she had a chance to answer. 'Well enough, thank you, cousin. She has a fine set of lungs on her, that is for sure. It is likely you could hear her from this distance if you listened carefully.'

'It is merely that she is teething,' Jane Pascoe protested softly.

'Teething? Has she been teething since she was born? No, my dear, you are naturally fond and do not see that you have bred a veritable termagant of an infant who whimpers even at a look. Why, it has been in me to farm the child out to some countrywoman to bring up as her own in order to relieve the household of her constant bellowing!' He laughed, inviting us to share his merriment, but I saw the flash of terror in his wife's eyes. Perhaps his unkind taunt was not quite the joke everyone else seemed to think it.

'She will grow out of it,' his father declared, stoutly.

'I remember you yourself were not the most amiable of infants but by the time you were out of petticoats you were bright and forward enough to have the ladies cooing over you, even if you drove the nursemaids to despair with your pranks.' He sighed. 'But then you lacked a mother's hand, she dying so untimely in your sister's babyhood.'

Blandford frowned, evidently less amenable to having his own shortcomings being exposed, but Lily coming in with the tea provided a timely interruption. He leaped to his feet in order to pass the teacups as Miss Olga poured.

I was relieved that he did not pursue his earlier questions. He might have remembered where he had seen me and I had no wish for the Misses Polsham to know that I had been wandering in places where I had no right to be. But my own curiosity was aroused, for I had recognised him as soon as I saw him. He was the man in the dandified yellow coat who had been in the close company of Nicholas Fox outside the Swan.

I wondered what business it was that drew them together.

Throughout the visit my grandfather spoke only when directly addressed. He sat balancing his cup and plate, coldly watchful, a great brooding hawk in stiff old-fashioned plumage, his frizz of white hair standing like a ruff round his head. For all his silence, his presence seemed overpowering, dominating. I knew quite well why he had come. To oversee my meetings with Ben. Mr Chadwick had said as much in his letter but I had chosen to hope that he would have a change of heart. As though he would! Seeing him again in the flesh reminded me forcibly that this was a man who would take no chances that his authority might be undermined. His distrust of me, his possessiveness of

Ben were powerful enough to bring him here to the city which Mr Chadwick had told me he much despised and had not visited in twenty years.

I had not thought beyond the delight of being again with Ben. Now I realised we were not to be left alone together and Grandfather's presence would not make for an easy atmosphere. Mr Chadwick had tried to persuade Grandfather that it might be in Ben's interests to stay in some quiet lodging but this idea had been brushed brusquely aside. 'The boy must learn to mix,' he had growled. 'He cannot be kept for ever secluded like a hermit.' So he had accepted Mr Pascoe's offer of hospitality in Birch House, his town residence close by the fashionable Northernhay Gardens.

Mr Pascoe seemed amiable enough, if rather vague, a man inclined to gaze round abstractedly as though his mind was engaged on more interesting matters – perhaps the horses he had left at Kingsbridge or the various enterprises in which he dabbled. Mr Chadwick, who was a quiet observer of human nature, occasionally graced his letters with witty little character sketches. He had told me that Mr Pascoe was a man known for enthusiastically taking up money-making schemes then abandoning them when his enthusiasm died. 'I understand that the buying of land in Plymouth and Exeter and the building upon it of cheap housing for rent to the labouring classes is his present interest,' Mr Chadwick had written. 'He has tried to persuade Mr Kerswell of the advantage and profit to be gained from such speculation but I think your grandfather is of a more conservative disposition and will not be tempted into any rash ventures . . .'

From my own observation I felt that Mr Pascoe would be kind in his vague way towards Ben, but of Susannah Pascoe I was much less certain. She seemed a shallow and superficial creature and there was a touch of unnecessary spitefulness in some of her utterances. Which seemed sad when she was blessed with the advantage of such a pretty face and figure. I could not imagine her being tolerant of Ben's shortcomings. As to Blandford Pascoe, I could only breathe a sigh of relief that he had his own separate establishment. I did not at all like the way he treated his wife, never missing an opportunity to contradict her or put her down and smiling all the while with the bland confidence of his own superiority. By the time the company rose to leave, she drooped in silence like a fragile leaf on a broken branch. It would be unbearable if Ben was afforded the same treatment.

'Goodbye, Miss Howarth. I am pleased to have met you.' Jane Pascoe's eyes were averted, her voice scarcely above a whisper.

I wanted to say something comforting, something to make her realise that I had seen how her husband treated her and sympathised. But all I could manage, awkwardly, as Blandford approached was, 'I am sorry we did not have chance to talk together, Mrs Pascoe. I feel that the afternoon would have passed pleasantly, for both of us, that is, had we been able to further our acquaintance.'

Her head lifted. Her large sad brown eyes looked into mine. I realised with a start that she was scarcely older than Susannah Pascoe. I had been deceived by the air she wore of a woman out of whom all youthful spirit had long since drained.

'Yes . . . yes, perhaps so.' A hesitant smile had scarcely time to curve her pale lips before her husband took her arm, crying, 'Come, Jane. You would tattle on and on without a thought that others might be waiting,' and the narrow shoulders drooped once more and she turned away without a further word.

Grandfather balefully supervised my leavetaking of

Ben. 'Come, shake your sister's hand, boy,' he ordered. 'And you, miss, will see your brother tomorrow, so there is no need for fuss.'

I gripped Ben's hand briefly and gave him a circumspect peck on the cheek before Grandfather waved him back. Mr Chadwick gave me a conspiratorial smile before he, too, shook my hand.

'I look forward to meeting you again, Miss Howarth, when I may tell you of your brother's progress these last few months since you left Falconwood.'

'I can already see that there has been much improvement,' I began, gravely, but Grandfather interrupted us.

'Yes, yes! You will have time enough tomorrow. Be ready and waiting by nine. I have hired a chaise to take us to Topsham where I have business and we will not wait on you should you be dilatory.'

'I shall be ready, sir,' I said, and to myself, grimly, when he had moved to take his hat from Lily, 'I should not give you the satisfaction of leaving me behind.'

In the event, Grandfather's frowning presence could not dull my happiness that week. I was determined to make the most of each moment that Ben and I were together and fortune smiled on us because the weather was perfect. Warm sunshine and blue skies accompanied all our outings. And even Grandfather could not supervise every minute of every day. When we went to Topsham he was a good hour closeted in the shipping agent's office while Mr Chadwick, Ben and I strolled past the quaint Dutch-style houses on the quay and out by the wide glittering mud banks of the Exe estuary, chattering fifty to the dozen to make up for the stilted conversation in the chaise. Grandfather louring at us from his corner and speaking only to curse each time the vehicle bounced over a pothole put a damper on anything more spontaneous, but once he had stumped off up the agent's office stairs with a final warning that we were not to go far, we were like persons released from a vow of silence with a thousand questions to be asked and answered.

And so it was on subsequent days. We viewed the sights of Exeter, with Mr Chadwick, as one born and brought up in the city, giving a learned and lively documentary on all we saw. We strolled in Northernhay Gardens and walked miles along the bank of the Exe and through the rich, summery lanes to the hills where we could see the countryside for miles around and the smooth coils of the river pouring towards the distant sea. There were always moments when Grandfather's attention was diverted and Mr Chadwick and I could converse privately or times when Mr Chadwick would fall in step beside Grandfather and Ben and I went ahead to enjoy the pleasure of being in each other's company without supervision.

I was always conscious of Grandfather's contempt for me, but I grew to understand during the week that his attitude to Ben was as close to benign as his embittered nature would allow. He watched Ben constantly from beneath frowning white brows, ready to admonish him for any transgression, yet his glance was often gentle, his tone unexpectedly tolerant though his words might be curt. And Ben, in turn, with the instinct that young children or animals often exhibit, having a sense that seems to see beyond mere words to the heart of the person, knowing whom to trust and whom not, appeared totally at ease in Grandfather's company. Tugging at his sleeves, calling his attention to something that took his interest – a flock of swans sailing majestically on the river, a cascade of scented roses spilling over a garden wall, a carving at the top of a pillar in the cathedral of a floppy-eared hound crouching at the foot of its master. 'See, Grandfather. See, Jo. Is that not pretty? . . . You know I have a puppy at home with ears just like that, Jo. His name is Nelson, for he likes the sea above all things.' He chuckled with delight. His face abeam with simple enjoyment. And Grandfather gravely attentive, his hand quivering at Ben's elbow almost as though he might touch the boy out of affection. 'I like the sea, too, Jo. I can swim bravely, can I not, Mr Chadwick?'

'Indeed yes, Ben.' And to me, quietly, 'The daily swimming has been one of the better notions the doctors have put forward. He has gained much in health and vigour through it, do you not think so, Miss Howarth?'

I nodded. I could see much more assurance in Ben's step. He did not stumble so much and his back was straighter, his shoulders broader. He looked well set up now, a far cry from the grubby, dishevelled boy I had taken to Falconwood. Impeccable tailoring, crisp white linen, a beaver hat set carefully on his neatly barbered hair, his smiling, open countenance had such an effect that it was not only Grandfather who regarded him with approval. I saw many a sidelong, even flirtatious, female glance as we walked through the town.

Ben remained unaware, thank heaven, but I felt a frisson of unease. The mind of a child in the body of a handsome young man might make for difficulties I had not previously contemplated. I could almost be glad he was soon returning to the safety and simplicity of a quiet country life.

Although I spent the days with Ben, I was escorted back in the late afternoons to Torre Crescent where the Misses Polsham kept me busy until bedtime. Miss Polsham had not the slightest interest in my outings beyond the inconvenience to herself, though Miss Olga would question me, frowning, before I set about my tasks, as though she had to be certain that Grandfather had not led me into unsavoury company or unseemly byways.

It was to a wide-eyed Lily that I poured out the excitements of the day as we curled up on my bed sharing whatever titbits she had sneaked from the kitchen. A few raisins, a scrubbed new carrot, a handful of raw shelled peas that tasted so sweet that I regretted that they must ever be treated to such a severe boiling by Mrs Caunter that there was little flavour left.

The evenings I had to spend away from Ben were galling because I knew he was staying so near. But I swallowed down my rebellious feelings, listened cheerfully to Mr Chadwick's accounts of the sociable evenings at the Pascoes' house and when Ben said, sulkily, 'I do not care for so many people. Grandfather says I cannot go to my room even when the noise gives me the headache,' I said, carefully, so that Grandfather might know that I was behaving responsibly, 'You will get used to it, Ben dear, and it is only for a short while. You will be back at Falconwood soon and think what tales you will have to tell Miss Lightbody and Mrs Beer.'

These ladies had apparently both grown attached to Ben. Mrs Beer had been so won over that she had felled a newly employed stable lad with a sweep of her meaty arm because he grumbled that Ben's growing menagerie of stray animals was a trouble to look after. Mr Chadwick had smiled wryly when he told me of Miss Lightbody.

'One never knows when she may take it into her head to visit the schoolroom. And when she does she either behaves with the grandeur of a visiting duchess or screeches round poking fun at what we are doing which is most unsettling to me though she makes Ben laugh. I cannot tell if she is fond of Ben but I believe she enjoys the measure of interest Ben has brought to her secluded life.'

She had sent me a gift. Grandfather had grudgingly thrust a package upon me with a curt, 'The old fool tells me it is some frippery that you might use, though I cannot see you have need for it.'

Inside was a collar of dirty, discoloured, but exquisite Honiton lace wrapped round the papery petals of a pressed flower that had once been a rose. Pinned to the collar was a note, abominably misspelled and written in an almost indecipherable spidery hand.

Yore Bro come of Best so far, I think you have
the Bad Bargin child, but Adversty ne'er broke
a strong Hart or Will or I sh'd be under the Sod
yers since. Yore time will com if yew wish it and
are Bold to take your Chans, as yore Waywood
Ma did, at the Rite Moment. She bein a Trew
Kerswell in Spirrit as I think yew are also.
Whate'er faults they was ever Fyters. Yore Bro
in his Pore Way also which I am diverted to see
how he does. I wood hope that Wat is Herein
mite be of use and bring yew Good Fortewn.
Both was give to me by a Nobleman and
Admirer and e'er browt me luck at cards.
    Yore Frend, A. A. Lightbody.

Another line, which appeared to be a dark warning of some sort, was added at the foot of the page.

Take heed. Wild Beests are not always to be
feered but Tame Ones may have evil harts.

I could not help but chuckle when I read it. The ill-spelled words and the hint of threat in the last line seemed to bring her tiny, malicious, yet vital little person right into the room. I was touched that she had thought of me, but that she now considered herself my friend was a surprise that I found quite in keeping with her eccentricity for I had had little inkling of it when I was at Falconwood. I penned a note of thanks for Grandfather to take back with him and put the brittle flower between the pages of my favourite volume of John Donne's poems before it disintegrated altogether, hoping that some hint of ancient luck might still cling to it.

The lace collar was soaked, washed and pinned out to dry. And now it had been stitched to the neck of the 'new' dark green linen dress contrived from one of Phoebe's hand-me-downs and let out with narrow bands of a paler green from one of Mrs Chadwick's bundles. The deep fall of creamy lace gave the gown a distinction it had certainly not possessed before. I blessed Miss Lightbody for her timely gift and for the acceptable thought that I might one day have a 'chans' to take.

This last evening of Ben's stay I was to dine at Mr Pascoe's house. Miss Olga had informed me that she dined with them at least once while they were in town and made it clear that she found it most irritating that I was to share this honour with her and that had it not been for the insistence of dear Cousin James and dear Susannah, she was minded to have stayed with her sister who had suffered badly with the palpitations that afternoon. It was highly inconvenient that I could not be there to attend to Fanny and she was sure that Lily would be unable to cope and the evening, of course, would be quite ruined with the worry of it . . .

There did not seem much sign of worry as we descended from the carriage Mr Pascoe had sent for us. Her cheeks were unaccustomedly pink with excitement and she rustled most importantly into the house to where Susannah and her father waited.

Though her elderly maroon crepe dress had been steamed over a kettle to freshen it and hung in the air for several hours, the odour of camphor had filled the carriage and now floated behind her like an invisible train. The smell did nothing to ease my stomach which fluttered unmercifully both with nervous anticipation and with the sad realisation that tomorrow Ben would leave Exeter and it was purely at the whim of our grandfather when I should be allowed to see him again.

Out of the corner of my eye as I greeted Grandfather and Ben I saw Susannah Pascoe's nose wrinkle distastefully as she pressed her soft peachy cheek to Miss Olga's parchment one. She exchanged a swift amused glance with her brother, who, as though at a signal, lounged forward from where he had been leaning against the mantelpiece, sniffed loudly and said, 'Has a tomcat got in? I declare there is a most odd aroma wafting about.'

Susannah tapped her fan against his waistcoat. 'Now do not be naughty, Blandford,' she said with a pretty laugh. 'Take no notice, Cousin Olga. He is merely teasing. The odour of camphor is quite refreshing and so sensible of you to keep the moth away with such vigilance, though I myself prefer my maid to use dried lavender or tobacco leaves which are less penetrating in their aroma.'

Miss Olga smiled uncertainly. Susannah turned her brilliant smile on me.

'Ah, Miss Howarth. We are so pleased you are come this evening. I told Mr Kerswell he was the veriest brute to keep you from us all week.' She pouted at him, fluttering her golden lashes. 'And you have not been kind, you know, letting the poor girl stay out in the sun all day on these tedious outings.' The blue

154

laughing glance swung back from Grandfather's stony face to me. 'With a colouring such as yours, my dear, you should never go out in the sun without a veil. Why, I declare your freckles have multiplied a hundredfold!' She lowered her voice confidentially. 'Our kitchen maid at home in Kingsbridge suffers in the same way but she has the most splendid receipt for a cream which guarantees to fade them in a most extraordinary manner. I shall send for it and you may have it for your own use. Now do come along, Miss Howarth, and sit by my sister-in-law. She needs someone to cheer her up. She is most doleful on account of little Ruth having a slight cough. No, no, Ben!' She waved him away as he made to come smiling after me. 'You must do as I instructed you and entertain Miss Olga very nicely, as a young man of excellent manners should learn to do. What say you, Mr Kerswell?'

Grandfather grunted noncommittally.

Bewildered, Ben hesitated then shuffled dumbly to where Miss Olga was seated. This evening Ben had no careful watchdog. Mr Chadwick had been given leave to visit his mother. Susannah had evidently set herself up in his place, for having disposed of the guests to her satisfaction she tripped to Ben's side where she sparkled vivaciously at him, occasionally putting in a laughing correction, as he and Miss Olga began a conversation that was stiff on her side, stumbling and blushing on his.

I could not watch. I felt Ben's distress as my own. Every trill of that pretty laughter rippled along my nerve ends. I saw how Blandford Pascoe from where he stood with Grandfather and Mr Pascoe glanced often towards her. The exchange of amused glances between brother and sister did nothing for my peace of mind.

'Your little daughter is unwell, then?' I turned

resolutely to Jane Pascoe. She looked paler than ever this evening. Her white taffeta gown gave a ghostly cast to her already ethereal looks. A sudden draught might have blown her away like a fluff of dandelion seeds.

'I fear the croup,' she whispered. Her scared brown eyes, her coiled mousy-brown hair were the only colour about her. 'Though Blandford insists it is but a cold. He would not allow me to send for the doctor though the roughness of her breathing was distressing me greatly, and the nursemaid is only a young girl. Oh, if only Blandford had allowed me to keep on my own dear nurse whom I could depend upon with my life . . .' She broke off with an anxious flicker of her eyes towards her husband. She gave a nervous laugh. 'Of course she had been Mama's nurse also and was quite old and grown slow, but Hannah was so practical in illness. Papa always said she was worth her weight in gold. And she was so loving and kind and I miss her so – and dearest Papa. If only . . .' Her voice wobbled precariously into silence.

If only her papa had not died and left her alone. If only he had not striven to protect her from fortune-hunters by settling her in marriage before he succumbed to his last swift and incapacitating illness. If only his illness had not made him exhausted and impatient, blinkering him to anything beyond the convenience of a comfortable arrangement with his old acquaintance James Pascoe who was eager to see his headstrong and extravagant son off his hands and conveniently married to an heiress. If only . . . if only . . . Blandford Pascoe had been someone gentle and tender that she could love and feel safe with . . .

I could only guess at some of the emotions bound up in those two words breathed out on a shuddering sigh. I knew the bare outlines of her story gleaned from Miss Polsham and Miss Olga. 'She has been very fortunate,' Miss Polsham had stated, 'to be gathered so timely to the bosom of such a good, old family when she had not a relative in the world to protect her. It was an excellent match for her, her father being a mere merchant in the cloth trade with a flare for making money.' She sighed at this indication of his unworthiness to be related, however distantly, with a genteel person such as herself. '*His* father I have heard was only a poor tenant farmer, but that is as maybe. The girl herself is well mannered, I grant you, and dear Blandford I am sure has no reason to be disappointed in his choice, though her nature must, by comparison, appear somewhat dull when compared to the lively intelligence and wit of Susannah, or Blandford himself. But then, breeding will out. She is so often sickly, too. I pray that neither she nor the child have inherited the chest weakness that carried off both her parents.'

I touched Jane's cold hand. 'Children's ailments often flare up and as suddenly subside,' I said. 'I remember that my own younger sister when she was small would run a fever and have everyone in a tizzy one day, then run round lively as a cricket the next.'

Her fingers latched onto mine as though desperate for reassurance. 'Oh, if that could be true of Ruth! But I do fear most desperately that it is not a passing illness, but something serious. And she is such a scrap. I cannot think she may be really ill and I not there to watch over her.'

'How old is she?' I asked.

'Eleven months and forward, I am told, for her age, though she is so tiny.' Her lips quivered to a tremulous smile. 'She will soon be walking. And her smile is so sweet. It breaks my heart to have to leave her. I would spend all day playing and talking to her if I could, though I know it would be spoiling her, and Blandford

157

forbids it, for fear I neglect my other duties, which is quite proper though difficult. I dote too much, I expect, but I never before realised what a depth there is to maternal feeling. It is the greatest blessing and yet the greatest worry, as you will find one day yourself, Miss Howarth . . .'

I sat and listened to the whispery voice that rushed on as though there were few occasions when she could talk about her child to a sympathetic listener. The tense fingers gradually released their hold on mine. By the time dinner was called I knew everything there was to know about Miss Ruth Pascoe.

'Oh dear, I am afraid I have bored you, Miss Howarth,' Jane said, the habitual worried look returning.

'Not at all,' I assured her and then added, quietly, 'I miss my own family very much. It has been a pleasure to share yours for a little while.'

'Then you must come and visit us!' Her brown eyes widened eagerly. 'Oh, please say you will!'

'What is this you wish for so fervently, my dear?'

We had not noticed the gentlemen approaching to escort us in to dinner. We both rose hastily, a flush rising almost guiltily under Jane's fine skin, though I could not think what she might have to be guilty about. 'It was just . . . I have so enjoyed . . . that is . . . I thought Miss Howarth might call upon us and see Ruth . . .'

A pair of pale, protuberant eyes swivelled in my direction. Then, slowly, Blandford Pascoe eyed me up and down.

He was scarcely as tall as I was. He tipped his head back to review my hair, my face, then his glance slithered down, lingering over my neck and bosom, crawling down over my homemade gown to my feet. It gave me the most horrible sensation of being naked in front of him. As though those watery blue eyes raked through the cheap material of my gown, through my chemise and petticoats and clamped obscenely on the flesh beneath. It was all I could do to stand there without backing off, my smile frozen, goose bumps rising on my bare arms.

'So you have made a friend, Jane, you sly goose,' he said, making it sound as though she had overstepped some invisible, forbidden boundary. 'And yet you pretend to be shy to the point where you sometimes cannot even hold a sensible conversation with those closest to you.' All the while he spoke to Jane, his eyes continued their salacious inspection of me. 'If Miss Howarth is so disposed, of course she must visit,' he said softly. 'I will welcome her most warmly. Most warmly.'

Grandfather bowed to Jane with stiff, old-fashioned courtesy. She managed to smile as she laid her hand on his black sleeve. I was no longer smiling. I felt a shiver of repulsion that I must go in to dinner with this unpleasant man.

'Come now, Blandford, Miss Howarth,' Susannah called from Ben's side. 'Do not dawdle or I shall believe you are engaged in a flirtation, you naughty creatures.'

My hot cheeks were more from rising anger than embarrassment. A flirtation? With this . . . this disagreeable fop? My thoughts were not ladylike when I found I was seated next to him with Grandfather on my other side. And during the interminable meal I scarcely tasted anything of the excellent food, nor took notice of the cool blue and cream ambience of the dining room. The house was airy and gracious and at any other time I should have surveyed my surroundings with interest. All I was conscious of was Blandford Pascoe's uncomfortable closeness.

Conversation rippled round the table. I tried to talk to Grandfather, but all he would favour me with was a grunt before he resumed his talk with Miss Olga and Mr Pascoe. It was to Blandford Pascoe I must listen and respond, sickened by the waft of the violet-scented pomade that greased down his hair and more so by the many times he seemed to have to touch me. His chair seemed uncomfortably close to mine. His elbow continually nudged me, his leg shifted and twitched against my skirt though I tried, discreetly, to rearrange it out of his way. His plump white paws, dainty as a woman's, fluttered against my wrist, rested briefly on my arm, brushed accidentally against my hand.

The meal seemed endless.

Across the table Ben had lapsed to silence, his face dull and uncomprehending, despite Susannah's chatter flowing remorselessly round him. I knew that look, though I had not seen it for a long time – and not at all this happy week. It meant that Ben had retreated into himself. It had all become too much for his under-standing. He was unhappy and bored and I burned with resentment on his behalf because it was so unnecessary. Had we not been manoeuvred apart by Susannah Pascoe – and I was sure now that it was deliberate – Ben and I would have enjoyed every moment. Instead we must each suffer unpleasantness at the hands of the Pascoe sister and brother.

When at long last Susannah gave the signal for the ladies to retire to the drawing room, I was so wound up with indignation that without pausing to consider I asked if Ben might join us.

'You would not mind, would you, Mr Pascoe? Miss Pascoe?' I said desperately. 'It is our last evening and time is so . . . so precious . . .' I faltered in the face of Grandfather's thundercloud of a frown but Mr Pascoe rescued me.

160

'Of course, of course. Had I thought of it myself I should have insisted on it, for Ben does not, in any case, care for port or tobacco. Go along with your sister, young man. You will enjoy being fussed over by the ladies.'

This time I would not be subject to Susannah's whims. I stuck to Ben's side and when Susannah, floating ahead of us in her rich, rustling lavender silk gown, turned to recommend the ladies where to sit, I was already sidestepping her and leading Ben to the sofa, where I determinedly sat, pulling Ben down beside me. Jane quickly seated herself on my other side.

We were cosy for a little while, and Ben began to smile again as I coaxed him into conversation and Jane shyly began to ask him about his menagerie of animals at Falconwood. Susannah, however, was sharp with the maids who filed in with the silver trays bearing the coffee pot and cups and there was something impatient about the whisking of her fan as Miss Olga, sipping coffee at her side, rambled on interminably about how the town was growing disagreeably crowded with traffic and how much better and quieter and more peaceful everything had been when she was a girl.

I felt mildly vindicated at Susannah's obvious displeasure, but all too soon the men returned, talking in heartily jovial voices about a forthcoming prize fight.

'Could you not return to Exeter for it, Frank?' Mr Pascoe asked. 'The bout between Caleb Smith and Mad Jack Barton promises well and the boy would find it lively sport.'

Grandfather shook his head. 'There is more craft and subtlety, to my mind, in good country wrestling. Which is why I have a mind to let young Ben have tuition from a retired champion we have living in Starcombe.'

'Ah, but if you had ever seen Daniel Mendoza

161

trounce Richard Humphries you would not say that. Mendoza's footwork enabled him to caper like a hunting cat round his opponent and I have never seen a pugilist with a more fearsomely fast straight left.'

'Bah! I saw Gentleman John Jackson fight Mendoza and a poor bout it was. Jackson only won because he held tight to Mendoza's hair while clubbing him brutally in the face! What craft is there in that? I have had more amusement from watching two fisher lads practising arm locks . . .'

I heard no more, for Blandford chose that moment to sidle over.

'And what do you think of prize fighting, Miss Howarth?' he enquired, breathing brandy fumes in a fruity cloud.

'I have never seen it and never wish to,' I said. 'It is a brutal business, from what I hear.'

'But exciting,' he breathed. 'At least, many ladies find it so. Such a display of male strength and determination seems to rouse the most turbulent and excitable feelings in the female heart.'

'Not mine,' I said coldly.

'How do you know if you have never seen a display of pugilism?'

'If there is such a thing to be held in Exeter, I am sure the authorities will move swiftly against it. I have heard that the militia is often called in to uphold the law.'

'But this bout will be held beyond the city bounds on land owned by a sporting gentleman who has the goodwill of the gentry and nobility for fifty miles round about. And the advertising of it will be discreet, though I reckon The Fancy in the whole of the county of Devonshire already knows and looks forward to it without even a single bill being posted.'

'I cannot see that any person of sensibility could be

162

amused by two men battering themselves to a pulp.'

'Then how fortunate it is that I have the means to widen your education. You must join us and our friends at the bout.' His glance slid triumphantly from me to Jane. 'I am sure my wife, who is also stricken with similar misgivings, would appreciate your company.'

'But you promised I need not go,' Jane burst out, twisting her fingers together. 'Not now . . . now that I am sure . . .'

'What fantasy is this, my dear?' he interrupted, silkily. 'I did not make any such promise. To be sure, to prevent you becoming over-excited I said I might consider leaving you behind. But think on it, my dear. You have a friend and ally in Miss Howarth who will surely be a comfort and support to you if you turn faint at the sight of blood.' He leaned over confidentially. 'Besides, if it is a son you are breeding this time it is only right that he should come under suitable manly influences from the start. Too much languishing at home in the company of a bawling infant will not make for the lusty heir I am hopeful of.'

I said, sharply, thankful to be on sure ground, for there was nothing I could think of more distasteful than to attend any event, let alone a prize fight, in the company of this man, 'Thank you for your invitation, sir, but I must decline. Miss Polsham and Miss Olga would never allow me leave to go.'

Blandford grinned knowingly. 'You think so? Oh, I am sure those dear ladies would not go against my wishes, especially when it is to the benefit of dear Jane.'

'Then my grandfather . . .' I began.

By way of an answer Blandford strolled across the room to where the men stood arguing amiably. A few moments' conversation, a disinterested glance at me from Grandfather, a shrug of his shoulders. It was done. Grandfather did not give a fig. Tomorrow he would leave with Ben. That was all he was interested in. All he wanted. He did not care what happened to me. If I ran to him now and begged his help, he would brush me away as though I was an annoying insect.

And suddenly I did very much want his help, his protection.

Oh, I hated the idea, true enough, of attending a prize fight. But that was something I could grit my teeth and bear. I could always close my eyes and refuse to watch if it grew too bloody and cruel. I liked Jane Pascoe, felt sorry for her, would be glad to give her my support. But Blandford Pascoe . . .

I shuddered. I not only disliked him. There was something else. I was not quite sure why or what sort of threat he represented, but it was there in his eyes, in his manner, in his knowing smile.

I did not frighten easily, but Blandford Pascoe scared me.

It was with a miserable, troubled heart that I went back to Torre Crescent with Miss Olga. As the smart equippage carried us through the dark streets, I not only mourned for the loss of Ben, I felt the stirrings of apprehension for what the following weeks might hold when Blandford Pascoe would be in Exeter.

Chapter Six

I had never seen such a throng of people and, despite my misgivings, I could not help being stirred by the excitement of the crowd pouring down the narrow country road. Donkeys, horses, carts and carriages of every sort moved haltingly forward amid a press of pedestrians who now and then burst over gates and hedge banks into the surrounding fields and ran on past the bottleneck, uncaring of crops and startled cows.

The open carriage was hired for the occasion, Mr Pascoe having persuaded Blandford that it was unwise to risk his own phaeton and high-mettled horses in the press. Now it jerked to a halt for the umpteenth time, to his curses. The driver cracked his whip over the heads of a covey of ragged boys who dodged away, whooping and jeering, almost under the legs of the nervous horses.

'Young devils!' Blandford cried, then to Jane, 'This is what comes of listening to your whining nonsense. We should have been here an hour since like the others.'

'I . . . I am sorry, Blandford . . . but I could not help it . . . I felt so sickly . . .'

'Aye, and I am even sicklier at your constant complaining!'

I could not stop myself. 'Mrs Pascoe is not well,' I

said coldly. 'She should have been left to rest quietly at home, as your father suggested.'

We had all gathered at Northernhay, Blandford and Jane fetching me from Torre Crescent on the way from their house near Magdalen Street. Miss Olga's dour warnings rang in my ears. 'Heaven knows what rough people will be about! On no account stir from the side of Cousin James and Cousin Blandford. It is in my mind now to withdraw my permission for you to go, especially since you have not finished turning out the attic and it is most disagreeable to have things left half finished. But I know Blandford would be disappointed that you could not attend upon Jane who seems for some reason to have taken a liking to you. But then, women in her condition often have odd fancies. It is kind of Blandford to humour her.'

I had not seen Jane since the night of the dinner two weeks ago and I was alarmed to see how ill she looked though her smile was eager when she saw me. Her head under its modishly plumed bonnet seemed almost too heavy for her slender neck and despite the sultry heat of the day, she hugged a pink silk shawl tightly about her shoulders as though she was cold.

Blandford handed me up into the carriage, his hand clinging damply to mine, and when I enquired in concern if Jane was feeling well he brushed my query aside. 'My wife is never *perfectly* well, yet nor does she ever seem quite *ill*. She is the same with the child. She has croup! She has congestion of the lungs! And all the time it is a mere cold, as I told her in the first place. You will have to learn to bear with this pretence of delicacy and weakness if you are to be her *friend*, as I, as her husband, have had to do.'

'Pretence?' I said sharply. 'I am sure Mrs Pascoe does not pretend. She looks very pale.'

'Because she does not set foot outside the door for

days! She cowers in the parlour feigning exhaustion when exercise and fresh air would be more beneficial.' He spread the tails of his green coat carefully before he sat himself opposite us. 'The physician himself recommends it. Does he not, Jane? Come now, speak up! You were there when he said so.'

'Yes,' Jane said, looking too frightened to say anything else, but in the clatter of our departure she whispered nervously to me, 'he also said that I should have plenty of rest and, if I went out, to avoid the hottest part of the day.' She stared hopelessly at the golden disc of the August sun from under the rim of her parasol. 'I . . . I hope you do not think me indelicate to speak of it, but I was the same when I was expecting Ruth. So very sick in the first months that I could hardly keep a morsel down. And I know if I should be left to please myself in my own way I will get through this distressing time and be quite well later on. I feel so tired and low today that I wonder if I am sickening for a summer fever.'

I wondered, too, when we entered Birch House to take light refreshments with the Pascoes and their friends before our journey. Jane turned faint and had to be led to a chair and revived with smelling salts.

Susannah fussed about her with an encouraging smile. 'It is the heat. The city streets are so stuffy. There will be fresh breezes when we are in the country-side. And so much going on that you will quite forget to mope! And we shall have a splendid picnic when the prize fight is over. Now do not turn up your nose at this lemonade. It is sweet and well chilled and will revive you admirably.'

Only Mr Pascoe seemed at all concerned that his daughter-in-law might find the outing too much.

'You are welcome to rest here, Jane,' he said, gruffly.

'Indeed, if you are unwell, it would do no harm to remain behind.'

'And I would be happy to stay with her,' I put in quickly, sensing escape.

'Nonsense!' Blandford said with hearty confidence. 'You are better already, are you not, Jane?'

She glanced up at him and opened her mouth as though to protest. Then she lowered her lashes and said, without expression, 'I shall be well presently. If I may just stay here in the cool for a while longer.'

'Of course you may,' Mr Pascoe said, 'though I think the rest of us had best make haste before the roads become too crowded. Do not delay too long now, Blandford.'

But we had and the delay had thrown us into the worst of the traffic and though the field where the bout was to be held came slowly into view across a stretch of rough common land, it was clear that it would be some time before we could reach it.

Had I not been in such uncomfortable company I would have begun to enjoy the good humour of the crowd out for a day's pleasure as we ground to a halt yet again. Children raced from the hamlet across the common to hop barefoot on the grass to country tunes played by a fiddler. Food sellers bawled their wares. Jugglers, an acrobat, a ponderous dancing bear had set up pitches, though few people dawdled. Most were intent on hurrying to get good places where the fight might be best viewed.

The ring itself was roped off in the centre of the field and the hillside sweeping away from it provided a natural amphitheatre, the grass already peppered with spectators. The area close to the ropes was tight-packed with bodies, the laden carriages and coaches of the gentry and nobility massed around them, providing excellent vantage points for silk-clad ladies and elegant gentlemen. I could not pick out Mr Pascoe or Susannah. But Blandford had seen a familiar face.

He let out a loud cry, stood up and waved his arms at someone standing by the entrance to the field where there seemed to be some commotion. 'Over here,' he cried. 'For God's sake, man, can you get us out of this press?'

I heard him but my attention was suddenly on Jane. She had become steadily more still and quiet and now had the strained look of someone struggling against waves of sickness – or pain. I watched her anxiously.

'We are late, dammit,' Blandford shouted to his acquaintance. 'At this rate we shall scarcely be at the gate by the time the fisticuffs are over. And I have important business to put in hand.' He patted his bulging waistcoat pocket. 'Mad Jack shall make me a happy man today. He has The Fancy's favour, d'you know. Oh, to be sure you must be loyal to your own man, but Smith will pay the price for his challenge. He is washed up! I'll not favour him with my guineas.'

Fortunes had been won and lost in betting on prize fights, as in every sport. Papa had been stoutly against it, indeed he had written a pamphlet on it, though I fancied the element of chance in his professional ventures was more than enough to satisfy any inherent gambling instincts he himself might have had. It was something that had both puzzled and intrigued me. How could any sensible person put all they owned, happiness included, in jeopardy on the toss of a coin, the fall of a card? It was irresponsible in the extreme. At least I had thought so until today, though I supposed Blandford had wealth enough and to spare. After all, according to Miss Olga, he had married an heiress.

Jane's pallor had deepened. I was about to speak to her when I heard the voice of Blandford's acquaintance.

I turned sharply.

Blandford, newly restored to good humour, was hastily stepping down from the carriage, calling back to us, 'Unfortunately, dear ladies, I have pressing matters that will not wait. We are likely to be stranded here for some while, so Mr Nicholas Fox here has kindly offered to escort you both to my father's coach. You will be perfectly safe in his hands. My wife, sir, and her friend, Miss Howarth.'

'Mrs Pascoe, Miss Howarth,' Nicholas Fox said, bowing gravely. Then he raised his head and looked straight at me.

It was a strange, unnerving moment. A picture dazzled in my mind, crystal clear, so that I could almost feel the snowflakes driven against my cheeks, smell that gruesome odorous *thing* that clanked its sinister message in the bitter wind. Hear his voice. *He was . . . my father. I shall be back to take my revenge . . .*

There was recognition and challenge in his sharp, intelligent grey eyes – and a warning that stopped my tongue before any impetuous words could be spoken. In the few seconds of unnatural silence that seemed to detach us from the heat and bustle of our surroundings, I could see, suddenly clear and visible in my mind, the tenuous link that had been forged by our meeting on that far-off winter's day. As though our meeting now was *meant* and before us the silvery chain that bound us stretched forwards into the misty future.

Then the pictures were gone, the cries of the crowd surged back. The moment might never have been.

Nicholas Fox smiled, that changeling smile that took the solemnity and harshness from his dark bony face and replaced it with sunny charm.

'I apologise for my dishevelled appearance, but I was called to help right a donkey cart that had overturned, blocking the gate.' He was bareheaded, coatless, his shirt sleeves rolled up over smooth brown muscular forearms, sweat plastering the tangled black curls against his forehead. 'Now if I may help you down, Mrs Pascoe, you have not far to go.'

For a moment Jane seemed as if she had not heard. Then, carefully, she began to raise herself from the seat, only to fall back again with a little moan.

'What is it?' I cried, breathless for some reason, as though I had been running.

Jane clutched my hand. 'I felt . . . I think there is something wrong . . . there is pain and . . . and . . .' Her horrified gaze went to her feet. On the white kid boots, on the frill of petticoat showing beneath her skirt were splashes of wet, running scarlet. 'The baby . . .' she whispered. 'I fear I am losing the baby . . . And here . . .' She stared round wild-eyed. 'I cannot . . . What will I do?'

I did not know. Panic swept over me. Jane could not have the indignity of miscarrying here in a hired carriage under the baleful gaze of a surly driver surrounded by the curious eyes of passers-by. And I did not know how to help her.

It was Nicholas Fox who acted, who leaped into the carriage, cajoled the driver into producing a grubby horse-smelling blanket from his box and who with great gentleness wrapped it round Jane, talking calmly and reassuringly the while and lifted her, a small vulnerable bundle, easily into his arms.

'Across the common,' he said to me, with a jerk of his chin. 'My lodgings.'

I stumbled in his wake as he elbowed his way through the crowd. Then he was striding strongly across the crushed grass, bearing his burden as though it were a parcel of feathers rather than one of flesh and bone.

'My landlady is a sensible woman. She has a great

deal of nursing experience. She will take care of you, Mrs Pascoe. I will find your husband and fetch him here directly.'

'No!' The word came out sharp and peremptory. Then, more quietly, in little gasps, 'I would prefer him not to know until the fight is over . . . if that is possible. Or Mr Pascoe and Susannah . . . I do not wish to spoil his . . . their enjoyment . . . They can do nothing . . . Will you stay with me, Miss Howarth?'

'Of course I will.' I forced a laugh. 'After all, I had hoped I would not be compelled to watch the prize fight.'

But not in this manner. I recalled how ill Mama had been once when she had miscarried. How the household had gone around on tiptoe while she lay white and feverish upstairs. It had been a long time before she regained her usual sturdy good health – and Jane was so small and fragile.

That other, secret, ambition I had harboured since I had known I was to come here today I pushed away. *Be Bold to take your Chance*, Miss Lightbody had written and I had proposed to take her advice. But it was selfish to think of myself at a time like this and in any case it would perhaps have not worked to my advantage, even supposing I had been able to put my plan into motion.

The hamlet was no more than a handful of picturesque cob-and-thatch cottages and an inn set around a stream that had been dammed to form a pond on which ducks quacked and squabbled.

Nicholas kicked open the garden gate of a cottage standing a little apart from the others and strode up the flagged path between neat banks of flowers.

'Martha Fitch! Where'm you to, my lover?' he called, his deep voice switching easily into the Devon dialect as he ducked under the low lintel of the open front door into a neat parlour.

A white-haired lady came from an inner room.

'What nonsense are you up to now?' she cried in a laughing voice, then raised floury hands in dismay. 'Mercy me, Nick,' she cried. 'Has there been an accident?'

He threw explanations over his shoulder as he began to ascend the narrow flight of stairs leading off the parlour. 'Our room, I think, Martha,' he said. 'Caleb and I can shift for ourselves in the stable if needs be tonight. This lady will not be for moving on, if I am any judge.'

A bulky fourposter and a smaller bed filled most of the space. Spare coats and shirts hung on pegs behind the door and several pairs of boots were ranged along the skirting. Shaving mugs and razors stood beside the jug and basin on the washstand. There was an air of careless masculinity about the room, though it was spotlessly clean, even to the starched white curtains billowing in the sultry breeze at the latticed windows.

Mrs Fitch, following us, thankfully took instant command of the situation as though young women in the process of miscarrying were brought into her best room every day.

'Put her down in the chair first, Nick. Carefully now! We'll have you out of those soiled clothes and into a nice comfortable bed in no time, my dear. Off you go now, Nick, back to your dreadful pursuits. We've work to do here and it is no place for a great useless male.'

Mrs Fitch gently untied the strings of Jane's bonnet. Jane's face had the dead-white pallor of a fish's underbelly. She groaned as pain convulsed her. Nick stood for a moment, shoulders hunched in the low doorway, his expression unreadable, watching her, his lips moving as though he cursed – or prayed – under his breath. Then he swiftly turned and went down the

173

stairs and I, realising that Jane was in good hands for the moment, saw one last desperate chance and flew after him.

'Mr Fox!'

He stopped halfway down the stairs.

'Well?' he said harshly, though I had the sensation that the harshness was not directed at me.

'Mr Fox, I have a favour to ask.'

'Of me?'

'You have been more than kind already, and were so once before, and I have nobody else . . . though I would have done it myself had I had the chance . . .' I was fumbling in the pocket of my green linen dress as I spoke, withdrawing the precious coins wrapped tightly in a piece of cloth. I held the package out to him. 'Sir, I beg you in the strictest confidence, would you find the best odds on Mad Jack Barton and put this money on for me?'

He looked at the package. Slowly he opened it and tipped the coins onto his palm. Then he looked up at me.

'Three pounds, Miss Howarth?' he said. 'On Mad Jack Barton?'

'He is bound to win, I have heard . . . Oh, I know it is a great deal – it is all I have, in fact, except for a little put by until my next salary is paid, but . . .' I took a deep breath, 'I have to trust someone . . . and . . . I think you are trustworthy, Mr Fox . . . despite . . . despite . . .'

'Despite having a father who was hanged for murder?' There was cold irony in his voice.

'No, no!' I said impatiently. 'Because you seem to be mixed up in this prize-fighting business, which is notorious for being peopled by rascals on the make and thieves and . . . and . . .'

'And the Nicholas Foxes of the world?'

174

'I said I trusted you whatever your involvement, though heaven knows why.'

'A great many people trust me, Miss Howarth,' he said softly. 'Their trust is not always justified.'

'There is no other way,' I said desperately. 'Believe me, if there were I would take it. I shall never achieve what I desire otherwise.'

His eyes were steady on my face. 'Whatever it is that you desire so earnestly, this is a risky way to go about it. Better that you give your sovereigns to the poor and ennoble your conscience if not your purse.'

'Mr Fox,' I snapped in an urgent whisper, 'I *am* the poor! And I can see no way of ever becoming rich unless I take whatever chance is offered to me to improve my situation!'

'And if your precious sovereigns are lost?'

'Then I am merely set back a few months, back to being entirely penniless and must start again, which I am quite prepared to do.'

He laughed suddenly. Amusement laced his voice. 'I admire your spirit, if not your reasoning. And I will do as you ask on one condition. That you take the greater risk – and the chance of greater gain – by backing Caleb Smith.'

'But Barton is the favourite . . .'

'He is younger, sprightlier and a deal more handsome than Caleb and popular with those who judge by appearances. But there are things that I know about him that will not be in his favour this afternoon.' His chuckle had a sinister ring. 'Nor should you know of them for you might immediately lose your ill-placed trust in my good nature. Caleb Smith, then, Miss Howarth?'

I sighed in exasperation. 'You give me little choice.'

His hand closed over the coins. I had the sensation of bridges being burnt.

'Forget you gave me this,' he said. 'Take care of that poor woman upstairs and let fate take its course.'

And he was gone, out of the door into the brazen sunlight, carrying my hopes with him.

'All is safely away,' said Mrs Fitch, peering at the bloody contents of the chamber pot. 'The Lord be thanked, for it would have boded ill for the poor girl if any part had been retained.'

Jane was past caring. The pains had been violent and she had lost what seemed to me to be a frightful amount of blood. She lay back, eyes closed, seemingly fallen to a doze now that she was released from the urgent strainings and retchings that had racked her thin body in waves of convulsive agony.

'She is still losing heavily,' I said, alarmed at the red stain steadily seeping through the cloths packed between her thighs.

'I hesitate to try leeches as her pulse is not robust, but I will sponge her down with vinegar and water,' Mrs Fitch said briskly, 'then apply cold vinegar and water compresses. That should do the trick.' She smiled at me warmly. 'You did excellently. I am sure Mrs Pascoe would not have borne up so well had you not been there to encourage and support her. She will sleep now, I think, and revive herself nature's way. Take yourself off into the garden for a breath of air. Perhaps you could take all these soiled cloths and her petticoats and drawers and put them in a tub of cold water to soak. There is some fresh drawn from the pump in the scullery.'

The air in the garden was sweet after the close smells of sweat and blood that had filled the bedchamber despite the open windows. When I had put everything to soak in the wooden washtub, I wandered between the rows of vegetables hardly seeing the fat cabbages and nodding turnip tops for going over and over in my mind all that Jane had suffered. And for nothing.

I thought of my mother with renewed respect. She had gone through this again and again, bearing four healthy children and miscarrying several. And I had only ever heard her profess joy in the experience of giving birth. No mention of the pain. And when young Rose had been born I recalled she was a whole day and half the night in labour. What could that have been like? She had never said, only laughed with happiness when we clustered about her as she sat up clean and bright in the tidy bed holding the swaddled new infant in her arms. Unlike many mamas, who fobbed their daughters off with silly fictions, she had been open with Phoebe and me when we had first experienced our monthly courses. Explaining with calm practicality what it signified, how our bodies were maturing to womanhood and the responsibilities and duties of marriage. 'And do not listen to silly ideas that some women put about that the marriage bed is a place of penance. What happens between a wife and a loving husband is a thoroughly natural and pleasurable experience, leading to the great joy of children.'

But then she was married to a man she loved. I could never imagine Papa being anything other than tender and gentle. Unlike Blandford Pascoe.

I cringed at the thought of how Jane must have suffered – and must go on suffering under the domination of her husband. Not only did he constantly demean her verbally, but now I knew of his physical cruelty. Had I not just seen the evidence for myself? The bruises on her thighs, on the small, blue-veined breasts; some faded purple, some livid and new. And the other marks, the still-raw grazes clearly imprinted, where teeth had sunk and bitten into soft, shrinking flesh. Neither Mrs Fitch or I had looked at each other as we gently removed Jane's clothing, though I heard the hiss of her sharply indrawn breath. We quickly covered her with an enveloping nightdress, hastily pulling it down over the ugly, shaming evidence.

Mama had said that the duties of the marriage bed were not a penance, but she knew nothing other than love. Jane, trapped in a marriage of convenience, fastened for life to someone she clearly feared, knew only the force of lust upon her helpless body and nothing at all of understanding and compassion.

The distant roars and groans of the crowd had been a continuous background sound all afternoon. Now there was prolonged cheering. The contest must be over. A contest I had once thought cruel and violent, but which now paled beside the one I had actually witnessed. If two men had battered each other to a pulp to please a bloodthirsty crowd, so be it. They had chosen to do it, for gain.

Poor Jane had had no choice. God alone knew how many more times she must go through the degradation of violation – rape – by her husband and the cycle of conceiving a child, giving birth or miscarrying. And there was nothing I or anyone else could do to protect her. If her health failed, if her mind and spirit broke under the harsh yoke of a brutal marriage, there was no escape for her. She was as much Blandford's possession as his horse or his dog. He had the might of law on his side. The right to her fortune, her body, her mind, her children. If she did not please him, he could punish her as he thought fit. Lash her with wounding words or kick and beat her into submission as he would a disobedient hound.

I drew a shuddering breath. For once I was thankful

that I was neither pretty nor possessed of a fortune that any scoundrel might see me as a desirable conquest. And for the first time I could see some benefit in Grandfather's harsh disposal of me. At least it was not into a premature and unwanted marriage. Life with the Misses Polsham might be dull and lacking in both affection and mental stimulation, but at least my body was my own and my mind free to plan a better future for myself. The need to make myself strong and secure without drawing attention to myself was more than ever paramount. Until I was of age I was still vulnerable to any whim of Grandfather's. Thank heaven the full weight of his aspirations seemed centred on Ben and, hard though it was to be separated from my brother, I now saw the sense in being a long way from Falconwood. Out of sight, out of mind. *Better by far with the old maids in town . . . you'll see* had been the last words Miss Lightbody had called to me as I left Falconwood. I had not heeded or believed them.

Now I did.

Jane slept heavily, blue smudges of exhaustion under her eyes. The room was pristine, smelling faintly of the lavender Mrs Fitch had burned on a shovel to dispel the less pleasant aromas. We removed all the signs of male occupancy, carrying the clothes and boots into the barn behind the cottage where a pair of sturdy horses regarded us with calm, inquisitive eyes. We spread blankets on the hay stacked sweetly in an empty stall which would provide a bed for the two men.

'It is only for one night,' Mrs Fitch said. 'They are planning to be off tomorrow and I cannot deny that I shall miss their company. They have been here for several weeks while Caleb gathered strength for today's ordeal. I had not realised that there was so much preparation. Up with the lark the pair of them to be out in the fields exercising and training, whatever the weather.' She shook her head, shuddering. 'I could not go and watch. Having cared for Caleb all this time, and grown attached to him as I already was to Nicholas, I should have felt each blow.'

'You have known Mr Fox a long time, then?'

'We met three years since – and a long way from these shores. In America.'

'You were in America?' I said, surprised.

'Indeed. And had my husband lived, I should doubtless have stayed there, content to be part of his happiness and fulfilment, though I was desperately homesick for my own dear country.' She smiled sadly. 'I was not fired, you see, with his burning spirit. He was converted, most powerfully, on hearing a follower of John Wesley speak and felt called to go and preach to the heathen. His intention was to travel to the interior in pursuit of the redskin Indians, but immediately we landed he fell in with people helping negroes fleeing from slavery in the southern states. And in helping them he found his cause – and, eventually, his death. It was a dangerous business, as Nicholas would tell you.'

'Mr Fox was involved?' I said, round-eyed.

'He was with a travelling fair, earning his money by taking on all comers in a boxing booth. On occasions he acted as a courier for the escape network and helped to bring a small party to a safe house in South Carolina where my husband and others were waiting to pass them on up the line. But it was raided by ruffians hired by the plantation owner. In the mêlée my husband was wounded and Nick it was who got him out of the house and, eventually, home to me in Baltimore, a journey of hundreds of miles and many hardships.' Her plump face was downcast. 'And alas it was in vain. My dear man died within days, for his wound had mortified and I believe it was only his strength of spirit that had kept him alive in order that he might be with me at the end. He died at peace, in my arms.' Her voice faded, her eyes stared into the distance. Then, with an effort, she smiled. 'But I've much to be thankful for. I have my health and means enough when all was sold up in Baltimore for my fare home and to rent this cottage in the village where I was born.'

'Do you have family living here?'

She shook her head. 'All gone now. 'Twas a great sadness to Mr Fitch and myself that we were not ourselves blessed with children – a lack I feel most strongly now that I am alone and getting old. Still,' she brightened determinedly, 'I have always had the greatest satisfaction in following the family tradition and seeing new life delivered safely into the world. My mother was the village midwife and nurse, and I went with her from an early age and learned everything that has stood me in such good stead wherever I have been. Most particularly on the long voyages across the ocean. The steerage passengers, in particular, suffer greatly from infections and poor food and the most dreadful conditions in bad weather when they are not allowed above decks.'

I regarded Mrs Fitch with renewed admiration and respect. She spoke in such a matter-of-fact way of considerable adventures and considerable distress.

'Were you not fearful of making the voyage alone?'

'I was lucky,' she said. 'Nicholas travelled back with me to Devonshire. He was a tower of strength. And I'm overjoyed that he's given up the fighting himself, as I urged him to so often, for he is a handsome lad and his looks would soon have suffered. Though he continues to make a living from the game. Perhaps in time he will see that there are other, more responsible ways to use his mind and his energy.' She absently stroked the soft, thrusting nose of the horse. 'Though there is a stubbornness in him and a strength of will that does not defer to persuasion, however well meant. For all that, I think he is a man who is capable of great sensitivity. I know my husband's death upset him and caused him to think deeply about his own situation. You see, he had become estranged from his father. I do not know all of it, but I think he was a clever, enquiring, but rebellious child who did not wish to follow in his father's footsteps as a blacksmith. When he found he had a talent with his fists I suppose it was natural that he saw it as a means to fame and fortune. But it was a troubling time for his father, who disapproved of such a hazardous way of life, he being strongly religious.'

'His father? Yet he . . . he was . . .' I stammered and stopped.

'Hanged for murder? Aye, indeed,' Mrs Fitch said gravely. 'Perhaps it was an injustice, perhaps not, but I know that guilt hangs heavily on Nick's shoulders because he was not here to support or protect his father in his hour of need. I think that deep down, though he had parted in anger from his father after a great quarrel and had not communicated with him for several years, he held an affection for him that he refused to acknowledge until he recognised the finality of my husband's death. When I decided to return, Nick determined to travel back to England with me and make his peace. But it was too late.'

'Yes,' I said quietly. 'I saw what Mr Fox had to face.'

I told her briefly how Ben and I had come in search of our grandfather and of our meeting with Nicholas Fox at the gibbet's foot. She looked at me with sympathy.

'An evil sight for two young people to come upon.'

'Worse for him.'

She sighed. 'The bitterness, the guilt is in him still. I have told him he should look to the future, not dwell on the past, but the wound is deep and raw and I fear that mischief will come of it. Why else should he befriend the husband of that poor child upstairs? A man he despises, yet pretends otherwise.'

I frowned. 'Blandford Pascoe?'

'He is laying plans. He does not speak to me of them, but he and Caleb have their heads together over secrets.'

'But what has Blandford Pascoe to do with Isaac Fox's death?'

'Why, nothing. I have not met the gentleman and I do not care if I never make his acquaintance, for I believe I should not like him.' We exchanged understanding looks. 'But he is innocent of any involvement, I'm sure.' She paused, then said slowly, 'It was his father, Mr James Pascoe, who was the magistrate who condemned Nicholas's father.'

'And through the son he somehow plans to take revenge on the father?'

She lifted her plump shoulders. 'He laughs away my concern and tells me he will go to the devil in his own way and in his own time. But I fear that he stores up trouble, not least for himself.'

It was a sentiment to ponder over as we returned to our vigil at Jane's bedside.

Whooping, excited yells drew us to the bedroom window. There was a brassy look now to the sun and heavy clouds loomed above the sizeable crowd advancing across the common. Out of the press emerged two men, one of them Nicholas Fox, the other, surprisingly, Dr Barlow, supporting a shambling figure with a battered swollen face split by a broad grin that revealed a bloodied gap where yet another tooth had been lost.

He was barely recognisable as the man who had been with Blandford and Nicholas that day when I had seen them outside the Swan.

'Caleb!' gasped Mrs Fitch, hurrying downstairs. 'By the sound of things he has won – but at what a cost! Oh, his poor head!'

They brought him into the parlour, the crowd still calling and cheering beyond the garden wall. He fell back wincing onto the sofa while Mrs Fitch fetched water and cloths and Dr Barlow poked and prodded at Caleb's bulky frame and declared him to be lucky for there were only a couple of broken fingers, a cracked rib and sundry cuts to attend to. For the rest there was nothing but the application of liniments. Time would do the rest. 'Though you will be a sight to frighten children with for a week or two yet,' he roared, as though it were the greatest joke.

Caleb laughed with him and groaned through split lips and laughed again. Nicholas only smiled wryly, though his voice was hearty.

'Mad Jack had more spirit than I thought, Caleb. To take you to thirty-four rounds was more than we bargained for. Still, you vanquished him soundly. It is a fitting reward that you take a handsome purse into retirement.' His eyes sought mine across the parlour. 'And you have well repaid those fortunates who had sense to back age and experience against brash youth.'

Of course! I had momentarily forgotten about my gamble. I felt a thrill of anticipation. Could I possibly have doubled or even trebled my reckless investment? What I could do with six or even nine pounds! Lily who was desperate to learn to read and write should have a copybook and slate and I should be able to browse in the booksellers for some new novel or book of poems – and I could treat us handsomely to a twist of toffee that we might nibble while we studied together. And there would be plenty left over to be secreted away for the future.

After Dr Barlow had attended to Caleb's battle wounds, Mrs Fitch took him on one side. 'I'd value your opinion as to Mrs Pascoe's fitness to travel. I feel that she should on no account be moved.' She paused, then said without expression, 'Her husband, who should be here shortly, may wish to remove her to Exeter which would be most detrimental to her condition and he might, quite naturally, not take notice of my advice.'

Dr Barlow nodded brusquely. 'My pleasure, dear lady.'

They had barely ascended the stairs when a thunderous-looking Blandford burst into the parlour with his anxious father in tow. Susannah, drifting in after them, managed to maintain an expression of sisterly concern, though her bright eyes raked the room with sharp interest, taking in the battered recumbent form on the sofa, then lingering appraisingly on Nicholas Fox's tall frame.

Nicholas, in a seemingly effortless sequence of moves, bowed courteously to the newcomers, slapped Blandford heartily on the back before he could say a word, congratulated him on losing so sportingly – 'It is the sign of a true gentleman to take defeat well. And I insist you take a glass of brandy with us before you visit your wife. The shock of learning of her unfortunate misadventure must be great' – and thrust a brimming glass into his hand. 'The doctor is with Mrs Pascoe now,' he added, 'so you may rest easy for a few moments more. She is in good hands.'

It was almost as if he put the correct procession of thoughts into Blandford's head; the scowl of fury lifted and Blandford looked merely ill tempered with the double blow of backing the loser and the loss of the hoped-for heir. He needed no second bidding to linger for a moment or two over the good brandy. He sipped the dark golden liquid with evident appreciation and made only the slightest of protests when Nicholas proposed a refill.

Mr Pascoe refused to drink. Indeed, once he learned that Jane was not in any danger, he began to fidget, as though wishing himself well away from this cramped room. And the company in it. Blandford Pascoe might consider Nicholas his friend. I did not think Mr Pascoe shared the same feeling, though he felt bound, stiffly, to thank Nicholas for his assistance to Jane.

Nicholas bowed, thoroughly at ease. 'It was nothing, sir. I was glad to be of service.'

The small parlour was getting steadily darker. Thunder rumbled distantly as Dr Barlow returned.

'Mrs Pascoe is resting comfortably. She has been seen through the worst by the skilled attentions of Mrs Fitch with Miss Howarth giving invaluable comfort and assistance to the stricken lady.' His eyeglasses masked the expression in his eyes as he turned to Blandford. 'It will be, I am sure, a great relief that you may leave her in such good hands. She must rest in bed for a week and not exert herself for a few further days after that. Indeed, if I were a devoted young husband such as yourself I would allow her a full fortnight's recuperation before I came to claim her back.'

It was Mr Pascoe who answered hastily, 'Of course, of course, we will do everything you advise, doctor. And you must not dream of fetching her in that phaeton of yours, Blandford, for it would not be at all suitable for an invalid. I shall send my carriage when we have word that she is fit to travel.'

Blandford drained his glass, then said, grudgingly, 'If that is the case, so be it.'

'And I would recommend,' Dr Barlow, added, 'that

Miss Howarth be allowed to stay and share the burden of the nursing for two or three days. I know how well she attends to Miss Polsham. I am sure that kind lady, though missing her ministrations, would most generously donate Miss Howarth's services in this emergency, especially as Mrs Pascoe has expressed a wish to me that she remain. I will fetch her back to Exeter myself later in the week.'

'That is no problem at all,' Mr Pascoe declared. 'I shall call upon my cousins once we are back in Exeter and explain the situation. And now, Susannah, I think we really must leave before the storm breaks.'

'Miss Howarth, it is most kind of you to stay with poor Jane,' Susannah said, 'I shall feel much happier knowing she has a friend with her. Why, I feel Jane's distress as my own, and I would willingly offer my own services, but through delicacy of nature I find the vapours of the sickroom intolerable, besides which I have many pressing engagements in the coming week and one does so hate to inconvenience friends.'

'Though I am sure you could find a few moments in your busy day to visit the Misses Polsham in Miss Howarth's absence,' Dr Barlow put in heartily. 'To have young people about is always a joy to the elderly. And I know how fond they are of you and your brother.'

'Quite so,' Susannah said, her expression unchanged, but her blue eyes hardening somewhat as she regarded the good doctor's blandly smiling face. By way of diversion, she leaned confidentially towards the crumpled figure on the sofa who had made only a token attempt to stand when the guests entered, before slumping back again. She widened her eyes becomingly and fanned herself with a pearl-handled fan that exactly matched the delicate shade of her muslin dress.

'Mr Smith, I do most sincerely congratulate you on

winning so splendidly. I have never before seen a display of pugilism, and it perfectly lived up to my expectations. I have to say I was quite thrilled.' She raised her long golden lashes and stared straight at Nicholas. 'And I believe we have you to thank for bringing such a display to our sleepy little corner of the world, Mr Fox.' The fan snapped shut. She smiled her sparkling, winsome smile. 'I find it most intriguing that you have chosen to return here. That is indeed the act of a brave man, when the countryside was agog so recently with the great scandal involving your father.'

The flicker of lightning was the only movement in the room. It played over figures suddenly frozen and attenuated, like a tableau sculpted from coloured marble. Mr Pascoe red-faced and frowning, Blandford grinning, Mrs Fitch distressed, Susannah, pink lips parted in anticipation, Nicholas, head bent, politely listening. He seemed the only person not taken aback by Susannah's oh-so-intentionally indiscreet remark.

'My father and I went our separate ways years ago, Miss Pascoe,' he said, smiling easily. 'Besides which, I was on the other side of the Atlantic Ocean when the unfortunate event occurred.' (Was I the only one, I wondered, to catch the ambiguity of the phrase?) 'Would you have me cower away from society because of something that was not my fault? I have my living to earn, my way to make in the world.' A small, smiling pause. 'And my way, I assure you, is not my father's.'

Susannah laughed merrily. 'Well spoken, sir. I have never myself given credence to the notion that the sins of the fathers must be visited upon the chil— Oh!' She let out a squeal as a loud crack of thunder made us all jump, spurring everyone to action. Mr Pascoe hastened to the window to peer at the gathering storm. Mrs Fitch escorted Blandford upstairs to bid farewell to his wife. Dr Barlow busied himself setting his surgical instruments to rights in his bag. Caleb Smith allowed his puffy eyes to close. I was the only one left to witness the little theatrical by-play enacted before my reluctant gaze.

Susannah somehow managed to trip over the hearthrug and fall gracefully against Nicholas. He steadied her, and for a moment her small, lace-mittened hands rested in his large brown paws. Blue sparkling eyes looked up into cool, steady, calculating grey.

'Thunderstorms always make me so very nervous,' she said, breathlessly. 'And I have dropped my fan . . .'

'Allow me.' He released her hands, bent and picked up the fan, examined it to make sure it was not damaged and presented it back to her with a polite bow.

'So kind,' she murmured.

'Not at all,' he answered.

And that was all. It was nothing, a harmless incident. A trifle.

So why, after the bustle of their departure, when Nicholas had helped Caleb to the barn and I stood alone in the middle of the parlour, did that one image, out of all the strange and painful images of that long day, return to my mind. And with it a sense of unease, of haunting threat that continued, like the storm rumbling round the distant hills, to hover on the edges of my consciousness long after the sultry afternoon tipped over into stifling, purple-heavy evening.

The troubling spell was still not broken when, as I sat quietly by Jane's bedside in the candlelight while she slept, the door creaked open to admit not Mrs Fitch as I expected, with the cool drink she had promised, but Nicholas Fox.

Without a word he crossed the room towards me, soft-footed, his long dark shadow shivering up the walls and, still silent, opened the bag he held in his hands.

I watched, open-mouthed, as the shower of coins

189

dropped heavily into my lap. More money than I had
ever set eyes on in my life! Candlelight twinked and
dazzled from the golden surfaces of the sovereigns. I
touched them wonderingly and looked up to thank
Nicholas.

But he was gone, the door closing softly after him
and, as though at a signal, the storm was suddenly
upon the house. A violent, wild, raging beast that
lashed at the thatch with torrents of rain, that sparked
lightning from its livid eyes and barked in great thunderous roars from its malevolent throat.

And the dark, haunting threat, whatever it was, or I
imagined it to be, lifted and was torn away into the
howling night by the wind.

Chapter Seven

The storm howled itself out in the night. I slept fitfully, rising several times to peep at Jane and once hastening to the window at the sound of voices. I feared drunken revellers might still be lurking but dawn was advanced enough to show that the common under the clear-washed sky was empty of stragglers. The man standing at the cottage gate talking to the cloaked rider mounted on a bay horse was Nicholas Fox.

As I watched, Nicholas tossed a small, heavy, clink-ing object up to the rider, who thrust it within his cloak, touched his crop to his wide-brimmed hat and swung his mount away. I sensed a furtive urgency about the transaction and wondered what secret busi-ness had brought the rider here in the quiet hours.

Nicholas seemed in no hurry to move. He watched the horse gallop away across the common, then stared about him as though enjoying these moments of solita-riness. He was coatless, shirt-tails hanging over his breeches, hair ragged. A man hastily dressed for a tryst that had dragged him roughly from sleep. Yet as he arched his back, stretched his arms wide, yawned hugely, then let his hands fall back to his sides, there was an air of relaxed, almost languorous satisfaction about him.

I was reminded, sharply, as I watched him, of a lean black cat that had lived with us on and off in

Manchester, wandering in from heaven knows where to be petted and cooed over by us girls on account of his amiable nature, then disappearing for weeks at a time, to return as though he had merely walked out for a stroll. Rose named the cat Velvet because of his sleek coat and cried whenever he left. Mama, once, in a temper over some domestic disruption, told her tartly that she was to dry her tears instantly. Cats were creatures unto themselves, self-sufficient and self-centred, dedicated to their own comfort, thinking nothing of attaching themselves to two households or more if it was to their convenience, which was why she had always preferred the devotion of dogs, though heaven knows she had not time enough these days to burden herself with pets when she had her own brood of contrary, unmanageable children to contend with, and besides, the wretched animal had scratched Ben only yesterday and drawn blood and was not to be trusted . . .

I had watched Velvet many times dozing on a sunny windowsill. Seen how, when disturbed, he slowly extended each finely muscled limb, stretched the plump, hard pads on his paws to show the full extent of his needle-sharp claws as though to warn the intruder not to take any further liberties. Then, having satisfied himself that there was no need to concern himself further, he would relax once more to boneless content. But however deeply asleep he appeared, his ears were always pricked to catch the smallest sound, his sheathed claws could strike swiftly and without a warning. As Ben, who teased him, soon learned.

I admired Velvet for his beauty and independence and even though I hated it when he brought in broken sparrows and still-living mice to torment under the kitchen table, I accepted it as part of his natural hunting instinct. But I did not allow myself to become attached to him. Perhaps I might have grown to love him had he stayed with us permanently. But, like Mama, I sensed in him a dedication to his own interests to the exclusion of all other considerations.

'Velvet, you are a rogue and a deceiver,' I would say sternly, tickling him under his chin. 'Poor Rose does not realise that you will be off as soon as you grow bored with us.'

The big cat would merely purr deep into his chest and gaze at me with such innocent guile from his golden eyes that I found it hard to be angry with him, even though I knew Rose would be heartbroken when he left.

Something of these emotions stirred in me as I looked down into the garden. I sensed in Nicholas Fox something of that lone cat's nature. The self-confidence, the relaxed, amiable, sleek outer skin that masked the inner dedication to his own purpose. There was secretiveness there. Maybe even something darker, more dangerous. A person it was wise to treat with wry respect, lest the couched claws sprang out and drew blood.

He turned on his heel, still without haste, and raised his eyes to stare unblinking and unsmiling at the window where I stood. I drew back, flustered and embarrassed to be caught spying on him, my hand clutching at the neck of my borrowed nightgown, though common sense told me that if he could see me at all in this light, it was a mere pale shadow through the lattice.

When I dared to peep again, he was gone.

Those few days I spent at the cottage made an idyllic interlude that was all too brief. The oppressive heat had gone. A fresh breeze from the south-west chased fat fluffs of cloud from the hills, across the valley and away. Cloud shadows raced over the bending grasses and bushes on the common, the wind set tree branches murmuring and clashing, even the sun seemed to dash with bracing haste across the blue and white heavens when all I wanted was for time itself to dawdle and allow me to make the most of each moment.

I had enjoyed the week with Ben, but this was different. I did not have to be on my best behaviour to please Grandfather nor watch every word in case I spoke out of turn. I could enjoy the luxury of being myself, with no one to scold or frown should I put a foot wrong.

Mrs Fitch was a comfortable person whose cottage breathed of the kindness trapped within its walls. Jane (for she asked me shyly if now that we seemed destined to be friends we might call each other by our given names) rapidly gained strength so that on the second afternoon Mrs Fitch thought she might be carried downstairs to sit, well wrapped, in a sheltered spot in the garden.

'Some people believe that the merest draught of air is disastrous to a convalescent,' she said, 'and so condemn their charges to lie abed in the close heat of sealed chambers. But 'tis my experience that this regime depresses an already weakened constitution. Far better that the invalid breathes fresh air and takes heart from absorbing the healing qualities of nature herself. Now lift her carefully, Nick, dear . . . that's the way . . . We have already set out a comfortable chair for you out of the breeze, Mrs Pascoe.'

I had expected the men to leave the day after the fight, but Caleb was too sore and stiff to do anything more energetic than hobble about the garden, peering about him through eyes like slits cut into his poor misshapen face, attempting to help me to pick beans, though his swollen, bandaged fingers had little grip.

I had thought his appearance battered enough when I had seen him before in Exeter with Nicholas outside the Swan Tavern, but heaven alone knew what he would look like now when the swelling subsided.

He grumbled as he tugged at a recalcitrant bean that he was perfectly able to sit his horse to Exeter where they had planned to take the mail coach to London, but Nicholas would have none of it.

'You have performed bravely, old friend,' he said, straightening himself from the self-imposed task of digging over a weedy fallow patch behind the cabbages. He laid a hand gently on Caleb's shoulder. 'You deserve a few days' rest before you face the rigours of the journey. Besides, I need time myself to recover from the sudden wealth I find I have amassed.' A sideways, teasing glance at me. 'And I think a few other people are in the same pleasurable state – those who were discerning enough to back a tried old battler, rather than a youngster of great strength but little cunning.'

'Not so much of the old!' Caleb said. 'I'm scarce a year ahead of you, Nick. Though, in truth, I feel an ancient bag of bones today. Still, I reckon young Jack'll be feeling a deal worse – and a deal poorer. I had it in me to feel sorry for the lad when I had him down for the last time. But he'll learn. Next time he won't be so foolish as to think he can meet a hardened pugilist without, er, the proper preparation and training.'

They both chuckled, as though at some shared joke, then Nicholas pretended mock humility as Mrs Fitch, who had been listening from the kitchen doorway and who never lost an opportunity to scold and chivvy them both on the foolishness and recklessness of their way of life, began a stern lecture. It was only cut short when Nicholas strode over, picked her up round the waist as though she was a slip of a girl instead of a large, plump woman, swung her round until her cap and hairpins flew off into the turnip tops, her grey hair came down over her shoulders and she squealed for mercy.

'You girt fool,' she cried, then giggled like a girl as he set her down on the bench by the kitchen window, retrieved her cap and hairpins and handed them to her with an extravagant bow.

'I declare I'm ruined for work for the rest of the afternoon,' she cried. 'Joanna, dear, would you be so kind as to fetch the pitcher of ginger beer from the pantry? He don't in the least deserve it, but supposing he begs my pardon, I might forgive Nick to allow him a glass.'

When I returned with the tray, he was bent over her hand, raising it to his lips, saying in a deep, throaty voice, 'Madam, I tender my deepest apologies, but in my defence I must insist that your comeliness, the saucy way you wear your pinafore, the tender and seductive manner of your recent speech quite overcame my gentlemanly instincts and brought on a fierce attack of unrequited love, so that my baser self was aroused.'

'Oh, stuff,' Mrs Fitch laughed. 'You see what I have had to contend with these past weeks, Joanna, while I have had this rogue under my roof? I never know when he might be taken by these mad moods. See how you have caused Mrs Pascoe to turn quite pale.' She leaned over and patted Jane's hand. 'He means nothing by his horseplay, my dear, except that his devilment sometimes gets the better of him. Be thankful that you have only to bear his company for a day or two.'

She smiled up at Nicholas with a tenderness, a wistfulness, that belied her words, so that I thought of her dead husband and the children she had not borne, and the empty ache that must always lie in her warm heart.

And whatever my private reservations about Nicholas Fox, I could only commend him for his evident affection for this kind woman and for the many thoughtful tasks I had seen him quietly perform about the house and garden. Not to mention the repairs Mrs Fitch had told me of. This winter she would not be troubled by the scullery door flying open on account of the broken catch, or have rain spilling into the parlour through a cracked pane of glass or need to worry about fuel for the fire. Caleb and Nicholas had gathered, split and stacked enough kindling and logs to see her through the whole of the winter.

'Nick declared wielding an axe was part of Caleb's training,' Mrs Fitch said, 'though I noticed he took turn and turn about until the sweat poured off him. Not that he would have any thanks or fuss. But that's his way.'

Later, after we had dined handsomely on mutton chops, tender new turnips and beans with a magnificent summer pudding awash with clotted cream to follow, I sat by Jane's bed while she yawned and dozed and fretted over the enforced separation from her little daughter.

'Oh, I do so miss her. There is no reason to suppose she will suffer from my absence, of course, but if only Blandford could think to bring her – but no, no,' she added hastily, 'I would not trouble him.' Nor wish him to disrupt the peace of her convalescence, I thought grimly. 'And he has much to do this week. He ... he has great plans for the Exeter house. He says it is sadly old fashioned and dreary, though Papa was proud of it and I myself feel more comfortable in it than when we are at Kingsbridge ...'

She rattled on in her breathless way, as she always did when we were alone, pouring out words, half-finished sentences, her mind skipping and leaping from

197

her troubles with the new servants Blandford had engaged in place of her father's old retainers to her worries about shaming her husband because she was such an inexperienced hostess and Blandford moved in sophisticated society.

Blandford. The conversation circled, darted, leaped aside and always, always snapped back to him as though, even in his absence, he kept her on a close chain. His moods, the implacable weight of his will marked her mind and spirit as clearly as the broad heavy band of gold on her left hand and the unspoken of, fading bruises marked her body as his.

Whenever she mentioned his name she smiled. That smile had nothing to do with gaiety. It was a nervous, brittle rictus. Always she smiled as she defended him, justified his actions, even when she related how he planned to tear apart the house in which she had been born and grown up – which she dearly loved – and construct in its place an expensive monument to his own vanity.

'It is to be in the classic style. Such noble pillars and ornament and quantities of furnishings ... And, of course, Papa's furniture will not be suitable and must go – but he chose with such care over the years and though it might not be modish, it is most comfortable.' Her haunted eyes above the smile pleaded, like those of a snared bird, for the comfort of release. 'Blandford says we shall have a house that will be the envy of all the country. Is that not splendid? Though I am not a splendid creature at all and feel quite overwhelmed at the prospect ... but I tell myself to look ahead to when Ruth grows old enough for parties and masques. Such a house will be a perfect setting for a beautiful young girl – oh, and she will be a beauty, I know it! She will not thank me if I cling to outmoded ideas and nostalgic thoughts ... Do you not think so, Joanna?'

There was so much I longed to say, to do. But I was as powerless as Jane herself and what use were easy words of comfort when I had no power to alter her situation? So I merely took her small, cold paw in mind and said, quietly, 'Indeed, that is most sensible, Jane,' and I felt that I betrayed her.

Long after she turned her face from me and closed her eyes, that feeling of betrayal clouded my thoughts.

Tomorrow my short idyll would end. Dr Barlow would visit Jane and take me back in his gig to Torre Crescent. I should be glad to see Lily, but the restraints of life with the Misses Polsham would be hard to bear after these few days of freedom. It was difficult to contain my restlessness as I sat in the candlelit parlour after supper. The men were locked in a contest over the cribbage board, with a slapping down of cards and cries of triumph or pretended outrage and what seemed to me – who had only ever played with Papa or Ben for spills – wildly extravagant stakes at five shillings a peg. Mrs Fitch was dozing over her darning so I quietly slipped from the room, wrapped the old shawl kept behind the scullery door round my shoulders and slipped outside.

The sky was still luminous with afterglow from the fiery sunset. I picked my way round the black bulk of the linney and out at the side gate, my eyes gradually adjusting to the darkness as I began to walk up the thread of a path that led between the shuttered cottages.

Beyond the hamlet the path followed the line of a hedge up the hill. I had seen men and women passing to and fro along it, though I had no idea where it went beyond the knot of ancient trees on the skyline. I did not care. I merely wanted the freedom to stride out strongly, shake off the gloomy shadow that had descended upon me when I thought of my return to

Torre Crescent, tire myself so that I should sleep dreamlessly and not fret about poor Jane's situation.

My skirts rustled softly against dewy grass and my ears caught the rustle and scutter of small creatures in the hedge. A disturbed blackbird piped and fluttered to silence. Somewhere far off a dog howled a protest to the brightening stars.

The hill grew steeper, but I did not reduce my pace and soon the pounding of blood in my ears, the harsh gasp of my breathing drowned all other sounds. It was only when I was forced to stop, catching at the stitch in my side, that I heard the footfall behind me and whirled in alarm. But the voice that called to me was a familiar one.

'You have a fine turn of speed,' Nicholas said, though sounding scarcely out of breath as he drew alongside. 'I had not thought to catch up before we reached the top of the hill.' He paused a moment, then said, softly, 'Forgive me. Do I intrude upon private thoughts? You wished for solitude, perhaps.'

'Perhaps I did,' I said. 'But no matter. I do not mind having my thoughts diverted to brighter topics.'

'Then your thoughts were sad ones? I suspected as much. You have seemed a touch down all evening. Come then, let us walk on and we will speak of cheerful matters. What shall it be?'

I was taken aback that he had observed me so keenly. Confusion made me speak more sharply than I had intended. 'Miracles and mysteries, Mr Fox. How three sovereigns may turn into over a hundred. And of an assignation with a man on a horse at a time when honest folk are still abed.'

He chuckled. 'Ah, but surely it is the nature of miracles that they are inexplicable. And life would be dull if there was not a little mystery to tease the intellect.'

We continued up the hill at an easier pace, the darkness cocooning us in an intimacy that, oddly, seemed neither awkward nor strange, though I straightway challenged him.

'How did you do it, Mr Fox? It seems to me that the odds must have been remarkable to achieve such a sum.'

'Remarkable, but not impossible.'

'Then what were the odds?'

'High.'

'Do I sense a reticence to speak plainly?' I waited for him to answer, but he merely stared ahead up the hill. I sternly regarded his hawkish profile, etched palely against the darkness. 'So I must assume that there is something you wish to conceal.'

He turned his head lazily. 'I had the sovereigns off fools with more money than sense, who like to gamble deep.'

'How?'

His sigh was pained. 'Such persistence! I had much rather hear how you propose to deal with your new-found wealth.'

'I will not rest until I have the truth, kindly do not try to divert me.'

'Very well, if you wish.' He sounded amused.

He recounted briskly, round by round, the side bets laid with various gentlemen, flown on wine and misplaced optimism, who could see no prospect of Caleb winning as the young, vigorous Jack Barton laid into his slower, older opponent. How by the twenty-fifth round, when Caleb seemed done for, there had seemed little risk in rising to Nicholas's challenge that the more experienced man would win. And as he talked, I could see it. How carefully, carefully he had laid the bait, bearing the prospect of loss bravely, seemingly intent on throwing good money after bad through sheer

201

loyalty to his man. In the thirty-second round Caleb, bloody and apparently weakening, had scarcely seemed to have energy enough to ward off Jack's blows.

'And that was when I made my own final, reckless wager. And yours, Miss Howarth.' His teeth flashed white in the darkness as he grinned. 'For every guinea down I would pay fifty if their man won. If Caleb won, of course, they would pay me.' He laughed aloud. It was a triumphant sound. 'They could not wait to empty their pockets and prove me deluded by false loyalty to my friend.'

I listened to him recount the events of the thirty-third round. How Jack Barton, the crowd behind him almost to a man, believed himself to be already the victor. 'He did not have the experience to know that an old battler like Caleb is at his most dangerous when he seems done for but is merely biding his time. And that stamina often counts for more in the end than dancing feet and lively blows in the beginning.' He paused as though reliving the scene, then said, with relish, 'Jack took his eyes off Caleb for a second too long. He was actually grinning to his howling supporters when Caleb's left fist drove into his ribs and his right landed square on his chin. He was down without knowing what had happened. And though he was soon on his feet and back in the fray, he was done for from that moment, though he was courageous and refused to give in until the thirty-fourth.'

We were close by the knoll of trees on the hilltop. As though by unspoken agreement, we stopped by the stand of ancient, twisted oaks. Above their dark, bushy shapes the stars hung like diamonds strewn on black velvet.

'You knew that you would not lose,' I said quietly.

'Nothing in this world is ever that certain,' he said, equally softly.

'The rider in the night. Was he some part of it?'

I hugged my shawl tight around my shoulders, conscious of the chill emanating from the dense shadow of the close-packed trees. Nicholas's words dropped into the damp air like stones into a still pool, fracturing the water into ripples that spread out and out into the far distance.

'He is a man who knows Jack Barton's tastes. In women. In brandy. He made sure Jack was short of neither in the last few weeks. The boy, you see, is young and headstrong. He had, until today, great confidence in his own natural abilities. He did not think a drunken spree or two would bring any great harm, though I understand his trainer was beside himself with rage when only two days before the fight Jack, in an advanced state of inebriation, had to be dragged – if you will forgive me speaking so plainly – from the bed of a trollop.' He hesitated, then said, too casually, 'Does that shock you, Miss Howarth?'

'The trollop? Or the fact that you . . .' The word 'cheated' hovered on my lips, died, because I was sensing again, strongly, that puzzling, invisible thread that linked my life to Nicholas Fox's and knew that what I said now was important, to him, to me. '. . . that you manipulated the result?'

'The trollop is of no consequence,' he murmured.

I looked deep and honestly into my mind and heart. Was I shocked? I once would have been. Now there was only an echo of the clear, black-and-white values of childhood. Too many harsh events had washed a layer of subtle colours over certainty. I might have condemned Nicholas Fox once out of childish prudery. But now I had my own secrets, my own purpose in life. Perhaps it was that which provided the link between us and however much I might cavil at his need for revenge, I could never forget our first meeting and his anguish at his father's cruel end. Perhaps, too, there was something of revenge in my own purposes. I wanted one day to be rich and powerful and that was a form of defiance against those who looked to crush me.

I let my breath out in a sigh. 'I am not shocked, Mr Fox, though I should be.' I hesitated. 'Was Blandford Pascoe one of the so-called fools who took up your challenge?'

'There are two names that are writ large in blood-stained letters in my heart,' he said. 'Kerswell and Pascoe. The bearer of either of them shall have no quarter from me, though Blandford Pascoe is a man who, even if I had not vowed vengeance on his name, would be easy to dislike. I warn you, Miss Howarth, be on your guard whenever you are in his company. And above all, never allow yourself to be alone with him. He is not to be trusted. Do you understand me?'

'All too well,' I said, incautiously.

His voice was suddenly steely. 'Why? What tricks has he been up to with you?'

'Oh, nothing, I assure you. But . . . he behaves . . . unpleasantly to his wife.' I was glad of the darkness that covered the embarrassed heat that flooded my face. I could not speak of the things I had seen, but perhaps the tone of my voice was enough.

'Ah, yes. Poor, sad creature. I fear she leads a miserable life.' A silence hung between us, then he said, slowly, 'That day you saw me in Exeter, outside The Swan . . . I should not like you to feel that I slighted you by not speaking. It was merely that I thought it best not to draw Pascoe's attention to you. Perhaps I hoped that you might avoid his company altogether, though I knew it was almost certain you would not be able to, with the Pascoes being related to your employers.'

'I had thought you ashamed to greet me when you

were in such grand company,' I teased, my spirits oddly lightened by his explanation.

'Grand company such as that I would gladly forgo for ten minutes' conversation with an intelligent and spirited young lady such as yourself.' It was his turn to tease.

'But I have Kerswell blood, have you not thought of that, Mr Fox? Or perhaps you remember it too well and mean to use me in some secret way as you use Blandford Pascoe. As a means of taking revenge on my grandfather.' The words came from nowhere. But perhaps they had been waiting in my head all along. Had to be spoken.

He went very still. I felt the newly lightened mood slipping away. The stir of deeper emotions was like the rustling of dark leaves above us.

He did not answer directly. 'How old are you, Miss Howarth?'

'I shall be eighteen within the fortnight,' I said, surprised to find this was so. I had given no thought to birthdays, once a time of treats and outings, now remarkable to no one but myself.

'Long before I was eighteen I was an usher in a gambling hell in St James's. My duties were to escort customers too drunk to find their way alone from the gaming tables to the place where – I beg your pardon – they could relieve themselves, or to light the amorously minded to upper rooms where the whores waited with open arms and painted faces to remove such guineas as they had left. It was a lowly occupation but better than previous jobs – sorting rags in a rag-and-bottle shop is one I recollect as being the most respectable, if the most noisome. At least in St James's there was a dry bed to sleep in and good food in my belly and the prospect, I hoped, of promotion to operator – that is to deal the cards if I learned the tricks and could cheat the dandies without any being the wiser – or even to rise to director and superintend the play. My companions were cardsharps and thieves and harlots, out to rook the rich and gullible, for it was a high-class establishment and the clientele was from the nobility and gentry. I hung around street fighters and pugilists in my spare time, and my companions there were no better and no worse.'

The night breeze gusted among the oaks and set the fringed edges of my shawl fluttering against my arms. I kept my eyes fixed on Nicholas Fox's profile, for it seemed he spoke to himself rather than to me, his gaze unfocused.

'It was a hard school for a raw lad up from the country, and the hardest lesson I learned as I scavenged a bare living in the pestilential alleys around the Thames and later when, by my wits, I prospered is that the gentler aspects of human nature – love, kindness, generosity – are constantly overridden by greed and selfishness. Self-interest always wins over self-denial. Once that is understood, the basic untrustworthiness of every individual never again comes as a shock. The only person one can truly trust and rely on in this world is oneself.'

'That is a cynical observation, sir!' It was also uncomfortably close to thoughts that I had in my darker moments, which made me perhaps sharper than I intended. 'And like to make for ruthlessness.'

'Ruthlessness? Perhaps I am ruthless.' He turned his head slowly and looked at me. His eyes glittered under their dark fringe of lashes. 'My father was a good, honest, God-fearing man. Over-harsh towards me through my headstrong youth, though perhaps he sensed in me a need for strictness, for discipline. If he stood before me now, he would no doubt maintain that his worse fears have been justified.' He gave a short, bitter laugh. 'Yet I know in my bones that I can survive in this world, whereas he, God-fearing and honest as he was, had his days cut short by the hangman's rope. And why? Because he trusted in his fellow men. Because he innocently believed that Frank Kerswell had long since forgiven him for daring to survive when his own precious boy had drowned, whereas the evil old schemer had held his grudge close and waited for the moment when he might take his vengeance on an innocent man.'

'Why do you tell me this?' My voice was not quite steady.

'Because there are those who sink under the blows life deals them and those who learn and are strengthened by them. You are, I fancy, of the latter breed. You are a survivor. You have learned already to bend to the wind instead of letting it break you by stiff-necked resistance. Yet I sense that resistance is there. A slow fire smouldering, waiting for the right moment to be fanned into hot flame. Am I right?'

For a moment I felt disturbed and exposed, as though he really had looked into my head and seen my secret thoughts. I brushed the idea aside. He was clever and manipulative. It was guesswork on his part.

'I do not intend to be companion to old ladies for ever,' I said tartly. 'I see no harm in hoping for something different.'

'Or setting that plan in motion,' he said.

'If you mean my impetuosity in asking you to gamble with my three guineas—'

'I mean that you are far too sensible to indulge in girlish daydreams about being rescued from a life of penury and servility by some handsome prince who falls instantly in love with you and carries you off to a life of wealth and indulgence.' There was amusement now in his voice. 'Fairy tales are not for you. You understand the real world. You intend to help fate as much as you can and you are far too wary, now, to be gulled by anyone. I understand you well enough now not to attempt it. Even if I did think I could deal Frank Kerswell a blow through you.'

'And, of course, I have no influence whatsoever with my grandfather,' I observed drily. 'Indeed, you know as well as I that he would not care if I walked to the edge of the world and fell off into a pit of monsters.'

His laugh rang out. A shout enough to carry clear across the dark valley.

'Who is the cynic now?' he asked, when he could.

'I am merely stating the obvious,' I said. 'And if you do not hush, we shall have the village out after us, wondering what mischief is afoot.'

'Not they. The Old Ones walk up here at night.'

'What old ones?'

'Legend has it that the trees grow twisted and gnarled like the limbs of old men because they feed off the bones of those who lived here when the world was young. They say that battles against giants were fought on this hilltop. And the earth is red because of the blood that stained it.'

The cool wind shivered down my back.

He put out a hand and touched my shoulder. His fingers felt warm and strong.

'Merely a legend,' he said, comfortingly.

'It is the breeze not some silly folk tale that chills me,' I retorted, though I was glad for a moment that I was not alone. 'Ghosts do not frighten me, Mr Fox. They have no power to hurt.'

'Bravely said, though I should not have expected anything other. You are not the fluttering kind to cower away from your own shadow. I think we shall do well in our future dealings together.'

I blinked at him. 'What dealings?'

'You are out to make your fortune, are you not? How do you propose to do it?'

I sighed. I was young, gauche, he could read me like a book. It was infuriating. 'I think you intend to tell me.'

'To place the alternatives before you,' he corrected gently. 'It is for you to decide whether to hide your money under a loose floorboard where it will gain nothing or place it in a bank at two per cent and watch it accumulate year by year until you are old and grey. On the other hand, you could invest in me, Miss Howarth, and reap a richer reward.'

'Give you my money to gamble away?'

'Would it reassure you to know that I did achieve my youthful ambition to rise to the top in a gambling hell before the wanderlust seized me and I took ship to America?'

'So you are an expert at card tricks.'

'Before I left I took a half share in a new gaming club which my partner ran most excellently in my absence. When I return to London I intend to become more than a sleeping partner, being tired of the fighting game and having a few ideas of my own I wish to put forward.'

'Mr Fox, this does not concern me.'

'I am prepared to cut you in on my share.'

'What?'

'You see, the lasting profit to be had in any gaming establishment comes to the owner. Oh, there may be nights, even weeks, when the bank appears to lose, though even that is no bad thing. A customer with a run of luck and a loose tongue is a considerable draw to others wishing to make the most of Dame Fortune's smiles. But in the long run it is the bank that makes the steady profit and the banker who ensures that it does if he is a shrewd and experienced man, as my partner is, and the business well run.'

'How well run, Mr Fox?'

'We relieve our customers of their money in such a painless and cheerful way, Miss Howarth,' he said modestly, 'that they return time and again for the joy of having their purses emptied by experts.'

'That I can well believe,' I said, a little grimly. 'But I should like to know precisely why you are making this heart-warming offer. It cannot be that you are in need of my guineas.'

'To be frank, Miss Howarth,' he said, 'I amaze myself with my generosity.'

'And the real reason?'

He tucked his chin down into his high neckcloth. The white linen seemed to reflect luminescence up into his face, accentuating the amused curve of his lips.

'I could say that it is a purely philanthropic impulse. That I see a courageous young woman caught in a trap of poverty and dependence and I wish to give her the means to escape.' He paused, staring unblinking into my eyes and for a moment I could almost believe him. Then he added briskly, 'But that would not be the whole truth, because I am as selfish as the next man and nothing I do is without calculation. You see, I think you may be useful to me. I intend to return to Exeter. I plan to open a gentleman's club. I already have a lease on one property and am negotiating another.'

'A gambling hell! The authorities would never allow it!'

'It will be a place of such respectability that not only will the good aldermen and retired generals press to become members, but they will bring their wives.'

'I cannot believe that possible! You have said yourself that such places are, well, dens of vice.'

'Up until now,' he said. 'But times are changing.

Some weeks ago I was talking to a man called Crockford, a fishmonger's son who has himself made a fortune from gaming. He is not generally liked, having an unfortunate, obsequious and oily manner, but he has a shrewd business brain that I have come to respect. He feels as I do. That there is a new awareness abroad, a certain hardening towards the loose morals of our capital, a wish for something different. Perhaps it is because its leader, our erstwhile Regent, has now become King and his high-flown cronies are scattered or ruined by debt. Perhaps it is merely a swing in fashion. Whatever it is, Crockford is making plans accordingly, though he is not the fellow to shout it abroad. He is quietly buying up leases on property in St James's with a view to the founding of a very different establishment.'

'And you propose to do for Exeter what Crockford will do for London?'

'On a much smaller scale,' he said. 'Nevertheless, I fancy our aims are the same. To open a select and thoroughly respectable club. There will be a fine dining room where members may invite their wives to partake of the finest food and wine in Exeter, a gymnasium where young bucks may be instructed in the art of fisticuffs and, at its heart, a discreet room where the gentlemen may chance their luck with a game of hazard or faro.'

'And where do I fit into this ambitious scheme?' I asked, reluctantly intrigued.

'I ask nothing more than that you keep your eyes and ears open and write to me occasionally, so that I may keep up with events in the town and with the doings of the Pascoes and your grandfather.'

'You are asking me to spy on them!'

'I do not ask you to creep about listening at keyholes,' he said. 'Just write to me as a friend, telling me

211

the gossip. For my part, I shall keep you informed as my plans advance.'

Was he my friend? Or I his?

Prudence battled with a reckless urge to throw caution to the winds. The man was a self-confessed scoundrel. He would take my money and lose it. He had as much as warned me not to trust him! My sovereigns would be far safer in my own pocket. I should sever all connection with him here and now. Tell him in no uncertain terms that I could not possibly consider writing to him. How dreadful if Miss Olga found out. Or Grandfather.

And even as these sensible thoughts paraded like upright soldiers through my mind, a silky, treacherous voice laughed them away. *Take a chance! You can do it. He has been lucky for you once. Perhaps he will be so again.*

'I do not move in society, remember,' I reminded him. 'Most of the time I am shut away with two elderly ladies.'

'Ah, but Jane Pascoe is now your friend. Who knows what possibilities that holds.'

'I will not manipulate a friendship in order to satisfy your curiosity,' I said sharply. 'And I do not want her harmed, whatever your plans are for her husband. Do you promise me that?'

'You know my feelings,' he said, with equal sharpness. 'I would free her from that gentleman tomorrow if I could. But as that is not possible, you may depend upon it that whatever scores I have to settle with Pascoe, I shall try to ensure that she does not suffer through it. Does that satisfy you?'

He meant what he said. I was sure of that. Less sure that he could keep to his word. Vengeance pursued upon Blandford would in some way reflect on Jane. But then, Nicholas Fox would go ahead with his plans whether I consented or not to be a part of them.

Perhaps I would serve Jane better by keeping in his confidence.

So I justified my actions. Had I thought longer and deeper, sensible argument might have overriden the seductive lure of intrigue and excitement offered by this near-stranger. But I did not want to think long and deep. It was as though, like the heroine of a fairy story that he was so sure I scorned, I had been imprisoned in a turret and he had opened a shutter and allowed me a glimpse of the world beyond my prison. I could not bear that shutter to be slammed shut again.

I did not tell him so, of course. He would only have laughed at such fancies from someone he evidently considered drearily practical.

We began to retrace our steps down the hill and before we reached the hamlet I had agreed to entrust a goodly part of my newly acquired fortune to him.

'You will not regret it,' he said confidently as we paused above the huddle of cottages where scarcely a glimmer of light showed. It was warmer here, out of the wind, away from the looming shadow of the ancient trees, mere picturesque black shapes now against the starry sky. Battles had been fought and lost up on that hillside, their bloody echoes ringing down the centuries. I had embarked on action of a different kind. Whether to be the winner or the loser I could not tell.

'I hope not, Mr Fox,' I said.

'We are partners now. Shall we shake hands on it?'

He held out his hand. I held out mine, felt it enfolded, held. It was not the mannered touching of polite, soft fingers. His grip was hard. I could feel the dry roughness of calluses against my palm, the wiry tautness of bone and sinew under my thumb and fingertips.

'I am Nick to my friends,' he said.

'Are you my friend?' I asked, quietly.

He bowed his head, regarding me steadily from under his dark brows. 'I shall prove it,' he answered. 'May I call you Joanna?'

'My friends call me Jo,' I said.

'It is a privilege I will do my utmost to earn,' he said solemnly.

He was still holding my hand. Now with an easy movement he lifted it and pressed it to his lips, then, almost lazily, he turned my palm and dropped a kiss onto the tender skin inside my wrist.

In a flash, my new-found excitement tipped into turmoil. That single, practised gesture sent a host of seething sensations into my mind, none of them pleasurable. He had spoken casually of the rowdy male company in which he moved. That gesture spoke of a different ambience than the fevered, wine-flown excitement of crowded gaming rooms where dandies jostled sweating tradesmen to gain space at the tables and greedy hangers-on flattered and tricked the gold from foolish pockets. It spoke of dalliance and coquetry, of scented boudoirs and assignations. Of jewelled, languid women, of spoilt, indulged beauties, of adventuresses. Women to be flirted with, lusted after. And ranged behind like a grinning, painted, sleazy frieze, those others – trollops to be bedded, for payment, in frowsty bedrooms.

I snatched my hand away. 'You do not need to waste your charm on me, Nicholas Fox,' I said sharply. 'I am sure there are plenty of London ladies who would be flattered by such tricks, but I prefer you to be straightforward in your dealings with me.'

He seemed, for an instant, to be taken aback. Then he chuckled, a deep throaty sound. 'I forget you are so young,' he said.

'If I were old and grey I should still prefer to be treated like . . . like . . . a . . . an intelligent person, not

214

a . . . silly miss without thought in her head beyond fripperies and flirtation.'

'I am sure you would,' he murmured. 'It was devilish unsporting of me to treat you like a woman instead of a . . . a person. But I assure you I meant no assault upon your honour. Or your sensibilities. I merely . . . forgot myself for a moment.' He bowed gravely. 'Pray tell me I am forgiven.'

He was laughing at me despite his grave demeanour, and I prickled with outrage. Mostly, I realised later, because I did not know how to answer with dignity. My sister Phoebe would have known, I thought crossly. My mother would have known. They were both born, it seemed, with a streak of feminine guile. No need for them to search frantically for some witty riposte or clever put-down. It would have come naturally to their lips. They would not have behaved at all as I did. If some gentleman had kissed their hand, they would merely have taken it as their due and forgotten about it instantly. They would not have taken it amiss, nor stood tongue-tied feeling unbearably embarrassed, before nodding curtly and rushing away with burning cheeks, leaving the gentleman to follow at his own lazy pace.

I went straight up to settle Jane for the night, thrusting aside the uneasy conviction that I had made a fool of myself.

I was almost restored, bustling about the candlelit room in an excess of efficiency, when Jane remarked sleepily, 'Have you hurt your hand, Jo?'

My fingers sprang from my wrist. I had unconsciously been massaging the spot that still, unaccountably, tingled from the burning touch of Nicholas Fox's lips.

'It is nothing,' I said, lightly. 'Nothing at all.'

I hoped it was the truth.

Chapter Eight

My return to Torre Crescent, though Miss Polsham and Miss Olga's company seemed dreary after Mrs Fitch's kindness, was not as difficult as I expected. There was Lily's ecstatic welcome to warm me and my secret plans to sustain me whenever my spirits flagged.

All the spare time I had in those hot August days was spent with Lily in the dusty attic, rearranging chests and boxes and furniture, scouring and polishing every spidery corner. With Miss Olga liable to sneak up at odd moments intent on finding us idle or gossiping, we were careful to talk in whispers and keep our hands busy, but these moments were the happiest in our day and we both savoured them to the full. I confided in Lily all that had happened while I had been away and shared with her the letters Jane sent once she was well enough to write. Miss Olga could scarcely deny me these and it was a relief to be open about them.

Nicholas Fox's letters were a different matter and I was obliged to ask Mrs Chadwick's help. It was fortunate that I only needed to give her the sketchiest of explanations. I had the greatest reluctance to talk about Nicholas Fox to anyone. Even speaking of him to Lily had been difficult. But Mrs Chadwick looked tired and distracted and had no time to linger to talk or question. 'My dear, of course you may ask any friend to write to you here, you never need to ask. I understand how you are placed. But you will forgive me if I make haste back to the workshop. My poor girls and I have worked all the night through to complete a large order for mourning dresses – a family of daughters whose father died suddenly yesterday . . .'

I retreated with all speed, glad that the matter had been accomplished so easily.

My eighteenth birthday was like any other day, except that I went about my duties with a heavy heart, unable to banish memories of happier times.

It was Lily who jolted me out of my attack of the miseries. She slipped into my room that night with a jug of barley water and a hefty wedge of the veal pie that had earlier appeared on the dinner table. Miss Olga had pared off two frugal slices and returned the rest to the kitchen to be served up tomorrow and probably the day after that. She would be aghast at the shrinkage of the pie.

Lily winked.

'Thieving cat got into the pantry this afternoon, when Ma Caunter was havin' a nap. I sent it packing wi' me broom but not before it had chewed most of the pie, a custard tart made specially for Miss Polsham and a cold mutton chop Mrs Caunter had set aside for her own supper.' She delved into the pocket of her apron and drew out the tart and the chop. 'Well, I never went to a birthday party in me whole life, nor 'ad one on me own account not knowing when the 'appy day is, so I thought it were time. An' you can't have a party wi'out proper things to eat, can you, Miss Jo?'

'Oh, Lily,' I said, 'what should I do without you?'

'Not been yourself all day, I could see that. So tonight we're not going to do any learnin', we're going to sit 'ere and pretend as 'ow we're proper ladies – not as you're not, miss, but fallen on 'ard times as you might say – and you can tell me all about the 'appy times with your ma and pa an' all. We even got a right good party lantern.' She jerked her thumb at the yellow harvest moon casting its limpid light through the small window and competing with the muted flicker of the candle.

'Will you share my birthday, Lily?' I said. 'I mean, make this your birthday too?'

Her face lit up. 'That'd be grand. I just wish I knew 'zackly how old I was, but I reckon I should be sixteen near enough.'

'Then sixteen you shall be this very instant,' I declared. 'So if you will pray be seated, Miss Walker, and partake of this magnificent spread, I will pour a little liquid refreshment for you.'

'Ta, Miss Howarth,' Lily said, and mimicking Miss Olga so precisely that I laughed aloud, she lifted her nose haughtily in the air, spread her skirts, and lowered herself to the bed. 'Ay'm obliged.'

We toasted our health, clinking together chipped kitchen cups that also appeared from Lily's capacious apron pocket. I choked when I sipped the barley water.

'Lily! What on earth is in this?'

'Oh, a bit o' this an' that to liven it up,' she said airily. 'A fair dash o' Mrs Caunter's gin as she keeps by 'er in case she comes over queer, the swillings out o' the Madeira bottle Dr Barlow finished last week, a sprinkling o' nutmeg . . .' She took a mouthful and smacked her lips. 'Sorta odd taste, but warmin'.'

Warming it was indeed. By the time we had emptied the jug, all tendency to tears had retreated under a rash of giggling. Lily had discovered from Mrs Caunter that Miss Polsham's mysterious and enervating illness dated from the day her engagement to a young gentleman was broken when he ran off with his mama's parlourmaid, was disowned by his family, and thereafter kept a common lodging house in St Sidwell's. 'Lived over the brush, they did, and could be seen any day bold as brass and 'appy as sandboys walking arm in arm through the town as though they was properly wed. Miss Polsham was so affrighted of bein' pointed at by folks as knew about it if she poked her nose out of doors – or, worse, meetin' the 'appy couple – that she took to her bed. An' her father and stepmama didn't help none. As long as they lived they blamed 'er for bringing disgrace on 'em, tellin' 'er the whole family was a laughin' stock through it. As though it were 'er fault, poor owd article. No wonder stayin' an' invalid an' seein' nobody seemed a much more satisfact'ry way of goin' on.'

Under the influence of the 'barley water', we found this unbearably funny, but when the candle burnt to a stub and the moon had lifted itself away from the window, shadows crept back into the room and we sobered enough to feel sympathy for the wretchedness Miss Polsham must have suffered.

'P'raps it'd been different if their real ma had lived,' Lily said.

'Or yours,' I said. 'Or mine.'

'Aye.' Lily's bright face saddened for a moment, but she was never downcast for long. 'Don't do to dwell on what's past,' she said cheerfully. 'An' besides, you've got your room looking proper grand thanks to the first Mrs Polsham an' her gee-gaws. I thought Miss Olga would've wet her drawers when she saw what you'd done. But she couldn't say too much, could she, havin' given you permission in the first place like you reminded her of?'

Miss Olga had caught me in the process of carrying the gilt-framed picture of the woodland nymphs out of the attic, but though she had insisted on finding what other treasures I had removed for my own comfort and pleasure, she had surprised me, after a short lecture on taking care of the valuable items that were graciously on loan to me, by grudgingly admitting that I had improved the look of my room.

I had felt several times since my return that there had been a softening in Miss Olga's attitude towards me. Not because she had missed me, I was sure, and I could only think it was because of Jane's friendship.

Jane had artlessly revealed in one of our conversations that Mr Pascoe owned the house in Torre Crescent, letting it to the sisters for a peppercorn rent and so enabling them to live comfortably within their modest income. So, apart from the blood tie, the sisters were bound to dear Cousin James in other ways. I could see that they would take care not to offend him or any of his family in case the matter of their rent came under scrutiny. Cousin James had called upon the sisters while I was still in the country, Lily told me, and spoken of me warmly. So, for the moment, I was regarded in a favourable light.

'Don't seem you done so much in 'ere, Miss Jo,' Lily said. 'Just shifted the bed under the window and put up those old pink curtains, but it looks real nice.'

I had found the curtains in a chest, mossy pink brocade faded in the folds and fraying at the hem, but carefully turned up and pressed they framed the small window and the plain white jug of grasses and leaves on the window ledge. The picture, glowing in its soft pastel colours, hid the cracked plaster above the tallboy. I had begun work on a patchwork quilt from scraps in which I planned to pick up the pastel shades of the picture and the curtains. It was ironic that with my ill-gotten gains I could afford to buy all the things I needed – a proper bookcase, a new rug, a few ornaments – but to indulge myself now would have drawn unwanted attention and awkward questions.

'One day we shall both have a place of our very own, Lily,' I vowed. 'And have exactly what we want.'

'Then I shall have a bed stuffed so full o' feathers I shan't want to get out of it,' Lily said. 'I'll lie all day looking through a big window at the birds and flowers – it will be in the country, won't it, this 'ouse?'

'Oh, yes,' I said softly. 'The house will stand four square on a grassy headland, with the fields and woods spread about and sea so close that you can hear the waves crashing against the cliffs. And Ben will be there and we shall never be separated again.'

For an instant, so strongly did the image of Falconwood rise in my mind that I was there drifting through rooms that were not dark and cold and empty as I remembered, but full of light and movement and laughing voices. And faces turning to smile as I approached. Familiar ones. Ben and Mr Chadwick, Mrs Fitch, Miss Lightbody, Lily. And unfamiliar, yet so much part of the scene that my mind did not question their presence, a young, grave girl who held her hands towards me, and the tumble of children playing like puppies at my feet . . . The deep sense of joy and contentment that filled me was to do with all these loved and loving people, yet they were only part of it. There was something – someone – else. Someone who even now rode into the stable yard, leaped from his horse and came striding across the cobbles. And I was no longer drifting but running into the garden over the trimmed lawns, between the beds of flowers, through air scented with lavender and roses. Running towards that someone, whose arms opened wide to enfold me . . .

'You all right, Miss Jo?' Lily's face peered anxiously into mine.

And the vision was gone. So abruptly that the sense

of loss was like a sick pain in my stomach.

'You're all pale and shivery.'

'I think perhaps that veal pie and your special brew do not quite go together late at night,' I said, struggling to pull myself together. I managed a smile. 'It is just that I am tired, I think. And you must be too. It is time we both went to bed.'

Lily struggled with a yawn. 'True, Miss Jo.'

'And thank you, Lily,' I said. 'It has been a lovely birthday.'

'It 'as, Miss Jo,' Lily agreed. 'Best I ever 'ad, seein' as I never did 'ave one before.'

I was still cold when I got into bed and the sadness that I had held back all day drifted over me like a grey, smothering cloud. And there was nothing at all I could do to escape it.

The day after my birthday Jane returned to Exeter and immediately sent a note asking me to call upon her, tactfully including Miss Olga in the invitation.

Jane's family home stood in a quiet cul-de-sac fringed by a once-neat garden that was now deep in builders' rubble and uprooted shrubs. Workmen swarmed over the cat's cradle of scaffolding that imprisoned the old rosy stone of what had been a plain and modest house. A new, classically pillared portico was rising round the front door, and either side of the house new foundations were being gouged out of lawns and shrubberies.

'It is all going ahead so quickly,' Jane said after the maid had shown us through to a small back parlour, where the noise of the workmen was less evident and the view of shrubberies sloping to a bluff above the river was still undisturbed. 'While I have been away, Blandford has put the alterations in hand. I was quite surprised to see how the work has advanced.'

She had assured us she was almost restored to health, but she looked fragile as a handful of bird bones, her shoulders drooping under the yellow silk of her fashionable afternoon gown, her face hollowed and pale.

'The house is to be almost doubled in size and will be quite magnificent, Blandford assures me, in the most modern architectural style.' She stared round wistfully at the comfortably cluttered parlour with its faded velvet curtains. The air was dustily fragrant with the potpourri heaped in bowls on the plain stone slab of the mantelpiece. 'Papa loved this room above all other. We rarely used the big parlour, though it catches the sun in the winter months. He said it was cosier in here and he never tired of the view. We would often sit comfortably here of an evening, he with his books, I with my embroidery . . . But Blandford says many of the interior walls will be demolished, to create large rooms where we may entertain grandly.'

'Dear Blandford was ever go-ahead,' Miss Olga twittered, exploring the room with bright, greedy glances, fixing all in her mind so that she could describe it to her sister later. 'How fortunate you are, Jane, to have so forward-thinking a husband.'

'My head aches from the noise,' Jane sighed, 'and there seem so many disagreeable decisions to be made. The rooms which are not to be altered must be refurbished, Blandford says, and I must convey my wishes to the architect. But I have no heart for it. I become so confused when first this suggestion then that is placed before me, and both seem to have equal merit. And I worry that if what I choose turns out badly, it will be a great deal of wasted expense. But it must be done before we leave for the country, which will be quite soon, so that when we return in the spring all will be ready for us . . .' She broke off, staring beyond me, her expression illuminated with sudden joy. 'Oh my pet lamb, there you are!'

She held out her arms to the small child borne in by her nurse. A solemn, plump infant, who was lifted onto her mother's lap and sat there, in a nest of white starched petticoats, her thumb in her mouth, and gazed steadily at the two strangers.

The mousy wisps of hair and the set of her chin were Blandford's, but the big brown eyes were her mother's, though as yet untainted by uncertainty and fear. It was not long before she began to wriggle determinedly until she was set down on the carpet. She crawled to Miss Olga and hauled herself upwards by means of a determined grip on the grey crepe skirt. Miss Olga's smile faltered when she saw the damp marks made by the small hands. Though she waggled her lace-mittened fingers and made a few nervous cooing noises, I could see she was made awkward by the child and was reluctant to pick her up in case further indiscretions were perpetrated on her best walking-out gown.

The nursemaid, a lumpish dull-eyed girl, was staring vacantly out of the window. Jane was too besotted to realise that not everyone could automatically share her delight in her offspring. Ruth gurgled at Miss Olga and a dribble made its way down her chin and suspended itself threateningly over Miss Olga's knee.

I leaned over and gently detached the clinging fingers, sweeping the child onto my own lap before the offending dribble could wreak further havoc on the grey crepe.

Ruth squared her mouth to wail, but I bounced her on my knee and launched ruthlessly into 'Ride a Cock Horse' until the protests turned to chuckles.

'A delightful child,' Miss Olga said, now she was suitably distanced.

I thought so. The warm wriggling body, the busy fingers tugging at my wayward hair that would be all of a tangle and loose from its pins when she had finished with it brought me to laughter which drowned the needle-sharp pain of remembering how once I had played so with my baby sister Rose.

'She takes to you,' Jane cried. 'Oh, but I cannot bear to despatch her back to the nursery so soon, though Blandford will not have her intruding upon adult company . . .' She hesitated then added boldly, 'But he is out visiting friends and is not likely to return until late, so I think this once we may be indulgent. I shall ring for tea and we will be thoroughly cosy together and forget all about those bothersome workers and their hammering and banging.'

We spent a comfortable hour over tea, Miss Olga nobly laying aside her rigid dietary rules and – purely out of politeness due to the absence of plainer fare, she assured me later – managing to consume a toasted muffin and two rich pastries oozing cream and jam. We were at ease, the child, crawling in exploration round the furniture or playing with her ivory teething ring, providing a focus for laughter and admiration. We fed her titbits from the tea table and sang rhymes to make her clap her hands and chuckle. Jane and I, reckless as to our gowns, were both on our knees playing peek-a-boo with the sofa cushions when the door opened, so softly that we did not hear it above Ruth's excited squeals.

'Well, well, such a bedlam of noise,' a voice drawled. 'For a moment I thought myself to be in a madhouse rather than the parlour.'

Jane froze, her cheeks blanching. Blandford Pascoe lounged against the doorframe, his pale, insolent eyes taking in our disarray, the fallen cushions, the now crumpled and crumb-covered infant.

'B . . . Blandford, such a surprise,' Jane stammered as we scrambled to our feet. 'We did not expect . . .'

'Not expect me, my dear? Come, come, I distinctly remember advising you that I should meet Mr Curtis here this very afternoon.'

Jane smoothed down her yellow skirts with suddenly trembling fingers.

'I . . . I must have mistaken your meaning,' she whispered, flickering a nervous, apologetic glance at the stocky man hovering at her husband's back. 'You said . . , that is I thought you were to be out all day.'

'But I specifically requested that you have ready all your ideas as to the decoration of the interior of the house by this afternoon at the very latest,' Blandford said, raising his eyebrows. 'Do you not recall? Have you not prepared anything?'

He is lying, I thought. Lying and enjoying every moment of his wife's humiliation.

Jane flushed. 'I . . . I have not quite yet been able . . .'

'Surely it would not have taxed your strength to try for once to please me.' His tone was pained. 'Mr Curtis, as you would remember had your mind not been set so securely upon your own affairs, has made a special journey to discuss your wishes.'

'My dear sir,' the architect said, 'another day or two will make no difference if Mrs Pascoe needs more time.'

'Mrs Pascoe has had time aplenty.' Blandford assured him. 'I can only apologise on her behalf.' He sighed, spoke man-to-man, amused, in a low voice we were quite expected to overhear. 'I fear I indulge my wife disgracefully. Perhaps I should be stricter, but the fair sex with all its womanly weaknesses has always appealed to the protective instincts in my nature.'

'One would not wish it otherwise,' Mr Curtis murmured stiffly.

'But tolerance has its limits.' He raised his voice. 'Mrs Pascoe has spent too many idle days lately, have you not, my dear? We can delay no longer. Decisions must be made.'

It irritated me beyond bearance that Blandford should represent Jane in such a blatantly false way.

'But Mrs Pascoe has not been idle from choice,' I said, stepping in front of Jane as though I could physically shield her. I held myself as tall and straight as I could and favoured the gentlemen with what I hoped was a calm smile, though irritation and distaste churned my stomach.

They gazed back at me, the one with questioning incomprehension, the other through narrowed, wary eyes.

I was suddenly terrified at my temerity, at how my defence of Jane might be twisted and used against her, but it was too late now to retreat.

'Mr Pascoe,' I said, my voice too high with feigned jocularity. 'You should not be such a tease. You know very well that Mrs Pascoe is barely recovered from her recent indisposition. It is the doctor who insists that she does not overtax herself. You must blame him if Mrs Pascoe has been unable to fulfil her commitments.' My smile felt rigid, but I dare not let it slip.

At my side I sensed rather than saw Miss Olga shrink back into her chair, waves of embarrassment emanating from the rustling grey crepe. I heard Jane's quick, scared breathing. Even little Ruth seemed to have caught the tension in the air and stopped her gurgling to stare round-eyed at the adults.

Blandford did not shift his languid stance. Only his pale eyes moved in lingering contemplation of my person, a look I remembered too clearly. I felt again the shivery sense of intrusion and disgust at his slithering regard. The sight of his tongue lapping out to lick his soft red lips before the discoloured teeth bared in a mirthless smile did nothing to steady my inner composure. Nor did his words.

'How very proper of you to reprimand me for my levity, Miss Howarth. I quite see, now that you have so clearly pointed it out, that I should not have treated my poor wife's state of health so lightly. I stand humbled by your censure.' He flourished a mocking bow, stepped forward, bringing a sickly waft of pomade and stale wine, and flapped a plump hand in my face. 'So what would you have me do, eh? Should we dismiss Mr Curtis, thereby causing further delay, while we attend upon my wife's full recovery? No, no, I think not. Time is of the essence. We return to Kingsbridge within the week and all must be put in hand before we leave.' He paused. 'So, Miss Howarth, both bearing as we do such a tender consideration for dear Jane's health, we must contrive together to relieve her of any distressing burden the doctor might disapprove of.'

Ruth chose that moment to bawl a protest at being ignored.

Without glancing at his wife or child, Blandford said, carelessly, 'Madam, pray have your daughter removed to the nursery.' He waited, tapping his foot impatiently, until the nursemaid had bundled Ruth off and her howls faded into the distance. Only then did he favour Jane with a sly and self-satisfied smile. 'So, madam, if you are not *allowed* to stir yourself to please me, then you may remain quietly with Cousin Olga while Miss Howarth accompanies Mr Curtis and myself on a tour of inspection. Come, Miss Howarth, take my arm. You are plainly a young woman of common sense and, er, good taste.' His eyes glinted with malice as they raked over my crumpled gingham gown and untidy hair. 'You may give us the benefit of your valuable opinion.'

Any idea I might have had of excusing myself faded

when I glanced towards Jane and saw only relief and pleading in her face. There was no support there. Jane – and who could blame her? – was only too happy to let me bear the weight of her husband's attention. If there were decisions to be made, then let someone else do it, for fear of later criticism.

I had manoeuvred myself into this awkward situation. Now I must make the best of it.

I ignored Blandford's proffered arm, swept briskly past him and fixed my attention on the architect.

'I am Miss Joanna Howarth,' I said, 'and my late papa, Mr Arnold Howarth, was interested in history and antiquities to the extent of having several volumes published on the subject. Perhaps you have heard of his *Rambles Round the Roman Walls of Chester* or *Some Ancient Houses of the County of Lancashire*? No?' I expected no other response. Papa's books had only ever found subscribers among his family and friends. 'His was an amateur's interest, of course, but he often regretted that so many fine, if neglected, old buildings of historic value were indiscriminately pulled down in favour of what was new and often inferior,' I went on with false, bright intensity. 'I naturally imply no criticism of your intentions here, but I would be most interested to hear your views as a professional gentleman.'

Mr Curtis took up the challenge as I hoped, looking, thank heaven, not a wit discomposed by being swept down upon by a somewhat breathless young woman almost a head taller than he was.

He bowed courteously. 'My views are not diametrically opposed to those of your father, Miss Howarth. We must indeed preserve the best of the past, but not at the expense of suppressing new, vigorous ideas, which would lead only to self-satisfaction and stagnation. This house, for example, is not unpleasing in its present aspect but it has no great architectural features or historical significance and therefore I have no qualms about improving it.' He tapped the roll of papers he held and added with a calm confidence that was, oddly, neither laughable nor boastful, 'I shall create here a jewel of form and proportion that will still be admired in a hundred, two hundred, years.'

His eyes were a piercing blue set in a square-jawed, ruddy-complexioned face. His solid frame was severely clad in black, relieved only by the stiff white points of his collar and neatly folded stock. He had the phlegmatic air of a man comfortable with himself and his purpose, yet there was impatience there. He was anxious to be about his business away from these distracting domestic squabblings.

I shared his impatience. And perhaps it was that shared emotion that struck a mutual note of concord from the first. Though I could not have guessed – how could I? – the surprising outcome of that chance meeting under Blandford Pascoe's lecherous eye.

There was a gentleman, one Dr Bowdler, who had earned the scorn of my papa and his cronies by publishing the works of Shakespeare in a version edited to omit any indelicate words and phrases that might have caused offence.

Dr Bowdler had a fine disciple in Miss Olga. I listened, that evening, to her account of the afternoon's events as she related them to her sister and was hard put not to smile. A picture emerged of Blandford and Jane as the most tender and devoted couple in all Exeter, their daughter the prettiest and most forward, their domestic arrangements singularly efficient. There was never a hint of Jane's distress at the upheaval; none at all of the moments of awkwardness and embarrassment. Even I was spared criticism. The rosy glow of

Pascoe approbation encompassed me and reflected flatteringly, or so Miss Olga fondly imagined, on herself.

We sat over the household mending, our chairs drawn to the window to catch the last of the light. Miss Polsham appeared to be dozing on her day bed but at the least hesitation on Miss Olga's part she stirred restlessly or cleared her throat or prompted with a 'You were saying, Olga?' in her faded invalid's voice until her sister took up the thread of her tale again.

When all had been recounted, and the final, astounding, piece of news related, Miss Polsham's eyes flew open and she said, quite forgetting to modulate her voice to its usual low, quavering pitch, 'Am I to understand, Joanna, that you have already agreed to take on these . . . these extra duties? And you, sister, have allowed it? What of her duties here? Really, that young man gets above himself!'

Miss Olga interrupted with a false laugh and a warning glance. 'Come, Fanny, you know I could not refuse dear Blandford when he put his request so charmingly. And Jane, too, is delighted that Joanna shows such a keen interest in the refurbishments of Roselawn. It is so convenient for her as she will be removed to the country for much of the winter and Joanna is on hand in Exeter to express Jane's wishes to the architect and to see that all goes according to Jane's orders.'

Miss Polsham subsided petulantly onto her pillows and Miss Olga, to put me firmly back in my place, criticised the quality of the darn I was finishing and demanded that I rip it out and start again. Whatever the sisters truly thought of the un-Bowdlerised version of events – Blandford's deliberate snubbing of his wife, his high-handed demands that Mr Curtis should consult me on the matters Jane herself should have attended to, namely the furnishings, arrangements and colour schemes for her boudoir and the principal guest rooms – was a matter for whispered conversations when I was out of earshot.

My feelings were mixed. On the one hand, I was intrigued at the prospect. On the other, that Blandford had called my bluff pleased me not at all, leave alone that I was now answerable to him.

I snipped, sighing, at the white threads I had painstakingly darned into the worn patch on an elderly table napkin, then rethreaded my needle.

The trouble was that, eager to remove myself from Blandford's side, I had shown far too much enthusiasm for Mr Curtis's ideas. Poring over the plans, seeing the narrow hall and stairwell as he saw it – widened to give a curving sweep of stairs up to a broad, airy landing. Picturing the low-ceilinged, haphazardly furnished upper rooms as they would be when fresh light spilled into them from the windows in the new façade. I clung close to Mr Curtis, as though for protection, as we progressed from room to room, Blandford trailing in our wake.

I felt the shade of my mother at my back as all the clever and successful ideas she had imposed on our various habitations spun through my head and spilled out, together with my own half-formed opinions, information garnered from books or excursions with my father into antique corners of old towns. My volubility caused Mr Curtis to pause in rattling off his somewhat offhand account, to regard me sharply, then to begin to listen to what I had to say and even to nod in agreement once or twice. Even Blandford wore a look of surprise and, by the time we returned to the parlour, an air of slyness. It was there that he stunned us all by his announcement.

'You will have no objection, of course, cousin, to allowing Miss Howarth such free time as may be necessary.' Miss Olga, flushing, twittered something incomprehensible. 'Ah, I knew you would be gracious.' Blandford was awash with oily insincerity. 'And how great a pleasure it will be for me, Miss Howarth, to know that we shall all benefit from your splendidly enthusiastic and artistic advice.'

'But you cannot expect—'

'Indeed I do!' Blandford interrupted. 'Why, the talent of my own dear wife in these matters is but a pale gleam against the illuminating radiance of your own profound knowledge. I would wager she does not know a Corinthian column from a cabriole leg, nor egg-and-dart moulding from a serpentine stretcher, do you, my angel?' Jane stared back at him in blank incomprehension. 'There, what did I tell you? But perhaps she feels that to be branded a blue stocking by too overt a display of intellect is not seemly in a wife. However, I readily confess that such trivial matters have never occupied me greatly either. Why should they when one pays others to deal with such detail? All I wish for is an establishment that will demonstrate to society that I am a man of position. Mr Curtis, whose reputation is beyond reproach, assures me that I shall not be disappointed and I expect the more formal rooms to reflect every nicety of current taste and fashion. But in view of my wife's ignorance, I could want for nothing better than that her newest and dearest friend' – how sarcastic the emphasis – 'should act on her behalf in the arrangement of the more private rooms.'

Blandford once more executed a deep and mocking bow, then turned his back on us and cried heartily to Mr Curtis, 'I pray you, my dear sir, take Miss Howarth into your complete professional confidence and give her the respect and assistance you would proffer my wife in similar circumstances.'

'Poor Mr Curtis looked most discomfited,' I hissed to Lily as I paced up and down my room that night. 'And who can blame him? Having me foisted on him! And having to stand for Blandford Pascoe being patronising and insulting while pretending to shower compliments. And it is all my fault! Pretending I knew so much, when I really know so little!'

'You'll manage,' Lily said comfortably.

'Hah! Much you know!'

'You're mekkin' a right fuss over nowt, I know that.'

'It's not nowt – nothing!' I swished to a halt and bounced down onto the bed beside Lily who was carefully scratching pothooks in her copybook, jolting her into giving me her full attention. 'It's embarrassing and . . . and scaring. Yes, scaring. There's a great deal of money involved – Blandford Pascoe's money! Not to mention Mr Curtis's reputation to think about. If I make a mess of it . . . Oh, if only I had not pushed myself forward!'

'If! If! If me auntie had balls she'd be me uncle,' said Lily rudely.

'Lily Walker!'

'Oh, come on, Miss Jo!' she grinned. 'Stop bellyaching! If it was me asked to tart up some fine lady's house, it'd be different. But you knows what's what. Look what you did in 'ere.'

'Oh, but—'

'Your ma could do it an' you got the knack an' all,' she said stubbornly. 'Anyone wi' half an eye can see. You could've taken 'owt from the attic but you picked out the bits as go real nice together. I can't see much difference wi' doin' the same for a bigger place.'

'Can't you?' Put like that it sounded so simple. I wished I could believe it, but I was still too keyed up to sleep after she had gone yawning to her bed.

I drew out pen and paper and wrote to Nicholas Fox.

It was a week since I had received my first brief letter from him with the address near the Haymarket where he and Caleb were now lodged and enclosing a document written in legal language which purported to give me a share in the Grey Cat Club. It looked official enough, full of fine-sounding wheretofores and hereunders, and sealed and witnessed. I had no way of knowing if it was genuine. I had to take it on trust, though in my heart I believed I had foolishly thrown away the money that had been so briefly mine.

But Nicholas had so far kept to his side of the bargain. I felt it incumbent on me that I should now keep to mine, though I had put off writing to him all week, for want of something interesting to say.

Now the events of the afternoon poured out and somehow committing the details to paper cleared and soothed my anxious mind. I daresay I said too much of my feelings, but as I wrote I felt I was actually speaking to him, which caused the words to flow with surprising ease.

I sealed and addressed the letter, sure there was nothing in it that he could find useful. But it was the best I could do. It was, as he had requested, a letter one friend might write to another. It had, however, helped me to put my thoughts in order and for that I was grateful.

I slept dreamlessly and woke to an easy acceptance of the challenge Blandford Pascoe had thrown me. And a fierce determination that I should do well enough to earn the respect of Mr Curtis.

Chapter Nine

The winter that year was a hard and bitter one. Rheumaticky old men groaned that the January weather was the worst they could remember and prayed for it to be over, while daring young ones persuaded nervous girls to tie skates to their boots and join them on the frozen Exe among the crowds of slithering, shrieking children. The sellers of hot pies and potatoes set up stalls around flaring braziers. The poor drifted in silent, ragged groups towards the source of the tantalising odours, the lucky ones snatching a few minutes to warm their blue fingers at the spitting blaze before the stallkeepers' oaths and blows sent them scuttling back.

The rich did not allow the weather to diminish their enjoyment of the season; indeed all the fashionable people congratulated themselves that they had managed to reach the Assembly Rooms for the Christmas ball. As January progressed, however, they kept more and more indoors as it became evident that they would be laying themselves open to chills or accident if they should venture out into snow or ice. They grumbled at the inconvenience, naturally, particularly at the lateness of the mails. None at all came out of Cornwall where a snowstorm was reported to have left drifts of up to twenty feet, the same violent blizzard causing many ships to founder along the coast.

The labouring classes had no option but to struggle

to their work over cobbles made treacherous by ice. Never had the local name of 'pitchings' for these stony surfaces seemed more appropriate. The steep streets and alleys were always a hazard to the pedestrian in the overcrowded lower reaches of the town, continually fouled as they were by the rubbish and ordure thrown into the central gutter or made slick with rain. Now the toll of broken limbs and sprains and bruises was heavy as boots and shoes lost all purchase.

The poor and destitute had no recourse but to fall upon charity and to be grateful for the gifts of coal and food donated from subscriptions hurriedly raised by kindly people about the town.

Memories of the dreadful journey Ben and I had made from the north revived each time I looked into the pinched faces of beggar children scavenging for scraps in the frozen mud of the High Street gutters long after the market traders had departed for comfortable, firelit homes. I had rubbed shoulders too closely in our journey with that tide of destitution ever to take for granted my permanent removal from it.

I might again be plagued by chilblains and the house so cold away from the sparse fires that I must break the ice on my water jug each morning, but I was no longer blinkered by my own misery into believing that my sufferings were unique. I knew myself to be fortunate on the days when I struggled out on some necessary household errand through snow that soaked my boots and stockings and caused the skirts of my gown to flap soddenly against my legs. I should return to a house that sheltered me from the elements, where I could rub Whitehead's Essence of Mustard onto my sore toes before putting on dry slippers and stockings. Where hot drinks and food, however plain, kept my stomach warm and full.

I had the luxury of being able to pause and admire

the snow-blanked spires and towers of the city locked in daytime crystalline beauty against a hard blue sky or silvered and serene under the glittering stars. I was comfortable in the knowledge that I need not seek shelter for the night in the doorway of some fashionable church whose ancient grandeur proclaimed God's glory but whose earthly guardians might be rigorous in sweeping any noisome vagrant from its sanctified environs. I was not put off from work and turned out of my lodgings for lack of wages to pay the rent because ice-locked rivers and snow-blocked roads slowed trade almost to a standstill. I did not have to find a squalid corner in the huddled alleys hard against the picturesque Roman walls where respite might be found from the searching claws of the east wind, or clench the muscles of my belly against the raging pangs of hunger that the cold made so much worse.

Good people helped where they could with many a private kindness to those who came begging at their doors. Even Miss Olga, in whom the spirit of charity burned with a modest flame, was moved to press a few coppers and a bag of shrivelled apples left from our own harvest on a ragged woman with a babe at her breast (rumoured to be a sailor's widow turned out of her parish before her lying-in for fear she and her infant should become a burden on the poor rate), who for several days haunted the snow-rutted alley beside St Perran's church. Unknown to Miss Olga, Lily gave her money from my own hoard and extra scraps from the kitchen, but it was too little and too late. After one night of intense cold – we later read in the *Flying Post* that the temperature had fallen to 13 degrees on the Fahrenheit thermometer – she and her babe were discovered dead and hastily removed for a pauper's burial.

Even Lily's ebullient spirits were quenched that day. In her eyes I saw reflected my own disturbed feelings.

Distress vied with guilt, sympathy with relief. We grieved for that poor woman, but silently rejoiced in our own security. So easily might things have been different had Grandfather closed his heart to Ben; had Lily's path not crossed mine. The cold that we felt came from within. As though we had both heard the chilly swish of Dame Fortune's careless passing and understood the precarious nature of her bounty.

Perhaps that reckoning put extra fire into our spirits. In the following days Lily's polishing had never been so energetic, her keenness to soak up every new piece of knowledge – from Mrs Caunter's method of making an economical broth to mastering the spelling of 'piece' as against 'peace' – so intense. I went about my duties with such energy that Miss Polsham said that she would sooner have a whirling dervish attend her and gave me a sharp rap on my chilblained knuckles with her hairbrush to emphasise her displeasure.

My enthusiasm extended to Roselawn as the thaw came and heavy rain cascaded down the streets, removing the last heap of dirty slush and making the streets passable again. My project there had taken a firm hold on my imagination, and I made every excuse I could to Miss Olga so that she might allow me to escape to Roselawn for an hour, even if I did not have an appointment to meet Mr Curtis there.

Mr Curtis was gravely tolerant of my presence and my enthusiasm and often questioned me on the books he had lent me or some newly finished aspect of the house.

'What do you think to that plasterwork frieze?' he would ask.

'The theme of fruit and wheatsheaves seems apt in a dining chamber and it is finely done.'

'Good, I am glad you approve.'

He meant it seriously. It was not his nature to joke or ridicule. If I did not like something but spoke in

240

vague praise, thinking to please him he seemed to sense it and would tell me straightly and without rancour to speak my mind honestly. His demeanour gave me the confidence to do so.

Another time, when the new staircase was installed, he held up a smooth curving 'S' of wrought iron. 'Tomorrow the men will begin on the balustrade for the stairs and gallery. What do you think?'

I examined it carefully. 'Simple and elegant, and in keeping with the shape of the staircase and the curving decorative pattern on the cornice,' I said. 'Which in turn will be complemented by the sweep of the mahogany handrail. Each element contributing to a pleasing and harmonious whole,' I finished, triumphantly.

'Good.' He nodded in his grave way, but I could see he was pleased that I had taken heed of the lectures he had given me on the subject. 'Within any interior, as with external architecture, one should always strive for balance,' he had told me, 'and for the inherent harmony of objects within each area of perspective. For the blending of colour and shape so that disparate items take on a particular quality to suit the style and intention of the room. For arrangements which will emphasise that which is excellent and minimise less fortunate aspects.'

I had taken it all to heart. Whereas Mama's way had been all flair and instinct and drama, his was the architect's approach of precision and calculation. Both, I could see, had advantages. But I saw, too, that taken to excess, one might lead to flamboyance and garishness, the other to an austere formality. What I must strive to do was to take the best from each and add something of my own.

That 'something' was the difficult part. All my ideas seemed dull and derivative when I put them onto paper.

When Mr Curtis was not present I wandered

aimlessly in and out of the rooms away from where the carpenters and masons and plasterers were working. The older craftsmen seemed wary of the presence of a young woman and some of the young apprentices tended to be cheeky or to pass ribald comments out of earshot of their masters. So I felt it best to keep out of their way, though I found it endlessly fascinating to watch objects of beauty form under the rough fingers of a craftsman, from a perfect joint in a piece of wood to a delicate swirl in a plaster frieze.

Apart from Mr Curtis, there were two people working at Roselawn who came to be my friends.

I was approaching the house one day, walking briskly as usual, when I heard my name called. I turned to find a young woman hastening after me.

'Miss Joanna . . . Oh, miss, 'ee takes such long strides. I thought I'd never catch 'ee.'

'Why, Emily!'

For a moment I did not recognise the maid who had worked for the Misses Polsham. Her face was wreathed in smiles as it never had been at Torre Crescent. She looked plump and bonny and drew back the folds of her bright, soft shawl to reveal the tiny infant snuggled within.

'Her's four weeks old now, miss. Good as gold. My Harry dotes on 'er. I'm just off to take 'ee 'is dinner. He'm workin' at the house yonder.'

'Roselawn?' I said in surprise.

'Thass it, miss. He'm doin' well,' she said proudly. 'Got men workin' for him, and 'prentices.'

We walked on together. I explained what my business was at Roselawn and realised that I knew the big, rough-haired man who was fitting out the grandiose library with cupboards and bookshelves, although we had not exchanged more than a 'Good morning' or 'Good afternoon'. I had admired his craftsmanship, though, and told Emily who immediately preened as though at a personal compliment.

'He'm clever, my Harry,' she said. 'Not a man as talks much, but thinks a lot.'

I wondered if Harry got chance to talk much, such a chatterbox Emily had turned out to be now that she was free of the restrictions imposed by Torre Crescent. But Harry, who was a good few years older than Emily, obviously adored her and the baby though he had a gruff, abrupt manner that masked a shy, quiet nature.

From the moment he learned that I was the Miss Joanna who had given Emily pennies to buy ribbons for her wedding, he went out of his way to be helpful in explaining the finer points of his craft and was never too busy to spare a moment to answer my questions.

My other friend was Timmy Whipple who worked for the upholsterer Mr Meredew.

Mr Meredew did not take kindly to my presence. He was a fussy little man with a shock of white hair and a perpetual frown and if our visits to Roselawn coincided, he followed at my heels like a snappy terrier. He refused to give me any advice or encouragement. He jealously guarded his professional secrets. If I wanted to know about the choosing, ordering or making of curtains and carpets, pelmets and bed hangings, blinds and cushions, and the best methods of covering walls with damask or Chinese papers, then I must find out by my own sharpness. He would not give me a ha'p'orth of help.

Fortunately, our paths did not often cross. It was Timmy who supervised the young apprentices and laboured from dawn to dusk on the beautiful fabrics that would grace the windows, walls and furniture of the house.

He was a God-fearing man of about thirty with a warm smile that illuminated his heavy features. He had a careworn air, which was hardly surprising when I learned of his heavy responsibilities. He was married with four young children and a father who could no longer work at the upholstery trade because of near blindness. His crippled sister also lived with them.

'She was stricken as a little maid by a terrible ague that left her without the use of her limbs. There are those that say 'twould have been better had the Lord taken her when He thought fit to strike her with such an affliction. But, as my ma used to say afore 'er passed away, there's a purpose in everything, though 'tis not for us to question it. 'Twill be in the next life when we learns the truth and poor souls like our Cissie gets their reward.'

Timmy was a great help to me, patiently explaining the measuring and cutting of materials, the fabrics that would gather well, or pleat nicely, which to choose for bed hangings as opposed to window curtains. I watched with respect the way his stubby fingers cut and pinned and tucked and sewed with swift and practised deftness.

If Mr Meredew also shared my respect, he did little to show it. He was quick to find fault with Timmy and rarely, and begrudgingly, gave praise. When I heard him tetchily scolding, I found it hard to hold my tongue as Timmy did. But then, Timmy had much to lose and little to gain by standing up for himself. He could not risk putting his job in jeopardy when there were so many people dependent on him.

Though I liked to watch Harry and Timmy, quite often I was content to drift round the house on my own, sniffing the sharp, clean aroma of damp plaster, admiring the way the new sash windows admitted the pale winter sunlight, drifting round islands of shrouded furniture, boxes of ornaments, pictures, which Mr Curtis had ruthlessly weeded out on Blandford's instructions. 'Nothing but the best has been kept. Nothing but the best will be added to it.'

I was in search of inspiration, and when inspiration did come, it was through one of these hidden objects. Yet it was quite by accident and at a moment I least expected it. It was like arriving at an unknown destination by a roundabout route and, upon arrival, recognising immediately that you were in the right place because the topography exactly matched the map you had been given. You knew also that though the signposts had led you through difficult country, they gave the true direction.

I had listened to Mr Curtis's lectures, I had studied the books he lent me, including the design books of Mr George Hepplewhite and Mr Thomas Hope who, I learned, were popular influences on current taste. From London had come sometimes scurrilous and often amusing comments from Nicholas on fashionable houses to which he apparently had entrée. I preferred not to think too closely of the how or why of his admission into London society. A man who lived by his wits, a man now substantially rich, a determined man who was not too scrupulous in the manner of his advancement might easily better himself, I fancied.

The town house of one Lady who considers herself the epitome of all that is grand is so overburdened with gilded flummery that one might imagine, like poor King Midas, even the food she touches must turn to gold.
Unfortunately, her overblown charms bely it ...

The passion for things Egyptian still rages. I dread the day when some fool, not satisfied with infestations of sphinxes and hieroglyphics, causes live camels to parade through his drawing room ...

I understand our noble monarch displays a
softening towards our late enemies across the
Channel now that they are duly subdued, and in
the interest of future harmonious relations
favours the styles of Louis XIV and XV . . .

I felt I should not chuckle over his disrespectful
comments, but I did. Nor should I feel grateful that
with every letter he bolstered my spirits. I knew he
only encouraged me because it suited his purpose for
me to be firmly ensconced in Blandford Pascoe's good
books. From the letter he had written in answer to my
first, and later regretted – so childish and feeble! –
outpourings, he was strongly insistent that I would
cope and cope admirably.

You are a sensible and capable young woman.
Do not let anything undermine your confidence
in yourself and your abilities. And never allow
private doubts to manifest themselves to others.
A confident and determined aspect will win
respect and reflect strongly upon your own
inner feelings.

His own philosophy?
I did not doubt it.
Contrary to the principles of submission and feminine docility that I was expected to display?
Most probably.
But the message struck home and gave me fresh
heart when I was feeling dejected and inclined to intro-
spection. At those moments I wondered why I should
feel it necessary to take so much time and trouble to
carry out Blandford's casually bestowed commission. I
had no need to go to any great pains to imprint my
own signature on Roselawn. Jane, had she been well
enough and interested enough, would merely have

made a few suggestions to Mr Curtis who would then have translated them as faithfully as he could. Blandford would never know, or care, if I aped the style of any arbiter of fashion. The house was meant merely to be a showcase for his own vanity.

For all that, I still felt driven to give of my best, to create something original, though for the life of me I could not express this in a practical fashion. Some element was missing. Some factor that I was not experienced enough to create or understand. It was very frustrating, not least because there was never time to concentrate my whole attention upon it. Though my duties at Torre Crescent were now second nature to me and I could often allow my mind to wander freely as I went about my tasks, I had precious little time to myself for serious study. I gladly helped Lily with her reading and writing and she was my dear friend and confidante, but I found myself on occasions begrudging her my attention, for I knew once she crept away to bed I would be too exhausted to do more than study a page or two of the design books before I fell asleep.

I felt a growing apprehension and irritability, which came to a head one morning when I was to meet Mr Curtis at Roselawn to talk over my final proposals. I had put down such ideas that I had in a notebook. Careful schemes that would be hard to fault and equally hard to enthuse over. I knew that they were not what I wanted, but the key to unlock the creative, original ideas which I sensed but could not grasp aggravatingly eluded me.

The faces of the stonemason's two apprentices goggling at me through the window of the grand new drawing room as I approached Roselawn did nothing for my temper, though I pretended not to have seen them.

They were two lumpish youths, who always made

free with their salacious comments when their master was not about. They were evidently alone, for their voices came loudly from the drawing room as I made for the stairs.

'Hair that red an' frizzy – 'tes a sign of 'ot passions,' one said.

'A devil between the sheets, d'you mean?'

'An' out of 'em! Ah, I like a woman wi' passions! Mind, one so tall and skinny and ill favoured is best got at when the candle's out. I've always found one whore's as good as the next in the dark...'

It was not only my cheeks that blazed. Usually I tried to ignore these gross asides, feeling myself at a disadvantage. But today I was in no mood for tactful retreat.

I whirled on my heel and strode savagely into the drawing room, my boots ringing loudly on the bare floorboards. Two startled faces turned to me.

'So that is how you pass the time in your master's absence! I'm sure he would be delighted to hear how *busily* you proceed with the tasks he set you.'

One of the lads, lolling by the fine new marble fireplace, hastily snatched up a broom and began vigorously to raise a cloud of dust around the hearth. The other, older, brasher, recovered his snag-toothed grin.

'Why, miss, we was only passin' the time o' day between ourselves as we worked. If you should have heard anything untoward, well, you shouldn't have been a-spying at keyholes.' Then he puffed out his cheeks, strained and let out a loud, rude fart. To the barely controlled guffaws of the other apprentice, he enquired innocently, 'What is it now, miss? Did you hear somethin' else not to your likin'? Me, I only heard the cry of a poor lost stinkbird a-callin' to its mate.'

This was too much for both of them. They fell against each other doubled over with laughter.

I would have banged their silly heads together had they not been poor targets, reeling about as they were. Instead I snatched at the nearest dust cover and flung it over them, together with a fine collection of dried plaster and wood chippings that had gathered in its folds.

Laughter turned to coughs and splutters. They fought to free themselves and emerged only to meet the knobbly fist of their master, drawn by the noise from the upper floor, who boxed their ears before turning to me for an explanation.

The apprentices stood red-eared, shamefaced, shuffling their boots, eyes sliding uneasily in my direction.

But my interest was so suddenly caught by what had been revealed by my cavalier removal of the dustsheet that I merely shook my head and said, vaguely, 'I think it was horseplay that got a little out of hand. Pray do not be too hard on them. I am sure it will not occur again.'

The astonishment of my tormenters would have set me laughing any other time, but I was too busy examining the elegant Pembroke table to take more note. I had scarcely noticed the table when it had been merely one object in the clutter of the old parlour. Now, on its own, in the clear wintry light pouring through the uncurtained windows into the room, I could appreciate why Mr Curtis had saved it from the saleroom.

Almost reverently, I blew away a scrap of sawdust that marred the perfection of the satinwood top with its flowing marquetry inlay of flowers and ribbons and in that moment all the knowledge that I had been acquiring, consciously and unconsciously, over past years from my mother and recent months from Mr Curtis seemed to merge into a single concentrated picture.

I saw the table in a setting that picked up the subtle

gold and bronzy-brown shades within the satinwood and the inlay. Velvety carpets, swagged curtains, a sofa and chairs upholstered in toning silk, grouped in an arrangement that was informal yet pleasing, the marquetry flowers and ribbons of the table repeated in the ornamental carved surround of a pair of matching mirrors and on the pilasters either side of the double doors . . .

'Allow me, miss.' The stonemason was at my elbow with the freshly shaken dustsheet. He laid it carefully across the table. 'Those young pups are in want of a good beating. But as long as no damage was done . . .'

'On the contrary,' I said cheerfully. 'I have reason to thank them for their intervention.' I gave the apprentices a brilliant smile that served only to increase their puzzlement and sailed triumphantly from the room.

The key had been there all along!

One object was all I needed. In a fever of excitement, I repeated the experiment in the upper rooms. Something large and elegant like the Pembroke table or the vast Tudor bed in the main bedchamber. Something as small as a china tray or a pair of ornamental candlesticks. Once I had this key, chosen from the disparate collection gathered in each room, its shape or its colour or its texture – I was not quite sure which – seemed to strike a response in my imagination. Ideas tumbled so fast that I could hardly contain them.

That first time, I stumbled over words when trying to explain to Mr Curtis why the bed hangings and coverlet in Jane and Blandford's room should be of a rich saffron to both complement and lighten the sombre aspect of the magnificent carved dark oak Tudor bed which had been in Jane's family for generations. And why the matching oak chest consigned to a smaller back room must be restored to its rightful place and why on no account should Chinese papers be considered in here, but the walls left plain.

Mr Curtis was patient. He heard me out, saying little as we proceeded from room to room. When we again emerged onto the gallery he nodded slowly. 'I should like you now to write down exactly what you have in mind, then make an inventory of what you believe to be necessary in each room. If you would be so kind, then, as to make a separate estimate of the amount of furnishing and curtain materials required, and perhaps a rough accounting of the other items, we shall go through it together at our next meeting.'

At our next meeting, barring one or two minor amendments, he gave my plans his unhesitating approval.

The winter and the early spring seemed to me to pass swiftly and not unhappily. I had believed myself doomed to dull drudgery when Grandfather despatched me to Exeter but though from necessity I was still bound to the elderly ladies, the ties now seemed less restrictive.

Whether this was due to a certain softening on their part or merely a reflection of changes in myself I could not say. Perhaps it was a little of both. Certainly my friendship with Jane and my involvement with Roselawn gave me a status in the ladies' eyes, and for my part I had grown used to Miss Polsham's self-centred ways and Miss Olga's scolding and parsimony. I might often be tired and irritated by their demands but there were occasions when I found myself actually warming to Miss Olga.

She preferred to do her own marketing if the weather permitted it, taking either Lily or myself to carry the baskets home. Never was she happier than when engaged in genteel haggling over quality or quantity with the butcher or grocer. She had a lightning mind when it came to adding a column of figures and heaven help the tradesman who thought to slip an extra farthing or ha'penny on to his reckoning. Nothing pleased her more than a bargain. Sallow cheeks flushed, she would emerge from the shop practically snapping the strings of her reticule over the saved coppers.

'One should never allow oneself to be bested when one's rights are clearly evident. Did you see the shifty way that boy of his weighed the sugar? You must always watch him. He never gives fair measure.'

She might haggle, the tradesmen might consider her a trial as I am sure they did, but she paid her dues promptly, in cash drawn from Brown's bank, each transaction necessitating immediate retreat to the dining parlour where she kept her account books in a locked desk, becoming exceedingly irritable if anything disturbed her until the necessary entries had been made and the books balanced.

Mama, I thought, would have been highly amused at such antics – and such principles. But the spectre of unpaid debts having troubled me through my growing years and culminated in my flight to Devon with Ben, I found this aspect of Miss Olga's character quite admirable.

When I considered my new challenging interest at Roselawn, the letters I might receive and write openly to Jane and the secret ones from Mr Chadwick and Nicholas Fox, and my tutelage of Lily, I could almost believe that my life had reached a satisfactory plateau after the miseries of last year. Indeed, though I was troubled by having to be underhand about some of my correspondence, this gave an edge to colourless days and a spice to my dreams.

I often regretted my foolishness in letting most of my ill-gotten guineas slip through my fingers into Nicholas Fox's, but on the drifting verge of sleep, imagination wove tantalising pictures of fortune and freedom. If in those sleepy moments Nicholas Fox's words rang true and his black-lashed eyes looked deep into mine with believable sincerity, with daylight common sense reasserted itself and I could smile and shake my head and resign myself to the notion that what I had so easily gained was likely to be as easily lost.

Each letter from Falconwood marked the snail's pace of Ben's progress in the more scholarly pursuits but there were compensations in other directions.

Our daily walks whatever the weather serve a dual aspect, *viz* exercise and learning. As Ben's interests lie in the natural elements, the flora and fauna that lie all around us, he has learned the names and habits of many plants and animals and birds almost without effort. He is now an excellent horseman and swimmer and his animals bring him great delight. It does my heart good to see him so content and happy.

And mine to know it.

Yet worrying undercurrents surfaced from time to time. Grandfather's impatience to force him ahead led Ben to occasional displays of stubbornness when he refused to study, once causing him to march out of the schoolroom. Matters came to a head when Grandfather, who had himself not ridden to hounds for many years due to his reluctance to mingle with local society, decided he must sacrifice himself in the interests of introducing his grandson to the thrills of the hunt.

It was a disaster.

All had gone well until the fox had been cornered and set upon by the hounds. Ben had witnessed the spectacle with horror, fetching one of the huntsman, intent on blooding him, such a buffet that the man was unseated. Mr Chadwick was spare with the details of the to-do, but I could well imagine Grandfather's chagrin and embarrassment when Ben, bawling tearful epithets, had turned his horse and galloped wildly home. He stubbornly refused to hunt again.

Grandfather's punishment was singularly unjust and the first I knew of it was on a day or two after I had received the letter, when Lily answered a knock at the door to admit Ben and Mr Chadwick. My surprise and delight was shortlived.

'I have a letter entrusted to me by Mr Kerswell to deliver personally to the Misses Polsham,' Mr Chadwick said with a courteous bow when he was shown into the parlour. Miss Polsham was not yet downstairs. Miss Olga had scuttled away at the sound of a male voice to change her cap and remove the cambric wrapper she wore to protect her dress. I did not care about my old faded house gown. I was too busy laughing and crying together and hugging my brother who looked so rosy and handsome and well grown.

'Oh, but why did you not let me know? Will you stay in Exeter long? Is Grandfather with you?'

'We leave for Bath within the hour,' Mr Chadwick said. 'We will stay a month for Ben to undergo treatment at the hands of a noted physician.'

I glanced at him sharply. 'You do not approve?'

'It would not be my choice.' He lifted his shoulders. 'But it is not my decision.'

'I hate to go,' Ben cried, his face crumpling. 'My dog Jess is to have pups any day and now I shall not see them. And the blackbirds already have eggs in a nest and I hoped to see them fly. And I shall miss Mrs Beer and Miss Lightbody.'

'Now, Ben.' Mr Chadwick laid a hand on his arm. 'We shall not dwell on that. There will be things to see in Bath that you will enjoy.'

'But it is a long way away, I do not know how far,' Ben said, truculently. 'I had far sooner stay with Jess.'

'The winter has been long and hard and of necessity we have been thrown much upon our own company,' Mr Chadwick murmured. 'Mr Kerswell feels that Ben has become somewhat, er, too set in his ways and would now benefit from a change of scene. He is confident that Ben will return in a more amenable state of mind.'

Mr Chadwick's words were diplomatic, as always, but his face was set and unhappy.

My joy evaporated. 'Do you mean that this . . . this visit to Bath is Grandfather's way of punishing Ben?'

Mr Chadwick looked uneasy but he did not deny it.

'The old devil!' I hissed. 'Ben is a person even if he is not quite like others, not some species of puppet that Grandfather can mould to his own will and image.' I paced angrily across the hearthrug. 'I am not surprised my brother hated to see a wild creature torn to pieces. I should not find the sight particularly pleasant myself. Why should he punish Ben by parting him from his friends and his pets and all that is familiar?'

But I had to suppress my rage for Ben's sake. Grandfather had decreed a visit to Bath. There was nothing Mr Chadwick or I could do about that. It was pointless to make Ben even more apprehensive. It was kinder to hold his hand and smile and reassure him that the time would soon pass and Jess's pups would be waiting for him on his return.

But perhaps Grandfather was not as stony-hearted as I thought.

Miss Olga returned to the parlour looking equally apprehensive at the unexpected intrusion into Torre Crescent's orderly routine. Her relief that the visit was soon to be terminated was quickly overshadowed by the prospect of more disruption.

When she opened Grandfather's letter she discovered that when Mr Chadwick returned from Bath I was to accompany him and Ben to Falconwood for a visit.

Spring surged into Exeter on a tide of pink and white blossom. The ever-present bells that had sounded with such hard clarity in the winter air now had a mellower ring as they boomed cheerfully over rooftops and chimneypots under a sky as blue and downy as a titmouse feather. Daffodils nodded under the apple trees in the garden where Miss Olga spent the lengthening evenings hoeing and weeding and planting.

My involvement with Roselawn was virtually over, though I called from time to time to see how work progressed, and with an increasing sense of dissatisfaction. My part was done, Mr Curtis had seemed pleased and that should have been satisfaction enough. Yet I felt that I could have done so much more – *wanted* to do much more. Planning was all very well, but how exciting it would have been to have carried all my ideas through to the finish. Visiting the warehouses and ordering materials, consulting upholsterers and carpenters, making any last-minute adjustments when it was evident that there might be a more pleasing arrangement, chivvying the workmen to give of their best. Reason told me I should never have had the time or the authority and, in any case, Mr Curtis was translating my ideas most faithfully. But I still felt as though I had only half completed the task I had been set.

Lily told me I was daft. 'You done enough for that old monstink Blandford. 'Sides, you'd be worn to a rag if you'd took on much more.'

Nicholas Fox was less blunt, but equally forceful. I must have been careless when writing to him and said more than I intended, though I sometimes had the eerie feeling that he had some sixth sense that saw through my actual words and picked up my thoughts.

> You have done well to get this far, though I know
> it galls not to see a task through to a satisfactory
> close. Think of what you have learned and not
> of what you have missed. It is no use fretting
> about the might-have-been. A chance could well
> arise in the future to use your knowledge and
> extend it. If not, at least you are the wiser for
> the experience. All knowledge, all experience, is
> riches and it is impossible to tell when these
> particular treasure chests might yield a greater
> bounty than can be anticipated at present.

As usual, he seemed to find the right words of reassurance, the right words to spur me on. Almost too perfect. A convenient knack, I thought in my more cynical moments.

But there were other matters to distract me as the one slow week followed another. Jane, to my great concern, had written to say she was again with child.

> This time I feel sure I will come to term, as the
> doctor here is confident I shall if I remain
> tranquil and in good spirits and to that end it is
> felt best if I do not remove to Exeter when the
> others do but remain quietly in the country until
> I am brought to bed. Oh, and I shall so wish for
> a son, for Blandford is more than ever hopeful
> for an heir and such good news that you are to
> come to Falconwood. I believe we are all invited
> to dinner to celebrate your dear brother's
> birthday, but as I will be unable to travel, I pray
> that you will find time to visit me.

For her sake, I hoped the coming child was a son. Then, her duty done, it might move Blandford to be kinder to her. Better, he might then leave her alone altogether and find his pleasure elsewhere, though I pitied any poor trollop who had to cater for his unpleasant tastes. Which were thoughts no young unmarried woman, gently reared, should have entertained, but then, as I increasingly discovered, there was an element in my nature that did not shy from facing plainly such crude subjects even if they might not be spoken of.

One other matter provided a diversion. In his letter, Grandfather had enclosed a draft for £10 on the Exeter Bank with the peremptory request that Miss Olga find a dressmaker and have me equipped with a new gown suitable for dining in company.

Miss Olga, whose last visit to a dressmaker had been more than three decades past, grew pinch-nosed at the prospect.

'Such extravagance! Why, for that money we could make several dresses.'

'But you have met my grandfather,' I put in hastily, then paused long enough to allow her to remember his towering, authoritarian presence in her parlour. 'Do you not think he might be offended if his express wishes were not carried out?'

'You may be right,' Miss Olga said after an uneasy moment. 'Though I shall have to enquire for a decent, reliable woman who will not overcharge.'

'But I know of just such a person! Mr Chadwick's mother!' I could not miss such an opportunity to set my acquaintance with Mrs Chadwick on a proper footing. 'She lives near the High Street and is, I believe, well thought of by a most respectable clientele. Should you like me to investigate further? Though of course I would not engage her until you have spoken to her yourself.'

Miss Olga would, so I made my first official visit upon Mrs Chadwick and she, forewarned of Miss Olga's delight in a bargain, promptly presented herself at Torre Crescent and gently agreed that ten pounds was an exceedingly lavish sum, but it was often the case that gentlemen liked to be generous with their womenfolk and she would be most economical so that perhaps a few extra, necessary items might also be purchased. She also added that from what she knew of Mr Kerswell through her son, he was a strong-minded and particular gentleman and the greatest care must be taken to ensure that what was created for Miss Howarth was both fashionable and agreeable in order to meet Mr Kerswell's exacting standards. Did not Miss Olga agree?

Miss Olga did, with the look of a nervous horse shying from an unknown object in its path.

Mrs Chadwick had, however, taken the liberty of bringing along a few samples of materials suitable for mild spring evenings in the country and if these could be agreed on, she would be happy to advise further on a modest style, bearing in mind that it must please the gentleman paying for it.

So I found myself in possession of a new gown, a pair of matching slippers and a fine Indian shawl.

Even I had been taken aback when I called at Mrs Chadwick's for my first fitting and she helped me into the silky folds of the soft green and ivory gauze with the clinging silk underskirt.

'It is quite beautiful,' I breathed. 'But surely something more serviceable—'

'There is no rule that serviceable cannot also be fashionable,' Mrs Chadwick said through a mouthful of pins. 'And really this new style with the lower waist and the piped seams might have been made for your figure.'

'But I cannot believe Miss Olga realised that the

little snippet of gauze you showed her would make up into something quite so frivolous.'

Mrs Chadwick's eyes twinkled. 'It is not Miss Olga we need to please but your grandfather, as I was at pains to point out.'

'I just wish I had the looks to justify the trouble you have taken. Now my sister Phoebe was so pretty she would have turned every head in a dress like this.'

'And you think you will not?' Mrs Chadwick said, crouching to tweak up the hem.

'I am sure of it! And I am used to it, so please, dear Mrs Chadwick, do not try to convince me otherwise out of mistaken kindness.'

'I would not dream of any such pretence.' Mrs Chadwick rose nimbly to her feet, took me by the shoulders and turned me to face the long mirror in the corner of her small, curtained parlour which served as a fitting room. 'Now, Miss Joanna Howarth, look closely at your reflection. What do you see?'

'Oh, I see the most beautiful gown,' I breathed. I swung the skirt so that the weighted ruffle at the hem swayed out and then fell back into the same perfect line.

'And the young woman inside this oh-so-beautiful gown?'

I dragged my gaze with reluctance to my plain and ordinary self. 'Still the same frizzy-headed beanpole, I am afraid – ouch. Oh, please, it takes an age to get my hair back tidily.'

Mrs Chadwick took no notice of my protests. Her fingers tugged fiercely at my hairpins, until my hair tumbled loose in a wild cloud about my shoulders.

'Look again, child,' she said. 'What do you see now?'

I giggled. 'Miss Olga would be horrified at such an untidy mop of hair and a dress that was cut so low.'

'Never mind Miss Olga!' I could feel Mrs Chadwick's impatience, but I did not know its source, nor what she expected me to say. 'What do you feel? What do you sense in your reflection?'

I shook my head, bewildered.

'You are not pretty. I agree with you there.' She shook me gently. 'But prettiness is transitory. You have something better. Your height . . .'

'Unbecoming in a woman,' I sighed.

'Your face . . .'

'Too like Grandfather Kerswell's.'

'Your colouring . . .'

'Unfashionable.'

'Perhaps you are too young to understand.' It was Mrs Chadwick's turn to sigh. Then she smiled and laid her hand against my cheek. 'Time is your friend. One day you will see what I glimpse now. You will have something far more interesting than prettiness, for you will become a handsome woman, my dear.'

'Will I?'

'And a passionate and maybe reckless one,' she added so softly that I wondered afterwards if I had imagined it as I peered doubtfully at my reflection, 'which is not an easy combination.'

Yet as Mrs Chadwick spoke, the girl in the mirror seemed for a moment to take on a different aspect. Neck and face gleaming pale against the cloud of red hair, tilted green eyes glinting under sleepy half-closed lids, hands composed tranquilly against the shimmering gauze of her dress . . .

Then I moved and the image moved too and with it the illusion. I was myself again. A tall, awkward girl ill at ease in her elegant gown.

Mrs Chadwick insisted on dressing my hair, damping and combing and pinning the springy strands. 'Now watch carefully. You should not force your hair into ways against its nature or strive to ape fashion

261

with fussy ringlets which would not suit you. Simplicity is best. If you pin the weight of it so, and let curling strands escape at your cheeks and neck to soften the severity – there, is that not an improvement?'

Somehow it was; though the difference was so subtle that not even Miss Polsham did more than frown and enquire if the wind had blown my bonnet awry as my hair seemed more than usually disarranged.

Nevertheless, I continued each day to practise pinning my hair as Mrs Chadwick showed me, until by the time I was ready to leave for Falconwood, Miss Polsham ceased to notice the change and I had begun to forget I had worn it any other way.

Falconwood. I had left more than a year since with tears as bitter and salt as the winter air.

Tears blinded me once more as I passed between the high gateposts on the plodding old nag allotted me. But they were tears of joy, of recognition, of gratitude.

Grandfather had relented. The exile was returned home.

My heart overflowed with happiness and optimism. I had been punished enough for the misdeeds of my grandmother, my mother, and now I was forgiven. I had hoped and prayed for it in the last weeks. Now, as we approached the house, I felt a surge of confidence, as though the very stone of Falconwood's sturdy walls, achingly familiar in the soft evening light, sent out their own unspoken message of hope.

I followed Ben indoors, to the loud and boisterous welcome from an assortment of dogs who scrambled over each other to reach him.

Harry Beer hauled in our bags. Mrs Beer, fat and smiling, cried, 'Why, Master Ben, you'm grown skinny as a starved hen. 'Tes well you'm back home to my good cookin'.'

And there was Miss Lightbody, trailing feathers and moulting velvet, a great cap askew on her impossible orange wig, reaching up to pinch Ben's cheek and screeching curses at the dogs and winking wickedly at me all at the same time.

Home.

The house folded me into its embrace. Amid the hubbub I seemed to inhabit a bubble of stillness. I breathed the remembered smell of old wood and stone, felt the security of sameness, endurance, seeping into my flesh, my bones, my heart.

Then the dogs suddenly fell silent, turning to look across the hall with cocked ears.

Grandfather's tread was clear and measured. His eyes were fixed on Ben.

For a moment he stood regarding Ben from under shaggy white brows, his harsh, beaky face expressionless. Then, slowly, he raised his hand and took Ben's.

'Welcome back, boy,' he said, but with so little expression and dropping Ben's hand so quickly that it was impossible to tell what emotion he felt at his grandson's return.

But there was no mistaking his feelings when he remembered my presence.

His eyes were as cold and hard as flint.

And though I curtsied and smiled politely and murmured some greeting, it was purely automatic. My optimism fell away, leaving a chill hollow of disappointment and resignation.

Whatever Grandfather's reasons for inviting me to Falconwood, it was not for reconciliation and forgiveness.

He despised me still.

Chapter Ten

I was several days at Falconwood before Ben's normal happy spirits resurfaced. Even then, at the least upset he became silent and withdrawn, with a wary, almost sullen air about him that I had never seen before. He had become very thin and pale. Whatever the treatment at Bath, it had clearly not suited him.

Mr Chadwick was at first reluctant to speak of it. But catching him alone in the schoolroom while Ben was out inspecting Jess's pups in the stables, I insisted on knowing the truth.

'The regime at Dr Roote's establishment is contrary to everything I believe in,' he began stiffly. 'Harsh. Unfeeling. Authoritarian. If not downright cruel! I wrote begging Mr Kerswell to remove Ben before too much damage was done to his mental and physical state, but he would not hear of it. He had it on good authority that Dr Roote was highly thought of for his treatment of idiots and persons with disorders of the brain and nervous system.' Bitterness rang in his now impassioned voice. 'I must not interfere on pain of instantly losing my position. As though I could have left Ben entirely friendless! I lodged outside, but I was, at least, allowed to visit him once daily and to reassure him that his trials would not last long.' He sighed. 'Some poor souls appeared to have been entirely forgotten by their relatives who had left them wholly at

Dr Roote's mercy, some for years, locked away.'

'Do you mean it was some kind of asylum?' I cried, aghast.

'In all but name,' Mr Chadwick said grimly. 'Oh, nothing to immediately offend the eye. Ben's room was small and spartan, but spotless, as was every room to which I was admitted. But the house is barred and locked and guarded as effectively as any gaol. Dr Roote himself is an affable, twinkling little man, but so adamant in his views as to verge on the fanatical and brooking no other opinion than his own.'

'Then you tried?'

'And got nowhere, beyond a lecture on his methods.'

'Which are?'

His hazel eyes were dark with anger and distress. 'He likens the patient to a distorted and dirty canvas which is in need of a thorough cleansing before a new picture can be painted upon it. The treatments are both violent and weakening. Castor oil glysters, purges and daily blood-letting are but the start, with nothing to eat or drink save spa water and dry bread. "To remove the poisons that cloud the brain and encourage the system to begin renewing itself." ' Mr Chadwick snorted. 'To make the patient too weak to rebel, more like. The next stage allows a low diet and a ritual of bathing and soaking – scalding hot baths, freezing cold ones, the application of ice packs to the feet and hot flannels to the head to draw the blood to the brain – and all manner of other foolish practices.'

He broke off to pace distractedly up and down.

'But perhaps the worst element was the isolation and the silence. The patients are kept apart, forbidden to communicate with each other, forbidden to read or be read to, to do anything other than lie immobile on their beds in their bare rooms when not undergoing treatment. The attendants never address a patient directly. Except for my one short visit and Dr Roote's daily examination, Ben was never spoken to. "It is important that the mental processes are not excited unnecessarily in order not to detract from the purification process." Bah! The man's a fool and a charlatan.'

'And if . . . if they . . . if Ben . . . should not willingly submit?'

His pacing faltered. I heard his breath rasp in his throat.

'Dr Roote does not allow for refusal.'

That bleak expressionless statement was chilling in its implications.

I closed my eyes. My poor, poor Ben. Torn from the comfort and security of Falconwood, held prisoner for what must have seemed to him an unendurable time, surrounded by strangers, unthinking strangers, silently imposing puzzling torments. Perhaps held under restraints, drugged . . .

'How can such things be allowed?' I burst out.

'Dr Roote claims great miracles stem from his treatment.' He flung out his arms in despair. 'Not instantly. Oh, no! That would be to invite ridicule. He has the gall to say that improvements might not be seen for many months. And he dispenses this . . . this nonsense with such assurance that it must give false encouragement to those gullible enough, or despairing enough, to believe him!'

'Those without hope might well turn to someone like that,' I whispered, remembering the black time after Ben's accident when we were grateful for every shred of hope the doctor – anyone – could offer.

'It was all so unnecessary!' Mr Chadwick cried. 'It has set the boy back! Physically he is worse than when he set out and all he has learned is distrust!' Abruptly he stopped his pacing. His arms dropped to his sides. 'Forgive me, Miss Howarth,' he said, making an effort to speak more soberly. 'I speak out of turn. I can see it is distressing you.'

'I am glad you spoke frankly. It is better that I know. I shall never forgive my grandfather for this. Never! To punish Ben so cruelly for refusing to do his will!'

After a moment Mr Chadwick murmured, controlled now, 'Perhaps we should be charitable. It might be that Mr Kerswell had a firm belief in the treatment and the timing was ... coincidence.'

But he averted his eyes as he spoke and I knew he was no more convinced than I.

Looking back it is easy to see the pattern of life as a meandering road. The straight easy stretches, the sharp bends round which shock and surprise lurk, the places where the road becomes fragmented and it is easy to take the wrong route, the clear rises to soaring heights, the deep dark plunges into frightening valleys. One can look back and say, 'Ah! *There* I made a mistake.' Or think with shame and anger, 'Why did I not make more effort to take this action, or that, and so prevent what happened later?'

At the time it is not so easy. One is swayed by emotion, blinkered by the trivial, restrained by bonds of necessity or fear or even love. One does not see or hear what is so clearly evident later.

Excuses? Perhaps. All I know is that it would have been difficult, then, to persuade myself into any other action than acceptance of my lot, and of Ben's. He was surrounded by affectionate care at Falconwood. He lacked for nothing. He was content. All this I saw and it was comfortable and expedient to believe that Grandfather's recent harsh treatment of Ben was an aberration, something that would never be repeated, nor anything like it ever again due to its evident inefficacy. Ben's place was here, in this quiet retreat, surrounded by all that was familiar and important to him.

Rage at Grandfather's treatment of Ben paled quickly to indignation, then was overwhelmed in the face of my unquenchable delight at being back at Falconwood. I was swept away with the sudden luxury of freedom. Drunk with it, made wild, like a leashed puppy suddenly released, that romps away in mad leaps and bounds.

It had been so long since all responsibility had been lifted from my shoulders. Years. Since Ben's accident. Ben was pleased that I was here, eager to show me all his favourite places and bring me news of his animals, but his day fell into a clear routine of schoolwork, exercise and leisure that I might join or not as the mood took me. I need not rise in haste, fearing to be late for morning prayers and so incurring Miss Olga's displeasure, nor spend the day running hither and yon at the demands of Miss Polsham's impatient bell. My day was empty of routine, devoid of duties.

Falconwood was a large house, easy to find an unused room or a hidden corner if one chose, though there was scarcely any need. The fancy grew on me that each person in the house, like the dancers in some complicated set, moved with solitary, pre-determined, self-absorbed steps about each other, circling, sidestepping, moving away and scarcely ever meeting. Into this curious pattern I inserted a few hesitant moves of my own, then, realising that no one, least of all Grandfather, cared what I did, I allowed myself to break into a more adventurous rhythm.

Grandfather still spent his day, as no doubt he had for years, going in silence about his own affairs, sometimes riding out early with his gun and his dogs and not returning until late, sometimes closeting himself in his study where Harry Beer would serve him his meals.

Each evening he would send for Ben and Mr Chadwick for a report on the day's activities, but I was ignored, as I had come to expect.

As long as I appeared at mealtimes and did not get under their feet at any other time, Mrs Beer and Bessy, now tolerably civil to me, accepted my presence without complaint and with little interest. Miss Lightbody, who came and went at the dictates of her own erratic impulses, certainly saw nothing odd in the fact that I might disappear into the countryside for hours at a time or feel the need to leave the parlour at dusk and perch on a fallen tree in the orchard to watch the stars brighten. If it had come to her ears that I had been seen running barefoot, my skirts hoisted above my knees, through the icy waters of the cove or climbing over fences and walls to investigate distant woods and fields, or dancing and singing in solitary abandonment on the cliff tops, I doubt she would have raised one painted eyebrow. Indeed, I almost collided with her one afternoon as I dashed into the house with scarcely time to tidy myself before dinner. She took no heed of my breathless attempts to apologise, nor of my dishevelled and wind-burnt state, but gave a tottering twirl, crying, 'Pray give me your opinion on this shawl? I have not worn it in an age and though it is a little damaged by moth, the colour is becoming, do you not think so?'

'Oh . . . why, yes . . . indeed,' I stammered. It looked no better and no worse than any other of her mismatched, decaying garments but I warmed with gratitude for her indifference to my wild appearance. How blissful not to be met with censure! 'It is a beautiful shawl,' I added. 'It suits you very well.'

And for a moment, as I fled up the stairs to my room, I could almost believe that the monkeyish, possibly mad, old stick of a woman with the rouged cheeks and impossible wig, pirouetting still at the foot of the stairs, had a wholly benevolent aspect.

I had forgotten – had I ever known? – such indulgence of the spirit and senses. Well fed on what seemed to be fatly sumptuous meals after the sparse fare at Torre Crescent, falling into a deep pit of dreamless sleep each night on a vast feather bed in a guest chamber, long unused but which Bessy informed me proudly had been polished and scrubbed and aired in my honour 'till all they ol' musty stenches was all washed away'.

My modest wardrobe occupied but a fraction of the giant press, even my new gown, still protected in a cotton wrapper and as yet unworn, looked lost in the cedar-scented space. The room was far bigger than the one I had slept in on my first visit, though I had somehow hoped that Mama's old room would have been prepared for me. But it was still locked. Mention of it brought the old hostile look back to Bessy's eye. "Tes none o' my business, nor o' yourn,' she said brusquely. 'Master says 'tes to stay shut. Thass all I knows.'

I was disappointed. I believe I had half expected Grandfather to indicate some change in his attitude to my mother. Some hint of forgiveness. It was all so long ago! And, after all, she had given him Ben, his grandson, so like his son who had drowned, who had come to be a consolation in his old age.

I said as much to Miss Lightbody as we sat late in the small parlour over the backgammon board. Ben had gone yawning to bed and Mr Chadwick, relieved that I was willing to take his place when Miss Lightbody demanded a game ('She cheats abominably!') had also retired. We had heard Grandfather bolting the front door, his footsteps clumping past the parlour and retreating up the stairs. He did not look in to wish

271

us goodnight or to reprimand us for staying up. He had no interest in conserving candles. Nor in us.

'Forgiveness? Tchah! It is not in his nature,' Miss Lightbody snapped. 'Apart from his Kerswell blood which has never been known for its tolerance of others' shortcomings, Frank was born under the Scorpion which, in its worst aspects, is a sign known to harbour and enjoy its grudges and never to forget a slight.' She shook the cup vigorously, spilled out the dice and swore roundly. 'God's blood, am I to get no doublets? What use is a one and a deuce when I am gammoned twice and like to be trounced again by a mere chit.'

'It is sad that he must remain so embittered,' I sighed. 'My mother perhaps was wrong to act as she did, but she was young and she truly loved my father.'

'Your ma's dead and gone,' Miss Lightbody said, cruelly. 'Forgiveness won't bring her back, nor bring comfort to Frank. He's too deep set in his ways.' She peered at me. 'When were you born, eh? Under peace-maker Pisces? You'll get no satisfaction in this house if you were.'

'August,' I said. 'Like my mother.'

'A fiery lion! I should have known. Lion and scorpion. There's an uneasy combination to be rubbing shoulders so closely. She and Frank were destined to be at odds. And you also, mayhap. Fire and water. Strong-willed both, each seeking to dominate, and should Mars make an unfortunate conjunction . . . Ah, there we have it! A five and a one.'

'That was surely a four . . .' I began, but she had swiftly whisked the dice back into the cup, moved her counter to take mine.

''Tis an easy mistake when the candles burn low,' she said blandly, 'but 'tis scarce worth lighting fresh at this hour. Of course, one cannot make fine judgments without knowing where the other planets lie within the natal chart. I shall need to know the day and time and place of your birth, child. And do not look so high-nosed. There's many a better and wiser than you who respects the wisdom of the stars.'

'Wisdom? I would label it superstition ... Oh, bother, double five and I cannot get off the bar.'

'Mock if you will, but I have lived long enough to see the truth of it. My mother gave birth to me in a rotting hovel with the Thames lapping its stink up against the walls at every tide.' Her bony little claws nipped at the counters. 'Had my stars been unkind I should have remained at her side to learn her honest if foul trade of pure-gathering, that is to say the collect-ing of dog turds for use in the tanning of leather. But an old crippled scholar who lived in the cellar and who taught me my letters drew up my chart and told me that the planets showed that I had the wits and the will to better myself. "Seize your chance," he said. "Your fifteenth year, your nineteenth and your forty-first will be the crucial times. Be bold then and take what opportunities come, for then the stars will favour fortune, but take heed of the lessons learnt and use them to your advantage in the future." '

Her words touched my memory. '*Yore time will com if yew are Bold to take your Chans,*' she had written. I reminded her of it.

'So I did. So I did. And would you if opportunity came? Or perhaps it has already.' Her little black eyes were sharp on me, almost as though they could see the golden stream of coins chinking into my lap from Nicholas Fox's hands and the cavalier way I had let myself be persuaded to part again with most of it.

I had taken my chance, much good would it do me. But under Grandfather's roof, to this indiscreet old woman, I would not speak of it.

I shrugged, smiled, said, to divert her, 'You wrote

also, most puzzlingly, of beasts wild and tame—'

'When I was fifteen,' she said abruptly, as though I had not spoken, 'I lost my heart and my virginity to a poor but handsome lad who could offer nothing but his penury, his hand and his member – a powerful, lusty and persuasive organ which I fancied might go on pleasing me for many a year. So I was married and mother of a brat and widowed and childless from a virulent summer diarrhoea all within a twelvemonth. But that year taught me that love and poverty are poor bedfellows and that I was pretty enough and forward enough to do better than tie myself to a poor man – or to any man – other than for gain, though I vowed not to sink to the level of a common doxy lifting her skirts for sixpence in a back alley.' She grinned maliciously. 'I make you blush, but think on it. 'Tis all part of life, and best spoke of without shame, even if you are yet a virgin, which is a tedious state. You are a virgin, are you not?'

'Miss Lightbody!'

'Do not pretend to be scandalised,' she said. 'You are made of stronger stuff than to swoon at plain talk, or I'm no judge ... So, by learning and scheming and seeking the company of those women who benefited from the favour of rich men, I was well rewarded. At nineteen I was spied by a minor sprig of the nobility who fell in love with my golden hair and my ripe bosom and set me up in my own establishment. After that I had many easy years and was still sought after when I was past forty, for I was still a pretty woman, easily passing for ten years younger. Then I met Frank, which was a time predicted by the old scholar, and high sport we had.' Her face crumpled to wrinkled wistfulness. 'Ah, if I had but met him before his faithless wife and his vagabond daughter and his drowned son had turned his blood to bile, then we should like to have been soul mates.'

Absently she shook the cup, spilled the dice, began moving her counters off the board.

'So your stars led you wrong,' I said tartly, still burning from her outspoken remarks. 'Surely you would have done better sticking to the life you knew in London rather than following Grandfather and allowing him to maroon you here for all these years, with no friend or neighbour or company other than servants.'

'You think so? Look at me, child. Is my hair the colour of butter? My skin as white as milk? My person scented and pleasant? Would I pass for thirty now? Or even a well-preserved fifty? I think not. I should be reduced to that most degraded and desperate of creatures, a burned-out whore.'

She threw a four and a five, I saw that distinctly, but I did not say anything when she removed her last four counters as though she had thrown a double. The game was over. I was tired and would be glad to go to bed. The fire was white ash, the candles guttering, the air sad with lost hopes.

'I stay close in his house because I am comfortable here. I have my memories. Besides, old age is a peaceful state to encounter after the ambitious burnings and amorous entanglements of youth. And there need be no tedium when you have a lively mind that rejoices in observing the foolish deceits and posturings of others.' She stood up abruptly, grinning slyly. 'I bettered you there, did I not? We shall play again tomorrow. Now I am off to my bed.' She scuttled to the door, loose fringes swirling around her. Her hand on the doorknob, she turned. 'Wild beasts are not always to be feared, that was what I wrote, aye. Did you not understand? I thought you sharp, chit. It was of *foxes* I spoke.' Her laugh was an eldritch screech. 'Or rather one fox in particular. An unusual fox. A fox with a black pelt. A sleek, handsome creature who could snap off an innocent chicken's head with the snap of his sharp white teeth or tear the pretty lamb to bloody shreds and hide his tracks so well that the outraged farmer and the huntsman and his hounds would not be able to find him.'

My cheeks burned again, but from the sudden shock of Nick's image springing into my mind.

'Better to be the fox's friend, I would have thought, than his enemy or his victim. That is what I meant, for I am sure such creatures may be come across in town as well as country.' Her beady black eyes glittered strangely. For a dizzy moment I was convinced she must see into my head and know all of my plans and hopes; then reason re-established itself.

'If you speak of *Nicholas* Fox,' I said, calmly, 'I have an acquaintance with the gentleman, as you may have heard. When Mrs Pascoe miscarried—'

'Tcha!' She waved her lace-mittened hands in the air. I could see the large rent in one palm. 'I care not the how and the where and the why. The stars intended it. So be it. I warned Frank 'twas no use to destroy the old dog and let the cub go loose, but he is bull-necked and thinks the matter settled once and for all by the hangman's noose. Ah, but what other did I say? A caution? Aye, a caution. I remember. Evil hearts, black hearts. 'Twas the spoiled and fawning lap dog I meant that chases at the fox's heels. You have met that creature, too, eh? A plump and lustful brute, cruel to the defenceless, that hides its true nature with licks and slobberings and pretences at civility. You have his mark? Ah, I see from your face you have. Good.' She opened the door and tottered out into the passage. 'I may be old and addle-headed,' she called over her shoulder, 'but I know and understand men. That one was ever foul-minded though he pretends otherwise. Such a one is best avoided, especially by a young bitch

276

who might unwillingly tantalise the lap dog's lowest instincts by the promise of untouched virginity.' She gave a loud cackle. 'But then, the lap dog is itself in danger if it chooses to run with the agile fox, for 'twill be outpaced and outwitted and one day the fox will surely grow hungry and pounce upon such a nice, plump morsel . . .'

She was mad, quite mad.

Yet when her untidy clicking footsteps had faded down the passage, I sat on in the chilly room and her words would not let me go.

The huge shadows from the draught-blown candle flames billowed and bent over the homely furniture. How often had my mother, my grandmother, the generations of women of my blood, sat late here, dreaming, talking, planning? Perhaps rebelling, plotting escape from some desperate entanglement. And was the anguish all for nothing?

I rose stiffly and went to the window to draw back the heavy curtain. The stars were a glittering embroidery of brilliants strewn haphazardly over the blackness of night. Did these far-off points of light truly plot our destiny? If so, why struggle against fate?

I let the curtain fall.

I snuffed out the candles, save one, wishing Miss Lightbody had not been so very definite in her convictions. I carried the candle upstairs, a warm circle of comforting light in the dark house, but I still felt, uneasily, that the old lady's talk of portents and planets had somehow set the future into a pattern that could not be changed.

The unheeding, drifting days came to an abrupt end one morning when I returned from a bracing walk across the cliffs.

Bessy met me at the door crying, 'Where'm you

been to, then? I've been lookin' for ee this past hour. Master's waiting on ee in 'is study.'

His mouth was set in a tight line. He waved me impatiently to a chair.

'Your brother,' he began without preamble, 'has an unfortunate streak of stubbornness.'

'My brother, sir,' I countered, gathering my wind-blown wits, 'has improved beyond anything I would have believed possible a year ago. It is entirely due to the sheltered life he has here and the care and love of those around him. You have been more than generous—'

'Do not butter me up, miss!' He stuck his great white-maned head forward belligerently. The two dogs who had welcomed me with thumping tails before sinking back to sleep woke again, ears pricked, eyes turning uneasily to their master. 'I have read another message in your demeanour these last days. You forget that I have an eye for deceit in women.'

I was taken aback that he had so much as noticed me. 'I spoke the truth plain for anyone to see,' I said. 'Ben has improved greatly. You have given him a fine tutor, fine clothes, excellent food. You have been unstintingly generous. That is fact and I would not wish to dispute it, but if you had allowed me to finish, I would have reminded you plainly that Ben is a person, with feelings, not a puppet that you can make dance willy-nilly to your tune.'

'You see! You disapprove of the discipline I must exert if the boy is ever to come to something.'

'Discipline! You call banishing him to Bath to be half starved and ill treated by a . . . a so-called doctor *discipline*? Why, sir, you would not treat your dogs or your horses in such a fashion! Yet you would foist such *discipline* on your grandson! Your own flesh and blood! And do not tell me it was pure coincidence that he

278

was despatched to this so-called clinic when he refused again to join the hunt, for I will not believe it.'

'If I did, that is my privilege. He must learn the value of obedience.' Red spots flared like alarm signals on his gaunt cheekbones. For a moment I feared he might raise his hand to me, so threateningly did he loom over my chair. 'He is no use to me otherwise!'

I stared at him, suddenly alert. 'What do you mean?'

He did not answer. He swung round so that his back was to me, not before I had seen his anger snuff out, to be replaced by another expression entirely. One so blank and guarded it was like a shutter closing on an open window.

'Obedience to one's elders,' he said flatly, 'should be learned in early childhood. Ben has forgotten that lesson if he ever learned it from his wayward mother. But he will.'

'By cruel means?' I cried. 'That is not the way! You must see that his incarceration at the Bath clinic has not improved him at all. And when you speak of Ben being of use to you, what exactly—'

'Enough!' He swung round on his heel, head lowered, threatening once more, the wily old eagle, ready for the attack, ready for the kill. 'You are impertinent! And too hot-headed and argumentative for your own good. I have had enough of that in my house.' He smiled then. It was not a kind smile. It alarmed me more than his anger or his bluster. 'When I sent for you I had some idea that you might be persuaded to speak to your brother and bring him round to my way of thinking. I had begun to believe, you see, that your sojourn in Exeter might have smoothed the rough edges from your character. Produced some evidence of true feminine docility. I observed some signs of it, I thought, when I was last in your company. But I was misled. You were play-acting, were you not? I might

279

have guessed that you had inherited your mother's guile as well as her temper. So I shall not offer you the hospitality of my house longer than needs be.' His rueful tone was gratingly false. I could see the satisfaction it gave him to have the power to withhold and deny. 'I had thought, out of kindness, to invite you to leave your employ and remove yourself to live here at Falconwood, to be a companion and comfort to your brother. Alas, I see that such a philanthropic action would be tantamount to taking a viper to my bosom.'

For a bleak moment I believed him. I felt myself cursed by my quick tongue. Why had I spoken too freely on Ben's behalf and thrown away any chance I had of staying at Falconwood?

'It is, as you know, Ben's birthday next week,' he said. 'I have decided on a small celebration. Among the guests will be the Pascoes. Mr Pascoe has kindly invited you to return to Kingsbridge with his party after dining here at the request of his ailing daughter-in-law who has some friendship for you, I understand, and has expressed a wish for your company for a day or two.' His manner betokened surprise that anyone should be so misguided as to favour me. 'I have accepted on your behalf. You may take the Exeter mail from there.'

He sounded almost jovial. I raised my head and stared at him. Cold conviction that he lied, that his pleasure lay in manipulating my emotions swept away my despair.

'You had no intention of keeping me here,' I said slowly. 'You planned for me to leave with the Pascoes from the beginning.'

He raised his shaggy white eyebrows. 'Had you shown some sign that you might fit peacefully into my household—'

'Stuff!' I cried, leaping to my feet. 'You talk of the

deceit and guile of your womenfolk, but you are a fine example of a man steeped in it!'

'And I would be like to see more evidence of this devotion you profess for your brother for the rest of your visit. It displeases me to have reports of you tramping like a hoyden about the countryside.'

I was incensed. 'You have spies watching me?'

He paced across the carpet, nudged a dog out of his way with the toe of his boot, leaned an elbow on the mantel.

'You are of little importance to me,' he said carelessly. 'Why should I need to employ spies? It is merely that one of my tenant farmers keeping watch for poachers saw you climb over a wall and enter his woodland. Thinking you to be a thieving gypsy he followed you to the stream in the woods where he derived a great deal of amusement from observing you remove your boots and stockings, hitch up your skirts and wade into the water. Fortunately he realised who you were – doubtless from the tittle-tattle that is prone to spread like a summer grass fire through the countryside – and decided to remove himself without setting his dogs on you.'

'Not soon enough!' My anger evaporated in a wash of indignation and embarrassment. 'A peeping Tom! That is intolerable!'

'And doubtless the tale will grow with the telling. I know the people hereabouts only too well. Soon it will not be merely your feet and ankles and petticoats that he saw, but a wanton display put on for his benefit.' Grandfather clenched his fist and brought it down with a crash on the mantel, making me jump. 'Pray keep within sight of the house in future unless you are escorted by your brother and his tutor. I will not have you the subject of scurrilous talk in every alehouse. Do you understand?'

I nodded, choked with misery. That I had been

watched when I thought myself blissfully solitary was a more distressing thought than Grandfather's assertion that I meant nothing to him, which I already knew.

'One more thing,' he barked. 'I forwarded money to your employers for a decent gown. I trust this has been used wisely and that you propose to make some effort with your appearance when we have company.'

'Oh, indeed yes,' I said bitterly. 'I shall take the greatest pains to impress your guests. I would not wish to embarrass you by looking as though I led anything other than an idle life of luxury.'

'Look at yourself!' he thundered. 'Mud and grass stains on your skirt, your hair halfway down your back, a rent in your sleeve! You look like a peasant who has just tumbled out of a haystack.'

'The wind . . . the path was muddy . . .'

'You have little enough to commend you. You could at least make an effort to be neat and tidy.' He flung himself into his chair, propped his feet on the hearth. 'I have no more to say. I shall not wish to see you again privately before you leave.'

Nor I you! I thought. Which was, perhaps, precisely what he wished. I went to the door, opened it. Yet I could not go without speaking what was in my heart.

'It could have been so different, Grandfather,' I said quietly. 'I . . . I would have done my best . . . to be what you wanted. To like you . . . to love you, even. If you had shown but the smallest hint of affection . . .' My voice died. He did not move. I do not know if he even heard me.

After a moment, I went out and closed the door softly.

The house was in a bustle of cleaning and polishing and airing for the two days before Ben's twentieth birthday. There were special deliveries of delicacies from Kingsbridge. Clouds of savoury steam and the vanilla smell of baking wafted constantly from the kitchen. Even Miss Lightbody darted about with sparky energy, hounding Bessy, poking her nose into the kitchen to screech orders and exchange insults with Mrs Beer, delving into cupboards and drawers in the dining room to bring out fine china, crystal and tarnished silver which she handled with surprising delicacy and deftness. She spent patient hours polishing and restoring the silver to brilliance, arranging compotes of fruit, garlands of trailing greenery twined with spring posies down the extended length of the table. She rejected my offers of help. 'Tush, girl, just keep yourself – and your great clumping brother and his tutor – from under my feet.' I saw that she was enjoying this brief spell of command and action, giving me a glimpse of the energetic woman she had once been.

Nothing had been done to alter the fabric of Falconwood since my last visit. There still hung about the place an air, not of neglect, for the house was ordered enough and clean, but of something missing – a loving touch, a truly caring hand. I had looked about me with eyes fresh from my recent experience at Roselawn, thinking how much I would like to bring all the lessons I had learned with Mr Curtis to bear on Falconwood itself. To sweep away dull drapes and unpleasing furnishings, to bring light and colour to gloomy corners, to spend time and thought reviving each room and passage to a warm and welcoming state.

I had a glimpse of how it could be when Miss Lightbody had finished her preparations. The table looked magnificent in its splendour of pristine linen and burnished sliver, dazzling crystal and pastel flowers. It sailed down the room like a bejewelled ship on a grey ocean, drawing the eye from worn brocade on elderly chairs, from faded curtains and sombre panelling.

'You have worked wonders, Miss Lightbody,' I said with genuine respect.

''Twill set our company by the ears! I find it exceedingly satisfactory that at my great age I have not quite lost all my talents, in which I was quick to find a tutor – a lady ruined by her love for the gaming tables – when I first set upon my career. For there is no whore more pleasing to a gentleman than one who acquires the manners and accomplishments of her betters for the drawing room yet is still able to match his lustful appetites in the bedroom. Now I shall tend to my own *toilette*, for I must play my part. I cannot appear at the festive board as Frank's doxy, even though 'tis an age since I shared his bed!' She gave a screech of laughter. 'Tomorrow you shall see me in a role I have not chosen to perform for many a year, for who has crossed our doorstep other than persons of no consequence, such as yourself?'

She was as good as her word. We – Ben, Mr Chadwick and I – had breakfasted early in the small parlour. We had presented our birthday gifts to Ben – a panel of flying swallows I had embroidered to brighten the wall of his bedchamber, a chapbook engraved with animals from Mr Chadwick – when this strange person tripped into the room and swept us a deep curtsy.

She had not been able to bring herself to discard the red wig, but she had managed to set it level, with a large plain cap covering most of it. The rest of her was entirely clothed in old-fashioned rusty black that creaked as she moved and cast off an odour of mould. Her face was as unadorned as the rest of her. No paint, no powder; not a frill, not a scrap of lace, and though she was heavily garbed from chin to toe, this absence of colour and ornament gave her a curiously naked appearance, as though she had been skinned.

'Shall I pass as a respectable housekeeper?' she demanded, jangling the keys bunched at her waist.

'Most respectable,' I said gravely. In truth I was surprised to find myself regretting the loss of that bedizened, bawdy little creature, and secretly pleased that by the wig and the manner of her tottering walk which indicated that her stiff skirts hid her usual rickety-heeled shoes, her true self was not entirely banished.

'Now 'tis your turn,' she said to me. 'Be off with you and get into your finery, else the company will mistake you for a poor scullery drab brought in to scour the dishes. As for you, my fine gentleman,' she said, reaching up to pinch Ben's cheek, 'you're a handsome sprig, even if your wits is sullied, and it pleases me to give you this as keepsake to mark the day. 'Twas given to me by a fresh-faced sailor lad who once took my fancy and who you remind me of somewhat, which gives me pleasure to remember when I look at you now.' It was a tiny bottle containing a miniature ship. 'See, boy, 'tis magical, for the ship sails on a blue sea, with all its sails puffed out, yet how did it get its tall masts within that narrow neck? If you should ever work out the hows and the whys of the magic, then perhaps it is that all your wits is not lost for ever.'

Ben was enchanted. 'I like birthdays,' he declared. 'So many fine things . . . And Grandfather, too, he is to give me a special present. He told me. Will it be soon?'

'Ha! It is impertinent to speak so!' She prodded him sharply in his midriff. 'Hold your tongue and be patient. There's pleasure in giving and pleasure in receiving, but the one sometimes demands a return and the other an obligation. Think on that while you wait!'

Ben smiled without understanding. 'Kind Miss Lightbody,' he said cheerfully.

She shook her head and hustled me from the room. "Tis sad, 'tis sad to be so,' she said, closing the door, then she stood on tiptoe and hissed in my ear, 'I fear Frank's hopes are misplaced, and when he finds out, 'twill put the cat among the pigeons. That will be the time for you and me and that sallow-faced scholar who watches over him to be on our guard, but that is not yet. Perhaps it will not happen . . . It is today you must be alert to possibilities, child. Frank does nothing without good reason. Remember that and be wary.'

And she was off down the passage before I could question her further, leaving me to repair with some mystification to my room.

I had one surprising memory of Ben's birthday to carry away with me when I left for Kingsbridge in the Pascoes' coach. It was both unexpected and strangely gratifying. I had an admirer!

Tom Davey was the son of Grandfather's lawyer, a shy youth whose hands and feet seemed too large and awkward for his gangly body. It was pleasing that Susannah, who felt it her due to be the focus of all male attention, however young and ungainly, could not wrest Tom Davey from my side the whole day.

We were a company of fourteen that sat down to an early dinner a little after two o'clock.

Apart from Mr and Mrs Davey and Tom, Grandfather had also invited Mr Aggett, his business partner in his Plymouth shipping interests, Mrs Aggett and their robust daughters of eighteen and twenty. 'It will do the boy good to mix with a few young people,' he had growled, adding ungraciously to Mr Chadwick, 'you may let him off the leash today. And you, girl, make sure they are kept entertained and from under the feet of their elders.'

Although Grandfather's thoughtful gesture in inviting the Aggett and Davey wives and children was for Ben's sake, not his own, he masked his true thoughts with an air of chilly reserve which did nothing to stem Mrs Davey's genteel but probing questions nor discourage Mrs Aggett's unashamedly wide-eyed curiosity. Kingsbridge drawing rooms would doubtless be entertained for weeks to come with details of a household that had been so long denied to female visitors.

Miss Lightbody came in for much covert scrutiny from the ladies, but even if the wig became somewhat askew as the afternoon drew on and her gait more uneven, she maintained a surprisingly dignified presence.

She was a monotone shadow of her usual gaudy self, chivvying Bessy in subdued tones, ensuring that there was no delay to the flow of dishes from the kitchen – steaming platters of lobster patties, roast ducklings, lamb cutlets and larded guinea fowls, deep bowls of green peas and sea kale, a vast ham garnished with watercresses, dewy jugs of sweet, smooth cider and home-brewed beer – and that empty dishes were borne away promptly. She might have had an invisible army of servants at her command so smoothly did the meal progress.

By the time a heavily breathing Bessy had staggered in with the last tray of custards, fruit jellies, rhubarb tarts and bowls of clotted cream, and port and Madeira were set upon the table, we were a flushed and merry company.

I was relieved at being placed between Tom Davey and Mr Chadwick. Mrs Davey and Sophia Aggett had the doubtful pleasure of being seated either side of Blandford Pascoe, whose laugh grew shriller and whose teasing of Sophia grew more exaggerated as the meal progressed. I could see that Sophia, a shy girl, did not know how to respond other than blush deeply but though I felt for her, I was not inclined to leap to her rescue, other than by an occasional sympathetic glance. I did not wish to draw Blandford's attention to me more than was necessary.

When we had assembled before dinner I had felt his pale eyes regarding me with a glance that had me drawing my shawl about my bare neck and arms. It was fortunate that, with Grandfather's wishes fresh in my ears, I could shepherd the young people away into the garden for most of the morning. Since Mr Chadwick conducted lessons out of doors when the weather was suitable, the garden had been somewhat trimmed and tidied and the rough grass set with wooden benches. At this season the drifts of colour from self-sown primroses, forget-me-nots and gillyflowers drew the eye from the neglected corners. Lucy Aggett even declared it to be 'delightfully Arcadian' and wished she had brought her sketching block to capture the 'charming arrangement of nature's artifice'.

The Aggett sisters, though not clever, were well mannered and eager to please and Lucy, the younger, earned my gratitude by chattering freely to Ben with never a patronising look or gesture. Susannah, elegant in sapphire muslin with matching ribbons woven into her golden hair, attempted to dominate the little group with a prolonged account of a visit with her friend Clarissa Alperton, daughter of Sir George Alperton, to Cheltenham, making much of the splendid establishment and superb water gardens belonging to the house of Clarissa's aunt.

Ben soon grew bored and fidgety, whereupon Lucy Aggett recovered his interest by whispering to him of the antics of her cat, while Tom Davey, seizing upon a pause in Susannah's retelling of the masques and assemblies she had attended, said quickly that he thought he had spied a rare form of honeysuckle among the common variety scrambling over the wall and might he point it out to me. It turned out not to be the fly honeysuckle which he thought it might have been – though he admitted afterwards that it only grew in chalky places in the south-east of the country – but it gave us an excuse to spend an agreeable time poking among the wild flowers while he explained to me with an amateur botanist's earnestness the difference between sublate and spatulate, peltate and pectinate leaves. This led naturally to the specimens garnered in his botanising walks around Cambridge where until recently he had been a student and to his future expectations now that he had joined his father in his Kingsbridge practice.

After such a display of disinterest in her doings, it was not to be expected that Susannah would let us escape without punishment. As we returned indoors she made disparaging remarks to the Aggett girls about the insularity and unfashionableness of Kingsbridge people who thought the world began and ended at Plymouth. To me, with her practised trill of laughter, she cried, 'A charming gown, Miss Howarth. So brave of you to have made an effort for this occasion, but it was quite wicked of your dressmaker not to advise you on a suitable style. That simple line and that particular shade of green is *so* difficult to wear.'

'But Miss Howarth looks delightful,' Tom Davey burst in, indignantly, then turned bright red, stuttered to a halt and was saved by Sophia's quiet, 'I agree with you entirely, Mr Davey. Indeed, I applaud Miss Howarth's good taste in choosing so springlike and delicate a colour.'

Susannah gave a contemptuous toss of her curls and swished ahead of us. It was gratifying to see her contradicted. Doubly gratifying to be championed, for it confirmed my own secret satisfaction with my appearance. For the first time ever, I think, I had this morning felt drawn to linger in front of the mirror and breathe thanks for Mrs Chadwick's advice and skill. The gown clung and flared and swirled as I turned this way and that and for once I did not rue my height, for I saw this gave a certain dignity to a style that might have made a shorter person seem dumpy. I had spent an age on my hair, trying to coax rather than force it into place and now the errant wisps that never would coil tidily away lay in springy tendrils against my cheeks and neck. Between the red of my hair and the green of my gown, my skin took on a pale lustre that made it look finer than it actually was.

And as I regarded my image, an interesting thought, borne of my experience with Roselawn, sprang into my mind. Just as I had sought one object in a room to spark my imagination into creating a whole scheme of colour and furnishings and ornament, might I not use the same practical method on my own appearance? Perhaps even to be outrageously bold and take one of my less pleasing features – my height, my red hair – as a focus. The thought was exciting. My imagination winged away in a dazzle of colour and drapings and jewels, then crashed to earth in a rash of giggles as I pictured Miss Polsham's reaction to having the peacock figure I envisioned living under her roof.

It was not likely that I should ever have the opportunity to exploit this fetching new idea, but the thought was very diverting.

'And so I would ask you to charge your glasses and drink the health of my grandson.' Grandfather raised his glass. He had made a short, formal speech before presenting Ben with a silver pocket watch and now, his eyes fixed on Ben, and with the first touch of emotion roughening his voice, he went on, 'My grandson who has been returned to me to bring comfort and delight

to my old age.' A pause, then, 'My grandson, who
from henceforth will rightfully bear the proud name of
his forefathers. I give you Benjamin Howarth . . .
Kerswell.'

'Benjamin Howarth Kerswell.'

'Benjamin Howarth Kerswell.'

Amid the surprised exclamation, the raising of
glasses, the return to general conversation, my gasp
of shock went unnoticed. I sipped my wine without
tasting it, then rose to lead the ladies into the parlour
where Miss Lightbody waited to hand round the tea
and coffee that I poured. I hoped the agitation I felt
was not visible.

I had a fierce pride in my father and it cut me to
the quick that Grandfather sought to overshadow the
memory of that gentle, kindly man. My first reaction
was that I should protest most strongly to him at the
first opportunity, but after a while I grew calmer and
with calmness came resignation. What was the use of
anything else? Grandfather would have his way, however I balked, and it would matter little to Ben, that
was for sure. His memory of the time before Falconwood was dim, as mine was not. The here and now
was all that concerned him. The addition of 'Kerswell'
to his name meant nothing to him and if such a small
thing pleased Grandfather, his benefactor – and might
well, I also realised, have gratified and amused Mama
– then I must accept it. At least it showed that Grandfather had truly grown to care for Ben, even if he had
contrived to drive another wedge into the gap between
Ben and myself.

Another small victory for Francis Kerswell. But one
day . . . one day I should not be so powerless. I must
hold to the thought that he was old and his powers
would fade. I was young. Time, if nothing else, was
on my side.

I turned my full attention to the ladies who were

agreeing that they would greatly appreciate a breath of fresh air before the afternoon grew too chilly. Would a stroll along the cliffs be possible if the path was not too arduous?

Out on the grassy cliff top the breeze cleared my head of the clinging wisps of resentment and hurt. The ladies exclaimed over the grandeur of the view, and would have me naming the headlands and other points of interest. Susannah, Sophia and Lucy had strolled ahead, and I was explaining that several of Dartmoor's tors were visible on a clear day when my eye was caught by a movement on the edge of the copse near the house.

From where we stood Falconwood was partly hidden by a fold of rising ground, and by the copse itself. The trees were not yet in full leaf and whereas in a week or two a horse and rider standing there would have been hidden, now it was possible to make out the smooth chestnut coat of the horse, the blue coat and dark hair of the bareheaded rider. As I watched, he raised his arm and put a spyglass to his eye.

'Would Hey Tor be in that direction I wonder, Miss Howarth?' said Mrs Davey. Then, after a moment, 'Miss Howarth?'

'Oh . . . yes, yes, quite so.'

I did not know the names of the tors. I could scarcely make sense of the question for the sudden return of agitation, though of a very different kind. Not laced with distress and resentment this time, but with an excitement that set every sense alert.

As I watched, the rider turned his attention from the house, swung the spyglass round as though tracing the path along the cliffs, then came to an abrupt halt, focused on the ladies. On me. I stopped myself in time from raising my hand, but I could not hold back my smile nor the rush of hot colour to my cheeks.

'I believe the coast of Brittany lies directly across the Channel from here,' Mrs Davey said, shading her eyes to stare out to sea.

'I declare I could never cross an ocean,' fluttered Mrs Aggett. 'I am a martyr to *mal de mer*, though to gaze on such magnificent waters and to breathe the salt air is most invigorating to the system. Do you not agree, Miss Howarth?'

'Indeed,' I murmured, not caring about Mrs Aggett's system nor anyone else's, but out of politeness I was impelled to glance at Mrs Aggett as I spoke and when I looked back at the copse, horse and rider had vanished as mysteriously as they had appeared.

Not my excitement though. I hugged it, hoarded it like a miser guarding secret treasure as I said my tearful goodbyes. Clung to it all the jolting way to Kingsbridge in the Pascoes' elderly coach.

Nicholas was back. I neither knew nor cared why he spied on Falconwood.

It was enough to know that he would be waiting for me in Exeter when I returned.

Chapter Eleven

The three days I spent at Kingsbridge were not pleasant and I was more than glad to be on the Exeter mail and away from the uncomfortable atmosphere of Brent House.

Susannah's was a capricious, shallow nature, and if she did not get her own way, she was inclined to take her spite out on whatever innocent person was closest. She had not been in the house ten minutes before she had boxed her maid's ears because she was tardy in answering her bell. But I believe that was more to do with Susannah's disgruntlement at not being the centre of attention at Ben's birthday rather than any negligence on the maid's part.

She was very high-nosed with the servants altogether. She even demanded that a gardener's boy be dismissed for leaving a rake on the path where she had almost tripped over it. Mr Pascoe was inclined to smooth over the incident, but Blandford added his voice to his sister's. The boy, he said, had a very cheeky manner and deserved to be made an example of so that the other servants would not get above themselves. I felt quite shocked that Mr Pascoe merely shrugged. 'Do what you will,' he said tetchily, 'I have far more important matters to attend to.'

It was just as Miss Lightbody had warned me.

'James Pascoe has always cared more for his horses

and his money-making schemes than for his own children. He was brought to fatherhood too late, I reckon.' She had laughed raucously. ''Twas a considerable shock when his wife found herself with child after twenty years or more of marriage, when she had believed herself barren. Then to breed a second child four years later, why, I vow, she upped and died from the surprise! As for James Pascoe, he was too set in his ways to wish his life disrupted by puking brats. They were left to the care of servants and nursemaids who petted and spoiled them in the interests of peace and quiet, or governesses too feeble to counter the whims of the little tyrants they soon became. Now he must reap what he has sown. His son mixes in raffish company and has a nature inclined to disreputable pursuits. His daughter, for all the advantages of her pretty face and the fashionable gee-gaws he indulges her with, fails to attract a suitor because of her shrewish nature.'

I had been inclined to dismiss most of this tale as being highly embroidered, but in those three days I came to believe that it was close to the truth.

To the casual visitor, Brent House might have seemed an idyllic residence. It stood a little outside Kingsbridge on a gentle south-facing slope, its grounds running down to a wooded tidal creek. The gardens, stables and glasshouses were well stocked and immaculate, the house itself, which had been new-built in the Palladian style some forty-odd years previously for Mr Pascoe and his bride, was spacious and comfortable. Only anyone obliged to spend a night under its roof could begin to appreciate the maggot of unease that gnawed constantly at the heart of such perfection.

The house was overly silent. Soft-footed servants went too swiftly and quietly about their duties, heads bent, eyes averted. A door accidentally slammed, an overloud footstep or inadvertently raised voice was a cause for hushings and nervous scurryings. The very air breathed tension. Hardly surprising when even such a minor offence as a forgotten rake could cause a lad to be turned off without a character.

It was not only the servants who had reason to be wary of Susannah. Jane was just as vulnerable to her sister-in-law's spitefulness. She lay in bed even frailer than when I had last seen her, her brown eyes wide with distress as Susannah merrily recounted the incident and how the head gardener had pleaded for leniency.

'He tried some cock-and-bull tale of the boy being the sole support of his widowed mother when I know for a fact that the town boasts a whole string of relations who are well capable of looking after their own. Blandford had to warn the fellow that his own position was in jeopardy if he did not hold his tongue, which he was then quick to do.'

'But could you not have given the boy another chance?' Jane sighed. 'It seems such a small misdemeanour.'

'And allow the other servants leave to think they may be lax and careless and we shall turn a blind eye? No, no, no! That would be quite wrong.' She wagged a finger playfully. 'My dear Jane, you will have to dispense with such extravagant ideas when you are mistress of your own establishment in Exeter. Servants are always quick to sense weakness and take advantage accordingly.'

Jane chewed nervously at her bitten lips. 'But I feel, Susannah, that I should not wish . . . that is I could not be . . . so arbitrary . . .'

'Arbitrary?' Susannah's voice rang with pretended outrage, but though her expression was affronted her beautiful blue eyes sparkled with satisfaction. 'Do you

297

not mean resolute or responsible?'

'Oh, of course, of course,' Jane said quickly. 'I did not intend to imply you had been over-hasty.'

'I should hope not!' Susannah smiled with exaggerated sweetness. 'Mark my words, Jane, my brother will be most displeased if the comfort he rightly expects in his own new house is in any way lacking due to slackness on your part.'

I could hardly bear to see the dumb terror that flared in Jane's eyes. I had a mad urge to slap that smug smile off Susannah's face. Instead, I said sharply, 'I am sure that Jane is properly grateful for your kindness in reminding her of her domestic duties, but I fear that Dr White will not be so well disposed towards you, Miss Pascoe, when he hears that you are disobeying his express orders.'

Susannah swivelled her head, fine eyebrows arched, as though noticing me sitting quietly by the bed for the first time.

'Why, Joanna – and you will allow me to call you Joanna, will you not, and you must please address me as Susannah now that you are a guest under my father's roof – what can you mean? Has that doddery old doctor set some tiresome new regime for Jane to follow?'

'Not at all. He says that Jane progresses well because she is physically and mentally at rest, but he was insistent that she should not be bothered by domestic trivia. Such matters, he explained, can loom large in the mind of an indisposed person, which may in turn reflect on that person's physical state. With unknowable consequences.' I paused, giving her time to reflect on this, then said with a smile as sweet as her own, 'Your brother would not be well disposed towards *you* if – all unwittingly, I am sure – harm was done to the expected child by an untoward word.'

Susannah's eyes narrowed as she weighed the threat in my words. 'You seem to have had an unconscionably lengthy talk with Dr White,' she said suspiciously after a moment.

'I was pleased to be here when he called but an hour since,' I said blithely. I did not add that the only words the doctor and I had exchanged were 'Good day' as we passed on the stairs. But there was no harm, I thought, in embroidering the doctor's ideas as I knew them from Jane's comments in her letters.

I had bested Susannah, but not for long. She left shortly afterwards, rising to kiss Jane's cheek and say with charming concern, 'I heard the nursemaid say that little Ruth was grizzly and out of temper this morning. I should hate you to be upset by her crying in case, as Joanna has reminded me, there should be unfortunate consequences, so I shall ask nurse not to bring her to visit you today. But I shall spend a time with the little pet myself, so you may rest completely happy in the knowledge that she is having every attention. No, no, it is not a trouble, I am thinking only of your wellbeing, Jane dear.'

And with a happy little wave she left Jane to fight weak invalidish tears at being denied her child and me to brood on whether by interference I had made matters worse.

Susannah's spitefulness was one thing, her brother's behaviour quite another. Susannah was shallow and self-centred, certainly, but in a curious way her spoilt nature, because it was open, was easier to tolerate. Blandford's nature was darker altogether and, to me, infinitely more sinister.

I already disliked him. That dislike intensified steadily in direct proportion to the flattery that he now chose to heap upon me.

We could not sit down to dinner or supper but that

he would call Mr Pascoe's attention to me for being so patient in sitting with Jane, and had he not observed me down by the creek playing with little Ruth? How kind I was to take an interest in a child who even a doting papa had to confess was grizzling and contrary. And as for my help with the refurbishment of Roselawn, when Mr Curtis had escorted him round the house on his last visit he had been extravagant in his praise of my assistance, for which he, Blandford, could not thank me enough.

I always answered noncommittally. I found it best. Susannah liked the conversation to revolve round herself and would quickly direct the talk away from me, though it did not distract her brother's eyes, which were for ever straying in my direction. I was always glad when I could politely excuse myself and hurry out of his company.

Away from mealtimes I did my best to avoid him, but his languid person seemed always to be idling towards me out of the shadows or his hand unexpectedly falling on my shoulder in some quiet room or his voice startling me when I thought myself alone. I even woke the first night and heard soft footfalls along the corridor – approaching, pausing, then moving on. Perhaps it was imagination that supplied the sound of breathing, the faint rattle of a doorhandle touched. Was it Blandford who stood outside and listened and not some servant about her late duties? I was out of bed with the key turned in the lock before the sound of footsteps died away and after that made sure that it was kept locked whenever I was in my room.

I only realised how tense I was becoming on the two occasions when I escaped the house altogether. Even though I had to tolerate Susannah's company, it was like having a weight lifted from my shoulders to be free of the threat of Blandford's presence for an hour or two.

We had been pressed by Mrs Davey and Mrs Aggett to call upon them while I was in Kingsbridge and this we did. Tom Davey contrived to be there on both occasions, gangling and awkward and touchingly eager to please. Ready to hand round cups and plates and shyly offering to accompany us back down Kingsbridge's narrow steep streets and as far as the creek road that led to Brent House.

It was a relief to be in comfortable, undemanding company. Tom's admiration was undiminished, which was pleasing, if incomprehensible, to me when I was so out-dazzled by Susannah's prettiness and elegance. He watched me with a calf-like expression that made me half sorry for him and half impatient. Before we parted, his face red, he asked if he might write to me to recommend a list of books for further reading on the subject of botany, which I would be sure to find fascinating.

I refused him as gently as I could, explaining that the ladies to whom I was a companion would not approve of me corresponding with a gentleman they did not know, but he looked so stricken that I added, 'Should you ever find yourself close to Falconwood I am sure my brother would be pleased to see you. His affection and interest, as you know, lie in the world of nature. With your knowledge of botany, you may be able to help and advise both him and his tutor.'

'I would be delighted, Miss Howarth,' Tom cried, grasping at this link to me, however slender. He turned back to Kingsbridge looking considerably brighter, leaving me to walk far less happily to Brent House with Susannah.

After Brent House, my spirits were quite buoyant at the prospect of returning to Exeter, but I found the house at Torre Crescent in a turmoil.

The previous evening Mrs Caunter had suffered a violent paroxysm of pain in her chest and arm while preparing milk toast for Miss Polsham's supper. Dr Barlow had diagnosed a serious ossification of the heart, bled her, ordered her to remain in bed and be dosed hourly with a medicine of camphor water and laudanum to relieve the symptoms, but an hour before I arrived she had suffered a further paroxysm and died.

Miss Olga was too distraught to do anything but welcome me back with relief. She had spent a night and day rushing between the old cook's bedside and her sister's room, Miss Polsham having taken a particularly bad megrim at the news from below stairs.

'Make haste and get changed,' she said. 'You may help me to lay Mrs Caunter out ... Oh, dear, there is so much to do ... funeral arrangements ... her relatives are all gone, no friends, so it devolves on me ... Then there is the expense, and my sister poorly ...'

So within half an hour of my arrival I found myself in Mrs Caunter's frowsty room off the kitchen helping Miss Olga to strip Mrs Caunter of her nightgown and many layers of grubby undergarments which she had refused to allow Miss Olga to remove when she had been struck down. It was not a pleasant task. It was a long time since Mrs Caunter's person had seen soap and water. Miss Olga's flared nostrils were the only sign that she was repelled by the sight and smell of Mrs Caunter's soiled body. Her composure helped me to control my own queasy feelings, for it was the first time I had ever done such a thing, the laying-out of my own parents and sisters being performed by a woman engaged by the doctor.

Oddly enough, I do not think it was through parsimony that Miss Olga personally performed this last task for her old cook. When we had finished, she stood back and surveyed Mrs Caunter lying clean in a crisp nightgown, hair neatly braided, limbs composed.

'It is like a last link to my girlhood gone,' she said

quietly. 'I remember her as a comely and energetic woman whose economy and piety pleased my papa. If I have tolerated a different mode of behaviour these last ten years or more, it is because of a weakness in myself. I could not put her off out of sentiment. Perhaps I was wrong.' She gave a quavering sigh. 'She is comely again now and ready to meet her Maker. Now, leave me, child, and attend to my sister.'

She drew a handkerchief from her pocket and held it to her eyes. It was the first time I had seen her overcome by emotion.

'Fancy 'er having a soft spot for the cantankerous old besom,' Lily whispered. 'I'd never have believed it. Nowt so queer as folk, is there, Miss Jo?'

But I thought perhaps it was that she grieved for the girl she had been and the stern papa she had loved and feared, and youthful hopes that had sunk away like an ebbing spring tide.

We slipped away quietly and left her to mourn in private.

Two days after Mrs Caunter was laid to rest, Miss Olga called Lily into the parlour.

'I understand you have been keen to learn such culinary skills as Mrs Caunter chose to impart to you.'

'Oh, yes, miss,' Lily said eagerly. 'I'm right keen on the cooking. Did most of it on the days when the ol' bes . . . er, Mrs Caunter wasn't up to the mark.'

'I have seen that you have coped tolerably well since her unfortunate demise and I am prepared to give you the chance to continue as cook, rather than bring in a stranger whom I should have to train up to our ways.'

'Oh miss, thank you,' Lily cried, clasping her hands in delight.

'There is the matter of your other duties in the house,' she added, thoughtfully. 'If I could be sure that there would be no lowering of standards, I would be prepared to adjust your wages . . .'

'An' me do both jobs?' Lily burst in. 'Course I could. Been doin' all t'donkey work for Mrs Caunter for ages.'

'I would be prepared,' Miss Olga added, more grudgingly, 'to employ a washerwoman once a fortnight to deal with the household linen.'

'That's very generous of you, miss,' Lily said, bobbing an energetic curtsy.

'Miss Joanna and I will oversee you, in the first instance, especially in the careful management of expensive items. I would ask you to bear in mind at all times that wilful waste makes woeful want.'

'For sure, miss. For sure!'

So Lily acquired status as a cook and Miss Olga achieved a saving in wages by employing one maid-of-all work to replace two servants.

It was an arrangement deeply satisfying to both parties.

Seeing Lily with fresh eyes after my absence I realised how much she had grown. Not upwards, for she would never be tall, but over the last year she had filled out. Her cheeks and arms and bosom were rounded, her fine hair still wispily straight, but glossy with health. The half-starved runaway urchin she had been was entirely gone. She reminded me of a little brown wren, always busy, bright-eyed and eager.

'Aren't I lucky, Miss Jo?' she repeated time and again. 'Who'd've thought that a year ago I was begging for me supper and now I'm queen of me own kitchen. Eh, I love the cooking and baking better'n anything. P'raps it's because I never 'ad much food in me belly whilst I was growin'. It feels like 'eaven to be dealing wi' it all day long. An' I'm setting myself to be a real good cook, an' all. You must tell me again everything you 'ad while you was at your grampa's. D'you suppose you could get that Miss Lightbody to write down some of Mrs Beer's receipts? Eh, I'm that happy.'

I was happy for her, but less so on my own account. As the days passed and I heard nothing from Nicholas Fox, I went from impatience to resentment that he had not got word to me, then to anxiety and finally to resignation.

The conviction that it had been Nick spying on the house wavered. I had been mistaken. I had been tricked by distance. He was probably still idling in London's fleshpots.

I was considerably cast down by this and cross with myself for being so affected. After all, I had quite made up my mind that I had nothing to gain from him or his gambling ventures.

All the same, it did not stop me from being watchful of passers-by as I walked through the town. Several times I thought I saw him and felt a leap of excitement that quickly dulled to disappointment when I saw that the stranger's height or dark colouring or turn of the head had deceived me.

Then, late one dustily warm morning, when Miss Olga and I were returning from the market through St Stephen's Bow, a low, covered stone passageway leading from Fore Street through to the cathedral yard, a man approaching us halted, blocking our path and said, 'Miss Howarth? Why, so it is! Good morning to you.'

And he was there, raising his hat, bowing, smiling the crooked smile that brought charm to his bony features, sleepily mocking dark-lashed eyes taking in Miss Olga's startled look, his conspiratorial glance inviting me to share his amusement in this piquant situation.

And how could I have mistaken all those boring strangers for Nicholas? One so much his own man, so ... so possessed of individuality, authority ... My mind groped for words while my physical body recovered from the tingling first shock of his sudden appearance and I hastily made the necessary introductions.

I heard my voice babbling childishly on, as though fearing silence. Heard how unnaturally it echoed back to me from the low arch of stone above us.

'. . . a friend of Mr Blandford Pascoe . . . you will remember, Miss Olga, I believe I told you how kind to Jane he was when she was taken ill . . . I had thought you still in London, sir, but I expect it is pleasanter to be away from the city now the weather is warmer . . .'

And on another level altogether, deep within, there was a flood of feeling so profound and disturbing that it was like an ache possessing my bones and running through my blood so that even my toes and the tips of my fingers felt the hot, weakening effects of it.

Then he was raising his hat again, murmuring that he hoped he would have the pleasure of meeting us once more. Perhaps at the rout Mr Blandford Pascoe was planning when his new house was completed.

Miss Olga had hold of my arm in a tight grip, hurrying me off, and I, helplessly, had no excuse – could do no other – than go with her. Away from Nicholas.

I glanced over my shoulder to see that he, too, looked back. He lifted his hand in a careless wave, then turned the corner and was lost to me.

We walked home briskly, Miss Olga questioning me suspiciously about Nick as we went. I had given her, she said, the impression that he was an older man, and she did not feel he was quite a gentleman, though he must be if he was a friend of her cousins. Nothing she could quite put her finger on, but he was altogether too, too . . . well, she found it difficult to express . . . dashing? No, perhaps *bold* summed it up. Not in his mode of dress, which was quiet, but he had an air that suggested recklessness. Did I know much about his background? And the name Fox, Fox . . . something she had heard . . . she could not quite place it . . .

Bold? Oh yes, *bold*. Bold and dashing. And devious and deep. And disturbing and . . . and . . . My mind teetered on the brink of some other reckless thought, and withdrew. Not here. Not now.

Did Miss Olga, dried-up spinster that she was, unconsciously respond to the pull of that strong, masculine personality, finding his boldness the only genteel explanation for faint, half-forgotten stirrings?

I answered her questions as shortly and unemotionally as I could. I watched her expression change from suspicion to alarm, to comprehension, to accusation.

'Born at Starcombe? Then he will be related to . . . to the murderer Isaac Fox! What? His son? Dear heaven! I remember now why the name seemed familiar. Cousin James was the magistrate who sent him to the assizes. Why have you not mentioned this before, girl? Why, you allowed me to believe that this man who . . . who lodged under the same roof as you and poor Jane was decent.'

'You did not ask,' I said simply. 'You did not seem interested before.' Which was true, but I had not wanted to offer information unnecessarily. 'And does it really matter, Miss Olga, when he was helpful and kind to Jane when she was in distress? I do not know what we would have done had he not been there.'

'My papa would have been scandalised,' Miss Olga cried in strangled tones. 'That I, a daughter of an elder of the Strict Followers, should spend even a moment in such a person's company. The son of a hanged man!'

'Who went to the gallows proclaiming his innocence! And surely Mr Fox cannot be held responsible for his father's sins. Besides, does not the Church preach forgiveness?'

We turned the corner into Torre Crescent, Miss

Olga's pace increasing all the time, as though she was fleeing home to shelter from that dire encounter.

'I knew he was not a gentleman!'

'A gentleman? Both Jane and myself received nothing but courtesy and consideration from Mr Fox. And as to who is a gentleman and who not, why Blandford is . . .' Just in time I bit off the words that rose from a passionate inner compulsion to defend Nick and to reveal to Miss Olga that her precious cousin had a far uglier nature. 'Blandford seems to consider Mr Fox a friend,' I amended lamely.

'Ah, but it is different for a gentleman. He may move in circles quite unsuitable for a lady without any fear for his reputation.' She flew up the front steps and whirled inside, gasping, 'A respectable unmarried woman must always be on her guard against any behaviour that might set tongues wagging.'

She came to an abrupt halt in the hall. I closed the door. She took deep, steadying breaths of the familiar lavender-scented air of security, safety, her shoulders relaxing. She turned to me, two spots of excited colour flaring in her sallow cheeks.

'I shall, of course, be obliged to cut him, should he be so . . . so forward as to address me in a public place again. I would recommend you to do the same, Joanna. If, on the other hand, your friendship with dear Jane and Blandford should lead you at some time in the future into the company of this . . . this *person*, I would suggest you are as cool to him as politeness to your host allows. And at all times be on your guard!'

I did not tell her that I had been on my guard since I had first met Nicholas Fox. Much good had it done me. I went up to my quiet room and, standing there, silent and alone, let my mind spin free. And this time I did not deny the terrifying and exhilarating intensity of the desire that roared into my head and sang in my blood.

And I whispered his name, over and over again, as though I was a sorceress weaving an enchantment to conjure him to my side.

'Nicholas . . . Nicholas . . . Nicholas . . .'

Such wild, unreasonable feelings were ridiculous, of course. Common sense told me that. Yet for a few giddy, unguarded moments I let my spirit float free, untrammelled by reason. I let the heady delight – so strong that it was almost painful – wrap me round in a glittering cloud of sensation, fizzing with unimaginable possibilities.

Then, sternly, I dragged my wayward thoughts earthwards. Back to my narrow room in this narrow house. Back to the reality of my situation. To the cold voice of reason which told me I was surely in the grip of infatuation which I had witnessed frequently in my sister Phoebe, who seemed to fall in and out of love as prettily and easily as she changed her gowns.

But I was not Phoebe and there was nothing pretty or easy about what I felt for Nick. If this was infatuation, I told myself, I should wake up one morning and find myself blessedly returned to my normal everyday state instead of being subjected to a constant torment of emotion every time I thought of him – which was too often and quite beyond my willpower to control.

But the days passed and all my mutinous efforts not to give in to this foolish fancy were mostly useless. I fell into daydreams so easily that Miss Polsham more than once had to repeat her orders to draw my attention. Alone in my room each night I read through his letters again and again, as though to draw fresh meanings out of the cheerful, inconsequential words he had written. I read poetry with new eyes, suffering over poetical lost hopes and faithless lovers. I shivered with pleasure at wanton phrases, previously unremarked, that now sprang out from seemingly innocuous verses.

In John Donne, in particular, there seemed a sensuality that set goose bumps prickling up my back. I learned whole stanzas by heart, chanting them to myself as I went about the house.

Come live with me and be my love,
And we will some new pleasures prove
Of golden sands and crystal brooks
With silken lines and silver hooks
There will the river whispering run
Warmed by thine eyes, more than the sun . . .

In my saner moments I felt like crying, 'Send home my harmless heart again!' Then laughed helplessly, for he could not. He was unaware and likely to remain so, for when we met again I must never, *never* allow him to see how I felt. I could not bear him to regard me as I regarded Tom Davey – with a mixture of pity and impatience.

Oh, but for all my resolution to be sensible I so much wanted to see him again. I went on solitary errands in a fever of hope. This time I would see him. He would be idling by St Stephen's Bow, or strolling through the market, or I might spy his tall figure passing the end of Torre Crescent.

He was never there. And the voice in my ear as I stood at the mercer's window one afternoon admiring samples of newly arrived summer toiles, though familiar, was not his but Caleb Smith's.

He cut a far more dignified figure than when I had last seen him. His dark blue coat, immaculate breeches and soft leather boots spoke of a man of substance, but no amount of expensive dressing could disguise his ugly battered face which broke into an amiable grin.

'Excuse me, miss, but I saw you just dropped this. Allow me.' I felt the weight of the packet as he dropped it into my basket, winking hugely.

'Th-thank you. Most kind,' I stammered.

He bowed, saying quietly, 'Nick says to tell you that the London partnership is now broke up. This is your share of it. There is an accounting enclosed.'

I was too stunned to speak for a moment. Then all I could think to say because it was the question nearest my heart was, 'Is Mr Fox still in Exeter?'

'Busy with his new venture, Miss Howarth. The building's going ahead at a great rate. He expects it all to be set up and running by the year's end. Oh, and he sends his apologies for not delivering this in person.' A kind smile, a crumb of comfort. 'He thought it best for you that he continue discreetly.'

Of course. Of course. Perfectly sensible. Perfectly reasonable. And miserably, *miserably* disappointing.

'Thank him for his ... discretion ...'

But Caleb was already moving away, to merge with the crowds milling around the market stalls.

I could not wait to go home to open the package. I found a quiet corner and opened it with fingers that shook more than a little. There was no personal note, as I had hoped. Only the stark figures – astonishing figures – totalling more than £200. It might once have thrilled me as evidence that my trust in Nick was not misplaced, but now it did not. I could not reconcile myself to the fact that Nick was in Exeter, so close, and yet we might have been worlds apart for all the chance I had of being with him.

Then a few days later word came that jolted me, guiltily, out of my self-absorption. Jane had again miscarried and her life was despaired of.

My memories were sharp of that stifling room in Mrs Fitch's cottage. The sights, the smells, the violent, bloody spasms that had reduced Jane to white

311

exhaustion. How much worse this time, with the pregnancy further advanced, and Jane, it had seemed to me when I visited her at Kingsbridge, frailer than ever, I could only imagine.

But within the week the news was better and by the time a cool and showery July was upon us, she was declared to be out of danger.

'She is so much improved as to be quite lively,' Susannah wrote, 'and is anxious that Blandford should not delay any longer his plans for introducing Exeter society to the splendours of Roselawn, which I am indeed quite eager to see for myself, having been confined here, though of course most willingly, with our dear invalid for so long.'

Our invitations came, considerably agitating Miss Olga who brought up the subject at every opportunity during the time it took her to make up her mind whether or not to accept.

'I feel that I should attend, out of courtesy to Cousin James,' she would say.

'Of course,' I would murmur.

'Yet as my sister so rightly points out' – Miss Polsham was being particularly sour and unhelpful, having suffered a weakening attack of palpitations following the arrival of the invitations – 'I am unused to attending large gatherings and might be overcome by the heat or the press of people.'

'Perhaps to an invalid like Miss Polsham such an occasion might seem daunting, but you are not an invalid, Miss Olga.'

'I do not dance or play cards.'

'There will be quiet corners set aside, I am sure, for ladies such as yourself.'

'But there might be unsuitable persons – I am thinking of that man Fox – whom it would be difficult to avoid.'

'Or easy, in a crowd. Besides, you would have the protection of other gentlefolk.'

'True. And at least I would not have the expense of a new gown. My good crepe has been worn so seldom.'

'And Mr Pascoe has offered to send his carriage for us. It would seem discourteous to refuse.'

'But we cannot stay long, or Fanny might fret herself into a nervous attack.'

'A soothing draught, perhaps, from Dr Barlow? Something to help her to sleep comfortably while we are absent? And Lily is very capable.'

'Ah, yes . . . Well, I shall give the matter further thought.'

So Miss Olga was persuaded – persuaded herself – that it was in order to attend the rout and perhaps to stay even so late as midnight out of respect for her Pascoe cousins. With memories of the attendant aroma of camphor and Susannah's spiteful remarks that had accompanied the maroon gown's last outing. I made sure that Lily gave it a good airing and pressing beforehand. It looked sadly dowdy even after that attention, and the colour, I knew, was not flattering to Miss Olga's sallow complexion. It was no use even trying to broach the subject of a new gown but I felt there would be no harm in trying to brighten the old one.

I had recently bought a length of fine cream muslin and made it into one of the new wide collars that were coming into fashion. It looked quite striking when I had finished embroidering the scalloped edge with tiny knots of flowers. I quickly added a few petals in the same maroon as Miss Olga's dress, swallowing a pang of regret as I did so – though the guineas in my hoard were a comfortable assurance that I would be able to replace the collar – and took it to show her.

'What do you think of this, Miss Olga? It is one of the new pelerines, very fashionable. Susannah tells me all well-dressed ladies will soon be wearing them. But now it is finished, I do believe it would be more suitable with your best gown rather than any of mine. Would you allow me to pin it on to see the effect? Then you could try it on, perhaps.'

The deed was done almost without effort. A show of reluctance, a frown on her part, 'It is quite unnecessary. I do not care to be too showy,' a little gentle pressure on mine, 'It will look perfectly modest, merely adding an extra touch of elegance.'

So she was persuaded, won, peering into the mirror, turning, looking over her shoulder. 'A new fashion, you say? I daresay it is quite . . . becoming.' Then, pursing her lips judiciously, a grudging, 'One must be prepared, I suppose, for dear James and Blandford's sake, to appear *au fait* with current style.' And almost a spark of youthful coquetry in the turn of her head, the lift of her chin, quickly disguised with an admonishing, 'I hope you have not been gulled into extravagance, Joanna. I could not be easy if I thought you had wasted money on fripperies.'

'Oh, it was quite a bargain,' I assured her, keeping my fingers crossed against the fib. 'The muslin was the very end of a bolt the mercer was keen to dispose of cheaply. And,' I added, quickly, 'it would please me very much if you would accept it as a gift.'

A small silence, a look that was both startled and – imagined, surely – warmly grateful, before she denied it with a tart, 'Certainly not. What use would I have afterwards for such an adornment? Remember I go to this rout only to do my duty by my cousins. Hark now. Is that my sister's bell? Quickly, girl, you have wasted enough of my time and yours.' And a hand touching my arm briefly as I passed. Her voice, quiet, sad, holding the echoes of lost hopes and empty years. 'It was a generous thought, Joanna. I am not . . .

314

unappreciative, but the time is long past when I might have . . . well, no matter. Hurry now. And . . . and thank you.'

The transformation of Roselawn was astounding.

Miss Olga and I both fell silent as we descended in the warm dusk from the carriage, climbed the wide, shallow steps under the new portico and entered the hall that was ablaze with light and milling with chattering guests. She was awed by the crowd, but I was overwhelmed by the beauty of the house. It was hard to remember the modest home it had been or even the confusion of builder's rubble, scaffolding and dust that had swamped it. Now it was a small masterpiece. Mr Curtis had said he wished to create a jewel and he had succeeded.

We moved slowly about the rooms, Miss Olga wide-eyed at the perfumed flesh on display, the silks and laces and floating gauzes and painted fans, the ear-bobs and necklaces and rings that flashed with the turn of every head, the gesture of every hand. But I looked above the bobbing ringlets, the satin turbans and nodding egret plumes and saw the perfect proportions of Mr Curtis's design, the calm elegance that complemented the vivid life beneath. There was an intense pleasure, too, in feeling that though it was the design of the upstairs rooms that I had been responsible for, I had also had some small influence on these lower rooms. In our discussions Mr Curtis had always been willing to listen to my suggestions. I felt thrilled that the friezes were picked out in the pale tints I had suggested, and that the velvets and brocades at the tall windows were not the aggressively strong and masculine colours Mr Curtis had first favoured, but of muted shades to allow the beauty of the Chinese papers on the walls to glow more vividly. I let my fingers drift to the silky top of the inlaid Pembroke table that had set off a whole chain of ideas; I noted how one grouping of sofas and chairs worked well, and with a critical eye saw that another did not and should be changed.

There was pleasure, too, in slipping quietly past all these bedecked strangers who, if they glanced at all at the tall, plain girl in the modest green gown, with no jewels to speak of except a childish gold necklace, dismissed her instantly as a nobody, someone's poor relation, perhaps, as the older woman with her most evidently was. They did not know that I had helped to create these pleasing surroundings which they admired and praised, and which, because the ambience did not threaten with over-stiff formality or jar the sense through a lavish use of harsh colour, allowed them to relax and be comfortable in Mr Pascoe's elegant new residence. And perhaps be impressed enough to remember the name of the architect, Mr William Curtis, when they wanted a grand new house or improvement made to the old.

This was probably just as it should be though I felt quite piqued that the excitement of the occasion caused Mr Curtis to be somewhat vague and dismissive with me. I caught him in a quiet moment to offer him my congratulations. He accepted them modestly, informed me that he was now engaged upon several important schemes in Bath and Bristol for a very influential landowner and begged to be excused. He hurried off to catch the ear of Mr Brown, the banker, leaving me feeling quite deflated. I quite understood that my own part in the creation of Roselawn was very small, but surely he could have spared a word of appreciation.

Which was why, perhaps, when Blandford breathed wine fumes down my neck, laid his hot, damp hand momentarily on my arm and said, 'You did very well for me, my dear. Far better than my wife could ever have done,' I answered coldly, 'It took a great deal of my time and much trouble.'

'I am deeply in your debt,' he murmured. 'Should you ever wish a favour, then do not hesitate to call upon me. I should be honoured to oblige you.'

'Indeed, sir, I may well one day call upon you to repay the debt you undeniably owe me,' I said, snatching my arm from his damp grasp. And with that I stalked away feeling considerably better for having allowed my feelings some expression.

I could not like Blandford, nor feel comfortable with Susannah, but there was nothing I could fault about the evening. Everything was organised with a lavish hand and no guest need feel bored for a moment, with an Italian tenor and a jolly magician to entertain and amuse at intervals, dancing for the energetic, card tables set up in a quiet room, and discreet corners sheltered by potted palms where the elderly might rest and gossip and sip a refreshing cordial. Supper was sumptuous, the table almost too decorative to spoil with swags of roses and ferns from which mounds of glazed hams, tender beef and garnished lobsters, epergnes of hothouse peaches and apricots and iced puddings rose in glistening mountains.

I congratulated Susannah on the success of the occasion as I collected a second plate of ice cream for Miss Olga – 'So cool and refreshing. I feel I might manage just a small helping more . . .'

Susannah had been at pains to remind us when she first greeted us that she, not Jane, had helped Blandford throughout. 'Jane's health was not up to it, you understand, and besides, poor dear, she had not the experience.' She had waved the languid hand of a woman of the world. 'When one has attended parties and balls in London and Cheltenham, one knows exactly how to proceed in order to impress *provincial* society.'

Now she tapped my shoulder playfully with her fan. 'You must take a little credit, dear Joanna. The decor is ... charming, though I have to say that my own taste is for the more striking, less retiring mode of decoration. But then I have moved in different circles.' Her bright, amused expression cast aside my part in the transformation of Roselawn as entirely unworthy. 'But Jane is well pleased.' *Too easily pleased.* 'And how has Cousin Olga enjoyed the evening? I fear she is quite out of her depth in a gathering of this kind.' *As you yourself are, Joanna, but then one has, unfortunately, to make a show of kindness to indigent relatives and their poor companions.* 'Oh dear, I trust you have not been too much of a wallflower on her account.' *Though I have done my best to ensure that you have been, for I have not forgotten how Tom Davey preferred your company to mine. I could not allow that to go unpunished, nor risk that some foolish young man here might equally decide to champion you this evening.* 'The ice is for Miss Olga? Yes? So generous of you to devote yourself to her comfort. Perhaps when you have completed that little commission, you might run upstairs and see if Jane's maid has removed the wine stain from Mrs Brown's gown. It is remarkable that in this crush there has only been one such unfortunate accident ... So kind of you, Joanna ...' A dazzling smile, her eyes, her attention already fixed on someone else, some other little matter she must deal with, and she swished away in a flurry of silver skirts and golden ringlets.

It was the pattern of the evening.

Whenever Miss Olga had settled to an amiable discussion behind the palms, of the shortcomings of modern youth or the disgraceful state of the streets with some like-minded matron, and I thought to slip

away to where the music beckoned, Susannah somehow always managed to waylay me, bearing me off to
meet some alderman or banker or retired military man,
each with a wife seemingly cast in the same stout,
florid, satin-draped and beplumed mould, who just at
that moment seemed in need of a quiet seat and someone to fetch a cold drink and a little something to eat.
And could I open a window – or close it against the
night air for fear of taking a chill? 'And perhaps, Miss
Howarth, you would be so kind as to sit with me until
my husband returns from his hand of whist, in case
this headache makes me a little faint and I need my
smelling salts.'

There were few occasions in the evening when I
was able to escape from the elderly ladies and avoid
Susannah's eagle eye, but I did manage a quiet conversation with Jane – fragile as a flower in stiff blue silk,
whose tense shoulders and over-bright eyes denied her
smiling protestations that she was enjoying every
moment – and then to slip among the guests, searching
for the one person I burned with impatience to see.

But did not.

Surely he had been invited! He had mentioned it
that day we had met in St Stephen's Bow. And Blandford's other cronies were here – mostly seeming to be
a raffish crew of young dandies who drank rather too
much and lounged about affecting a patronising air
of boredom.

Nick did not come. And it was late now. Too late,
surely.

I walked slowly up the curving sweep of the stairs
in search of Mrs Brown and her wine-stained skirts.
Miss Olga would be wanting to go home soon and I
would have to leave with her. My spirits began to
droop. I did not care a fig that I had been closeted
with old ladies all evening. I did not care that my

graceful green gown and my simple gold necklace were cast into the shade by the shining silks and glittering jewels on display. Nothing mattered but that I should see him. If he did not come in the next half-hour, the evening was dust and ashes.

I reached the galleried landing Mr Curtis had created above the hall and saw Mr Curtis himself in earnest discussion with a group of gentlemen.

I stopped, put out my hand to the banister, my legs being suddenly less than steady.

He was there.

For a moment the buzz of voices rising from below, the sound of fiddles striking up a jig faded away. I seemed locked in a profound silence into which carried only the deep murmur of his voice. I was unobserved. I was glad of it. I stood there trying to breathe steadily, trying – and not succeeding – to make my heart beat calmly, my pulse to stop its mad pounding.

'Ah, Miss Howarth.' It is Mr Curtis, flushed now and expansive from the wine he has consumed, who breaks the spell, beckoning me forward, so that I must move and smile and tear my gaze from Nick's face and pretend a look of polite enquiry towards Mr Curtis. And on no account look again at Nicholas, beyond a brief impersonal glance, the coolest of acknowledgements, for fear I betray myself. Fix, instead, upon what Mr Curtis is saying. Now he is all compliments. 'Miss Howarth has a keen eye . . . an exceptional aptitude . . . a feeling for colour and form . . . to be congratulated, most sincerely, for her part . . .' Try for modesty now, the disclaiming gesture of a well-brought-up young lady. An act, merely. The words flying about meaningless, not registering.

And here is Mr Clarence Brown among the group, banker of this city, whose wife had the unfortunate accident with a glass of wine and who even now, emerging from Jane's room, is bearing down on her husband. She, too, is full of complimentary words. 'Mrs Pascoe's boudoir . . . so charming . . . quite the prettiest . . .'

And Nicholas's voice dropping as a pebble drops into a pool of still water, setting ripples dancing away to the farthest weedy reaches.

'I believe several leading ladies of this town are already of the opinion that no one but Miss Howarth will do to advise them on improvements they are making to the decor of their homes. She will be quite the rage very soon.' A lazy laugh, a teasing, encouraging *flirtatious* look from under those thick, black lashes, so that a portly, grey-haired grandmother feels suddenly seventeen again and bridles and trills with laughter.

'Why then, Miss Howarth, I insist that you call on me this very week! Perhaps a boudoir such as Mrs Pascoe's – I am so very taken with the notion – might be contrived. Now our youngest daughter has fled the nest, we have plenty of room and to spare, do we not, Mr Brown? You shall give me your opinion, Miss Howarth!'

And her pompous husband, flown with good wine, nodding indulgently, sealing the arrangement with a careless, 'You may have a boudoir for each day of the week, my love, if it gives you enjoyment.' Which causes the other gentlemen to be amused – perhaps their laughter a little sycophantic, for it is always best to keep on the right side of a man who owns a bank and is known to lend a sympathetic ear to those gentlemen blessed with clever ideas but not necessarily the means to put them into practice. 'Ladies will have their little extravagances.'

And Nicholas bending to whisper some nonsense to Mrs Brown that makes her giggle and flutter her fan, then glance at me a little coolly as she sweeps past and say, in a crisp manner, 'I shall expect you at Mountwood House at ten o'clock precisely on Thursday next, Miss Howarth.'

The dream, for it is a dream, surely, continues, for I am floating, with Nicholas down the stairs. His hand warm on my elbow, his voice laughing in my ear, 'She would have had you running at her beck and call for nothing, but I told her that your fees were very reasonable.'

'Nicholas! How could you? Surely it is not proper!'

'You see! You must be saved from yourself. Your services have a value. Remember that.'

'But it seems less than . . . well . . .'

'Genteel? Ladylike? My dear girl, there is many a titled lady with the ear of someone of influence who earns a decent living by charging fees for those seeking a favour. Society does not frown on that, any more than it should on you. But come, are you engaged for this dance? I must make up for lost time. It has been a day of problems and delays, as seems usual when one is beset with builders. Now I shall forget them for a while.'

And if I had a problem in the world, I did not know it or care about it as Nicholas swept me into the dazzle, the laughter, the music.

Chapter Twelve

Those few apparently casual words Nick had dropped into the conversation with the banker and his wife set me on a course that jogged me out of the low spirits that took hold after the rout.

I had stayed long enough afterwards to see and understand with a deep and chilling clarity that however I might hope and wish it otherwise, Nicholas treated me as he treated every other female he spoke to. I saw how he bestowed that lazy smile, that intent, caring, *admiring* look on Susannah, on a covey of her pretty acquaintances, on a formidable matron or two. I could not tear my eyes away, yet it was quite unbearable to see how easily they succumbed, how their eyes brightened, their cheeks flushed – and how eagerly their hopeful glances followed his progress round the room. I was not the only fool to be beguiled by his practised charm.

For practised it was. And calculated. Done for a purpose. He had confessed it to me as we danced.

'Do you think I shall succeed, Miss Howarth, in making a fortune from these good Exeter folk? Do you suppose the gentlemen will oblige me by bringing their wives to dine and later chancing a few guineas at my gaming tables while their sons think themselves fine dogs to be going a few rounds with some slow old battler in the gymnasium? Will Reynard's become a fashionable success?'

We parted, turned, rejoined hands, advanced down the room.

'I expect it will,' I said, coolly, though my fingers burned at his touch and I was more breathless than the sedate dance occasioned. 'You seem to me a gentleman with determination enough to make it succeed.'

He nodded. 'Indeed. Tonight is the start.' His slow, crooked smile was, for a moment, not charming at all, but dangerous and cruel. 'I am an unknown quantity to these innocent people. They have heard of me. They certainly know about my unfortunate father, for scandal will always spread itself about as generously as a rampant weed. But I have also made sure that clinging to that vigorous weed were other seedlings which I hope have fallen on fertile ground. If so, they are now halfway to believing that I am not only wealthy, but that I have moved in fashionable London circles, that I have been honoured by the friendship of some of the highest in the land and may even be on easy terms with that person of great good taste and unfortunately gross appetites, King George himself.'

'And how much is the truth?' I asked, a little too tartly, perhaps, for his glance was lazily mocking as he answered.

'Enough to make me less of a liar than you appear to think me, Miss Howarth.'

Embarrassment, the welter of despairing emotions I must not show, lent my words an ever sharper edge. 'So you intend to establish yourself as a thoroughly respectable person, to be admired for rising above misfortune.'

'Exactly so. And to that admirable end I shall defer courteously to the superior opinions of any gentleman who engages me in discussion. I shall impress the mamas with my good manners, play the cheerful good fellow with their sons and the respectfully ardent admirer with their daughters. In that way I mean to pursue the great and good of this town and in due course, when Reynard's is ready, there may still be a few who might feel it proper to refuse my invitation to its grand opening, but many more who will feel privileged to accept.'

'And what then?'

The music ended with a triumphant chord. He kept hold of my hand, bowed low over it and when he straightened, the ghost of that cruel smile lingered in his eyes.

'What then, Miss Howarth? Can you not believe that that would be triumph enough for the son of a poor blacksmith who was hanged for murder?'

I shook my head. I should have snatched my hand away but a weakness I could not master welcomed the warm firm pressure of his fingers. 'You have revenge in your heart, Mr Fox,' I said quietly. 'I think it is a harsh and powerful taskmaster – too powerful perhaps for your own good.'

'You understand my purpose, Joanna,' he breathed softly. 'As I understand yours. Shall we let the matter rest at that?'

'No,' I burst out. Then, quietly, 'No.' It seemed suddenly important that I speak, as though the thoughts, the words had been forming for a long time and now must be said. 'I understand the depths of your . . . your hurt, Mr Fox . . . Nicholas . . . But is all that you have achieved so far, and will achieve, not enough? Without bringing harm to other people? I saw you at Falconwood, watching the house. I can only guess at your reasons for making that journey to the place which must hold such bitter memories. Was it to keep alive that burning for vengeance which surely must sometimes flicker and weaken to allow gentler intentions to take hold?'

His grip tightened on my fingers. There was no desire to charm now. The raw emotion in his narrowed eyes chilled me to the bone. He did not look at me with kindness or smiling tolerance, but with anger, barely controlled.

'Is it not right that justice should be served on those who manipulated an injustice?'

'But it will only foster more vengeance, more unhappiness. Can you not see? My grandfather's quest for revenge has not brought him comfort in his old age. Far from it!'

'Ah, you soften towards the old monster. For shame. I had thought you possessed of more spirit.'

'No, no, no! I merely regret the time and energy he has wasted on a silly feud. Time that could have been spent in fostering friendships and goodwill – not least within his own family! Instead he has trapped himself in a miserable snare of his own making, isolated and unhappy and unloved.'

'And in his pride and arrogance thinks himself safe. Which I assure you, he is not.'

'Oh, there's no talking to you!' I wrenched my hand away, angry, confused, upset. I could not speak what was truly in my heart. That I was stricken with fear for him. Fear that, in his single-minded pursuit of revenge, he would bring some terrible fate down on his own head. I knew nothing of what he planned; perhaps he did not really know himself except that he would seize the moment when it came. But in some deep recess of my mind I felt a shivery stir, as though whatever it was already cast a shadow before it.

'No talking to me at all, I'm afraid,' he said, the old, lazy mockery back, though anger still simmered in his eyes, etched itself in his deep frown. 'But if it will humour you, I swear to do my best to avoid a loveless and friendless old age.'

'If you live to see it,' I said tartly. 'Which I seriously begin to doubt.'

He shrugged with the air of a man impatient of an irritating fly. 'Do not set yourself to be my conscience, Joanna,' he began harshly, then, his eye caught by something – someone – more soothing and pleasant than me, the hard lines of his face smoothed, his flash of temper instantly smothered.

'Miss Pascoe,' he said, bowing. 'How very charming you look this evening.'

Susannah's rustling, laughing intrusion was, for once, a relief. The evening for me was over. The others might dance on until dawn, but for me the gaiety, the rich promise, had dissolved to a sad disillusion.

'Ah, Joanna, there you are,' Susannah cried. 'I believe Cousin Olga is fretting to be off and you have kept the carriage waiting these twenty minutes!'

And as I hastened away, her tinkling voice carried back to me, 'So generous of you to take pity on Miss Howarth, Mr Fox. I am afraid she has been something of a wallflower this evening.'

And Nick's own deep, treacherous, conspiratorial chuckle followed me – haunted me – all the way home.

Nicholas had joked that my ideas might become all the rage and it was an exaggeration to say that they did, but from that first, nervous if excited visit to Mrs Brown's expensively furnished town house grew a steady flow of requests to advise ladies similarly taken with the idea of providing themselves with an elegant boudoir.

I had quailed at the thought of asking a fee for something which was so enjoyable, but when I was admitted to the town house by a loftily patronising butler and saw the opulence of the interior, I did not think she would balk at a guinea, though, as became a banker's wife, she made sure she got value for money.

The bank must make handsome profits, for the Browns lived in some style. The grandeur of the rooms somewhat reflected Mrs Brown's own strong and florid personality, though she had firmly decided that her boudoir should imitate the gentle pastels and feminine frills of the pretty, restful room I had created for Jane. It took a great deal of patience to persuade her otherwise.

Apart from Mrs Brown's own personality, the sunless northern room chosen to be her boudoir called for a very different treatment. After a great deal of rewriting of my proposals we settled for the warm, bold, oriental colours of her favourite Kashmir shawl and plain, sturdy, walnut furniture instead of the fragile gilt pieces she had initially insisted on. And though she employed her own decorators, carpenters and upholsterers, she would have me visit several times to ensure that all was going according to my plan.

It was a success. And success brought its own demands.

Several of Mrs Brown's friends and acquaintances, having seen the usefulness of such a cosy, private retreat away from the demands of children, servants or even husbands, wished to consult me with a view to my recommending something original – that was always emphasised – for themselves. And, though never openly expressed, it was nevertheless understood that it could well be more expensive, more *enviable* than anything Exeter had seen before, though entirely within the bounds of good taste, of course. Oh, and it was such an advantage to be able to explain one's ideas to someone of the same sex who did not become overbearing or patronising when one perhaps did not quite comprehend, say, the mode of hanging wallpapers on framed canvas but was willing to explain the details clearly; who was understanding of the many tiresome little discomforts of female life which could be soothed by resting peacefully in a favourite chair or napping on a comfortable sofa, if either of these useful items could be included in the overall plan . . .

They were mostly the wives of Exeter's prosperous traders and businessmen who in the manner of those newly come to wealth were not ashamed to make a show. They themselves might have been born and raised in humble circumstances but that was now discreetly put behind them. They lived in the new rosy-brick terraces and crescents in the pleasanter parts of the town, with maids and footmen running to do their bidding, governesses to groom their daughters for good marriages – the prettiest maybe even to catch the eye of some younger son of the gentry or nobility who might be prepared to overlook the connection with trade should a lavish dowry be provided – and good schools for their sons who would go on to even greater achievements in their father's business or a well-paid profession.

They were ladies who craved to acquire gentility and surely there could be no more evidence of genteel good taste than a boudoir – and how delightfully sophisticated it sounded when spoken of casually in conversation . . .

I was learning as I went. Learning which workmen were pig-headed and uncooperative, which were willing to listen. Learning, most valuably, from mistakes – both my own and those of men who had served long apprenticeships and saw no reason to trust my judgment against their own experience. I learned to apologise sincerely when the fault lay with me and to smooth bruised male pride with some face-saving remark in the interest of future peaceful working relationships.

And the most useful lesson I learned was that there

was a great deal more money to be made than I had expected.

Quite early I realised that Nicholas was right and I should not undervalue my services. I tentatively raised my fee to two guineas, then, daringly, to five. It was a risky and decisive move. The lady to whom I presented my account had been difficult from the first, so querulous and demanding and ill tempered – stripped of her fine clothes and carefully cultured tones it was easy to imagine her exchanging insults over a fish barrow which rumour had it she had pushed through the town as a small girl – that I came to dread my visits and wished I had never started. But I steeled myself, kept my own temper under control and in the end the boudoir – all showy gilding and rich, dark colours – was completed and declared quite passable. Surprisingly, she paid up without a quibble, then took immense satisfaction in grumbling to her friends about the extortionate cost of it all, so ensuring that everyone was suitably impressed at the extravagant lengths to which a doting husband might go in order to please his wife.

As summer rolled into a wet and windy autumn, Miss Polsham grew more tetchy at my absence. Miss Olga, on the other hand – and surprisingly – grew more accommodating. She had imperceptibly drifted into an alliance with Lily and me to keep Miss Polsham not exactly in the dark but protected from any day-to-day irregularities that might have upset her constitution or her temper. Miss Olga still scolded, still chivvied us in case we wasted a moment that might be usefully occupied, yet our misdemeanours, and my requests to leave the house, were seldom relayed to Miss Polsham as they once had been.

'Really, Joanna,' Miss Olga would snap, 'my dear sister will be most aggrieved. This is the second time this week and you were gone a whole two hours on Tuesday. Who is it this time? Mrs Brown's sister recently returned from India? Well, I suppose, I should not wish to be responsible for disappointing that good lady but what I shall say to Fanny I cannot think . . . though perhaps if you make sure to be back before she wakes from her afternoon nap, we may not have to trouble her at all . . .'

'The old girl's got a soft spot for you,' Lily said, nodding sagely. 'Not that you'd've known it this morning when she was giving you a right roasting for cutting up that old petticoat for dusters instead of patching it up.' She giggled. 'You'd have thought you was destroying your best partying dress instead of sommat more patches than 'owt, mean old cat. Still, for all that, she talks different when you're not there. Why, the other day I heard her telling Miss P. when she was moanin' on about you not being here to rub her achin' back how lucky they was that you came to them. Spoke proper sharp, she did. Said havin' someone young and energetic about the place brightened the house, and Miss P. should be grateful you wasn't some flibberti-gibbet wi' nowt on her mind but prinkin' in front of the mirror.'

I was touched, but I thought that if Miss Olga found the house brighter, then it was probably more to do with Mrs Caunter's demise and Lily's cheerful command of the kitchen than anything else. As time slipped by it was clear to see how much the old cook's gloomy and bad-tempered presence had poisoned the atmosphere. The kitchen was a different place, scrubbed and bright and welcoming, though Lily flatly refused to move into Mrs Caunter's old room when it was cleared out and whitewashed. 'I likes my little room in the roof. I can look out and feel I'm a princess in a tower! But maybe I'll put that old rocker in here and I can sit and put my feet up when I've got five minutes.'

Even Miss Olga ate more heartily these days, tempted by Lily's tasty offerings. Perhaps that alone was enough to improve her temper. Perhaps, indeed, the previous rigidity of diet had been her way of coping with the awfulness of Mrs Caunter's cooking.

Lily quickly learned that the cheapest cuts of meat, the stringiest fowl, could be turned into tender stews and hearty soups with long, slow cooking. She had mastered the art of tackling pastry with a light hand and learned to bully the bread dough into rising into smooth floury mounds. There was always a savoury pot enriched with herbs and vegetables simmering on the fire, a pie or a pudding sending its tempting aroma from the black depths of the oven, and now that Papa's tobacco pouch was exceedingly weighty, I could add my own little treats to liven mealtimes, explaining them away with a light, 'Oh, but it was such a bargain, the farmer's wife was anxious to clear her stall and be off home before dark.' I bore home the bilberries brought down from the moor that morning, the slices of best quality gammon, the pound of finest butter, the dozen new-laid eggs, small deceits which gave me quiet pleasure, though the bigger deceit, the source of my money, made me uneasy. Sometimes, encouraged by the kindlier atmosphere, I toyed with the idea of taking Miss Olga into my confidence. But I knew she would be shocked at the thought of ladies paying me to give them advice, even though she took pleasure at being associated at a distance with people of influence and always pressed me for every detail of their houses, their clothes, their servants. 'It is not out of idle curiosity I ask, Joanna,' she would say, primly denying the avid gleam in her eye, 'but I have a duty to your grandfather to ensure that you do not set foot in any establishment he might consider unsuitable.'

Any mention of my grandfather always brought me quickly to my senses.

As to my other investment, with Nicholas Fox, that was quite beyond the pale.

I was angry and distressed when I learned that Grandfather had actually visited Exeter in early September to discuss the building of houses on a piece of land Mr Pascoe owned. He had not called to see how I fared or to bring news of Ben and I did not learn of the visit until he had returned to the country.

Grandfather, Jane told me, had decided against the venture. 'I believe my father-in-law was quite down about it. There is so much demand about the town for property of all classes that he fails to understand why Mr Kerswell will not see the advantage of the investment. Or so I heard him telling Blandford.'

I did not care about Mr Pascoe and his building activities. I cared only that Grandfather had chosen to ignore me.

I had seen with distaste the cramped double row of dark, unsavoury little boxes Mr Pascoe had built for cheap rental in a marshy hollow not far from the coal wharves. I thought them gimcrack and most dangerously liable to be flooded when the Exe was in spate and felt sorry for the families forced to occupy them. He had recently bought a pair of old large houses in the cramped alleys of the lower town which he was busily dividing up to create a tenement. There was evidently profit to be made from packing as many poor people as possible under one roof, but I suspected there would not be much comfort or convenience for any tenants by the time he had finished. His enthusiasm, fired by this success, had led him to buy several plots in St Thomas's across the river where more cheap little rows might be crammed in. I wondered if he had

333

perhaps overstretched himself that he now needed to encourage Grandfather to invest in his schemes. If he had, he must have found some other financial source for he was soon surging ahead with his plans. But I did not give Mr Pascoe's schemes more than passing attention. I was more concerned for Ben.

I knew from Mr Chadwick's letters that Grandfather's grip on Ben had steadily tightened since my visit in the spring and Ben was slowly, sometimes painfully, being shaped to suit his status as Frank Kerswell's grandson.

There had been no more incarceration in the dreadful institution at Bath, but the threat was used more than once when other lesser punishments – confining him indoors, placing his beloved pet animals out of bounds, forbidding him the pursuits he loved, swimming, walking, riding – failed to win him instantly to Grandfather's scheme of improvement.

So Ben learned to accept that if he was truculent with the dancing master who rode in twice a month from Plymouth, if he sulked when visiting the Aggetts or Daveys at Kingsbridge, or refused to hand out cups to the ladies as a gentleman should when taking tea with them, retribution would fall swiftly and inexorably when he returned to Falconwood. If he behaved himself and did as Grandfather told him, it was a different tale. There would be a fine surprise – a dovecote, complete with a pair of turtle doves set up in the garden below his window, a handsome new coat, a trip to Plymouth to take dinner with the master of one of Grandfather's schooners and to view the great warships in the Sound.

So, by carrot and stick, Ben was driven and coaxed to conform to the standards Grandfather had set. Sometimes I thought in despair that Ben, my Ben, was slipping further and further from my reach, becoming more Kerswell than Howarth as surely Grandfather had intended when he changed his name. But the more Grandfather's influence over Ben grew, the more my resolve strengthened that he must not be allowed to win the battle for the heart and mind of my brother. One day I should have the means and the opportunity to remove my brother from his clutches and to give Ben a comfortable, secure life, free from cruel threats of punishment and surrounded always with love.

In my darkest moments, when determination wavered, I thought that my only ally was time. Ben and I were young and Grandfather could not live for ever. But mostly I kept myself hopeful. All things were possible with hard work and willpower and I was comforted by the knowledge that Mr Chadwick kept my memory fresh in Ben's mind as would, I hoped, Tom Davey who now called regularly at Falconwood. He seemed to have a genuine fondness and sympathy for Ben and Ben looked forward eagerly to his visits. Indeed, both the Aggett and Davey families, young and old alike, were kindly people who would be understanding of Ben when he visited them, which went a great way to tempering my anxiety, as did the realisation that there was no more talk of forcing Ben to go hunting.

In late September, Mr Pascoe, the tenement finished, his other building activities left in the hands of an overseer, with Mr Brown the banker to keep a watchful eye on matters, decided that he might profitably extend his little empire to Plymouth. With this in mind, he closed up the Northernhay house and returned to Kingsbridge. Susannah elected to stay with her brother and his wife at Roselawn.

'Jane needs me rather more than Papa does, she being so unversed in the art of managing a household,' she sighed, with a martyred air. 'Blandford, indeed, was quite desperate that I should stay to help and guide her and one must do one's duty.'

Unfortunately, Susannah's idea of duty was to take the reins of Roselawn from Jane's hands and, with her brother's complete approval and complicity, set about turning Roselawn into a hub of social activity. Released from whatever restraints she endured in her father's houses in Kingsbridge and Exeter she greedily embarked on a lavish round of entertainment and being entertained.

Jane trailed unhappily in her wake. She had never fully recovered from the last miscarriage. She had days at a time when her energy seemed to desert her altogether and she was forced to rest. That was when I was glad of the care I had put into designing her retreat, her boudoir, where she spent countless solitary hours, for Susannah paid no more than token attention to her and Blandford was scarcely at home unless his presence was needed to host some function arranged by his sister. When Jane's energy was at its lowest ebb, she was even too enervated to bear the company of little Ruth for long.

Sometimes I wondered at the depths of Blandford's purse. He had married Jane for her fortune, but with the vast cost of refurbishing the house and the rate he and Susannah were living, money must be swilling away like water down a drain. Gossip was plentiful about the band of roisterers Blandford mixed with. Whispers went about of young bucks indulging in riotous parties which spilled drunken noise and upset into some of the most respectable streets of the town, of gambling with shockingly heavy stakes (one young buck was reputed to have fled the country because he could not honour his losses) and of a sordid incident when a group of the town's dirtiest and most diseased whores was smuggled into a private soirée and revealed themselves, bawdy and half-naked, to a scandalised group of churchmen and their wives. Blandford had not dared to tarnish his social standing by being privy to that particular event, but it was common knowledge that wherever gentlemen gathered to carouse and play cards, young Mr Pascoe, with money, apparently, to burn, would be there, the last to leave the tables, excessively generous and open-handed when he won, sportingly careless of his losses.

Blandford grew plump and flushed that autumn. Plump with good living, flushed not only with the fine wines and brandy he consumed, but with the success of his house, the entertainments and the grand dinners to which no one refused an invitation due to the prowess of his chef, lured from one of the great London houses by an excessive salary.

My meetings with Nicholas were few. Twice we met when I was taking tea at Roselawn in the company of other people, with no chance to speak to him alone, which was for the best and also a great grief. I buried hurt, tender feelings ... love ... deep. Bound it in chains of common sense. Weighted it down with the uncompromising knowledge that I was nothing to him, nor ever would be. I was as coolly civil to him as he was to me. I stood straight and smiling as he bowed over my hand and held the same polite smile as Susannah and her friends clustered in a charmed and charming circle around him, their laughter falling like cold rain on my heart. But I saw, too, glimpses of a different Nicholas in his dealings with Jane. How his voice, his smile, warmed and softened whenever he spoke to her and how deftly and apparently carelessly he distracted Blandford each time he seemed about to make some derogatory remark to his wife or draw unnecessary and unkind attention to her – playing the jovial good fellow, throwing his arm about Blandford, drawing him away. I recognised the gesture. He had done the same that first time I had seen him in Exeter when by denying me recognition he had defended me from Blandford's curiosity.

I tried, and succeeded I think, not to envy Jane those moments when he showed his concern, his protective kindness, but I was also saddened that this gentler side to his nature was all the time overridden by more reprehensible traits fostered by his need for revenge. Traits, I believed, which could be mastered, subdued, if he would only allow his innate common sense and good nature to have full play.

But perhaps I deceived myself, blinkered by this foolish, unbiddable, painfully raw and tormenting emotion that was infatuation.

Or love.

On the third occasion, Jane and I were walking in Northernhay Gardens well wrapped up against the cold October wind. Whisking in fresh and tangy from the moors, the wind had brought colour to her pale cheeks, its wild buffeting seeming to infuse her for once with an almost feverish energy. But the sparkle in her eyes was more due to the rare pleasure of having Ruth all to herself rather than the effects of fresh air. The nursemaid was kept indoors having turned her ankle on the stairs, Blandford and Susannah were out in the town about their own affairs and, fearful that they might return and deny her this unexpected treat, Jane had hustled me out as soon as I had arrived.

Ruth was over two years old now. A quiet, biddable little girl. Too quiet, I thought, too quick to obey, as though silence and obedience were already a shield against the uncertainties created by the adults who surrounded her: the rough nurse who constantly grumbled and slapped, the papa who remained a distant, scornful presence, the mercurial aunt whose teasing sometimes frightened more than delighted, the

338

mama whose love overflowed in frantic kisses and hugs and fussing, but who was all too seldom there to defend her from the nursemaid's bullying and who was so often closeted in her room, wan and weak and unapproachable.

Ruth trotted neatly between us as we strolled under the bulk of Rougemonte Castle, throwing us solemn, watchful glances from under the rim of her bonnet. When we stopped to admire the view across the deep combe below, with the thread of the Longbrook running down to the Exe and only the sinister bulk of the prison and the army barracks beyond to draw the eye from the panorama of market gardens and fields and farms rising to the distant, encircling hills, she obediently stopped too. I expected any moment she would tug away from our hands and skip ahead, as my lively sister Rose most certainly would have done, but Ruth only continued docile. Even the little gloved paw resting in my hand did not cling or fidget but lay passive and undemanding.

'Is she not a good little thing?' Jane said, her eyes glowing with love and pride. 'I am the luckiest of mamas to have such a sweet-natured child.'

'Indeed,' I murmured. I bent to draw Ruth's attention to the animals grazing in a field below. 'See, sweetheart, there are sheep and what else?' I waited. There was no reply. She might never have seen a donkey. Or a flock of geese. 'The big birds. Do you know what they are?'

She shook her head.

'Why, of course you do!' Jane cried, encouragingly. 'Nurse brings you here often.'

She shook her head again and I had a quick vision of the surly nursemaid giving the child the prescribed amount of bodily exercise with never a thought to wakening her mind. Ruth was cloistered away most of the time with this bumpkin. The nursery itself was spotless and airy, but singularly devoid, now I thought of it, of the clutter of battered, much-loved toys and books that I remembered from my own childhood. None of us – Phoebe, Ben, Rose or myself – had ever lacked for someone to tell an exciting story, to sing a rhyme to make us laugh or a lullaby to send us to sleep. There was always someone on hand to point out the wonders on every side – the iridescent sheen of a starling's feathers as it preened itself, the way the rain made pretty patterns on a windowpane or the sun illumined the veins of a leaf. Someone, always, to answer the thousand questions that a child must ask if it is to learn and understand. Ruth had nothing of this in the care of an ignorant nurse whose only talent lay in keeping her charge shiningly clean and beautifully dressed and ensuring her dolls, which sat in a pristine row on the top of a high cupboard, were kept in the same immaculate state. Ruth was always holding one of these exquisite creatures when I visited the nursery, but I had the sad feeling that once Mama and her friend had left, the doll would be removed and placed out of harm's way.

Something of this must have occurred to Jane. She sighed and said, wistfully, 'I wish my dear nurse might have stayed. She would have been so . . . so devoted to Ruth, as she was to me. We used to have such fun on our walks.'

'Well, we shall have fun today,' I said cheerfully and, swinging Ruth's hand in mine, I launched into 'Goosey, goosey gander'. Jane soon joined in and our walk from then on was accompanied by laughing choruses of all the rhymes and songs we could remember.

Ruth's eyes did not stay solemn for long after that. After urging us on to our third chorus of the rhyme with 'Doosey again, Mama', she began to chuckle and when a deep baritone voice behind us added a harmony to the last line, it was her mother and I who were momentarily startled to silence, not Ruth, who instantly demanded another chorus.

It was I who in a sudden, trembling confusion bent to retie Ruth's loosened bonnet strings, Jane who turned with a pleased smile to Nicholas. 'Mr Fox, what a pleasant surprise! Oh dear, we thought ourselves alone. I hope the noise of our singing did not carry too far. What will you think of us?'

'Merely that I am lucky to have this dull afternoon brightened for me by meeting three such happy ladies,' he said gravely.

I straightened, hoping that if my cheeks were flushed it would be attributed to the cold wind or my ministrations to Ruth. My voice sounded cool, the words more hostile than I intended, as I said, 'Good afternoon, Mr Fox. We did not realise we were being followed. Have you been watching us for long?'

'Not long, Miss Howarth,' he said and by the careless tilt of his smile I could see my accusatory tone did not trouble him in the slightest. Rather it amused him, as the sight of the three of us caught singing and unawares amused him. This stung me more than if he had been defensive or angry and I stayed cross and silent as the other two exchanged the comfortable pleasantries of people who are perfectly at ease with each other.

'Doosey again, Mama!' Ruth tugged impatiently at her mother's skirts. But it was Nicholas who bent to tickle her gently in the ribs until she giggled, then swung her up into his arms, unmindful of her small kicking feet making dusty marks on the smooth dark broadcloth of his cutaway coat, or the clutching fingers tugging the crisp white folds of his cravat. 'Doosey again!' she squealed.

Completely relaxed and cheerfully unselfconscious,

he began to chant the rhyme, bouncing Ruth in time to the music then tossing her into the air and catching her when he came to '. . . and threw him down the stairs'.

'Again!' she demanded. He obliged, laughing, and Jane, watching them with fond eagerness, whispered, 'He reminds me so much of my dear papa when he plays with Ruth. He too was a man at ease with small children, which I think is rare in gentlemen. Mr Fox never fails to ask after Ruth when he calls and enjoys it so much when Blandford allows her to be brought down so that he can spend a few moments with her. And she, bless her, as children will, seems to sense it and is never shy with him.' Then she added, wistfully, giving an unbearable wrench to my already tormented emotions, 'I hope he does not leave it too long before he finds himself a good woman for a wife, for he will make a splendid father.'

I instantly pictured him smiling down at a hazy collection of small children tumbling round his feet, his arm round the tiny, elegant waist of a dainty creature who leaned against him, looking up trustfully into his eyes. I could not see clearly the features of this woman – this unknown wife – but I knew she must be everything I was not. Beautiful, sweet-tempered, perfect in every detail of form, face and temperament. She would adore him, as he would cherish and love her for as long as they lived.

I loathed her with every fibre of my being.

Ruth tired at last of the game. Nicholas put her down where she immediately took advantage of being, for once, the centre of loving attention and began to hop about, loudly chanting her own version of the rhyme.

While I still stood dumb with despair and jealousy, Jane tore her eyes away from her beloved child to ask

Nicholas if he was yet through with the builders.

'Very nearly,' he said. 'But there is still a long way to go if Reynard's is to open in January. New year, new venture.' There was a hint of weariness in his voice. I raised my head sharply and for the first time studied his face. There was a sallow tinge to his skin, a bruise of shadow under his eyes, as though he had been working late and long. I quelled sympathy. This was what he wanted. He had set his own course. It was no business of mine whether he wore himself to a shadow.

But the next moment it was my business and I do not know whether I fell into a trap he had set or he into one hastily arranged by me out of frustration and longing and desire.

'It is a pity,' he said, smiling lazily, 'that Miss Howarth could not apply her talents to the public rooms of Reynard's as she did to Roselawn.'

Equally carelessly, the words springing unbidden to my lips, I said, 'Are you so overstretched, sir, that you could not afford my price?'

'Which is?'

'Offhand I could not possibly say. I should have to visit the premises and make an estimate.'

'Of course. Name the day and the time.'

I took a deep breath. 'And I should wish a free hand to employ the workmen I know to be reliable and co-operative. And to order furnishings and fabrics from whom and from where I choose.'

It was no longer a game. The lazy smile was quite gone. The grey eyes quickened with interest. Had his teasing been meant to spark my contrary reaction? Or had I taken him by surprise? Hard to tell. All I knew was that I had been spurred to fling down a challenge.

I waited. I was the one smiling now, afire with exhilaration, with no thought to the consequences but that

343

he should take up that challenge.

The seconds of that brief pause seemed like minutes.

Then, coolly, 'Very well. I . . . look forward to receiving your estimate and your ideas. You will send a note when you are able to come to Reynard's? Good. Caleb will escort you there.'

It was only after he had gone that I came down to earth with a sick bump and wondered how in heaven's name I was going to explain this away to Miss Olga.

I had a restless night, but by morning I had worked out my strategy. Blandford Pascoe owed me a favour. I detested the thought of having to ask his assistance, but I could see no other option. Miss Olga would be shocked into certain refusal if I asked permission to do anything for Nicholas Fox. The request – the command – coming from dear Cousin Blandford, whom she would not, dare not, cross, would ensure me the space and time I should need to tackle Reynard's.

I had to have this commission. And not purely because I fancied myself in love with Reynard's owner. There was a small, bright ambitious flame within me that had been steadily growing over the months. Sparked by the hunger for independence, ignited by the unexpected opportunity that was presented to me at Roselawn, fanned by the smaller successes that followed, it now burned clear and strong and compelling.

It was time to put into practice all I had learned – from my mother, from Mr Curtis, from books, from Roselawn and from the houses I had visited since in the course of helping genteel ladies to create the perfect boudoir. I had kept my eyes and ears open. I knew which craftsmen were open to ideas and which would grumble and question every order; which skimped on materials to gain an extra profit and which took pride in giving of their best. I knew where the most sumptuous selection of fine furnishing brocades and satins might be viewed, where the importers of carpets from China and India and Arabia had their warehouses and the dealers in expensive wallhangings and papers had their stores.

I also knew that these people made money out of each other. That was the way business worked. It was like a cake made in layers. At the bottom were the manufacturers of these goods, at the top the person of fashion waiting to be persuaded that his parlour, his drawing room, his dining room was sorely in need of some frippery thing in order to be *à la mode*. And in between were all the people making a profit out of the people on the layer beneath. The craftsman from his apprentice, the mill owner from the workman, the shipping line that brought the merchandise across the seas, the carrier who carted the bales and the chests to the wholesaler, the owners of the warehouses, the retailers, or someone like Mr Curtis whose professional advice came at a price. For seeing the work was thoroughly done, for taking the bother of choice and the harassing business of dealing with tradespeople – from his client, he could round up his account with a nice plump profit.

That profit could be mine.

I would *make* it happen if I possibly could. I would not think of failure, or of all the obstacles that stood in my path. Reynard's would be a beginning, a showpiece, with no one else to take the praise or blame, and the whole world – or the small piece of it that came to wine and dine and lose money at the tables – would know it, because I should insist upon it.

And if I had to swallow my distaste for Blandford Pascoe in order to ask him the favour he insisted he owed me, then so be it.

Perhaps the power of thought and will had some

influence. I dreamed of it by night and thought of it constantly by day and I willed Blandford to be there when next I called on Jane. Perhaps Dame Fortune heard and was in a generous mood. Whatever it was, he was there, on the point of departure, his groom waiting with his showy phaeton and high-mettled horses at the door as the butler showed me in. Ordinarily I would have politely removed myself as quickly as was prudent into Jane's company. Today I nodded graciously. 'If you have a moment, Mr Pascoe, I should like to speak to you privately.'

Luck was again smiling over my shoulder. Blandford was in an expansive mood which I later learned was due to a handsome win at the tables the previous evening. He waved the butler impatiently away and if I had to stand my ground while he came too close, so that I was overpowered with the sickly violet scent of the pomade that slicked his thin hair to the carefully arranged Byronic locks he had taken to favouring recently, and if I must try not to flinch away from his slimy glance which slid over me like pawing hands, it was worth it. He agreed, his words amiable, his tone managing all the same to be suggestive.

'Why, Miss Pascoe, I am your servant to command. I feel humbled you should ask this trifling favour of me when I am so deeply in your debt. I shall approach my cousins this very day. It will take no more than a few moments of my time which, though valuable to me, is as nothing set against my ... *desire* ... to see you content.'

I did not imagine the pause, the emphasis, the way as he spoke the word his mouth slackened and his pink tongue flickered out to wet his lips.

'Thank you, sir,' I said, stiffly. 'I ... I am obliged to you.'

His whisper was soft, sibilant, wrapping us in hateful

intimacy. 'I am glad, my dear, that you are grateful. Gratitude is such an ... agreeable bond between friends, is it not? Perhaps, in the future, there may be further occasions when we may express our *gratitude* to each other.'

By a great effort of will I managed not to reveal by a word or a glance the revulsion that seized me. I wanted the commission for Reynard's too badly. But as he bowed and left, managing in passing to let his gloved hand linger for an instant on my shoulder, I vowed to myself that this was the first and last time I should call upon Blandford Pascoe's assistance.

I would sooner have dealings with a cageful of venomous snakes.

Miss Olga was waiting for me in the parlour when I returned.

She was seated solemnly in her father's chair, an ominous sign. She usually only repaired to it when she wanted to add extra authority to a scolding. My heart sank. I could not imagine her refusing any request of her Pascoe cousins, but if I was to be given my head over Reynard's, by heavens she was going to make me suffer for it.

I was so convinced of this, so instantly fired with defensive indignation, that it was some moments before I took in what she was saying or even noticed how her hands were twisting together in agitation.

'... I have sat this hour since Cousin Blandford left, examining my conscience ... and I must speak to you plainly, Joanna. You see, my cousin can be so forceful that I felt bound to agree to his request, but I would not ... that is, I would very much like to know your feelings on this matter. You see, however Blandford might insist, I must know if this ... this connection with the man Fox is agreeable to you.' She leaned forward, a sallow, dowdy figure in a faded snuff-coloured gown, yet in that moment possessing both dignity and bravery. 'If it is some fancy of Cousin Blandford's and you yourself are against it, I shall . . . defend your right to choose. You must not consider yourself under any obligation to my cousin or his friends.'

Indignation swilled away. I regarded her in stunned silence. I knew what it must have cost her to make that decision, to go against her upbringing, the long years of bending her will to masculine authority and to mollifying the Pascoes who had the terrifying power to raise the rent, thereby paring her frugal means to the bone.

And I also felt shame in that moment. Shame for the deceits that I practised, must continue to practise if I was to achieve my goal. Shame that I had still continued to judge her with the clouded vision of my first months of banishment to Exeter, and to believe that her attitude to me remained unchanged. Of course it had changed, as Lily had told me. I only realised how much in that moment when Miss Olga made the offer to sacrifice herself on my behalf. And sacrifice it was. Challenging Blandford's orders, an unpleasant prospect for anyone, would be a terrifying confrontation indeed for Miss Olga.

But I could be honest with her in one respect.

Impulsively I crossed the room, knelt by her chair and took her hands gently in mine.

'Miss Olga, I am sorry you are distressed and it is all my doing, which I truly regret. But before I explain, there is one thing I must say.' The words did not come easily, because only now did I realise the truth of them. 'I . . . I was forced to come here by my grandfather and I stayed because I had little option to do otherwise if I wanted to see my brother again. But now, if Grandfather – anyone – ordered me away from here tomorrow, I should feel sad. You see, I have grown to respect you, Miss Olga, to feel secure here, yet . . .' I stopped. Impossible to explain the contradictory emotions that warred in my heart. How in one sense I felt stifled by this narrow house and by the demands of the sisters, yet in another, knowing how stark and unloved their lives had been, I was moved to sympathy and an odd sense of protectiveness towards them. There was even a growing affection, particularly for Miss Olga, that the ambitious, independent, reckless side of my nature urged me to deny. 'Yet, what I have done . . . am doing . . . is because I must provide for my future. I can have no claim on my grandfather, you see, who disowns me entirely.'

'And I cannot keep you here for ever, I know that.' She spoke quietly. 'Nor should I expect to. What life is there with two old maids for a bright young person? But you will marry, I'm sure.'

'I doubt that, Miss Olga,' I said frankly, with a fleeting, searing, image of the paragon whom Nicholas would wed, so that my voice sounded harsh for an instant. 'After all, I have no looks, no fortune – nothing, in fact, to recommend me.'

Miss Olga sighed. 'Let me tell you something, my dear. Looks and fortune mean nothing. It is for your nature, your character – for your *self* – a man will love you. I know. I was loved once, and I was never pretty like Fanny, but quiet and shy.'

'But you did not marry.'

'My sister had formed an unfortunate . . . attachment . . . to a blackguard, which caused a scandal. When the truth came out, she fell into a decline, from which she has never fully recovered. Papa and Stepmama were deeply distressed by . . . by the incident and it was thought best that I, as the younger sister, should be protected in future from undesirable outside influences.'

'And your young man?'

'Pronounced quite unsuitable. A youngest son with no prospects. A captain stationed with his regiment at the barracks. I was introduced to him by a mutual friend just before Fanny's . . . misadventure.' She gave a short, dry laugh. 'Had we met earlier, with time to establish himself as worthy and sensible before . . . Well, it might have been different. As it was, our . . . courtship . . . was so happy, but oh, so brief. I was not allowed out for many weeks after Fanny's disgrace unless I was accompanied by my father or stepmother and he was forbidden to call. There were letters, but Papa intercepted them and called me and my step-mother in so that he could read out selected paragraphs before he put them on the fire. They proved, he said, that Rupert – Captain Gibbs – was a frivolous man, intent only on pleasure. Yet it seemed to me they were innocent accounts of happy occasions. It was very . . . painful to me to hear his words, private, loving words, read out so coldly. Then the regiment was sent to India. There were letters from there, too, but they stopped after a while. He never married, I understand, but died a bachelor five years later of a fever . . .'

The story had tumbled out, bleak and sad. Bland words of comfort did not seem appropriate. Miss Olga had lived all her adult life with the consequences of the deliberate, selfish cruelty of her father. Her life blighted into subservience to him and now to her sister. Nothing I could say was of any use.

She cleared her throat. 'Dear me, how did we get to my affairs? It is all so long ago. In the past and done with and probably for the best. I should not have liked the heat of India, I am sure. Though perhaps if I had my time again . . .' Her hand came out and touched my hair. 'You have a vivacity and eagerness for life, child, that will serve you well, whatever you decide to do. I confess I did not think so when you first arrived, but time has proved different.' Then, softly, 'If I should have married Captain Gibbs, if I should have had a daughter . . . Well, no matter. To hear happy voices in the house, yours and Lily's, has become a pleasure to me, reminding me of the time when my mama, my real mama, was alive . . . Now, what are you thinking of, girl, get up from your knees this minute,' her tone was again tart and scolding. But it no longer seemed of consequence. Some barrier had been breached today that would not be re-erected. As though the years between us had shrunk in number, bringing us closer together. 'You will be crushing your good visiting gown abominably. Seat yourself properly and try to be lady-like for once. Now, explain yourself properly.'

So I did.

Chapter Thirteen

I told Miss Olga the bare bones of my plan and I realised as I spoke that I was not appealing to the person who sat opposite me, this frugal twig of a spinster, but to the other Miss Olga, the spirit of that long-lost eager girl who, in different, kinder circumstances, might have gone happily into a freer existence at the side of her husband. To her, to that young woman whose life was irrevocably blighted and restricted from the day of her sister's disgrace, I spoke of the great need I felt to make my way in the world. To be free of the necessity to be dependent on anyone, man or woman. How I saw that the way to achieve that independence was to use what intelligence and talents I had to better my prospects.

'And I do have talent,' I said, abandoning false modesty in my eagerness to convince her, leaning forward, willing her to understand, losing the careful cohesion of my argument because beyond the prim, disapproving expression was a gleam of empathy. 'You have seen for yourself what I did at Roselawn. The work I have done since – if you speak to any of the ladies, I believe they would commend my efforts. And now, to be in charge and take full responsibility at Reynard's . . . Oh, it is a chance that might never come again.' And a last appeal, this time to the Miss Olga who knew, because she had to, the value of every penny and who had never had the luxury of being careless or generous with her money because there was never enough spare to be careless with, 'I think there will be a profit in it for me, and for you too, Miss Olga.'

'Profit? What are you talking about, girl?'

'I did not work for the ladies for nothing,' I said boldly. 'I asked a small fee for my services.'

'Joanna!'

'And I didn't mention it because I thought – I knew – you would not think it proper. But I cannot feel guilty about it because I am proud that I gave of my best and the result pleased the ladies. And why should I not be paid a fee? A gentleman in the same circumstances would not hesitate. And it is not menial work, nor degrading. After all, the great London architect John Soane, with whom Mr Curtis was a pupil, speaks of the "poetry of architecture" and my papa always said that the best architects, those who create a fine building whether it is a modest house or a great palace, were and are artists as great in their way as Titian or Rembrandt. And in the work that I have done and will do I hope I shall enhance that poetic vision by beautifying and harmonising the interiors. Which is a perfectly proper occupation for a lady, is it not?' Uncertainty warred with interest in Miss Olga's expression. I pressed on urgently with the crucial point. 'If, with your permission, I am allowed to take on this commission at Reynard's, it will be far more profitable than anything I have done before. It will also take up a great deal more time.' Now I played my last card, tossing it temptingly before her. 'I could not possibly expect you to continue paying me a salary for the time I am out of the house. Indeed, if all goes to plan, I will be able to contribute to the housekeeping – or even to engage someone to take my place while I am absent.'

354

I stopped. She looked stunned. The silence lengthened. Then she ventured, hesitantly, 'This man Fox . . .'

'He may not have the background of a gentleman,' I said, carefully, 'but I would consider him more trustworthy than many a one. Jane has the greatest regard for him.' I paused, then added, 'Do you not think it would be more charitable to commend rather than condemn him for rising above misfortunes that were not of his making?'

'But your grandfather might not care for you to associate with such a person. Or to undertake these duties.'

'My grandfather cares not a hoot for me!' I cried passionately. 'Ben is the only one he has feelings for. Sending me here was a convenient way to rid himself of a nuisance! If you had beaten me and locked me away to starve in an attic he would not have raised a finger to help. Look how he came to Exeter recently and did not even care to call and see how I did or to pay you a courtesy visit! If he has heard from Mr Pascoe or anyone else of my doings – as he most probably has – he has chosen to ignore them.'

'Yet perhaps I should write . . .'

I was unable to contain my impatience. I jumped to my feet and paced the length of the room and back. 'And what communication have we had from him since the spring? Nothing! I doubt if he would bother to answer if you wrote. And in the meantime I lose my chance at Reynard's.' I flung my arms wide, beseeching her with every fibre of my body. 'Miss Olga, if you have any feeling for me, allow me this opportunity.'

She frowned, then said, in a cold, dry voice, 'I do believe, Joanna, that had acting been a respectable profession you might have had some success on the stage. A most unseemly display of histrionics! Thank goodness dear Fanny has retired to her room and is not a witness.'

My heart sank. I had overstepped the mark. I felt suddenly too tall, too gauche, my feelings too exposed as I stood awkward now in the middle of the Turkey carpet. She was going to refuse. Of course she was going to refuse. Why had I ever believed she would do otherwise?

'Pray seat yourself in a sober manner. That is better. Now, let me make myself clear. I could not possibly allow you to visit this place, this Reynard's, a young woman, alone. Quite out of the question.'

Excitement drained away. I gripped my fingers tight together. I would not accept this without a struggle, it meant too much. I would fight . . . fight . . .

'So, you will take Lily with you as a chaperone and I shall instruct her to stay by your side at all times.'

'Oh, Miss Olga!'

'I am trusting you to be discreet and ladylike and to conduct yourself in proper manner, do you understand that?'

'Of course, Miss Olga.'

'I shall quiz you both as to your activities and behaviour on your return and expect frank and honest answers.'

'Yes, Miss Olga.'

'If the slightest hint of anything untoward comes to my ears, I shall immediately order you to give up this . . . this foolhardy idea, even if it went against Cousin Blandford's express wishes.'

'I would expect nothing else, Miss Olga.'

'Very well.' She stood up and walked straight-backed to the door, where she turned, her expression no longer grim and forbidding, but unexpectedly serene. As though the making of such a momentous and unusual decision had released some source of calm strength.

356

'All that remains, child, is to wish you good fortune in this enterprise.' Her voice was stern. 'And I look forward to hearing more of this profit you talk of, otherwise I shall think my trust entirely misplaced.'

I could almost imagine she smiled encouragingly as she left the room.

I wasted no time in writing to Nicholas. Two days later Caleb presented himself at Torre Crescent and if Miss Olga seemed unnerved by her first glimpse of Caleb's battered features, his quiet, polite demeanour soon reassured her, not to mention the handsome new carriage at the door. Miss Olga could not fail to be impressed, as I was myself, as Caleb handed me up the steps. And Lily, rising to the occasion, stepped up and seated herself with such an air of self-possession that she might have ridden in such an equippage every day of her life.

Only when we were safely within did she break into a broad grin.

'Eh, Miss Jo,' she said. 'Isn't this grand? Just fancy! Lily Walker travellin' like a lady.' She sniffed appreciatively. 'Smells all lovely and new and leathery. Not like that ol' wagon we was took up north from the poorhouse in, which was the only other time I can remember not havin' to use me two own legs to get anywhere. Stank of rotten straw and horse, that did, and worse wi' all of us childer packed in like eggs in a basket an' some of 'em sick wi' the jogglin' and bouncin' an' the little 'uns doin' everythin' under 'em – oh, beggin' your pardon, Mr Smith, sir,' she said, as Caleb climbed in and settled himself next to her. But she was completely unabashed and far too excited to stop talking. Lately she had begun to smooth the rough edges from her speech. 'Now I'm a cook, I've got to learn to speak proper ... properly. One day, perhaps, I'll be a cook in a big house with scullery maids doing all the rough work and I'll need to set an example.' But now the words fell out in a rush with no thought to grammar or diction. She pressed up to the window, exclaiming at the sights and asking questions which Caleb, thoroughly amused, answered gravely. I could see she was greatly pleased because he addressed her courteously as 'Miss Walker' which I do not think anyone before ever had.

I had no need to talk. I leaned back against soft black leather as the carriage jounced through the streets and thought that Nicholas was indeed flying high with this elegant carriage, drawn by matched chestnut geldings, the coachman liveried in the same chestnut with cream trimmings. Chestnut? The bright rusty-brown of a fox's coat. Cream? The soft light fur beneath its throat and the tip of its brush. Black? The paws. It scarcely needed the inlaid motif of a running fox twisting cleverly through the intertwined letters N F on the inner panel of the doors to proclaim whose carriage this was.

Nicholas Fox. Reynard. The thief who stalked on silent paws in the night in pursuit of the unwary rabbit, the fat, complacent pheasant on its roost. Who dared the gun of the farmer, the snare of the gamekeeper, the teeth of the slavering pack to slip and slide and dance within an ace of danger in search of his prey. There were few who loved him for his bravery and many who hated him for his cunning, and at that moment, closed up in this carriage that spoke overwhelmingly, boastfully even, of Nicholas Fox's spirit, his pride, his vengeful intent, I shivered with the uncertainty of not knowing on which side my loyalty lay. Did I love him as I thought I did, or was it merely virginal curiosity and desire, by its nature unslaked and unsatisfied, that kept me tormented? The dark, tempting attraction of the unknown. Did I admire him for his intention to wreak rough justice on those who had betrayed his father, or fear him because I did not know what form this revenge might take and what innocent persons besides those who might deserve punishment would be swept to ruin with it?

I feared *for* him, that was for sure. No good had come of the feud between the Kerswells and Foxes, only heartache and distress. But he would not listen. He was too blinkered to see that he might be sowing the seeds of his own destruction. 'For they have sown the wind, and they shall reap the whirlwind.' Miss Olga, who was inclined to enter with more than spinsterly relish into her biblical readings when it concerned the Lord wreaking His wrath on wrongdoers, had dwelt dramatically on that phrase from Hosea only a few days since. It had lodged, just as dramatically, in my mind.

Nick would call down the wind to break and batter and sweep away his chosen victims, but the uncontrollable force of its passing might sweep Nick himself to destruction, and others, myself included, might well feel the violence of its passing.

It was a short journey. Not as far as many of my journeys around the town, comfortably walked, as Nicholas well knew. The sending of the carriage was a deliberate gesture, a statement both of reassurance and establishment. *See, this is my carriage, bearing my insignia. These are my fine horses, my coachman, wearing the livery I have chosen. Take heed! I am proud of what I am, what I will be. I am a person to be reckoned with. This fine equippage is but a start.*

I should walk in future. The carriage wrapped me round too sensuously. It was too full of him, of his desires, his ambition, his spirit. I wanted to rest my head back against soft, padded leather and close my eyes and let my limbs melt into languid acceptance of what he was, of what I felt and desired . . .

So I sat up the straighter, tense, stiff, unyielding. And when the carriage stopped I could barely wait for Caleb to alight, following him out before he had time to turn and offer his hand, glad of the damp, bracing wind on my face, glad that there was no need to excuse myself for such a hasty, unladylike exit. Caleb would merely think I was eager to be about my work, eager to assess the façade of the building while Lily chattered on excitedly and the coachman turned his horses under the arched entrance to one side, hooves and wheels echoing loudly and hollowly for a moment or two then subsiding to a muted clatter in an unseen stable yard.

The street lay close enough to Southernhay with its theatre and baths and subscription rooms to be drawn into its fashionable orbit, yet discreetly tucked out of sight of the main thoroughfare. A street of quiet, professional respectability where solicitors and attorneys had their offices and the frontage of Brown's bank directly faced the modest doorway.

Nick had chosen well and I saw with a sense of relief – for I had expected something more flamboyant – that the exterior was as plain and businesslike as any of the others. A small, gilded, running fox above the bell pull of the door was the only clue to the building's purpose.

He was waiting inside, looking dishevelled as though he had hastily pulled on his coat over a workmanlike shirt and breeches. But in command of himself, bestowing his crooked, charming, devastating smile on me, on Lily who bobbed so prompt and deep a curtsy, from which she rose pink-cheeked and breathless, that I knew she had responded wholeheartedly to his charm. My own smile froze. It was all so false, so practised, and Lily so grass-green she could not see it! Any woman was fair game to him. Even a little dumpling of a maid with a coarse brown shawl flung over her cheap lilac cotton dress, whom no real gentleman would have deigned to notice, let alone to include in his welcoming words. These ungracious thoughts swamped the saner, fairer voice that urged me to be pleased that he saw Lily as a person and not as a mere faceless servant. I spoke sharply, cutting short his unnecessary politeness.

'I have promised Miss Olga we shall not be too long, Mr Fox. Perhaps you would be kind enough to show us round without delay.'

'Of course.' His dark eyebrows lifted just a fraction. He responded in equally businesslike tones. 'Shall we begin in the dining room? Through the arch here.'

We had scarcely explored the ground floor before the enormity of the task before me squeezed out all other considerations and brought me up short in fright. This was nothing like Roselawn with a nucleus of furniture and ornaments to guide my vision and a kindly architect to teach and encourage and ultimately to take the responsibility. Nothing like creating a pretty boudoir for a bored lady, where I might suggest, advise, comment, but in the end I could turn my back and leave it in the hands of others to carry out the schemes. Everywhere was bare and stark as the builders had left it. Not a piece of furniture, a drape, a picture interrupted its plain, scrubbed, pristine newness. It was a blank canvas on which an artist might paint a masterpiece – or an amateur scrawl a laughable daub. Despite the unused chill of the rooms, I felt my armpits damp at the thought that wilfulness might have caused me to have overestimated my talent, which in that moment seemed a frail thing indeed.

Nick had bought the leasehold of three terraced houses. His builder had been skilful in turning them into one building. Inner walls had been removed to make a reception hall, a reading room, a dining room.

Smaller, more intimate areas that might be booked for private parties lay at the back behind oak doors, linked by a corridor that ran to the kitchen and pantries which were set on two sides of the cobbled yard at the rear.

'This is the public face of Reynard's,' Nick said carelessly when we returned to the hall with its circular stair rising to the upper floor, 'into which a man may safely bring his wife to dine or where business may be done over a glass of fine claret. I leave it to your good judgment as to what constitutes a suitable background for such activities. The basement stair is through there,' he gestured towards a closed door. 'But that is Caleb's domain and you need not concern yourself with it.'

Caleb's battered face crinkled to a grin. 'There's naught flowery and genteel about teaching young bloods the art of fisticuffs and ladies won't be venturing down there. A practice ring, a few plain benches and a gallon or two of embrocation to rub on sore heads and limbs will suffice.' He roared with laughter and Lily giggled, shooting him a cheeky glance.

'Ladies, maybe, but what about me? I wouldn't mind an eyeful o' t'quality sportin' themselves.'

'You not a lady?' Caleb said gallantly. 'I'd not have said that, Miss Walker. Well, I daresay for a friend, we can arrange a peep or two . . .'

Their chaffing talk drifted after us as they dawdled up the stairs. Nick led the way with long, quick strides so that I had to hurry to catch up with him on the landing. He caught my elbow, drawing me towards a plain oak door. 'This, Joanna,' he said, softly, 'is the heart of my enterprise.' He put his free hand on the brass handle and slowly turned it. 'This is where more blood and tears and sweat will be spilled than ever is lost in the ring downstairs.' He flung open the door with a showman's flourish. 'The gaming room.'

I stepped inside. A room of modest size, divided by

arches into three separate areas, the long wall pierced by sash windows that overlooked the street. Polished oak boards shone silkily beneath my feet and there was furniture here shrouded under dust covers.

'This is the temple dedicated to the Goddess of Fortune,' Nick said. 'And this her sacrificial high altar.' With mock reverence he drew the cover off the largest of the shrouded shapes. 'The hazard table.'

I stared uncomprehendingly at the oval mahogany table, its green top marked with yellow lines.

'Here and here,' he pointed to an indented space either side of the table, 'my croupiers will stand.' He smiled at my blank expression. 'The men who supervise the game. Men who have to be trustworthy, for they regulate the stakes and pay and receive the money. And they must know all the tricks a desperate player might use.' From his pocket he drew a pair of dice and dropped them into my palm. 'Ivory. Brand new at a guinea the pair. And these,' into my other hand he placed another pair, 'look just as new and clean, yet throw them onto the table and they will reliably turn up a four and a three.'

I examined them. 'I can see no difference.'

'They are well crafted. Many that have been tampered with are crude and easily spotted. Yet the skill lies not in the dice themselves, but in palming the good dice and replacing them with ones with a six either side, or those that have been weighted or altered in some way. A little bevelling of the edges, or the insertion of a pig's bristle in one corner can have interesting and rewarding effects.'

He took the dice off me, scooped the good ones into a small leather box which he shook before spilling them out onto the green table. Time and again they threw up an assortment of numbers, then suddenly it was the three and the four and the three and the four again, before the flow of haphazard numbers returned. Throughout he wore an air of completely relaxed detachment, his hand moving smoothly over the table, without any unexpected twitch or gesture to give himself away. But, with a shocking and practised ease, the switch had been made.

At least, I told myself it was shocking. I told *him* it was, at which he grinned lazily and said, 'You are not shocked. You merely feel you ought to be. You were intrigued. Admit it.'

'Intrigued by the skill, yes,' I said. 'That does not mean to say I do not condemn the immorality of the act, nor fear for the innocent gentlemen here who may be gulled—'

'Oh, ho! I seem to recall you had no difficulty with your conscience when you were afire to gamble on Caleb's fight.'

'That was quite different.'

'But to accept your winnings when you knew there was a measure of, shall we say, adjustment involved? Come, come. That surely speaks of a less than noble conscience. As does your share in my London gaming house. I have noticed no qualms in reaping a little profit there.' His eyes glinted. 'I seem to remember we had a conversation such as this one moonlight night on top of a hill. We reached a certain understanding then, or so I thought.'

I felt my face grow hot. And it was not my conscience delicately protesting, but a lucid memory of the way he had held my hand, turned it over, dropped a light – a searing – kiss on my wrist. If there was a moment when my body, my heart, had known what my head still continued to deny, that was it. And I could not stop the question slyly insinuating itself into my thoughts: how would I react now if he should do such a thing again?

'Is it come too close to home, Jo?' he said softly. 'Did your conscience lie easy when strangers in far-off London were being gulled? And does it now stab you uncomfortably at the thought of someone you know being fleeced almost on your doorstep?'

His words stirred in the air like the dust motes moving in the watery prisms of sunlight slanting from the windows.

'Perhaps there is truth in that,' I said quietly. I walked to the window. I could not think clearly or breathe evenly when he stood so close. 'There are so many half-truths and evasions in my life nowadays that I wonder what sort of a person I am becoming – have become – and whether my dear papa would now recognise his own daughter, or approve of her.'

'Because you have chosen not to be trodden down, by your grandfather or anyone else? Because you have fought back and begun to make something of the very poor lot fate has awarded you? Surely you cannot think he would condemn you for that. And your mother was a Kerswell through and through. She let nothing stand in the way of what she wanted. She would surely have understood.'

I could not help the bitter laugh that escaped me. 'Oh, Mama would not have cared. I was not her favourite and she never forgave me for Ben's accident which ruined his life and hers . . .' I could not finish.

There was a small silence, then he said, softly, 'And yours – or so you think. How old were you then?'

'Thirteen.'

'And you are still blaming yourself? Punishing yourself?'

'Who else is there to blame? If I had not gone with him that day, if I had done as Mama had told us and stayed at home instead of allowing myself to be persuaded out . . .'

Suddenly, violently, his hands were on my shoulders, spinning me round. 'How could it have been your fault? You were only a child! If anyone was to blame it was your brother himself!'

'It is cruel to say that! He has suffered so much.'

'Christ in heaven, girl!' For some reason he was angry. 'Your brother knows nothing of suffering beyond what is physical and of the moment. He lives, he breathes, he eats, he is comfortable, he is happy! It will always be so. It is you who are the true victim of that accident. You think and grieve and torture yourself still, because your mother made you a scapegoat! Made you believe yourself responsible. And your father allowed it to happen which causes me to think him a poor, weak vessel.'

'No! Not Papa. He was always kind and loving, to us all.'

'Then why did he not stand up for you?'

'He did. He did . . .' But my words faltered. How many times had my father's gentle protests been turned aside by my mother's anger? How often had he retreated to the comfort of his books and his writing and his lost causes, leaving me to face Mama's cold scorn alone?

'Kerswell blood and Howarth blood. Strength and self-will and passion mingling with . . . what? What manner of man was your father?'

I saw his dear, kind, loving face and felt my throat tighten. 'Gentle . . . bookish . . . a man of dreams and hopes and . . . and disappointments, I think, for so few of his schemes ever came to anything. Yet resilient, too.'

'And in you these elements war, do they not? The wilful self-seeker against the gentler side of your nature that torments you with doubts and apprehensions.'

His hands were still on my shoulders, heavy and warm. We faced each other in quietness. There was no background chatter from Lily and Caleb. They had vanished. We were alone.

'There is no reason,' he said, still urgent, 'why you should not make the most of what nature has bestowed on you through both your parents. I think you are already doing it, wrapping your dreams in strength and determination, pushing on, forcing yourself into a new role. Think how far you have come from that grubby, bedraggled, hungry child who dragged her helpless brother half across the country in search of sanctuary. And, not finding it, how you have coped since to wrest the best from what fate has thrown at you. You are winning, Jo! Do not for a moment feel daunted by what you have to face here at Reynard's, as you did a few moments since. You will cope and you will cope splendidly.'

I blinked up at him, startled. 'How did you . . .?'

He touched my face with his fingertips. 'You have an expressive face. You have not yet quite learned the knack of covering your feelings. And besides . . . perhaps I should not say this, for I have told you the manner of my life and my aims, neither of which have any claim to respectability, but I feel that there is something in us that calls, like to like, some inner quality which from the first we have recognised . . . in each other . . .'

His words grew slower, drifted away, but his eyes, grey and clear, held mine – held me – transfixed in his glance, like a fly locked and bound in a prison of amber. And he was held, too. As though between one second and the next, in that scrap of time, in that infinity of breathless space, there was some deep and fundamental change.

The fingers against my cheek were no longer those of a friend, an ally, a comforter. They slid silkily against my skin, tracing along the line of my jaw, moved in among the errant wisps of hair that were for ever escaping from the confines of my bonnet.

I did not think. Mind and thought and reason had no place. I did not care when he undid the strings of my best bonnet and let it fall; when, with infinite slowness, those same warm, searching fingers twined into my hair so that pins scattered with small clattering sounds around my bonnet on the glossy floorboards.

And my own hands rose like pale moths in the dusty, sunlit air, seemingly beyond my control, to cup themselves either side of his face and begin their own exploration. I felt the bones hard under my palms, the faint harshness of dark stubble rasping against my skin, the crispness of the black curling hair at the nape of his neck.

'God Almighty,' he whispered. 'No . . .'

Then nothing. No more denials, mine or his. Pure sensation. Purely animal, instinctive. To touch, to taste, to drink in the scent of him, that hot tang of male flesh; to taste his lips, his tongue; to know the power of desire let loose. An ecstatic fire. Pain laced with pleasure, heat in the belly and a sensuous softening of the flesh.

I do not know how long we stood there. Too long. Not long enough. Or what broke the spell. Hooves clattering below the window. A distant voice. A flurry of church bells striking the hour. Anything. Something.

We moved apart. Moved like automatons, he to pick up my bonnet, I to gather the fallen hairpins. A door opening, footsteps approaching – that was what had alerted us. By the time whoever it was came into the room, we were standing calmly by the window and I was saying, in a rush, 'I see you are well placed for depositing your profits in Brown's bank, being directly opposite.'

And he, carelessly answering, 'Brown's? Convenient,

yes, but not my choice. Clarence Brown is a man who lives too well and courts the custom of too many fly-by-nights for my liking. I feel my money to be safer with the Sparkes brothers in the General Bank—'

'Joanna, my dear!'

The familiar voice surprised me. I spun round, hoping the hair I had hastily crammed back under my bonnet would not tumble out.

'Mrs Fitch!'

She came beaming across the room and folded me into a warm embrace.

'Did Nick not tell you? He sweet-talked me away from my cottage with a tale of being so desperate for a housekeeper he was nigh on ready to throw himself into the cut.' She chuckled. 'But truth to tell, Joanna, I found myself overly quiet in the village after the excitements of travelling with my husband. And last winter was a hard one and lonely. Perhaps it was a mistake to bury myself in a small place. I felt a stranger there after so long away. I made my mind up straight off when I was asked by this rapscallion. I reckon there'll be excitement enough in a place like this to keep me from sinking into boredom in my old age. But come, the pair of you. 'Tis cold as charity in here and I'm sure you'll be getting chilled, Joanna. I've a good fire going in the parlour and hot chocolate waiting.'

She tucked her arm in mine and led me along the passage to the door at the end, keys jangling at her waist. She unlocked the door which led to a short passage.

'The private quarters,' she said. 'My room is at the end there, by the stairs. The maids will sleep on the floor above. I already have my rooms very comfortable. I am afraid I cannot say the same about Nick's parlour.'

'Give Martha Fitch a bunch of keys to mark her

status and she turns into a terrible scold,' Nick growled.

'Stuff and nonsense. Just because you won't spend a ha'penny on making yourself a nice cosy retreat. No time! Too much else to do, he says.'

Nick's small parlour was spartan. There were neither rugs nor curtains or covering of any sort. It contained several mismatched Windsor chairs pulled to the fire and a small deal table littered with books and papers. Caleb and Lily were toasting themselves before a bright blaze, Lily's cheeks nearly as scarlet as the coals.

'Not even a decent set of china,' Mrs Fitch said, handing round flowery pink cups brimming with frothy chocolate. 'These men have been making do with such a collection of cracks and chips, 'tis a disgrace to call it pottery. And as to bringing it out for company, I have tossed the lot to the rag man! These are from my own tea set. Nicholas and Caleb have been living like gypsies for so long they've forgot how to make themselves comfortable in a decent house.'

'About which I'm sure you mean to nag us incessantly,' Nick said, putting his arm round her stout waist and placing a smacking kiss on her cheek which made her shriek with laughter and push him down into a chair beside Caleb.

'Here, have a morsel of my apple cake, and stop your nonsense. Now, Joanna, tell me your plans for Reynard's.'

Reynard's. I pulled my hot and heady thoughts away from Reynard's owner, though my glance had a wayward tendency to drift in his direction. And all too often he was looking at me, his expression unreadable.

'Oh, I shall have to give it a great deal more thought,' I said. 'Light and formal probably for the downstairs rooms. A warmer, more intimate feel for the gaming room . . .'

'To make the gamesters believe themselves cosy and secure?' Nick said. 'Good. It may encourage them to open their purses wider as my generous provision of free wine and food for the players is also meant to do.'

Mrs Fitch tut-tutted, but Caleb laughed.

'I've heard talk already, Nick. Some grand folk are got all excited about the club and wondering why such a useful meeting place hasn't been thought of before. Why, you're set up to be quite a philanthropist in their eyes!' The gold in his teeth flashed cheerfully. 'Little do they know that the club stands or falls by the success of the gaming room. That fine food and excellent brandy partaken in the dining room, or a peaceful hour's nap over the *Flying Post* or *The Times*, are meant merely to fuel them with the strength and inclination to climb the stairs and chance a guinea or two at the tables.' He nudged Lily with his elbow. 'That's not to be known beyond these four walls, of course, Miss Walker.'

'Mr Smith! As if I would!' Lily declared, her cheeks even fierier, but her broad grin denying her attempt at indignation. She was enjoying every moment of her unusual morning out. We would be reliving it for days!

I looked at Nicholas. 'So, you would lure them to the fox's lair,' I said softly. 'And what then, Nicholas? Will you deal with everyone honestly? Or will you gain from the clever tricks you play so well?'

He looked relaxed, his long legs stretched to the fire. At ease, despite the uncomfortable smallness of the chair. In control of himself once more. As he had not been for that short breathless space in the watery, dusty sunlight. . . .

'In this business,' he said, 'it is an advantage to know all the tricks. Not to use oneself, but to spot trickery in others. Reynard's will, I assure you, be as meticulously and fairly run as any religious institution.' A smile, cool, remote. Not touching his eyes. 'My role will be merely that of – well, shall we say, a benevolent but strict abbot? Whose rule will be discreet but firm.'

'With the object of his devotions the pursuit of worldly pleasures rather than spiritual grace.'

A pause. Our glances holding across the small, warm space.

'Indeed.' His voice was light, teasing, but his narrowed eyes, that cool smile, countered its careless tone. 'I shall, like any abbot, strive to provide an orderly and tranquil haven for those in search of such an amenity. Yet with enough novelty and excitement to tempt the more adventurous. You see, even the pursuit of pleasure may pall and grow stale with familiarity, as the routine of the monastery must surely do even to the most devout monk.' Another, lengthier pause. Then, offhand, almost as though speaking his thoughts aloud, 'Yet there are times when one may be surprised and diverted by some new and unexpected ... amusement ... which could prove quite refreshing and stimulating. For a little while at least. Until the novelty palls. Then one must cast around for further diversion.'

We were not speaking of cards and dice. He knew it. I knew it. He was cautioning me as clearly as if he had spelled it out.

For an instant my hand froze on the pretty china cup. Then, slowly, I replaced it in its saucer, my mind leaping first to words of indignant protest then sobering to prudence.

I was innocent in these matters as he was not. But I was no fool. The power and intensity of feeling that had caught us up was not the product of my imagination. He had been overwhelmed, as I had been. Totally. Now he was denying it.

How could he talk himself into believing it was

something less than it was? How could he now, treacherously, wish to wound me when so short a time ago his fingers on my face, my hair, had moved with a tender, searching reverence. When his kisses, not tender at all, had awakened such a riot of sensation within me that even now my body shivered with pleasure. How could he belittle all that?

Because, for him, you are unimportant, a distraction, set against his greater ambition. It is not in his nature to acknowledge any undermining, weakening emotion in himself.

I set down my cup carefully on the table. I smiled warmly at Mrs Fitch and thanked her. I ran my hand over the back of one of the Windsor chairs which though disgracefully battered had most pleasing quality in its shape and which would bear closer examination at a later date. I gathered Lily. I walked to the door. Only then did I turn and speak to Nicholas directly.

'Would Friday morning be convenient for me to call upon you again? Good. I shall bring you my proposals. But I warn you not to expect anything in the way of cheap novelty such as you just spoke of – in a different context of course. That would be quite the wrong approach for something as important to . . . to me as to you – Reynard's.'

That was as close as I dare go to what lay in my heart. I was unaccountably close to angry tears. I turned away swiftly without waiting to see how he took it, or even if he understood, saying abruptly, 'Until Friday, then.'

'I await your proposals with pleasure,' he said to my retreating back.

It did not at all help my overwrought state that he sounded as if his mind was already on other matters.

If I had taken Nicholas at his word that he would

receive me with pleasure when I arrived again at Reynard's, I should have been gravely disappointed. It was an uncomfortable meeting. Or perhaps I was unduly sensitive to the constrained atmosphere brought about by my own determination to be rigidly correct in my manner and in the presentation of my ideas.

The intervening days had given me time to think more deeply of what had happened between us. I had faced the fact squarely that, love him as I did, I had not one advantage over any other woman who caught his eyes. In truth, I was severely disadvantaged. Apart from my lack of influence and money and my connection to a family he had every reason to detest, Nicholas Fox was a man of experience where women were concerned.

I was ignorant, green as grass in affairs of the heart. And therefore vulnerable. I had no kind and protective mama to shelter behind. No worldly woman friend to give me advice. I was like a traveller trailing barefoot and unprotected through unknown territory, while he was armed and booted and knew every inch of the path. I had only my wits to rely on and they were telling me strongly now that I should tread carefully.

Nicholas might have been momentarily disarmed by the emotion he felt for me but he had quickly re-erected his defences. I could hardly bear to remember *how* swiftly he had recovered himself. How quickly, how *humiliatingly*, he had turned from a warm and tender man to one prepared, in his own interests, to wound someone he had held so passionately a short while previously.

Was it a game to him perhaps? Was this the way the game was played in sophisticated circles and I too raw and inexperienced to understand the nuances of blowing hot one moment and cold the next to tease and provoke?

No!

I would not believe that! He *had* for those few vital moments been totally sincere. Unthinking, blinded, abandoning himself, as I had, to whatever it was – this attraction, emotion, call it what you will.

That had been true.

The other was false. The denial. Born of reason and common sense and all those other rational virtues. The same ones that I now drew upon deeply for my own protection. Keeping Lily by my side all the time I was in Nicholas's company; not by a stray unnecessary glance or movement of my body or hesitation in my voice giving him the slightest reason to believe I saw him other than just another client with whom I must deal in a businesslike way.

It was painful. I wanted him. Oh, how I wanted him! But on my terms, not his.

Truth to tell, I was not sure what my terms were. The phrase sounded grand but I was incapable of forming any clear idea of how I should proceed, beyond being resolved not to show myself as a foolish, simpering, silly creature, trembling for a fond look, a kind word. Someone who could not glimpse the harsh bony curves of cheek and brow, the tumble of black locks against smooth brown skin, the sensuous sweep of curling lashes – too beautiful, too gentle in that hard, handsome face – without being possessed of a melting, languid wash of desire.

I was that creature. Willing to take my heart, my blood, my life and lay them at his feet – when I was sure that he would not treat these gifts as temporary offerings to be laid aside when a more costly and opulent prize presented itself.

So, I held my back stiff as my resolve, kept my mind on curtains and colour schemes, carpets and costs and did not hold back in argument when my sketches and samples came under his critical eye. He had strong opinions, especially about the way the gaming room should be displayed.

'Green and gold, Joanna? A dark crimson red would be more to my taste.'

'As is normal – one could say tediously so – in other establishments?'

'It gives a close, warm feel to make the players relaxed.'

'But clashes with your chosen livery, you will agree. Your croupiers and servants in chestnut and cream would vie disagreeably with crimson. No, we must be clever and pick up a richer, deeper shade than the table tops for the curtains and valances. I have brought samples which may be suitable, with gold tassels and ties. A toning pastel green for the walls against which plain gold-framed mirrors would look elegant.'

'Mirrors? Would you help every cheat in the county to spy his neighbours cards? No mirrors.'

'Then a few well-chosen watercolours. Nothing heavy. Gilded candle sconces on the walls.'

'For ornament only, if you must. The light must be clear and concentrated over each table.'

'Ah, of course.'

'And while you are making notes, add that the chairs in here must be plain and comfortable. I'll not have anything with devilishly awkward ornamentation to torment a man's spine every time he leans back. A player suffering so will not linger longer than need be.'

'Comfortable chairs were already in my design. See in this woodcut, these chairs after the style of Thomas Sheraton have padded backs and seats which would be upholstered in some hardwearing fabric to complement the curtains – striped plush, say, or rep. I know an excellent cabinet-maker who could make them up locally at a reasonable cost . . .'

So we argued each point and each left satisfied that

over Reynard's at least we had reached agreement in most particulars.

As to the other, that still remained fraught and shadowy and painful. I was glad that in the coming weeks I should not have much time to dwell on it. Reynard's, not its master, would claim my full attention.

Chapter Fourteen

I worked hard and long in the following weeks but sometimes the frustrations and delays seemed unbearable and I lay sleepless, tossing and turning, wondering if I had taken on too much, whether it would all be done in time, whether the estimates I had laboriously calculated and to which Nicholas had agreed would be grievously wrong when the final accounting came.

At such low times I thanked heaven for Timmy Whipple and Harry Drew, whose practical good sense was a calming support. I had sought out Harry in his workshop in St Thomas's as soon as I knew what I had to do at Reynard's. Emily came rushing out from the adjoining cottage to show me how the baby had grown and insisted I go inside for a dish of tea and homemade scones.

While we ate and Emily chattered nineteen to the dozen and the baby gurgled and crawled around us, Harry calmly browsed through my sketches and the woodcuts.

'I should wish your estimates as soon as possible,' I said urgently. 'And there is a very elegant comb-backed Windsor chair I should like you to look at. I feel it would make an excellent pattern for the dining room chairs. Mr Fox acquired it when he was in Norfolk and I understand it is a style made locally somewhere in the east of the country. I should like to know if there is a chairmaker capable of copying it in Exeter or if we must order it from elsewhere. There is so much I should like your advice on, I scarcely know where to start. Oh, and do you know where I might find Timmy Whipple? I heard that Mr Meredew had died and if Timmy has not found other employment, I could offer him work.'

Harry shook his head. 'He used to live down to Bonhay, but 'ee moved. Somewhere behind Butcher Row, I 'eard. Reckon 'ee was hard hit when his master was took. Couldn't find no one to take him on. Tried to set up on 'is own account, but wi' all they mouths to feed at 'ome ... Well, 'ee fell behind wi' the rent and 'ad to look for a cheaper place.'

When he learned I was intent on searching Timmy out, Harry insisted on accompanying me. 'No place for a lady on 'er own,' he said, and truth to tell I was glad of his protection as we ventured into the noisome streets of the west quarter.

I had been to Butcher Row often enough at Miss Olga's request in search of poultry bargains, though I had never cared to go far beyond it. Behind and below the narrow street was a maze of alleys and courts winding down to where the old West Gate had stood and falling steeply again to the timber yards, warehouses, cloth mills and their drying racks on the stretch of land called Shillhay on the banks of the river. These ancient ways were lined with equally ancient, and once fine, houses. The gardens to the houses had long disappeared under infillings of cheap and rickety dwellings. Somewhere amid these dank courts and their dark little tunnels of entrances the Whipples now lived.

The task of finding them seemed daunting, but we were fortunate in that when we made enquiries among the shopkeepers in Butcher Row we found one who knew the family.

'Mrs Whipple was a good customer when they were to Bonhay, but since they moved down-along 'tis usually the li'l maid comes wi' 'er granfer – he'm blind, poor soul – for a penn'orth o' scraps an' bones. Try askin' bottom end o' Smithern Street. Thass the way they comes up.'

It was a raw, drizzly morning which mercifully subdued the worst of the smells but made a horrid slime of the rubbish strewn over the cobbles. After almost catching my foot on a dead and rotting cat I tried not to look too closely at the foul heaps piled into the central gutter and took care to lift my skirts well clear when we had to step over them. But soon we had to abandon the luxury of a cobbled way as we picked up the trail of Timmy Whipple's daughter and her blind old grandfather.

People here were not disposed to talk to strangers. Slatternly women standing at doors, knots of men huddled at corners melted away at our approach. But a small, ragged boy overheard us questioning a milkwoman easing her yoke and milkcans through a narrow entry and tugged at Harry's jacket.

'I knows who you mean, master! 'Tis worth a penny at least if I show you,' he added cheekily, holding out a filthy paw.

'When you've proved to be honest,' Harry growled, catching him by the scruff of his shirt and propelling him forward.

The boy earned his penny. I made it two when the door on the topmost floor of the squalid tenement opened and an astonished Timmy Whipple looked out at his visitors.

The boy scuttled off with the speed of a black beetle from the light of a candle in case I changed my mind and Harry and I went in to the room that the Whipple family now had to call home.

They had done their best with it. It was as clean as they could make it, but nothing could disguise the grey crumbling plaster on the walls, the green, mouldy patches on the ceiling where the damp had got through, the cracked and broken glass in the windows, the gaps patched with tarred paper and, above all, the smell. The stench seemed soaked into the very brick and wood of the building. A compound of human ordure, rot, unwashed clothes and bodies, and the ripe waft from the pigs squealing in a pen in the court below and the steaming midden standing next to it.

In this small, odorous space, four adults – one old and blind, one crippled and lying on a cot in the corner – and four young children must live and sleep and work. Timmy and his wife Zillah sat in the poor light filtering through the window finishing a pair of curtains, the fine gold velvet carefully arranged on a clean sheet.

''Tis for an old customer of Mr Meredew's,' Timmy said, his nimble fingers never stopping as we talked. 'But 'tis all the work I have on at present, so whatever you wants, Miss Howarth, I'm free to start.' He beamed at his wife. 'You see, Zillah, I told ee the Lord 'ad us under his protection. Our prayers 'ave been answered. Miss Howarth is His messenger, for sure. Come to lead us out of the dark valley back to the green pastures.'

Zillah, small and wiry with eyes shadowed with tiredness, shot her husband an exasperated look that seemed to say, 'Not before time.' To me she gave a relieved smile. 'Oh, miss, 'tis good of you to think of my Timmy.' She looked around wistfully. 'P'raps we'll be able to save a little now an' move back to where there's grass an' flowers an' fresh air. 'Tis terrible bad for the little ones here. They'm always ailin'.'

Hardly surprising, I thought grimly. Aloud I said, 'The good fortune is on my side, for I could not think how to proceed without someone so able and experienced at my elbow. Now, Timmy, please present yourself at Mr Fox's sharp at nine tomorrow, if it is convenient. No, please do not get up. Harry and I can see ourselves out.'

But they insisted on Maggie, the bright-faced eight-year-old, accompanying us down the broken staircase.

I could not wait to remove myself from that foetid room, from the warren of squalid alleys. It grieved me that the child, and the other children, must remain there. The memory of her shy smile as she waved us goodbye haunted me for the rest of the day.

My encounter with Timmy's family made me even more determined to make a success of Reynard's. Such success could not help but reflect on Timmy. His face lit up when he saw the amount of work I was putting his way, though he was somewhat daunted in the matter of giving an estimate for his services, for that had always been Mr Meredew's province.

Together we worked out a system and I was thrilled that out of my hoard I could offer him an advance. 'This is a deposit, to ensure your goodwill and to assure you of mine,' I said crisply, to remove any hint that I might be offering charity. 'If it suits you, we shall work out an accounting each month, as I shall do with Mr Fox, and when you present your final account, you will deduct this sum from it.' I smiled at his worried face. 'Once we get into the way of it, I am sure it will work very well. Perhaps Mrs Whipple will be able to begin looking for fresh lodgings soon.'

Timmy nodded somewhat cautiously, but his wife lost no time in taking action. With the prospect of steady work through the winter, she had the family transferred to a small cottage off Longbrook Street within the month.

Which was a great relief to all of them. And to me.

Harry Drew helpfully reminded me that there were bargains to be picked up at house sales. He often looked in to find items suitable for restoration. 'I was over to a gentleman's residence at Heavitree only yesterday. I recall a pair of good cane sofas and a pair of library steps. They could be got up for this reading room you speak of. Mr Fox might care to view 'em.'

He did not care to view. 'Take Harry or Timmy with you. They're the ones to give you advice if you need any.' He spoke coolly. 'I have a great deal to do on my own account so I would be glad if you would not bother me with details. I rely on your good taste and acumen, Joanna.' His smile was fleeting. A brief glimpse of warmth withheld. On purpose? Or because he genuinely did not have the time to spare? I tried not to be concerned. I did not want to be concerned, though it was not easy. If I was not on my guard, even the sound of his footsteps somewhere near where I was working at Reynard's – and I knew his footsteps above all the others in the place – was enough to create an inner disorder that was almost like a sickness. I trained myself not to stop what I was doing and turn to watch for him and not to hope that he would find a moment to come and talk to me. To continue, smoothly, whatever discussion I was having with Timmy or one of the workmen; not to let slip the armful of brocade I was trying against the window . . . But oh, how difficult, how frustrating, how wearing on already overstretched nerves; but necessary if I was to guard my pride and my conviction that this was the right way.

So Timmy or Harry escorted me to house sales and offered their quiet professional advice. It was Harry who turned me from the cane sofas which were somewhat unsteady on their legs to a set of mahogany wing chairs, heavy and old fashioned, the chintz covers threadbare, but undeniably comfortable, with frames that were solid and without worm. Then to the unexpected bonus of a fine library table which, under the dust, had the deep gloss obtained by years of care and polish, and the set of library steps.

We set our top price and I left him to do the bidding while I watched, learning how the bids went, how to catch the auctioneer's eye and how not to let enthusiasm outrun my purse, which happened I fear to two gentlemen who were intent on a rather handsome cheval glass, the winner of this war of bids paying well over the odds for his victory and looking rather abashed when he had gained his booty.

It was a wild, wet morning which was in our favour. The crowd was small and we got all we wanted at a bargain price. It gave me the greatest satisfaction to draw my purse from my reticule and pay the clerk without a second thought. It was an independence that pleased me deeply and boosted my confidence.

Which I needed, for it was not all smooth going. The wholesalers were suspicious of a woman calling herself a decorator. Were there not enough good, honest upholsterers in the city? Not to mention master builders and architects, men of long experience and good taste upon whose opinion and skill the nobility and gentry relied for the adornment of their houses? No, it really would not do for a young woman of such limited experience, as any woman must be, to push herself forward in this manner.

In consequence I was sometimes denied access to the warehouses or, if I was admitted, left kicking my heels until someone could be found, often the most junior clerk or warehouseman, and patronised abominably.

Their attitude unsettled me. I found myself becoming defensive, hesitant, perhaps even beginning to feel that they were right. But I kept doggedly on, searching always for the right materials to clothe my ideas, refusing to concede that it would be much easier if I shelved my pride and begged Nicholas to speak to these men on my behalf. Or even to ask Timmy to accompany me. Sheer pig-headedness, I suppose. I was not yet ready to concede that I could not manage without a man to smooth my way. And feeling, also, that if I gave in now, I would never forgive myself for being so weak-kneed.

Matters came to a head when I came to place my first order.

The wholesaler was a ferrety man whose warehouse lay behind his mercer's shop in North Street. In the shop I had been treated civilly enough, but once I had outlined my purpose and been shown into the warehouse crammed from floor to ceiling with bolts and bales, his obsequious manner was cast aside as he tried to sweep me hurriedly up the narrow aisles towards a dim corner where I could see that odds and ends of broken and soiled bales lay. But I would not be hurried and with delight I spotted exactly the plush I wanted for the gaming room, as well as a good serviceable Manchester stripe in dark green and cream that would be ideal for re-covering the reading room chairs.

I told him my requirements and, a trifle embarrassed, enquired diffidently about a discount, about credit. He hummed and hawed, did a sum in his notebook, then remarked with a sneer underlining every word that he might possibly allow a two and a half per cent discount. 'For cash, naturally, unless you have a bank to provide a reference, Miss, er, Harmsworth? No? I supposed not.'

He smirked as though he knew that I had visited every bank in the city and all had politely but firmly refused to allow me to open an account. 'Miss

Howarth, you are under age and therefore cannot be held responsible for any debts you might incur. Although we are sure you are perfectly trustworthy, we cannot, indeed we are not allowed, to take the risk.'

'You see,' the mercer went on, 'with times being what they are with so much distress in the countryside, not to mention the outrageous rates and taxes I must pay, I could not possibly afford to take a chance on such a large order, though I would of course be willing to present myself to Mr Fox in an effort to iron out this little difficulty, gentleman to gentleman.'

'That will not be necessary,' I said, still willing to placate him. 'I am engaged by Mr Fox for this work but I am quite independent of him, as any upholsterer might be. And the quality of your goods – this plush is excellent and of the exact shade I have searched Exeter for – will mean I shall probably be able to place other orders. Perhaps a small deposit—'

'But you fail to understand my difficulty, miss, er, Gawsworth,' he interrupted. His eyes moved scornfully from my unfashionable bonnet to my darned gloves and my shabby old cloak. 'You have no credentials. You have walked in off the street. Why you could be any riff-raff come to gull me out of my profits. I am used to dealing with sound men of business. Men of some standing in this town. The small deposit you propose would hardly compensate if you made off with my goods. No, no, it will not do.'

It was as much as I could do not to knock the self-satisfied smirk off his face. I said not another word to him, clamped my teeth over my wild rage and stalked out. I marched straight to Mrs Chadwick's arriving breathless and fuming, so much so that I was perfectly high-handed in my demands that she do something, anything, and quickly to turn me into a lady of quality so that I should not be sneered at by some upstart of a tradesman, probably bred in the gutter, for he had grease spots on his waistcoat and enough dirt under his fingernails to grow potatoes in— I clapped my hand over my mouth.

'Oh,' I said, my temper cooling, 'I am sorry, Mrs Chadwick. I had not meant to burst in on you so . . . so rudely. Please do not be offended. Though he really was a most obnoxious little man! And it is the principle of the thing! If he had not stocked a quality plush of the exact shade I have looked all over Exeter for I should not have stood for him treating me like . . . like . . . a dolthead, like an inferior being, a child who should know its place in the nursery, not bothering grown-up men when they are about their important affairs!'

'I fear that is an attitude you must be prepared to encounter regularly,' Mrs Chadwick said dryly. 'However talented or clever a woman may be, even the most stupid man will consider himself her superior. I have seen it all too often. Protest otherwise or, worse, show the world that you have brains and are prepared to use them, and you only lay yourself open to abuse.'

'I will have credit off him! I swear it. It is the way business is run and I will run mine properly and pay him when my own accounts are settled.'

Mrs Chadwick smiled. 'At least in Mr Fox you seem to have found someone who is willing to give you a chance to air your talents. So be thankful for that, Joanna, and be resilient in the face of other slights you are bound to meet. Now, I have some plates of winter fashions just in. Cast your eye over them while I get one of my girls to make tea for us, and I would suggest that you think in terms of a walking dress and mantle. A French velvet would look well but perhaps more sensible, for you are about in all weathers, would be a good quality merino. There is this rich chocolate colour . . . No, I have a fine slate-grey – where is that width? Ah, here – which looks splendid when it is made up. It would be particularly striking with your colouring. There, hold it to your face and look in the glass. You see, it does not deaden the skin tones as it does on so many people, indeed it enhances the quality of your complexion and the extraordinary drama of your hair. A bonnet in, say, *gros de Naples* in the same shade with a cluster of silk roses under the brim – no! Better one curling plume, of a silver shade to match the silver chinchilla trim on the mantle. Gloves in doeskin . . . and half-boots are the mode this season, I understand, though of course I should not urge you to even more expense . . .'

'Everything!' I said fiercely. 'I shall have everything. And it must be of the best. I have the money saved, Mrs Chadwick. I had not intended to spend it on myself, but now I see that it is imperative if I am to command respect.' Especially from ignorant little men with greasy waistcoats and dirty fingernails, I thought angrily. 'I will show them . . . show them all!'

Mrs Chadwick, dear lady, had all ready within the week, by which time I had bought gloves of such quality that they felt like a smooth second skin, been measured and fitted for a pair of half-boots, and a bonnet had been delivered from the milliners.

Miss Olga regarded me quietly when I stood before her ready to go out in my new outfit. Indeed, she had been calm and amenable with me since I had begun my work for Nicholas. Listening to my accounts of each day with such rapt attention that her ever-busy fingers grew quite still over her crochet or darning. Colouring with pleasure when I asked her opinion. Accepting unquestioningly that we should engage the daughter of our washerwoman, Widow Pierce, to come in by the day and help Lily.

Mary Ann was a shy and willing twelve-year-old, desperate for a place to help support her tribe of small sisters and brothers, and upon Mary Ann Miss Olga now poured all her energies, scolding and chivvying her round the house, watching her every move exactly as she had once done with me.

Miss Olga and I, it seemed, had reached a certain level of understanding, of acceptance. No longer well apart behind the clearly delineated lines of employer and servant, but circling closer in a warmer, more agreeable space.

By contrast, Miss Polsham fretted and fumed and never lost an opportunity to cavil at her sister's leniency. For Miss Olga's sake – the constant complaining must have been a sore trial – I did my best to smooth her ruffled feathers, surprising her with gifts of the sugared comfits she loved, spending as much time as I could with her, but I despaired that anything or anyone would ever serve to please her. Self-pity was too ingrained. Invalid selfishness had become a way of life and it was far too late to hope for any improvement.

'You look . . . very well, Joanna,' Miss Olga said after a long thoughtful moment. She cleared her throat. 'I have, as you know, always derided extravagance in dress. That is, I followed the precepts of my papa who detested above all things vanity, pride and forwardness in young girls, which of course are always unseemly attributes and liable to foster waywardness and attract the wrong sort of worldly person – I believe I have read you his tract on the subject. In consequence, Fanny and I were raised strictly. Yet even so, for all Papa's caution, Fanny fared badly, when other girls, whose parents were lavish and by Papa's standards exceedingly lax in discipline, made good, sensible marriages . . . Oh dear, now I am rambling on and it is of no interest to you, though I think of it often enough. And I know that life is so often unfair and seems to reward those who do not strive too hard for godliness, though perhaps in the next it may be different – to be sure, it *will* be different. But more and more lately I have wondered that God, having created something beautiful – a flower, a glorious sunset, a child in His own image as we are all children in His image – means us, surely, to look upon His work with . . . with delight and pleasure, not condemnation. I . . . I would not spoil my roses by allowing them to be swamped with weeds or try in any way to make them look less than they are, but to set them off so that they show themselves at their best. As do children . . . young people . . . shown more . . . more attention, more loving kindness than perhaps my father, my stepmama, thought desirable.' She drew a deep, trembling breath. 'That has been in my mind for a long time but I cannot, you see, speak such sentiments to my sister, who was always closer to Papa, more obedient, than I. Yet I cannot help but feel disloyal . . .'

She glanced almost fearfully at her father's chair as though the spectre of that stern tyrant might rise from its depths to order some dire punishment.

'If you are disloyal, Miss Olga,' I said quickly, 'then so must I be, and most of the population of the country. For much as we love and admire our parents, the time must come when we have to think independently and form our own opinions, which is surely how civilisation advances.' The troubled frown was not dispelled. I pressed on, firmly, 'Miss Polsham may not see that so clearly. She has been confined to the house, an invalid. But you, Miss Olga, have been about far more, which must give you an advantage, making your opinions more . . . more relevant and lively than those of someone who has been shut away for so long.

Did you not tell me yourself that you would once have been prepared to go to India? Such courage! Why, I am sure even your father would never have dared to contemplate taking such a bold step. Yet you, a young, innocent girl, would have gone out into the unknown with a brave heart!'

I held my breath for a moment for fear I had offended her by referring to her sad romance, but I could think of no other way to boost her fragile self-esteem. No argument, no other opinion than the Elder's had ever been allowed to flourish in this house. She had grown old and grey under the threat of that authoritarian presence, which still held the power to frighten her.

But I had not offended her. She looked again at her father's chair. Not in a nervous way, but considering it. Perhaps not seeing it at all but staring beyond it, into the distance, to the young girl who had dared to love a dashing captain.

'India?' she said, after a moment. 'Yes, I would have gone. It held no terrors for me. Not with . . . well, no matter.' She gave herself a little shake and, for a moment, seemed to straighten and grow, holding up her head with a touch of defiance, saying in her usual firm voice, 'Dear me, I have gone the long way round, Joanna, when all I meant to say was that you pay for dressing, indeed you do. Why, child, I should scarcely have known you had I met you in the street! You look quite . . . handsome. It is your bearing, of course, being so uncommonly tall, and you do not bow your shoulders to hide your height, which so many girls would do. And though that colour is perfectly restrained and sober, the effect most certainly is not. It is most becoming. Most becoming. Now be off with you. I cannot think why you keep me chattering here when I have a thousand things to attend to . . .' The ghost of a smile hovered to take away the sting of her dismissal.

I carried her heartening words with me, along with the astonishing image I had seen in my looking glass, to North Street where I proceeded, with a great deal of satisfaction, to revisit Mr Oliver, the greasy little mercer.

After that I never allowed myself to have doubts. I no longer asked, I demanded, and made it clear that if my demands were not met, there were other wholesalers who were waiting to give me excellent terms. I chuckled to myself sometimes, being strongly reminded of scenes I had witnessed many times when my mother had set shopkeepers running to do her bidding. She had an authority that was born and bred in the bone. She never questioned her right to command nor the obligation upon other people to respect that right. Such an attitude came less easily to me, but when I saw how confidence in my appearance, in myself and my aims bred respect – if grudging on occasion – and civility rather than suspicion in others, then I felt it was a lesson well learned. The Mr Olivers of this world would not easily browbeat me again.

Autumn rolled on. Days of exhilaration and activity, of excitement and worry and exhaustion until, gradually, Reynard's began to take on the appearance I had planned. There was no time for socialising. I had to turn down Jane's requests to accompany her to an exhibition of paintings at the Subscription Rooms which I should have liked and to view the 'Wild Brazilian Venus' displayed at the Swan Tavern which I think I should not have enjoyed.

'It was most amusing,' Susannah said, trilling with laughter. 'So hunched and brown and ugly a creature with great wooden pegs in her ears and lips and dressed in nothing but a shift and a great weight of beads and feathers. Yet she is considered a great beauty in her tribe and is the wife of a chieftain. We went with the Alpertons and Clarissa turned quite white when Gerald poked the creature hard with his stick while the keeper's attention was diverted. She was terrified the so-called Venus might turn vicious. But do you know, the creature winced exceedingly and Blandford lost his wager with Gerald that she was quite without feelings.'

'I thought she had a sad, gentle face,' Jane murmured. 'The keeper looked a kind man and he said he will return her eventually to her people, but how can we be sure? I do not think she is happy travelling from place to place to be exhibited before strangers.'

'Nonsense, Jane,' Susannah cried. 'Were you not listening when Gerald explained? The heathen savage, he said, though it will have a reaction to pain or cold or heat or hunger, as would any animal, does not have the thought processes or the mental capacity of a civilised person which are, naturally, much more sensitive and refined. She probably understands her situation no more than ... than that strange little Java sparrow which picked out cards with its beak. Gerald said that it was but a clever trick, though he intended to work out the method of it, and the bird had no intelligence at all.'

I was getting a little tired of Gerald Alperton's pronouncements. Susannah had quoted him extensively during the past hour. Always in glowing terms and always loudly, so that Nicholas and Blandford, following behind through Reynard's almost finished rooms, could not fail to hear.

Gerald, the brother of Susannah's childhood friend, Clarissa, had recently returned from a long stay in Italy, where his parents, Sir George and Lady Alperton, had despatched him two years since after a congestion of the lungs had aroused fears of a consumption setting in. He was a tall, angular, opinionated man of five and twenty and, according to Susannah, had become her helpless admirer.

'I cannot believe how his sojourn on the Continent has so refined him. Of course he has travelled and read extensively and has studied the great masters of Italian painting and speaks French and Italian with great fluency . . . Oh, and his manners are exquisite. He treats me like the most delicate flower and makes every other gentleman of my acquaintance seem a perfect bumpkin. I declare I am quite swept away by his courtliness.'

I wished Gerald Alperton *would* sweep her away. It would be an excellent match for her and Jane's life would be a good deal more comfortable without her sister-in-law for ever interfering and criticising. But I had the feeling that I would be disappointed. Susannah's admirers, apparently numerous and drawn by her undoubted beauty, seemed remarkably adept at avoiding making a declaration.

'Susannah is too choosy, I am afraid,' Jane had whispered only recently. 'Mr Pascoe has confided that he would like to see her settled, he being over sixty, and one never knows at that age . . . Susannah is almost twenty now so it is high time that she made up her mind.'

Choosiness? Or was it her sharp tongue and shallow personality that caused her would-be suitors to have second thoughts? Perhaps I should be charitable and believe it to be the former, though by the time we had climbed the stairs and approached the gaming room, exasperation was the only emotion I could muster.

They had walked in with Nicholas, having encountered him in Southernhay, one afternoon in early

December. My good dress was enveloped in a large apron and I was standing on a ladder helping Timmy with the last dining-room window. I stood on one side and Timmy the other while he carefully swathed a length of green and gold damask over the pole to match the apparently careless drape over the other windows.

I was particularly pleased with the dining room. Its airy proportions were enhanced by the cream, gold and green colourings that I had chosen to be the scheme throughout Reynard's. The tables and chairs were already in place, the set of framed prints of picturesque scenes around Exeter were waiting to be hung, and the gold-framed mirror which would be placed over the severe but elegant marble mantelpiece to complete the decor would be delivered within the week. In my mind's eye the room came alive. Silver clinked on china, steaming trays of food were borne from the sideboards by smiling servants, fashionable people sat at the tables – my tables. I felt a surge of pride. It would look splendid and it would be all my work. The pictures I had envisaged in my head, sketched in my notebook, were all coming to vibrant life.

Timmy tweaked the last fold into place, clambered down the ladder and stood back to cast a professional eye on the other windows. "Tes a proper job, Miss Jo,' he said with satisfaction. 'They French-draw curtains hang true as a die. My missus'll be thankful to know that, her was worried about the weight causing hems to sag a bit, but as I tells her, you can't go wrong wi' double linings once you got the measurements and the cutting right in the first place.'

'You do not think I should have had more formal pelmets?' I asked anxiously.

He shook his head firmly. 'Myself, I likes the freer headings, providing 'tis nicely done.' He grinned. 'And I reckon they drapes is as pretty as any I've seen.'

At that moment Susannah's trilling laughter startled us. 'Why Joanna, how extraordinary you look! Oh, pray do come down! I declare just to see you perched so high makes me turn quite giddy.' Her small hand in its pale kid glove fluttered out and sought the support of Nicholas's arm. She closed her eyes and swayed gracefully, her expression charmingly distraught as I stumped none too pleased down the ladder, aware that I was probably showing far too much ankle to eyes that were not Timmy's unheeding ones.

My pleasure in the room diminished knowing that in its unfinished state with the tables and chairs stacked at one end, the walls bare, the carpet hidden under drab drugget, the chandeliers still swathed in their wrappings, no visitor could share my vision. What could Nicholas be thinking of! He had particularly said that he would not admit sightseers. The element of surprise was important to give extra piquance to the night when Reynard's doors would be flung open for the first time.

I glared at him but he did not even look at me. He was watching Susannah with an expression of dry, faintly ironical amusement. Telling her now that she could open her eyes. Miss Howarth was safe on the ground. As he spoke he patted the hand that still clung to his sleeve.

Blandford was looking at me, though. Swaggering into the room, the peacock of the party, casting even Susannah's pastel prettiness into the shade, with a bright blue cutaway coat so outrageously puffed at the sleeves and tight at the waist that I wondered if the turquoise, red and purple embroideries on his waist-coat concealed the lacings of a corset. That he had noticed my ankles was certain. That he enjoyed the sight of me hastily removing my apron, smoothing my hair, evidently put out that I must prepare to be polite, was equally obvious. His pale eyes glittered as they charted the contours of my body.

'I fear we have discommoded you, Miss Howarth,' he drawled, 'but our curiosity overrode all other considerations.'

'And I am entirely to blame!' Susannah trilled, fluttering her eyelashes at Nicholas in mock contrition. 'Oh, say you will forgive me for persuading you, Mr Fox. But I am an inquisitive little minx, as Papa has so often told me. I am teased most unbearably in my mind if my curiosity is not satisfied, and we were so near when we met, it seemed such a shame not to take the opportunity. I do assure you we shall be the souls of discretion. We shall not utter a word to anyone!'

'Think no more of it,' Nicholas said, smiling. Charmingly at his ease, as though he had not grumbled to me, laughed with me, at the ploys by which several acquaintances had sought to be invited in. And been, in the politest, most skilful manner – for they were, after all, potential members of Reynard's – refused.

But he had not refused the Pascoes, which was galling. And incomprehensible. Yet, as he turned to Jane, whose features were pinched and pale under the weight of a mauve satin bonnet heavy with silk roses and crystal beading, and said, gently, 'Do you feel a little warmer now you are indoors, Mrs Pascoe? I swear the wind comes from the North Pole today,' not perhaps so incomprehensible after all.

Jane looked up at him gratefully. 'It does indeed, Mr Fox. I should have put on my heavier cloak had I realised . . . and we have been outdoors longer than I anticipated. But I am becoming warm and comfortable again now, thank you.'

'Shall we then make a brief tour of the premises before we repair to my parlour for refreshment? I have warned my housekeeper to expect visitors, which has whirled her into a frenzy and called down reparations on my innocent head because all my energies have been poured into Reynard's and I have not yet had time to attend to the comfort of my private quarters. Now, Miss Howarth, would you be so kind as to explain your scheme for this room?'

So, smiling, he effortlessly removed himself from Susannah's hand, shepherded me to Jane's side, fell in beside Blandford, engaging him instantly in a conversation that drew his attention away from me. All so cleverly done that it might not have been contrived. Or perhaps it was my overheated, oversensitive feelings towards Nicholas that deceived me into believing it was contrived, to give Jane, and myself, some respite from Blandford's company and to prevent that small, gloved, demanding hand from reasserting its place on his arm.

Susannah was not so easily deterred. She drifted slowly through the rooms, never allowing us to get too far ahead of the men, turning her head so that her beautiful profile was outlined against the light of a window, lifting her arm gracefully to indicate some feature she might praise or, more usually, criticise, aware always of the pretty picture she made. If the men dawdled, she drew them towards her with questions, with teasing laughter as though she had them on invisible reins, tossing the name of Gerald Alperton, her admirer, into the air so that they, and we, might know how lucky we were to be favoured with her company when she might at this very minute have been off on some far more interesting outing with Gerald and his charming sister Clarissa.

There was now only the gaming room to view. Once we had seen it, I planned to make my excuses and escape, but at the top of the stairs Jane, who despite her protestations still looked chilled and pinched, turned a sickly grey and reached suddenly for the banister. I caught her round the waist.

'What is it, Jane? Do you feel faint?'

'Just a little breathless,' she gasped. 'I shall be well in a moment.' She swayed alarmingly, her slight weight tipping against me. I looked round for assistance, calling, 'Mr Pascoe, your wife . . .'

But it was Nicholas who bounded up the stairs two at a time. Nicholas who slipped a supporting arm round her until she steadied and the dizziness passed. Nicholas who said she must rest until she had quite recovered.

And Blandford, her loving husband? Oh, Blandford did not hurry at all, but sauntered to where his sister stood at the gaming-room door crying, almost accusingly, 'Jane, what is it? Oh, you will give us these frights! Why did you not say you felt faint?' Blandford, the gaudy peacock, whose attention was not to be diverted from the gaming room by something so trivial as his wife's indisposition, pushed past Susannah, calling carelessly over his shoulder as he entered the room, 'Do not upset yourself, Susannah. You know how my dear wife is when she is breeding. All vapours and tremors and dramatics. She will be right as ninepence presently. Would that these dramatics came to anything but I do not hold out much hope of ever having a son and heir.'

I scarcely heard Jane's halting, embarrassed, 'It is only just certain . . . I am so sorry . . . upsetting everyone . . .'

I was watching Nicholas.

He had slowly raised his head to stare at the Pascoes. Blandford and Susannah. Brother and sister. Blandford had his back to us. Susannah was endeavouring to contain her impatience and pretending to be concerned over Jane's sudden indisposition. Neither noticed the look on Nicholas's face. A look which froze my hand, my body, my mind. A look of such pure venom and loathing that for a moment it seemed to swamp the very bones of his face, turning the harsh, handsome angles into ugly black pits.

It was gone almost before I recognised it. He was himself again. Charming, concerned, gentle with Jane, supporting her to the door of his private apartments where Mrs Fitch and a snapping fire and reviving refreshment awaited her.

But what awaited Blandford? Susannah? Not today, or tomorrow, but sometime in the future when all the ugly weight of hate that Nicholas harboured could no longer be contained?

I could not think about it too deeply. Not now. The chill of that glimpse into Nicholas's heart seemed to have slowed my blood. It was all I could do not to shiver as Jane did.

I was not sure that I clung to her fragile hand to comfort her or myself.

The next day Dr Barlow ordered Jane to rest. 'Just to be on the safe side,' he told her cheerfully. 'And I am sure the sacrifice of missing the Christmas and New Year festivities will be a small one compared to the joy of bringing your child to full term.'

But to me, when he made his weekly visit to Miss Polsham, he was less sanguine.

'She should not have been put through this again,' he said bluntly. 'If I had attended her at Kingsbridge when she miscarried last, instead of that old fool White, I would have spoken to her husband straight.'

'Would he have listened?' I said sharply.

'When Mrs Pascoe is recovered I must do my best to make him listen,' he said. 'In the meantime I have warned him that should he so much as disturb her, in

401

any way, I shall not answer for the consequences.' He coughed and looked at me over his eyeglasses. 'Forgive my frankness, my dear. I forget your youth, your unmarried state. It is not a subject your employer would care to hear us discussing. However, I believe you understand her situation more than most. You were present at Mrs Pascoe's first unfortunate miscarriage and you are her friend.' He paused and then said, gruffly, 'She has need of a good friend. Visit her when you can and keep her cheerful. It will do her more good than any physic I could prescribe. A person bright in mind though frail in body will often come through an ordeal where a doleful one will succumb.'

As the days shortened towards Christmas, Jane did begin to improve. By day she was carried to the sofa in the quiet privacy of her boudoir, there to lie in a nest of lacy pillows while the dancing firelight brought a touch of transient colour to her cheeks. By night she slept peacefully and alone in the big old bed that had been in her family for generations. Blandford, it seemed, had taken Dr Barlow's strictures to heart. Not, I was sure, for Jane's sake, but for the child she carried which might, this time, be the son he desired. Blandford slept elsewhere in the house and saw no reason to play the solicitous husband when there was a household of servants to attend to her needs and he had pressing engagements elsewhere.

Susannah made a great show of concern towards Jane. For ever swishing in and out of the boudoir, chattering in a bright patronising tone of nothing at all, fussily rearranging pillows or summoning a maid to build up the fire or remove a tray or bring refreshment. And never failing to make sure that Jane appreciated the sacrifices being made on her behalf.

'I am so glad when you are able to sit with me,' Jane confessed one grey afternoon as we sat in her boudoir listening to the rising wind howling in the chimney. I had reassured Susannah at least three times that of course she must go and take tea with Clarissa as she had promised and she had, at last, left us alone. 'It is so much more . . . restful to be with you.' Jane nestled back against the pillows and with a shy, conspiratorial smile whispered, 'And perhaps now we might send for Ruth. Susannah only allows me to see her once a day, and for such a little while. She says anything more would tire me, which is not at all the case, but I have delayed today's visit just so that I may indulge myself.'

So Ruth was fetched and her nursemaid dismissed and the three of us were together as the grey daylight faded. Ruth, solemn little thing that she was, scrambled onto my lap and nestled down, thumb in mouth, as I told her stories and softly sang the little rhymes and catches I had once sung to my sister Rose.

Jane watched us, sometimes humming as I sang or reaching out a thin hand to stroke her daughter's soft fine hair.

'Do not send for candles,' she said, dreamily, when I shifted Ruth's drowsy weight against my shoulder and screwed up my eyes to see the time on the tiny gilt case clock on the mantel. 'It is so magical and peaceful in the firelight. I can feel that we are marooned on a little golden island in a dark, dark sea. I should like to stay here always. Warm and safe and content.'

'It is almost Ruth's teatime,' I reminded her. 'Her nurse will be here any moment to fetch her away.'

'And Cousin Olga will expect you back soon,' she sighed. 'I know. But you will come again tomorrow, Jo? Now that your work is finished at Reynard's, promise you will come every day?'

'I will do my best,' I assured her.

'Then I shall have something to look forward to.

Now, let me kiss Ruth before the nurse comes.' She eased herself up on the pillows. 'Come to Mama, my little lamb. There.'

The tableau in the apricot flush of the firelight unexpectedly caught at my heart. Ruth leaned against the sofa, burying her face in Jane's shoulder, her little starfish hands clutching the falls of lace round Jane's neck as though she never wanted to let go. Over her head Jane's glance met mine.

For an instant something strong burned in her face. She held out her hand. When I took it, her grip was almost feverishly powerful.

'Thank you for being my friend, Jo,' she said. 'It has meant so much to me. And knowing that you understand how I feel for Ruth, how important it is that she has someone who loves her, gives me great comfort.'

There was a rap on the door. Jane's face crumpled with distress as she sank back on the pillows. The nursemaid came in and claimed Ruth who whimpered only once into her mother's breast, the mewling of a kitten which senses it is to be abandoned, before she allowed the lumpish nurse to bear her away.

Candles were brought. By their light the delicate tones of the room I had designed especially for Jane sprang into focus. But the colours seemed drained and pallid to my eyes after the glow of the firelight.

It was the warmth and colour of Jane's magical golden island that I carried with me on the breezy journey home.

The roar of the gale made sleep uneasy that night. Later we were to hear of its hurricane violence that had cast ships at Plymouth adrift, turned the River Exe at Topsham as rough as any sea, and thrown chimneypots and slates down upon the heads of passers-by in the town.

I was woken in the small hours by a violent banging

on the front door. I flew down the stairs scarcely hearing Lily's sleepy cry of, 'Whatever is it, Miss Jo, at this time o' night?' echoing down the stairwell.

It was Nicholas, grim-faced, rain streaming from the capes of his greatcoat, scarcely needing to bark out his message, 'It is Mrs Pascoe – Jane – very ill and calling for you. Hurry, Jo! Hurry! There's little time.'

But I was already flying back up the stairs, throwing on my clothes with fingers that fumbled at buttons and hooks, pulling on boots, finding a cloak, a bonnet. Then down again to the hall where Miss Olga's shocked face stared up at Nick's in the light of Lily's candle. She seemed unaware that she was barefoot, in her nightdress, and that it was the wicked Mr Fox who gently held her hand as he quietly spoke to her. There were tears in her eyes as she said, 'Take care, Joanna. I shall pray for her . . .'

The wind was like a wild thing, lashing the rain horizontally along the crescent. Nick almost threw me up into the phaeton – Blandford's phaeton, I noticed, with the bit of my mind that was still coherent.

He drove like a demon. We lurched and clattered and skidded through the silent town. I hunched against him, turning my face into his shoulder as the rain drove in under the skimpy hood tearing my bonnet back on its strings and soaking my hair. And all the while, in fragments, shouting above the cacophony of our passage and the howl of the rain-sodden gale, Nicholas told me how he came to be driving Blandford's phaeton to fetch me in the middle of the night. The phrases were disjointed, disconnected, shocking in their frankness, as though he could not contain them and had forgotten that I was there at all.

The bleeding began with a terrible violence and swiftness just as the maid was settling Jane down for the night. The child had been aborted before

Dr Barlow could reach Roselawn, and though he had worked with every possible method at his command, Jane continued to haemorrhage. At midnight, grim-faced, he had told a near-hysterical Susannah that there was nothing more he could do, that it was a matter of hours and Jane's husband should be sent for immediately.

All that anyone knew of Blandford's whereabouts was that he had driven, earlier in the day, with his friend William Fortescue to a cockpit out on the Honi-ton road. But William Fortescue was not returned home either. The pair might be anywhere about the town drinking away their winnings or drowning their sorrows.

Servants were despatched to all their likely haunts. One astute stable lad, who had already found it rewarding to keep his eyes and ears open and his mouth shut while learning as much as he could about the household's business, slipped away to the one person he knew was sure to have a good idea where his master might be. He received yet another shilling to add to the coins already carefully stored under the thatch of his mother's cottage against the day when he might one day own his own livery, for Mr Fox was generous, and he knew a great deal more of Bland-ford's habits, and tastes, than Blandford could ever realise. He also had the ear of a few people who had cause to regret ever meeting Mr Blandford Pascoe: a tavernkeeper in Bridge Street whose daughter had damn near had the dress torn from her back and been handled as though she was a common whore when she had taken food to a party of drunken young bucks in the private parlour; a pert young harlot frequenting Stepcote Hill who had been so damaged by Blandford's attentions that she had not been able to earn for a month and still bore the scars and the pain; a watchman down by the docks whose old dog had been beaten and kicked because it had dared to growl at three roisterers relieving themselves into the river . . .

So within a short time Nicholas was in a house in Cowick Street hauling Blandford out of the large soft feather bed which he was presently sharing with his friend William and a startled lady of uncertain age whose sea-captain husband was presently engaged in sailing a cargo of tea and spices from the East Indies. The men were so fuddled and drunk they scarcely knew where they were or who it was interrupting their sport. The phaeton and the tired, wet horses still stood outside the door, guarded by the woman's boot boy. Nicholas had bundled Blandford up into the seat and raced him home, manhandling him into the house, only to meet Dr Barlow about to despatch a servant to fetch me. It seemed, to save time, that the exhausted horses must make one final journey.

I heard it all and I did not care that the terms Nicholas used, the oaths and curses that the wind spun away, were not those that should ever sully a lady's ears. They seemed in keeping, somehow, with the primitive force of the storm and the urgent headlong force of our flight.

And was I too late, after all?

Lights poured from Roselawn's windows, as though to welcome guests to a party. Eager hands steadied the horses. Nicholas lifted me down from the phaeton with as little ceremony as he had put me up, his arm about me as we hurried into the light and the warmth, his hands at my throat untying my wet cloak, my bonnet, throwing them to a maid, then his hands beginning to unfasten the buttons of his greatcoat and suddenly stopping. He blinked at the light, as though all at once realising that his part was done. There was no more need for haste.

I flew up the stairs to Jane.

Someone had burnt lavender in the room. Its smell, summery and clean, hung about the rich brocade hangings of the bed.

She was nothing more than a handful of fragile bones which scarcely mounded the bedclothes. Her hair was a light brown cloud against the starched pillow. The only colour in the waxy whiteness of her face was the fan of her eyelashes, the fine trace of her brows.

Susannah wept quietly on the other side of the bed. Somewhere in the shadows Dr Barlow waited. Blandford was nothing more than a stertorously breathing hump of dishevelled clothes slumped on a chair in a corner. I sensed more than saw any of them.

I gently touched Jane's face and spoke her name.

Her lids lifted slowly. 'Jo . . .?' Her voice was no more than a breath.

I leaned close.

'Jo . . . please . . . Ruth . . . you are the only one I trust . . .' The breathy whisper faltered, gained strength once more. 'Promise me, Jo . . . that you will love Ruth . . . and . . . and protect her. Promise . . .' Her brown eyes burned into mine.

'I promise,' I said. 'Of course I do.'

'Love her, Jo . . . please love her . . . and let her . . . remember me . . .'

She gave a little gasp then. No more than a sigh of contentment.

The air about her was suddenly very still. And the scent of lavender was the scent of twenty summers burnt and gone to a wisp of fragrant smoke.

Chapter Fifteen

When I came downstairs Nicholas was waiting.

Dr Barlow had long gone, called away by his man with an urgent message to attend a patient taken with a fever. Susannah had allowed herself to be led off to bed and soothed with a hot posset. Blandford, grey-faced, eyes bloodshot, still unsteady on his feet, had been removed by his valet to sleep himself to sobriety and the realisation that he was left a widower.

I had stayed on at Jane's side alone. Wanting a quiet interval to calm the sudden trembling that had taken hold of me and to allow the tears to flow. Not for Jane, tranquil and peaceful in death as she had never been in life, and whom I could not in all conscience wish back to resume an existence in which there had been little happiness and much suffering – but for myself. The night's events had inevitably stirred raw memories for the other people I had lost. Papa, Mama, my sisters. And Ben, who now, despite my hopes and the strength of my purpose, seemed as far removed from me as ever.

Presently the trembling ceased and my legs felt capable of bearing me away. I became aware that the house, so lately full of bustle, had hushed. I felt forgotten. A minor character in the drama that had been enacted through the long night. Too unimportant for anyone to bother about and no matter if I felt desperately alone and bereft.

One sleepy footman jumped to attention as I descended the stairs, but a taller figure moved from the door of the drawing room, took my cloak and bonnet from the footman and dismissed him with a curt nod.

'You should not have waited,' I began.

'I could not have left you,' Nick said.

He wrapped my cloak round my shoulders. Gently, with great care, he buttoned it at my throat. He lifted my hair free. I only now remembered that it was loose. There had been no time for pins or ribbons. Remembered, too, what a shaming sight I must look with my red, swollen eyes and my horrible frizzy wild hair and tear-streaked face.

I turned my head from his gaze, lifted my hands to my hair to twist it back into a plait, but he caught at my arms and once more drew the cloak round me. Tightly, this time, trapping my arms helplessly within it. Then he put one hand under my chin and turned my face towards his.

'There is no shame in grief and tears,' he said softly.

His kisses were light. Butterfly touches, soothing, gentle. His arms slid round me and I went into them with a sigh, the strength and security of his embrace slowly warming that cold, frightened space in my heart where I was not the grown-up, capable Joanna Howarth but a child crying for comfort.

I do not know how long we stood there but when he released me, handed me my bonnet – my best one, snatched in haste, now ruined and bedraggled with rain – I found I could manage a rueful smile at my scarecrow reflection in the imposing hall mirror.

'You have beautiful hair,' Nick said, watching me. 'It is a shame you must hide it under a bonnet.'

'Beautiful? Oh, come now! There is no need to stretch kindness that far.'

'Kindness?' He looked at me in a puzzled way. 'Why should I be kind?'

'Because I was upset . . . but I am recovering . . .'

He gripped my shoulder. His face was taut and serious, the grey, black-lashed eyes dark and intense. 'I mean it, Jo. Your hair is extraordinary. It crackles with life and energy and colour. It should be left loose about your shoulders, free and untrammelled, not bundled up and contorted into some frigid style considered fashionable. In some way . . . I feel that . . . it reflects your . . . your own inner spirit.' He seemed strangely at a loss for words. His fingers touched one loose frizzy length that still untidily escaped my bonnet. 'This strand, for instance. Stubborn as its owner. Defying the hand that wishes to control and twist it awry. See, I crush it, and it does not subside to limpness, but springs back, undefeated. That . . . that is the spirit that I see in you, Jo. The same vitality that shines in your eyes, even now, and gives your face an animation that . . . I admire . . . that draws me, even against my will and knowing that I must not be distracted.'

His kiss this time was not meant to comfort. Nor did I wish it to. His words dazzled in my mind with the clarity of diamonds. This was not a man playing the charmer with clever deceits and smiles. Here was the truth and I rejoiced in it.

All the recent grief, and the old grief, were momentarily forgotten, overriden by the urgency of my response to him. Not this time the languid, weakening, breathlessness of those other snatched moments at Reynard's but something more forceful, more demanding and infinitely more reckless.

A clock chimed somewhere within the house. Six o'clock. Boards creaked overhead, voices whispered in the distance as the household began to stir itself to face the new, difficult, different day, though it was dark

411

still and the night's candles guttered low in their sconces.

We let ourselves quietly out of the house. The rain had stopped, the wind had lost its power. We picked our way round the puddles, walking slowly, talking little, uncaring of the lights going on in windows, the first carts rumbling noisily over the cobbles, a few men and women already clattering to their work.

We heard nothing of them, saw nothing of them. We walked entwined. We paused to kiss, to touch, to explore. Those searching lips and hands were all that mattered. I scarcely knew where we were. Once, in deep shadow, he unhooked every fastening in the bodice of my dress and the touch of his hands and lips on my cool, bared, willing flesh seared like the touch of a desert wind. When I opened my eyes I saw that we stood in the black shelter of a great buttress. High above our heads the grimace of a gargoyle, beyond again the soaring carved outline of a tower against clouds that were tearing raggedly apart to reveal a few paling stars. It did not seem wrong or sacrilegious that we stood here and discovered each other. There was no guilt or fear, but rather a sense that these ancient stones, which had observed for centuries every frailty and ecstasy of human life, would shelter us now from all harm and condemnation. Indeed, had he laid me down on the wet grass and taken me then and there, I think they would have soaked up my joy and set the great bells ringing in celebration.

But that was not to be.

Nicholas was, after all ... Nicholas. Not for him some brief, uncomfortable coupling because his emotions had temporarily bettered his common sense. Not for him the unplanned, unlooked for, maybe disastrous action which would unhinge his carefully worked out schemes. All this I realised, bitterly, later. Then, I only saw his consideration, the tender way he loosed me, kissed me, drew me down to reluctant reality from the heights of uncaring passion.

We walked the remainder of the way to Torre Crescent as decorously as if we had only the most formal acquaintance. I did not even take his proffered arm when we came to patches of slippery mud swilling over the cobbles. I dare not. I could not risk even the slightest touch which might shatter the fragility of the composure I now drew about me as tightly as any protective cloak.

I tried to hold that sense of wonder, of delight, but already it was diluting in the flood of returning grief for Jane, dejection that I must soon part from Nicholas and a dreadful, shivering exhaustion that made every step an effort.

Lily and Miss Olga must have been watching for me. The door flew open before Nicholas knocked. One look at my face was enough for them to know. I tumbled inside. Amazingly, it was Miss Olga who steadied and soothed me and spoke words of comfort in the kindest of voices and through her own tears.

My recollections after that are hazy. I remember the sickly way the flame of Lily's candle dazzled then retreated into a tunnel of blackness, voices that thundered in my ears but made no sense. Then nothing until the most dreadful pungent smell made me choke and gag and open my eyes. I was lying down – hazily I saw it was my own room, I had no idea how I had got there – Miss Olga holding a smoking feather under my nose.

'Thank heaven,' she cried. And then to someone else, far distant in the swimming rainbow fog, 'She has the most dreadful colour. I think perhaps Dr Barlow—'

'I will fetch him at once.' Was it Nicholas who spoke? My darling Nick, who loved me . . . I wanted to giggle.

How outraged Miss Olga must be that he was in her house, in my room. But I was too tired even to smile, let alone speak to either of them.

I slept for many dreamless hours. I woke feeling weak but thankfully without the swimmy feeling of imminent faintness.

'It was the shock of the events of the night which overwhelmed the system,' Dr Barlow said. 'I would recommend that you remain in bed for tomorrow at least, when we may be sure all the nervous symptoms have subsided.'

'But how can I?' I protested.

'Quite easily, my dear, if you give your mind to it,' he said, smiling.

'Of course you will remain in bed if Dr Barlow has ordered it,' Miss Olga put in sternly.

'A light, nourishing diet devoid of stimulants except for one glass of sweet wine into which an egg may be beaten to be taken at mid-morning and mid-afternoon, if you would be so kind, Miss Olga. And ensure that a hot brick is kept to her feet at all times. And you, Joanna, must help yourself back to full health by sleeping as much as you can. Sleep is a great healer. All your wearied functions will soon be restored to full elasticity and strength if you follow this regimen. Good morning to you, ladies. I will look in again in a day or two.'

It was a relief to lie back and let everything, for once, drift by me. When I ventured downstairs two days later I had the scratchy throat of an impending cold and Dr Barlow insisted that I must remain indoors until my system was fully restored to normal health. Miss Olga was soon sneezing and blowing, too. There was no question of either of us attending Jane's funeral and I felt guiltily relieved.

I had said my private goodbyes to Jane. I should

have hated the mockery of mourning that the Pascoes would exhibit. Mr Pascoe, who had arranged her disastrous marriage to his son purely with an eye to her fortune; Susannah, who had never really been kind to her, but would shed many pretty tears and look enchanting in the finest black silk and lace. As for Blandford, I felt sick to my soul when I thought of him dragged drunk from another woman's bed while his wife lay dying. He had killed Jane by his cruel and lustful depredations on her frail body as surely as if he had stabbed her in the heart with a knife.

The Pascoes arranged for Jane's body to be interred in Exeter. A matter of expediency, not sensitivity. Mr Pascoe, summoned urgently to Exeter, had had a slow and difficult journey from Kingsbridge through floods and the detritus of the storm. It was thought better – more convenient to all concerned – to lay her to rest with her parents in their tomb in the Trinity burying ground. At least, in death, she would be with those who had once loved her. There would, of course, be a showy memorial erected later among the rest of the deceased Pascoes in Kingsbridge church. No doubt full of flowery phrases: 'Dearly beloved wife . . . paragon of gentleness and womanly virtue . . . this memorial erected by a grieving, inconsolable – lying – husband . . .'

On the shortest day of the year, Miss Olga and I, muffled against the cold, gathered the first violets that were showing among their heart-shaped leaves in the shelter of the garden wall. We fashioned them into a posy, binding the stems with purple ribbon and gave them to Nicholas when he called on his way to the funeral, to lay on Jane's grave.

When he had gone, Lily and Mary Ann were summoned to the parlour and Miss Olga conducted a short, dignified service of remembrance. We all agreed it was far more personal and moving and suitable to someone of Jane's retiring nature than any ceremony held under the eyes of a fashionable crowd of strangers.

The head cold, as head colds will, infected all the household. Within days of Miss Olga taking it from me, Mary Ann and Lily were red-eyed and red-nosed and dosing themselves liberally with the essence of coltsfoot that Mary Ann's mother swore by. Miss Polsham was the last to take it and the worst affected. The cough settled on her chest. She gave us more than a few sleepless nights as she wheezed and gasped the dark hours away. The affliction did little for her temper, or for anyone else's. We were all out of sorts and irritable.

Nick's visits were the only relief. He brought with him a sense of life beyond these restricting walls, a life whose threads I should soon have to pick up again. For the present, though, I was content to let myself drift, unwilling in my convalescent state to face either the cold streets or the problems inherent in Jane's final request that I protect and love her daughter. I had made her a promise, but there was little I could do about it at the moment. Mr Pascoe, having got wind of the scandalous manner of his son's behaviour on the night of Jane's death, had acted with determination. He insisted that Roselawn be closed up. His son and daughter and motherless grandchild were hastily removed to Kingsbridge, out of reach of prying eyes and gossiping tongues. Ruth was temporarily quite beyond my reach.

Nick spoke of their flight in the most courteous tone, the underlying irony only discernible to the sharp ear.

'The family wishes to bear its grief in decent and perfectly understandable privacy in the tranquillity of the countryside.'

'Cousin James was ever a man of common sense,'

Miss Olga agreed, nodding sagely over the fine embroidery that was whisked out whenever a gentleman, that rare and strange animal, called. I wondered how much, or how little, she had understood of Blandford's behaviour from the bare bones I had given her. But discretion – blindness – over family failings was too ingrained for her to speak aloud any suspicions she might harbour.

What was clear and surprising was her attitude to Nicholas.

Miss Polsham certainly had a great deal to say on the wisdom of admitting such a person to a respectable parlour. But Miss Polsham was still confined, feverish, to her bed. She had not experienced Nick's masterful charm which Miss Olga had been subjected to in full measure.

For once I could not view his performance with jealous condemnation. I was too delighted with the result; that when he called to enquire how we invalids did, he was invited in and offered a glass of the precious Madeira. This he accepted with grave consideration, sipping it with reverence, as though conscious of the honour bestowed upon him.

'I think I have misjudged Mr Fox,' Miss Olga said, thoughtfully, to me. 'He proved himself to be very strong and capable that dreadful night Jane was taken from us, yet never in any way overstepped the bounds of good manners, where a less sensitive person might have been more overbearing, impatient, with the natural confusion and nervousness of us ladies. I believe it would be unchristian of me to taint the young man with his father's crime, when he is clearly a . . . gentleman.' A blush suffused her sallow cheeks and she added, hastily, 'Dr Barlow, whose opinion I value, also assures me that there could be no possible detriment to our reputation if Mr Fox chooses to call upon us. Rather to the contrary. Apparently, he is well thought of in his dealings about the town, an honest man, evidently, and a charitable one. Dr Barlow informs me that Mr Fox has subscribed most generous sums to several societies which provide the indigent and industrious poor with cheap winter coal, clothing and blankets. I believe he had gracious notes from both Lady Acland and Lady Northcott in consequence. And if Sir George Alperton, who comes from a very old and distinguished family, can see his way to becoming patron of Mr Fox's new establishment, then I feel it would be wrong of me to withhold the common courtesies due to someone held in high regard by people superior to myself.'

I agreed, gravely. 'My own experience with Mr Fox has shown him to be a man eminently courteous and honourable. As you know, he has settled my accounts for Reynard's with commendable swiftness. I believe that the prompt manner in which I have been able to pay my suppliers and contractors in consequence can only augur well for future business now that I have their trust.'

So the civilities were justified, maintained. I hugged to my heart what else I knew of Nick. The real Nicholas Fox. The vengeful, cunning, passionate man whom I loved and desired. Who, most importantly, loved and desired me. That knowledge alone enabled me to be content with so little – an exchange of glances as we sat speaking pleasant nothings in the parlour, a touch – trivial, accidental – in passing. In his eyes I saw reflected the same overpowering need as in my own. A hunger that gnawed and would not be assuaged, that drove him here to this old maids' parlour when he had a hundred pressing matters to attend to with Reynard's grand opening almost upon him.

I smiled to myself thinking of Susannah who must

be mortified at being cloistered in the country, in mourning for the sister-in-law she despised, when she might have been at the event that promised to outshine even the splendour of the Christmas balls.

Miss Olga and I had a private invitation to take tea at Reynard's and view the premises with a small group of selected guests, which was far more pleasing to me than having to jostle at the crowded opening and a source of great excitement to Miss Olga.

'There is no question! You cannot accept!' Miss Polsham rattled her lungs with a cough that sounded not a little forced. She was almost recovered but she refused to believe Dr Barlow when he pronounced her fit enough to go downstairs. 'We are a house of mourning. It would not be proper!'

Looking at her plump and petulant in her comfortable bed, the colour back in her cheeks, the empty tray denoting a greedily consumed luncheon, she seemed far more healthy now than Miss Olga and myself. We were washed out, weary with the broken nights that still continued. Miss Polsham was not one to suffer even the briefest bout of sleeplessness alone when she could have us dancing attendance to plump her pillows or remake the bed or fetch her a hot drink.

'We should not be long . . .'

'You will not go, Olga, and that is that! What would Papa have said? I will tell you, he would have been as shocked as I am. That you could leave your ailing sister to frequent an establishment where all manner of drunken riff-raff might ogle you—'

'Fanny! We are to meet Sir George and Lady Alperton privately. There is no question of drunken riff-raff!'

'You are being led astray by evil influences!' She glared at me. 'Since this young madam came to the house we have had nothing but disruption. Half the time she is running looseshod through the town about her own affairs when her place is here, with me. I have told you time and time again that your hand is not firm enough, Olga. Young people need strict discipline. It was one of dear Papa's strongest precepts. Laxity can only lead to self-will and vanity.'

'Joanna works hard and does not neglect her necessary duties here.'

'She clearly does, Olga. She is neglecting them now. Wanting to drag you off to enjoy yourself when I am so clearly in desperate need of attention.' Miss Polsham was beside herself with temper, her face as red as a turkey cock's. She played her trump card. 'I will not stand this neglect a moment longer. I shall write to her grandfather. Fetch me a pen and paper, instantly! I will put an end to Miss Joanna Howarth's roisterings.'

The ultimate threat, which might once have made me tremble in my shoes and which, from the triumphant glint in Miss Polsham's eye, was exactly the reaction she expected. Why then did I feel so calm? So indifferent?

'No, Fanny. I will not allow that.' Miss Olga's voice was firm.

'Olga! What can you mean?'

'You are being unfair.'

'Unfair to demand what is rightfully mine? Joanna's complete attention and devotion to duty?'

'She has brought more than cold duty to this house, Fanny. Perhaps you are too bound up in your ailments to notice the difference. There is a lightness about the place that has not been here since we were very small. I remember – and you must too, for you are the elder by eighteen months – laughter from that time when our own mama was alive. I remember sunshine in the house, pretty dresses and flowers. Even the furniture seemed like trapped sunshine with its golden gilding. It all disappeared when she died. The furniture was put away. It was as though . . .' she hesitated, frowning, searching her memory for tantalising glimpses of a time so long ago it had the quality of a dream. 'As though Papa and our stepmother needed to banish her completely. In case, perhaps, we made unsettling comparisons? Or was it because it was easier for them to rule by fear and harshness and we could not be allowed to believe there was a . . . a different, gentler, more loving way?' She shook her head, then said in a voice that trembled slightly, 'Fanny, things could have been so very different . . . these years, all wasted, when we have been trapped here. I have pondered this a great deal lately. I think that in what time is left to us we should not be afraid to . . . to remember Mama, who believed in love and kindness. And to admit into what remains of our lives the vigour, the enthusiasm, all the pleasure that youth . . . that Joanna will continue to bring. If we allow it.'

Miss Polsham stared at her sister in shock and disbelief. Then she fell back on the pillows with a shudder. 'I feel quite faint. You know I cannot stand disagreements.'

'Because you will brook no opinion but your own,' Miss Olga said, tartly. Then with the air of someone voicing a discovery, 'You are exactly like Papa in that. And in the matter of allowing nothing to interfere with your own comfort.'

'That I should live to hear you speak so slightingly of your own flesh and blood,' Miss Polsham moaned. 'Quick! My smelling salts, Joanna. And pour me a glass of water, though I do not know if I shall have the strength to drink it.'

Miss Olga caught my arm. 'Your smelling salts are on the table at your bedside, Fanny. As is the carafe of water. You have only to reach out your hand. Perhaps you may regain your strength the quicker if you

421

wait upon yourself for a while. Joanna and I have other, more pressing, matters to attend to. When you are more composed, you may like to venture downstairs, as Dr Barlow has suggested. Please ring if you feel able.'

As soon as she was beyond the door, the enormity of what she had done set her quivering. 'I . . . I have never spoken to Fanny like that before,' she whispered, her expression anguished. 'We have never had a true argument over anything.'

'Because you have always deferred to her,' I said softly.

'I have never liked to upset her for fear her delicate constitution might be overset, but today I was carried away. I do not know what overcame me. We are sisters . . . so close. The shock might truly be too much. Perhaps I had better go back . . . Perhaps she is right and I am being selfish.'

'You are not the selfish one,' I said gently. 'You have devoted your whole life to caring for your sister. You are to be praised, not condemned.'

'Do you think so?' She was desperate for reassurance.

'If we give Miss Polsham a little time to reflect on how lucky she is to be so devotedly looked after, then she may realise you deserve to be allowed a little recreation outside these four walls.'

We tiptoed away like conspirators. Downstairs, Miss Olga busied herself setting out paper, pen and ink, recovering herself in these small, familiar activities, then suddenly blurting out, 'I would like you to know, Joanna, that I meant what I said to my sister. This house is a different place since you came to it. That is all I wish to say on the matter, but you may take it that no word of complaint will go to your grandfather.' She cleared her throat in embarrassment. 'Now, when I have penned a note to Mr Fox accepting his invitation, I should like you to come up with me to the attic. There is something I wish to search for among my mother's things.'

We made several trips up to the attic that afternoon. Mary Ann, coming in to light the parlour candles, stared in surprise at Miss Olga seated on a gilt chair which we had placed opposite Mr Polsham's across the hearth. Her taper twinked light off unfamiliar objects on the mantel. An enamelled box with a design of white peacock feathers, a pair of blue and gilt Staffordshire candlesticks and, finest of all, a magnificent green and gold potpourri jar, decorated with tiny birds and trees. 'Mama's wedding present, I understand, from one of Grandpapa's Guernsey captains. It is Sèvres. *Vaisseau à mât* I believe it is called as its shape has the likeness of a ship with a mast. My stepmother thought it sinfully ornate and could not bear to look at it. I was always sad that it had to be banished to the attic.'

We sat at our darning that evening in the same meagre candle and firelight that was all Miss Olga allowed. Yet it seemed that the room was not so dim as usual.

Miss Olga's glance strayed often to the mantel. I had the fancy that something golden in the fine glaze of the potpourri jar reflected on her contented face and lightened the parlour's bulky shadows.

Three days later Miss Olga and I climbed into Nick's carriage and were whisked to Reynard's.

Tomorrow the doors would admit the cream of Exeter society. We should read about it in the paper: the eminent guests, the excellence of the quadrille band, the wonderfully dramatic readings from *Hamlet* and *Macbeth* by Mr Macready fresh from his acclaimed season at the theatre, the performance of the glee singers, the lavish supper. For a moment I envied those who had the right of entry and who were not restrained by ties of mourning.

But I thought no more of it once I was inside. I felt only pride and delight.

In December I had felt well satisfied with all that I had achieved at Reynard's. Yet the rooms then had been echoing, cold and empty. Now there were blazing coals in every grate. A bustle of liveried servants scurried about preparing for tomorrow's opening. It was not merely a building with decorated walls and furnished spaces, but something that lived and breathed, that had life. And, as if the gloomy January afternoon had been specially ordered, the chandeliers were lit early to add an extra shower of brilliance and sparkle.

If I had created Reynard's public face, Nick was its beating heart. His vigour and enthusiasm seemed almost to crackle in the air as he led us from room to room and finally back to where tea awaited us in the dining room.

He looked devilishly handsome in a dark green cutaway coat, with a lighter, revered, silk waistcoat underneath. Tight white nankeen trousers curved to his strong calves and emphasised the length of his legs. His dark hair was meticulously groomed, curling smoothly back from the high stiff collar of his shirt. He was showing himself off as much as his establishment.

We were an exclusive party. A brace of aldermen and their wives, Sir George and Lady Alperton, Mr Thomas Sparkes the banker, Mr Cornforth the lawyer. Miss Olga was a little breathless at being surrounded by so many gentlemen, but Lady Alperton, a large comfortable talkative woman with an extraordinary quantity of blue plumes nodding from her bonnet, swept her along with a stream of kindly comment until she had recovered enough to respond.

I was not allowed to hover in anyone's shadow, Nick

saw to that. Nor did I wish to. This was not Roselawn and I had learned so much in the intervening months. Not least that if word was to be spread about my ambitions as a lady decorator, then I had to be bold. Shrinking violets were for the drawing room. To impress prospective clients I had to put myself forward as a showier bloom. To this end, my elegant slate-grey dress and mantle were now set off with a new and much more dashing Spanish hat in the rich purple called amaranthine. The effect with my height and my red hair, which I had pinned more loosely than usual, was dramatic and startling. For the first time in my life I turned heads and it gave me a strange sense of power to see the appreciative alertness of the gentlemen, the sharper, more critical wariness in the eyes of the ladies.

That Nick was determined that I should gain every possible advantage from this afternoon was outrageously clear from the start. One of the aldermen had a puddingy wife, given to an over-abundance of gushing compliments. She fell into a positive ecstasy over the curtains in one of the small rooms – and straight into Nick's all too ready hands. 'That shimmering gold effect is exactly what I would wish to achieve in my music room. Pray, what material is it?' Nick smiled so charmingly, so steadily upon her that from her heightened colour and the fluttering of her sparse lashes, it was evident she thought herself to have made a dazzling conquest.

He said, shrugging, his tone a caress, 'I am a mere male, Mrs Acton, helpless in these matters. I have been fortunate to be able to call upon the talents of Miss Howarth.' He acknowledged me with a polite but distant nod as though he could scarcely bear to withdraw his attention from the damnably fine woman fate had thrown in his path. 'You will know, being at the heart

425

of Exeter's lively society, that Miss Howarth is skilled in the subtle arts of the decorator.'

'Oh . . . indeed,' she agreed, with an uncertain glance in my direction. She had clearly never heard of me before today.

'She is exceptionally talented in this perceptive and delicate art which is shared by so many of your sex.' His admiring glance indicated that she, the pudding, was naturally included in this selected band. 'I was fortunate to obtain Miss Howarth's services as she is much in demand by forward-thinking individuals who wish to bring a modern and fashionable flavour to their houses.' He lowered his voice. 'Why, Lady Nugent whose recent masked ball at Teignmouth was quite a sensation – you may have read an account of it in the *Flying Post* – is considering a consultation with Miss Howarth. I speak in confidence, naturally.'

'Oh, I would not breathe a word, Mr Fox,' exclaimed the pudding, already anticipating the pleasure of passing on this interesting snippet to her friends and acquaintances.

'I say this merely to explain my good fortune in wresting a promise from Miss Howarth that she would defer her many other projects so that Reynard's might be put ready for the date I had planned.'

The fluency of these untruths held me between shock and the giggles. I had not even heard of Lady Nugent, let alone her masked ball. As for the 'many projects' I was supposed to have in hand, I only hoped nobody pressed me to name one.

Nick turned his helpless expression on me then. Except that I could see the amusement flickering in his eyes, I too might have been taken in.

'Miss Howarth, perhaps you would be so good as to explain to Mrs Acton the exact nature of the curtains.'

'Certainly,' I said crisply, keeping a tight hold on a

threatening chuckle. 'They are of merino damask with a lining of glazed stuff. You will see that I have used the same damask in the upholstery of the chairs. The colour is picked up again in the pattern of the Axminster carpet, though the overall effect there is green rather than gold . . .'

When I stopped speaking I realised that everyone had paused to listen. After that it seemed accepted that I should give a short commentary on each room. There was much lively questioning and my opinion was, flatteringly, sought and reflected upon. Did I intend that the carpets should be removed, as was customary in many households, for coolness and freshness in summer? Did I believe that the present craze for gas lighting in the streets would ever be extended to private houses, considering the recent unfortunate experience at the theatre when a leaking pipe caused a dreadful effluvia throughout the building and decided the management in favour of reverting to patent lamps and wax candles? What was my opinion of fringes, of machine-made lace? Were elaborate pelmets truly out of fashion?

By the time Miss Olga and I climbed into Nick's carriage in the twilight for the journey home, I was as wrung out as an actor must be after a performance. For performance it had been. Reynard's was my stage and I had been called upon to give an entertainment for which, I hoped, reward would come in due course. There was already a hint of it.

Mr Sparkes had murmured of a widowed lady, recently out of mourning, who had only the other day consulted him on the financial aspects of a planned move from a quiet country property to Exeter's livelier surroundings. 'She is without a relative in the world and I feel she might benefit from the advice of a capable lady such as yourself. Would you allow me to mention your name, Miss Howarth?' I would indeed.

Mrs Acton, delicately skirting the question of Lady Nugent, was tenaciously curious on the manner of furnishings favoured by the nobility. Her daughter, it seemed, was to marry a young man with a connection – remote but nevertheless lifting her socially into an excitingly elevated sphere – of the Duke of Somerset. It was so important, was it not, that her fine new establishment at Heavitree should be laid out in perfect taste in case His Grace should ever deign to honour the house with his presence?

I thought quickly and imaginatively, then showered Mrs Acton with a cascade of glittering possibilities which greatly increased her bewilderment. It was the right moment to present her with my card, hint vaguely of the private commissions I was presently engaged upon – at which she gave a knowing and conspiratorial nod – but assure her that I would always find time to help and advise any genteel persons of my acquaintance who wished to place themselves in the forefront of fashion.

The seeds were laid. I hoped they would grow into sturdy plants. As the carriage pulled away up Southernhay, I was still borne up by the exhilaration of being flattered, of knowing that my contribution to Reynard's success was not inconsiderable.

I was looking out of the window unseeing, scarcely hearing Miss Olga as she related all that Lady Alperton had said to her, when the carriage gave a violent swerve. Another equippage dashed past, taking up most of the road. I caught my breath at the closeness. A roar and clatter of wheels and hooves, a white flash of a horse's wild eye, a glimpse of the grinning driver wielding his whip in the juddering light of the carriage lanterns, and it was past us and Miss Olga was crying, 'Heaven forfend! Whatever was that?'

'Oh, some young blood showing himself off to be a reckless fool,' I said grimly.

'Reckless indeed!' Miss Olga cried. 'He will kill somebody if he goes about the roads at such speeds.'

I clamped my teeth over the words that sprung to my lips, that the man, in my eyes, was already guilty of murder, though there was not a court in the land who would convict a poor bereaved widower whose wife, like so many, had died from the natural and hazardous process of childbearing.

Blandford Pascoe had, it seemed, already tired of playing the grieving widower. He was back in Exeter and, if I was not mistaken, heading for Reynard's and a reunion with his good friend Nicholas Fox.

My fears were confirmed the next morning. Blandford paid us a visit, swaggering in on a waft of sickly pomade which mingled unpleasantly with the heavy odour of the cigar he lit without so much as a by your leave. He would not sit, or take refreshment. He had come, he said, merely in the capacity of messenger, to pass on letters from his father and sister.

This duty done, he stood with his back to the fire, coat-tails spread, ignoring Miss Olga, fixing his pale glance on me.

'I tender my congratulations, Miss Howarth, on the fine decorations at Reynard's. And to think I played a small part, though I am sure not overlooked or forgotten by your charming self, in assisting you to your triumph, by persuading Cousin Olga here that you should be given your head. Quite the bold and clever miss you are turning out to be, eh?'

I controlled a sharp answer with an effort and said, turning the conversation with chilly politeness, 'I thought, sir, that you intended to remain in the country until Easter.'

'My father will. And Susannah, at his insistence,

429

though she rails, as I do, against the bumpkins she must cultivate if she is to have any social acquaintance at all.'

'With so recent a bereavement in the family,' I said sharply, 'I should have thought that the least of her concerns. Or yours.'

His smile was a brief, unpleasant baring of his discoloured teeth. 'On the contrary, Miss Howarth. I find the company of the Daveys, the Aggetts and their ilk a veritable drain upon my constitution. I need, in my time of grief, to be distracted by more congenial pursuits than countrified dinners followed by the caterwaulings of the Aggett girls performing duets upon the piano and fiddle.'

'And what of Ruth? Is she well? Have you brought her to Exeter?'

'Certainly not. She has her nurse. Susannah is there to oversee her. A child of that age needs nothing more.'

'I would not dismiss a father's love so lightly. Ruth must greatly miss her mother. Surely she would appreciate visits from her papa.'

'Then she will have to do without.' His eyes mocked my concern. 'Any daughter of mine must learn early to adapt to the will and wishes of her father. I have always told the nurse to be as strict as need be, though my wife over-indulged her whenever she had chance. Now, without her mother's undermining influence, the child will grow up docile and disciplined. I maintain that these are the finest traits a father can encourage in his female children so that when the time is ripe, they may be married off advantageously without the risk of disobedience, or kept at home to look after him in his old age, whichever is most suitable.'

'That is a calculating and unloving attitude, sir, towards your own flesh and blood!'

'But practical.' He threw the wet stub of the cigar

on the fire where it hissed and flared and died to black ash. 'However you might rail against it, my dear Joanna, you must know in your heart that it is a woman's lot to be submissive to a man and to acknowledge him to be her master.' His gaze slithered down from my face to my neck and lingered insolently on the swell of my breasts. 'My daughter is luckier than many, in that this lesson will be learned early. Too many grown women foster the notion that they are man's equal.' He sighed, licked his tongue slowly round his lips. 'Which makes their inevitable humbling all the harder for them to bear . . .'

The taint of his cigar hung about the room long after he had gone. As for the pictures raised by his unpleasant ideas on child-raising, they spun in my head for the rest of the day, fuelling my guilt and frustration.

If Blandford chose to keep Ruth secluded in the country, there was nothing I could do about it. Ruth was his child, to be disposed how and where he wished.

And it was no use at all wishing that, lulled by firelight and friendship, I had not made my promise to Jane. I had. The words could not be taken back and the weight of them seemed to hang round my neck like a necklace of lead.

Chapter Sixteen

The days lengthened. Along the garden path pale snowdrops gave way to the sturdy spires of purple and white crocus. Before February was out, daffodils, early because of the mild winter, were a blaze of dancing yellow under the fat-budded apple trees. The old damson threw out a frosting of white blossom amid which the blackbirds fought noisy territorial battles. A pair of robins nested in the thicket of winter jasmine growing against the privy wall and sparrows scrambled and squabbled in the house eaves. The promise of the season surged in every hedgerow and wood in the surrounding countryside, in the moist, plum-red furrows of newly turned earth, in the deep wooded valleys, the distant green hills. A promise that drew Miss Olga out to her beloved garden in every spare moment, there to hoe and prune and sow the precious seeds hoarded from last year's harvest.

My own harvest had already ripened to a different cycle.

The widow of Mr Sparkes's acquaintance, Mrs Eleanor Barton, asked me to wait upon her in the house she had leased near Bedford Circus. She was a willowy, serene, childless woman of about forty who had been married to a man considerably older than herself. He was a nabob who had made a fortune in Bengal and returned to Devon when the Indian climate had broken his health in order to find a suitable wife to care for him in his retirement. Introduced by a mutual acquaintance, Miss Eleanor Livesey, the daughter of the late Reverend Livesey, a country parson, was a most harmonious choice.

She had been a companion and housekeeper to her father until his death after a lingering illness. She was quiet, conscientious, practical in all domestic matters, experienced as a sick nurse and deeply grateful to be rescued from the prospect of eking out her small annuity with fine sewing which was all her father, over-generous to others, had bequeathed to her. So, with gratitude and respect, she had devoted herself tirelessly to her husband. After his years in the crowds and heat and colour and noise of the East he wanted nothing more than the tranquillity and isolation of a bleak and lonely valley at the moor's edge and a restful companion who would not irritate him with intrusive chatter or demands of her own.

Mrs Barton had sheltered him in his growing reclusiveness, nursed him through frequent bouts of fever, run his household with calm efficiency and never once hinted that she felt lonely or frightened in such a remote and unfrequented place. In death, as in life, she had respected him. She had lived out the time of her mourning in the dismal, rambling Jacobean house he had furnished with all manner of bizarre curios and mementoes of his life in the East. But now, her dues having been paid in full, and with a considerable inheritance as her reward, she had decided that after all the years of devotion to other people, the time had come to further her own interests.

'And do you know, Miss Howarth, I am not entirely sure what those interests might be. It is sad, is it not, to be in such a case?' she said cheerfully. 'I shall have to try so many things before I can decide in what manner

I wish to spend my declining days. Think of it. I shall have to put myself to visit every exhibition that comes to Exeter, to attend all manner of lectures, to read books on many subjects – indeed quite frivolous novels of which my papa or my husband, being superior and upright persons, would never have approved – to patronise the theatre ... So very tiresome, but necessary, I suppose.' Her smile broadened. 'And I must begin with this house. I have no mind to carry the past with me into this unknown future, beyond, naturally, one or two small mementoes of my father and my husband. Things that I may look at from time to time to remind me of those two persons in whose worthily solemn shadow I spent so many years.' She sent me a mischievous glance. 'I fancy from the splendidly bold and frivolous hat you are wearing, Miss Howarth, that worthy solemnity does not figure strongly in your character, for which I am indubitably grateful. It gives me leave to believe that we shall do very well together.'

Mrs Barton was a delight to work with. She had a child's eagerness to see, to learn, to understand, coupled with an engagingly dry sense of humour. She had clear ideas of what she wanted. 'Warmth and light and comfort above all and no dark corners in which might lurk collections of poor, sad, dead butterflies or stuffed animals or dusty tomes in Latin and Greek. And I have always felt that multi-armed goddesses and gods with elephant heads should never have been removed from the places where they are venerated in the first place, as their only function in these cold climes seems to be to frighten the maids out of their wits.'

Mrs Acton's daughter was of a different mettle. She was a fickle miss of no great intelligence but much self-importance.

'Pray, Miss Howarth, understand that I will tolerate

nothing about me but that which is the best and finest. My nature is such that any imperfection in my surroundings is an agony to my sensitive nerves. My fiancé, Mr Cutler, being eager to set our life together on the most harmonious footing, is anxious that I shall have my way in everything. Are you not, dearest?'

'In everything,' Mr Cutler replied, in a pale voice.

I quickly discovered that two words seemed to be the limit of his conversation and these were usually emitted to mark his full agreement with everything Miss Acton proposed. Miss Acton proposed a very great deal and was just as likely to change her mind completely within the hour, the day or, worst of all, the week.

I dreaded the arrival of a note from Miss Acton. She was insistent on having carpet fitted to cover the floors of the downstairs rooms, then, 'I have had a sleepless night thinking of the hygienic aspects. All manner of creetures might be harbered. I have quite decided that a square of carpett of a size to allow a generess area of polished owk surround to be visible is best. And in the bedchambers only small carpets that might be taken up and beeten daily . . .' Two days later she had changed her mind again. 'Think of the danger to any guest if these small carpetts should slide underfoot. My nerves truly could not stand the wurry of it. I think there shall be no carpetts at all. However, I must insist on some generess quantity of carpetting being retayned in the main bedchamber for I am too prone to take a chill in winter otherwise.'

So it must be bare polished boards upstairs in the guest chambers and cold comfort for any chilly naked foot venturing upon them in winter. It was the same with colours. Blue was 'so perfect, so charming, my most favrite shade which you must use wherever possible', only to be declared, after several nights of torment on Miss Acton's part, to be 'prone to give one of the hedache if it is too much in evidence'. So we went through a rainbow of colours before once again deciding that perhaps blue would predominate after all.

Then, of a sudden, Miss Acton, growing bored with household furbishment, was diverted by the swift advance of her wedding and the myriad worrying details about her gown, her trousseau, the wedding breakfast and the invitations which she must instantly attend to if all was to be perfect. It was a great relief to be set arbitrarily aside upon my promise that the house would be as magnificent as I could make it by the time the happy couple returned in June from their post-nuptial tour of the Continent. With a sympathetic thought towards the dressmakers and milliners about to be tormented, I began the pleasurable task of sorting and selecting the finest pieces from the vast quantity of furniture Mr Cutler had inherited from a spinster aunt and which were already stored and shrouded in the smart new outbuildings of the stuccoed villa.

Those early months of 1824 were full of satisfaction and promise. I felt within myself a flowering of confidence. Each day held fresh challenge – some difficulty with a supplier, a workman to be reprimanded for cutting corners, a bolt of material proving to be seriously flawed so that an alternative must be sought, estimates to be drawn up, justified, discussed.

I did not shrink from any of it and I found firmness, plain speaking and persistence in all my dealings to be very valuable. I also learned when a conciliatory word served better than confrontation and to judge the moments when it was best to hold my tongue altogether. And all the while I had a growing awareness of the niche I was carving for myself and the need to present a self-assured face to the world. A shrinking violet, as I had realised previously, could not be my style.

Just as that first glimpse of the Pembroke table at

Roselawn had provided the key to a particular method of working, so my extravagant Spanish hat served to inspire my methods of dressing.

I decided my dress must be simple to the point of starkness in muted shades of slate, deep sage green and dark chocolate. No girlish pastels and never a frill or flounce to break the lines of gown or mantle.

There was no disguising the colour and wilful springiness of my hair, so I gave up trying unsuccessfully to bundle it away under a bonnet. Instead, I showed it off boldly, complementing its liveliness with the most dazzling hats ordered from Miss Sprigget, a young milliner recommended to me by Mrs Chadwick.

She was a talented young woman who had learned her trade from her widowed mother who had recently died. She was, in turn, teaching two younger sisters the rudiments of the trade and struggling to support several younger siblings. She had none of the fixed ideas and pompous manner of many older milliners, a wonderful eye for colour and form and pure magic in fingers that could, with a length of plain satin ribbon, a handful of seed pearls, a scrap of tulle, turn an ordinary hat or bonnet into a thing of great originality and style.

The total effect was dramatic. The dark colours and plainness of my dress made me look taller, more slender and certainly older than I was. The dashing hats, confections of straw or silk or gauze, combined with my red hair to look all the more striking against the muted tones of the rest of my attire.

It is always hard to see oneself as others do, but I fancy that my image grew as a somewhat daring innovator in independence. Perhaps people did not totally approve of a young woman setting herself up in a position traditionally held by male upholsterers, but then I was not exactly an upholsterer, was I? I could almost hear the drawing-room chitchat.

'A lady decorator? Do you think that is quite the thing? I understand she is related to some squire in the South Hams. An old family, to be sure, yet she herself comes from the north, where perhaps there is more freedom in these matters. One must certainly admire her forthrightness and I have heard nothing derogatory about her work, on the contrary, but she goes about town in a very bold fashion and looks, well, quite . . . different to other young women. I wonder if it sets quite the best example to our daughters, though I confess I have thought of consulting her over the nature of some alterations I propose to the guest wing. In confidence, my dear, I wish to set those patronising cousins of mine by the ears when they visit me next. I would show them that we are as forward thinking in Devon as ever they are in Highgate . . . Perhaps I shall send her a note and arrange a meeting when Amanda and Lizzie are not at home . . .'

So the notes arrived in a persistent trickle that showed no signs of drying up. I had more work on hand than I could comfortably cope with alone. Domestic arrangements would have to be altered.

Miss Olga's jaw dropped.

'You wish me to take over your accounts? But surely, Joanna, I am not experienced—'

'You are just the person,' I said. 'What does it need more than a head for figures, common sense and honesty, all of which you have in good measure? You have managed the household affairs since your father died and never allowed a debt to accumulate. I should like my business accounts to be treated in just such a straightforward fashion, for I am afraid they are in a most lamentable state at present.' I flourished a handful of assorted papers from the heap I was trying to sort on the dining table and said, with feeling, 'I shall smother under all this paper if I do not get it into some sort of order. Oh, please say that you will, Miss Olga, for I would rather have you than any stranger.'

She wavered. 'Of course, I should like to help, but . . .'

Forgetting to be cool and businesslike, I cried with excitement, 'Oh, Miss Olga, I do believe I am set to be a success. I am making more money than I could ever have dreamt possible and have the prospect of much more, but I do need some assistance. You see, as I go on I find I am fully taken up with the artistic and creative side. I am beginning to neglect the day-to-day running. I entirely miscalculated an estimate the other day because I was rushed and shall have to bear the loss, and that I cannot afford to do. I need someone practical and reliable at my elbow who can attend to the accounting ledgers and the bills. Who better than you?'

'Well . . .'

'Oh, you will! Miss Olga, I shall be eternally grateful.' I enfolded her in an impulsive hug.

Pink-cheeked, she said, tartly, 'There is no need for an unseemly display, Joanna.' Nevertheless she began inspecting the papers on the table, exclaiming, 'Why, this account is dated February! How could you be so lax! You may well be talented and clever, but bear in mind the parable of the house built on sand. I see that despite my better judgment, I must involve myself.'

'I cannot tell you how grateful I am.'

'Save your thanks until you see if I can make head or tail of this muddle.'

'And I have also been wondering,' I said, more tentatively, 'if I might use part of the attic. I have so many sample cards and drawings that must be kept that my room is becoming very crowded.'

'I was about to speak to you on that very subject,' she said, frowning. 'My sister is not best pleased to see so much evidence of this . . . this occupation of yours about the house, especially as you tend to be careless in the manner of the disposal of your effects. Only this morning she almost fell over a bundle of velvets you had left lying about.'

'Those velvets were missing when I got to Alphington!'

'They were, for some unaccountable reason, residing on the lower landing.'

'I must have dropped them when I was carrying my samples downstairs. I do apologise.'

'I have returned them to your room, though where to find space to place them was a problem. Indeed, child, I am in some confusion as to how you reach your bed through all that clutter. I have the greatest dread that the tide of paper and materials will swamp the house like the Exe in flood. The notion of the attic had already occurred to me. I think we must investigate.'

Whereupon she rang for Mary Ann and marched ahead of us up the stairs.

Within the hour Mary Ann and I had hauled back the lumber to leave a good floor space. We left a few useful items. A battered but solid table, a pair of cane-seated chairs and a five-branched pewter candelabrum that would furnish a good light.

'My studio, Miss Olga,' I said, with satisfaction. 'See, if I throw dust covers over those boxes they make a level surface to lay out the samples and sample cards and sketching papers neatly. Reference books and ledgers will have to be stacked in that corner for now, but I will ask Harry Drew to set up some shelving on the wall there. The table can sit this side to catch what light there is by day from the little window.' I beamed at Miss Olga. 'Now we may both work here in privacy and Miss Polsham need never be disturbed.'

Miss Polsham was less and less vociferous as the days passed.

Lily put it succinctly. 'Nowt for her to bellyache about, is there? She's warm, comfortable and well fed, 'as lots of attention from Mary Ann. What more could t'owd besom want?'

There was that, of course. We never lacked a fire in the cool spring days and meals had taken on a new and flavoursome aspect. The house was undeniably more comfortable now. We could have a generous blaze in every necessary fire grate for I had placed a regular order for best coals. Lily, on nodding terms with all the servants in the terrace, had struck up a friendship with the fat cook of the retired old sea captain next door, who was glad of the chance to pass on knowledge gained in a lifetime of service in grander houses. The captain, she complained, liked everything plain and simple.

'He'm set on mutton chops, boiled greens and rice puddens. 'Tes terrible frustratin'. Never gets chance to show off my queen o' puddens, or my orange cream wi' brandy. But you gets that book o' yourn, young Lily. I'll give you the receipts an' you've only to knock if you wants a' 'and wi' the makin'. I'm stretched none since missus passed away, wi' only one quiet gentleman to please.'

The plain, hearty food Lily had learned to make now took on a subtler quality as, in her quick way, she absorbed the methods acquired over the years by her generous friend. Even Miss Olga looked forward to some new culinary achievement – a spicy sauce, a savoury tart, a light-as-air pudding, daintily presented – at dinner or supper.

But the change in Miss Polsham, I guessed, was

more due to the fact that for the first time in their life together, Miss Olga no longer meekly acquiesced with her sister's wishes. She had defied her over the visit to Reynard's, and had insisted on receiving Nicholas in the parlour as though he were a true gentleman, even allowing him the honour of sitting in Mr Polsham's sacred chair. She had refused point blank to allow any word of complaint about me to be sent to my grandfather. All these things had given Miss Polsham pause to consider her position. The balance in the household had swung away from her. If she did not accept these changes, there was every likelihood that her sister might choose to draw further away from her, perhaps ignore her altogether.

Miss Olga not only encouraged me but had become herself more outward looking. She went out more, indeed she was mistress, now, of the meaningful hint.

'Such a bright afternoon. I could quite be persuaded to take a stroll, though I really have so many pressing duties,' or, 'It seems such a waste to hire a hackney coach for one person, though of course you must if the rain shows no sign of letting up . . .'

She was particularly taken with Mrs Barton's house, the plan of which was not unlike her own, yet so different in atmosphere. She saw the house at different stages, from its somewhat neglected and shabby beginnings to the warm, airy, comfortable home it became. Once Mrs Barton knew we lived but a few moments' walk away, she warmly invited Miss Olga to call whenever she wished.

Miss Olga found Mrs Barton as engaging as I did and her good humour refreshing, especially as she insisted on living on the premises while the painters and carpenters worked round her, which was no comfortable matter.

'It is entirely selfish of me to stay, I assure you,' she

insisted. 'How could I leave my dear house to the mercies of these rough men when I fell in love with it the moment I saw it? I could sooner have left my respected husband in his final hours. No, I think it is the greatest pleasure to watch how it returns to its former elegance by the day. Besides,' she added blithely, as a tiny girl staggered in under a tray weighted with cakes and pastries, 'I have to keep a sharp eye on my little maid that she does not flee back to the poorhouse whence I removed her. I fear she finds me shockingly lacking in the stern methods employed there. Her constitution might never recover. I must regularly threaten her with a whipping and a diet of bread and gruel in order to encourage her to stay. Is that not true, Matilda?'

'Yes, ma'am. I mean, no, ma'am,' Matilda giggled as she carefully put down the tray.

'You see, the child is undoubtedly still confused by the unfortunate change in her circumstances. When you bring the teapot, Matilda, pray do not weep at your ill luck in fetching up here with me, condemned to sleeping on a feather mattress and eating a hearty dinner every day. You might dilute the tea, which would be most impolite to my guests.'

The maid went off still in fits of giggles. Mrs Barton beamed. I chuckled. Even Miss Olga smiled broadly.

They were pleasant visits which I regretfully had to abandon once I became busier, though I was pleased when Miss Olga began, independently, to make her own calls upon Mrs Barton. Then, greatly daring – and after a few acrimonious exchanges with Miss Polsham – she invited Mrs Barton back to take tea with her and her sister. I was relieved when I returned home to find that she had even managed to charm Miss Polsham who had threatened to retire to her room should Mrs Barton outstay her welcome. But she had not gone.

'An', d'you know, Miss Jo,' Lily said, wonderingly, 'Mary Ann swears she heard Miss Polsham laugh. And more'n once an' all. It must be the first time since 'er was a babby. Reckon we must look to see if 'er face 'as cracked wi' the effort.'

I believe, in those months, I was as happy as I ever had been in Exeter. Only when Mr Chadwick's occasional letters came, only when I wrote back, did nostalgic images of Falconwood seep treacherously into my mind to unsettle me. But Grandfather seemed not to be pushing Ben beyond his limits, which was a relief, and Ben had become accustomed to the little amount of socialising that Grandfather insisted upon.

Through all these busy days, like a constant singing note under my thoughts, my actions, my words, ran my love for Nicholas.

I scarcely saw him. I could not walk into Reynard's now as though it was my right. That time was past. I was a visitor, calling upon Mrs Fitch, slipping quietly through the private door at the back, reached through the central yard and up the stairs to her comfortable room at the foot of the narrower stair which led to the maids' attic rooms. Her windows overlooked the yard. The menservants were housed in rooms on the other side of the stables where Caleb had his quarters. Between them, they maintained the scrupulous respectability that Nick insisted upon.

'There must be no hint of lax behaviour. It is all too easy for an establishment to gain a bad reputation which is not easily got rid of. Slovenly, dishonest servants are rightly seen as a symptom of uncaring, slovenly and dishonest employers. And remember this. Once any member of this club, or his guests, enters the premises, they must be welcomed with a smile and treated with civility no matter how rude or inconsiderate they may be. Though one hopes that with such impeccable, willing service, the excellent food and wine

445

obtainable at such reasonable prices and the favourable air of calm comfort in the house, there will be few grievances and complaints.'

Mrs Fitch had settled energetically to her new role with the maids, rosy-cheeked young girls from the country mostly, some of them away from home for the first time.

'They all seem good girls. If they do their work well and keep to the house rules, then all I ask in return is that they say their prayers each night, go to church or chapel each Sunday and don't let their heads be turned by city ways.'

I visited Mrs Fitch, listened to Mrs Fitch, talked to Mrs Fitch, but it was news of Nicholas, a glimpse of Nicholas I yearned for.

Chance encounters were rare these days. His concentration, his hopes were set upon Reynard's. He was up before the maids and to bed only after the gaming-room door was closed behind the last player, and all the hours in between he was busy about the place, for nothing must go wrong in these early days and if by chance it did, he must be on hand to put it right.

Mrs Fitch's room was a few mere yards from Nick's. But he was seldom in the private quarters and then only to snatch a moment's respite or to settle out some back-scenes problem.

I went at the quietest times, in the morning, always hopeful, often disappointed. When I did see him, we were never alone and he was in a hurry and in consequence disappointingly polite and distant.

Once only was it different.

I was hastening up the back stair quite early, and he was running down, his long legs taking the stairs two at a time. I stopped short. He halted several steps above me. The stair was windowless. The outside door below was closed, the only light filtering from the door opening onto the floor above.

I caught my breath, suddenly bereft of air, bereft of words.

He came softly, slowly down towards me. I watched him with a joy and longing in me that was surely as fierce as that felt by a starving soul set before a banquet, my whole body urgent with the pleasure and pain of it.

He looked weary, the dimness accentuating the hard, handsome lines and shadows of his face. His rough black hair was untidy, his chin dark with stubble. He wore no coat, only a crumpled white shirt open at the neck to show a vee of smooth pale skin, an unbuttoned dark waistcoat over it, trousers that had seen better days.

'Joanna,' he said. It was no more than a whisper.

He came slowly down to my level. We stared at each other wordlessly. Then he sighed, stepped down another stair and very gently, like an exhausted child, laid his head against my breast.

His arms slid round my waist. I closed my eyes and let my fingers slide in among the tousled, black curls. I could smell the muskily warm male scent of his body, feel the palms of his hands, one above the other against my spine, the pressure of his cheek against my breast. Yet there was a curious innocence about it, a need to comfort and be comforted, given and taken with deep, quiet understanding.

So we stood.

And the moment when it became other was clear and natural also. When his head turned and I felt the heat of his breath piercing through the silk of my bodice and the lawn of my chemise to the deep, hidden cleft between my breasts. When his hands moved down my thighs and the slate-grey folds of my skirt crumpled under his fingers and my whole body leaned, yearning and seeking, to his touch.

'Oh, my dearest Jo,' he said. His voice was so achingly sad that it doused the heat of my desire like water dashed on a blaze. 'This cannot be. You deserve better.'

His lifted his head and straightened and when I would have caught him back he imprisoned my hands on his own.

'No,' he said gently. 'This nonsense must end . . . all that has happened between us . . . I have been thoughtless and selfish.' He shook his head as if to clear it. 'Forgive me, my wits are addled. I cannot remember when last I was abed before four in the morning.'

'Forgive? Nick there is nothing to forgive! Why, that would be to cheapen what we feel!'

He looked at me for a long moment. The sadness was still there, yet it seemed something harder, more resolute veiled his eyes. When he spoke it was brusquely and without emotion.

'What you imagine you feel is your own affair. Do not ever make the mistake of crediting me with similar emotions.'

'But you . . . you care for me! I know it and I lo—'

His hand clamped over my mouth. His eyes were two grey flints. 'Do not say the words. Do not even think them! That way lies pain and disappointment. Do you hear me, Joanna? Whatever . . . weakness I have displayed in the past, you must forget it. It will not happen again. I have nothing to offer you. Now or in the future.'

I tore his hand from my mouth. 'You cannot mean that!' I gasped.

Steadily, deliberately, he said, 'There is no room for you in my life. Understand this and you will save yourself much anguish. And someday when you are happily settled with a good sensible husband and a brood of children about your skirts, you will thank me for what I do today.'

I was beside myself with pain and rage. 'How dare you tell me what I must feel and think and do! Who are you to know that I can dismiss what I know to be true so lightly! You know the truth in your own heart, but you prefer to lie to yourself . . . to me . . . to deny your feelings.'

He shrugged. 'You have a right to be angry. I admit I might have misled you into believing that you held some attraction for me beyond the ordinary, which was wrong of me. But in the circles in which I have previously moved . . . well, such flirtatious advances are not taken seriously. They are merely a pleasurable way of filling a few idle moments.'

'It was not like that!'

'You see, I quite forgot that you are not a woman of the world. Such . . . dalliance . . . in more sophisticated society is but a frivolous, inconsequential thing. My dear girl, you have taken a few kisses and caresses far too seriously. Treat the whole episode as a lesson learned. I am not the man for you. I never was. You will realise that in time and be grateful.' He flourished a sketchy bow. 'Pressing matters await me. The chef, superb in culinary activities, is extraordinary in the number of people he offends with his sharp tongue. I must settle an argument between him and his assistant before kitchen cleavers begin to fly.' He ran lithely down the remaining stairs.

I might have believed him. The doubt was there along with hurt and the green-eyed spectre of jealousy which was never far away at the suggestion of other women. Had I clung to my pride and my dignity and allowed him to go without another word, then maybe, in time, I would have resigned myself painfully to the inevitable. Who knows, it might have been better – for me, for him – that way.

But there was something, some instinct. Perhaps an unnatural tension in Nick's shoulders, a sense of wrongness in the patronising, mocking tones he had used. As though he would convince himself as much as me.

When he reached the foot of the stairs, I said quietly, 'Nicholas.'

He hesitated, his back to me. 'I have nothing more to say to you.'

'Nicholas,' I said again. 'Look at me.'

For a moment I thought he would refuse. That he would walk out of the door and close it without looking back.

Then he turned very slowly. His expression was grim and defensive and it took an unconscionable time for him to raise his eyes and look into mine.

'I once saw a strange thing.' My voice was barely above a whisper. 'I once saw our two lives as silvery threads. They twisted together like the links of a chain stretching into the future.' My words sighed down the stairwell. 'I think . . . I believe that chain to be our destiny.'

'No!'

'I think . . . even that first time, in the snow and the cold when I was a poor bedraggled waif and you a man mourning at the foot of a gibbet, there was an inevitability in our meeting that we both recognised.'

'Foolish fancy!'

'You have a strong will. But willpower alone may not be enough to defeat this stronger . . . emotion that binds us.'

'Joanna, I am not worth the candle—'

'I know.' I was suddenly very calm and very sure. 'You are deep and dark and secretive in your inmost heart. You are possessed of a charm that is not always true. You bend people to your own purposes with flattery. Now you mingle with those who consider themselves superior and, like a chameleon, you have put on their colouring – a false colouring because you are not like them, you are your own person, and you use these new acquaintances to your own ends.'

'Then why do you not go away and forget me?'

'How? By taking a butcher's knife and cutting out my own heart? For that is the only way.' I smiled. 'No, Nick. Because I see the good in you also. And because whatever you are, whoever you are, I love you. I am helpless against it.'

All colour had drained from his face, leaving it ashy white. He put out his hand to the banister rail, as though for support.

'Jo . . . Jo, you will understand in time . . . why I do this. It is for your own sake.'

'Your justifications do not interest me, Nick, and I do not wish to know what tricks and plots and connivances you have in your mind.'

'Then what is it you want of me?'

'Do you not know?' I said softly.

I waited and the silence grew and swelled until he burst out, 'Damn you to hell, Joanna Howarth! I do not want to love you. You are not beautiful and delicate and amenable which are the most desirable assets of a female. You are plain and bold and spiky-natured! But . . .' He took a deep breath and when he spoke again it was as though he picked the words, wondering, from the depths of his being. 'You haunt my mind and my heart. I close my eyes at night and you are there with your wild red hair and your sharp green eyes. I look each day at charming, pretty misses admirable in every way and find I am comparing them to you and seeing them as insipid. They do not have your smile that comes, like true beauty, from the heart. They do not have your pride and your perverse, unwomanly manner of striding about as though you care not a fig what people think of you. They do not have your strength and determination. They are not you and, God help me, it is you that I love . . .' His voice died to silence. Then, bitterly, he said, 'Is that what you wished to hear?'

I nodded, my throat suddenly tight with tears.

'I will tell you this also. I wish to God that I had never set eyes on you!' He turned away and strode to the door. 'But I have thought myself in love many times before and sooner or later reason reasserts itself. I will certainly have no truck with silly fancies of linked destinies and silver chains. Life is what you make of it. My life's pattern is setting in the way I wish it to go. It does not include you, Joanna Howarth, desirable as it seems at this moment. Do you understand that?' Again he spoke as though to convince himself rather than me.

I said nothing.

The door slammed after him. Cool air gusted up the stairs and stirred against my face. My body still clamoured, unfulfilled, for his touch but my heart sang with the knowledge that he loved me.

With that certainty to cling to, I could face anything.

I closed my eyes on a deep, exultant breath. Behind my lids I saw the silvery chain, strong and clear, weaving away into the infinite, unknowable distance. Binding me to Nick with the untarnished unbreakable bonds of true love.

Our ways might part temporarily at Nick's insistence but he would be drawn back to me. It was inevitable. I would wait with what patience I could muster until he returned to me. Then we should be together always. So, in my youthful, romantic innocence and ignorance, I believed. And made no allowance for human will and human folly.

In late April Susannah returned to Exeter and to my delight she brought Ruth with her.

'Papa would not let me come before this, and only now because I insisted Blandford should shoulder his responsibilities towards Ruth,' she said when she called upon us. She sat in the parlour like a pretty, sulky butterfly. 'I have been so shut away and quiet in Kingsbridge, for Papa is away more than at home since he is building houses in Plymouth.'

'And how is Ruth?' I said eagerly. 'What a pity you did not bring her, for I should dearly love to see her again. Is she well? Is she much grown.'

'I suppose she is. I am no judge of infants,' Susannah said grudgingly. 'You must call at Roselawn and see for yourself for I quite draw the line at dragging her out and about the streets of Exeter. I had enough on the drive from Kingsbridge. She was grievously sick with the jolting of the carriage. The stench was dreadful and the velvet trimmings on my new gown were totally ruined. I cannot bear to think of it.' She waved her hand dismissively and stared, frowning, round the room, at the chairs and the ornaments. 'You have made some changes here, I see. And new curtains, too. Do you not think the colours overbright, Cousin Olga?'

'I find the pattern quite pleasant,' Miss Olga ventured nervously. 'And Joanna says the stuff will wear well.'

'Ah, Joanna.' Susannah found amusement in this. 'I suppose, being among the trade, as it were, you obtained some disregarded bolt end cheaply.'

'Not at all,' I said calmly. 'Miss Olga is ahead of this summer's fashions. We chose it from some newly arrived samples. That particular chintz, the red roses on a cream background, I find very pretty.'

Susannah's smile sharpened. She leaned confidentially towards Miss Olga. 'You know, cousin, you should not let yourself rely too heavily on Joanna's word. She has some very odd ideas of propriety. Why, Clarissa Alperton told me only yesterday that Joanna goes about the town dressed in a shockingly unsuitable manner for a young, single woman.'

'I believe I have not set eyes on Miss Alperton these last three months,' I said in the same light tone. 'Which means she must be relying on hearsay. How sad for Miss Alperton that she has so little to occupy her mind that she must rely on spreading silly gossip among her acquaintances.'

Susannah tossed her head. 'Her brother Gerald saw you, if you must know. He said he could not believe his eyes when he saw you alighting from a chair in Paris Street. He was forced to cross the road to make sure it was you.'

'Ah, yes, I do remember the occasion. He almost tripped in his haste to offer me assistance with my sketching case and kept me talking an unconscionable time in the wind. I believe I was wearing this gown. Do you find it, then, too striking, Susannah?'

She looked at the severe sage-green lines of my high-necked, long sleeved dress, its only decoration Miss Lightbody's cream lace collar. 'It would not be my taste, of course. That dark unbecoming colour . . .'

'Not too florid, then? Or alarming in any other way? Pray do tell me frankly if you think it is over-ornamented.'

I knew, with delicious malice, why she hesitated. Why it was impossible to fault my dress, yet how its clever lines emphasised my narrow waist and strongly revealed the shape of my breasts and shoulders and arms. How its subtle, sombre colour made my skin take on a translucent whiteness, my hair a rich confusion of fiery red so that my bold Kerswell nose and unfortunate features seemed to blend to a satisfactory harmony.

'No . . .' she said, uncertainly. 'But there was mention of a hat . . .'

'Ah yes, I think it would have been the cream straw with the topaz and vermilion ribbons.'

'An unfortunate choice of colour with your complexion,' she sniffed.

'I do not *think* it was the amaranthine, which is quite my favourite.'

'Amaranthine?'

I smiled in a kindly fashion. 'The colour has become very fashionable this season in Exeter. You are, perhaps, a little out of touch, Susannah, after your country sojourn. You will find fashions quite changed. Your bonnet, for example. Perhaps the crown is a little shallow and the drape of the scarf not quite . . . Well, allow me to recommend a splendid milliner I have discovered. Miss Sprigget will, I am sure, be happy to acquaint you with what is *à la mode*.'

Susannah almost choked on the biscuit she was nibbling. But she quickly recovered. She was far more adept than I was at aiming darts where they would hurt most.

'We had a most interesting and enlivening day at Falconwood only a week ago,' she trilled with a sweet smile. 'What a shame that you were unable to grace the company to celebrate your brother's coming of age. We had a most excessive luncheon and a fiddler to play afterwards so that the young people might dance. It was quite droll to see how your brother performed. Particularly with Lucy Aggett who steps about like a clodhopper. Between the two I was hard put to hide my laughter.'

I had not been invited. I had not even known there was to be a celebration. But I had not been able to let my brother's coming of age pass without some acknowledgement. I had bought a splendid silk waistcoat, wrapped it and sent it to Grandfather, along with a note begging him to give it to Ben, with my love, for his birthday gift. There had been no reply.

'It is such a pity,' she rattled on, merrily, 'that Mr Kerswell persists in making your poor brother such a laughing stock. If Ben has dancing lessons until doomsday he will still cut a hopeless figure! And as for all his other plans, why, they will surely come to nothing.'

'What plans?' I said sharply.

'Oh? Did you not know? Of course, Papa as his oldest friend and business partner has tried most tactfully to advise him, as has Mr Davey, his lawyer, but Mr Kerswell still believes your brother will one day regain his wits, which is clearly not the case.'

I choked back my impatience. 'There is no reason to suppose that Ben will not continue to progress.'

'But never to the extent of becoming a responsible person, able to conduct business affairs. Your grandfather these last weeks has taken Ben everywhere. The shipping offices in Plymouth, the farms to meet the tenants. He says the boy must know and learn of all this if he is to inherit . . .' She paused, her pretty head cocked on one side, eager for my response.

I kept my polite little smile intact. 'It is gratifying to be reminded that Grandfather's kindness to Ben continues.'

'A kindness, you think? When Ben is clearly unfitted to anything beyond the simplest of tasks? But then I suppose as his sister you must stay loyal. However, you must be a touch concerned about the business of Lucy Aggett . . .'

'What business?'

'Lucy is so dull and countrified. Even so, I cannot help a twinge of pity for her situation with your grandfather having selected her as a suitable wife for your dull-witted brother.'

'Wife?'

Susannah's eyes sparkled happily. 'Oh, you did not know? Forgive me if I have sprung the news upon you too suddenly. You have gone quite pale. Her sister, Sophia, was I believe Mr Kerswell's first choice, but she has recently become betrothed to the captain of one of her father's ships. So Lucy it is to be, and I believe your grandpapa has only to speak to her papa and the matter is quite settled. I understand Mr Kerswell is most eager, in view of his age and his health which has not been robust this winter, to see everything swiftly arranged and will make a generous settlement upon the happy couple.' She lowered her voice to a confidential whisper. 'It is the matter of an heir, you see. He is quite desperate to ensure the continuation of the Kerswell line and name. Though one would doubt your brother's . . . abilities in that direction.'

Miss Olga gave an embarrassed cough. Susannah fixed me with her bright malicious gaze, eager to follow every nuance of my shocked response.

I made sure I disappointed her. I leaned towards her and patted her hand warmly. 'I am so grateful for this happy confirmation of my expectations, Susannah,' I lied.

'Oh?'

'I see that surprises you, but I have the greatest regard for dear Lucy. She has a quality of warmth and kindness that would make her an ideal wife for my brother and a mistress for Falconwood. I confess,' I said, piling lie upon lie without conscience, 'that when I saw Ben and Lucy so tender together last year, I harboured hopes of just such an alliance.'

457

'Last year?'

'Did you not notice? Why, Susannah, I thought you far more perspicacious in these matters than I. But perhaps you were too intent on trying to catch Tom Davey's attention to notice. Now, do give me your advice, for I am really too excited to make sensible judgments. Would it harm, do you suppose, to drop a sisterly note to Lucy, offering my good wishes?'

'Oh no!' Susannah said quickly. 'That would not do at all!' She stopped short, flustered, before recovering and adding lightly, 'There is nothing *official*, you understand. It would not be tactful . . . or indeed proper to speak of . . . of any betrothal before Mr Aggett had sanctioned it, for it may be that in the circumstances he might be against the match.'

'Oh, I do hope not,' I sighed. 'But I suppose I must continue to be patient, which is most trying when one is so far away.' I brightened. 'Do Lucy and her family come often to Exeter? Perhaps I could write and invite them to call. It would give me an opportunity to speak privately to Lucy. To give her my blessing.'

'They never come to Exeter,' Susannah declared, rather too hastily. 'If Mrs Aggett takes the girls anywhere beyond Kingsbridge it is to Plymouth to visit her sister.' She rose in a flurry of lavender skirts. 'I must take my leave, for I promised Blandford to return early. We have scarce had chance to exchange two civil words since I returned, we are both so much out of the house.'

It was gratifying to have called her bluff so satisfactorily. But I was not yet finished.

'How is Blandford?' I enquired in a sympathetic voice. 'There is talk about the town that he has been somewhat overstretched. It must be a worry to you, Susannah, that your brother gambles so heavily. Why, I even heard a rumour that he has had to reduce his household—'

'Who told you that?' Susannah interrupted sharply.

I shrugged. 'I forget. Is it not true?'

'Of course not! It is just that while he was alone, it was sensible to close up rooms and reduce the number of idle maids. Now that I am returned to Exeter, we shall be making plans for some grand entertainments.'

When she had gone I went up to my room and sat on my hard little bed, staring into space.

I had vanquished Susannah and it was gratifying to have seen her alarm when I mentioned Blandford and Roselawn. I had no doubt that his behaviour must be causing the family some distress. Mrs Fitch had told me that he was heavily in debt.

There was little that went on at Reynard's that she did not know about. Though servants were never allowed in the gaming room when play was in progress and the croupiers were a close-mouthed breed, there was plenty of gossip among the gentlemen afterwards for an attentive and soft-footed maid or footman to glean.

Most of the gentlemen who frequented the gaming tables looked merely for an occasional pleasurable evening's entertainment. To a hardened few it was a deadly serious business. Mrs Fitch shook her head and whispered of the prospect of ruin that faced the foolhardy.

'It seems to me a sorry affair that a man can be parted from his fortune by the turn of a card. But Nicholas, who can be the kindest of men, has no conscience on this score. On the contrary, he laughs at my concern and says that he does them a favour. If Reynard's was not here, he assures me, they would find somewhere far worse where they would be cheated and lose their money even more quickly.' She sighed. 'Which unfortunately is true, and I do believe him when he assures me that the gaming is conducted strictly and honourably and he is always on hand to prevent any sharp practice, yet I cannot but feel a pang for the innocent wives and children who must suffer . . .'

But sitting there on my bed it was not the Pascoes' problems that troubled me. I was afire with far less worthy and charitable emotions.

I had no doubt that Susannah exaggerated in her account of Ben's prospects. She had hoped to amuse herself at my expense. I had not crumbled under her assault, as she expected, but had attacked and routed her. Nevertheless, I realised that there was probably a strong element of truth in what she had told me. It was logical to suppose that Grandfather wanted an heir. Why else should he take such time and trouble over Ben who had the likeness of the son, our uncle, so tragically lost? And if Ben, for all the money spent on him, the doctors consulted, the experimental treatments tried, could not be returned to full intelligence, what then?

Ben must breed. If he was capable – and doubtless Grandfather had the opinion of the finest doctors – then he must mate, like a valuable hound in its prime, in order to continue the blood line. The child, given a mother of sturdy, fertile stock, would be healthy and intelligent and a worthy successor to carry the Kerswell name and lineage on to future generations.

Lucy Aggett was perhaps the girl chosen by Grandfather, as Susannah had said. If not, some other girl, or even some woman of experience willing to overlook Ben's handicaps and instruct him in the duties of the marital bed. Her reward: to be mistress of a fine house and a comfortable life for herself and whatever children she would bear.

And once Grandfather had died and his stern rule was over, then this unknown woman, Mrs Benjamin Howarth

Kerswell, would reign supreme over Falconwood.

I sat there in the bedroom I had tricked out with all the art at my disposal. The furniture arranged to diminish its ungainly length, the pink curtain at the window that caught the colour in the patchwork quilt and the new rug under my feet. The pretty painting of bathing nymphs hiding the crack in the wall, my books of poetry and essays, my work basket, an ornament or two prettily arranged in a sturdy rosewood bookcase Harry had made for me. A room that, despite every effort, would never look anything but what it was. A cramped sleeping place entirely suitable for a worthless paid companion. The destiny to which Grandfather had despatched his only granddaughter, careless of the fact that in her veins the Kerswell blood ran as vigorously as it did in her brother's.

I burned with resentment.

Why should it be? Why might Ben be forgiven so readily for the sins of our mother and grandmother? I was just as innocent of any crime against the Kerswell name, yet I was condemned to exile and exclusion. Why did the world turn so hardly against a female child when a male child, even a damaged one, was deemed more worthy to love, to cosset – to inherit – than a female?

All the old pain and frustration bubbled up in a choking lump in my throat. I squeezed my eyes shut tight against angry tears. Hating Grandfather, despising the unknown woman, Ben's future wife, who would enter Falconwood at Grandfather's express wish and invitation, and become its chatelaine. Despising, for a moment, even Ben, whom I loved, because he did not realise how fortunate he was.

Falconwood.

I clasped my arms tightly across my breast, rocking back and forth in an agony of longing.

I wanted to be there. I *should* be there. It was my right. I was a Kerswell, by birth, by blood. *She* would not care for Falconwood as I could. She did not love it, as I had from that very first day, wanting to bestow my love like a gift in every shabby room.

Behind my screwed-tight eyelids I saw its stout walls and jutting chimneys, the glitter of its windows in the sun, its wild gardens and orchards spread around it like untidy skirts.

I stood in brilliant sunlight by the sturdy front door and heard the greedy sea roaring and pounding and the sea birds mewing and shrieking under lean, grey clouds, which streamed from the western horizon like a silent invading horde, trailing purple rain shadows in their wake. The sun was high, but moving swiftly westwards so that the cloud shadows changed direction, running ahead of the clouds now, touching the house with sudden chilling darkness.

The door opened easily and I moved inside. Others followed. I could not see, but I knew them. Their voices, soft and sibilant, welcomed me in. Their butterfly fingers touched my shoulder, my waist, my hair. The women of Falconwood. I felt the generations of happiness, of grief, of suffering, of contentment that crowded at my back.

'*You are stronger than I supposed, child. We are proud of you.*' My mother's voice.

Then another, and another, in a babel of sound, rising and falling, so that I caught the words haphazardly out of the air. '*—We need you . . . Take care . . . take care . . . our blessings . . . but we are helpless . . . We cannot prevent . . . take care . . . Falconwood is your destiny . . . not easy . . . not easy.*'

And my mother's voice again, rising above the babel. '*When the storm comes, bow your head and bend to the wind, child. That way you will survive. That is how you* will gain what you most desire. But not without suffering.' Her voice ebbed away, rose again. 'We shall watch for you. We are always here.'

And she was gone, they were all gone, streaming past in a rustle of silky mist that dissolved into nothing even as I saw it.

Rain beat on the roof. The wind howled round the eaves. I moved through rooms that were filled with warmth and light. The golden glow of lamps and candles dispelled every shadow, fires snapped in every grate. Here a table recently vacated, homely with crumpled napery, half-emptied glasses; there an embroidery frame in a spill of rainbow silks, a book open at a well-thumbed page, a scatter of children's toys abandoned on a hearthrug. They were so near, the ones whose faces I ached to see. I could sense them, ahead of me, always ahead. In the next room, the next. A door flew open and voices burst out in an explosion of laughter. I laughed with them, feeling their joy as my own, running towards them, but I could not reach the door before it banged shut. And I was outside the house once more, shivering in the dark. Yearning to be beyond those lighted windows, back in the warmth. Back where I truly belonged . . .

In the blink of an eye the picture in my head was gone. I stared around in a daze. The narrow walls of my room shut me in. I was alone, cold, with Mary Ann tapping on the door, calling, 'Miss Jo, Miss Olga's waiting dinner for you.'

'I shall be there in a moment,' I said in a voice so calm and ordinary that she could not have known that I was wracked with shudders as though taken with a violent ague.

For in my mind I still stood outside Falconwood's closed door and the chill darkness held me a prisoner of loneliness.

Chapter Seventeen

My feelings were in a stew in the following days. There were moments when I dreamt, as I had so often in the beginning, of snatching Ben from Grandfather's clutches and escaping with him to some distant place, where I could devote my life to his welfare and comfort.

But the arguments against such reckless action were more powerful because I had far more to lose. I had friends I would miss. I would be haunted by guilt because of my promise to Jane, for I would have to sever all connection with Ruth. I would dearly miss my occupation as a lady decorator. I was proud of the small niche I had carved for myself but I recognised that as nearly all my commissions had come about through the influence and recommendation of satisfied clients, it would be well-nigh impossible to start afresh in a new town, a woman alone, without introductions and connections.

And Nicholas, my Nicholas, bound to me by invisible bonds, who loved me, who had admitted he did, and who chose out of stubbornness to deny that love. How could I go away? I must be here when he came to his senses. Oh, he was obsessed with Reynard's at present, which I understood, for he had much to lose if the enterprise failed. But it would not be for ever. The time would come – a few weeks, a few months –

when Reynard's would demand less of his attention. That was the moment I must patiently wait for.

Yet behind these explanations, which appealed to my reason and my heart, there was another.

Falconwood.

If I took Ben away, we should both of us lose all hope of ever setting foot in Falconwood again.

And that was as convincing an argument as any.

I lost no time in visiting Roselawn, anxious as I was to see Ruth, and I was distressed to find a shocking air of neglect hanging about the house.

The low shafts of morning sun showed up starkly the weeds in the unraked gravel of the garden paths, the shaggy lawns and unkempt borders. Indoors, all was dim and silent. No footmen hovered, no maids scurried soft-footed about their duties. A young, uncertain parlourmaid, cap askew, led me into the drawing room, swept a dustsheet off a chair, begged me to be seated and scuttled away to inform her mistress of my arrival.

I stared around in dismay. So much effort had gone into producing a house as fine as any in Exeter where people might be entertained on a grand scale. Indeed, the elegant proportions of the drawing room, of the house itself, on which Mr Curtis had lavished all of his talent could not be concealed. But the shrouded furniture, the smeary windows, the closed-up smell spoke as clearly of abandoned hopes and expectations as if Blandford himself had stood in the middle of the drugget-swathed carpet and announced them.

I had not been in the house since the stormy night of Jane's death. An unremarked and unremarkable life had been extinguished that night and it occurred to me, as I waited, sad and uneasy, for Susannah to appear that the spirit of the house had been extinguished too. Like a candle briefly lighted then snuffed out. Beautiful still, but quite, quite lifeless.

'That wretched girl!' Susannah swept into the room, skirts swishing, her face thunderous. 'That she should bring you in here, Joanna, when I told her that any callers must be shown to the small parlour! I swear I do not know what Blandford is thinking of to engage such a half-wit! But then, he is so rarely in the house.' She was very angry. Far more than the misdemeanour of a maid warranted. 'I find this room depressing in the extreme,' she snapped. 'It was never to my taste, but now it is a positive mausoleum. I swear I shall not set foot in here again until Blandford returns from the country and orders the house to be opened up properly.'

'Your brother is gone away?' I said, with some relief.

'He sprung it on me only this morning! Here am I left quite alone with hardly a servant to attend me and only a puking child – *his* child – for company. And he *promised* when I returned all would be as it was before and we should be lively and entertain. It is no use for him to run to Papa for help. I told him, but he would not listen. All he will get is a flea in his ear. Papa complains that he must draw in his horns until his schemes at Plymouth are completed, leave alone having spare—' She brought herself up short, her lids fluttering down over angry but suddenly nervous alert blue eyes. Her fingers were still locked tensely together, but she gave a little false laugh, followed by the pretence of a ladylike yawn. 'Dear me, I was up so late last night I fear I have quite got out of bed the wrong side this morning and I am pressed for time, for I am to drive with Clarissa and her mama. Pray, Joanna, take no notice of my maunderings. Why, it is probably for the best that poor Blandford has gone away for a visit or we should have been out of temper with each other for days.'

'I have an engagement also,' I said briskly, 'so do

not let me keep you, Susannah. You said that I might visit Ruth.'

'Of course, of course. I shall accompany you to the nursery myself. Now, let me tell you of the splendid soirée I was at last evening, a most lively company, and Gerald Alperton so attentive that I had to be quite brusque with him for monopolising my attention. Another month and I shall be out of mourning – though to be honest I find the lilac and lavender shades with the white love ribbons so fetching that I shall not discard them out of hand...'

She led me away, chattering of nothing, with no pause into which I might throw an indiscreet question. Had she but known it, I had no inclination to pry further. The neglected house, the lack of servants, Blandford's hasty flight to Kingsbridge confirmed all that I had heard, of a man heavy in debt with creditors pressing.

I felt a fleeting sympathy for Susannah, a pretty, silly butterfly left to flutter uselessly in this big empty house. But what met us in the nursery drove any kind feelings towards Susannah out of my head.

The room was preternaturally neat. Barred windows with white muslin curtains, scrubbed table and chairs, polished floorboards, a strip of dark carpet set squarely before an unlit fire which was protected by a large brass guard. A range of plain cupboards down one wall, a door, firmly closed, leading to the smaller night nursery. No toys, no books, no voices. No evidence at all of a small person busily occupied.

I felt disappointed. The nursemaid perhaps had taken Ruth for a walk and I should not be able to see her. But then the nursemaid herself rose from a seat in the shelter of the chimney corner with some shapeless grey knitting hanging from her big red hands.

'Where is Miss Ruth?' Susannah enquired.

468

The girl stared at us from under fuzzy black eyebrows, sketched a lumpish curtsey and said, "Er had to be punished, miss.'

'Oh dear,' Susannah said, with an exasperated sigh. 'What is it this time, Sally?'

"Er wet the bed again, an' you know, miss, I can't abide no dirty 'abits.' She glanced proudly round the immaculate room. 'Like 'er pa, Mr Pascoe, says, 'er has to learn to be a little lady and little ladies don't act like they ol' pigs in a sty.' She thrust out a fist. 'An' see what I gets for my pains. 'Er can be proper vicious, kickin' and bitin' when 'er has a mind to it.' There was a faint arc of tiny indentations on her thumb. 'I'm like to be marked for weeks!'

'Yes, yes, but if you have confined the child to her bedroom, would you be so good as to fetch her out?'

The girl made no move. "Er's not dressed, miss,' she said, stubbornly. "Er's not ready for showin' to visitors.'

'Then pray bring her as she is,' Susannah snapped. 'It is no matter that she is still in her nightgown. I have not all day to waste, nor has Miss Howarth who has called especially to see Miss Ruth.'

The nursemaid still hesitated. 'Very well, miss, though I'd rather . . .'

Susannah's foot tapped impatiently. The girl's mouth clamped shut. She glared at me before doing as she was bid.

The words I had heard hung in the air like a warning, alerting some primitive instinct that propelled me after her. She was through the night nursery door and closing it quickly in alarm when she saw me. I put my weight behind it, thrusting her backwards.

'You've no right in 'ere, miss!' she cried.

'Where is she? What have you done with her?'

The room was empty. The narrow cot freshly made

up with crisp white sheets. A plain ewer and basin, a candlestick, neatly folded towels on a marble-topped washstand. The nursemaid with her back to a tall cupboard, her arms spread as though protecting it.

''Er had to be punished if 'er did any wrong. 'Er pa told me when I first come.'

Then I heard it. A mewling noise that set the hair prickling at the back of my neck.

I gripped the maid's shoulders, flinging her away so that she fell against a corner of the washstand with a cry of pain. I turned the key and pulled the door wide.

The smell came out first, a hot and ammoniac blast. Then a tumble of sheets, some still sodden, others patched with yellow stains. And the child, making that frantic, pathetic mewling, her eyes screwed shut, her arms going up as though to defend herself against blows.

I caught her and held her tight, pinning the flailing little fists with one hand, desperately trying to soothe her.

'Hush, hush, sweetheart. You are safe now. I've got you. Don't cry.'

But there were no tears. Just that dreadful, desperate keening and a body rigid as a board, inconsolable, in my arms.

'What *is* going on?' Susannah peered round the door.

'I was only doin' what was needed!' the nursemaid bellowed. 'An' she've hurt me real bad.'

I swung round on her, scarcely able to find my voice for the terrible rage that possessed me. 'You . . . you evil crow. You should be whipped through the streets for what you've done to this child.'

''Er pissed the bed! Thass not right. 'Er's got to learn—'

'How long has she been in there?'

'Dunno. Miss Pascoe,' she whined, 'tell 'er I done nothing wrong.'

'How long? An hour? Two?'

She shrugged. 'I s'pose.'

'And from the disgusting state of these sheets, not for the first time.'

''Er's got to be learnt.'

'By terrifying the wits out of her? By tying her up in wet and stinking sheets and leaving her locked up in the dark?' I was shaking with the horror of it.

Susannah chose that moment to say, 'You see, Joanna, how Blandford plays on my good nature. He leaves all these tiresome domestic upsets for me to deal with and I find them very trying.'

'How very difficult for you, Susannah,' I said through gritted teeth. 'And how do you propose to deal with this particular situation? Shall you turn this . . . this evil creature off without a character?'

'She shall be reprimanded, of course. But Blandford thinks highly of her.'

'Ah, Blandford. The grieving widower, the considerate papa. I can see that he would think well of such an excellent disciplinarian.'

Susannah frowned. 'Sally has overstepped the mark, true, in this instance, but she is clean and trustworthy—'

'And cruel and ignorant.' I suddenly thrust Ruth towards her. Susannah averted her face and quickly stepped backwards. 'You may well turn your head. She stinks, does she not? Her nightgown is soaked. See how her skin is raw and chapped with the wet. And these . . . what are these? Welts, if I am not mistaken, across her legs. This clean and trustworthy person has taken a stick to her.'

'She bit me, Miss Pascoe! Thass not to be stood for!'

I swung round on her. 'You would bite and kick if you were a helpless infant and knew you were going to be shut in a cupboard and left for hours at a time . . .' I stopped, hot anger suddenly dying. I looked at the faces of these two young women. One dull and sullen, the other full of sulky distaste. Justifiably angry I might be, but I had no rights in this house. Ruth was not my kin. If I was to help her I must tread with caution.

She was a stiff, dead weight in my arms. The dreadful keening had stopped, but her eyes were still tightly closed, as though she could not bear to open them upon fresh horror.

'You have an engagement which you must keep, Susannah,' I said, choosing my words with care. 'Mine is not so pressing. So I would be willing, if you should be agreeable, to stay awhile and see that order is restored here and that Ruth does not give her nurse any more trouble. Then you may go with an easy mind.' I managed a small, sympathetic smile. 'I do believe I have not fully understood until this moment how worrying it must be for you to be here without the support of your papa or your brother and with Ruth to care for.'

'I find it most disagreeable to be put upon so,' Susannah said petulantly.

'Men believe their affairs to be far more important than those that occupy mere females. Yet what can be a more demanding and responsible task than caring for a poor motherless child in the absence of her papa?'

'As I have done all these months. And not a word of thanks.'

'You have borne up wonderfully. I am sure both Mr Pascoe and Blandford will grow to appreciate your selflessness. As will Ruth herself when she becomes old enough to understand.'

For a second Susannah's glance was uncertain as it rested on her soiled, terrified niece, as though unaccustomed doubt fluttered in her shallow mind. Then, with a toss of her head, she gathered her self-centred justifications around her like a shield.

'It is most unfair that I should be forced to worry over Ruth when I have so looked forward to driving with Clarissa and her mama. And it is every day the same. Always some tiresome problem with which I must deal. Still, as you are here, Joanna . . .

It was done. I felt myself sag with relief. I had gained time. Not enough. Not nearly enough to undo the harm that had been done to Ruth in the past months. But a brief respite in which to try and ease the child's present terror.

As soon as Susannah had gone, I asked the nurse to fetch out the bath and bring hot water and towels. 'And be sharp about it,' I added as she limped off, rubbing her hip and muttering under her breath.

I did not give a hoot for her bruised hip or her bruised feelings. I paced the room, rocking Ruth against my shoulder as though she were a baby, crooning the little rhymes that she had once loved to hear, willing her to emerge from the terrible locked-away state of terror.

Presently one small damp paw moved and fastened itself into my hair. She would not let go, even when the bath was ready. In the end I had to take off my hat and unpin my hair, so that she could cling for security – and painfully – to the same wiry strand as I lowered her into the comforting warmth of the water. Only then did she open her eyes and go limp as a rag doll.

When she was bathed and clean, I dressed her and set her on my lap. I brushed her soft hair until it stood about her head in fine damp tendrils. And I talked to her. Nothings. Soft, coaxing words until, at last, she began to answer.

We sat there for a long time. Too late I remembered I should have sent a message to the serge maker's wife who had requested that I call to discuss the decoration

473

of her summer parlour. It had seemed important when I set out this morning. Now it did not. If I lost the commission, it was not the end of the world. What mattered was Ruth. What mattered was that her ignorant nurse should not ever again treat her in such a violent fashion.

The nursemaid finished clearing away the soiled sheets. I made her scrub out the cupboard and leave the doors open to air. When she had finished, I called her out of the night nursery. I indicated a chair. 'Please bring it and sit by me.'

She looked surprised at the unexpected request and perhaps, too, at the politeness of my tone.

'Tell me, Sally,' I began, 'where did you work before you came here?'

Her heavy features shifted uncertainly. 'Afore this, miss, I was near two years at a tavern down Idol Street.'

'And your duties?'

'I wasn't one o' they doxies as worked there,' she said quickly. 'Proper 'spectable, I was. Missus 'er said 'er'd never had anyone kept the place as clean. Master never liked me, though. When missus brung me home from the poorhouse, he boxed her ears. Said she'd picked the ugliest, stupidest brat just to annoy him. But I was glad I worn't pretty like Alice nor Meg nor any of they others he'd took in. After he done wi' beddin' they, they was put to earn their keep wi' the payin' customers. I was kept to do the rough scrubbin' and cleanin' which pleased me best.'

'He did not touch you?'

She glared defiantly. 'Nothin' I could do 'bout that. But it was just a few times. In the beginnin'. So I reckon that don't count. Alice'd warned me not to scream and make a fuss, for that was what 'ee liked best an' I didn't want to please he, on no account, for he stank like an ox and what 'ee did give me bellyache somethin' terrible.'

I stared at her dull, heavy face in sick comprehension. The words spilled out, flat and slow, without thought. No shame, no shock at what had been done to her. Nor even the intention to shock me. She was telling it as it had happened because she had neither the wits nor the sensitivity to do otherwise.

'And how . . . how did you come to be removed from this place?'

'Why, Mr Pascoe, o'course.' She brightened at the memory. 'Missus run off after master give 'er a good hidin' one night when he was drunk. Master, 'e was in a right temper. Drags me out an' shouts as he'll give a glass of his best brandy to anyone as'll take this last reminder of his missus off his hands. Mr Pascoe was there with some friends an' Mr Pascoe he asks, "Is her clean and obedient?" and master says, "They learned 'er obedience well in the poorhouse. As for the other, 'er be too clean by 'alf an' I'm not a man as takes much stock by that, findin' a mite o' muck more natural to live with. But her's never 'appier than when her's up to her elbows in soapsuds or a-polishing some innocent bit o' furniture. Why, 'er'd polish your bleedin' dick if you left it lyin' about!" Mr Pascoe, he laughs fit to bust an' says I should suit 'im well, for he could see as I'd got the sort've qualities as'd be useful in his pursuit of domestic contentiement.' Her thick brows came down in a frown. 'He often talks in big words, Mr Pascoe, bein' a gentleman, so's sometimes I 'as to think 'ard about 'is meanin'. But I does know this.' She thrust out her heavy jaw belligerently. 'He'm never 'ad cause to find fault wi' me.'

'No,' I said quietly. 'I am sure you have been . . . everything he would have wished.'

A dull, stupid, mistreated creature. Doing her duty in the only way she knew how.

'Sally, one more thing. The poorhouse. How did you come there?'

'I don't properly remember. I was there a long time. I had a ma once, but 'er died.'

'And did they treat you well?'

'If we was good we 'ad mutton and pudden' twice a week and cheese on Fridays and clean frocks on Sundays.'

'And if you were bad?'

'We 'ad to be punished, miss. Course we did. 'Tes only natural. Mrs Taylor – 'er was the one as looked after us – 'ad a big cane. Her broke it over my back once. For I could never learn letters, as we was s'posed to. Then for upsetting Mrs Taylor particular, like not scrubbin' in corners, or fallin' asleep when the reverend come to read from the Bible, then us must do wi' half rations for a week. Terrible hungry times they was. But if it was somethin' really wicked, like doin' everything under you in the bed, or soilin' your drawers, which the little ones was particular prone to, then you was put in the shed.'

'Shed?'

'Out in the yard. Locked up there summer or winter, stiflin' hot or bitter cold, to think about the sinfulness o' dirty 'abits. Couldn't stand no dirty 'abits, Mrs Taylor. She learned me good about that,' she added proudly.

Easy to understand now, that by Sally's lights she was doing nothing wrong. She knew no different. She was merely passing on all she had ever experienced herself.

My arms tightened around Ruth. She lay inert and sleepy against my breast. *Please love her . . . protect her . . . promise me . . .* It was barely six months since I had promised Jane and already I had failed. I felt the weight of that promise, the weight of my neglect, however justifiable. Against that, there was the rage I felt towards Ruth's papa and aunt. Blandford who, in order to humiliate and distress his wife, had dismissed Jane's old, loved nurse and replaced her with this thick-witted bumpkin. Susannah, too caught up in her own selfish pursuits to notice what went on under her pretty nose. Or to care if she did.

But what to do now, in whatever time there was before Blandford returned?

Sally still sat there, heavy as a sack of coals, big red hands slack in her lap.

Such a chasm of understanding to be bridged.

I smothered a sigh and began.

It was a week before Blandford returned. I arrived at Roselawn on a clear warm morning to take Ruth for a walk. The door was open. I peered into the hall to see Susannah wringing her hands, the parlourmaid saucer-eyed and Sally, the nursemaid, leaning over the banisters to gawp at the dishevelled figure sprawled on its back at the foot of the stairs.

I would have discreetly retreated if it had been possible, but Susannah spied me and snatched me inside, slamming the door shut as though she feared a gaping crowd might assemble.

For once she seemed at a loss for words. She stood there staring helplessly at her brother, as we each did. Four women in a frozen tableau round the sprawled figure.

The smell of brandy was very strong. It dribbled from the bottle Blandford clutched in his hand and when he lifted it, tilting it waveringly to his wet mouth, more slopped down over his chin and ran in rivulets over his cheeks to the matted hair that straggled round his ears.

He threw the bottle from him. It crashed against the banister rail in a splatter of glass and spirit, so that the parlourmaid squealed and edged into the

477

protection of the drawing room door.

'Nothin',' he hiccupped. 'Bastar' gimme nothin'...
own son... own son... bastar' miser...' He swung
his head round, unfocused eyes squinting. 'Bastar'
females... useless... standin' there... useless
bitches...'

His hands scrabbled on the stairs. Slowly, he pushed
himself to a sitting position. His once dandified yellow
coat and green trousers were smeared with filth, as
though he had been crawling in the gutter.

'No use t'any man... bastar' females...'cept on
their back wi' their legs open...'

'Blandford!' Susannah's voice came out as a horrified squeak. 'You forget yourself!'

'F'get mysel',' he mimicked, swinging his head from
side to side in an attempt to focus. 'Don' get... high
horse wi' me, li'l sister... my house...'member that.'
He groped for the banister and hauled himself to his
feet, eyes screwed to piggy slits. 'An' you... red-haired
bastar' bitch... take that look off y'r face... you
hear?' He staggered forward. 'Need a lesson... clever
bitches same's any other slut... Need showing who's
master.' He bared his teeth in a leer, his hand fumbling
obscenely at his crotch. 'I'll 'ave you beggin' for it...
on your knees... See's I don'. Red-haired slut...'

His knees buckled suddenly, his eyes glazing. He
crumpled to the floor, where he stayed, setting up a
loud snoring.

Susannah gripped and ungripped her white-
knuckled hands.

'We cannot leave him there! Suppose someone calls
and sees? But how shall we get him upstairs? There is
not a manservant left.'

'The drawing room?'

'Between us... perhaps... we could lay him on the
sofa until he recovers.'

478

We were whispering. We still whispered as we dragged his leaden weight into the shrouded drawing room, though he was so deep in his drunken stupor I do not think he would have heard if we had let off firecrackers in his ears. It was more seemly, somehow, to whisper. As though the hushed cadences of our voices might force the ugly vibrations left by Blandford's words to retreat.

But it was hard to escape from them, even when Ruth and I walked in the brilliance of a summer sun. For each time I looked into the solemn, wary face of Blandford's little daughter, it was to be reminded of the shadow that encompassed her.

The long days brought a spell of hot, dry weather. Miss Olga's roses, at their best, hung fat and fragrant against the mellow stone of the garden wall in swathes of deep crimson and saffron-hearted white. The first strawberries ripened, were tasted and pronounced excellent. The old damson dropped the excess of its plentiful crop, littering the ground with small hard bullets which Miss Olga tidied into the compost heap each evening.

The streets were breathless and dusty. People with leisure to spare sought open spaces on the heights of the town where a welcome breeze might be caught. Even the Exe coiling its length below the ancient walls looked listless, the city's refuse turning turgidly in its oily currents.

I was glad that Timmy and his family were no longer living in the lower town where the stinks from middens and cesspits and pigsties of its residents grew daily more noisome, an assault to the nostrils of any sensitive soul forced to pass through the narrow, dark alleys, and a breeding ground for summer fevers and agues. The roads beyond the city were busy with equippages bearing family parties to scenic spots for picnics. Those especially fortunate and able to be careless in the matter of paying – so Miss Olga informed me, aghast – as much as twelve guineas a week for decent lodgings removed themselves entirely to quiet and refreshing watering places such as Exmouth and Dawlish or Lyme Regis.

Business slackened, for which I was not ungrateful. I worried that I had little work to offer Timmy, though I knew he had built up a fair trade on his own now, word having got about of his excellent craftsmanship and modest charges. I felt, quite proudly, that his association with my various projects had gone a long way to setting him on his feet. On my calling to see him and finding him out, his wife assured me cheerfully that they had orders enough to see them over the coming weeks. 'Timmy was only saying this mornin' that he should soon have to think of taking on an apprentice. As 'tis we can just about manage, for our Maggie's beginning to be useful with a needle. Aye, he'm set fair to being in as good way o' trade as his late master. God rest 'im.'

Miss Olga's meticulous ordering of my accounts had freed me from a tiresome burden and her growing friendship with Eleanor Barton had brought a lively new interest to Torre Crescent. Mrs Barton called often with some thoughtful gift for Miss Polsham and took a keen interest in the garden, seeking Miss Olga's advice on the refurbishment of her own neglected plot. Miss Olga warmed to this attention, pressing upon her visitor seedlings and cuttings and keenly following up their progress by visits of inspection. Perhaps Miss Olga glimpsed in the younger woman someone she might have become had she ever been released from the burdens of obedience and duty. Mrs Barton, grateful for the abundance of her good fortune, possibly saw in Miss Olga a woman to whom she could freely extend her understanding and compassion without the leaden weight of responsibility. Whatever it was, the friendship was genuine and warming to see.

Lily and Mary Ann between them ensured that the household ran like clockwork. Even Miss Polsham had grown less demanding of me. She often compared me, unfavourably, to Mary Ann. 'You are so hard-fingered, Joanna. You have such bountiful health yourself you have no comprehension of the delicacy of the invalid constitution. Mary Ann, untutored as she is, has far more delicacy.' To Mary Ann I overhead her say, 'Take care, girl! Oh, if you had but half a grain of Miss Joanna's good sense you would be the better for it . . .' It was a little game that gave her great satisfaction.

I had leisure for the first time in many months. It enabled me to devote myself to Ruth, though each time I called at Roselawn my heart was in my mouth in case I should meet Blandford. But he was seldom at home and when he was, the parlourmaid ushered me inside nervously, her frightened eyes telling me more clearly than words to be quiet and quick. I would slip to the nursery, thanking heaven that it was at the other end of the house from Blandford's bedchamber where he would be snoring off the drunken excesses of the previous night. Only once did he rouse himself while I was in the house. Hearing him stumbling and cursing down the front stairs, I spirited Ruth down the back stairs and escaped through the kitchen door.

Sometimes the nursemaid accompanied us, dragging reluctantly behind, for she saw no merit in long unnecessary walks. Nothing I did or said seemed to penetrate the dense wall of her understanding. Her untutored mind was set in its narrow limits and nothing could persuade her to look beyond. She was employed to look after Ruth, but saw her merely as an object to be kept as clean and polished as the furniture.

Within those limits she was exemplary. The nursery was a sanctuary to cleanliness, Ruth herself was kept as neat and shining as a new pin. It was easy, when one understood this, to imagine the genuine horror that Sally must experience when any activity threatened to spoil such a pristine image, be it an out-of-place toy, a soiled pinafore or – terrible in the extreme – a wayward bladder. Easy to understand, but impossible to condone or forgive the harsh methods which were all Sally knew of discipline.

I did, however, extract from her a reluctant promise that there would be no more incarceration in the cupboard for Ruth.

'Thass all very well, miss, but 'ow'm I to learn 'er?'

'With kindness, Sally. The more you frighten the child, the worse she will be. And you must not leave her so long. Before you go to bed yourself, rouse her and put her on the pot. And get up half an hour earlier and take her from her bed before she has chance to wet it. Will you try that, Sally?'

'More trouble for me, I see that.'

'For a while, but I'm sure it will help. Promise me you'll try.'

A hostile look from under fuzzy brows, a slow duck of the head – that was as much as I had come to expect in the way of willingness, for she viewed me as a nuisance who unsettled her charge by indulging her with noisy romps and encouraging activities with books and dolls that created unnecessary mess.

I kept Ruth out as much as I could, returning her with reluctance. It grieved me to leave her in that desolate house. Even Susannah seemed affected by the haunted silence which hung over the rooms, the brief, disruptive interludes when the master of the house was at home only serving to emphasise the deadly quiet when he was gone. It was scarcely an atmosphere in which a child could thrive, let alone one left to the ministrations of a rough nurse.

Susannah was more and more with the Alpertons, kindly Lady Alperton apparently sympathetic to the girl's somewhat irregular situation. Though perhaps Sir George was less so. Gerald, to Susannah's chagrin, had been summarily despatched to their Yorkshire estate on some urgent but unspecified business that would keep him conveniently absent for several weeks.

'I might as well be back in Kingsbridge,' said Susannah crossly, 'there are so many people out of town.'

Out of town. Of course. And such tiresomely enervating weather for those who remained. Quite the best thing to stay indoors out of the dust and see only one's closest friends. Quite the best ... And the whispers? Those soft and insinuating murmurings drifting and weaving from one shaded parlour to the next?

'My dear, the brother ... most unfortunate ... One feels sorry, naturally, for the girl ... but for the moment unwise, do you think, to include her?'

Well, they were of no account. Bored ladies will always find something to gossip about. If Susannah preferred to blame the weather for the few invitations she now received, who was I to contradict her? If she chose to ignore the swish of silk skirts briskly withdrawing, the snap of fans opening to mask averted faces, it was not my place to interfere.

And if I had? If I had put it persuasively, 'Susannah, you are not happy rattling about in this big house on your own. Why not take Ruth back to Kingsbridge? Just for a little while until Blandford feels able to open the house properly. Perhaps it will not be for long. A few weeks and you will return feeling perfectly refreshed ...' Would it have made any difference to the outcome?

There have been times when I have tortured myself with that thought.

But now ... now I know that it is far easier, and

483

infinitely more comforting, to look at the wheeling stars and be lulled into believing that they drag along each helpless human soul in a relentless bondage towards a predicted destiny.

The hot weather lost its grip. We woke one morning to the dismal sound of rain drumming against the windows.

'Thank heavens,' said Miss Polsham as I helped her downstairs after breakfast. 'I find the heat weakens my system excessively. I have felt quite feverish these last days.' She leaned heavily on my arm to emphasise her frailty and added. 'Of course, Joanna, you will not have had the time to remark my sufferings, you are so busy with your own affairs.'

'There is half a gale blowing,' sighed Miss Olga staring gloomily out of the parlour window. 'The roses will be quite spoiled.'

'I shall take a cooling powder.' Miss Polsham settled, plump and pink-cheeked, onto the day bed. 'You may bring it in ten minutes, Joanna, when I have recovered my breath . . . No, no! The cushion in the small of my back, *not* under my shoulders. Mary Ann has just the knack. I despair that after all this time you still have not learned—' She broke off as a door slammed somewhere in the house. 'I trust no one has left a window open to cause a through draught . . .'

The parlour door burst open.

A moment's shocked silence, then Miss Olga, recovering, said faintly, 'Why, Blandford . . . such a surprise . . . I did not hear your knock . . .'

'Let myself in, dear coz,' Blandford said. 'Door on the latch. No reason to stand on ceremony . . . thought to drop in on my way home . . . need a little rest before I pr'ceed further.' He swayed in the doorway. His face was a sickly grey. His eyes were two sunken pits in which small fragments of colour glittered.

'Are you ill?' Miss Olga's hand fluttered anxiously to her cheek.

He swung his head round slowly, pinning her with a mad, cruel smile. 'Ill? No, not ill. Merely ruined.' A laugh bubbled wetly in his throat. 'Ruined beyond all hope of recovery.'

He was drunk, but not to the stage of incoherence. He was still – just – in control of his speech, of his limbs. And the more dangerous for it.

'Well? Are you not going to ask the manner of my ruin? But first,' a grotesque, staggering bow, 'I have this terrible thirst. Is there brandy in the house? Or that . . . that bug-piss Madeira?'

'Tea,' Miss Olga whispered bravely, her hand quavering towards the bell. 'Perhaps tea would be best. Or coffee.' She swallowed. 'Pray, seat yourself, Blandford, I shall ring . . .'

His lip curled. ' "Tea would be best",' he mimicked in falsetto. Then, roaring, 'Shit on your tea! What use is tea to me, you dried up bag of gristle?'

He lurched into the room knocking against a small table that rocked perilously, causing Miss Polsham to squeak in alarm. He swung towards the day bed and leaned over it, thrusting his face close to hers.

'Cousin Fanny . . . fat and feeble Fanny,' he hissed. 'How kind . . . how kind to be upset over my downfall when you have troubles of your own. Having to go through life unwanted, a useless jilted bitch . . . Never to know the thrust of a man's prick into that tender . . . tender, desirable orifice . . .'

He could not continue for a fit of lunatic laughter. Miss Polsham's lip quivered. Two fat tears gathered and slid down her scarlet cheeks.

'Sister,' she moaned. 'My heart . . . the pain . . .'

Miss Olga edged from the window, trembling, to

485

clasp her sister's outstretched hand. Beyond her, Mary Ann's frightened face glimmered momentarily in the doorway. I heard the patter of her footsteps as she ran – for Lily, I prayed. For someone sensible and strong and unshockable.

Swiftly, I stepped behind Blandford and said, clearly, 'Mr Pascoe, pray be seated. I will have wine fetched.'

His laughed choked off. He turned.

'Ah, the trio complete . . . the red-haired whore herself . . . *You'll* be d'lighted to hear my news, won't you? High-nosed slut! I'm ruined. Everythin' gone . . . No money, no horses, no house . . . all gone. Fortune's a bitch, I tell you. Gulls a man into b'lieving the dice are with him, then turns cold and proud and ruins him. Fortune's a bitch . . . hazard table's a painted, deceiving whore . . .'

'Take that chair, Mr Pascoe,' I said in as level a voice as I could muster. 'I shall sit here and we may continue the conversation more comfortably.'

'Comf'table?' he giggled, his glittery eyes almost disappearing into the dark pouches above his grey cheeks. 'Not comf'table now . . . Cir . . . circumstances all changed. Numbers runnin' my way all night, d'you see, then no more . . . All gone, main and chance . . . Nick . . . Ol' Nick – devil himself – took the lot . . .'

A flicker in my mind. Dice falling this way, that. Long, hard fingers scooping them up, tossing them down in careless, practised deception. I thrust it aside. No time to think of that. How was I to get Blandford Pascoe out of the parlour? Out of the house?

Lily appeared in the doorway, Mary Ann hovering at her shoulder. I took courage.

'I . . . we are very sorry to hear of your misfortune.' I must not antagonise him. I must remain calm, pleasant. 'You must have had a . . . a wearying night. Indeed you look exhausted. If you do not care to sit

486

down, then perhaps I should send out for a cab to take you home.'

'Have no home . . . jus' told you . . . Shall stay here's long as I please . . .' His giggles died. Something sly and leering seeped into his expression. 'You'll not say me nay, Joanna Howarth, will you? Need . . . need you to be kind . . . very kind . . . need somewhere to rest . . .'

His hands groped out. I sidestepped, smiling. 'Of course I shall be kind to you. If you will come this way, Blandford, I will find somewhere quiet where you may take your ease.'

Get him out of the parlour, away from the two frightened, bewildered ladies. Get him into the hall where, between us, Lily and Mary Ann and I might be able to persuade him – force him – out of the house.

He leered at me, then stuck his tongue out, waggling it obscenely between his lips. 'Bitch on heat. Ready for it, eh? Always had a fancy for you, y'know. Pretend to be hoity-toity . . . but I see that you're hot for it . . . Like all the rest . . . whores, sluts . . . panting to be on your back with your skirts up . . . Somewhere quiet, thass it . . . I'll teach you who's master . . .'

It was intolerable, but it had to be borne. Keep the smile fixed. Hold his attention. Edge him past the day bed and the two ladies. Try not to listen to the stream of foulness that spewed from him.

And we were almost at the door when he stopped so suddenly I nearly cannoned into him. His hand groped out. This time it caught at my skirt, twisting deeply into the silk, tugging me forward. I pulled back, snatching at my skirt to release it. The sharp movement was my undoing. My heel caught against the edge of a chair and I staggered off balance. He leapt at me then. I caught a glimpse of his glazed, intent, triumphant expression as we fell and knew the horror of

487

being momentarily helpless as he landed heavily on top of me, pinning me to the ground.

Somebody screamed. Mary Ann? Miss Polsham? I had knocked my head sickeningly against the corner of a cabinet. I fought against weakening blackness, aware that it was important I did not succumb to it yet barely able to comprehend the reason. It was a moment or two before understanding came back and with it blind panic.

I felt hot wet lips slobbering against my neck, heard the rip of nails against silk as a hand kneaded my breasts, felt the other hand thrusting up my skirt, tearing at encumbering lawn and lace and seeking the flesh between my thighs.

I tried to heave him off, but he was a dead weight. 'No!' I cried. 'No! Please!'

His lips crawled wetly to my mouth. I twisted my head away. He laughed and the laugh held cruelty and pleasure combined. 'Submit, bitch,' he hissed. 'Or you'll have to be taught . . . a lesson.' His nails sunk into the tender flesh of my inner thigh.

I tried to kick out. Failed. His nails dug deeper, moved higher.

Lily was at his back now. Pummelling and pulling at his shoulders, screeching, 'Gerrof, you brute! Leave 'er be. God 'elp us, he'll rape her else. Mary Ann give us a hand. No! Run and fetch help. A chairman, errand boy – *anyone*!'

The hand at my breast squeezed so hard that, try as I might, I could not hold back a cry of pain. He liked that. I was dizzily aware that my struggles, my fear, increased his frenzy, but the instinct to resist was stronger than reason.

Then as quickly as it had begun, it was over. Blandford's weight suddenly lifted from me. There were other voices, familiar, welcome. Someone smoothed down my skirts, I was helped to my feet, a chair brought.

I blinked to see Caleb holding Blandford up by the back of his coat. He dangled, choking and kicking, from Caleb's hands as though he had no more weight than a plump puppydog. Nick faced him. With a movement so fluid that it appeared effortless, he swung his clenched fist at Blandford's jaw. Blandford's face registered an instant's surprise before he slumped unconscious between Caleb's hands.

Nicholas turned swiftly to me, his face as ashy white as Blandford's had been, the bones sharp-etched under his skin. The night, the many nights leading to this last one, had taken its toll of him, too.

'Jo, I did not realise – forgive me. We were to see him safe home but he slipped our guard.' He took my hands tightly between his own. 'Are you hurt? Did he . . . harm you?'

I shook my head and stared at my hands locked in his. Mine trembled. His were rock steady, the skin callused, the nails roughly clipped. Hands that dealt in deceit but felt warm and comforting. Blandford's hands were plump and soft and cared for, yet I felt myself soiled and grubby because they had touched me. I wanted to hide myself away and strip off my clothes and scrub away every trace of his vile assault.

'Jo . . . I would not have had this happen for the world.'

I raised my head and looked him in the eye. I was awash with shame and embarrassment, but there was growing anger there, too.

'Would you not? Did you not plan to remove Blandford from his fortune?'

'I did not know he would turn on you. How could I?'

'Sometimes our actions have consequences we cannot foresee.'

'Spare me the sermon. You know my mind. Nothing you or anyone else can say will alter that.' He was tight-lipped now. His anger leaping to match mine. No one was close enough to hear our urgent whispers. Caleb was hauling an unconscious Blandford down the hall. Mary Ann was fussing over weeping Miss Polsham, Lily holding smelling salts under Miss Olga's nose.

'Oh, Nick . . . Nick, please reconsider. There is too great a pain in all this . . . and you have so much. Will you not be satisfied?'

He dropped my hands. Stepped back. Bowed.

I heard then what he had heard. A voice crying out in the hall.

'I am pleased you are not too badly shaken, Miss Howarth,' he said, formally. And turned in time to catch in his arms the person who came flying into the room.

'Oh, is it true?' Susannah sobbed, beating her fists against Nick's chest. 'Is he ruined? Have you taken everything from him?'

'I am afraid so, Miss Pascoe,' Nick said gravely.

'Oh, why did you let him? You knew he was hard pressed . . . to take all that he had left . . . the house . . .'

She slumped against him, wracked with sobbing. He held her gently, saying in a quiet voice, 'It was his choice. His own decision. His friends cautioned him. I tried to reason with him. But he would have none of it. Luck was with him earlier in the evening.' Nick shrugged. 'It failed him at the most critical moment. He is not the first to stake recklessly, nor will he be the last. But all was fair and honourable, as those who stayed to witness your brother's misfortune will testify.'

'To lose everything,' Susannah moaned. 'What will Papa say? And what shall I do now?'

'Miss Pascoe . . . Susannah, I am sorry that you must

490

suffer for your brother's losses, but please understand that you may stay at Roselawn until your father makes the necessary arrangements for you to return to the country. I shall not press for your departure.'

Tears trembled on her long lashes as she gazed up at Nick. Her golden curls were in disarray about her tear-stained cheeks. A maiden in deep distress. Genuine no doubt. How could any red-blooded male resist the urge to console and comfort?

Nicholas certainly did not. He took her hand, patting it gently. 'My carriage is outside. You will allow me to escort you and your brother safely to Roselawn? Good. You may rest assured, Miss Pascoe – Susannah – that I will do my best to make this difficult time as easy for you as is possible.'

He said his farewells to the ladies and withdrew. He did not glance at me again. His attention was all on Susannah. Pretty, addle-headed Susannah, who went with him like a lamb, and did not hear the warning rattle of weighted dice.

The carriage clattered away down the crescent. Somewhere a church bell tolled its funereal message into the wet grey air. I shuddered. I felt cold and sick, as though the doleful pronouncement of one unknown death in this busy city had special significance for me.

Perhaps others, too, heard that fateful bell and felt its dismal resonance. Later to shake their heads and wonder if its ominous tolling had been a portent of their own personal tragedy.

For the following day Brown's bank failed. Against that greater disaster, Blandford's downfall and disgrace slid into insignificance.

Chapter Eighteen

Eleanor Barton brought us the news, breezing in with an armful of flowers for Miss Polsham. 'Are they not beautiful? I could not resist the impulse to show you how my garden surprises me every day. Marigolds and stocks and the good Lord knows what else have seeded everywhere and I have forbidden the gardener under pain of death to remove one single weed until we are quite sure it is not something entirely beautiful that must be preserved. In consequence, he thinks me a perfect dragon, and is so bowed down with misery at being beholden to such a virago that even an extra sixpence does little to alleviate his distress.' She beamed at us. 'And, Miss Olga, I would beg a favour. I was at a bazaar yesterday held in aid of some deserving charity or other – distressed archbishops or downtrodden princesses, I forget which – and felt bound to purchase something for I feared that Lady Alperton and her committee might have locked me in until I did. This little watercolour of pink roses took my eye, but truly I cannot find a place to hang it. Could you find a nook for it somewhere as a small return for the positive cornucopia of cuttings you have given me for my weedy plot?'

The watercolour was charming in its oval velvet-frame. Miss Olga, after a moment's blushing hesitation for form's sake, accepted it with delight. And so the cheerfulness Mrs Barton always seemed to bring with her caught us up, dispelling some of the nervous atmosphere that had hung over us since yesterday's unpleasant events, though we had spoken little of it. The ladies, I think out of embarrassment and shame that such a dreadful scene had been enacted by one of their own kin, here in their own parlour, myself because I shuddered away from all remembrance of Blandford's assault. I even forbade Lily to mention it though she overflowed with sympathy and indignation. 'Best to forget it ever happened,' I said wearily. 'Just make sure that the door is kept locked as long as he remains in Exeter.'

Mrs Barton, kind, shrewd Mrs Barton, who had hurried here in order to prevent the news reaching us by some more dramatic and shocking method, made sure we were comfortably seated, then told us so quietly that for a moment Miss Olga still held the smile she had worn since her friend had arrived.

'I believe the doors are locked and a notice posted to the effect that the bank has ceased trading,' Mrs Barton went on in the same calm, reassuring voice. 'I could not get near enough to read it myself, for the crowd was too dense, but a kind man who had done so told me. Now, dear ladies, I shall beg your indulgence for putting myself forward, but I propose that we ring for refreshment. There is nothing more that can be usefully done at the moment and a cup of freshly brewed tea I always feel to be most restorative in moments of crisis. Certainly, I should recommend you not to make representations to the bank in person. The crowd assembled there was very angry and upset, as might be supposed, which, though it may relieve pent-up feelings, serves not the slightest purpose otherwise. The important thing is to stay composed in order to make a rational assessment of the situation as it may affect you and to decide what may be done for the best.'

I rather felt that this was the manner in which Eleanor Barton had met the crises in her own life and her calm example had its effect on Miss Polsham. She, no doubt, would have made a great to-do had we been alone, but with a glance at her visitor, she restrained herself to throwing her head back dramatically against the cushion and closing her eyes. But I wondered if Miss Polsham had truly grasped the situation. For most of her life she had taken refuge in invalidism. She had grown old in the comfortable conviction that the world circulated round her person and would go on doing so whatever happened beyond these four walls. It was Miss Olga my heart went out to. Miss Olga, who by the day, the week, the month, kept scrupulous account of the household budget and knew exactly what the failure of Brown's bank meant.

All colour drained from her face, leaving it tallow-white. It was the only sign that she had heard. Sitting there motionless, erect, as composed as Mrs Barton would have wished, she said, after a moment, 'Troubles never comes singly. Blandford ruined and now this. Poor Cousin James. It will hit him hard.'

And that was all.

She rang for tea, poured it with a steady hand, enquired civilly after Lady Alperton's health and whether the bazaar had been well patronised, from which Mrs Barton took her cue. She kept the conversation flowing on these innocuous matters until Miss Olga lost some of the stunned look in her eyes and her colour began to return. Mrs Barton took her leave then and I saw her to the door where we held a whispered conversation.

'My dear, one does not wish to offend by enquiring

too deeply of their circumstances, but is all their capital bound up in Brown's?'

'I believe so.'

'Dear heaven! Then you must promise that you will acquaint me if there is anything, any way, I can help.'

'You are very kind.'

'Merely practical. What relatives do they have apart from this cousin?'

'None that I know of.'

'And the cousin – I gather he has problems of his own. Is he likely to offer any assistance?'

'I believe he, too, was heavily involved with Brown's bank. This house is his. It may be that he will be forced to raise the rent if he is in difficult straits himself.'

She nodded briskly. 'Is it not his son – the ruined son – who gambled away his house at Mr Fox's establishment?' She smiled at my surprise. 'Lady Alperton's committee was a-buzz with it. Exeter, for all its size and its splendour, is no better or worse in this respect than any small place. I find these good ladies are as gossipy as the cottagers' wives in the villages where I have always lived, particularly enjoying the comfortable superiority of having biddable offspring who are unlikely to blacken the family name . . . But I will not keep you. Miss Olga will have need of you. Thank you for your frankness. I shall not abuse your trust.' She shook out her umbrella. 'I shall call again in the morning. Good day, Miss Howarth. Let us hope that it leaves off raining soon. Bad things always look worse when the sun does not shine.'

When the sun did come out, it scarcely improved matters.

Miss Olga sat for a long time over her account books, then called me into the dining parlour. We sat either side of the table, the polished oak surface bare save for an open book in front of her. It was the big family

Bible which she had removed from its lectern. As soon as I was seated, she began to read.

' "But they that will be rich fall into temptation and a snare, and into many foolish and hurtful lusts, which drown men in destruction and perdition.

' "For the love of money is the root of all evil; which while some coveted after, they have erred from the faith, and pierced themselves through with many sorrows." '

She closed the Bible carefully, resting her hands upon it as if to draw up warmth and comfort. The lines in her sallow face seemed to have deepened to indelible scars. She had aged ten years in a morning. She looked a tired, bowed, defeated old woman and it brought a lump to my throat and a welling resentment against those who had connived or mismanaged or downright cheated two innocent ladies out of what was rightfully theirs.

'It behoves us well to remember these words of St Paul at this troubling time,' she said. 'And a text that has hung above my bed these many years has also come into my mind today. "Lay not up for yourselves treasure upon earth, where moth and rust doth corrupt and where thieves break through and steal." ' She sighed. 'I stitched that sampler when I was six years old, yet here am I, into my sixty-fifth year, and only now brought to understand the truth of it. I have nothing but a few shillings in my purse. The rest of our money has gone, just as though thieves had made off with it. And the worse thing is, Joanna, that I do not think I can stand the shame and distress of telling my poor helpless sister how we are brought to the brink of destitution. She has trusted in my good judgment and my management of our affairs since our father died and I have failed her.'

'Fiddlesticks!'

'Joanna!'

'If we are apportioning blame, let us at least be honest, Miss Olga. Miss Polsham, as the elder sister, should rightly have taken all the responsibility for the household. Instead she chose to lead the life of an invalid and let others wait on her hand, foot and finger.'

'Chose? Joanna, I will not have that. She has always been delicate.'

'Before or after she was crossed in love? Oh, yes, I know all of it. I daresay she was hurt and ashamed but then you have been in love, too, and were dreadfully distressed by the outcome. You did not take to your bed.'

'That was different.'

'And tell me this. How many bills do you have outstanding in the house?'

The change of tack bewildered her.

'None, thank heavens.'

'And you think this is failure? To be so scrupulously honest and prompt in your dealings that no tradesman ever has to come begging for his account to be settled? I would say that was excellent management. And believe me, I know about people who are careless and forgetful in these matters, for my own mama and papa were so inclined and my brother and I suffered greatly after their death in consequence of all the debts that had accrued.'

I could not contain myself. I stood up and strode back and forth across the carpet.

'Miss Olga, you should not be putting on a hair shirt for your own supposed shortcomings, or even wasting time getting angry with those who truly deserve it. We have a problem and we must think how best to tackle it.'

'That is all very well for you to say. You are young,

full of energy. It is not so easy when you are old and tired, and it may be . . . may be that even the roof above your head is not secure, leave alone how we are to manage for housekeeping.' Her voice wobbled treacherously.

I spun round. 'No! You must not even think that, do you hear?' I swallowed hard, for what I had to say next was difficult. And inevitable. I had known that from the first. Once the words were spoken, I could not draw them back. But I had to speak. Out of conscience, out of respect, the sympathy – the affection, I admitted now – I felt towards Miss Olga I could not let the moment go, even though the rebellious, angry, determined streak in me shrieked against it. 'I . . . I have some money put by,' I said. 'We can survive on that for a while.'

'Oh, my dear, I could not let you . . . and what little you may have would be soon swallowed up.'

'It is not such a small amount,' I said. 'Do not forget that my business has thrived this twelvemonth.' And there was that other, the wager with its reward of golden coins tossed into my lap by a careless hand, the further reckless hazarding that had doubled the original harvest.

'I cannot accept charity.'

'Miss Olga, I have lived here for nearly three years. I cannot see that there is anything charitable about helping to maintain what I have come to regard as my home.'

I saw for the first time a spark of hope in her eyes.

Relieved, I went on crisply, 'I shall be continuing with my work as a lady decorator, which means that I shall continue to need your help with the bookkeeping. Perhaps we may come to some financial arrangement over that, which will not in any way be charity. And I could not see Lily put out on the street, and Mary

Ann and her mother need the work.' My nest egg, my precious nest egg would be plundered, scattered to keep the household running . . .

Best not to think of it. Best to consider only the practicalities and be glad that Miss Olga's shoulders straightened a little and she brightened.

'And there may be things we can sell,' she said. 'I shall look in the attic. Some of those chests have not been opened for years. There may be an oddment or two that might have value, though Papa sold Mama's silver toilet set and her jewellery before he remarried, my stepmama having no liking for reminders of her predecessor, even her children . . .' She broke off with a gasp. 'That was unworthy! Oh, dear. Pray, Joanna, disregard what I have said. I am all at sixes and sevens.' She cleared her throat, collected herself and said, in her usual sharp manner, 'You may go now and reassure my sister that all is well.'

But I had scarcely reached the door when she said, clearly, 'She was a hard, unfeeling woman. Why should I go on denying it? I hope God will forgive her, for I cannot.'

And she squared her shoulders and challenged the empty room with a bold and daring glance, as though courageously facing an invisible enemy.

Miss Olga, her confidence somewhat restored, wrote a note to Susannah that afternoon. 'Mary Ann shall take it. In the normal way, Joanna, I should either go myself or ask you to make a personal visit, for it is at times of trouble that families should offer support to one another. However, I am sure that Susannah will understand that we have much to do here, and we could not leave my sister to fret alone when she is so deeply upset by today's dreadful events. I have told Susannah we shall remember them all in our prayers.'

So she tiptoed carefully round the true reason for

not wishing either of us to go to Roselawn. I was deeply grateful for her timidity. Much as I worried about Ruth, I still felt bruised, mentally and physically, from the encounter with her father. My skin crawled with loathing when I thought of his groping hands on my body. I neither wished to talk about it nor risk the possibility of another such drunken assault. For once, I was content to stay indoors and busy myself helping Miss Olga to investigate the contents of the attic chests.

Alas, as Miss Olga had predicted, there was no secret cache of treasure. She sighed over her mama's faded silk dresses. 'I remember this – and this. How pretty she looked in it. It is called a sack-backed gown, because of the long pleat hanging loose from neck to hem. If I shake it out you can see. Is it not quaint? And there is a little of the original colour in this fold, such a pretty cornflower blue. And here is Papa's wig stand and a box of powder ... and his very bagwig! That? Oh, it is what Mama called a crasset. It is a crude type of oil lamp common in Guernsey, I believe ... This cane walking stick must have been Papa's, though it is not his style. Far too dandified with that carved handle and scarlet tassels. Perhaps in his youth ...' And our task was made the slower because each object must be examined and spoken about before it was set aside to be sold or carefully returned to the cedar-scented darkness of the chests.

The cane walking stick with its tarnished silver handle was, alas, the most valuable item. I feared the whole collection would not fetch more than a few guineas, but Miss Olga was heartened by this practical activity and moved on to contemplate her mama's pretty French chairs.

'I could not bear, Joanna, for some rough man to treat them carelessly or for them to be displayed to the gaze of all and sundry at a public auction.' She gazed

501

at me hopefully. 'Do you suppose that a private buyer might be found? A genteel lady refurbishing her house, perhaps. Someone with a large enough drawing room to set them out to their best advantage? If in the course of your work you should come across such a one . . .'

'Then I will guide her to your chairs, Miss Olga.'

Satisfied, she once more draped them in their dustsheets and closed the door gently on memories of her far-off childhood.

Mary Ann returned from Roselawn with a dramatic note from Susannah.

> I cannot tell you how this latest Dreadful News
> has sunk me in the Utmost Gloom. There is as
> yet no word from Dear Papa, though I expect it
> Hourly and Dear Brother Blandford is in such
> Distress that I Fear for his Health. What I would
> do without the Comfort of Good Friends I do
> not know. Would that I were little Ruth, an
> Innocent Child, who I think is the Only Person
> in the House who is sangwin, out of ignorance
> of the Sore Events that bring us such Great
> Grief.

'Poor Susannah,' Miss Olga sighed. 'One feels so helpless to advise.'

Selfish cat, I thought. Never a word of concern about her elderly cousins. As for Blandford's 'distress', if his head suffered as a result of his drinking I hoped it was exceedingly painful; if he was distraught because of the loss of his house, then I wished him a prolonged and agonised spell of torment.

The note told us little. Mary Ann, sharp child, had gleaned a great deal more below stairs while she awaited Susannah's answer.

''Tes such a great house,' she said to Lily and me, her eyes round. 'Why, this liddle kitchen would scarce take up a corner o' theirs, and so many cupboards and pantries I should never remember which from t'other – and a scullery big as a barn and every sink having its own pump, so no water need be carried—'

'Did you see Miss Pascoe?' I interrupted gently.

'No, miss, but they said in the kitchen as 'er'd had the vapours and was lyin' in the parlour wi' the blinds down on account of Mr Blandford 'ad locked himself in his bedchamber wi' a bottle of brandy. And he was cussin' inside and smashing things and making a terrible commotion.'

'Was he indeed,' I said grimly.

'Even Mr Fox couldn't persuade he to give up.'

'Mr Fox?'

'Yes, miss. And Mr Caleb. They was both there else I think the maid and cook both would have packed their bags and gone for fear Mr Blandford might break out and do them a mischief.'

What would I do without the company of Good Friends . . .

I said sharply, 'Lady Alperton, her daughter Clarissa, were they not there?'

'Heard no mention of it, miss.' She was agog to relate the more dramatic details. 'Mr Fox, he set Mr Caleb by Mr Blandford's door and said no one was to go near and Mr Blandford would come out when he was hungry and thirsty enough and Mr Caleb would know how to deal with him.'

I was sure he would.

'Cook says as 'ow Mr Fox, being the rightful owner now, wants to make sure his property's not damaged afore the Pascoes move out which she hopes'll be quick, for there's wages owin' and Mr Fox 'as promised to make it up to any servants who've stayed loyal,

503

which isn't so many as far as I can see, being but the cook and the parlourmaid and a scullery maid and a boy as cleans the boots and brings in coals.' She paused for breath, rushed on, ' 'Er says like as not there'll be more arguing and carrying on when Mr Pascoe comes up from Kingsbridge, for he'll not like what Mr Fox done to Mr Blandford. But 'er do like Mr Fox a deal better'n her likes any of they Pascoes, for all his pa was hung from a gallows-tree. He'm kind and generous, 'er says, and a natural gentleman, whereas Miss Pascoe and Mr Blandford is terrible short on both accounts.'

'Yes, yes, but what of the child, Miss Ruth!' I said, suddenly and perversely impatient with hearing Nicholas's praises sung. I had no need to hear of his charming ways. I was well aware of them. And, as others were not, of how that charm masked a darker and far less engaging streak in his character.

Mary Ann shrugged. 'Nothing of 'er, miss.'

Poor child. It seemed her lot to be put away and forgotten. But perhaps, at present, it was for the best with all the upset in the house.

'I just hope that wretched nursemaid is being good to her,' I said.

'Nowt you can do about it at present,' Lily said stoutly, 'so no use mitherin'. Now, out of me way, Miss Jo. I've a stockpot to put ready for simmerin' for tomorrow's mutton broth an' I thought I'd make some cheese tartlets, which Miss Olga's partial to, to go with a salad of lettuce and chives for supper. Cheer her up a bit. Even if the old girl pretends pastry's a bit weighty near bedtime, I notice she manages to gobble 'em up pretty sharpish.'

I did not tell Miss Olga any of Mary Ann's revelations. It would only have distressed her unnecessarily. Nicholas called upon us late that afternoon and was, thankfully, equally discreet.

He would not sit. He had merely called as a friend, he said, to enquire after the health and welfare of the Misses Polsham on a day which had brought sad tidings to a great many people. So, tactfully, he left them the choice of confiding their involvement with Brown's bank or retaining their privacy over these intimate financial matters.

Miss Polsham removed herself straightaway from the responsibility of choice.

'My poor health, as ever, is a cross I have learned to bear with fortitude, Mr Fox,' she said in a frail voice. 'Though it is courteous of you to enquire. With regard to other, more worldly matters, I do not have the strength to concern myself with them. My sister, who has the good fortune to enjoy all the benefits of a robust constitution, may be able to offer an opinion, for she is constantly out and about in Exeter.'

Miss Olga said, carefully, 'One has the greatest sympathy for those in desperate need. We . . . we have suffered somewhat through our connection with Brown's but I believe we may overcome our present difficulties.'

'I am pleased to hear that,' Nicholas said gravely. 'But I hope, Miss Olga, that if these circumstances change, you would have no hesitation in calling upon me. I should be honoured to assist you in any way I can.'

'Thank you, Mr Fox.'

'Not at all, Miss Olga. And as I have just this moment come from your cousins, may I reassure you that an atmosphere of calm now prevails at Roselawn. A message from Kingsbridge arrived just before I left. It seems that Mr Pascoe hopes to return tomorrow.'

He was very tall, very vigorous, very masculine in that shaded, female parlour. He did not look at me beyond one cool glance, a curt dip of the head when

Mary Ann showed him in. His coldness did nothing to counteract the surge of those riotous feelings which were inevitably stirred by the sight of him. I seemed incapable of controlling that physical, almost painful turbulence, though I masked it well enough, I suppose, taking refuge in stiff-backed silence. If that was the way he wished it, I could play that game too. If he could pretend to be indifferent, so could I. I certainly would not simper and fawn upon him in order to win his favour, as Susannah did. Such posturings were the prerogative of shallow, empty-headed creatures. I would not join their ranks.

Lofty enough sentiments. But after he had gone I fell into a melancholy mood. Doubts and regrets circled endlessly in my head. To counteract them I excused myself and retired to my studio under the roof tiles.

But the lift of the spirits that I usually felt as I busied myself with my drawings and samples did not come. I was too restless to settle and was relieved when Mary Ann called me to supper and this long troubling day drew to a close.

Mr James Pascoe returned to Exeter, but he did not immediately pay a formal call upon his Polsham cousins, nor did any further word come from Roselawn.

'I should hope Cousin James would let us know soon if he proposes to raise the rent,' Miss Olga said anxiously several times a day.

'Perhaps there will be no need,' I comforted her and hoped fervently I was right. The summer slackness in business which I had welcomed earlier now took on a more serious aspect. There was an air of caution about. A feeling that it might be prudent, even if one was not directly affected by the failure of Brown's, to take stock, to curtail any unnecessary expenditure. The merchant who had wished to please his wife by refurbishing her summer parlour now discovered that his wife grew sentimental over the Chinese papers and fading furnishings she had lived with all her married life. 'A woman's prerogative, eh? To be fickle?' he twinkled. 'But perhaps we shall have the pleasure of speaking to you again on the matter at some later date. May I keep these clever drawings of yours to hand, and the estimates? I shall produce them the minute she shows signs of a change of heart.'

Worse, I became a direct victim of Brown's failure when a bill I had presented to a lady for the redesigning of her bedroom remained unpaid. Calling to press my case, I found the house shuttered and silent. An old man guarding the gate told me that the family had fled in the night to avoid their creditors. I was twenty-five guineas out of pocket and it was a hard blow.

I began to realise that I should have to take serious stock. To dip into my nest egg for gowns and hats and boots and Mary Ann's wages and the many little treats and comforts for the ladies, when it was continuously topped up by my earnings, was one thing. To have to run a complete household with the prospect, seemingly, of a much reduced income was quite another. I asked Miss Olga to prepare a full account of the household's expenditure and we went over it together to see where economies might be made. But it was a household where little was wasted; Miss Olga saw to that. I tried not to let my worries show.

'We shall manage for now,' I said cheerfully. 'And let us hope that by the autumn everyone will want their houses done up in time for the Christmas festivities.'

But at the back of my mind lurked the ominous thought that if business did not pick up and Mr Pascoe raised the rent, we should be in difficult straits by Christmas.

Mrs Barton brought tales of people far worse off

than ourselves. Even one sad case of a desperate man unable to face his creditors casting himself into the Exe, his poor drowned body fetching up at Countess Weir.

'As for the Browns themselves,' she added, 'they have not been seen since Mr Brown left the bank premises the evening before the closure was announced. But rumour has it that they have sensibly taken passage to a happier land *on* the water, not under it.'

'They have run off?'

'To Topsham in a closed carriage that very night and thence aboard a ship that sailed on the morning tide. Narrowly ahead, one hears, of those who would have detained Mr Brown to face charges of misappropriating the bank's funds.'

Miss Olga's eyes widened in disbelief. 'He has caused so much grief, yet he goes free . . .'

Mrs Barton patted Miss Olga's hand. 'That is debatable. I would not have his conscience for all the tea in China. I should not care to have a man's death haunting me or a widow's tears washing through my dreams even if I had carried off enough gold to keep me in comfort for the rest of my days.'

' "Vengeance is mine; I will repay saith the Lord," ' Miss Olga sighed.

'Quite so,' said Mrs Barton briskly. 'Perhaps the Lord will send a particularly violent storm to harass them all the way to Constantinople or Cape Town or wherever they are bound. Or send a giant whale to swallow them up. Mrs Brown, I feel, would make particularly choice dining for a hungry sea monster, do you not agree?'

So she coaxed a wan smile from Miss Olga, who prayed mightily before supper that night for those storm-tossed on the oceans of the world and on the need for forgiveness. Almost as though her own conscience was pricking her on certain, relevant matters.

Mr Pascoe and Susannah arrived one morning just after Mrs Barton called. She had been carried off into the garden by Miss Olga to admire an exceptional show of arum lilies which had found the summer this year particularly to their liking.

'If you would be so good, Miss Howarth, as to summon my cousin indoors,' Mr Pascoe said in a curt voice, 'I should like to speak to her and Fanny in private.'

There was an ominous quality about the statement and in his demeanour. He looked as though his body had shrunk within his clothes. The flesh of his face seemed to have slid away, leaving weighty bags under his eyes and sagging folds under his chin. His usual air of vague joviality was quite gone, replaced by a sullen aspect in which I recognised for an instant a look of peevish sourness I had caught often on Blandford's face.

'Of course,' I said quietly. 'Susannah, perhaps you would care to take a turn round the garden while your papa is engaged?'

I was sorry to interrupt Miss Olga's pleasant interlude with Mrs Barton. Alarm flared in her eyes and she hurried indoors. I made the necessary introductions, and Mrs Barton after a polite exchange of civilities made to go.

'Oh, pray do not leave on my account,' Susannah said pettishly. 'We do not intend to stay as we have several more calls to make. And I am forced go with Papa, it seems, for I am to be treated like a child and *ordered* to accompany him, whether I like it or not. It is perfectly intolerable of him to treat me so!'

I had been so concerned that Mr Polsham's visit heralded bad news that I had not taken much note of

Susannah. Now, this unmannerly outburst made me look at her closely. She wore a wide-brimmed straw hat with, unusually for her, a length of pink gauze swathed across it and pulled down as though to shade her complexion from the sun, though it was a cloudy day. Behind the veiling her expression was mutinous and there was a distinct reddening and puffiness about her eyes. I had never known Susannah shed tears other than to make a calculated effect of helplessness that left no unpleasant trace. Something beyond the ordinary had upset her this morning.

'There is no secret about what Papa is telling Cousin Olga,' she said, the words bursting out as though she could not contain them. 'It will soon be common knowledge that he is to sell all his Exeter properties, including this one.'

'Selling! But what of Miss Polsham, Miss Olga?' I cried.

She shrugged. 'This house has always been a millstone, he says, because our cousins have never paid an economical rent and it was his kindness that allowed the arrangement to continue. For myself, I believe it would be more natural in a father to bestow such kindness on his own children rather than on a pair of indignant old women, but in this I have been sadly misled. His innocent daughter, who by the nature of her sex must rely on the goodwill of a parent, must suffer. And Blandford, who brought ruin on himself and deserves punishment, will scarcely be punished at all. Indeed, he will come off best. It is so unfair!'

I stared at her blankly. Her words made no sense. Indeed, I was not paying much heed to them. Whatever squabble she had with her father, it was unimportant compared to the fact that this house was to be sold. At the least that meant a rise in the rent. At worst someone might buy it who wanted the property for his own use and the ladies could be put out of their home.

Mrs Barton cleared her throat, adjusted her bonnet strings and murmured, tactfully, 'I really must not take any more of your time, Miss Howarth. I shall call again, tomorrow, as usual. Do give my regards to Miss Polsham and Miss Olga and beg their forgiveness for not making my adieux in person, for I believe I will leave by the garden gate which will shorten my journey home. Miss Pascoe, I am quite charmed to have met you. I have heard much about you and find it most, er, pleasing that the reality of your presence quite matches up to the sentiments expressed by your many acquaintances.'

The dry tone of her voice was lost on Susannah who, reacting automatically to any suggestion of a compliment, turned on a sweet smile which was instantly switched off as Mrs Barton left us. She glared at me.

'Papa is also advising our cousins that you are to accompany me back to Kingsbridge tomorrow,' she announced. 'Your grandfather will have you met there and taken on to Falconwood.'

'Falconwood?' The surge of joy I felt was instantly dashed. How could I leave the ladies at such a worrying time? They needed me here. Grandfather had ignored me for all these months and now this peremptory command. 'But there is hardly time to pack my bag and make the necessary preparations!'

'Do not look at me as though it were my fault!' she snapped. 'The wishes – the *orders* – of our elders and betters must be obeyed. You are no better off in that regard, Joanna, than I am, for all that you set yourself up, quite foolishly, to be independent of authority. Striding about town as though you were the equal of any man! Most unbecoming.' For a moment her expression was sly and knowing. 'Perhaps Mr Kerswell means to put an end to such unfeminine activities, which cannot reflect well on him.'

'Hah! He has not shown in the past that he cares a fig for me. Why should he bother himself now?'

'Oh dear, you have gone quite red in the face! You should endeavour to remain calm at all times, Joanna. Such a choleric effect is most unbecoming.' Having needled me to crossness cheered her a little. She now proceeded to try to irritate me even further. 'And if I had any idea of the whys and wherefores of this whim of your grandfather's, I am afraid I am not at liberty to disclose them.'

'I should not dream of asking,' I said, through gritted teeth.

'Men will have their own way, whatever *our* opinion,' she said. 'It is the way of the world.' Then with a touch of her usual pertness, she added, 'Mind you, one is able on occasions to pull the wool over their eyes. Like tonight when . . .' She stopped short. 'Well, no matter, it is merely that . . . that I have persuaded Papa to allow me to visit the Alpertons for one last time. It is to be a quiet musical evening. Among friends.' Her glance slid from mine. She reached out, snapped the head off a perfect white rose and began, viciously, to dismember it, petal by petal. 'Papa thinks, you see, that I should not be too much on public view at this particular time. As though it were my fault that he is rendered insolvent and Blandford is ruined. *Particularly* I must be removed from what he calls "bad influences" which *I* do not consider *bad*, nor does Exeter society. "Blood will out," he says. But it is pure spite and envy on his part because of Blandford's disgrace, which reflects badly on us all . . . Oh, if only the wretched bank had not failed, if only Blandford had gambled away his property to someone other than Nicholas, it would surely not have come to this!' She threw down the now naked rose stem and ground it under her heel

512

into the old red brick of the garden path. 'That is what I think of Papa's stupid pride! His treatment of me! I will not submit! I will not be condemned ... and ... and used to suit his purposes, and Blandford's purposes ... and to have no say ...' She broke off on a wrenching, ugly sob. 'How can I bear it? To be taken away from him like this.' The face she turned on me was pitiful in its naked emotion. 'I love him ... I have never felt like this about any man ... I think from the first there has been an attraction between us ... though it is only recently that he has dared to allow his ... his affection for me to show ... and I have recognised the depth of my feeling ... and now we are to be torn apart ...'

I said, through a throat suddenly tight, 'This ... this person is ...?'

'Nicholas Fox of course. Have you never noticed the many little attentions he pays me? The ardent glances? And these last few days he had been a rock when all about me has crumbled to ruin.' She sought a handkerchief in her reticule and mopped her face. In a somewhat calmer voice, she said, 'You cannot understand how these things are, Joanna, I realise that. You have no experience. But I assure you it is no light matter to be in love at all, let alone with a person disapproved of by one's father ...'

'Miss Pascoe, Miss Pascoe.' Mary Ann scurried from the house, bobbed a curtsey. 'Mr Pascoe's waiting on you, miss, ready to go.'

Susannah carefully replaced her handkerchief in her reticule, shook away the rose petals scattered on her pink muslin skirt, looked about her as though seeing the garden for the first time. Then she adjusted the veil over her eyes, gave me a slow, gracious nod.

'I do agree that the garden is looking perfectly delightful,' she said, in a loud, clear voice. 'It is a pity

I must leave, but Papa will not be kept waiting. Good-bye, Joanna dear.' She leaned forward and kissed the air somewhere near my cheek and hissed, 'Say nothing! Do you understand? Nothing. To anyone.'

Her dainty pink heels tapped away up the path in Mary Ann's wake and I was left alone with my thoughts and the fragments of a once-beautiful rose.

The little attentions he pays me ... the ardent glances ... The phrases ran round my head like rats in a cage. They beat a tattoo at my temples as Miss Olga explained in a thin, unnatural voice that the house was to be sold over her head. They thundered in my ears as I read the letter from my grandfather which Miss Olga handed to me, because her voice would not quite hold steady enough to read it aloud: 'I regret the haste ... the convenience of travelling with Miss Pascoe ... Please accept my apologies ... an urgent matter or I should not have sought to inconvenience you ...' And that strong, hard signature. *Francis Kerswell*

What urgent matter? I thought vaguely.

Ardent glances ... the little attentions he pays me ... On and on and on, numbing me to everything else. To Miss Polsham's attack of palpitations, to Miss Olga's misery, to the urgency of sorting clothes to be packed for the visit to Falconwood. Somehow the hours were to be got through. Silent hours. As though an odd sort of hush had descended on the house so that each slow beat of my heart sounded unnaturally loud in my ears.

I did all the right things. Consoled Miss Olga, calmed Miss Polsham with camomile tea and soothing noises. Was brisk and practical in the matter of packing my bag and tidying my studio and advising Miss Olga if any enquiries were made for my services, she was to make sure that the person knew I would be pleased to wait upon her or him the moment I returned.

514

'To be sure, Joanna, I shall do my best, though I would hope for such a one to be a lady, for I never quite know what to say to a gentleman . . . Oh, but I wish it was not now that you had to leave us. Perhaps it will only be for a few days,' she added hopefully.

'Do not fret, Miss Olga. Grandfather will not keep me longer than is necessary. He has no love of me. Nor I of him, if the truth were known.' I managed a smile. 'He will send me packing as soon as maybe.'

'Then let us hope nothing . . . nothing *definite* occurs until you are back. Cousin James said there may be people wishing to view the property – all manner of strangers – and there may be lawyers to deal with, which would be a great trouble . . .'

'I cannot think that a great deal will happen in the short time I am gone,' I said.

'You think not?' She brightened. 'Well, I shall take heart from that and shall pray, Joanna, that you travel safely and return to us swiftly.'

I was glad I had offered her some comfort. I only wished that someone would do the same for me. But I had no escape from the words in my head and no way of knowing how true, or how false, they were.

The journey to Kingsbridge was as safe as Miss Olga would have wished. The day was fair, the horses sturdy, the Pascoes' carriage comfortably sprung. Other travellers on the road were few and considerate. There were no delays or inconsiderate jostlings at toll gates or narrow bridges. No farm carts or herds of cows or strings of pack horses lumbering from field tracks to block our way. Our wheels kept clear of ditches, no horse lost a shoe or went lame. The views of the hills and moors and the distant, sparkling sea, when we were not tunnelling through deep lanes, were wild and splendid.

And inside we were as quiet and still as the jolting and rattling of the carriage would allow. Sally sat in the far corner and stared dully out of the window. Susannah, unusually pale, unusually silent, sat opposite me. Ruth lay curled on the seat beside me in a dead slumber, her head in my lap. "Tes a cordial cook told me of,' Sally had said proudly. ''Tes proper good 'er said for dosin' liddle ones as is fractious. Sets 'em to sleeping proper peaceful. An' Miss Pascoe, 'er didn't want no journey same as we had up to Exeter, wi' the maid bein' sick somethin' terrible.' She held up the bottle. 'Godfrey's Cordial, 'tes called. Druggist do say 'tes very pop'lar.'

It was most efficient. But I felt uncomfortable at the way the child slept. It was too deep, too unnatural. She had scarcely roused when she had been lifted into the carriage, had smiled blurrily at me and instantly dropped to sleep again.

But I wished I could take a dose of the magic cordial and join her. Instead I must sit here and think of Susannah and Nick together and wonder if he had been at the Alpertons' last evening. And if he had, had he spoken to her? Touched her hand? Smiled at her with the smile that broke women's hearts? *The little attentions he pays me. . . . the ardent glances . . .*

'Did you have a pleasant evening?' I asked, could not help but ask, with cool, stiff politeness as we rattled across the Exe Bridge.

Her eyelids flickered down, smooth ivory over blue. 'Most pleasant.' A soft, secret smile curved her lips.

'The company was agreeable?'

'Most agreeable.'

'Were there many people present?'

'Something above twenty.'

'And . . . nobody there that your papa might have . . . disapproved of?'

She did not answer. Her glance slid to Sally, unheeding in her corner, then back to me. Her smile deepened before, almost dreamily, she turned back to the window and gazed, as the carriage took a bend in the road, upon the distant prospect of the great cathedral on its hill, with the huddled roofs of the city spreading around it and down to the curving arm of the river.

It was all the answer I needed. I knew, with cold certainty, as we left the city behind and the red dust of our passing trailed us along the highway, that she and Nick had met together last evening, and whatever had transpired had swept yesterday's distraught, tearful outburst, at least temporarily, from Susannah's memory.

Harry Beer brought the ancient Falconwood chariot to meet me at Kingsbridge. I kissed Susannah who said, 'It will not be too long, I think, before we meet again.' And smiled that enigmatic, secret smile that tore my composure to shreds. I kissed Ruth, now awake and inclined to grizzle, and hugged her and promised, as she blinked the sleep from her eyes, that I should come and see her as soon as I could.

I would not pause for refreshment. We had drunk ginger ale from a travelling flask and nibbled at cold chicken as we journeyed. I wanted to be at journey's end. I was impatient, now, to feel that sense of homecoming, feel the strength and solidity of the house about me. Within Falconwood's walls the turbulent spirit would find calm, the hurt would heal.

The last jolting mile seemed endless. I wished I could leap down from the carriage and run direct across fields and woods instead of meandering to and fro in the deep winding lanes. We came out at last on the final stretch, a thread of red dust slicing through the green grass of the headland, the deep indented cliffs stretching away to distant Start Point which jutted like a blue smudge on a child's painting into the glittering sea. On the other side the ripe, rich curves of wooded hills and fields. And Falconwood ahead, snug among the mounded trees, a thread of smoke drifting up from the kitchen chimney, windows glittering in the evening light. Waiting for me. Waiting to welcome me home.

There was a stinging behind my eyelids as I stepped down stiffly from the chariot and went up the steps to the front door. It opened almost before I could knock, as though someone had been watching out for me. A whoosh of barks and yelps and wagging tails as the dogs bounced out. Bessy Beer, holding the great door back, gaping at me, then belatedly dropping a rough curtsy, and Ben was behind her, beaming shyly, as he dropped a kiss on my cheek and Mr Chadwick taking my hand and shaking it warmly. A flutter of ancient lace and trailing taffeta click-clacking down the hall and Miss Lightbody's voice crying, 'I swear I had forgot that you were such a great height! Nor do I recall such elegance! Such a splendid hat! Why, 'tis a fine lady now, not a drab child that comes a-visiting.' And in my ear, the hiss of her whisper, scarcely audible, like the hint of a storm to come in the stirring of dry dust on a balmy summer's day. 'Be ready, child. He means mischief. I mislike the omens . . .'

I shrugged the whisper aside. I let the house take me in. The door clanged shut behind me, my life in Exeter was far away, sliding back into memory and taking the heartache with it.

I was home. I was safe. It was enough for the moment.

Bessy Beer was toiling up the stairs with a message from Grandfather as I came out of my bedroom, washed, refreshed and changed into my favourite sage-green gown, Miss Lightbody's lace collar at my throat, my hair coiled and pinned in the way I was now able to keep it controlled, yet allowing its natural exuberance to give it life and movement.

'Please, miss, master'll see you in his study after supper.'

'Thank you, Bessy.'

She stood aside to let me pass. There was a grudging respect in her manner. Very different from the previous occasions. As though there was some change in me that held her back from the rudeness she had previously had no difficulty in displaying. Indeed, she seemed a little in awe of me.

I would have been amused, had I not begun, as I dressed, to think about Miss Lightbody's whisper. What had she meant? What mischief? There was little on the surface that indicated trouble. Ben was well and happy. Mr Chadwick his usual gentle, amiable self. We were a cheerful company assembled for supper and Miss Lightbody gave no hint of anything amiss as we ate and talked.

But perhaps that whisper of warning did something to prepare me when I went into Grandfather's study. Or maybe I was older and wiser than the green girl who had stood here, shocked and distressed at being parted in such a cruel manner from her much-loved brother. I no longer trusted blindly to the goodwill of others. I particularly did not trust the tall, beaky-nosed man with the mane of rough white hair who stood astride the hearthrug, his hands clasped behind his back, staring at me from under his shaggy brows.

'Grandfather,' I said quietly, dropping a curtsy.

'Joanna.' Then, after a long, regarding moment, awkwardly, as though dragging up the memory of old-fashioned courtesy, a stiff little bow. 'If you would care to take a seat.'

'Thank you, sir, but I think I should prefer to stand.'

And so, facing each other across the brown and faded spaces of the room, he told me how he and James Pascoe had laid their plans.

Grandfather would pay off Blandford's debts and settle him into a steady marriage in exchange for a certain favour whereby James Pascoe could rid himself of his pretty, spoilt and now dowerless daughter. With those two problems solved, James Pascoe would be able, just, to steer through these troubled times, making many economies but salvaging his Kingsbridge house and his pride. And Grandfather would have the prospect of his most cherished desire. A grandson to carry the Kerswell blood to future generations.

So I listened as Grandfather laid the future before me. A future mapped out by these two gentlemen for their convenience and satisfaction.

Susannah was to marry Ben. And I was to become the wife of Blandford Pascoe.

Chapter Nineteen

There had to be more. Must be. He was too calm, too sure of himself.

I said, 'And if I refuse?'

He lifted his shoulders. 'You are under age. I have the authority to decide for you. However, I hope you would not go against my wishes.'

'I have no choice?'

'Of course. Though you should realise that if you do not marry young Pascoe, then the bargain is broken. Susannah will not be obliged to marry Benjamin.'

'What then?'

'Ah, you have come straight to the crux of the matter and I shall be equally direct. If this marriage between Susannah Pascoe and Benjamin does not take place, I shall have no other course but to send Benjamin to the clinic in Bath where he previously had a short sojourn.' He picked a sheet of paper off the mantel-shelf. 'I have Dr Roote's letter here. He is convinced that in a year, perhaps two, the improvement in Benjamin's mental processes will be great. The boy will, of course, be left completely under Dr Roote's control for as long as is necessary. Should you like to read it?'

I made no move to take it. There was no need. Grandfather was not lying.

'I have made an appointment for Benjamin for a date two days after that fixed for your wedding. If the wedding does not take place, I shall dismiss Mr Chadwick and will accompany Benjamin myself to the clinic.' A pause to allow this to sink in. 'If, however, you agree to marry Blandford Pascoe, the moment the ceremony is over I shall write to Dr Roote and cancel the course of treatment. There will be no more talk of doctors and clinics. I shall then do everything in my power to ensure that in my lifetime and, through my lawyers, after it, Benjamin will remain here for as long as he lives surrounded by his animals, wanting for nothing, with servants to look to all his needs.'

'And suppose Susannah refuses to marry Ben?'

'She has not refused. What young woman in her position would? She is a shallow, silly girl but she has seen the sense of it. Her father can no longer afford to keep her in fashionable clothes and pretty trinkets, with servants to run after her. She will have all she wants or needs here. She will be mistress of a fine house, she may engage what servants she wishes, make what changes she likes, providing I, or my trustees if I should die, approve. She may entertain her friends, put on as bold a show as she pleases and once she had produced an heir, a pretty sum will be settled on her for independent use. Until that time she will remain at Falconwood. After that she may do as she pleases. The child, the son, will have every possible advantage heaped upon him, and, at his majority, will inherit this house, the farms, the shipping interests, everything, to guard and, in turn, pass on to his son, the next Kerswell. You cannot say that is an unfair bargain.'

'But this . . . this child, this heir you so desire may be a girl.'

'Susannah is young – healthy, so I am assured. She will breed easily, I think. Motherhood is, after all, the natural inclination for a woman. The supreme reason for her span on earth. Sooner or later there will be a son.'

'You are very sure. Have you not thought that Ben might not be capable . . . of . . . marriage?'

He gave a snort of laughter. 'Do you take me for a fool, girl? Of course I have made sure he is capable of bedding a woman. Though doctors have assured me he is physically mature and sound, I have taken no chances. I have accompanied him several times to a woman of my acquaintance, a clean, decent, discreet widow, who has obliged me by teaching him his duties. She assured me he performed well and enjoyed the task. In that at least,' he added with satisfaction, 'he has the inclination of a true Kerswell.'

Once Mama and Papa had visited some duke's great seat in Derbyshire. While they were shown round the grand rooms, we children were left to lose ourselves in the gravelled walkways of a yew-hedged maze. I now had the same feeling that I had then as again and again a promising way out ended in a high, frustrating barrier.

There was nothing left for me but to appeal to what scrap of human sympathy might remain under that hard, unforgiving shell.

I said, controlling the tremor in my voice, 'Are you aware, Grandfather, what you ask of me? Do you know what manner of man this is that you would have me marry? He is . . . corrupt. Cruel.'

'And ultimately a weak, vain, stupid fellow.' Grandfather's smile held a hint of complacency. 'You will manage him well enough once you have his mark.'

'Manage him!'

'And then there is his daughter. I believe you have some fondness for the child and she for you. You should make her a splendid stepmama. I am sure that your friend Jane, who died so untimely, would have approved.'

It was as though he had studied all the vulnerable

aspects of my character and meant to be relentless in his attack upon them.

He turned to his desk. From a dusty bottle he poured a generous measure of liquid into two plump glasses. He handed one to me and took the other himself, holding it up to catch the candlelight as he spoke.

'You may have thought yourself comfortably out of my sight in Exeter but I have made it my business to acquaint myself with your progress.' The heavy liquid tilted against the cut crystal in rich amber-dark swirls. He brought the glass to his nose and drew in a deep, satisfied breath. 'Cognac. The best. Mature and smooth. Our former enemies may be a cunning race of flea-ridden peasants who had discriminately lopped off the heads of their aristocracy and are known to dine on frogs and snails, but their brandy is the nectar of angels ... Yes, child, I know far more than you think. In the beginning, perhaps, I thought to put a stop to the correspondence you set up with my grandson's tutor—'

'You knew?'

'No harm seemed to ensue, so I allowed it to continue. It has given me some amusement to watch the way you contrived to deceive me. And then, I confess it, I grew interested to see how you would proceed. What you would make of yourself and if you would turn the less than auspicious circumstances in which you were placed to your advantage.'

'And ... and your conclusion, sir?' I said, taken aback by this turn in the conversation.

'It was far beyond my expectations. I think that you will not be a milksop of a wife to Blandford Pascoe, as was his first. Indeed, I have it in me to feel sorry for him, though he himself is eager for the match. But as I said, he is a fool.'

'And a bully and a lecher. You would condemn me to the . . . the humiliation of submission—'

'Submission? You? Hah! I would sooner expect a cornered tiger to submit. You stand before me, a strong-willed, resolute woman with a generous inheritance of your mother's boldness – perhaps even a little of her waywardness though it is tempered with a shrewd intelligence peculiarly your own – and you speak of submission?'

'If you think by flattery to win me round—'

'Flattery?' he roared. 'Great God, those are the characteristics that I least appreciate in a woman. They have been the downfall of the men of this family. Strong, cunning women who do not bend easily to a man's will. Who connive and cheat in order to follow the cravings of their sensual natures. I do not like you, Joanna Howarth, any more than I did. You are too independent in your thinking and there is too much anger burning in your soul. A dangerous combination. No, I do not like you, but I say this. If your spirit and character were evident in the grandson who bears my name and my hopes, I should be a happy man today and would die a content one.' He thrust his glass towards me. 'A toast.'

'I have nothing to celebrate!'

'To a bargain, then, even if you think it now a bad one for yourself. It is an excellent one, you must agree, for the weaker vessels whom we strong ones must protect. Benjamin, Ruth Pascoe, even that silly girl Susannah who shall lack nothing her shallow nature desires. So, you keep your part and I shall keep mine. You have my word.'

Our glasses chinked. He drank deeply. More slowly I raised my glass. The cautious sip I took slid like velvet fire over my tongue. Then I took the rest, feeling the heat burn down, down towards the icy waste where my heart had once been.

I accepted a second glass of brandy before I left the study. Then, boldly, asked for another, meeting Grandfather's cynically amused glance across the rim of the glass. He was the first to look away. Was it the contempt in my eyes that confused him? I did not care. I craved only the strong spirit's comfort, understanding for the first time in my life its seductive attraction. How quickly it blunted the sharp edges of shock. How easily it blurred the emotions so that even the most harrowing circumstances might be viewed with a wholly illusory calmness.

I drifted on unsteady legs back to the parlour. It was fortunate that Mr Chadwick and Ben were already preparing to retire, for speech seemed to slide in an ungainly fashion from my tongue. I feared to let slip an incautious word. There was a time and place for Ben to be told. Not now, blurted out with brandy-inspired clumsiness.

I sat on by the empty hearth. There were footsteps at first. The sound of bolts being secured. Then all fell silent so that I could hear moths fluttering against the windows, pale ghosts drawn from the dark, warm night to the spurious enchantment of a candlelit room. My thoughts were maudlin. Even if in their persistence these foolish, helpless creatures found an open casement and danced towards the light, what was their reward but singed wings?

Clumsily I rose to my feet. Slowly and carefully I snuffed all the candles, save one to light me to bed. The moths could go free now. I had released them from their bondage to the flame to live out the span of their small, secret lives.

'Take care for predators, though,' I said aloud, soulfully. 'The world is full of them, great birds of prey that will gobble you up if you are not on your guard. All little creatures should beware. Partic'larly. . . .' A giggle rose in my throat as my tongue stuttered over the word. 'Partic-u-larly, female creatures . . . The great hawks are hovering all round, and just when you think you are safe, that is when you should be most on your guard . . .' I stopped. Caught my breath. Raised the candle towards the door, the shadows bending and twisting as the sudden draught caught the flame. 'Who is there?'

The door creaked again. An impossibly gigantic moth fluttered in the slice of darkness beyond the door.

'Miss . . . Miss Lightbody? Is that you?'

A clawed hand detached itself from the wings that were not wings but the billows of a pale shawl.

'Come, child. Bring the candle. Follow me.'

She darted ahead of me down the dark hall, then whisked up the stairs. A night creature, I thought as I stumbled after her, my feet finding it difficult even with the benefit of the puddle of light from my candle. Cat's eyes to see in the dark. Or an owl's. I wished I had her vision. It was so far . . . up and up. And should we not stop on the first landing? My room lay along the passage. But no, we must make haste up another flight, Miss Lightbody turning to urge me on, and follow her along an unfamiliar corridor which turned sharply, down two steps, up three, and to a door to be unlocked and a room beyond.

The door closed behind me. I blinked at the light within. Candles everywhere. Bracketed in elaborate, tarnished holders, sprouting from the necks of bottles, askew on pieces of broken china, all near drowned in oceans and rivers of congealed wax. And the sight they revealed was extraordinary.

Colour and clutter and richness and squalor burst around me in a rolling tide. My decorator's eye, functioning in spite of the brandy, applauded the sumptuous, reckless abandon of it all, even as my skin crawled from the overwhelming closeness of the atmosphere.

A fire, despite the summer night's warmth, crackled in the grate. Uncleared ash from many such fires spilled out in a soft grey hillock over the hearth. Heavy crimson velvet curtains, swagged with blackened gilt, covered the three windows which I suspected, judging by the stale atmosphere redolent of old lady within, were rarely opened. The rest of the room drowned under the weight of garments strewn across chairs, hanging from hooks and rails round the walls, tumbling out of half-open presses, piled on the yellow coverlet of the half-tester bed. Lace and multicoloured satins; rich brocades and fine, floating gauzes; shawls of cobweb fineness and petticoats crusted deep with frills; towers of caps, jumbles of stockings and fans and gloves and slippers. And jewels! Pearls, entwined crystal, amber and jet and amethyst and shining gold in careless heaps, necklaces, brooches, ear-bobs, rings, buckles . . . All such a confusion of colour and glitter that at first the eye did not catch that everything was as wrinkled and threadbare and ancient as the elderly sprite whose room this was. And that the jewels were paste, their glitter meant only to deceive.

'Shall you sit, child?' the sprite enquired sweetly, as though the pair of us, alone in this gaudy, grubby chamber, constituted some formal company. But her eyes sparked black and malicious in her wrinkled face as she swept an armful of scarves and shawls off a chair drawn to a small table and took a seat close beside me, scrabbling her little mittened claws among a pile of scattered grubby papers.

''Tis a pity your brain is addled with brandy,' she began, 'for I had hoped to explain the charts precisely.'

'Charts? What charts are these?'

'Questions before I have even begun!' she snapped. 'Hold your tongue! I cannot abide a chatterer.'

'But why have your brought me here?' I shook my head to try and clear it, to try and make sense of the strange circles and symbols on the paper in front of me. 'What is the writing? I cannot make out—'

She slapped back my fingers. 'It is enough that I brought you here, for there are few that I allow in. Never the sluts, for they whine about dirt and fleas and spiders, and I had sooner allow a pack of scavenging dogs to disturb my treasures than those fools. And never your poor witless brother and his long-faced keeper, though if Frank had asked me to teach the lad all the wicked pleasurings of the bedroom, then I should have gone about it with a will. Aye, the will is there, if not the fleshly qualities that made me the whore I was. So the widow woman had the advantage of me. Pah! I would have torn out her eyes and boiled them for breakfast had she challenged me once.' She cackled loudly. 'Frank, if he wished still, I would allow in to my bedchamber for the sake of the pleasure we once had of each other. But he does not wish and, perhaps, no more do I. So it is you, beanpole, I have invited, out of some misbegotten impulse. We shall not call it sympathy. Or kindness.' She thrust her face into mine. 'Do you think me capable of those gross emotions? Eh? Eh?'

'I . . . well, I think you try to be . . .'

Again that cackle of laughter.

'I try to be nothing that I am not. And I am not kind. Or sympathetic. I merely take amusement where I can find it. And it amuses me at the moment to take your part against the machinations of these foolish old men.'

'You know – you must know, for you hear everything – how I am trapped by what Grandfather and

Mr Pascoe have set up.' Maudlin tears prickled my eyes. 'Marriage to that . . . despicable, loathsome, vile creature.'

'Oh, pray spare me your virginal whinings,' she snapped. 'It will be no better and no worse than many are brought to. And if there is no love on your part, then you must look upon it as a benefit. For 'twill enable you to keep a cool head and use his passions to your advantage.'

'He is cruel and a bully,' I moaned. 'Why, you yourself once cautioned me against him.'

'Did I? More fool I, for his destiny meets yours.'

'My destiny? But I hate him, he is a brute!'

'Then you must make him docile.'

'Oh, you are no better than my grandfather!'

'Ah, good. I had sooner see that spark of anger in your eye than watch you wallow in a slough of self-pity, though I feel it is the brandy that has been speaking rather than your true inclination.' Her black eyes glinted at me. 'Or perhaps there is another reason that makes you mislike this marriage more than necessary, eh? Well, miss? Would you deny it? Or call Venus a liar for she told me of it long before you knew it yourself.'

I put my head in my hands. I could not think clearly for the strange way the room began to circle slowly about me, the gaudy colours running and merging together in the brilliance of countless shimmering candles.

'You talk in riddles,' I said in a muffled voice.

'And you, child, must learn not to drown your wits in strong spirits when above all else you need a clear head.' Her hand shot out, talons fine as a cat's claws raked my wrist. 'Wake up and listen! Frank thinks he has set the course, but the stars tell me what they have ordained and the two do not tally.'

'The stars . . . the stars . . . such nonsense . . .' My

eyelids were so heavy I could barely open them against the swimming light. 'I need to sleep . . . I need . . . my bed . . .'

The voice, sharp and hissing, a serpent's in my ear. 'What is it you wish, child? Think on it. Your position is strong. Mars and Jupiter favour your lion now, while they hang at this moment contrary to Frank's scorpion.' The little clutching claw on my arm, shaking me to wakefulness. 'You will not change the greater destiny, but you may still achieve much to give you strength and resolution, then you may bend to the gale that sweeps over you, knowing you will survive.'

Familiar words. A different voice, a different dream than this.

'They have you trapped, aye, but snares are set for them also. They will not escape. None of them. Even the black fox who runs like the wind and has long evaded the hunter and thinks himself too clever and too cruel to be caught. Remember this, child, when you wake. It will give you courage.'

The sensation was strange. Of drifting from the brilliant room into the dark. Of floating down the stairs. And I was back in my own room, in my own bed. Buttons and laces to be undone and stockings to be removed and pins to be taken from my hair, and all was accomplished by hands other than my own. Brisk little hands which raised the comforting sheets gently round my shoulders.

And that insistent voice again, that dream voice. 'Sleep well, child. You will need it, as we all shall in the days that are to come.'

Then I dreamed the brush of lips on my forehead, the soft click of the door closing and the fluttering of moth wings beyond the casement.

I woke to sunlight pounding against sluggish eyelids. I had a raging thirst and throbbing head and a clear certainty as to what I must now do.

Sometime in the night, troubled and restless as my sleep had been, resolve had come to me. If this marriage was to take place, and I could see no escape from it, I should not go to it in ignorance.

I washed and dressed with great care, then opened the window wide and breathed deeply of the cool, sweet, salty air. The throb in my head was easing, my resolve strengthening. Today there was much to be discovered, much to plan and decide. Was it Miss Lightbody who had said the advantage was mine? Now I knew that to be so. My recollections of last evening were fuzzy. Though I knew she had taken me to her room, I could not clearly recall why, except that her weird talk of planets in my favour hung sharp in my mind. Such a strange creature she was. She meant well, I supposed, though she had lived so long cut off from the world in this house that I guessed she was more than a little touched in the head.

She was not down this morning. I breakfasted with Ben and Mr Chadwick, then Ben and I walked to the stable yard. As always, a straggle of dogs, sniffing and bounding, went with us. Cats came yowling out of the stable to wind themselves round Ben's boots, though they shied away from my strange presence. Doves fluttered to his hands for the handfuls of grain he held and the horses hung their soft noses over the stable door and whickered with pleasure to see him.

He had names for all of them, even the hens clucking over the cobbles, a broken-winged jackdaw who hopped and squawked with them, the shadowy barn owl perched up in the gloom of the stable rafters and a pair of herring gulls who observed us through yellow eyes from the stable roof.

Ben looked very handsome as he petted and stroked and talked to his family of animals. No longer a boy, but a fine, strapping young man, glowing with good health. Only a simplicity of speech, a childishly guileless quality in his manner betrayed someone who would, perhaps, never now be quite as others. It was unutterably sad. Yet when I remembered the days and weeks when he had lain uncomprehending on his bed, the shambling youth I had dragged half across England, I beheld a miracle.

'Ben,' I said impulsively, 'do you remember our life before this, before we came to Falconwood?'

He frowned. 'I remember . . . I remember we were cold, Jo, and unhappy. And we travelled very far.'

'We did, Ben. From the north. And do you remember Mama and Papa and our sisters, Phoebe and Rose?'

'They all went away, Jo,' he said slowly. 'You said they went to a better place. But I wished they had not left us.'

'We could not go with them, Ben,' I said sadly. 'Sometimes people have to be parted. As we are so often.'

'But you come back to me, Jo,' he said, eagerly. 'I like it when you visit. I can show you my animals and you shall come to the cove and watch me swim. It makes me happy when you are here.' His beaming smile twisted suddenly to a sullen grimace. 'I do not like to go away. I like to be at Falconwood. Everyone is kind here. I went away once, Jo. There was a man there who hated me. His name was Dr Roote.' He spat out the name. 'I hated him, too, Jo. He locked me up and hurt me. I wanted to come here to see Jess's pups and he laughed at me and called me bad names. I will not go visiting there again!'

I put my hand on his arm. 'No, Ben,' I said quietly. 'You shall never go there again. I give you my solemn word.'

Grandfather was in his study when we returned to the house. I went straight to him, hiding my apprehension under an air of calm composure. I knocked briskly on the door, not even waiting for him to call before I entered.

He made to rise, frowning. 'What is this? I do not care for interruptions when I write my letters.'

'We must talk, Grandfather. There is much to be discussed. Pray be seated. I shall draw up this chair.'

We faced each other across the desk.

'What discussion is this?' he asked warily. 'I said everything that was to be said last night.'

'Indeed, no. I have many questions and wish you to speak plainly. For instance, you tell me Ben and I are to be married but when is this to take place and where?'

There was a look of relief in his eyes, quickly masked. What had he been expecting? Anger? Tears? Rebellion? I felt a rush of confidence. *Mars and Jupiter favour your lion . . . They hang contrary to Frank's scorpion.*

He said, grudgingly, 'The banns will be called for the first time this Sunday. The date is set for three weeks from Friday, at noon at the church here in Starcombe. I should have hoped that it would be a double wedding, and my grandson married in the church where so many of our ancestors lie, but Susannah insists she will be married at Kingsbridge church, and her papa is disposed to please her in this small matter. So that event will take place the following day.'

A twinge of compassion for Susannah. All she had said in the garden in Torre Crescent, her hints to me on the journey to Kingsbridge, meant that she had been told of her fate that day in Exeter. Yet her tears and her protests had meant nothing to her papa. Such arrogant creatures these men were, thinking that they had the last word in the ordering of their womenfolk! *Knowing* they had, for who, legally, could gainsay that authority? All the same, Susannah would have Falconwood to do with as she pleased. Why should I feel sorry for her?

'And the remaining days between now and the wedding? What plans have you for me during this time?'

'There is no necessity for you to make the tedious journey to Exeter again. I shall write to the Misses Polsham to explain the circumstances. And of course I shall be generous with you in the matter of fripperies you will need to order for your wedding. I believe there are good dressmakers to be had in Kingsbridge.'

'And the marriage settlements?'

He frowned. 'The lawyers will attend to those.'

'Of course. But I should like to know precisely the nature of these settlements.'

'What is there for you to know? I shall pay young Pascoe's debts and you will live quietly at Brent House once you are married. After that, your future, as is perfectly proper, will be directed by your husband. If he chooses to return to his dissolute life, then I fear his father will wash his hands of him completely. If he is as repentant as he claims and is sincere in his attempts, as many have done after a misspent youth, to apply himself rigorously to more worthwhile pursuits under his father's direction, then the Pascoe fortunes may well be restored. A sensible, far-seeing wife will be a great asset for one in his position should she have the inclination to put her mind to the task. Benjamin's future, as I have already informed you, will be assured here. He will be comfortable and cared for. Edward Davey will see to it that all the legal niceties are observed. Benjamin's lack of mental capacity will be taken into consideration when appointing suitable trustees – sound professional men – to manage the assets Benjamin's son will inherit, in the interim between my death and the coming of age of my heir.' There was a hint of melancholy in his smile. 'If I could live to see that day, I would, but I fear another score of years would be too much to expect.'

'There is some comfort for me in that I shall be living close to Falconwood and Ben,' I said quietly. 'However, I have given a great deal of thought to all you told me last evening and there are certain . . . requests . . . No, let me put it more strongly, certain conditions that I wish to lay before you.'

'Conditions!' His shaggy brows met angrily over his nose. 'You have agreed to be married, that is enough.'

'Is it?' I clasped my hands and set them firmly on the desk. I sat bolt upright, my gaze unswerving. 'Grandfather, I shall marry Blandford Pascoe. I do not wish it. It will make me exceedingly unhappy. But you have left me no other recourse because the wellbeing of my brother and to a lesser degree the welfare of Blandford's child, who is sadly neglected, depends upon it.'

'So?' he growled.

I went on in the same level voice, 'I see that there are two ways for me to approach this situation. You have said that I am self-willed and determined and bold. Perhaps I am. I also have a strong sense of justice. You, my own grandfather, have taken your own spite out on me for events that happened before I was even born. You turned me from your door when I was most in need of kindness and help, you separated me with unnecessary harshness from the brother I loved and have chosen to ignore me over these last years, uncaring if I was lonely or miserable or even half-starved – as I was for a short time. You have manipulated me into this position where I must marry a man I loathe. I think I have every right to feel badly used.'

His glance flickered away. Was that a hint of guilt, of sympathy there? I had to believe it.

'I had no obligation—'

'As I have no obligation to make the way to this marriage, and beyond, easy and comfortable for you.'

'Tchah! What nonsense is this? You have made your bargain.'

'And I shall keep it. As I expect you to keep your side of it. However, the manner in which I shall keep it remains entirely in your hands. If the simple conditions I shall put to you are met, then I shall be as sweet and yielding and agreeable as you would wish a granddaughter to be and do everything in my power to please you. If you choose not to agree to these requests, then I shall be as disagreeable and uncooperative as I can make myself, both now and in the future. And who knows what the future holds? There may come a time when it would be to your advantage to have me as an ally. We both wish the best for Ben, do we not?' I paused, then said, 'The choice is yours, Grandfather. Shall we be friends or do we needlessly continue as enemies?'

He pushed back his chair, walked to the window, stood with his back to the room, hands clasped under his coat tails.

'And these . . . conditions?'

'In the first instance I should wish to return to Exeter to settle my affairs there and to bid goodbye to my friends. My second condition is that you appoint me as one of the trustees who will guard Ben's welfare and the Falconwood estate in the event of your death until your heir comes of age and inherits.'

There was a long, tense silence. Or perhaps the tension was just within myself. Grandfather did not move. His study window held a view across the orchard to the cliffs beyond. I caught movement there. Ben on his fine chestnut gelding moving slowly and easily out onto the cliff path. Man and horse as one, peaceful and content, under a summer sky.

The horse broke into a canter as it breasted the first low rise to the cliff top, then we lost it from view behind a clump of wind-twisted thorn bushes. Only then did Grandfather speak, his back still towards me, his shoulders bowed under the old-fashioned cut of his coat, as though a sudden burden came upon them.

'My hopes, my desires are bound up in that boy,' he said in a slow, weary voice. 'He is the very image of my drowned son Philip. I had . . . great hopes that his damaged mind would heal and . . . and – such a foolish fancy I realise now – my reward would be to have my beloved son returned to me, full of youth and vigour and strength, to make me young again and take all the bitterness away. To shoulder the burdens that, with growing age, seem weightier with each year.'

I stood up and went to him. I had a moment when I thought to lay a sympathetic hand upon his sleeve, but I feared the rebuff such an intimacy might provoke.

'If you had asked my help, Grandfather, I should have given it gladly,' I said quietly.

He sighed. 'Perhaps I have been . . . too narrow in my views. But then, you are your mother's daughter and you have a look of my own faithless wife, Harriet. How could I trust you?'

'I am like my grandmother?' I found the thought pleasing.

He shrugged. 'I catch her in you sometimes. Something about the colour and shape of eyes, the cheekbones. A watchful quality, though she was softer, rounder, smaller than you. Very handsome.' His voice deepened harshly. 'Very . . . desirable – and very treacherous.'

'So because I have something of her likeness, I must

538

necessarily have her character?'

He did not answer directly. He swung away from the window, brushed past me, crossed to the desk.

'I think, I believe, that you have a genuine regard for your brother. That will keep you careful not to harm his interests. The other trustees will not allow you to overstep the mark.'

I had it! Yet so tenuous and fragile a link to Falconwood's future that it scarcely seemed worthy of the leap of spirits I experienced.

'And I see no harm in your visiting Exeter, provided you are back well within the due date of the wedding.'

And again that leap of triumph, quickly suppressed. I said, meekly, 'Thank you, Grandfather. I think it best if I go to Exeter tomorrow. A week or so will be sufficient for me there.' I curtsied deeply, the very image of the agreeable, dutiful granddaughter I had promised to be. 'I shall order a wedding gown from Mr Chadwick's mother, who is the finest dressmaker in Exeter. I shall not disgrace you at the wedding.'

'I did not think you would,' he said dryly.

We eyed each other. We both smiled. Cautious little smiles, that masked the complex, busy working of our minds. But smiles, nevertheless.

It was enough for the moment.

I had one more preparation to make for my return to Exeter. I went in search of Miss Lightbody. She was not about the downstairs rooms. I went softly to the upper floor, crept along the passage, retracing a journey I had only the vaguest memory of, down two steps, up three . . . yes, that was the door. I tapped. Then again, louder. The sound of a key turning and a bright black eye at the crack of an opening.

'Miss Lightbody, may I enter?'

'No, you may not!' she screeched loudly. 'You have no business here! I allow no visitors.'

I held my finger warningly to my lips. 'Please, I do not wish anyone to know I am here. I need your help.'

Her little monkey face creased to a grin. 'Ah, that is different. Why did you not say so?'

She bolted the door behind me. The room was all gloom, save for one sliver of sunlight where a curtain had been pulled back an inch or two. There was a glow of embers in the hearth. The heat and the odour pressed down like a heavy hand.

'Well? What do you want of me?'

'I need a disguise.' I said. 'I need, for a short while, to be unrecognisable. Someone other than Joanna Howarth.'

'So, mischief is afoot! Good! Good! My bones ache for a morsel of intrigue. What are you planning, minx?'

'A little masquerade. Quite harmless. Nothing that need concern you, Miss Lightbody.'

'You lying troll!' she cackled. 'You mean mischief to someone. I catch a wonderful waft of deceit about you. Who is to be the victim, eh? Frank? Susannah? That foppish knave you will marry? Or perhaps all three?'

I said, 'I cannot think what you mean. I have some unfinished business in Exeter which I must go about . . . prudently. That is all.'

'Prudence that needs to go in disguise!' she cackled happily. 'What a fine jingling hypocritical sound that has to it. Well, my feet have ever danced merrily to the music of deception. How can I resist this particular tune?'

She teetered among the jumbled heaps of her finery, small hands darting about like little bony fish in a murky pool.

'What will you be? A painted courtesan in rouge and patches and powders? Now where did I put those mouseskin eyebrows . . . A duchess? A princess?'

'Something simple,' I said firmly. 'I need to cover

my hair and mask my face. And dark in colour, for it will be night-time. I have a hooded cloak which would have done, but I did not bring it, the weather being so warm.'

'Better and better! This *prudent* business does not take you, then, straight back to the bosom of the worthy spinsters to retrieve your good warm cloak, but you must stay out secretly in the dark? Methinks I like it more and more.' She screeched with laughter, and flung aside a drift of tawdry yellow satin and a jumble of cracked slippers to produce a dirty tumble of grey curls. 'Here! A grand wig to cover that fiery mop. I should not think it still lousy after all this time, though fearsomely itchy it was once. I have not worn it in thirty years.'

I declined the wig. And the offer of various more excessive gowns. 'They would not fit,' I said politely. 'But is that a mobcap?' I dived among a clutter of caps, sadly in need of the goffering iron. 'And that black shawl, might I borrow it? And the mittens, and the poke bonnet. Oh, and that grey stuff skirt.'

I took the booty back to my room, Miss Lightbody's gleeful cry, 'I shall demand to know the whys and the wherefores when you return,' ringing in my ears.

With the door safely closed, I tried the effect. The mobcap covered my hair, the concealing wings of the battered poke bonnet shaded my face. I tied the skirt round my waist over my dress and once the shabby silk shawl was draped round my shoulders and the holey mittens covered my hands, my transformation was complete. I smiled with satisfaction when I looked in the mirror. Perfect. A poor woman whom no one would look at twice. If I drooped my shoulders, kept my head down and shuffled rather than strode out as I usually did, I was surely unrecognisable to anyone in Exeter. If I was noticed at all.

541

My smile faded. I narrowed my eyes at my reflection. It was a gamble I took. A gamble that, if I won, would help me to face the detestable marriage I was being forced into. Once, I had been rewarded handsomely by being so reckless. Nicholas had poured gold coins into my lap. Would he be so willing this time to allow me my reckless way? For it was not money I wanted of him. But that which would turn me from a maid to a woman.

Men prized virginity in their brides. To a man such as Blandford Pascoe, the bedding – the rape – of a tender, frightened virgin must be a most desirable prospect. Grandfather and James Pascoe, with their convenient agreement, had offered me as a sacrifice to Blandford's perverted tastes. Grandfather had spoken airily of my 'managing' Blandford. So easy to say! Well, if this was scarcely the 'managing' he had envisaged, it was a start. I should not go to my marriage bed an innocent, trembling victim.

Behind the rage that sparked in the depths of my eyes there was the shadow of bewilderment, of pain, even of fear. But I could not, would not, think about the years ahead that I must be bound to that despicable man. I must think only of the here and now. That way I should survive and not succumb to the bitter encroachment of self-pity and despair.

For a plan hastily conceived and swiftly put into action, the first part at least ran with remarkable smoothness. I took with me from Falconwood only my small carpetbag, easily manageable. In it were the garments borrowed from Miss Lightbody. There was no one I knew on the coach. I travelled from Kingsbridge in my green gown and splendid hat, holding myself very stiff and proud so that the other inside travellers – a farmer's plump wife and a dowdy elderly

542

lady, terrified of the spanking pace and inclined to yelp at every bend and pothole – were wary of striking up a conversation, leaving me to brood and worry in peace.

I had requested that I be set down at a spot some two miles before the village of Alphington. Once the coach had rattled off, it was very peaceful. My head still jangled from the clatter and bouncing of the coach, but the hedges and fields, rising tranquil to the rounded hills on either side, soothed with their silence. Once I was sure I was quite alone, I gave up my pretence of waiting to be met by another equippage. I walked to the nearest gate, picked up my skirts and, feeling a child again, climbed the gate and dropped into the field.

The corn was breast high, ripening fast, the breeze sighing over it with a dry rattling sound. Under the hedge I donned my disguise, regretting that I must lay my beautiful hat in the bag where I feared it would be crushed. I pulled on the mobcap and poke bonnet and pinned the shawl so that the bodice of my green dress was not visible. The grey skirt hid the rest. My good boots I could not compromise on. I did not wish to hobble on blistered feet into Exeter, but a liberal spattering of red mud hid the quality of the leather.

The stale odour rising from the shawl and the skirt, the dinginess of the garments gave me an odd sense of being cast back in time to when Ben and I had travelled the long wintry road south to Falconwood. We had been two of the many poor people trudging the roads, shifting streams of humanity, respectable, hopeful, hopeless, helpless, all seeking something better, or different, at the next village, the next town. In these garments it was not difficult to remember how I had felt then. How curiously invisible to ordinary, settled folk we had been. If they noticed us at all, it was only to watch this gawky girl and shambling lad out of sight to make sure we were not up to mischief.

I hoped, dingy and shabby as I looked, that I should pass similarly unnoticed today. But it was too early yet. I must sit here in the shade of the spreading ash tree, fan away the hovering flies, and wait until dusk.

I was not disturbed. Carriages, carts, horses went by on the road beyond the hedge. Sometimes there were footsteps, voices. They passed, diminished and I was snug and undetected in my sanctuary. And even if the farmer had come upon me, I had my story ready. I was only a poor woman, up from Plymouth in search of work, resting her feet before the trudge into Exeter.

The sun went down trailing a finery of gold and red clouds and I made my move.

I went slowly and steadily and, though I knew I should keep my eyes down, it was difficult, for a huge yellow harvest moon rose to light my path. And it was so achingly beautiful, casting its pale radiance over the silent countryside, that I could scarcely turn my eyes from it.

It was an odd journey, curiously detached from real life. Grandfather assumed I was back at Torre Crescent. The Misses Polsham thought I was still at Falconwood. Instead I was footloose, unencumbered by anyone or anything.

Only when I crossed the Exe Bridge, with the reflected lights of the city breaking and dancing round the broken globe of the moon in the river's troubled surface, did the sense of being free and unencumbered diminish. Now I must take care to keep to the shadows and avert my face from anyone that passed. The nearer I got to Reynard's, the more danger there was of being recognised.

But luck was still with me. I reached Southernhay and turned off down the narrow street towards

Reynard's, turning my eyes from the shuttered windows of Brown's bank that brought guilty reminders of Miss Olga. I slipped through the arch into the yard, my luck still holding. Crockery clattering, raised voices, a hot steamy waft from the kitchen. Voices, too, from the stables, and shadows cast by a lamp moving within. But no one in the yard as I sped across it to the door at the foot of the back stairs. I caught my breath in case it was locked, but it gave under my hand. I was in and up the dimly lit stairs in a twinkling.

I was almost at the top when a plump figure barred my way, lamp aloft, crying, 'Well, madam, and where do you think you're going?'

My heart sank.

Mrs Fitch. Guardian of the stairs and of the honour of the maids. I might have known that she who had an eagle eye for the comings and goings would scarcely miss a stranger hot-footing it into the house.

'Well?'

I raised my head, pushed back the wings of my bonnet.

She thrust the lamp forward. I heard the quick intake of her breath.

'Joanna? Is that you? And at this hour? But come up, my dear. Is something wrong?'

I could do nothing but fling myself on her mercy. 'I have come to see Nicholas. Dear Mrs Fitch, I *must* see him, and please, the utmost secrecy, I beg you. No one must know I am here, not even a maid. Please, let me go to his room and wait. Forget you have seen me. I will explain, but not now . . .'

She frowned, puzzled, as she took in the shabbiness of my clothes. But the urgency of my tone impelled her to action. Without another word, she beckoned me forward, looked both ways down the passage, then stood back to let me pass.

'His room is not locked,' she said quietly. 'Go quickly now.'

'You have not seen me,' I breathed. 'Promise? And no word to Nicholas, either. He must not know – yet. Let him return in his own good time.'

She opened her mouth, to caution me perhaps against such reckless disregard of my reputation, but something in my face seemed to make her change her mind. Her glance softened. 'I always thought you had a sensible head on your shoulders. I will not question you, for I am sure you have your reasons. Good reasons. Quickly now. I shall be discreet.'

She watched me go. A brief nod, a smile as I reached the door and she turned away. I slipped inside, leaned back against the door, heart thumping, waiting for my breath to slow and for my eyes to adjust again to the not quite dark of moonlight spilling through the crack in the curtains. Then, stepping carefully round the furniture, I moved across the room to the door of the inner chamber where I had never been. The bed-chamber. Then I went in and closed the door behind me.

I had been borne up on a strange, feverish tide of excitement. Now it evaporated with a rush as the latch clicked behind me, fastening me in what seemed to be total blackness. The enormity of what I did suddenly overwhelmed me. How could I do this? How could I present myself to a man and demand to be instructed in those intimacies that should only be contemplated by any respectable woman within the privacy of marriage? It was certainly not a woman's place to make such an outrageous proposal, yet here was I in a man's bedchamber in the dark of night, about to beg him to deflower me.

I groped my way forward, my outstretched hands encountering the curtains of a bed and jolting back as though they touched something on fire. *His* bed curtains, sheltering and ornamenting *his* bed. They moved, whispering, at my touch, and a scent masculine and musky stirred in the air.

His presence was so strong in this room that I half expected to hear his deep voice ringing out in challenge and shivered, remembering his coldness the last time I had seen him. The other memories, of the kind, generous and tender man I knew existed within his complex character, the image I had clung to these last days, disappeared and I remembered only his duplicity, his vengeful scheming, his easy charm, his self-interest.

That Nicholas would listen to my request and decide, coolly, what advantage, beyond the mere fleshly encounter offered to him, could be wrested from the situation. But the other Nicholas, the one who had driven recklessly through a wild night to take me to the bedside of a dying woman and who, in those dark hours afterwards, had held me fast in his arms with a tenderness and passion that made no attempt to mask his true, deep feelings, the Nicholas I loved seemed far away from this room, this building. A faint, shadowy figure hovering behind the powerful image of the man who had ruined Blandford Pascoe.

I stood there, torn with indecision, with desperation. And shamed by the clear and certain knowledge that my desperation sprung from a deep need to see Nicholas, to touch him, to hold him, whatever the cost in pride and self-respect.

I did not care why he would choose to take me to his bed. Only that if he refused, I did not know how I could go on living.

Voices. Muffled voices. They murmured to me out of the darkness, bringing me out of the daze of indecision. Not in the room, beyond it. Beyond the far wall. And the room not so dark after all. An odd chink of yellow light, high up.

I moved cautiously towards it and nearly tripped over what I felt to be, bending to touch the obstruction, a wooden box of some sort placed conveniently against the wall. I stood on it, curiosity overcoming caution, raising myself on tiptoe to put my eye to the place where the light came through. A peephole, no less, where Master Reynard could spy upon his prey!

And now I played the hunter, for I looked down the length of the gaming room. Not the neat, empty room I knew but crowded as I had never seen it. Each table with its clusters of players and observers, hands dipping among cards and dice. Frowning faces and laughter and one man, ridiculously, wearing his coat inside out for luck, but his face doleful as the dice pronounced him the loser and a groan of sympathy went up from his friends. And at the far end of the room at a tall desk was Nick himself, seemingly absorbed in conversation with a group of men, yet I could see how his glance flicked constantly over the tables, missing nothing, noting everything.

Except for the watcher spying on him from his own eyrie. A woman who gazed at him, washed anew with longing and burning with love and desire.

I was not long at the peephole. When I stepped down, I was composed and resolute once more, refusing to admit to shame and doubts. Indeed, having seen Nick, I was now emboldened to the point of recklessness. Having come so far along this wayward path, it was pointless now to give in to maidenly modesty.

Quickly, before my nerve deserted me, I began to take off my clothes. As I peeled away the layers, even though it was dark, I felt increasingly vulnerable, and increasingly audacious. When I had removed my chemise and drawers, I fumbled hastily in my bag for my nightgown then, abandoned creature that I seemed to have become, I let it drop from my fingers. I slid between the cool linen sheets of Nick's bed, naked as the day I was born. The linen was newly laundered, crisp, the pillowcase smelling of the sunny outdoors. I had no idea of the time. All that I knew was that because it was Saturday, Nick would close the gaming room promptly at midnight. It was the house rule, strictly observed. Play was not permitted on Sunday. It could not be long before he came to me . . .

I awoke, shocked and confused, a light flaring in my eyes, dreams of floundering in a turbulent sea full of invisible monsters ebbing away.

'Great God in heaven! Joanna! What the devil are you doing here?'

Nick's face, all hard planes and black shadows, swam at me. I blinked, raised myself on one elbow, then remembered and clutched the sheet back round my neck. But not quick enough. I heard the sharp intake of his breath, saw his eyes narrow.

'Mother-naked in my bed, Joanna Howarth?' he said softly. 'What devilment is this?'

The words I had prepared were all in my head. Words to explain, cajole, persuade. But they fled, died and I could not speak at all. Instead one great, dry, wrenching sob broke from my throat. Just one. Then silence. Yet that silence, that stillness, was full of some communication beyond mere speech. We stared at each other, soundless, breathless, held by a compulsion that was both inexplicable and infinitely full of meaning.

Then, slowly, he moved . . . or I moved. It did not matter. His hand reached out to touch my face and mine forgot the necessity to hold modestly to the sheet, but lifted as if by some urgent, primitive command to clasp his neck.

The light flared and trembled as he set the candlestick down roughly. And with the same instinctive urgency that compelled me, he pulled me towards him, burying his face first in my hair, then his mouth seeking my cheek, my neck, my lips, my breast. A storm of kisses, rousing in me a raging surge of pleasure that was near to pain in its intensity.

He spoke then, groaning out the words against my throat, even as his fingers – and, shamelessly, mine – tore at shirt buttons, trouser buttons, 'Jo . . . I should not . . . you deserve better . . .'

'How could anything be better than this?' I whispered. 'Nick, my darling, I want you, need you . . .'

We wasted our breath with words. They had no power. We were far beyond them, flesh against flesh, triumphant, in a place somewhere without reasoning or common sense. A place where bodies and souls, emotions and feelings merged and became a single, powerful, driving force that blinded us to everything but the pursuit of mutual delight.

Afterwards we slept, awoke to explore each other with wonder and tenderness and to make love once more. This time, all urgency gone, to a slower, more languorous and, subtly, even more pleasurable rhythm.

Nick fell asleep, his fingers tangled in my hair, his head on my shoulder. The candle had long since burnt itself out, but there was already lightness in the room that spoke of dawn beyond the heavy curtains.

I lay drowsy, sated, and unutterably sad. If I turned my head just a little, my lips would touch Nick's forehead in the lightest of kisses. If I moved my hand, I could feel the smooth skin of his chest and the firm strength of healthy muscle and bone beneath. If I shifted my knee I could feel the roughness of his thigh, the secret bush of wiry hair, the slackness of manhood spent. All this, the most natural and tender of intimacies, was mine. But for so short a time. So pitifully short a time.

This room was my bridal bower, this bed my bridal couch, but the man whom I loved and who lay deep in sleep beside me was not my husband.

And though I wished he were with all the power of love in my heart, I knew I must face up to the cold, clear light of dawn and prepare to leave him.

Chapter Twenty

The sonorous clang and clatter of Sunday bells summoning Exeter's citizens to worship roused Nick finally from sleep. From the chair where I sat, I watched him stir, move his arm languorously as though to caress the space where I had lain, blink awake. 'Jo . . . ?' The slow, sleepy, smile when he saw me broke my heart. 'But you are already dressed. Why did you not wake me?'

'I must leave, Nick,' I said, quietly. 'I stayed only to bid you goodbye.'

It was the moment I dreaded. In the dark hours it had been easy to turn his questions aside with kisses, caresses, murmured words of love. I did not wish to break the spell that held us. Indeed, there had been some magic, some enchantment, woven about us that made explanations irrelevant. We were two lovers lost in each other. He had accepted the gift of my presence, my love, as freely and unquestioningly as I accepted his.

But that time was over. Now we were back in the real world where questions must be answered and explanations given. And as I spoke, in the same quiet, unemotional voice, of what had happened and what I had to do when I left him, I must watch the expression of the man who had woken vulnerable and gentle change and harden.

He made to speak once. Out of anger, perhaps, or distress, but I did not allow myself to falter in my tale. I spoke on rapidly, compelling him to listen. He bit back the words to hear me out in an increasingly grim silence. I was filled with pain, torn with grief, as I watched his expression change and saw the cold protective mask clamp down. But I must show nothing of it. Nothing. Give way to sentiment, to self-pity, and I was lost. I must stay calm, resolute, cool in order to boost my fragile self-control.

Yet, if he had spoken then, if he had leapt from the bed and taken me in his arms, shouting defiance to all that had been planned, I think I should not have had the strength to do other than let him take the burden of choice and responsibility from me. And I should have given myself, weakly, to the foolish, selfish dream that the love we shared was more important than anything else and that together we would miraculously overcome all problems.

But he did not and the moment, if it had ever existed, was lost. The austere voice of duty was free to summon me in the direction I should go, the importunings of Nick's own dark plans to draw him inexorably in another.

Slowly and deliberately Nick took up his dressing robe and, carefully ensuring that I should not glimpse his naked body, drew it on and knotted the sash tightly round his waist. It was a gesture that told me as clearly as if he had spoken that the abandon of the night was totally over and must now be forgotten.

He paced to the window and pulled the curtain back, staring out into the street, his back to me.

'So that is the way of it,' he said, in the same unemotional, controlled tone that reflected mine. 'It is . . . unfortunate that your grandfather has pledged you in marriage to that particular scoundrel, but I have to say it is no more than I could have expected of him. Frank Kerswell is a man untroubled by conscience. However, Joanna, I think you have shown yourself more than capable of turning any ... unfortunate situation to your advantage.' The indifference in his tone cut me to the quick. 'I cannot say I am ... ungrateful ... for the bed sport we have enjoyed, even if your intention was to spoil Blandford Pascoe's expectations of a virgin bride, rather than favour me with that privilege. Indeed, had you chosen to inform me of your reasons for stealing into my bed – which I took, quite amusingly I see now, to be because of some grand though misguided passion you held for me and to which some unfortunate weakness in my own character responded without a thought for the consequences – the night's activities would have had an extra piquancy. However, I congratulate you on your ... foresight and the subtle way you have set about besting your future husband.'

Such cold, bare, unembroidered facts, starkly related. They denied all the love we had shared for those few hours, all my feelings towards him and his towards me. Protests rose to my lips and faded there. What was the use? It was the truth. Leastways, one aspect of the truth. But whatever I said in my own defence now would only make parting the more agonising. Better that he protected himself by staying remote and indifferent. Recriminations and anger would be the worse to bear for both of us.

'I shall leave now,' I said.

'It would be best if you waited in the parlour until I have dressed,' he answered. 'Then we shall consider how you may leave the premises discreetly. We must take care to guard your reputation, must we not? Or is being seen leaving my rooms part of some other tactic about which you have chosen not to inform me?'

He still had his back to me. He could not see the hot colour flood my face at the cutting edge in his voice. My own voice was controlled, but only just, as I said, 'I would wish to be discreet, of course. And, Nick, I . . . it is not . . . Oh, no matter.'

I fled into the parlour where, unable to control the distress, the frustration of my feelings, I paced up and down, up and down until a scratching on the outer door brought me up short.

It was Mrs Fitch. I drew the bolt and let her in. She was carrying a tray. A pot of chocolate, rolls and butter, boiled eggs, a plate of ham. She set it on the table, saying loudly, 'Your breakfast, Nicholas,' and in a whisper, 'I thought you must still be here, my dear. There is plenty for you both. Most of the servants are out now at church and chapel and the rest about their duties. I have pleaded a headache to stay behind in case I may be of help to you.'

I could have flung my arms round her, laid my head on her comfortable bosom and wept at the kindness of her tone. But there must be no weeping.

'Thank you, but I am not hungry. If perhaps we could go quickly to your room . . . it would be better for me to leave from there. It . . . it will look then, if anyone does see me, as though I have called upon you, as I sometimes do . . .' I was jabbing pins into my hat as I spoke, gathering up the bag that held Miss Lightbody's old clothes, as desperate now to get out of this room, away from Nicholas, as I had been to find him last night.

Blessedly, Mrs Fitch did not question me or hesitate. She moved quietly to the door, opened it, peered out, then beckoned me forward.

'Make haste,' she cautioned.

'Joanna!'

I froze halfway to the door. Nicholas had emerged,

now fully dressed, from the inner room. His face seemed to have taken its unnatural pallor from the white linen shirt he wore.

'Joanna,' he repeated. His voice was strained, husky, as though he struggled to overcome some inner conflict. 'I . . . I spoke harshly just now, out of . . . pique. I should not have done . . . to send you away without hope. When, if my plans come to fruition . . . Well, no matter. I should better have given you some prospect of deliverance.'

I scarcely heard what he said. I was only aware of the width of the room between us, a chasm of space echoing with regrets, with longings, with words that could not be spoken now.

'I . . . I must go,' I whispered. 'Goodbye, Nicholas.'

I turned away, my eyes veiled with tears that he must not see and walked away from him. Out of his life and towards the one that lay bitter and unwelcoming ahead.

I owed Mrs Fitch an explanation and was determined to be honest with her, but the moment I began, she said firmly, 'My dear, you have no need. In fact, I should like it best if we talked generally and comfortably together as we always do. I'm always delighted to see you, as you know,' her smile held such genuine warmth and understanding, that it was hard to cling to my composure, 'so it is an unexpected pleasure that you have called this morning. Why, my headache has quite lifted at the prospect of a pleasant chat. Now, I shall make hot chocolate and I insist you eat something – a little bread and butter, perhaps, and a sliver or two of ham.'

The sliver of ham was a hearty chunk. I nibbled at it to please her and drank the hot chocolate gratefully. It at least slid down easily, offering a superficial warmth, though nothing could touch the block of ice that was my heart.

So the awkward moment passed and presently I was able to brace myself to see the shock in her eyes when I told her of my forthcoming marriage. She, who had cared for Jane the first time she had miscarried, knew better than anyone the manner of man I was marrying. But, taking her cue from me, we went through the motions of pretending an interest in wedding gowns, though we neither of us seemed to be able to summon up a great deal of enthusiasm for the subject and quickly passed to other matters.

I stayed with her until the maids returned from church and chapel. Their cheerful voices came echoing up the back stairs, voices from a different, saner world.

When I said that I must go, Mrs Fitch put on her bonnet and gloves and declared her intention of taking a little air which would clear away the last of her headache. 'If you can bear my company a little longer, Joanna, I believe I may stroll with you up Southernhay.'

So she ensured that no salacious interpretation could possibly be put upon my exit from Reynard's. My secret was safe and there was only my own body, which ached still from unaccustomed lovemaking, to remind me of a lost maidenhead and a lost love.

I was welcomed back to Torre Crescent as though I had been away for a month rather than a few days.

'My dear,' cried Miss Olga, 'I am so glad your grandfather has not delayed you too long in the country. There have been two enquiries for refurbishments to old properties, one of which is most promising. And we have some most excellent tidings—'

'Sister! Allow Joanna to remove her hat and tidy herself,' Miss Polsham interrupted, but she spoke without the usual whining note in her voice. Indeed there was even a genuine smile. 'Then she may return to the parlour so that we may sit and talk in a civilised manner.'

Lily, who had found some pretext to come above stairs and caught the end of the conversation, shook her head at my raised eyebrows. 'Don't look at me, Miss Jo. I don't know nowt . . . nothing, 'cept that Mrs Barton was here this morning for a good long while.' She beamed, her mind instantly turning to matters more important. 'I've a fine sirloin roasting and 'taters crisping in the dripping tin and an apple pie to follow. Like as though I knew you'd be back today, for I know 'tis your favourite. So I hopes you has a good appetite after all your journeyings.'

When I returned to the parlour, Miss Olga could barely control her excitement. She was dying to speak, but had to be content with sending her sister encouraging glances. Miss Polsham was not to be hurried. She fussed with the shawl round her shoulders, requested that I plump up the cushions and rearrange the rug that covered her feet. Only then did she deign to inform me that Mrs Eleanor Barton had called this morning with important news.

She lifted her hand in a weak, martyred gesture. 'I do not normally care to involve myself with financial matters. The general delicacy of my health decrees that I must take care not to overheat my mind with day-to-day worries of this nature. A healthy and vigorous person cannot know the extreme fatigue and debilitation pain causes to an invalid when a calamity such as the failure of Brown's bank occurs, with its consequential effects upon our finances and those of Cousin Pascoe. I have been wracked with grief. Wracked,' she repeated, closing her eyes in enjoyment of the word.

'Yes, yes, dear,' Miss Olga put in, as the dramatic silence lengthened, 'but that worrying time is over. You have no need now—'

'Thank you, sister, I do not care to be interrupted!' Miss Polsham's eyes snapped open at the threat of having her moment of glory snatched away. 'As I was saying, Mrs Barton did us the honour of taking us into her confidence over . . . certain personal matters. She has, it seems, a considerable fortune inherited from her late husband, the nabob, which she is in the process of investing in property in Exeter.' Miss Polsham, irritatingly, paused again before her last triumphant announcement. It was all I could do not to go over and shake her. 'Among these properties are two in Torre Crescent, including, Joanna,' she concluded dramatically, 'the one in which you are yourself seated.'

I blinked in amazement. 'Mrs Barton now owns this house?'

'The legal papers are being drawn up and will be signed this week,' Miss Olga said, beaming, 'and she has no intention of raising the rent. Is it not splendid news?'

'Splendid,' I echoed faintly.

'The other property she has purchased is the captain's house next door,' Miss Olga said. 'The old gentleman, who is becoming increasingly incapacitated, has decided to remove himself, finally, to his daughter's house in Crediton.'

I hated to have to dampen their spirits with my own tidings, so I sat quietly for a while, stretching out the moments, listening as they praised Eleanor Barton and her kindness. I felt deeply relieved that she had sprung to their rescue and felt it was out of the goodness of her heart rather than a burning need to invest her money in property. I would ask her, privately, to keep a watchful eye on the ladies after I had gone. Which still did not solve the problem of an income for them. They could not live on air. But I must think about that later. I now had to brace myself to break my own news.

I told them of Ben's forthcoming marriage, of mine, as gently as I could. I spoke positively, emphasising the alliance of the two families as being a sensible proposal. I commended Grandfather's generosity in settling Blandford's debts upon my marriage and made much of Susannah's good luck in being presented with such a favourable and secure match when her prospects were sadly diminished by her papa's misfortune.

Miss Olga paled, her hand went to her throat. 'You will marry *Blandford*?' she said, faintly. 'Oh, my dear . . .'

I interrupted quickly, fearful of my fragile composure dissolving, saying with a bright, false smile, 'I shall be your cousin by marriage! That is a happy thought, is it not, that we shall be related, however many times removed?'

'Oh, yes . . . to be sure,' said Miss Olga in that same faint voice, 'but . . . marriage . . . I am quite . . . overcome. I had not thought, you see, that your grandfather had plans to . . . to take you from us . . .' Her eyes pleaded with me. 'I trust it . . . it will not be for some time yet.'

I swallowed. 'I promised Grandfather I should be back at Falconwood no later than ten days' time.'

Once I should have been glad to leave Exeter, leave these old ladies. Not now. Not like this.

'That is no time at all!'

'And my affairs, all my affairs in Exeter, must be settled by then. I am sorry.'

Silence. My face ached from the effort of keeping my expression bright.

Miss Polsham rescued me. She flung her head back against the cushions. 'My smelling salts,' she quavered. 'Quickly, Joanna. Such palpitations, I am like to faint right away.'

She did not faint. Her cheeks remained a healthy pink. The palpitations had no apparent effect on the vigorous and regular pulse I could feel under my

561

fingers as I chafed her limp hand. But she provided a welcome distraction. And perhaps it was not all play-acting. When she was coaxed out of her dramatics she was genuinely anxious, so much so that for a few moments she forgot her role as a frail invalid untroubled by worldly concerns and revealed that she had a sharp awareness of household affairs.

'But what is to happen to us, sister, now we have no money? We have come to rely on Joanna's contribution. If Joanna goes, we shall have no income at all. We shall be lost. And it is worse, now, than once might have been the case. We have more to lose than when we had a ... a plainer, quieter way of life.'

In the sisters' frightened eyes I saw the house as it had been when I first came here, with the evil-tempered Mrs Caunter reigning over the kitchen, the dreadful food, the harsh influence of the late Mr Polsham hanging like a baleful presence over his daughters. His presence was still here, of course, but it had become muted, softened, largely ignored. Even his much acclaimed diet was rarely spoken of these days. Miss Olga occasionally murmured a guilty protest when Lily sent up some particularly ornate dish to surprise us, but she would manage to put her doubts aside in order to sample it and pass judgment, and somehow, quite absently, she would thoughtfully munch her way through a substantial portion. The house had laughter in it now. Life. There was a sense, particularly for Miss Olga, of new vistas opening beyond its narrow walls. New friends. New experiences.

I said, lamely, 'Let us not be too pessimistic.'

Two faces turned towards me, hopeful, trusting, but I could think of nothing more useful to say. I was glad that Mary Ann's entrance and her announcement that dinner was ready forbade further discussion of this private and delicate subject.

One week.

One week in which neatly to tie up all the loose ends of my business. To write innumerable letters. 'I shall move to the country on my marriage and consequently regret that I shall not be available for further consultation ... If you should require the services of an excellent upholsterer, Mr Timothy Whipple of Longbrook Street, whose good services I have often called upon, would be pleased to wait upon you. I would also recommend for any cabinet or carpentry work Mr Henry Drew of St Thomas ...'

One week in which to consult with Mrs Chadwick and set her into a frenzy among her fashion books and patterns. 'It will be a rush but never fear, your wedding gown will be ready in time. Though I wish you would consider the ivory satin instead of this grey shot with midnight blue. You would look so elegant and regal, but then as you say, one has to be practical. The blue will be more suitable for quiet country living later, especially with the matching long pelisse. You will choose the shoulder capes and Brandenburg fastenings for the pelisse, will you not? The very newest of fashions, my dear, and the very thing for walking out on inclement days. And you wished other gowns for the coming season? Your grandfather has been most generous! This fine merino is of the best quality ... or there is the damask silk. The green striped with russet would be becoming ...'

Better I had chosen deepest, darkest mourning for the love that I had lost and the marriage that I must endure. Or scarlet, for the fallen woman that I now was. But I could say nothing of this to Mrs Chadwick.

Only insist on the darkest colour, the richest colour, for my bridal gown, for I would not go to this wedding draggle-tailed and meek, but proud and fine and bold. I should spend every last penny of the money Grandfather had carelessly bestowed upon me for my trousseau. It left my other money, my secret money, free for me to use as I wished.

One week in which to say goodbye to friends and acquaintances and to seek a few private words about Ruth with Dr Barlow when he called. A man who had observed human nature at its best and worst and was unshockable on both counts, he answered my questions with brisk frankness. 'In the matter of bed-wetting it has been my experience that the harsh treatment you describe only serves to exacerbate the condition which in itself is sometimes brought on by some upsetting event in the child's life. Many authorities decry the idea that a young child is capable of any depth of understanding, but I would suggest that the cause might stem from the sad loss of her mother.'

'And the Godfrey's Cordial?'

'If the child has the griping pains of an irritable or inflamed bowel, it is an excellent medicine when properly prepared by a reliable druggist. How could it be any other with a digest of such excellent ingredients as ginger, sassafras chips, coriander, which is boiled and added to treacle with a due proportion of laudanum? In the correct dosage and judiciously used it cannot be bettered. But its general use as a regular soporific is not to be recommended. It is much favoured by the poorer classes of women who use it indiscriminately to keep fractious infants sleeping while they go about their work, but it saps the general health and when the taking of it becomes a habit, there is much distress to the child when the medicine is withdrawn. Indeed, there have been cases when an infant has died without wakening from its unnatural sleep.' He shook his head. 'In the case of the Pascoe child, it is not cordials and potions she needs but affection.' His bushy white eyebrows met in a frown. 'Who is there in that family to give it to her? Certainly not her remaining parent! If I am to be honest with you, I think that for you to become her mama and love her as your own will be the saving of her.'

One week, too, to practise shutting out the memory of the night I had spent with Nicholas. One week to walk about Exeter and prevent my heart from leaping each time some man bore a vague, passing resemblance to him. One week to adjust to the prospect of becoming the wife of Blandford Pascoe.

But in these last three, I was singularly unsuccessful.

The days moved by, too full, too fast. Fittings for my gowns, for my hats, for new boots and shoes. Visits to Timmy and Harry to bid them goodbye. Eleanor Barton proved more elusive. I called twice and each time she was not at home. On my second visit her little maid informed me that her mistress had scarcely been in recently. 'Er'm always gaddin' lately,' she said with the cheerful honesty that gave Mrs Barton much quiet amusement, but would have mightily shocked a less amenable employer. 'So 'tis no use you waitin' on 'er, for I don't knows myself where 'er's to and how long 'er'll be.'

I had to settle for sending her a note, giving her my news and telling her of my relief in knowing that I might leave Exeter assured that the Misses Polsham had so good and kind a friend.

My last day in Exeter came. I had planned to spend the morning packing. I felt very low and inclined to indulge in gloomy thoughts as I sat in my attic studio sorting out sketches. It gave me no pleasure, today, to think of people, long after I had left Exeter, continuing to derive satisfaction from some harmonious blending of colour or form that I had created. The sketches, still with the snippets of materials pinned to them, seemed sterile and dull. It was hard to recall the enthusiasm and eagerness I had brought to each individual plan. It all seemed so useless now. Best to destroy the lot and forget I had ever thought myself to be possessed of any talent.

A tap on the door and Lily appeared.

'There you are, Miss Jo! I been looking all over,' she hissed, tiptoeing in an exaggerated manner across the bare boards and wincing as her boots squeaked. 'Mary Ann's busy bottomin' Miss Olga's bedchamber an' the ladies are in the parlour, so's if you come down quick to the kitchen, miss, no one'll be any the wiser.'

'Wiser about what?' I asked, startled.

'Caleb – Caleb Smith wants a word quiet-like.' Her eyes were round with excitement. 'Oh, miss,' she burst out. 'Do you suppose it's some message from Mr Fox with a plan as'll rescue you from marriage with that dreadful—'

'Of course not!' I interrupted crisply, sharp to deny the jolting leap of something close to hope at the mention of Caleb's name, quickly dashed. There was no running away from my situation. Ben would be the one to suffer if I did. 'It is quite likely to be a message concerned with . . . with Reynard's. There was a problem, I understand, with some curtaining that had begun to fade,' I improvised quickly.

Lily looked crestfallen. 'Caleb didn't say anything of that.'

'Is there any reason that he should?'

'No, but . . .' she hesitated, 'Well, Miss Jo, he usually talks pretty open with me.'

'Does he indeed?' I said, with a smile. 'And where do these open conversations take place?'

She stuck her nose in the air, her cheeks pink as peonies. 'Now, Miss Jo, don't go getting daft ideas. You knows very well I been once or twice on my half day to see the young bloods at their fisticuffs down at Reynard's, at Mr Smith's invitation.'

'Nothing more?'

'It may be that he's stopped by a few times, in passing,' she said, indignantly. 'And I might have just been taking the weight off my feet for a minute and he may just have sat hisself down, bein' not pressed for time ... And I could not have let him go wi'out some refreshment, could I?' She frowned with pretended crossness, hissed, 'If it's a message about curtains, my name's not Lily Walker, so if you want to find out, you'd best make haste to my kitchen, for I can't waste time a-persuadin' of you when I'm in the middle of bakin'.'

Caleb rose to his feet as I came into the kitchen. His masculine bulk seemed incongruous in the little kitchen, yet he moved as one thoroughly at home and familiar there and the look he cast at Lily as she bustled ahead of me was certainly not that of a polite stranger. And Lily, for all she immediately set about a vigorous pounding of the bread dough that she tipped out of its warm earthenware crock onto the floury kitchen table, could not prevent a small, smiling glance at Caleb.

So that was the way of it. I felt a pang. Partly it was due to a sense of exclusion. Once Lily and I had been close, sharing our secrets and hopes. We had been like children, clinging together in our loneliness, for comfort. But now we were grown and we had secrets it was not possible or necessary to share.

She had grown bonny. A small, round, bustling young woman unrecognisable as the scraggy waif who had dragged at my arm in a crowded street and begged for work. Lily had found her niche in the world. And perhaps she had also now found love. The pang I felt also combined wistfulness. This gentle giant of a man with the battered face and the fists like hams would be kind to her and she, in turn, would lavish upon him all the devotion waiting to be released from her starved little heart. But above all I felt envy. For there was no one in the world with the power to say them nay.

'Well, Caleb,' I said briskly. 'You bring a message?'

'I bring the good wishes of your friends at Reynard's upon your forthcoming marriage,' he said carefully. 'Along with a token of our regard.'

With a bow he handed me a package.

Inside was a handsome silver filigree cake basket with a card signed by Mrs Fitch and Caleb. The third bold, black signature was that of Nicholas Fox.

I carefully lifted the basket from its wrapping. It was then that I saw the reason why Caleb had been bidden not to come to the parlour with the gift. I glanced at Caleb but his face was impassive. Did he know? Had Nick confided in him? Impossible to tell.

'It is beautiful, Caleb,' I breathed . . . 'I shall write, of course, but would you convey to Mrs Fitch and . . . and Mr Fox . . . my most sincere thanks? I am deeply touched.'

I returned the basket to its box and left Lily to bully Caleb into accepting a slice of lardy cake, hot from the oven, and he, grinning, to sink meekly and easily back into the chair.

On the back stairs I once more removed the basket and snatched out the other card that lay buried in the wrappings. Two words only in the same bold hand. *Have hope.* And coiled, serpent-like at the bottom of the box, a fine silver chain, no more than a thread, glinting in my trembling fingers. At either end a clasp in the shape of a tiny, fragile heart.

I closed my eyes. Behind my lids the silver cord I had dreamed linked Nicholas to me glittered as strongly as the one between my fingers.

He had remembered.

Have hope.

For the first time I dared to do so.

I had scarcely time to compose my thoughts and settle to my sorting when I was summoned downstairs again. Eleanor Barton had unexpectedly arrived.

'My dear Miss Howarth,' she said, 'thank heaven you have not already left. You will have thought me most negligent not to have answered your note, but I have been so occupied. However, I determined to see you in person.' She hesitated, then said in the same level, light tone, 'To congratulate you, of course, on your forthcoming marriage . . .' adding with barely suppressed excitement, 'but also to acquaint you with . . . certain plans of mine.'

'Pray do not tell me you have been purchasing more houses!' Miss Olga cried, throwing her hands in the air in mock horror. 'Why, you will own half Exeter soon.'

'Such energy,' sighed Miss Polsham. 'I declare, Mrs Barton, the very thought of dealing with lawyers and leases makes my poor head throb.'

'It is the lawyer you should feel sympathy for,' Mrs Barton said, beaming. 'His head must ache abominably. I believe if he sees me knocking on his door once more he will instruct his clerk to turn me into the street, for I have driven the poor man to distraction and ignored all his sensible advice. But no, I have not bought even one more brick or scrap of mortar, I promise you. It is what I intend to do with the premises that I already now own that has caused my lawyer such grief and confusion.' Her eyes sparkled. 'And now I intend to make you both regret that you ever allowed me over your doorstep, for I have a proposal to put to you, Miss Olga, which, if you refuse, I do solemnly swear might cause me to hurl myself into the Exe the next time it is in flood, my poor corpse to be washed away and never to be seen again!'

Miss Olga chuckled, though Miss Polsham felt duty bound to disguise her smile by pursing her lips and saying, in a faint, reproving voice, 'Mrs Barton, my sister has many worries at present. Not the least the loss of Joanna, which will place extra duties upon her. I trust you do not intend to add to her burdens.'

'Unfortunately, I do,' said Mrs Barton, sounding more cheerful than ever. 'And I am afraid the remuneration I am proposing will in no way compensate for the tiresome duties I shall hope to lay upon my dear friend.'

Miss Olga quivered to attention. 'Duties . . .?'

'Remuneration?' Miss Polsham said, looking alert. 'If you would be so good as to explain . . .'

'My school! And my Home for Distressed Women, a true home not a place of rules and frowns, where women fallen upon hard times may take shelter – and there are many quietly despairing, having lost everything in the recent bank failure. Oh, I have so many ideas I believe my brain will burst with them! And without Miss Olga, who is so accomplished at bookkeeping and so level-headed and practical, I do not believe I shall be able to achieve half of what I set out to do.'

The ladies were too astonished to speak. I was openmouthed myself.

Mrs Barton, having taken the wind completely from our sails, proceeded to tell us that now she had the freedom to do anything she wished, she had begun to feel, lately, the lack of some purpose in her life.

'Although I was invited by Lady Alperton to join

various charitable committees, all most worthy, my eyes have a distinct tendency to close when it comes to the solemn business of debating with a dozen other persons the spending of ha'pennies here and three-farthings there and upon whom to lavish this bounty. I found myself once or twice terrified in case I lost myself so far as to snore, which would have caused Lady Alperton to swoon dead away with horror. So, having the money and the time, I thought it would be amusing to set up some worthy causes on my own account.' For a moment flippancy slid away and she said, quietly, 'Heaven knows there is need wherever you look and charity sometimes has a forbidding face. A private person might tread lightly and discreetly where a committee would go heavy-footed. Besides,' she added, with a return to gaiety, 'I am so full of quite daring ideas that no responsible committee would countenance half of them.' She smiled at me. 'I am afraid, Miss Howarth, you must bear some of the responsibility for setting me on this wayward course. I have watched you with interest. You have talent and you have used it to great effect to become a lady decorator, a most unusual course for a young woman. It set me to wondering if it would be possible to set up an institution to educate clever girls beyond the ordinary run of schools. There are many excellent academies for boys, but so few for girls that cater for anything beyond preparing them for the marriage market.'

'You would encourage them to be blue stockings?' queried Miss Polsham, frowning.

'I would encourage them to think for themselves,' said Mrs Barton stoutly, 'and to use the brains and talents God gave them. And if their enthusiasm is fired by the geometrical theorums of Euclid or translating from the Latin or . . . or learning the anatomy of the human body, then I shall hire someone to teach it to them in a thorough manner.'

'But I see no use in that,' said Miss Polsham, looking puzzled. 'For a young man who may go on to be a lawyer or doctor, it is one thing, but how shall it benefit a young woman whose duty lies in the home, with her family? Besides, the strain of so much brain work might be injurious to her health. It is well known that a woman does not have the same intellectual capacity as a man.'

'Does she not?' Mrs Barton said dryly. 'It seems from my observation that women manage very adequately when they are allowed. Have you not thought that men have the advantage of encouragement? A woman under the rule of a man, be it her husband or father or brother, is actively *discouraged* to think beyond the drawing room and the nursery. I should like, in some small way, to redress that balance. To give women the chance to prove that they are capable of independent thought. Besides,' she added with a beaming smile, 'who knows, it may be that a future generation of women will demand the right to become doctors or lawyers or even the prime minister of England! Such teaching as girls ordinarily receive would scarcely fit them for such eminent careers.'

We laughed at her nonsense, as she intended, and the uncomfortable moment when she had seemed quite steely instead of her usual good-humoured self dissipated.

Miss Polsham, still peeved that her views had been challenged, said, 'We were taught at home, perfectly adequately, by our stepmama. Indeed, the excellence of our handwriting has often been commented upon, has it not, sister?'

'To be sure,' said Miss Olga, staring vaguely at the embroidery on her lap. 'We were modestly schooled in reading, writing, some small use of the globes . . . But do you not remember, Fanny, how quick I was at numbers, which our stepmama most certainly was not. I could add and subtract and divide great numbers at ease in my head. Papa for a while took some pleasure in devising all kinds of problems with which to test me.'

Miss Polsham frowned. 'But was there not some trouble with the elders of the chapel over it?'

'Papa had some measure of amusement in my skill. Once, when the elders came to a meeting at the house, he invited them to pit their ability with numbers against mine, but the outcome was, I think, not what he expected.' She jabbed her needle into the fine lawn of the handkerchief. 'These grown, grey men were shocked, not amused. They thought it unnatural and perverse that a small child should best them. They spoke severely to Papa. Such demonstrations, they said, would only lead to worldly vanity and a corruption of the intellect. They prayed long and loud over me that day, saying that I must never again allow the devil to tempt me into displaying further evidence of the precocious and immoral taint that was clearly evident in my character.' She sighed. 'I cried a great deal, as I remember, which pleased them. Yet my distress was more for the loss of any further arithmetic lessons than for fear of the devil. And thinking of it now leads me to believe it was the vanity of those foolish men that was piqued.' She looked at Mrs Barton and said quietly. 'I believe that had I had the opportunity to attend such a school as you envisage, Mrs Barton, I should have found it deeply satisfying to be encouraged, rather than put down.'

'Then you will be willing to help me in my venture?'

'It would give me great pleasure,' said Miss Olga.

'And you will not be disturbed to know that I plan this school of mine in the premises adjoining this house?'

Miss Polsham gasped. Miss Olga looked surprised,

but after a moment's thought she shook her head. 'I believe I find that quite an enlivening thought.'

'Then it is settled!' declared Mrs Barton. 'Oh, we have so much to talk about – how many boarders, how many day girls, how many free places to offer to bright girls of humble means, for though it will be politic to have a sprinkling of daughters of forward-thinking eminent families, my principal aim is to foster excellence even if it is found in a crossing sweeper. There will be tutors to be interviewed and engaged, the premises to be assessed and alterations made, and all will have to be costed, Miss Olga. I shall rely on you entirely for that for I cannot add two and two without it making five.' She turned to me, her voice regretful. 'I am sorry that you will not be here in person to advise us, Miss Howarth, on furnishings and decoration, as I expected you would be when the idea first came to me. I do regret that a talent such as yours, though it will be dearly appreciated by the good folk of Kingsbridge, should now be lost to us in Exeter. But not entirely perhaps?' She paused, her eyebrows raised over her intelligent eyes. 'The house next door is the twin of this one, though some alterations will have to be made when the old gentleman moves at the month's end. If you would care to consider posting some suggestions as to decoration, once you are settled in your new home, it would be the greatest help.'

A short while ago I had considered tearing up my sketches, seeing no prospect beyond the grim one of marriage to Blandford Pascoe. My mood was very different now. Two words had changed that. *Have hope.*

'I should be honoured,' I said.

I had one last duty to perform before Miss Olga and I, the rest of the house silent and sleeping, finally retired to bed.

I had sewn a small linen purse. Into this I put the money I had left – much depleted now – saving but twenty sovereigns to carry with me in my father's old tobacco pouch. I reflected, wryly, that I was leaving Torre Crescent scarcely richer than I had entered it. But wiser, far wiser.

I pressed the purse into Miss Olga's hands. 'I will take no refusal,' I said. My voice wobbled. 'It is for my sake as much as yours that I beg you to accept this small gift. I wish to go away knowing that this house, that all the people in it, are provided for when I am not here. Yes, I know, you will have the most generous remuneration from Mrs Barton, but this will be a little nest egg ... against ... against ... Oh, pray do not cry, Miss Olga, for I shall be quite undone.'

There was no going on. But after a little while, when we had managed to collect ourselves, for we were both of us women who were ashamed to give in too easily to sentimental tears, we took up our candles and I followed Miss Olga for the last time up the dim, narrow stairs of the house that had, finally, become a home to me.

Chapter Twenty-One

'Married in grey, you'll rue the day,' chanted Miss Lightbody. She teetered round my bedchamber like a seedy sprite as I laid my bridal clothes out for her inspection.

'My dress is more blue than grey,' I said.

'But so dark! 'Tis a dank and dismal drab you'll look tomorrow, to be sure. Like a winter ghost crept out of the shadows to fright an August day.'

'There is, of course, the hat,' I said, drawing it from the press.

'Hah! Better!' Her little claws nipped greedily among blue ribbons and flowers. 'A bold conceit! 'Twill give you the pretence of a queen of ice and snow rather than a spectral shade. And what flowers will you carry, Miss Snow and Ice?' She peered up at me with bright unwinking eyes. 'Lilies? For purity and innocence? Or will it be poppies, scarlet as blood – and sin?'

'You overstep the mark, Miss Lightbody,' I said tartly, but I turned away from her to hide the colour that came up hot in my cheeks.

'And come too close for comfort, eh?' she tittered. 'Well, if you will not say, as you promised, what you was about, dressed as a drab to go on secret dealings, then I must guess.'

'I recollect no promise on my part, merely a demand on yours,' I said.

577

She ignored me. 'You did not return straight to the bosom of the old maids, for you told me so yourself. But where did you go, and for how long . . . and with whom? I ask myself these teasing questions over and over.'

'And find no answer, nor will!'

Ever since my return from Exeter she had been like a terrier needling and nipping at my heels. I had finally submitted to her curiosity about my wedding gown, though I had locked it away determined not to lay eyes on it until it was necessary to do so. It reminded me too strongly of what I must endure. But I could not, would not, speak of what she most burned to know and I was exasperated beyond endurance at her persistence. I whisked the hat out of her fingers and replaced it in the press, slamming the door closed.

'Oh, the answer comes readily to one who knows human nature and human lusts and conjoins this knowledge with the track of Venus in the heavens, and a certain look about a maid who has become a woman . . . Well, you were pale and mopish from the bellyache a few days since, so at least he did not get you with child . . .'

'Miss Lightbody!' I whirled round. 'You forget yourself! And . . . and I will not stand for this . . . this interrogation a moment longer! Please go away!'

'Hoity-toity, such a temper,' she said, spreading her wilted skirts daintily and seating herself on the bed. 'Well, 'tis to be expected in one who will be a bride on the morrow, and the groom not the man who has taken her fancy and mayhap her bridehead. I shall forgive you, in this instance.'

'I do not wish for your forgiveness,' I said, through gritted teeth. 'Merely your absence.'

'What? When I came out of charity to give you sound advice?'

'I cannot think there is any advice you could usefully give me.'

'Perhaps you have a wish, then, to be like the jacka-nape's first milksop wife, for ever breeding. For myself, once was enough. I did not care to go again through the trouble of childbirth and was equally loathe to tangle with the methods to rid oneself of a tiresome encumbrance. I have known too many poor whores bleed their life away in agony and fever after the knitting needle or the sliver of glass had been mercilessly used to roust out the impediment.'

I shuddered. 'Please, Miss Lightbody.'

'Unpleasant, is it not? But a woman's lot is not an easy one and it behoves us to make the most of every opportunity to improve it. Well,' she demanded, 'am I to stay here all day until you deign to listen to me?'

I sighed. She was quite capable of it. Besides, my curiosity was caught. Could she truly know a way to prevent a child being conceived? How useful a trick if it were possible.

It was a matter, she said, of a piece of sponge soaked in vinegar and placed so as to prevent the man's seed reaching the womb. 'For if it does, it will root and grow to be a babe, as would any common weed seed put into rich ground. You must of course take care to use the chamber pot and remove the sponge soon after the sport has been enjoyed, but remember that a young man, newly wed, is lusty and may be roused frequently to further demonstrations of his prowess.'

I was too interested to blush. 'And will it not . . . well . . . be noticed by the man if . . . if there is an impediment?'

She screeched with laughter. 'If his member is aroused, it scarce notices the nature of the orifice it enters, leave alone the geography of the place. Besides, the sponge mimics the silken surfaces it protects. I should particularly commend this course of action midway between the monthly courses, which seems the most like time for the seed to fall on fertile ground, though there are those who insist it is a different time of the moon. I can only say that this method served me faithfully over many years. I learned it from a French courtesan who had similarly escaped the chains of childbearing – though unfortunately it did not save her from the pox which carried her off in her prime.'

I busied myself smoothing out a crease in the skirt of my wedding gown. 'Thank you for the advice,' I said a little stiffly.

'Make sure that you take it,' she snapped, 'unless you wish to be brought to bed every nine months until you are worn to an old woman before your time, for he has proved himself well capable.' In her unpredictable way, she suddenly whisked off the bed, crying, 'You keep me here chattering and I have a thousand things to do. There is the silver to be got out and the sluts to chivvy, though 'tis scarcely worth the bother with only the Pascoes to sit down to the wedding breakfast.'

She scurried off, mumbling and cursing under her breath. I put away my wedding gown and took myself out of doors. I needed air, space, sunlight.

I was grateful to Miss Lightbody for the surprising information. But she was like a thorn in my flesh, constantly jabbing me with her questions and insinuations. I found her almost uncanny ability to sense what was in my head unnerving, her talk of planets and portents disturbing. It seemed that when I most needed to be distracted from thoughts of my future she appeared at my elbow to remind me.

Hatless, bare-armed, for there was no one to see and disapprove, I walked out onto the headland. There was a hot breeze out of the east, bringing with it a bluish haze that blurred the distance and hung like mist over the water. A long swell heaved the sea towards the cliffs and flung itself in a ceaseless, rhythmic lather of foam on the rocks. I turned in a circle. There was no one else in sight. Nobody came riding towards me along the cliff road. Nobody stood within the shelter of the woods, waiting to hail me. All that moved was a pair of hawks, circling lazily in the eddies of hot air above the cliff edge. Peregrines. I watched them wheeling effortlessly, the afternoon warm, their bellies full so that they remained oblivious of the frightened calling and fluttering as small birds flitted nervously into shelter.

Have hope.

I had hoped . . . for what? Nicholas to appear on a white charger to carry me off? For some messenger to bring news of an ingenious way of escape? Common sense had surfaced time and again to dash away the ever-present fantasy spun by my imagination. I could not expect to escape. It was impossible. If I ran now, the hawk who ruled Falconwood would swoop and mercilessly destroy my brother and in so doing destroy me. For how could I live with myself if I allowed such a thing to happen?

Yet I still looked for someone, some sign that might indicate an alleviation of my predicament. Something to make the way forward easier, kinder . . .

Two people were coming up the path from the cove, a scatter of dogs loping and bounding round them. Mr Chadwick and Ben, figures too familiar to raise any false hopes. I could not distinguish their features from this distance yet I knew that Ben would be smiling, skin healthily glowing from his swim, his eyes guileless and innocent and unaware. Oh, he knew that tomorrow I should be married and the day after he would be married, but he accepted the facts now without distress. He had been troubled at first, but Mr Chadwick and I had worked patiently to reassure and calm him, emphasising over and over again that the ceremony would be simple and after it he would be staying at Falconwood with his friends and his animals and nothing would be changed, except that he would have a wife to care for him and love him. Even Susannah, when she had visited Falconwood last week, had put herself out to foster this impression. She had been most agreeable to him. And Blandford, wearing the palpably false smile of a man who has glimpsed the chasm beyond the brink and knows that he has no other option but to submit to the heavy grip of the rescuer, had surpassed himself with a hypocritical fawning over Ben and excessive politeness to everyone else.

The Pascoes had visited us in order to make the final amendments to the marriage settlement with Mr Davey and Tom. Tom had grown to be a personable, sober young man, his puppyish admiration of me long put aside. He was past the age of instant and temporary infatuation. Time had changed us both. Yet there was a hint, still, of warmth in his manner that I was grateful for on a day that was difficult for me. He was easy, too, with Ben, borne of his many visits to Falconwood. What had begun as a tenuous link with me had long since progressed into a genuine friendship, for its own sake, with Mr Chadwick and Ben. I was thankful for it as I watched them together. Tom did not patronise Ben, but treated him with consideration and kindness, which boded well for any future legal dealings with Falconwood in which Tom was involved.

But it was not Tom who came to mind or even Blandford as I stood on the cliffs waiting for Ben and Mr Chadwick to reach me. It was Susannah. I did not wish to feel concern about her, but I could not help myself. That day at Falconwood she had looked dazzling, a sparkling vision in sugar-pink flounces, her ribbon-threaded curls glossy and perfect. She had laughed, pouted winsomely, teased; she had set herself to charm. And it was all totally false. The brilliance of her eyes had a febrile quality, the snap of her fan was like the snapping of over-taut nerves. She had undeniably lost weight. Had she been older she might have looked haggard, but in one so youthful and smooth-skinned, it merely gave a hint of shadow under her cheekbones to emphasise the pretty contours of her face. Every now and then I intercepted a glance between father and daughter. Hers begged release. '*Is this really what you want of me, Papa? I am doing my best, but it is so very difficult.*' And his encouraged. '*It will not be so bad as you fear. You have much to gain, as we all have.*'

She was playing her part in this masquerade to the best of her ability, as I was myself, but it was costing her dear.

'Susannah?' said Blandford, vaguely, when I enquired. We were walking in the garden, Ben and Susannah ahead, Mr Chadwick a little apart with the air of a man wishing himself elsewhere, the other gentlemen having retired to the study to sign the documents. 'Susannah? She is perfectly well, why do you ask?'

'She seems a little . . . overwrought.'

He shrugged his plump shoulders. 'I have not noticed. I believe it is natural in a bride to be anxious.' He sniggered, said in a soft, suggestive voice, 'As you must be yourself, my dear Joanna.'

I had laid my hand lightly on his sleeve, keeping as much space between us as I could while maintaining an attitude of polite attentiveness. Now he put his damp, hot hand over mine, pulling me close. 'This is the first time we have been alone together. I do not wish to discuss my sister, but to talk of you, and to express my pleasure at our forthcoming union.'

'But she may be sickening for something,' I said, somewhat desperately, too aware of his fingers stroking my wrist, of his other hand slipping round my waist and moving lightly and deliberately upwards to come to rest where it must contact the swell of my breast as I moved. 'It would be . . . be too unfortunate.'

'She is healthy enough. Indeed, she has energy to spare, for when she is not indoors closeted with the dressmaker, she is for ever taking long solitary walks. I fear she has quite shunned her Kingsbridge acquaintances, feeling some shame is attached to the decline in the family fortunes and her present situation. She has the worst of it, I agree.' He pressed his mouth to my ear, whispering, 'Your brother, I fear, will not be the . . . adequate and ardent bridegroom that I shall be.' He nuzzled my ear. 'You have a lot to learn, my dear, not least in the matter of pleasing a man, which I think will not come too easily to your proud nature. But it is greatly to my satisfaction that I am to be your tutor.'

The thought of his drunken assault on me in the Torre Crescent parlour rose up to taunt me. I barely controlled a shudder.

Susannah saved me then, twirling round, calling, 'Do catch up, you pair of turtle doves! For we are none of us wed yet and must chaperone each other properly.' And again there was that high, desperate edge to her voice that made me think that even these few moments alone in Ben's company were a torment to her.

So I stood now on the cliffs and I wondered how she felt today, with her wedding so close. As I waved to Ben, who broke into an eager jog-trot, beaming delightedly because I had come to meet him, I found it in me to hope that she was not shedding too many bitter tears and that eventually she might find some comfort and consolation in her situation. For as I had learned myself, there was nothing she could do to alter it. And the sooner she accepted that, the better.

Dreams. I was trying to run for the Kingsbridge coach on legs that floundered in mud. I was desperate to reach it before it left, but the coachman was Blandford who, when he saw me coming, laughed and cracked his whip over the horses' backs and sped them away. Then Mrs Chadwick was stitching me into a tight white dress that bound my arms to my sides and constricted my breathing, saying, 'A perfect fit, my dear, it will show you off to great advantage . . .' Only it was a shroud and I knew if I could get to Nicholas he would tell them that I was still alive. I could hear him calling me, but there was a barrier, a deep, wide river full of evil-looking fish, upon which I was floating swiftly towards a great chasm into which the water dropped with a roar like thunder . . .

I awoke gasping, sweating, tangled in the bedsheet. The roar of the waterfall faded to the faint beat of rain against the window.

I disengaged myself from the sheet and went to throw the window wide, letting the rain splash in on me while the pounding of my heart quieted. The shower was passing. The dawn clouds were pink against a fragile blue sky. There was the moist, cool smell of earth newly refreshed.

My wedding day. But the sensation of being held in that tight, constricting shroud stayed with me long after I was dressed and ready to meet my bridegroom.

The Pascoe carriage was expected around noon, when the Pascoes and Ben would proceed immediately to the church, Grandfather and I following in the ancient Kerswell chariot. We should return to Falconwood for the wedding breakfast and later Mrs Blandford Pascoe would travel to her new home, Brent House, with her new family. Tomorrow the happy couple would make their first public appearance as man and wife at the wedding of Miss Susannah Pascoe to Mr Benjamin Howarth Kerswell.

That was how I felt about it. Detached, impersonal, as though it were all happening to someone else. Even my wedding finery did nothing but make it seem more unreal.

Both weddings were to be quiet, family affairs, as was suitable in the circumstances. Blandford, though his behaviour since Jane's death had been execrable, was by rights still in mourning and even if his natural instincts led towards an excess of show he must bow to the judgment of his father and my grandfather who wished all to be got through as swiftly and discreetly as possible. It was my heartfelt wish too. I could not have faced a throng of smiling guests intent on pressing their congratulations and good wishes upon me.

I sat quietly in my room waiting for Bessy to call me, the glass of wine and almond biscuits she had brought up earlier standing untouched on the dresser. Round my neck for all to see I wore Mama's pretty necklace. Under my gown, lying lightly against my skin, was the silver chain that Nicholas had sent me. I had worn it day and night, but now I reached up and unclasped it, separating the two hearts. I held it for a moment to my lips, then tied it in a handkerchief and slid it into Papa's old tobacco pouch, along with the twenty sovereigns. I could not take it with me to Brent House where Blandford might find it. I should leave it here in the only place I could think of where no one else would look.

It still wanted half an hour to noon. I went in search

of Grandfather, finding him in his study looking uncomfortably formal, his cravat starched and high and his old-fashioned black coat and white breeches pressed to perfection, buckled shoes glossed to a deep shine. I had never before seen him turned out so immaculately.

He frowned at me. Not a frown of disapproval, but of assessment. After a moment, he cleared his throat, said, 'You look very fine, Joanna.'

'And you, Grandfather,' I said, making him a little curtsy.

He bowed in return, smiled, and it was possible for a fleeting moment to sense the handsome, debonair young man he had been before tragedy and unhappiness had embittered him and the years had carved the deep lines in his face, bent his shoulders and frosted his hair.

And something else caught at me, something not quite recognised, a thought darting away before I could catch it . . . There were other, more pressing matters that must be attended to.

'Grandfather, I have a small favour to ask.'

'And think to find me in a mellow mood, and unable to refuse you, eh? Let me tell you, child, there is nothing more likely to set me in a temper than being forced into dressing up like a popinjay – and not just today, but tomorrow must be tolerated as well!'

'You cannot lay the blame at my door,' I said equably. 'It is all your own doing.'

'Always a ready answer,' he growled, but it was a half-hearted growl. He was well satisfied that his plans were coming to fruition. 'Well? What is this favour?'

I looked him straight in the eye. 'I should like your permission to go into my mother's room. The one you keep locked.'

He was taken aback and his frown this time was the

genuine article. 'Why?' he demanded.

'Because I am my mother's daughter and she is not here to see me married. I . . . I should like, for a few moments, to . . . to feel close to her . . .' I stopped, because it was suddenly true. It was more than wanting to hide my money and my necklace, it was as though that thought had come to me, borne on the other, hidden need. 'It . . . it is not easy to ask, Grandfather, nor, I know, for you to grant me this favour, when you would prefer to forget all she once meant. But it would mean a great deal to me . . . I should only be a few moments . . . If I might ask Mrs Beer for the key?'

His face was as hard as flint.

'No, you may not.' Silence. A silence so cold that I felt the goose bumps come up on my skin. And that chill was the chill of final, uncompromising defeat. I felt the strength go out of me. The unreal, detached state of mind went with it, my last protection.

'There is no need to trouble Mrs Beer. I have a key.'

Had I heard right? He was rummaging in his desk, flinging the key at me as though it burned his fingers. 'Go, if it means so much. But you will not find her there.' He turned away and stalked to the window. With his back to me, he added in a harsh whisper, 'I never have.'

They were the saddest words I had ever heard him speak.

Grandfather was right. Mama was not there among the dust and cobwebs. The room was exactly as it had been the morning when Mrs Beer had locked me out of it. A young girl's room, frozen in time. But the girl she had been, that I had been, had long gone. It was smaller than I remembered and the prettiness, still evident, despite the neglect seemed fussy and overblown.

I hid the tobacco pouch at the back of the deepest drawer in the clothes press, under a pile of petticoats.

A smell of mould came up. There were black speckles on the once white, now yellowed, lawn. Decay and death. The room itself, I realised, exuded an overpowering aroma of it. I closed the drawer quickly, all the suffocating, frightening sensations of my dream returning in full strength.

I regretted I had come. It had been a futile exercise. There was no comfort, no consolation to be had here. Only a reminder of the inexorable passage of time that turns all things to dust.

I left as though the devil himself were at my heels.

And perhaps he was.

Bessy pounded into my room, breathless from the stairs, and the importance of her news. 'Mr Pascoe, he'm took bad.' My heart rose at the possibility of reprieve, then plummeted once more. 'Mr Blandford's come alone as Miss Susannah's 'ad to stay behind to see to 'er pa. 'Ee been purgin' somethin' terrible . . .'

'Thank you, Bessy,' I said, briskly cutting short further revelations.

She curtsied, sullen at being denied her moment of excitement. 'You'm to come down right away, miss,' she muttered. 'Mr Blandford's already left for the church, along o' Master Ben and Mr Chadwick.'

'Very well, Bessy.' I rose calmly and went to the mirror to put on my hat. 'Tell my grandfather I shall be down in a moment.'

I took my time pinning on my blue hat, gathering up the small posy of wild flowers I had picked in the fringes of the garden this morning. White, yellow-eyed daisies, a cornflower or two, a few sprigs of lavender from bushes that had seeded themselves under the dry protection of a wall. I had bound them with damp moss, tied them with a long blue ribbon that matched those in my hat.

'Weeds? You carry a bunch of weeds?' Miss

Lightbody said, teetering in her rusty black house-keeper's disguise at the foot of the stairs.

'They please me,' I said shortly. I wanted no exotic blossoms. I felt it was symbolic to carry these hardy flowers that were so tenacious and lusty of life.

She screeched with laughter. 'Then my offering will not look amiss in that sorry company. Here, take it for luck. A Romany woman once gave it me when I rescued her brat from a stinking mob that had caught him thieving from a market stall. He deserved to be caught, but it is my contrary nature to be whimsical in these matters and I liked the cheeky cut of his jib. The Romany woman pressed upon me this sprig of heather which she spoke some spell over. I believe that while it was still fresh it had some potency, for I won handsomely at the tables whenever I remembered to tuck it in my bodice. I had not seen it for an age until it came to my hand when I was searching for a brooch I thought to wear today.' She thrust it into the posy, a twig as shrivelled and dry as herself. 'For luck,' she repeated, then, softly, 'you have need of luck. The planets move in dark and dangerous patterns. All that is certain is uncertainty.' Her unwinking gaze was extra bright. I realised she looked at me through tears. 'The pattern is strange and terrible. We shall none of us escape the shadows that wheel and turn and cast us into confusion.'

She spun on her heel and was gone, tottering away on uncertain legs as Grandfather strode into the hall and summoned me impatiently.

I left the sprig of dried heather in my posy, incongruous as it was. It ill behoved me to dispense with even this poor, weak symbol of good fortune.

A long day. A day to be got through, moment by heavy moment.

I made my vows. I promised to love and obey a man I despised. I spoke clearly and held my head high and thought the vicar looked a sick, frail man. I worried, distantly, that he might fall in a faint before completing the ceremony and watched his grey, thin face with concern, but he did not and I walked from the church on the arm of the man who had been joined to me for life and whom I should now call husband.

The wedding breakfast must be enjoyed. I must eat, if only a little, I must smile, I must acknowledge the toast that Grandfather made. I must not shrink from the little touchings and pressings of knee against thigh, of fingers against flesh that my husband bestowed upon me, as was his right.

I drank deeply as my glass was refilled. Wine blurred the edges of feeling. I have no recollection of stringing words together. I heard others speaking. Grandfather's concern at his friend's sudden ailment. His hopes that he would be well enough to take his part in tomorrow's ceremony. Blandford's ready assurances that should his father still be indisposed, he would readily step in to give his sister in marriage . . . I remember nothing else except deeply envying Susannah her one extra day of freedom, even if it was spent at the bedside of a sick man.

The afternoon wore on. Presently, it was time for the Pascoe carriage to be brought from the stables and my boxes and bags loaded upon it. It was time for goodbyes. Ben's eager hug. Mr Chadwick's formal bow and good wishes. Grandfather taking my hand and unexpectedly pressing a kiss on my cheek with a murmured, 'Your conduct has been pleasing, child. I wish you . . . contentment.' Not happiness. How could he wish me that when he knew that happiness was the least likely component of this marriage? Mrs Beer waving, Bessy Beer enthusiastically hurling a handful of rice that clung to my pelisse like pearly teardrops.

The Pascoes' coachman was a gnarled, dour man, with a mouth tight and close as a rat trap. He handed me silently into the carriage. Blandford followed me in, sitting in the opposite corner so that he might smile his farewells as we moved away down the drive.

I cast one, last despairing glance back before we turned into the lane. The little knot of people on the steps waved, Ben standing tall as Grandfather and handsome as he must once have been. But the picture I carried with me was of Falconwood itself. The sun was lowering. Light drenched the westward-facing walls and dazzled from the windows. For a moment the house gave the illusion of being theatrically unreal, as though it floated, a golden mystical vessel among waves of mounded greenery.

Then the view was cut off by the high wall as we rounded the gateposts, to reappear when we crested the cliff road. Falconwood was itself again. Solid, sturdy, drawing steadily back from us to merge and blend with the land from which its stones had been hewn.

And I was alone for the first time with the man who was my husband.

It was dark when we reached Brent House. The wine had long since ceased its fizzing in my head and a chill desolation had settled on my heart. The sight of my new home did nothing to alleviate it. The shutters were drawn over whatever rooms were lit inside. One lantern burned low in the porch and there was no one to welcome us, not even a maid scurrying to fling the door wide to the new mistress.

Blandford handed me down. I was stiff with the jolting. Much of the road from Falconwood was bad, the winding lanes strewn with ruts and potholes. It had been a slow journey, but at least it had saved me from Blandford's attentions, for it was imperative for us both to cling tightly to the straps in order not to be thrown about. Conversation had lapsed and died after a while. Blandford watched me, his sly smile flickering occasionally at my endeavours to keep upright as the wheels rolled into some extra deep pothole. Once or twice he appeared to doze, his chin on his chest, but his eyes never seemed quite to close. I pretended to be deeply interested in the view beyond the window. When it grew too dark to see I, too, closed my eyes, though it was impossible to rid myself of the feeling of his gaze constantly and unpleasantly upon me.

The housekeeper, Mrs Jenkins, who met us in the hall, was middle-aged and silent. I remembered her from my previous visits and smiled, but she did not respond. She carefully lowered her eyes, curtsied, and said, to Blandford, 'Supper is laid in the dining parlour, sir, whenever you and Mrs Pascoe are ready.'

'Mrs Pascoe is exhausted from her journey,' Blandford said, with pretence at concern. 'We will take some refreshment in our room. Nothing heavy, you understand, a little cold beef, a pastry or two. A glass of claret to put some colour into her cheeks.'

'I am really not at all tired, Blandford,' I said, desperate to delay the moment when I must climb the stairs with him.

He ignored me. He waved Mrs Jenkins away with a brusque gesture.

'But what of your papa?' I said, quickly. 'And Susannah. Should we not enquire . . .?'

'They are long abed, I am sure,' he said. 'There was scarcely any sleep for us last night, remember.' He moved closer, ran his hand down my cheek and down, down to my breast, stroking, pressing. 'Nor tonight, for us, my dear wife.'

'Please, Blandford, not here. The servants . . .'

He smiled unpleasantly. 'Servants? What are they but a class as low as pigs. They will take no heed of a man paying attention to his wife, for they themselves are like to fornicate where and how they will.'

'Blandford! For shame! That is a dreadful thing to say.'

He thrust his face close to mine. 'Do not contradict me, madam. I will not have it! Remember where your duty lies. You are bound to obey me now, not the whims and fancies of your own conceited nature. From now on you will do as I tell you and speak only as I tell you, do you understand?'

I gritted my teeth against the hot words that rose in my throat. I must strive to be calm and civil. Antagonising him now would do no good. I was trapped and must submit to my captor until I had learned the best way to make my captivity bearable. I bowed my head silently so that he would not see the anger and frustration in my face.

His mood was restored by my apparent acceptance.

'Continue to bear these precepts in mind, at all times, Joanna,' he said jovially, 'for in a wife there is nothing more agreeable than a desire to please and serve her husband. After all, he is the one set by nature to be her master and guide in all things.' He laughed softly and drew me towards the stairs. 'And I may say it pleases me greatly that we are now wed. I have always felt drawn to you, Joanna, and have often had the notion that it would be . . . rewarding . . . to have the mastery and taming of such a bold spirit. Besides, it is well known that the temperament that goes with such fiery locks tends towards an insatiable lewdity between the sheets that can be exceedingly pleasurable to a man.'

I kept my head averted. If he thought it was through

embarrassment or fear, so much the better. It was not. It was because I felt a little leap of jubilation. The night's events could not be avoided, but I knew now how they might be managed to give my new bridegroom the least possible satisfaction.

I had known, so briefly, the powerful delight of love shared by two people caught up in mutual passion. I had experienced the tenderness of a lover who had tempered his ardour to my inexperience and who had wished to please me as much as himself.

I thanked heaven for it, for now I discovered the dark side of human passion, when it is lust rather than love that rules and the desires of a spiteful nature are wrought upon the object of that lust.

There were times in the night when I thought of poor, fragile Jane going through this same violation, other moments when I found the words of Ruth's nursemaid, Sally, running through my head: Alice warned me not to scream and make a fuss, for that was what he liked best . . .

So I lay inert, as passive as I could make myself, never once wincing or shrinking or protesting. It was not easy, for my very passivity roused him to frustrated anger and therefore to further attempts to goad me into a response. But I succeeded and it was a small triumph that added to the inner core of strength that I hugged to my heart. Strength already fostered by the knowledge that I had denied him the taking of my virginity and, God and Miss Lightbody willing, the chance of a child.

I was allowed, at last, a respite and fell into an exhausted sleep. When I woke it was full daylight and something had disturbed me. The sound of hooves on cobbles? Raised voices?

Susannah's wedding day, I thought bleakly. The

house would naturally be astir with preparations.

Blandford still snored. He lay on his back, slack mouth agape, his flabby white arms hugging the bed-clothes to his crumpled, sweaty nightshirt. Thankfully he stayed so until I was washed and dressed. I took pains to be quiet. The privacy afforded by the small dressing room seemed very precious.

My face in the mirror was pale. I pinched my cheeks and composed my expression so that I did not look so strained. A calm demeanour was essential. I must show no weakness. Blandford would be alert for it and seek to play on any vulnerable emotion that I displayed.

I hoped I would be able to remove myself downstairs in search of Susannah before he stirred, but as I was tiptoeing across the bedroom, there was a hammering at the door and a loud voice, Mr Pascoe's voice, bellowed, 'Blandford! Unlock this door!'

I hastily slid back the bolt which Blandford had secured last night, sneering, 'See how I do everything in my power to preserve your modesty, my dear. Though there is not a servant in the house who would dare to disturb his master on this particular night.' But I had felt it was more to shut me in than to lock anyone out.

Mr Pascoe burst into the room. Not a man weak from a violent illness, but a man who had been out riding hard. He was still in mud-splattered riding clothes, red-faced from the exercise.

And very, very angry.

He ignored me, beyond one choleric glance. He strode to the bed, raising his riding crop and bringing it down hard across the bedclothes mounded above Blandford's stomach. Blandford yelped.

'You damned fool! You young nincompoop! You married her and now there is nothing! Nothing!' he screamed. 'The settlement is null and void! Frank

Kerswell will be beside himself with rage when he knows! And we might have salvaged something, snared you someone rich, if only you had done as you were told for once instead of tying yourself to a millstone!'

Blandford made an effort to rise and yelped again as the riding crop swished down.

'It is not my fault,' he whimpered, wriggling to dodge further blows. 'It is that cheating blackguard's!'

'You blind . . . stupid . . . disobedient oaf!' The crop rose and fell on each word. 'I should . . . have done this . . . years ago!' Then Mr Pascoe turned and in a final fury of anger smashed the crop on the window ledge, breaking it in two and sending the potpourri bowl flying in a cascade of scented petals and shattered china.

For a moment there was only the sound of his harsh breathing, then Blandford whined, 'But I thought you would have caught up with them, brought her back. They had surely not been gone long.'

'Long enough.' Mr Pascoe sat down heavily on a chair and put his head in his hands. 'They were seen to take the Plymouth road. That is all I know. I have had notices posted there, but I have little hope. He has spirited her into thin air.'

I found my voice at last. It came out high and desperate, with a terrible keening note. 'What . . . what has happened, Mr Pascoe? Please. . . . please tell me what has happened.'

But I already knew before he spoke the words. My heart beat heavy and thick with the anguish of it. Every nerve in my body quivered with pain.

He raised his head and looked at me with cold distaste.

'Nicholas Fox has run off with my daughter. She has ruined herself and it seems that her brother and father will now be brought down, too.'

'But surely,' Blandford put in eagerly, 'Frank Kerswell will see us right. His granddaughter is my wife, we are kin now.'

'You have not the sense you were born with,' his father said with withering scorn. 'Frank cares only for his idiot grandson. The girl is nothing to him. The contract was off the moment Susannah disappeared. The lawyers have it all written in wherebys and theretofores. If you chose to ride to Falconwood to marry the chit instead of relaying the bad tidings and calling off the wedding, then you must take the consequences. She has no dowry and you are not free to seek a more suitable wife. We are in a worse case than before.'

And neither of them, caught up in their own snare of trouble, spared a look or a word for me. It was too late now to prevent Grandfather from leaving Falconwood. There was nothing else to do but prepare ourselves for the distressing interview that would be forthcoming. Mr Pascoe ordered us curtly to be in the drawing room within the hour where we would await the arrival of the bridal party. 'We must do our best to retrieve whatever is salvageable from this mess. Though I fancy there is little now to be gained.' The bedroom door slammed after him.

I remained where I was. I did not move because, for the moment, I could not. I felt that my flesh was turned to marble and that if I tried to move, my body would crack and splinter and fall to fragments like the broken potpourri bowl.

Blandford threw back the bedclothes and scrambled from bed. He had been humiliated and someone must suffer for it.

'This is all your doing, madam!' he snarled. 'You snared me with your whore's tricks.'

This was so palpably untrue that it was amusing. And how comical he looked, dancing about on his skinny white legs, his plump belly jouncing underneath his nightshirt.

He raised his hand and struck me across the face. I blinked, swayed. Yet the sting was nothing. Somewhere there was a hurt so great that this minor injury made no impression at all.

'I forbid you to laugh!'

I was in my heeled slippers. He was barefooted. It meant that he was forced to look up at me. That was amusing, too.

'You will suffer for this! By Christ, you will!'

It was all very silly. Did he not realise that his threats and posturings meant nothing? Who or what could make my situation worse than it already was?

I said, pleasantly, for it was always best to show tolerance towards those whose intelligence could not encompass too much deep understanding, 'Blandford, I have things to do before my grandfather arrives. Might I have your permission to set about them now?'

His hand, raised to strike again, hesitated. Uncertainty chased surprise across his features.

'And you have but a short time yourself, to get ready,' I went on, encouragingly. 'It would not do to keep your papa waiting, would it? Shall you go down for breakfast? I will have a tray sent up if you prefer.'

'What things?' His voice was an irritated squeak. He cleared his throat, tried again. 'What things? Come, answer me, madam!'

'Why, as the new mistress I must ensure that such a difficult day as this promises to be runs as smoothly as it is possible to make it. Whatever else your papa holds against me, I should not wish him to find me wanting in this particular. I must acquaint myself with all the domestic arrangements. For instance, has the vicar been informed? Should a note be sent?'

'That is all attended to. Now listen to—'

'With this . . . this upset there is doubtless anxiety below stairs as to how they should proceed. I shall see Mrs Jenkins and cook straightaway. And of course, Blandford, you will not wish me to hesitate in introducing myself to Ruth as her new mama.'

'What? I give you no such—'

'And I do think it inadvisable for you to stand about dressed only in your nightshirt. The day is overcast and there is a damp draught coming from somewhere. I should not like you to catch a chill. There is trouble enough in the house.'

He glanced down involuntarily at his naked feet, shifting them uneasily on the polished floorboards.

'I feel no draught.'

'But it is quite strong. A veritable breeze.' I shook out a gather in my skirt as though the imaginary draught had disturbed it, so drawing his attention to my appearance which until that moment I think he had not properly observed.

The comparison was not favourable to his own frowsty, unwashed state. I had put on, in honour of Susannah's wedding, the grey-blue gown which I had worn under the matching pelisse for my own wedding yesterday. Very dignified and imposing in the richness of its heavy silk. I felt gratified that it suited me so well.

'Come now, Blandford. When you are dressed perhaps you might discover the source of the draught – an ill-fitting window sash, I would judge. Then we may see about having it repaired.'

'You are . . . are presumptuous, madam!' He seemed to have difficulty in spluttering out the words.

'Is it presumptuous to be concerned with the well-being of my new family?' I said in a tone of gentle reproof. 'I am afraid I cannot agree with such a sentiment, husband. However, I do realise you are labouring under the strain of . . . of recent events.

Accordingly, I shall this once forgive you this bad-tempered outburst.'

'Forgive me . . .?' He was dumbstruck. He had set out to humiliate and dominate me and instead by some means he could not quite grasp I had eluded him.

I did not quite understand it myself, except that all hope had fled and the pain of deception and betrayal was so great that I felt nothing else would ever again have the power to wound me. Least of all the ineffectual buzzings and stingings of the strident little bluebottle who was my husband. Because he could no longer hurt me, his power over me had diminished. Later, perhaps, rage would come. Against him, against Nick, against Grandfather, the three men who between them had torn my life apart. Not now. Now, there was a terrible dark weakness engulfing my emotions. All I could summon up from that black place was a kind of amused contempt to combat the posturings of this plump little fly. And somehow that had proved more effective than any outburst of rage could possibly have been.

As I went about my self-appointed tasks, I pieced together the details of Susannah's flight, from the whisperings of maids before they realised I was within earshot, a tumble of excited words from Sally, eager to acquaint me with the awful excitement of it as I sat hugging Ruth in the nursery. Already there was an embroidery of myth. A masked man on a black horse seen lurking night after night down by the creek, lovers' trysts in the woods by day, and strange omens that had not been heeded – a single magpie circling the house in an ominous manner, an elder bush uprooted by a foolish gardener without the necessary precautions, for everyone knew such bushes belonged to witches and trouble would surely follow if the bush was not placated with the correct charm . . .

The truth was that no one had seen or suspected anything. Susannah had crept downstairs, slid back the well-oiled bolts on the front door, walked out into the night and disappeared. It had happened before the hour of two in the morning, when the groom, who had been sitting up with a sick horse, strolled out for a breath of fresh air and discovered the front door to be standing open. He had raised the alarm, but all that was missing from the house was Miss Susannah, leaving a note for her father expressing her delight at being rescued from an unpalatable marriage by the man she truly loved. Menservants had been sent off in all directions, Mr Pascoe himself taking the Plymouth road as being the most likely. Blandford had been left with instructions to cancel the marriage arrangements then ride immediately to Falconwood to acquaint my grandfather of the unpalatable facts. Blandford had chosen, as so often in his spoiled life, to bend the instructions to his own wishes.

There had been the slenderest chance that he might have been thwarted, that a rumour might have reached Falconwood first. But fear of Blandford, and the certain dismissal that would have followed had anyone in his employ defied him, had prevented it.

Mrs Jenkins, hovering in the dining room as I made a pretence of eating breakfast in solitary state, said quietly and quickly, 'Forgive me, ma'am, for speaking out, but Brookes – the coachman – wished for me to give you his apologies.' She glanced nervously at the door. 'He's a religious man, ma'am, a Methodist, an' he thought 'twas a wrong thing that he was made to keep silent when he brought Mr Blandford to you yesterday, for he would have spoken out about Miss Susannah. But he has four young children, ma'am, and a sick wife, and Mr Blandford . . . well, he made him swear . . .' Her voice tailed off, she edged back from the table. 'He didn't want you to start off thinking badly of him, ma'am, that's all.'

'Thank you, Mrs Jenkins,' I said. 'I . . . I appreciate his . . . his concern. Will you tell him he must not reproach himself? I quite understand his position.'

And before she dipped her head and bobbed a quick curtsy, I saw in her face that she understood, and sympathised with, my own sorry situation.

That morning marked the coming of old age to my grandfather. He walked into the drawing room of Brent House a vigorous man, eager to see his ambitions come to fruition, his will strong and certain. He left very differently. Drained, tired, morose.

He had taken the news in silence, and it was this very silence, I believe, that disconcerted us all. I, for one, had thought there would be a dreadful scene. I believe Mr Pascoe expected a great outpouring of rage and was braced to defend himself.

But there was no need. Grandfather went very pale. He groped blindly for a chair and fell heavily upon it. Brandy was brought, but he waved it away. He continued to sit there with his head in his hands, while Mr Pascoe launched into explanations, apologies, lamentations. He raised his head only once, when Mr Pascoe was deploring his son's acquaintance with Nicholas.

'. . . I should have put a stop to it. But there it is, Blandford is of age and young men must be given their head to make their own mistakes. Though I warned him often enough that there was bad blood in that blackguard Fox – as you know to your cost, Frank. In the past the breed has cost your family dear. Now, it seems, the whelp of that name has brought ruin to mine.'

Grandfather spoke as a man in a dream from which

he cannot waken. 'Fox? Aye, the sins of the fathers, we cannot escape them . . . mine . . . his . . . I should have known better than to try . . .' He covered his face again.

Ben, who had been staring round in puzzlement, said, 'Grandfather? When will I be married? Is Susannah here? Do we go to the church soon?'

Mr Chadwick touched his arm, with an anxious look at me. I rose quickly, saying, 'Refreshments are ready in the dining room and then we will fetch Ruth and walk outdoors a little. Come, Ben. If you will excuse us, gentlemen.'

I was glad to go. There had been times when I should have wished to see my proud, arrogant grandfather brought low. It brought me no comfort now. It merely added another facet of sadness to a day already overburdened with it, and moved me to a comparison I did not wish to feel.

Grandfather would not stay and Mr Pascoe did not press him. He was relieved, I think, that there had been no violent scene and that the way was still open for later discussion upon the delicate matter of my dowry. I think, too, that there was genuine concern for his old friend. Grandfather did not recover his colour. When the carriage was brought round and we assembled to make our farewells, the sunlight limpid in the clearing sky emphasised the greyness of his pallor. He seemed to stagger a little as he went down the steps to the drive. Blandford put his hand out to help him. Grandfather shook it off brusquely. 'I have no need of your assistance,' he growled, with a touch of his old manner. 'It is merely a little dizziness.'

'Doubtless the shock,' Blandford murmured with an ingratiating smile, hastily adding, 'that is, the shock of my sister's treachery. For my own case, I must cast myself upon your generosity and beg forgiveness for

604

allowing myself to be swayed by the importunings of Venus in the matter of your granddaughter. I humbly beg that you give us your blessing, sir, and that we, my dear wife and myself, might have your permission to call upon you in a few days to pay our respects.'

Grandfather's glance was hard and unforgiving. 'You are a fool,' he said. 'A fool, a cheat and a liar. If you ever try to set foot in my house again I shall personally see to it that you are thrown into the midden, which is the place I perceive to be closest to your natural element.'

It was Blandford's turn to blanch. 'But, sir,' he cried, seeing the prospect of any settlement slipping from his grasp, 'your granddaughter . . . my wife . . .'

'If you think to press your case through her you will be disappointed. She will tell you herself that there is no love between us, nor ever has been.'

Blandford opened his mouth to protest, then closed it as his father motioned him angrily to silence for fear he should damn his case completely.

Grandfather went slowly to the carriage. He paused before he mounted the step and beckoned me over.

I was holding Ruth by the hand. She walked gravely beside me, clinging tight, fearful perhaps that I might be going to leave her when I had promised her I would not. In her short life, nothing had ever shown itself to be that certain.

Grandfather looked at Ruth for a long moment. There was something wistful in his eyes. He touched her fine brown hair. It was almost a caress.

'At least the child comes well out of this,' he said heavily. 'You have some affection for her. That is to the good. The only good, I fear, to come out of this sorry day.' He sighed and shook his head as though to clear it. 'You know my nature, Joanna. It is not in me to admit my own faults and I am too long in the tooth to confess them now. But I think you understand that I . . . that you . . .' He cleared his throat. 'If you should ever find yourself of a mind to visit us at Falconwood, I . . . should not turn you away.'

I had once likened him in my thoughts to a great powerful eagle. Now that eagle was old and tired. It was the moment to strike. When he was injured and defenceless and could be overpowered.

But there had been too much pain, too much bitterness. I could not encompass more.

I looked into his eyes, said quietly, 'If I may be spared from the threat of the midden, then perhaps I shall.'

The ghost of a grim smile hovered on his lips. It reflected mine.

He climbed into the chariot without another word. Harry Beer whipped up the horses. I did not care to watch the carriage go.

I walked back into the house with Ruth and left my husband and my father-in-law to pick over the bones of the day and feed their hopes on such scraps as could be salvaged.

Chapter Twenty-Two

I could stand the days. Even if Blandford pettishly forbade me to go beyond the grounds. 'I will not have you parading yourself boldly as you were used to in Exeter. And you are to receive no callers, do you hear? The Aggetts and Daveys and their ilk are only out to spread gossip.'

No one save Mr Davey and Tom called. I did not have a chance to speak to either of them. I was in the drawing room working on my sketches for the decoration of Mrs Barton's school, Ruth playing at my feet, when they arrived. But they were shown straight into the library and left after only a short interview. From Mr Pascoe's long face and Blandford's sulky one as we sat down to luncheon, I gathered that the meeting had not been to their liking, though they did not bother to acquaint me of it and I did not choose to ask.

Yes, the days I could tolerate. I could assume the cloak of light, detached tolerance that kept Blandford warily at bay, though he watched me slyly, creeping about soft-footed whenever he was at home. On the occasions when Mr Pascoe, still intent on keeping his son to the straight and narrow path of duty, had taken Blandford off to Plymouth and I was free of his presence, it was as though a great weight lifted from the house, which even Ruth seemed aware of. There was laughter then and I could romp with her, toss her squealing into the air, kneel on the rug and play counting games, curl on a chair and tell her stories while she watched me with her solemn brown eyes, thumb in her mouth, ready to beg, shyly, 'Another story, please, Mama,' whenever I stopped. If Blandford was home, we escaped into the grounds to watch the gardeners at work in the walled kitchen garden, to wander among the shrubberies and across the lawns and down to the creek to spy herons and feed the fussy mallards with crumbs begged from the kitchen. She, above all things, kept me sane, I do believe, and prevented me dwelling on the loss of my love and my freedom.

My first action as a stepmama had been to dispose of the remnants of the bottle of Godfrey's Cordial, which I demanded from a puzzled Sally. ''Tis terrible good, ma'am, for soothin' 'er when 'er's 'aving a tantrum.'

'I am here now, Sally, to deal with any of these so-called tantrums,' I said sharply. 'Though it seems to me that these do not occur without cause, for she is a docile child. Far too docile for my liking. However, I shall keep Miss Ruth with me as much as I can. And there is no use in putting on a long face. I am pleased with the way you have obeyed my instructions with regard to the bed-wetting. You see, it was not so difficult, was it? And the situation is much improved, you will agree.' She nodded mulishly, but brightened a great deal when I added, 'And of course, if I take charge of Miss Ruth, it will leave you free to give the nursery a thorough cleaning and polishing.'

Sally asked me anxiously several times if her place was safe. 'For t'other maids is full of talk that master's like to close the house and move away, for all his fortune's gone.' I soothed her fears, but the truth was that I did not know.

Mr Pascoe always brushed my questions impatiently

aside. 'Everything is uncertain. Pray do not bother me now. You shall know in good time.'

I knew better than to question my husband. It did not take much to displease him and his displeasure was likely to manifest itself in unpleasant ways. He was cautious, though, by day, acting the model of tender solicitude, particularly when his father was near. As though he must justify the wilfulness that had prompted him to take me in marriage. Once the bedroom door was bolted at night, he shrugged off that pleasant veneer as a snake sloughs its skin and allowed his vicious passions full rein.

Against them I had no defence except passiveness. Once, goaded beyond endurance, I cried out, 'Why, Blandford, did you marry me? For it seems that you have no love or kindness in your heart.'

He flung himself off me with a snarl. 'The devil alone knows. He is the one who laid this trap for me. He has always looked at me out of your eyes, you bitch, and tempted me beyond reason with lustful imaginings. And now I know it was all a mirage, for you are nothing but a prick-teasing shrew! A lump of female flesh that promises all and gives nothing. But by the devil himself you shall suffer for this deception. I will find ways to make you pay.'

I shuddered as I lay there in the dark, listening to his breathing subside to a bubbling snore. My body throbbed and stung from his brutal penetration and the smell of his flesh and his juices was rank in my nostrils. And it was then that the images I could hold back during the day broke through and tormented me as they did each long night.

I would live through every moment of the hours I had spent with Nicholas, and despair and jealousy would battle for supremacy as I thought of Susannah with him, sharing the intimacies and delight that I had known. Nicholas had ruined the well-laid plans of my grandfather and Mr Pascoe, but he had brought this terrible living nightmare down on me in his quest for revenge. Worse, each night I had to face the fact that had he truly loved me he would not have allowed it to happen. I was expendable, a mere pawn to be sacrificed in a cruel and relentless game.

Yes, I could suffer the days, but the nights were well-nigh unbearable.

No word came to Mr Pascoe from Susannah. I had a faint, irrepressible, unworthy hope that by some other means – word from Mrs Barton or Miss Olga – I might hear that Nicholas had cast Susannah aside as cavalierly as he had carried her off. I had not expected to hear anything from Grandfather, though I found myself hoping for a note, a message from someone at Falconwood, when Harry Beer rode in to Kingsbridge, which he often did. I believe Mr Pascoe, too, expected some communication from Grandfather, for I over-heard him grumbling to Blandford that he had not softened. 'He refuses to answer my notes and I had hoped for some sort of reconciliation by now, some suggestion that he would settle a decent sum on his granddaughter. But Davey says he is adamant.'

No news arrived from Exeter either.

I had exchanged letters with my Exeter friends while I had still been at Falconwood. Now there was silence. The days ticked over, became a week, two, three. I had written to each of them, Miss Olga, Lily, Mrs Barton, skimming lightly over my situation, though they would read enough between the lines, and finding some ease in describing the pleasant time I spent with Ruth. I had despatched my suggested designs for Mrs Barton's school, placing them with the other letters on the tray in the hall to be taken to the Post Office. I discovered the reason for the silence one breakfast time.

Blandford and I were alone. Jenkins brought in the salver bearing the morning's mail and Blandford slowly picked over the letters, laying those for his father carefully to one side.

'Ah, one for you, my dear,' he said, with a smile.

'At last,' I said, lightly. 'I had begun to think I was quite forgotten by my friends.'

'Not forgotten yet,' Blandford said jovially. He broke it open.

'Blandford! That is my letter.'

'And you are my wife. I have every right to supervise unsuitable correspondence from this . . .' he turned the page and read the signature, '. . . this Eleanor Barton.'

'Mrs Barton is not unsuitable! She is a most worthy person, you know that very well.'

'Worthy? When, in black and white, she admits to encouragement of those unseemly activities that personified your conceited character when you were in Exeter?' He skimmed the page, then read aloud. ' "I trust that nothing is amiss that I have not heard from you since your marriage . . . I eagerly await the arrival of your sketches and designs for my school . . ." ' He flicked his nail disparagingly against the letter. 'It is clearly her intention to lead you to defy me.'

'No! You have never once said—'

'As to this school of hers, I cannot believe that anyone could have the audacity to consider that girls may be educated to be the equal of their brothers. Nature intended the female sex to be weak and inferior. Their role is to obey and honour their menfolk, to be the vessel of procreation and to nurture their offspring. Nothing more. To fly against that natural law would bring shame and discredit on their families.' He flourished the letter. 'And by any civilised standard, Mrs Barton condemns herself out of her own mouth.' Slowly and deliberately he ripped the letter into shreds.

I gasped and half rose.

'Pray seat yourself, Mrs Pascoe,' he said. 'I do not care for histrionics at breakfast.'

I looked at him in disbelief, a sudden suspicion chilling me. 'My sketches . . .'

His smile deepened. 'You left a package to be posted. That is not to say I permitted it to leave the house.'

I sank back to the chair. 'You . . . you kept it back . . . and my other letters? Where are they? What have you done with them?'

'The gardener's boy created a conflagration that I observed to be most thorough. After all, had such rubbish not been dealt with correctly, it would have bred unpleasant possibilities, as a piece of offal left in the sun breeds stinks and maggots and must therefore be disposed of promptly.'

I knew that to respond to his goading only added to his pleasure, but I could not help myself.

'You had no right!'

'I had, and have, every right. I am your husband and master. Any friendship you may aspire to, any correspondence that you wish to take up, must from now on first pass my scrutiny.' He picked up a piece of toast and chewed it reflectively. 'You see, I fear that I was lax in that matter with my first wife. Had she not invited you into my house, I should not have come under the influence of your whorish tricks.' He dabbed at his greasy lips with the napkin. 'And therefore, my dear, I should not now be regretting what my father calls "the millstone" that I have hung about my neck.'

There was a young maid standing by the sideboard ready to attend to us should our cups or plates need replenishing. A mere piece of the furniture in Blandford's eyes and to be totally ignored. I had no doubt her ears were sharp enough. I felt myself colour. To be called such names in the presence of another person, however lowly, filled me with embarrassment. I gripped my hands together in my lap, striving for control.

'Blandford, if I must ask permission to write to Mrs Barton,' I said in a low voice, 'then I ask it now.'

'Regretfully I must refuse. And as my spinster cousins are unfortunately in the woman's pocket, I forbid all correspondence with them also.' He pushed back the chair and stood up. 'I shall make it my business to call upon my cousins when I am in Exeter. I shall be accompanying my father on a visit in a day or two in order to finalise the sale of his properties. I shall explain the situation so that they will not pursue the matter further.' He added, jovially, 'And pray do not think to defy me in this, Mrs Pascoe. Every servant in this house will be watching out for you with instructions, on pain of dismissal, to report to me any indiscretions. If you disobey me, then you may be sure I shall find some . . . suitable method of punishment.' He added, casually, as though the idea had just come to him and had nothing whatsoever to do with the conversation that had gone before. 'I believe I shall favour the nursery with a visit this morning. It is as well to keep the nursemaid on her toes. I should not like her to become in any way slack or slovenly in her supervision of my daughter, especially as you, my dear, her stepmama, are so inexperienced and rather too inclined to be over-indulgent with the child.'

The subtle threat in those final words alarmed me more than all the ones that had gone before. And even though it galled me to do so, I determined to keep a firm hold on my words and my demeanour until Blandford left so that he could find no possible fault.

My husband and father-in-law would be away for the best part of a week. My relief was tempered with caution. Until they were actually gone, I could not allow myself to believe that there would be so many nights when I should be allowed to sleep in peace.

The night before they left, Blandford was particularly forceful and prolonged in his attentions. I closed my eyes and endured until he had finished. After he had thrown himself panting onto the other side of the bed, he suddenly lashed out with his fist, catching me a blow in the ribs that made me gasp with pain.

'You will have to do better than this, my fine lady,' he hissed. 'You have as much life in you as . . . as a bolster! And I do not care for it. I do not care for it at all.' He rolled back towards me, spitting his wine-laden breath into my ear. 'You must learn to please me, do you hear?'

'Why should I?' The words were out before I could stop them. 'You tricked me into this unnecessary marriage!'

He clamped his hand over my mouth, his nails biting into my cheeks. 'You are too full of clever words and conceit, madam. You fancy yourself superior to me, but I have every intention of bringing you low. I will make you beg and crawl for my favours before very long, believe me. Remember this, do you hear?' He sniggered, venomously. 'When I return, if you do not voluntarily give me what I ask, then I shall find some way to . . . persuade you.'

He released me then, turned his back and slept.

I curled up away from him, my arms round my knees, hugging my misery, and though I tried my utmost to hold them back, the bitter, frustrated tears slid down to wet my pillow.

Mr Pascoe's farewell was a curt bow, a dutiful peck on my cheek before he climbed into the carriage. He had not yet been able to forgive me for my unwelcome presence which had signified the dashing of his hopes. Perhaps he never would unless Grandfather relented and furnished me with a dowry. A remote possibility, indeed.

Blandford tipped my lowered face to his and kissed me lingeringly on the mouth. An ardent, loving husband reluctant to part from his adoring wife, the solemn child clinging to his wife's skirts and looking up at them both with big brown eyes. Such a pretty tableau for the servants to observe.

They could not know how painful was the pressure of his hand under my chin, or see how my compressed lips resisted his open mouth, the flickering of his tongue. They could not hear how he spoke, this loving husband. 'Do not think to be rash or to disobey my wishes in any way while I am absent. Occupy your time instead, madam, in contemplation of what I told you last night. When I return, I expect to find in you a willingness to learn what is expected of an adoring wife. Do you understand?' All this spoken with a jovial smile, the same smile he turned on Ruth. 'Such a charming little creature she is becoming. And you are devoted to her, are you not, Mrs Pascoe? And she to you.' He sighed and shook his head. 'It would be such a pity if I had to deny you both the privilege, for privilege it is, which I have been pleased to grant, but I regret that I shall be most sadly forced to withdraw it if you continue to displease me, my dear wife. You would do well to think on that, too.'

I watched the carriage go. Ruth slipped her warm little hand into mine.

'Shall we feed the ducks now, Mama?' she asked, timidly.

'Yes, my love,' I said.

'And then will you tell me a story?'

'I will tell you as many as you like.' I swooped her up in my arms.

'A princess!' she squealed. 'Tell me about a princess who was rescued from a fiery dragon by a handsome prince . . .'

'And went to live in a palace of gold and lived happily ever after,' I said. And I hugged her tight, burying my face in her fine brown hair so that she might not catch the echoes of the grief and despair that filled my heart.

I thought a great deal about Jane in the following days. She had been such an easy victim for Blandford. Gentle, timid and ultimately too frail to withstand the demands he had made upon her. Rebellion had not been in her nature, yet even if she had challenged Blandford, what chance did she have of gaining from it? Very little, I told myself gloomily. Although I was very different to Jane, with a stubbornness, a determination in me that would not let me sink under completely when Blandford issued his threats, I could see no way of easing my lot. No way to fight, particularly if by doing so I caused him to take out his spite on Ruth.

All the same, this respite from his attentions, so that I could spend my nights in blissful, restorative slumber, and the golden September days when I could be out of doors with Ruth, restored a certain optimism. As my body recovered from Blandford's bruising love-making, so my mind regained some of its resilience. How often in my early days at Torre Crescent had I believed my world had crashed about my ears, never to be rebuilt. Yet, in retrospect, Grandfather's banishment of me to Exeter had been a different sort of beginning. Perhaps I should look to this unwanted marriage in the same way. I was down in the depths once more, but it might be that I could find a way to claw myself up.

That was a heartening thought and the oasis of these quiet days gave me the time to look outwards, beyond my own troubles. I thought wistfully of my Exeter friends. I longed to know how Mrs Barton was progressing with her plans and if Miss Olga was finding satisfaction in her new role. And Lily and Caleb. How were they? And Ben. I prayed silently that Grandfather, now that his plans were dashed, would not turn his bitterness upon my brother. But surely not, surely he would not be so cruel. Ben was responsible for none of this unhappy mess.

It was while I was thinking of Falconwood that I remembered Mr Pascoe was still hopeful of a dowry for me. That sparked off an interesting train of thought. Grandfather had barred Blandford from his door. He had not barred me, though I had not mentioned it to anyone at Brent House. Could I now hint to Mr Pascoe that I would be prepared to visit Grandfather to beg him to reconsider? There was little likelihood of Grandfather relenting, I felt, but at least to show willingness to help my father-in-law might be to my advantage. Blandford could hardly protest if his father decided to let me try where all else had failed. And if I failed, it did not matter. The situation would be no worse than it had been and I should have gained by an outing to Falconwood, reunion with Ben and some news of the outside world. If I succeeded, then I should most certainly improve my standing with Mr Pascoe who would be a useful ally against Blandford.

The peaceful nights and golden daylight hours held only one irritating facet. Except when I was in my bedchamber at night, I was constantly watched. In the garden there was always a gardener making a pretence of weeding or hoeing. Inside the house one of the maids, if she was not making some excuse to come into the room where I was, would be hovering beyond the door as though on guard. Worse, I was encumbered all day with Sally.

'Master Blandford 'ee said partic'lar that I wasn't to leave Miss Ruth,' she said mulishly when I tried to coax her away with hints of urgent dusting to be done in the nursery.

'But surely, Sally, you can see we can come to no harm sitting here on the grass making daisy chains.'

''Tis not my choosin', ma'am.' She glared at me as though I was to blame. 'For I should sooner be indoors than out here wi' nasty wasps and gnats an' all manner of biting creatures. But master said I was to do my duty by Miss Ruth, as I was paid to do, and stay with her at all times while 'ee was gone, an' if I didn't do as I was bid, he'd turn me off when 'ee got back.'

So I had to put up with Sally who kept up a constant grumble about grass stains on her pinafore and Ruth's hair needing brushing and the inadvisability of spending too long breathing damp air from the creek, for everyone knew that miasmas rose from mud when the tide was out to bring all manner of ills.

Sally pined for her pristine nursery and I fretted for freedom from these petty restrictions by which Blandford reminded me of his hold over me and kept me fast.

On the morning of the fourth day I awoke with a strange feeling of anticipation, almost of excitement. There was no sense to it. Perhaps it was merely that the restful nights and days now were reflected in a return to my normal robust spirits. Mist was lying still and milky round the house. I dressed quickly, went outdoors and ran down to the creek, uncaring that the hem of my skirt was soon darkened and wet from the dew-heavy grass. The house, the formal gardens were blanked off by the mist. I could see only a few yards across the still water, a few fallen leaves on its surface moving up the creek on the tide. Somewhere a jay chattered. A fish plopped in the water. And I was quite alone. I had no doubt been seen to leave the house but no word had yet got to a gardener to find me. The mist embraced and hid me. I breathed deeply of the earthy scents rising from the ground, the tang of salt water wafting from the creek. I took this moment of freedom and held it close. A moment when there was no past, no future, and the world was reduced to this little space of quiet detachment.

Then I remembered the dream that had slipped away when I woke. I had been walking on the cliffs near Falconwood in a dense sea fog with the waves crashing against the rocks far below. I had been searching for my silver necklace with the clasped hearts which Susannah had stolen but I could not find it and now Blandford was close on my heels and I must hide. I was near to the house but I could not find the path. I could hear people urgently calling to me, Grandfather, Ben, Nick. Mama's voice was strongest of all. 'Come, child, we have waited a long time. You have not far to go . . .' And all the time I could hear Blandford's horse pounding relentlessly towards me.

I stared at the shrouded water. For an instant I was awake in the same dream, the voices calling me, the clattering hooves, and there, in the swirls of mist, tall shapes moving . . . Grandfather and Mama coming to fetch me to safety, and surely that other figure following behind them was Nick. I reached out my hands, relief and joy swamping my heart. Thank heaven, I was to go home at last . . .

Voices. I turned sharply, the dream – the vision – fractured. The voices were real, raised in some argument. The sound of hooves on gravel came loud through the fog.

I obeyed a sudden compelling instinct and began to move towards the sound. I cast a last glance across the water but there was nothing save the bland wall of mist flowing over the unruffled surface and the dead leaves drifting on the tide.

The horse and rider came into focus as they approached the drive. A big, solid chestnut gelding, the rider trying to urge it forward while a gardener clung protesting to the bridle.

'You'm trespassing! You'm not to go to the house. Master's orders!'

I hitched up my skirts and ran, sliding and slipping on the wet grass.

'Harry! Harry Beer!'

He turned a relieved face towards me. 'Miss Jo! Thank the Lord. I knowed you was here, though this ol' toad tried to tell me different. I 'ad to get a word to 'ee. Mr Chadwick told me particler.'

I looked up at his grey, unshaven face. 'What is it, Harry?' I whispered, filled with dread, 'Is it Ben?'

He shook his head.

''Tis master . . . your grandfather, miss. He'm been took mortal sick with an apoplexy. Doctor's on his way now. I been to roust him out. Mr Chadwick says master's been calling out for you and he may not last many hours.'

'Then I must go at once.' There was no hesitation. I did not stop to think of the restrictions laid upon me. 'But I shall need transport. My husband and father-in-law have taken the carriage.'

'I'll ride back to Kingsbridge,' he said eagerly. 'Hire you a nag.'

'No.' I was suddenly cool, my thoughts quick and lucid. 'I am no horsewoman . . . and there will be someone else with me. Get me a chaise, a gig – anything. The carrier's cart if needs be.'

The gardener was still clinging to the bridle. He was an elderly man, bent and gnarled from his years of outdoor life. He made immediately to protest. I drew myself up to my full height with all the authority I had learned to produce in my dealings in Exeter.

'Release your hold immediately! Mr Pascoe himself would not deny me leave to go to the bedside of my dying grandfather.'

I stared him down. He reluctantly let go the bridle, muttering under his breath, but clearly taken aback. As though a harmless insect he meant to squash had jumped up and bitten him.

I could spare no time for his offended sensibilities. I hurried to the house, leaving Harry Beer to clatter off to Kingsbridge. I must be ready by the time he returned. And so must Ruth.

Ruth would go with me. I knew that without question. I could not leave her just as she was coming to trust and rely on me. Nor could I allow her to be unprotected against whatever mood her father was in when he returned and found me missing. But it was deeper than that. A compulsion. Like the necessity to cram all the possessions that I could into my bags. As though a voice somewhere ordered those preparations.

Sally started to wail and cry when I told her to get Ruth ready and pack a bag of necessities. 'But master ordered me to stay with Miss Ruth. He'll put me off. What'll I do?'

I stared at her dull, pasty face. I did not want to feel sympathy for her. She had been hard and unfeeling to Ruth. But the stupid creature could scarcely be blamed when her own life had been shaped by unthinking cruelty.

'Oh, very well. If you will not stay, you must come with me,' regretting as I said it the impulse to saddle myself with an extra encumbrance. 'It is for you to decide. I cannot waste time persuading you. Make haste or I shall leave you behind.'

Mrs Jenkins surprised me by being entirely co-operative.

'I've kept my eyes shut and my ears blocked for

too long in this house, madam,' she said, dourly. 'I've nothing to lose now. I shall give my notice when Mr Pascoe returns. I've some savings. My sister's been widowed recently and her and me's to set up a lodging house in a nice respectable part of Plymouth. But even if I wasn't leaving, how could I in conscience stop you visiting Mr Kerswell your grandfather when he's mortal sick? 'Twould be against all natural feeling.'

I scribbled a note to Mr Pascoe and left it with Jenkins. I gathered my bags, my stepdaughter and a still blubbering Sally and herded them out of the house. I smiled wryly at the significance of the conveyance that Harry Beer had rounded up for us. It was a farm cart driven by a fat, ruddy-faced farmer. I climbed aboard remembering a cart similarly smelling of pigs.

'Tis not too grand,' Harry Beer apologised, 'but Jack Woods 'ere, he was just settin' off back 'ome an' was willin' to go by Falconwood . . .'

I cut short his apologies. 'I was once grateful for a kind farmer who took pity on a penniless young girl and her brother one winter's day and took them aboard his cart. I am just as grateful now. Now, up with you into the back, Sally, and do stop snivelling and complaining. Think of the pleasure you will get from scrubbing the straw from your clothes later.'

I took my place beside the farmer, Ruth on my lap, Harry Beer riding his tired horse slowly along with us.

So we journeyed to Falconwood. A very different journey to that first one, for this time I knew that the voices that called me back would not let me go again so easily.

Grandfather was grievously ill.

'He has not been the same since we returned from Kingsbridge,' Mr Chadwick told me quietly. 'I think the shock undermined his health. Once or twice he complained of pains in his head and seemed quite confused. He was not well again last night and Miss Lightbody, looking in on him in the small hours, found him stricken.'

'It is fortunate,' Dr White said, in his fussy way, 'that by the time I arrived he had regained his senses. Those who lie insensible for more than a few hours are liable never to recover. I have bled him and applied leeches to his temple, which has eased his breathing somewhat, and administered a black draught to free his bowels. I would advise that you continue with the cold compresses to the head and mustard plasters to the feet. The next twenty-four hours will be critical. I shall call again tomorrow. Good day to you, Mrs Pascoe.'

We took it in turns with Grandfather through those twenty-four hours and the twenty-four hours after that. Myself, Mrs Beer, Mr Chadwick, Miss Lightbody whose eccentricity seemed, for once, to be muted to a tender concern for the man she had once loved and, I think, still did. Only once, on the second evening, was there a hint of the old Miss Lightbody when she clutched my arm and hissed in my ear when I came to relieve her in the flickering candlelight of Grandfather's bedchamber. 'I think his time is not yet. The pattern of his stars speaks to me.'

I shook her off a little impatiently. 'If he recovers it will be entirely due to careful nursing and his own strength of will.'

'Ah, yes, but 'tis the scorpion that gives him the will to live.'

'Miss Lightbody, I cannot believe in this talk of scorpions and lions and destinies.'

She sighed. 'Had you the interest, I would teach you the science and practice of it. Then you would understand for yourself.'

'I have neither the time nor the desire.'

Her black simian eyes glinted in the candlelight. 'So be it. Perhaps it will fall to some other child of this house to be curious before I die and take the secrets with me.'

We spoke in whispers but Grandfather heard and stirred restlessly. 'Ellen?' His voice was slurred. Half of his body and face was paralysed, though the apoplexy had not taken his speech entirely. He was still confused and mistook me sometimes for my mother.

I went to him. 'It is Joanna, Grandfather, come to sit with you awhile. Are you comfortable? Shall I shake up your pillows?'

'Ellen,' he said. 'Forgive me.'

'You are forgiven,' I said gently. 'Now try to sleep.'

Sometimes it was Joanna he begged forgiveness from. Reassured, he would doze, to waken again with the same request. I smoothed the sheets and settled his nightcap on his head, shaven now, at the doctor's insistence. There were angry red marks on his temples where leeches had been applied. His bold curved nose stood out gaunt in his twisted face. I felt compassion for this man whose life had been torn and broken by an inability to forgive and could only beg forgiveness of others when he was old and ill and it was far too late.

Miss Lightbody was still standing in the shadows. She was wearing her housekeeper's black as though, for all her talk of the time not being yet, she was already in mourning.

'Call me,' she said, 'if there is any change.'

'Of course.'

She shifted uneasily. 'There is one more thing and this is not the planets that speak, so hear me out.' Her skirts rustled with a sound like dry leaves. 'This I dreamt, and dreams are truer sometimes than black marks on white paper. Your brother, you must guard him.'

'You are tired,' I said, trying not to let my impatience show. 'You have had nights of broken sleep. Sometimes the imagination takes curious flights.'

'A waking dream, a sleeping dream. It is all the same. I think you know a little of it, do you not? This house, it is full of the dreams of many women who reach out and touch those who live here now.'

The flesh on my back went cold. This uncanny knack she had, as though she could look into my head and know my thoughts, stilled the quick answer that rose to my lips.

'You cannot deny it. You hear them too, those women. Ellen is sometimes very close to you.'

'My mother?' I said, through dry lips.

'Aye. She came to me in my dream. "Watch for Ben," she told me. "There is a final danger. Save him and guard him well and when the danger is past the future is safe for those who belong in this house." '

'Danger? Miss Lightbody, what danger did she mean?'

But the old lady had gone in a shiver of draught from the closing door, leaving me to watch over Grandfather and quiet my perturbed thoughts.

When the doctor came the following day, he pronounced himself pleased with his patient's progress.

'It will be a week or two before we may be sure of a recovery, but I think, Mrs Pascoe, we may be more hopeful. We must now think in terms of aiding his digestive system and adopting such means as may tend to ward off future attacks.' He frowned at me. 'I think, like most gentlemen, he is given to the enjoyment of fine wines and spirits. Well, there must be none of that now until his health is restored. Nor any animal food. Egg beaten in milk, taken in small quantities, will be sufficient at first. As his appetite improves you may add vegetables to his diet. I shall leave a mixture of mint water, tartar emetic and tincture of digitalis. This will keep down the circulation.'

He promised to call again in a few days and I mentioned to the doctor, as I pressed him to the refreshment that Mrs Beer had prepared, that my husband and father-in-law would be back from Exeter by then and would be anxious for news. Almost before I could frame my request he had volunteered to call and inform them personally of Grandfather's progress.

'There is a small matter of an account outstanding for some months. I should welcome the opportunity to remind Mr Pascoe of it. I am sure that it is merely an oversight on Mr Pascoe's part, but he has been so occupied lately it has been difficult to find a suitable time to call.' He cleared his throat, delicately. 'Perhaps, Mrs Pascoe, I might ask that if it were possible, you might bring the matter to Mr Pascoe's notice if it slips his memory again.'

'Of course,' I agreed. 'I should be happy to do so, though as you say, it is most assuredly an oversight on Mr Pascoe's part.'

Poor Dr White. I feared his journey would be as useless as my promise to jog my father-in-law's memory. Harry Beer had told me that there was a great deal of gossip in Kingsbridge about the Pascoes. The gates of Brent House were barred to anyone without a good reason for entering. ''Tis said they owes money everywhere. They'm frightened in case 'tis people turning up on their doorstep dunnin' 'em for their dues.' No wonder there had been no visitors to Brent House. Blandford's strictures to me were merely an extension of those general ones imposed upon the whole household.

If I had needed any confirmation of the grave state that the Pascoes' financial affairs were in, it was provided the next day.

Tom Davey rode to Falconwood, bearing sympathetic messages from his own parents and the Aggetts and a basket of hothouse grapes for the invalid.

'If there is anything at all we can do,' he said, formally, 'please do not hesitate to advise us, Mrs Pascoe.' Then, with a shy smile, so that the boyish eagerness showed through the acquired grave lawyer's manner, 'I am pleased to find you well. I . . . we were a little, er, concerned . . . that is, the unfortunate circumstances surrounding your marriage . . .'

'Most unfortunate,' I said dryly.

'And when we called, my father and I, at Brent House we did not have the pleasure of seeing you, though of course,' he added hastily, 'your husband assured us you were in good health when we enquired.'

'But you could not bring yourself quite to believe him?'

He blushed. 'I put that awkwardly, Mrs Pascoe. Pray forgive me.'

'For implying the truth? No, no, Mr Davey, there is nothing to forgive. My husband's word, I fear, leaves a great deal to be desired when it comes to speaking honestly. I know that to my cost. And now we have that perfectly straight between us, I would appreciate your frankness on other matters.' I smiled. 'I am quite out of touch, you see, with Kingsbridge gossip. But first, you shall have a glass of claret and a piece of Mrs Beer's excellent squab pie before we go in search of Ben who has taken my little stepdaughter to look at the horses.'

During the hour or two that Tom Davey was at Falconwood I learned much that was common knowledge in the town. That the financial situation of my husband and father-in-law was indeed precarious. Mr Pascoe's creditors were pressing, and Brent House itself had been heavily mortgaged in order to clear all Blandford's debts. I felt Tom's withdrawal once or twice when my questions were too pointed, but I sensed he was being as honest with me as he dared within the limits imposed upon him by professional discretion.

And I learned, too, things I did not wish at all to touch upon and had fought most desperately to avoid mentioning. Yet when he spoke the names I dreaded to hear, every fibre of my being cried out with the urgency of wanting to know. And I listened politely, my fingernails digging into my palms to counter the anguish in my heart.

'The elopement is considered most romantic by the young ladies of the town, I believe, though their mamas are decidedly *not* in favour. Rumour has it that Mr Fox carried Miss Pascoe off to Bath . . . but I expect,' he added hastily, 'that you had sooner hear about Sophia Aggett's wedding plans . . .'

I heard nothing of them, though I believe I made admiring noises at the right intervals.

I could only think of Susannah and Nicholas spending the days together among the many diversions that fashionable city had to offer. And their nights. The long, warm nights spent in the intimacy that Nicholas and I had known so briefly.

I recovered enough to speak plainly to Tom Davey before he left. Indeed, perhaps the mention of Nicholas and Susannah had resurrected the bitterness I had tried to suppress and that made me less inclined to guard my words that I might have.

'For my own part, I do not care about a dowry,' I said. 'But Mr Pascoe will doubtless wish me to plead his case. I should be grateful if you or your father, as Mr Pascoe's lawyers, would emphasise that I must tread lightly and that any interference would be unwise. It might be better if he and my husband, particularly my husband, kept away from Falconwood for the time being.' I looked at him squarely. 'It is not purely my dowry that I think of, Mr Davey, but myself. I did not wish to become Mrs Blandford Pascoe and I should not have done, except for his deception. However, I find myself in the intolerable situation of being married to a man I mistrust and dislike and who cheated his own father and my grandfather as much as did that . . . that rogue who carried off Miss Susannah. I have to say that I welcome the time that I spend apart from him.'

He did not look shocked, merely for a moment very young and very sad. 'I . . . I understand, Mrs Pascoe,' he said quietly. 'I shall do my best to see that your sojourn here is uninterrupted. With the utmost discretion, of course.'

'Thank you, Mr Davey.'

'Mrs Pascoe, I . . .' he hesitated, moved his hand as though to reach out to me, then snatched it back, gathered up his hat and bowed. 'I must be on my way,' he said briskly. 'The clouds are beginning to look threatening. I will bid you good day and, if you will allow, I shall call again in a few days to see how the invalid does.'

'I look forward to it,' I said. 'And thank you, Mr Davey.'

Storms blew in from the west and south in the days that followed, sending the gulls wheeling inland to find respite and drowning the landscape in sheets of rain. Lanes and bridle ways turned to quagmires of sticky red mud. Branches and leaves flew from trees that groaned and creaked in the gale. It was a time when those who had no immediate necessity to turn out stayed indoors.

I felt cosily marooned at Falconwood, the life of the house flowing in a steady, comfortable rhythm within its walls. Grandfather continued to make progress and those who nursed him were united in their concern for him. Even Mrs Beer did not eye me suspiciously as she had used to do but looked to me as being in charge of the household now that my grandfather was no longer in command.

I was amazed how quickly Ruth had settled. I had thought that she might be fearful of strange faces and a strange house and fully expected her to remain shy and silent. True, the first day she clung close to me, watching all around her with her big, solemn eyes. But what she saw were people who smiled, who did not get cross if she dirtied her pinafore or skipped instead of walking sedately. They were prepared to listen to her timid questions and furnish pleasant answers instead of frowning and waving her off. They took her into the great warm kitchen and fed her with new bread crusted with jam and thick yellow cream or let her play with a litter of plump black puppies in a basket by the fire. They did not speak harshly, but called her a dear little maid and there were friendly dogs willing to have their ears gently pulled and cats who were obliging enough to be teased with a pretend mouse Ben made of a screw of straw tied to a string. As the days went on, she became Ben's shadow as much as the dogs and cats that trailed him, drawn to him by that same unspoken, inexplicable magnetism that the animals trusted, and he treated her in the same gentle, undemanding fashion as he did his dogs.

Sally and Bessy Beer had struck up an immediate friendship based on love of elbow grease and, I suspected, a companionable distrust of me. I had told Sally briskly that Blandford's orders had no jurisdiction here and that Ruth would come to no harm in a house where everyone would look out for her. 'The child needs to be free of petty restrictions. If you feel yourself in need of occupation you may offer your help to Bessy who will be glad of it with Mrs Beer taking her shift sitting with Mr Kerswell. You need have no idle moments.'

Nor did she. Nor, I think, had she been more content. I left her, as I did Ruth, to find her own niche. I think it was as much freedom as either of them had had in their lives and both began tentatively to blossom under it.

The thought of returning to Brent House and my servitude to Blandford grew daily more repugnant. I tried not to think of it but to live moment to moment, but as the storms abated and Dr White once more made his way to Falconwood, I was relieved to hear that Mr Pascoe and Blandford had not yet returned to Kingsbridge.

'Some delay due to the carriage being damaged by a falling chimney pot in the recent storms. However, I shall make it my business to call upon them immediately I hear of their return, when it is possible that I may be able to give them better tidings of Mr Kerswell's progress.'

Grandfather's improvement was painfully slow, to be measured in small things. A grateful look, a squeeze of his good hand for some small service that had brought him comfort, a word spoken clearly, the moments of confusion growing less and the times of awareness becoming longer. But he was getting stronger, day by day, inch by inch, so that we all began to feel more cheerful and inclined to tell ourselves that he would surely now make a full recovery.

When Tom Davey called again he carried letters from Mr Pascoe and Blandford.

To his old friend, Mr Pascoe wrote a bland note full of polite sentiments which I read out to Grandfather. Grandfather listened unsmiling, then turned his head

631

on the pillow and closed his eyes. Presently he held out his good hand and I took it. 'Sad,' he said. 'Sad.' But whose sadness concerned him – mine, Mr Pascoe's, his own – I did not press him to reveal.

The letter to me was cautiously worded, expressing encouragement in my aims to be reconciled to my grandfather.

> Blandford is as anxious as myself to see you returned to Brent House, but of course we should not wish to deprive your grandparent of your tender ministrations. Pray do not think to leave Falconwood until my dear old friend is returned to good health when I trust we may once again renew the ties of friendship that have always existed between our two families.

I crumpled the letter and threw it aside. I had bought myself, and Ruth, time. That was all I needed to know.

Blandford's letter expressed equally encouraging sentiments, but with an underlying reminder of his hold over me.

> I hope Mr Kerswell will make a swift recovery, for it grieves me deeply to be separated too long from my loving wife. As to you having carried off my daughter, I confess I feel some disquiet that you found it necessary to remove her from the bosom of her loving family. That girlish tendency of yours to act impulsively must be moderated, my dear wife, or sooner or later it will surely bring grief . . .

Loving family, indeed! I tore it fiercely into shreds, scribbled two similarly bland and polite notes in reply for Tom to take back with him and put the Pascoes from my mind.

Grandfather's advances marked the passage of time. The day when he could sit up in bed, when he first was allowed to sit in a chair looking touchingly frail and shrunken amid the swathing rugs, when, with Harry Beer's strong shoulder on one side and Mr Chadwick's on the other, he attempted a few steps. His speech improved and his brain seemed clear again, but his paralysed arm and leg remained floppy and useless. We began a daily round of stimulating treatment to the affected limbs, massaging with liniment, vigorous brushing with a flesh brush and the application of stinging nettles, which Dr White had great faith in.

With each stage of his recovery I felt a dwindling of security. Soon there would be no good reason for me to stay. I had bought time with vague and probably quite hopeless promises about the restoration of my dowry. But as Grandfather grew stronger, I still could not bring myself to broach the subject for fear of spoiling the trust, the acceptance, that had imperceptibly grown between us. Or, indeed, setting back his steady recovery. I told myself the right moment would present itself. Until then . . .

Until then, with a lightening of spirits as Grandfather improved, we might snatch moments of enjoyment. Ben had kept up his daily walks to the cove to swim. Sometimes, Ruth and I accompanied him, to remove our shoes and stockings and paddle in the surf, or we would stroll the cliff path, or spend an hour gathering blackberries from the bramble thickets in the lane. Mr Chadwick would accompany us and, once or twice, Miss Lightbody. I realised I had never seen her outside the house before. I had associated her always as an indoor creature who thrived in the candlelight and shadow of stuffy rooms. Out of doors, she seemed strangely reduced and nervous, clinging to my arm, her black eyes darting about like those of a frightened horse ready to bolt at the slightest untoward movement in the grass. She kept up a stream of grumbles, too, her sharp little nails digging into my arm as she teetered along. The breeze was too strong, too fresh, the sunlight too dazzling, the path too stony and she was like to break an ankle. In exasperation I asked her once why she had come.

'Cannot a body take a breath of air without a mort of questioning from a silly young chit?' she snapped, but her glance darted away to where Ben and Mr Chadwick swung Ruth between them, her excited squeaks of 'Again, again' carrying back to us.

I frowned, touched by a sudden chill. Surely she could not be thinking of that dream about Ben. Surely she had not appointed herself as a sort of watchdog. It was a ludicrous thought. I dismissed it. Let Miss Lightbody believe what she would. I could not spoil these precious days with worrying about nameless fears dreamed up by a foolish old lady.

So the days drifted on, broken only by Tom Davey's visits, by the doctor's calls. And I lived cocooned in this calm little world that was Falconwood until one gentle autumn afternoon my husband rode in and, like a sudden harsh storm, brought fear, violence and death in his wake.

It began a day like any other, pleasant in its orderliness. The house hummed with the sounds of activity. Bessy and Sally chattering as they worked, the rich, yeasty scent of Mrs Beer's baking wafting through the house. Even Grandfather caught it and thought he might fancy a slice of a crusty new loaf with blackberry jelly, which pleased us all for his appetite was still fickle.

A little after two o'clock, Miss Lightbody, Mr Chadwick, Ben, Ruth and I settled in the dining chamber to a hearty dinner of steamed turbot, boned and larded hare with mushrooms, braised ham and buttered leeks. We watched with amusement as Ruth, perched on cushions, her head still barely above the table, sturdily tried everything. She was very different from the pale, silent child I had brought here. Her cheeks were rosy from the hours spent out of doors and her eyes were beginning to lose that careful, watchful look.

'What shall we do afterwards?' I asked her as she spooned in the last satisfying mouthful of damson tart and cream. 'Should you like to sit quietly and I will read you a story?'

She shook her head. 'Pick mushrooms,' she said. 'With Uncle Ben.'

'But that is best done in the morning,' Mr Chadwick said gently.

'Mushrooms,' she said, showing a stubbornness that made us smile.

'That is what I should like to do also,' Ben said amiably.

'An' all the dogs, too,' Ruth insisted. 'And the pussycats.'

'Such a caravan of clumsy creatures,' Miss Lightbody grumbled. 'Mark my words, one day I shall break my neck over one of the great lumps and it will be your fault, Benjamin Kerswell!'

Mr Chadwick volunteered to sit and read to Grandfather while we were out.

'We shall not be long,' I promised him, 'then I shall relieve you.' It did not, at the time, seem a difficult promise.

I fetched my shawl and bonnet and a basket and followed the others out. We walked without haste, Miss Lightbody fussing and fretting at my side, through the orchard to the cliff path. There on the slopes, behind clumps of brambles, were sheltered spots where fat white mushrooms thrust up through the rabbit-cropped grass. Ruth ran ahead, eager to be the first to spot them, and as she did I saw something moving far off along the cliff. I halted, shading my eyes against the sun. A horse and rider. For a moment I thought it might be Tom Davey, but he had told me it would be Sunday before he returned. A passing traveller, that was all. I thought no more of it and wandered on, to where Ruth was holding up the first mushroom.

It was a little while before I realised Miss Lightbody was not with me. I looked round. She was standing a little way off, her mittened hands clasped tightly together at her breast watching the rider approach. Then, turning sharply, so that I could see the fear etched deeply into the wrinkles on her face, she said in a strange, whispery voice, 'He has seen us. It is too late to hide ... too late ... and even if we ran, who knows ...? That, too, might be our destiny ... We cannot escape. I know it.'

'For heaven's sake, Miss Lightbody,' I said in a low voice, bustling over to her. 'What is this nonsense? You will frighten Ruth and Ben with this foolish ...' My voice died as I looked beyond her to the rider. This time I saw clearly who it was. He wore his dandified yellow coat and tall hat and he lolloped in the saddle, swaying loosely with the movement of the lathered horse.

Blandford. And, if I was not mistaken, Blandford drunk.

I found myself clinging to Miss Lightbody's hand and it was as though all time was suspended for the two of us. Ben and Ruth were still bent over the mushrooms, the dogs ran to frisk and sniff at the strange horse's heels, but we two were frozen together in a terrible waiting stillness.

'Well, what've we here?' Blandford cried, snatching at the reins to halt the horse. 'My beloved wife, my ever-loving, dutiful, bitch of a wife come t'meet her husband.'

His words unfroze us. I took a step forward and felt, rather than saw, Miss Lightbody slide away from me to stand back, an observer at the drama.

'Blandford,' I said. 'We . . . I . . . did not know you planned to visit us.'

'And what would you've done, bitch, if I had, eh?' He thrust his head forward. A bubble of saliva stood at the corner of his wet mouth. 'Well, sh . . . speak up!'

'Why . . . why, welcomed you, of course, sir.' My brain raced. I must placate him. Get him to the yard where Harry Beer and the stable lad could deal with him. Out here there was no one to protect us. I had a sudden image of his drunken assault on me in Miss Polsham's parlour. Not here. Not here. I could not bear it if he tried here to foist himself upon me, within sight of Ben and Ruth. I smiled, put my hand on the bridle. 'You must come inside, Blandford. You will be tired and hungry after your journey. There will be refresh—'

I did not see the blow. The crop caught me viciously across the cheek, sending me staggering.

'Get your hand off, madam. Don' presume to touch my horse without per . . . permission.' He swung his head round. 'You!' he yelled. 'You, child . . . c'me here to your . . . papa.'

Ruth moved nearer to Ben and slid her hand into his.

'Come here, I say! Run wild too long . . . Teach you a lesson . . . Teach her a lesson.'

It could not be happening. Not on this peaceful autumn day with the sun gilding the sea and the soft breeze stirring the grasses, warm and gentle as a mother's caress. But Blandford was real. The ugly violence in his voice was real. The stinging pain in my face was real.

And real, too, was a weird and catastrophic sense of

time slipping, sliding away from me. Of events moving inexorably towards some predestined climax.

Danger . . . danger . . . Watch for Ben . . .

The words shrieked in my senses.

Blandford wrenched the horse's head, kicked it forward. Iron hoofs danced nervously, carving crescents of blood-red earth in the green turf.

'Leave go of that idiot boy's hand,' Blandford snarled, 'or by Chris' you'll have a beating you'll not forget!'

I felt rather than heard Ruth's terrified whimper, Ben's distress.

'No!' I screamed. 'No! Blandford, please!'

I was moving forward, and it was like the worst of nightmares. The terror, the feet and limbs clogged to a terrible slowness, knowing that I could not get there in time, that something dreadful, dreadful could not be prevented.

It was over in seconds. Each separate action melding fluently together.

The shadow of horse and rider fell like a curtain across Ben and Ruth. Ruth cowered back. Ben looked up at Blandford in fear and bewilderment. Blandford's arm lifted up. It was black against the sun but the low mellow rays gilded the edges of his yellow sleeve, the clenched fist, the thin crop.

At that instant a dog, sensing danger to its master, streaked forward, barking, under the horse's nose. The horse whinnied, shied. The crop whistled down, missing its target by an inch.

Ben caught Blandford's arm and wrenched it down. There was a flare of sullen anger in his face. Blandford squealed with pain and fury and tried to free his arm. But a man flabby with drink and years of indulgence was no match for a healthy, well-muscled young man. He lost his balance, toppled forward.

His squeal of rage and fear was cut off abruptly as he thudded, twisting, to the ground. And with the thud came another sound that brought bile into my throat and made me want to stuff my fingers in my ears.

The sickening crack of breaking bone.

Then silence. And stillness. Even the dogs standing motionless, ears cocked, noses forward, pointing at the man who hung by one booted foot from the stirrup, his head at an unnatural angle on the turf, his eyes wide and staring in his dead face.

Miss Lightbody was the first to move, pushing past me, taking Ben by the arm and tugging him round so that he was no longer blinking helplessly at the man – the body – at his feet.

'Move, blast your eyes!' she shrieked at me. 'You must take the boy! Save Ben! Remember? Those were her words. Save Ben.'

I shuddered. I wanted to be sick, to vomit up the bile that clogged my throat.

'Save Ben,' I whispered. 'Yes . . . yes.' Automatically I held out my arms. Ruth flung herself into them. I lifted her up and buried my face in her neck. 'You are all right, my lamb. There is nothing to fear. Nothing at all.' I did not know if I was reassuring her or myself.

Miss Lightbody jostled Ben forward. 'Go with your sister! Go on! Back to the house with you. All of you.' And standing on tiptoe to breathe in my ear, 'Do not look back! You have seen nothing. Heard nothing. He was never here. Do you understand? Impress it on the boy that he must not speak of it!'

I nodded numbly. She gave me a little push and slowly, then quicker, I began to stumble away, carrying Ruth on one arm, clasping Ben's hand with the other, dragging him back to Falconwood and safety.

I disobeyed her. I glanced back once, in time to see

her pulling the horse round so he faced westward. Then, with Blandford's riding crop, she thwacked its withers, so that it reared and whinnied and galloped wildly off along the cliff top, dragging with it by the foot still caught in the stirrup the mortal remains of my husband.

Five days later Blandford was laid to rest in his mother's grave in the churchyard at Kingsbridge. There was no suspicion that anyone else was involved in his accident. Indeed, there were a dozen witnesses to the fact that he had spent the morning drinking brandy in a tavern down by the quay and should never have gone chasing across the countryside in such a state. He had been found by a ploughboy two miles from Falconwood, his boot half torn off, but still twisted firmly into the stirrup.

It was clearly an accident. Tragic, of course, but then young Pascoe had always been foolhardy. It was those who were left one felt sorry for. The widow, the child – and particularly the father. A ruined man in every way. Become something of a recluse since the last unhappy event. Cared about nothing. Not the daughter-in-law, not the grandchild. The daughter whose elopement had caused such a stir was rumoured to have made some efforts towards a reconciliation when she heard of her brother's death, but he would have none of it. So the widow had retired to her grandfather's house, leaving the old man to brood alone. Every servant sacked, horses sold, save for one old hunter he spent his days grooming, house closed up except for a couple of rooms. Only a close-mouthed old woman going by the day to make his meals. He had disposed of the last of his business interests in Plymouth which had given him, it was generally understood, the means to continue to exist, barely, at Brent House.

It was all very sad.

And standing in my window at Falconwood, watching the last leaves tear from the trees in a November gale, perhaps I was the only one who made the connection between that embittered, ruined old man and a gruesome relic who had swung from a gibbet in the snow.

Chapter Twenty-Three

Those autumn days shortening steadily into winter were a time of renewal.

For a while I was numb and exhausted, sleeping badly and wakening suddenly with that sickening snap of bone ringing in my ears and Blandford's dead face before my eyes. I still feared that Ben or Ruth might inadvertently let slip the truth about what had happened. I had managed to treat the whole incident lightly, as a silly game Ruth's papa had played, sensing that to show fear and shock would serve to impress it indelibly on their minds.

To Ben, later, I said that Ruth's papa had gone away now, like our own papa and mama had done, and would never, ever return. 'People do not like to be reminded of friends who have gone away for ever. It makes them very sad. So, my love, it is best to be kind and not speak of him to anyone but me. Will you remember that?'

He agreed solemnly. 'I like it best when everyone is happy.'

Ruth herself clung to me like a little frightened shadow for some days. But my reassurances that her papa would never come back gradually comforted her and there were so many exciting new things to do, like learning her letters and gathering pretty autumn leaves to press between the pages of the heavy old Bible from

Grandfather's study and, best of all, Ben putting her up on the jenny donkey and leading her gently round the stable yard. The incident on the cliffs was soon overlaid by all these diversions and forgotten.

'We saved the boy,' Miss Lightbody whispered, some days after the funeral. 'Ellen is content. We did as she asked. She will do her part also. She will be there in his dreams to soothe away his remembrance. Rest easy, Joanna. Our secret is safe, I know it.'

I wanted to cry, 'I will not listen to this foolish talk of dreams and spirits!' but I said nothing, for in my heart I knew that it was not foolish at all.

There were happy things to divert my mind, too, as the days drew away from that terrible one. The enormous relief that there could not now be a child of Blandford's to remind me of my brief, disastrous marriage. I was truly free of him. There was the renewed correspondence with my Exeter friends and Grandfather's steady improvement. Above all, there was the feeling that I was my own person once more, beholden to no one.

Grandfather could hobble about now with the aid of a strong shoulder, though he dragged his leg and his arm hung useless. Harry Beer would carry him downstairs each day and he would spend an hour or two in his study where I helped him to put his sadly neglected papers in order, enter the ledgers and write his letters.

Between us now there was a growing trust and affection. When he learned of Blandford's death he had said, gruffly, 'There is a home here for you, where you belong. And the child also. I find it comforting to hear a child's voice in the house again. I have missed that. And I think, now, the boy will never ... Well, so be it.' The lopsided grimace that passed for a smile flickered briefly. 'I find calm and quiet a more enticing prospect these days than strife and struggle. When one has stared death in the face it alters one's perception of what is desirable.'

It was the time of year when the tenant farmers came with their rents and their complaints. I sat with Grandfather, entering the amounts in the ledger, making a note of any repairs or alterations that were sanctioned and being introduced to each farmer in turn as, 'My granddaughter, Mrs Pascoe, who is literally my right hand.' This acknowledgement warmed and pleased me and when the men had assembled in the parlour for the ale and cider, cold beef and ham and hog's pudding Mrs Beer had prepared for them, I told him so.

He looked at me sadly. 'Your mother always enjoyed this particular task. I have been reminded of her a great deal today.'

He turned away, but not before I had caught the glint of tears in his eyes.

Regular letters came from Exeter. Lily sent a few painstakingly penned lines, Miss Olga wrote formal little notes in her neat hand, Mrs Barton's were long and gossipy, making light of all the frustrations and setbacks of setting up her school. It was from her that I learned that Gerald Alperton had found himself an heiress, that Miss Olga was proving a whirlwind of industry and enthusiasm, that Susannah and Nicholas had now taken up residence at Roselawn.

Though there was at first a great deal of ruffling of feathers and cries of 'Disgraceful! A Scandal! Cut them Dead!' I do believe that Society – an animal whose curiosity often seems to override its scruples – is inclined to favour assessment rather than ostracism. Indeed, I have a suspicion that a certain gentleman's club has had a rush of new members eager to witness at first hand – and condemn roundly – any further iniquitous behaviour on the part of its owner. As to the invitations to musical evenings and card parties at Roselawn, I fear the ladies suffer greatly at having to accept every one in the cause of evaluating the respectability of their host and hostess.

Now, my dear, as soon as you feel up to the journey, your friends would welcome you and little Ruth most heartily for an extended stay. We are quite prepared for any severe lecture you may wish to deliver when you see how amateurishly we have set about the execution of your delightful designs . . .

It was an invitation impossible to accept. How could I, when Nicholas and Susannah would be so close? To meet either of them now would be opening myself to further injury when the wounds I already bore were still raw and bleeding.

Yet I had enjoyed reworking the sketches Blandford had destroyed and I caught myself more than once looking about me at Falconwood and thinking of improvements that could be made. It was like having an inner eye that had been opened and now refused to close. Whatever my mood, any house that I visited, even Brent House where I had been so unhappy, seemed to come under the scrutiny of that inner eye and in my head I refurbished and reshaped and redesigned the rooms. I knew I could make Falconwood beautiful. Nothing drastic, nothing too modern, but a gentle, gradual revival to a perfection I began to glimpse as the weeks passed.

In an idle moment I sketched a few ideas for the dining parlour and showed them enthusiastically to

Grandfather. He looked them over carefully, then sighed. 'I would not care for it, though I daresay it would look very fine.'

'The curtains are very shabby,' I began, hopefully.

He shook his head before I could go on. 'No, child. No. If they are shabby to your eyes, to mine they have the merit of being familiar. I am too old to crave change. When I am gone will be time enough.'

Through my disappointment I felt a quiver of excitement. It was as close as he had come to admitting that Falconwood would one day be mine. He had told me, shortly, after one of Mr Davey's visits that Ben and I need have no more worries for our future. He had put all his affairs in order.

'I intend to spend the time left to me with an easy mind, knowing that I have done my best to protect those that need and deserve protection and to prevent those who come after from the taint of discord that has lain over this family for too long. I . . . I hope there will be peace within these walls at last.' He took my hand in his good one and gripped it tightly. 'Joanna, you are strong-willed and proud, as I was myself once and like many others have been in this family. God knows, there are times when such strength is necessary, but there are others when forgiveness and tolerance is best cultivated. But say you will try not to allow that strength and pride to become too unbending. Allow the womanliness I see in you, the source of the kindness and gentleness that is also in your nature, to balance your will. I think, I believe, my own life, and that of others, would have been very different had I been given such advice, and taken it, when I was twenty.'

I could only nod and grip his hand the tighter. It had taken great courage for a man so stiff-necked to make such an admission and we sat on for a while, locked in our own memories, in a silence that was filled with unspoken regrets.

I had hoped – we had all hoped – that Grandfather would gradually be restored to his former vigorous self. But he reached a plateau of recovery beyond which, despite our continued attempts to bring life to his paralysed limbs, he could not proceed. His appetite was improved, he put back a little weight, but there was still a gaunt, frail air about him and he tired very easily.

But the change in him was more than physical. As though conscious of what he had denied himself all these lonely, embittered years, he was greedy for company, soaking up the experience of being part of a family again, however fragmented and disparate.

Ben and Ruth gave him particular pleasure. Without the urgency of his ambitious plans for his grandson to colour his vision, he now grew to appreciate Ben for the person he was. He had grown tolerantly fond of Ben before his illness, but now he came truly to love this handsome, gentle grandson who did not, could not, bear malice, but reflected back the kindness and goodwill shown to him. Such simple goodness, child-like and uncomplicated, was a balm to his troubled soul.

Ruth, Ben's shadow, also had a child's simple acceptance, showing no fear of the old man who clearly meant her no harm. She, remembering how she had addressed that other elderly gentleman, Mr Pascoe, called him Grampa, which amused him greatly, and brought treasures to show him – empty snail shells, pretty pebbles from the cove, a doll Bessy Beer had made for her out of a clothes peg.

He grew to enjoy playing backgammon with Mr Chadwick, though after a couple of acrimonious games with Miss Lightbody he refused to play with her again. 'You still cheat abominably!' he growled. 'I've not lost my wits, you light-fingered bawd! I saw you twice bearing off an extra man you were not entitled to!'

"Tis not that I cheat, Frank Kerswell,' she cackled, 'but that you cannot bear to be bested!'

'Lying trollop!'

'Pompous son of Satan!'

Later, she said happily, 'But for his poor wasted body I could have believed myself back in the old days. 'Tis a long time since he spoke so lively. I could almost believe the spark in his eye spoke of lusty appetites revived. I must look to please him for, who knows, it maybe that this bag of old bones will once more be regarded with favour.'

After that she appeared each evening in such an extravagance of lace and plumes, with so many glittering brooches and beads attached to her person that we blinked at the dazzle. And she lost no opportunity to needle her old lover into an exchange of acrimonious backchat that gave them both a great deal of satisfaction.

But most of all, Grandfather enjoyed reminiscence. At first it was a mere crack in the gate of his memories, then a positive flood poured out to whoever showed an interest. Stories of his boyhood and youth, of his own father, of my mother. I heard many of them as I sat with him before he slept.

When Harry Beer had carried Grandfather upstairs and helped him to bed – for as soon as he was able he had dispensed with the fussing of women about him – he liked me to fetch him the nutmeg-scented bread and milk the doctor had recommended and to sit with him until he was ready to settle to sleep.

'If I must have this invalid's pap,' he grumbled, 'then I need some distraction to help it down.'

We would talk quietly and easily in the candlelight, the warm blaze crackling in the fireplace sending shadows swaying and flickering across the bed hangings. One night, I was feeling tired, my thoughts for once inclined to drift from the long rambling anecdote about my great-grandfather who had been a wild rip in his youth. Ruth, who slept in a small room next to mine, had been whiny and miserable for several days with a bad cold. I had been up several times the night before to see to her and now I was thinking longingly of my own comfortable bed.

The name brought me up with a jolt.

'Fox, did you say, Grandfather?'

'Jem Fox, aye. Their fathers, as I said, arranged the marriage secretly . . .'

He had, I realised, been talking about his own father. I groped for the threads of the story.

'You mean my great-grandfather fell in love with this village girl and when she found she was having his child she was secretly married off to the blacksmith's son, Jem Fox?'

'I think it near broke my father's heart. It was his own father's deception as much as anything. My father had been sent off on some cock-and-bull errand to Plymouth. When he returned it was to find the deed done and the new bride moved into the blacksmith's cottage. The blacksmith was given a handsome purse for his pains, the child a name that was not Kerswell which left my father free to make his choice from among the suitable young ladies my grandfather had selected for him.'

'Then . . . then the Foxes are related to us . . .'

'Tied by blood,' Grandfather said somberly. 'And by friendship that has always seemed destined to turn to hatred. My half-brother, Matthew, who was scarcely a year and a half older than me, was my friend through our growing years. He was never acknowledged publicly by my father, but once Grandfather died and he came into his inheritance he took it upon himself to encourage the boy. He paid for him to go to school, allowed him freedom of the books in his study, made sure the whole family wanted for nothing.' His eyes were unfocused, he spoke half to himself. 'He was a handsome lad, dark, like his mother who had been a foundling, taken in by a rough but kindly fishing family. Some said she had Spanish or Romany blood. Some said she was a by-blow of the fisherman himself. Whatever the case, she was a pretty, black-haired, unruly child who grew to a beautiful, olive-skinned woman with a terrible sharp tongue on her. She ruled the great, docile giant of a blacksmith and the handful of daughters she gave him with a rod of iron. There was only Matthew, whom she adored, could charm her out of her spleen.'

'Did ... did he, Matthew, look like you, Grandfather?'

'Red hair, green eyes. Black hair, brown eyes. That was all that separated us in looks. Our natures were very different, but we were almost of a height and build. My features mirrored his.'

I had it then. That moment when I had glimpsed in Grandfather the debonair young man he had been.

'Nicholas ... Nicholas Fox,' I breathed.

He nodded, slowly. 'He favours his grandfather rather than his father. Though I suspect he does not have Matthew's sunny disposition, but more of the gypsy woman's nature. Or perhaps the Kerswell blood runs true in the veins. It has a powerful, wilful influence.' He stared into space. 'I think my dear Harriet loved Matthew for his gentleness, his ability to see the good in people and not the worst.' His voice sank low. He looked infinitely weary. 'After ... after I suspected her infidelity with Matthew, everything that was good in me seemed to turn sour. Some said I had a hand in

651

Matthew's death. I had not. But I believe if I could have overcome my jealousy, my anger, and the need to punish her with coldness for the pain she had given me, she might not have gone into the decline that robbed me of all that I knew, too late, I held most dear.'

A log crackled in the grate behind me. The spicy scent of applewood wove about the room. Grandfather closed his eyes. His voice was faint as a sigh.

'Harriet, my dear Harriet. Perhaps I shall learn one day if she has forgiven me.' His face contorted briefly, as though some inner struggle tore at him. 'Young Isaac, too . . . suffered . . . the sins of the fathers . . . And all so . . . so . . . useless . . . Forgive . . . Forgive . . .'

I snuffed the candle and tiptoed away. But I lay awake for a long time that night, unable to rid myself of the sadness of his words and remembrance of the tears that had slid from under his closed eyes and made long untidy trails down his gaunt cheeks.

I thought of the silver chain Nicholas had given me many times in the following days. The chain of love, I had thought it. The chain of blood, also, I saw now. Had Nicholas known all along? I guessed that he had. And hated that knowledge. Poor Nick. Locked in a vengeful way of life that would bring him no happiness. He had only to look at Grandfather to see that. He had married Susannah not out of love, but out of a need to hurt and destroy those he considered his enemies. How could a marriage with such a grievous foundation possibly bring satisfaction? No good would come of it. He and Susannah would both suffer. For the first time I found my hurt and anger deflected. I found it in me to be sorry for them both.

Christmas was drawing close. Grandfather had been speaking wistfully of childhood Christmases and I determined that we should make this a happy time. The years at Torre Crescent had seen Christmas come and go with hardly a variation in the day-to-day routine, except that Miss Olga would bear me to Butcher Row late on Christmas Eve to view the seasonal array of poultry in the hope of a last-minute bargain and Miss Polsham complained about the noise of carollers staggering back to the cathedral under her window in the small hours. The late Mr Polsham had eschewed Christmas as a pagan festival. The day, therefore, was marked only by extra prayers.

This year would be very different.

On Christmas Eve Harry Beer brought in a yule log and we lit it with great ceremony. We dressed the house with evergreens and hung a kissing bunch of mistletoe and holly in the hall. Bessy and Sally, giggling, made their own kissing bunch which they hung at the back door in order to take advantage of Billy, the lanky youth who helped Harry Beer around the stables, and the lad who came up from the village to deliver the fish. We sang carols round the fire after supper, and on Christmas morning there was an excited exchange of small gifts. Mrs Beer, who had spent the morning in a cloud of pudding steam and savoury smells, emerged from the kitchen triumphantly bearing a magnificent roast goose. A plum pudding dancing with blue brandy flames was borne in afterwards with equal ceremony.

Much later, when Ruth, exhausted from the excitement of the day, had been put to bed, the adults sat round the parlour fire while Ben roasted chestnuts on a brass shovel and Miss Lightbody heated a poker ready to plunge into a secret mixture of brandy, rum and wine which she declared to be the finest punch to be had in the whole of the country.

The poker went into the mixture with a great sizzle.

Miss Lightbody stirred the brew, muttering to herself, like a Macbeth witch. She was particularly ornate tonight in a skirt and bodice of rich scarlet overlaid with red net which clashed alarmingly with her wig. The bodice with its yellow fichu was scattered with an assortment of paste brooches. Three great white plumes and a jet comb hung askew from her wig. A weight of amber beads hung from her ears.

'There!' She removed the poker from the jug and poured a glass each. 'Sup up! If it is not the best you have ever tasted, my name is not Amelia Alice and I shall be hung for a lying bitch!'

Before we could venture to sniff the brew, Grandfather said quietly, 'A toast, I think, to round off the day.'

The candles had burned low and the fire had fallen to brilliant embers. Grandfather sat to one side of the fireplace, his two old dogs, Jupiter and Rex, grey-muzzled and stiff-limbed now, sprawled sleeping at his feet. I had a friendly tabby cat curled on my lap, an aloof tortoiseshell condescended to perch on the arm of Mr Chadwick's chair while he absently stroked her ears. A pair of black and white kittens hunted and pounced on each other under Ben's chair and a ragged mongrel, nose to the fire, twitched and yelped in sleep as he chased phantom rabbits. It was a homely, comfortable scene. Grandfather paused, looking round, as though savouring the ordinariness – the extraordinariness – of it all.

Eventually he raised his glass. 'I drink to the future,' he said. 'May this day be a symbol of the harmony this house will know in the years to come.'

We clinked glasses and swallowed the hot and heady brew.

Harry Beer came in then to help Grandfather upstairs. The dogs climbed to their feet and followed.

They were not allowed in the upper rooms and usually they padded off to Grandfather's study where they slept.

Tonight they were sitting at the foot of the stairs when I went up to say goodnight to Grandfather. They were still there, ears cocked, noses pointing upwards, when I returned.

I shooed them away. They went reluctantly.

In the night I dreamed that Mama, young and smiling, stood on the cliffs outside Falconwood and Grandfather, restored to health and vigour, walked towards her with the dogs racing back and forth between them. He held out his arms and she ran into them and the dogs set up a great barking at the joy of it.

I awoke suddenly. The dream spun away. Had it been the barking of the dream dogs that had roused me? I heard, then, the long low howling coming from below. Then silence.

In the morning we learned what the dogs already knew. That their master, Falconwood's master, had died peacefully in his sleep.

Grandfather was buried in the family grave on a grey morning with a wind like a knife coming out of the east to set a skin of ice on the puddles left by overnight rain. Miss Lightbody huddled against me, for warmth or comfort I could not tell, as we stood in the windswept churchyard. A forlorn red curl escaped through a tear in the dark veil she had thrown over her black bonnet. Ben was at my other side, blinking back tears as the coffin was lowered. Mr Chadwick stood with bowed head. Beyond him and in a half circle, the wind whipping their coat-tails and the black bands on their hats, were Mr Aggett, Mr Davey, Tom Davey and Harry Beer. At a respectful distance stood a silent crowd of villagers and farmers.

The wind caught the vicar's words and tossed them over the lumpy grass and between the leaning gravestones so that I seemed to catch only a few phrases.

'Man that is born of woman hath but a short time to live . . . he fleeth as it were a shadow . . . deliver us not to the bitter pains of eternal death . . .'

The roar of the sea, the howl of the wind, the sharp, stony clatter as handfuls of earth rained down on the coffin.

'. . . earth to earth; ashes to ashes . . .'

Miss Lightbody sobbed uncontrollably. I put my arm round her bird-thin shoulders. If anyone looked askance at this foolish old woman who purported to be a servant – though the world and his wife knew she had been the mistress of the old man – taking such a prominent part in the ceremony I did not care. She had loved him and she grieved for him and, above anyone else, she deserved to be allowed to toss a last nosegay of flowers down onto his coffin.

'. . . raise us from the death of sin into righteousness . . . receive the kingdom prepared for you from the beginning of the world . . .'

It was over. The vicar, looking as though the next gust of wind might tumble him over, murmured his few practised words of comfort in my ear, excused himself from returning with us to Falconwood as his wife would be anxious for his return, for those who were wise in the way of weather said there was snow to come. He scurried in the direction of the vestry and I gently urged Miss Lightbody towards the waiting chariot. 'For if we do not get out of this wind, we shall all surely be stricken . . .'

The words died on my lips. I stopped, all the use suddenly going out of my legs.

'Mrs Pascoe, do you feel faint?' Mr Chadwick caught my elbow and looked anxiously into my face. 'You have lost all your colour. Such a strain, and the cold . . .'

'No,' I said. 'It was nothing . . . As you say, the cold. Would you see Miss Lightbody to the carriage? There is someone I must speak to.'

I walked steadily forward towards the one mourner I had not noted, who perhaps, until now, had not wished to be seen. He stood alone, very tall, very still. I stopped in front of him.

'Joanna,' he said.

'Nicholas,' I said.

I looked into his eyes. He looked into mine. And all around us was a curious silence into which I could hear the slow, thick beat of the blood in my veins. He held out his hands and mine went into them. And in that moment I forgot everything that had ever kept us apart and that would go on holding us apart. Because time meant nothing at all.

'You will come back with us to Falconwood?'

'If I am invited.'

'I invite you, Mr Fox.'

'Then most certainly I accept, Mrs Pascoe.'

All was bustle and warmth at the house. Mrs Beer's last tribute to her late master was a magnificent spread which all the gentlemen tucked into with a will, appetites sharpened by the cold. I could not eat. Neither could Nicholas, though he made a pretence of it. We adjourned to the parlour and I tried to keep my eyes from him, concentrating on what Mr Aggett was saying or Tom, who was eager to press upon me assurances that anything he – or his father, naturally – could do to spare me worry at this difficult time . . .

'You are most kind,' I said, cutting him short as politely as I could, regretting to see the disappointment, quickly masked, that replaced the boyish eagerness, but wanting so desperately to go to where Nicholas stood with his back to the window, a little apart, wearing the puzzled air of a man who finds himself overtaken by events that have set him off balance.

'Mrs Pascoe, might I have a word?' Now it was Mr Davey infuriatingly at my elbow. 'I took the liberty of informing Mr Fox of Mr Kerswell's demise and requested his presence here today. Might I now ask that he adjourn with us for a few moments? Somewhere quiet, where we might talk in private.'

'Of course,' I said and now it was my turn to be puzzled.

We went into Grandfather's study. Candles burned within to dispel the growing darkness outside though it was still early in the afternoon. The fire was lit, Rex and Jupiter lay before it, lifting their heads in sharp anticipation as the door opened, then settling back with resigned sighs.

I had not been in here since Grandfather's death and I felt much as I felt the first time I had entered it on that snowy day with the master not yet returned. An intruder. The room spoke so clearly of Grandfather, his character, his personality, that it seemed almost sacrilegious to be here when he was not.

Nicholas felt it too. He hesitated in the doorway, his body tense, his eyes narrowed as though he expected something dangerous to leap out at him. Then he stepped inside and the tension slid out of him. He smiled, a wry twist of the lips. It was just a room, after all. Shabby, smelling of dogs and ancient tobacco and Macassar oil.

I perched on the upright chair, waving Mr Davey to the seat behind the desk. Nicholas moved naturally and easily to Grandfather's comfortable wing chair. In one fluid movement he leaned back, crossed one long leg over the other, stuck his elbows on the arms of the chair and linked his fingers together across his chest.

For an instant it was so clearly Grandfather settling back into his chair that I was taken aback at how blind I had been not to make the connection before.

Mr Davey cleared his throat to get our attention. He had brought a document out of some inner pocket. He settled his eyeglasses on his nose.

'The late Mr Kerswell's will,' he said. 'If you will permit me, I will give you the gist of it, rather than reading it in its entirety.' He glanced apprehensively at the window. 'I believe there are a few flakes of snow already in the air and we are anxious to set off before the storm breaks.'

Nobody had been forgotten. There were small bequests for Mrs Beer and Harry and Mr Chadwick, 'In the hope that they will continue to live and work at Falconwood where I believe they have been content.' Miss Lightbody was provided for with an annuity.

Mr Davey looked at me over his spectacles and informed me of the very generous amount Grandfather had settled on Benjamin and myself. 'You and your brother are to remain at Falconwood as long as you wish. The house will be held in trust during the lifetime of Benjamin Howarth Kerswell, you yourself, Mrs Pascoe, to be one of the trustees.' He transferred his gaze to Nicholas. 'You, Mr Fox, inherit the bulk of the estate. On the death of Benjamin Kerswell, the house will pass to you or your male heirs.'

I burst out, 'But I . . . that is . . .' I broke off. I meant to say 'unfair' but the word would not come out. I loved Falconwood. Grandfather had known that. But Grandfather had also wished more than anything to have peace within Falconwood's walls. To right the wrongs of an unforgiving past.

The chain of love . . . The chain of blood.

Both men waited. Nicholas's face was paper-white with shock.

I said, carefully, 'I think that my grandfather has dealt fairly with us all. Thank you, Mr Davey.' From somewhere I found the strength to stand up and smile calmly. 'And now, pray do not let me detain you further. The weather is indeed closing in. I shall join you shortly. Mr Fox, could you spare a moment or two? I should like a word.'

The door closed softly behind Mr Davey.

'Believe me, Joanna,' Nicholas began harshly, 'I had no idea . . . I do not know if I can accept this . . . from my enemy.'

'You must take it,' I said. 'It is your due. And he was not your enemy at the last. He wished to put an end to the cycle of revenge. And to acknowledge your right to his estate. I wish it, too.'

'Then you know . . .?'

'That you have Kerswell blood? Grandfather told me the truth of it. You have a look of him, as he once must have been. Does that upset you?'

He thought for a moment, then shook his head. 'Once, perhaps. Now, I am too . . . too stunned to know what to think. Except,' his voice dropped to an agonised whisper, 'except that it is all much too late for us.'

The width of the room was between us. And yet no space at all.

'Oh, my dearest,' I cried. 'Why? Why did you marry Susannah? It was so cruel, when you did not love her.'

'But I did not intend . . . God forgive me, I meant only to ruin her. To live with her for a little while and then cast her off. You see, I wished to save you from that blackguard Pascoe by foiling all their plans. Do you not understand? Susannah had told me of the contract whereby you and your brother would be married off. And I thought to rescue you by removing her

660

and at the same time throwing those I most hated into confusion. Your marriage, then, could not possibly go ahead.'

Have hope. Have hope. Of course!

He sank back into the chair and put his head in his hands. 'When I heard the truth of it, I swear I near went mad.'

Out of the torrent of words I caught like a drowning woman at a straw, at the one possible hope. 'You meant only to ruin her . . . not marry her . . . then . . .'

'There is to be a child,' he said bleakly. 'I married her as soon as I knew. I have many failings, but I could not knowingly allow an innocent child, my child, to bear the stigma of bastardy.' He looked at me with all the weight of his despair – his hunger – darkening his eyes. 'I have gained what I wished and lost everything, Joanna. Without you, there is nothing . . . nothing left that will bring me any joy.'

There was a fluttering, soft as feathers, at the window. Snow was blowing against the glass. Already there was a white tracery along the edges of each pane.

I went to Grandfather's desk, opened the drawer and took out the key of my mother's room. I laid it softly on the arm of Nicholas's chair.

'Will you stay tonight, Nicholas?' I asked softly.

Then I left him to ponder on what he should answer.

It snowed all night. By daybreak deep drifts buried the lanes and hedges. Tree branches groaned and broke under the weight of it. The whole world, it seemed, was transformed to a pristine expanse of glittering white.

Ice and snow without.

Fire and heat within.

Then the wind blew soft from the west and the thaw set in and released the land from the stony grip of the bitter cold.

In that span of days the old year died and a new year began.

A new beginning.

A new life.

The household was not astir when Nicholas left. I stood at the window of my mother's room and watched him ride out from the stable. He looked up as he passed below the window. He raised his hand in farewell, then the dank foggy morning swallowed him up.

I turned back to the tumbled bed. Papa's old tobacco pouch lay on the coverlet. It held, still, the sovereigns I had saved and which I would never now need. I moved my hand to the flatness of my belly. I should buy something for the child, if there was to be one. I hoped that there was. I believed that there was. Our son. Nicholas's and mine.

I had assured Nicholas that I had the means to keep us safe from such eventuality, but deliberately, secretly, I had chosen not to use it.

A final deception. But out of it would come joy not sorrow. The joy, I prayed, of a new and wanted life.

The silver necklace was no longer in the pouch.

Sometime in the night Nicholas had clasped it round my neck. Two hearts, joined for ever. Whatever distance of time or space that destiny intended to put between us now, nothing could ever truly separate us again.

I walked across to the door. I made to close and lock it, but instead I left it open. There would be no forbidden rooms from now on. Let the light and the air dispel all the sad shadows.

Falconwood would be beautiful again. I would make it beautiful and dignified and desirable.

For myself. For Nicholas. And for all those who would come after us to seek peace and hope within its walls.

Epilogue

Extract from the Exeter *Flying Post*. August 1832.

The malignant epidemic which has afflicted so many citizens continues to rage unabated.

At her home in Exeter on Saturday last, of the cholera, lamented by all who knew her, Mrs Nicholas Fox, together with her new born son. Daughter of Mr James Pascoe of Kingsbridge. Her grieving husband, well known for his many charitable works in the district, is understood to be retiring, with his young daughter, to live permanently on his estates near to Kingsbridge.